Praise for Nikki Moore

'I know that Nikki Moore is an author that I can trust to deliver the feel good factor in whatever she writes … definitely one of my top author finds of the past year!'
Lisa Talks About

'I loved every single minute of this fun, flirty romance … the perfect read for your boring commute to work.'
Bookaholic Confessions

'Uplifting and at the same time thought provoking too. I guarantee you'll be hitting that button on Amazon to order the fourth book in the #LoveLondon series as soon as you've finished this one.'
Dawn, Crooks on Books

'Game, Set and Match to a lovely romantic story full of sensuality, poignancy and humour … This short story flowed like a novel and the ending was believable. A lovely summer read.'
Jane Hunt Writer Book Reviews

'A sweet and flirty short story, I really enjoyed it. I can't wait to see what Nikki comes up with for the next book in the series.'
Sky's Book Corner

'Whoever said romance was dead has clearly never read a Nikki Moore book'
Rachel's Random Reads

NIKKI MOORE

I've adored writing and reading since forever and have always been a sucker for love stories so I'm delighted to be part of the fabulous HarperImpulse team! I write short stories and fun, touching, sexy contemporary romance and really enjoy creating intriguing characters and telling their stories.

A finalist in writing competitions since 2010, including Novelicious Undiscovered 2012, I'm a member of the fantastic Romantic Novelists' Association. I blog about three of my favourite things – Writing, Work and Wine – at www.nikki-mooreauthor.wordpress.com and am passionate about supporting other writers as part of a friendly, talented and diverse community, so you'll often see other authors pop in!

You can find me at https://www.facebook.com/NikkiMoore Author or https://www.facebook.com/NikkiMooreWritesor on Twitter @NikkiMoore_Auth to chat about love, life, reading or writing … I'd love to hear from you!

The Complete
#LoveLondon Collection

NIKKI MOORE

Harper*Impulse* an imprint of
HarperCollins*Publishers* Ltd
1 London Bridge Street
London SE1 9GF

www.harpercollins.co.uk

A Paperback Original 2016

First published in Great Britain in ebook format by Harper*Impulse* 2015

Cover images © Shutterstock.com

Nikki Moore asserts the moral right
to be identified as the author of this work

A catalogue record for this book is
available from the British Library

ISBN: 978-0-00-816784-4

This novel is entirely a work of fiction.
The names, characters and incidents portrayed in it are
the work of the author's imagination. Any resemblance to
actual persons, living or dead, events or localities is
entirely coincidental.

Automatically produced by Atomik ePublisher from Easypress

The #LoveLondon series has been a fantastic journey – one that wouldn't have been anywhere near as much fun without such incredible people supporting me. This collection, along with a massive thank you, is therefore dedicated to:

My wonderful family

My lovely friends and work colleagues

My amazing editor Charlotte (rightly nominated as Editor of the Year in the Love Stories Awards 2015)

All my fabulous fellow HarperImpulse authors

The warm and dedicated HarperImpulse team

All the fantastic readers, reviewers and bloggers

And especially,

Cara, Finn & Mark xxx

Author Note

Dear Reader,

When the first in the #LoveLondon series – *Skating at Somerset House* – was released in December 2014, I had no idea of the wonderful, dizzying journey that lay ahead of me.

Writing a set of romances that could be read as stand-alone stories that were also linked was a challenge I was more than up for. Five novellas, one novel and a hundred and eighty thousand words later, here we are!

This series is my love letter to London. It's a city I never get tired of with its varied architecture, amazing buzz, vibrant communities and diverse beauty. Even if I spent every day of the rest of my life exploring it, I don't think I would discover all of its secrets.

During the writing of the series, every couple in every one of the stories became my friends and I was rooting for them to get their happy ever after. I hope you feel the same way.

I could never have predicted the way readers, bloggers and reviewers would take #LoveLondon to heart and I've been truly overwhelmed by the support, be it a tweet, a Facebook post or a lovely review. What's been even more humbling has been readers contacting me to say a story touched them, or made them laugh, or how they wished they weren't saying goodbye to the characters – and is there a follow up please? I have spent a lot of the last year with a smile on my face …

So now, as we're approaching the end of the year, it feels only right to put the whole series together in one collection. I really hope you enjoy it, and I hope you grow to #LoveLondon as much as I do.

I would love to hear from you, so please do get in touch via Facebook or Twitter.

Love, Nikki x

#LoveLondon Series

Skating at Somerset House
New Year at the Ritz
Valentine's on Primrose Hill
Cocktails in Chelsea
Strawberries at Wimbledon
Picnics in Hyde Park

Skating at Somerset House

Noel Summerford hated Christmas.

The intense, harried craziness drove him half nuts every year. The pressure to buy everyone presents they didn't want and would never use. Shoving, rippling crowds on the streets forgetting their manners, desperate to cross every item off their shopping lists. People parting with their hard earned cash at rip-off prices that would reduce to near zero as soon as it hit Boxing Day. Endless turkey dinners with dry overcooked white meat, lashings of sickly cranberry sauce and stodgy stuffing. Unwanted, twee greetings cards with their cutesy reindeer or Santa cartoons. Cheesy, artificial music piped into every shop for months, seasonal tunes playing on every radio station until he thought his ears would bleed, especially as the girls in the office insisted on turning the music up to near deafening volumes. His female colleagues wearing silver bauble earrings and pressuring the men to dress in novelty ties and festive knitted jumpers made him grind his teeth, but worse was how they clambered up on desks in ridiculously high heels to hang decorations from the beige walls and white-tiled ceiling. It was an annual health and safety nightmare, given that he was the Corporate H&S Officer for a high-street retail giant.

Yes, Christmas was definitely his least favourite time of the year, and his preference would be to hide in his man-cave for the whole of December. He therefore couldn't think of anything worse than ice skating – or in his case falling on his arse countless, humiliating times – at Somerset House. It was London's favourite outdoor ice rink according to The Evening Standard magazine, or so Matt had informed him. He could admit that the main sandstone neoclassical building, set in a square shape around the central courtyard, *was* quite impressive with its graceful columns, Victorian style black lampposts, mini white-encrusted trees in massive gold leaf pots and grand entrances on the Strand and the Embankment. Right now that was contrasted against the modern single-storey, white-framed, temporary buildings that housed Tom's Skate Lounge, the Cloakrooms/Box Office and main skate entrance. Mint green and teal SKATE posters were displayed prominently and matching Fortnum & Mason flags flapped in the winter breeze. You couldn't deny there was a great buzz to the place with all the noisy, excitable visitors chattering and skating, both locals and tourists from the sounds of it. But Noel was a disaster on the ice, and the giant Christmas tree in a huge wicker hamper was overdecorated and overdone … as well as a sharp reminder it was only a few days until the dreaded C-day. There was no escaping it.

Leaning up against the transparent waist-high wall guarding the rink, taking a much needed break from skating, he shivered and shifted from one foot to another. Cold vapour formed in a puffy cloud in front of his face as he exhaled. It was seriously bitter today. He checked the watch that'd belonged to his grandfather; rectangular face, brown leather strap, built to last. It was three in the afternoon, so it was only going to get colder and bleaker. Although, if he froze to death, at least it would be a merciful release from this ice-encrusted hell. This was the last time he was doing a favour for a friend. Not that refusing had really been an option, given the favour was to carry out perfectly reasonable god-fatherly duties for Jasper, whose dad Matt was Noel's best friend.

Teeth chattering, as he watched people - including Jasper - whizz around the ice, he decided he was going abroad for Christmas next year. Somewhere he could sit on a beach, dewy beer bottle in hand and read a crime thriller while soaking up the sun's rays. Because even though he was wrapped up in black jeans, a long sleeved top, thick green jumper, woollen winter coat, scarf, thermal lined gloves and a beanie hat pulled right down to cover his hair, he was still bloody freezing.

As if the weather wasn't bad enough, every time he got on the rink four year old Jasper skated rings around him. It was embarrassing to be a thirty year old guy with no sense of coordination who couldn't push away from the wall, stop, or glide along the blindingly white ice without falling over ... but it was mortifying that Jasper, who'd only skated once before (or so he claimed) was showing Noel up with such natural talent. Already having taught himself to do some kind of spinning stop, he was currently attempting to skate backwards, forcing his heels together then apart in curved S shapes. The kid had absolutely no fear, throwing his little body around like it couldn't be bent or broken. But that was kids for you. They were resilient little things, unlike some adults.

No. Not today. There were other things to worry about, like looking after Jasper, which was why he'd fought the temptation to dive into the Skate Lounge with its windows overlooking the rink and rainbow coloured assortment of round paper lanterns hanging from the ceiling, and was staying put. He should probably get Jasper to calm down a bit, stop with the tricks and skate in nice sensible circles holding Noel's hand instead. That was what the H&S part of him would do with a potentially dangerous activity; minimise the risk. Except:—

a) the kid probably wouldn't listen to a word he said,

b) Jasper was always on the verge of hyperactivity so it made sense to tire him out,

and most importantly,

c) it was probably safer for Jasper *not* to hold his hand.

The little tyke came hurtling towards him in an expensive blue

5

ski suit, stopping with a scrape and spraying ice up into Noel's face.

'Jasper!' he snapped, scowling and scrubbing the sharp ice crystals off with his gloves.

The boy's round-cheeked face fell, eyes widening. Noel sighed, feeling like a complete bastard. It wasn't cool to upset Jasper, just because *he* wasn't enjoying himself. Besides, he was genuinely fond of the little whirlwind and loved being his godfather.

'Never mind,' he joked, forcing a grin and stretching over the wall to straighten Jasper's hat, 'it's only a bit of ice. I was getting bored anyway, needed something to wake me up!' Rolling his eyes in an exaggerated cartoon character way, he crossed then uncrossed them, making the boy giggle. 'How's it going? Enjoying yourself? You're doing some good stuff out there, Jay.'

'Uh-huh,' Jasper nodded, dark head bopping up and down like the dog in the insurance ads, 'it's really, really awesome. But it would be better if you were skating with me "ncle Noel.' He beamed, showing a gap where his two front teeth should be, reminding Noel of the carol, *All I Want For Christmas* …

The hope that Jasper might be ready to go after nearly three hours of skating died, and the boy's expression became pleading as Noel fell silent. The rest of the day would be spent with a storm cloud of guilt hanging over his head if he said no. Jasper had been bugging Matt about skating at Somerset House for months, ever since one of his friends had mentioned going the year before.

Time to do his duty. Careful to keep the dread off his face, Noel nodded. 'Sure, I'll give it another go.' *My seventh one today.* 'Be right there.' He clomped through the skate entrance building and stepped on to the ice. Clutching the wall for support, trying to balance on the metal blades, – stupidly risky if you asked him, who would think to put knives on a pair of boots? – He pulled himself over to his godson, sure his knuckles were not just white but positively glowing beneath his gloves. Perhaps he could manage a circuit without making an idiot of himself this time.

Nodding at Jasper, 'Come on then,' he smiled bravely and

carefully pushed off from the side. Walking/wobbling more than actually skating, arms extended like a pair of crippled wings, knees shaking, doubt flashed through his head. *There's a snowball's chance in hell of me not landing on my arse again.*

Holly Winterlake loved Christmas.

The chaotic, festive madness of it all thrilled her every year. The delight of spinning and dodging around people in shops to grab the best bargain to cross off her gift list, bought with her Christmas slush fund which she saved up towards monthly. Scrumptious turkey dinners with moist white meat, lashings of fruity cranberry sauce and fragrant, tasty stuffing, not to mention crispy butter-slathered roast potatoes. Exchanging cheery greetings cards featuring cutesy snowmen or North Pole cartoons, watching the assorted envelopes dropping onto her parents' doormat every morning. The jingling, jingly, upbeat tunes playing everywhere to get everybody into the Christmas spirit, which she turned up to maximum volume on the radio while she and her mum bopped around the breakfast table each morning. Having the perfect excuse to wear her favourite tiny silver snowman earrings. Hanging the circular red berry foliage wreath on the front door, set off perfectly by the green ivy twined around a wire topiary frame. The optimistic pining for snow and a white Christmas. Catching the tube with her mum's favourite metal tray if it did snow (more fun than a sleigh because you had to cram your legs onto it, tuck your chin into your knees and hope for the best) to slide down a steep Hampstead Heath hill.

Yes, Christmas was definitely her favourite time of year. In fact, Holly's preference would be to celebrate it every month, and pretend that summer with its muggy, prickly heat and scorching sun that burnt her fair skin and bleached her blonde hair lighter didn't exist. This December she couldn't think of anything better than ice skating for a living. It was a dream come true to be an Ice Marshall at Somerset House, being paid to loop the rink to make sure members of the public were safe, providing them with help where they needed it, issuing skates on request and helping the Ice Technician clean the ice when it became dented and scarred from use. The skating test before the job offer had been as easy as breathing, she'd completed the training at the beginning of the previous month easily and she was lucky enough to have picked up five shifts a week, working up to eight hours a day. Her mum might be worried about her overdoing it on the ice but the money would all definitely add up towards her start up fund. Come the New Year, she was going into business.

She glanced around, grinning. The forty foot Christmas tree near the North Wing, sprinkled with twinkling lights, gorgeous silver, gold, white, bronze and teal baubles and miniature Fortnum and Mason hampers, was an exciting reminder that it was Christmas Eve the next day.

Letting out a small squeak of anticipation, and checking she had enough room, Holly did a quick one foot spin, the first she'd learnt as a child. Starting with arms outstretched and pushing off with her right foot, twirling around she brought her arms in and her foot up against her knee, then span back out, ending with her arms crossed over her chest, both feet planted. Laughing, she did it again, joy and exhilaration zinging through her as the familiar move brought back a thousand happy memories of her professional figure-skating days. Those years had been filled with hard work, endless hours of practice, more bruises, grazes and sprains than she could count, and little time for friends or hobbies, but had also included some of the best moments of her life. When you got it right, it felt like you were flying.

It was a shame she could no longer do a Lutz or Axel as easily as a one foot spin, but she couldn't take the risk.

When she came to a stop, a small boy with big green eyes and a mop of brown hair peeking out from under a winter hat was staring at her. Steady on his feet, he looked more comfortable on the ice than the majority of adults. She'd seen him earlier, confidently gliding along. He hadn't needed her help and she'd been busy helping a family with twin girls, blonde hair in matching plaits, so she hadn't had a chance to tell him how well he skated.

'Wow,' he breathed, showing off a massive gappy grin. 'That was sooo good. You're a really cool ice person.'

'Thanks. I'm Holly, one of the Ice Marshalls.' Rather than someone who sounded like they were actually made of frozen water. She smiled. He was adorable. All massive eyes and cherry red cheeks. 'What's your name?'

'Jasper.'

'Well, I'll let you into a secret Jasper.' She scooted a little closer to him, bending down to his height. 'When I was only a tiny bit older than you, just after I started school, I started skating. I was in competitions, and won things. So I've had a lot of time on the ice.' Before the injury. When her world turned upside down. 'How long have you been skating? A few months?'

'Nope,' shaking his head, 'this is my second time. Daddy works a lot and Melody has gone home for Christmas. But she'll be back as soon as she can and she promised, promised, promised to bring me lots of presents and hugs. She said I'm a busy boy who keeps her running around but I'm on Santa's good boy list.' From the way he said it, he'd heard it a lot in the past few weeks.

'I'm sure you are,' Holly agreed, amused at his babble. 'Melody sounds cool.' Who she was, Holly wasn't quite sure of, obviously not the boy's mum, but would his Dad's girlfriend really disappear off for Christmas? 'But is this really only your second time? You're very good you know.' She paused, 'Do you want me to show you a few tricks a bit later on?' Strictly speaking she was here to help the customers who needed it but she could wait until the end of the afternoon, when it got a bit quieter, to spend some time with him.

'Would you?' he jumped, heels to his bum, and landed perfectly again on both skates, which was harder than it looked. 'That'd be super cool!' he paused, expression dropping. 'I have to ask if it's okay though.'

'Ask who?'

Spinning around in a perfect one eighty, he glanced around the rink. After a moment he extended a podgy finger, glancing at her sheepishly. 'Him … he's not very good.'

'I'm sure he's not that bad—Oh.'

They watched in silence as a man wrapped up to the max with a face like a British thundercloud under a beanie hat slipped and lurched around the rink, arms flailing, even though every few feet he was using the wall to steady himself.

From the look on his face, Jasper was embarrassed. Heck, Holly felt embarrassed, but it was for Jasper's dad on his behalf, rather than not wanting to be seen with him. 'Well, at least he's trying,' she said from corner of her mouth, 'he might get better.'

'Ummm …' the boy gave her a doubtful look.

But bless, you had to give the guy points for being here for his son, and making a bit of an idiot of himself in the process. Maybe he just wasn't very fit. He looked a bit bulky and soft around the middle. Or perhaps he didn't have good balance. Shame he wasn't a child; otherwise he could use one of the penguin skating aids available for the younger skaters in the separate area down the South Wing end.

Right. Two birds with one diplomatic, tactful stone then. 'Come on,' she gestured the boy to follow her, 'let's go ask him about you trying something a bit more adventurous.'

'Hi, there!' Her tone was friendly as she skated up behind the man, but unfortunately it unnerved him. Whipping his head round, his feet scissored, arms wind-milling. Trying to find his centre of gravity but failing, his legs started to slide in opposite directions. 'Oops!' Acting on instinct, Holly moved in, threading her arms under his to hoist him up, leaning forward for balance. 'Woah, there you go. I've got you.'

Practically spooning the guy upright wasn't the most professional way to help and she might get a telling off by the Front of House Manager, but it was the best she could do at short notice.

He didn't reply, just made a grunting sound and shook his head.

With his back plastered to her front and bum tucked into the curve of her hips, she realised he wasn't as bulky as he first seemed; it was the never ending amount of layers he was wrapped in. No wonder he was having issues, his upper body was totally constricted. No, he wasn't soft around the middle; he was actually quite nicely built.

'Okay?' she asked a little breathlessly. Untangling their arms, she steadied him with a firm hand and glided them over to the side, checking to make sure Jasper was still with them. The little boy gave her a reassuring nod, keeping pace.

'No, I'm not okay,' the guy spat as soon as he was hanging on to the wall, 'you scared the crap out of me!'

The girl took a step back at his tone, emotions flickering over her face; astonishment, irritation, simmering anger, settling at last on blank politeness. Pale blonde hair tied back in a high ponytail, she had glacier blue eyes, creamy skin and was girl next door pretty, but everything about her screamed winter. He preferred the hot Latin type. Women with curves and smouldering dark eyes. Not women who looked like Taylor Swift's slightly taller twin. The loose purple tabard - *Ice Marshall* in white script across the front - worn over some kind of waterproofs was hardly sexy. She could be straight up and down under there. Not that it mattered.

'I'm sorry if I startled you,' she said, every word coated with frost. 'But perhaps I can talk you through some skating tips?' Looking pointedly at Jasper, who was gazing up at Noel with a puzzled expression.

Noel realised what he'd said and the way he'd said it, and gritted his teeth. First he'd had to be publicly rescued, then he'd spoken to his rescuer like a spoilt five year old. That wasn't okay. Frustration tumbled through him. He wasn't getting any better at skating. And there was a funny hitch in his stomach at having a woman plastered up against him for the first time in two years, since- Stop. There was no way he was going to think about *her* now.

'I'm sorry if I was rude,' he glanced at the girl apologetically. 'And thank you for the offer …?'

'Holly.'

'Holly. But I'm not interested in getting any better.' Shaking his head. 'I might be here tomorrow, but after that I don't plan to come near an ice rink for a *really* long time.'

She giggled, then bit her lower lip, teeth straight and white except for a slightly crooked canine. It was a tiny imperfection, but somehow appealing.

He cleared his throat, raising one eyebrow, 'Are you allowed to laugh at customers?'

'S-sorry,' she choked, covering her mouth, 'probably not, I just—ahem,' she dropped her hand, smiling, 'you just sounded so pained. I had a fleeting thought … I wondered if you were traumatised.'

'Yeah,' he drawled, elbowing aside the mental note his treacherous brain had made about what an appealing shade of pink her lips were, 'I'll be seeking compensation from Somerset House to fund some counselling sessions.'

Her smile widened, eyes twinkling. 'It would be a conflict for me to give evidence on your behalf,' she joked, 'but you definitely seem like you could use them.'

'I'll let you know how I get on,' he grinned back, then fell silent. Why was he flirting with her? She wasn't his type, and the last thing he needed was a woman complicating things. 'Anyway,' he muttered, 'I'd better get on.' He turned away to pull himself along the edge of the rink using the wall. 'Come on, Jay.'

Jasper frowned but nodded, obediently skating a few metres ahead, near enough that Noel could keep an eye on him, but not so close that he'd be in the danger zone if his godfather fell over.

Noel was surprised when Holly stayed with him, matching pace.

Taking a breath and winking at Jasper, who'd turned to watch them over his shoulder, she lowered her voice. 'Look, I am sorry if I surprised you, and if you don't want my help that's fine, but

I'd actually come over to speak to you about something.'

He nodded, trying not to think about what he was doing with his feet. The more he thought about it, the more likely he was to fall over. 'I see. And what's that?' he'd caught the look passing between Holly and Jasper. They were obviously up to something. No wonder Jasper was staying close, rather than zipping around like he had done earlier.

'I'd love for Jasper to stay on so I can teach him a few moves later. He's a natural.'

'I'm not sure that's a good idea. It sounds sort of dangerous.' He risked taking his hand off the wall and moved faster, trying to remember to slide his feet in turn, instead of walking on the ice.

'I know what I'm doing and would be with him the whole time,' she said earnestly, accelerating to keep up with him. 'It's no more dangerous than a lot of other childhood activities; riding a bike, swimming in the sea.'

'I wouldn't know,' he dismissed, then stumbled on a groove in the ice, and started going down, arms flailing. She was there immediately, slipping her right arm around his waist and fitting neatly under his left arm to steady him, as if they were a couple, like they'd been doing this for years. He could feel the warmth of her body up and down his side. Smell strawberries in her blonde hair, her glossy ponytail swinging against his cheek. Their faces were so close he could tilt his head and kiss her if he wanted to. 'Thank you.' He straightened up abruptly, got his balance, feeling his face go red. 'Like I was saying,' he continued gruffly, 'I really don't know that much about kids.'

Holly squinted at the guy, aware of her hand clutching his waist, and the way she could feel his minty breath on her cheek. 'Pardon?' How could he not know about childhood activities, or kids? 'But you're got one!'

'What? What are you—? Ah.' Letting out an exasperated sigh, he gently disentangled himself from her, and hobbled back over

13

to the wall. 'Jasper,' he called, 'come here please.'

Jasper waved, and started back toward them.

Pulling his hat off, Jasper's dad scrubbed a tanned hand through his thick dark hair, which was starting to curl. She did *not* want to run her fingers through it. Okay, maybe she did a tiny bit, because he was kind of cute when he wasn't frowning, scowling or grumbling, and he had lovely long eyelashes, but he wasn't really her type. She preferred blond sunny guys with open expressions and the preppy college look. Grumps need not apply.

'Well,' she tried to hide her confusion behind an uncertain smile, 'I suppose a lot of parents go through a steep learning curve.' She had two nephews who'd definitely put her older sister through some challenging times.

'He's not mine.' He explained, putting an arm around Jasper's narrow shoulders as the boy appeared beside him. Looking down, his wry smile communicated *you little tinker*. Jasper pulled a *you got me* face and smiled back hopefully. 'I'm his godfather, Noel.' He explained, looking back at Holly. 'And while I spend time with him whenever I can, I'm hardly an expert when it comes to kids.'

'Oh, right.' She paused, something in her melting at the affection between them. Noel clearly hated skating but had brought Jasper here anyway. Perhaps he wasn't so bad. *Irrelevant, get back on track.* 'Well in that case maybe you can ask his dad? Or I can talk to him? If he understands how talented Jasper might be-'

'That won't be possible.' His face settled into a blank *Keep Out: This Ski Trail is Closed,* expression.

'Why not?'

'He's working.'

'We could call him—'

'Pleeeeasseee.' Jasper tugged on Noel's jacket, eyes wide and bottom lip stuck out. 'Please can you phone Daddy-'

'Nope. Sorry. Not now, kid. He's not available. The best I can do is try and talk to him tonight and see if he'll let you try some stuff tomorrow, if we come back.' He glanced down at the boy, his expression softening. 'Why don't you skate a bit, Jay, while Holly and I talk. Stay close, okay?'

'Kay,' grinning mischievously, Jasper started skating in a semi-circle, pushing himself off the wall behind Noel, flying past them to touch the wall a few feet beyond Holly, turning and launching himself back to the wall beside Noel again.

'Look, I'm sure he'd enjoy learning from you,' dropping his voice, Noel looked down at Holly and she realised with a flutter in her belly that he must be well over six foot, given he towered above her. 'But Ma- my friend isn't usually keen to let Jay participate in risky stuff. He's very protective.'

She gave him a quizzical look.

'Jay's mum died in a car accident.' Noel expanded quietly. 'Jasper and his sister were in the car when it happened.'

'Oh. Wow.' Holly tucked her hands into her trouser pockets. 'Poor things. It must be awful to lose a parent so young.'

Face tightening, Noel's voice dropped a few octaves. 'Yes. It is.'

'Still. It's really not that risky, learning a few spins. He's out on the ice anyway-'

'I get it, but it's not my decision to make.' He cast a look over at Jasper, who was still skating around them, getting closer but still not quite in earshot. 'Like I said,' he spoke quickly, 'I'll talk to his dad this evening and if he's okay with it, I'll bring Jasper back tomorrow and you can show him a few tricks then.' He looked positively depressed at the prospect.

'Thanks, I guess I'll have to be happy with that for now.' She paused, 'I take it you don't like, or enjoy, skating?'

'Hate it,' Noel agreed flatly, staring around the ice rink accusingly like it was a living thing.

'It's not the ice's fault!' she protested lightly.

'Obviously.' He turned his attention back to her. 'But I'm rubbish, that's all there is to it.'

'You're still learning—' she began.

'I know I'm a paying customer,' he said, dark brown eyes

amused, 'but come on, be honest.'

''Ncle Noel, 'ncle Noel!' Jasper paused, stomping his skates on the ice, 'I can stamp out the tune to the Teenage Mutant Ninja Turtles movie!'

'That's great kid,' Noel gave him a thumbs up, 'but be careful please.'

Holly smiled and picked up the ribbon of conversation as Jasper resumed skating in a half-moon around them. 'Well, you could definitely use some practice …' She backtracked at the glowering expression Noel gave her, 'Okay. Truthfully? You're not good. And I know you said you're not intending to work on your skating, and I get it, but it's still nice to be here, surely? It's so lovely and Christmassy,' she breathed, grinning, throwing her arms out. 'It's such a great atmosphere. Everyone's in a fantastic mood. Well, almost everyone.'

He studied her, eyes narrowing. 'Personally I can't think of anything worse than all this,' he edged forward as Jasper narrowed his semi-circle, getting closer to Holly and Noel each time he tapped the wall, 'festive rubbish. I'm just here for him.'

'Festive rubbish?' she squeaked, 'You don't like Christmas either?' she could hear the horror coating her voice and this conversation was probably getting too personal, but she couldn't leave it there.

'It's an expensive exercise in commercialism,' he replied. As she opened her mouth to respond, he held up a hand, palm out. 'Before you say it, yeah, I'm being bah-humbug. Guilty.'

'I don't know what to say. That's really sad. I just see it as a time of giving, fun and spending time with friends and fam—'

'I can do without the lecture, thanks, but generally speaking people are in a great mood because it's an excuse to drink alcohol, eat lots and have time off work.'

'Woah. That's a bit strong. Maybe you just need to experience the joys of Christmas.'

'See the wonder of it through a child's eyes, you mean?' he quipped, unzipping his coat.

Obviously this guy had a cynical streak a snow-covered mountain-peak wide.

'Perhaps.' She muttered, gliding nearer as Jasper brushed her arm. 'Or maybe … is there a reason you don't like Christmas? Are there bad memories, or—?'

'It's really none of your business, and please don't psychoanalyse me. Despite us joking about counselling, I don't need therapy. I don't mind other people enjoying Christmas, I just don't want to be forced too as well. I mean,' he pointed at the enormous Christmas tree, 'look at that. Is it really necessary?'

She flushed. This guy was deeply unhappy about the whole thing. Well, each to their own, and he was right, he was a customer – the last thing she wanted was a complaint. She was enjoying this job too much. 'Maybe not necessary, but it's tradition, which to some people is important. Anyway, I'm sorry. I didn't mean to upset you.'

'I'm not upset. Don't worry about it.' He waved off her apology. Rubbed a hand along the back of his neck. 'Oh, man,' he muttered under his breath, 'I'm being an idiot.'

A waft of sexy male aftershave hit Holly at the same time as his admission, and something tingled in her belly. She realised how close they were, only a foot spanning the space between them, thanks to Jasper's game. Her eyes wandered over his face, noticing that actually he had a lovely firm jaw line, with a slight coating of stubble. She gulped. Shame he was such a Scrooge. Not that she was really into dating at the moment. She planned to be immersed in her new business for the next few months, or years, if that was what it took.

Noel suddenly lurched toward her, as Jasper ran into the back of him. 'Oof! Jasper!'

He grabbed Holly's shoulders so as not to crash into her, and she braced her hands against his chest so that they didn't head-butt each other. She caught another waft of sexy aftershave.

Jasper giggled and skated away in a figure of eight.

'I am so …' Noel trailed off as he stared down at Holly.

She held her breath, aware of the firmness of his chest under his woolly green jumper, the way her fingers were clinging to the soft material.

Shaking his head, looking confused, he tried again. 'I'm sorry. He's a handful sometimes. And I'm sorry I snapped.' Stepping back carefully, he made an effort to smile, and the corners of his eyes crinkled slightly. 'It's not you at all. It's completely me. I shouldn't have spoken to you like that. It's just that I've had the same conversation with people for years. It's getting boring. Not to mention frustrating. Christmas just stresses me out.' He touched her arm, and she swore she could feel the heat of it through her waterproof top, which should *not* be possible.

She dropped her arms and tucked her hands in her trouser pockets. 'Fair enough.'

'Really?' he looked surprised, quickly followed by suspicious.

'It's your choice.' Holly shrugged. 'And I get it; people going on at you about the same thing over and over can drive you a bit barmy. My mum does it all the time about the skating. I've just learnt to listen, nod in the right places and then do my own thing anyway. Works wonders for my stress levels.'

'Maybe I'll try that,' he mused. 'But I mean it,' he insisted. 'I am sorry. And I'm not like this about everything, honest. You should see me in the summer. I can tell jokes with the best of them.' He smiled. 'I know a good one about a health and safety officer who walks into a bar—'

'You don't have to convince me of your comedy value,' she shook her head, 'it's fine. Hopefully Jasper can come back tomorrow, but if he can't, he can't. Enjoy the rest of your afternoon.' She'd done all she could, and would just have to see if they'd show up the next day.

'Wait, I—' he caught hold of Holly's sleeve as she went to skate away backwards.

Jasper appeared next to them, stopping with a spray of ice.

18

'Can we go have a hot drink 'Ncle Noel? I'm cold.' He chattered his teeth to demonstrate how much. 'Pleeeeease.'

Despite her desire to leave, and that she should be asking Noel to let her go, Holly smiled. The little boy was a real cutie.

'And can pretty Holly come with us please?' He turned to her, eyes bright. 'I want you to say about ice skating. And your cups and trophies.'

'I—'she gazed at Noel over the boy's head. *Oh, help*. 'I'm sure you can manage without me. I'm due a break but—'

'Please join us.' Noel said, to her bewilderment. 'If you can.' *I'm exhausted*, he mouthed, rolling his eyes. 'The drink is on me.' *Please*, his brown eyes begged, in much the same way Jasper had pleaded with him a moment before. He obviously wasn't used to looking after kids, and needed a break from Jasper's steady stream of random chatter and demands. 'I'll be nice,' he promised.

She decided to take pity on him. But only to make his godson happy. 'Okay.' *It's at a price*, her eyes sparkled back. 'They do a nice hot chocolate or cream tea in the Fortnum's Lodge.'

'Yay!' Jasper hopped up and down, 'Yay, yay, yay.'

She noticed Noel swallow at the brand, and could almost see a cash register in his brain ringing up the bill, but to his credit he simply nodded. 'Sounds good to me. The lodge is in the West Wing right, just behind us?'

Nodding, 'Have you been here before?'

'No, I looked up the floor-plan online.'

'You're a guy who likes to be prepared.'

'I don't like the unexpected.' He said, looking serious. 'I like to know where I am, where I'm going, what's happening.'

Holly stared at him. 'Sounds like you're talking about more than maps of Somerset House. But surely you can't always know where you are, where you're going or what's going to happen.'

'I don't see why not.'

'Life isn't like that,' she shook her head, 'it's messy and complicated. You can never know what's around the corner.'

19

'I can't think like that. I couldn't think of anything worse.'

'But,' she drifted closer to him, 'the unexpected things are the best parts.'

'They are? Why?'

'Because they usually end up being the fun or exciting bits, or the times you learn the most about yourself, or your friends or family.'

'That's very idealistic,' he replied, his dark gaze fluttering over her mouth before returning to her eyes, 'but an interesting way of looking at it.'

Feeling her cheeks warm, she grinned to hide how flustered she felt. 'You know I'm right, despite that lukewarm reply. Now let's get going, I can't be too long.'

Signalling to a fellow Ice Marshall colleague that she was taking a break, Holly tapped on the face of her sports watch and held both hands up twice. He nodded in reply and waved back at her, grey hair catching the bluey-purple spotlights spanning the rink.

Spinning around, she got off the ice and took a seat in the Skate Entrance building, Noel and Jasper following close behind. Rapidly unlacing her skates, she encouraged Jasper to do the same. 'Come on, the quicker we get our shoes on, the quicker you can have a hot chocolate. Race you.'

'While you two do that, I think I'll get rid of a few layers.' Noel said above her. 'I'm sure it'll be a lot warmer inside the main building.'

Holly heard rustling and when she straightened up, skates in hand, her eyes widened. Who'd have known he'd have such gorgeous broad shoulders in that clinging green jumper and amazingly taut, muscular thighs in snug black jeans?

'If you come back tomorrow,' she muttered, 'you might want to try wearing trousers that aren't so …' she got her breathing under control with a effort, 'tight.'

Huh. It was obviously too long since she'd pulled if she was finding the Grinch of Christmas Present so damn attractive.

A few minutes later, Holly lead Jasper over to grey double doors with a red sign hanging above it, *Fortnum's Lodge at the Christmas Arcade* in bold white lettering. Noel was trailing a few feet behind. He loved Jay, but his boundless energy could be challenging. At least Jasper was practically attached to Holly's hip, giving Noel a break.

'Thank you for saying I'm pretty, Jasper,' Holly pulled the door open for the boy, motioning him ahead of her, 'it was very nice of you.'

Swivelling his head, Jasper gave her a toothy smile. 'S'okay. You are. Melody's pretty too, but she has darker hair. You look a bit like Rapunzel out of Aimee's book but I don't think your hair is long enough.'

Holly ran a hand down over her pale blonde ponytail, which reached the middle of her back. 'My hair is long, but I agree a prince couldn't use it to climb the side of a tower. Who's Aimee?'

Scrunching up his face like he'd eaten something icky, 'My big sister.'

'Oh,' she bit her lip, 'I see. Right, go and pick a table.' She gestured around the wooden floored room they'd stepped into with its high square tables and bronze effect metal stools with rectangular backs. It was connected to another space that was meant to be a pop-up version of the Fortnum and Mason store in Piccadilly, fresh nuts and fruit arranged next to neat rows of green and teal boxes of tea and other dried goods.

'Cool.' Jasper raced over to the corner of the room and clambered up onto a stool.

'What a charmer.' Holly smiled at Noel. 'Sure to be a heart-breaker.'

'Yeah, he's much better with the ladies than I am,' he joked, but knew there was an edge to his voice, 'takes after his dad and uncle.' Matt and Stephen were usually the ones who got the girls. He was the wingman, the quiet afterthought. Matt had told him to try smiling more, engage in conversation. Stephen, younger and brasher, had taken a different tack. 'If you stopped scowling

21

and looking so flipping miserable, you might get more action.'
Thanks so much, mate.

He did all right if he wanted to. He just wasn't that bothered most of the time. He liked being alone. Avoid the complication, minimise the risks.

'So.' Holly said as they threaded their way through the tables. 'Pretty ironic that someone who hates Christmas is named after it.'

'Hilarious.' Noel dead-panned, sliding onto the stool next to Jasper, trying to work out how to avoid the questions she was sure to ask. The air smelt of cinnamon, and the steam rising from jugs of hot milk staff members were heating up and pouring into mugs. The clatter of cutlery and conversations created a lively din.

'So, one of your parents must have liked Christmas?' Holly prompted, sitting down opposite him.

Yep, just as he'd expected. He shifted in his chair and picked up a menu. 'What's good in here?'

Holly blinked at his deflection, then shrugged. 'You can make it merry; they do a mean tipsy hot chocolate, or there's mulled cider, and you can get champagne and truffles or cream tea as part of Skate Extra,' at his blank look she explained, 'packages you can book. And their signature drink is the Fortnum's Bees Knees cocktail I think … but seeing as it's only half past three it's probably a bit early for that.'

'Yeah, and you're also showing what you spend your evenings doing,' he replied cheekily, 'but what else is good?'

'Everything really. The standard hot chocolates are nice; you can add whipped cream, chocolate shavings and marshmallows.'

Jasper started humming noisily and swinging his legs, attracting attention from the family at the next table who were feasting on a delicious looking chocolate fondue.

'What are you going to have, Jay?' Noel asked. 'Hot chocolate?'

Jasper nodded, his humming increasing. Then he stopped. 'What is there to do in here? Are there any toys?'

Noel hesitated. Come clean or try and fudge something? 'No,

not really, this is a café really but—'

'I'm bored, did you bring my iPad?'

'No, because we came to skate,' Noel said patiently.

'But Melody always—'

'Why don't we order and then we can—' his voice broke halfway through the sentence.

'Have you ever seen this before?' Holly exclaimed, pulling a smartphone from her pocket and quickly tapping the screen. 'Look at this cool app.'

'What is it?' Jasper scooched nearer to her.

'It's a tracker for Santa. On Christmas Eve you can see where he is as he travels around the world delivering presents.'

'Woah, really?' he bounced up and down in his seat, using his new favourite word. 'Cool.'

Noel rolled his eyes at Holly. 'Now you've done it,' he murmured in a low voice.

Holly carried on what she was doing but to his surprise stuck a small pink tongue out at him. 'Yep, really.' She turned back to Jasper, 'And you can even see where he is now, at his home in the North Pole. Look,' she handed the phone over, showing him where to press for more information, 'but it only works for good boys and girls. So you need to let your uncle sort out the drinks nicely.' She threw a look at Noel and he got the hint. She was good. He went and spoke with a member of staff and within minutes they each had a luxurious hot chocolate in front of them, the heat of the milk quickly melting the generous lashings of whipped cream.

Noel wrapped his hands around the drink and chilled out while Holly and Jasper chatted about ice skating. It would soon be time for him to take another turn on the ice before taking Jay home, giving him dinner and trying to wrestle him into bed at a sensible time. At least he was going to be doing it at Matt's pad in Knightsbridge rather than attempting to somehow shoehorn Jasper into his tiny flat in Camden.

'So, what do you like most about Christmas?' Holly was quizzing

Jasper as Noel turned his attention back to their conversation.

'I like the tree, and decorations, and sweets and presents and games and being with Daddy! And sometimes Aimee when she's not reading, or telling me what to do.' The boy rocked back and forth in his chair, a cream moustache coating his top lip. 'What about you?' he asked Holly.

Noel swore he could already see devotion in the boy's eyes, as Jasper waited for Holly's response.

'I like crackling log fires,' Holly replied, face glowing, 'and drinking eggnog. Being with my family to see them open their gifts, then watching Bond films and Disney classics on TV, cracking open nuts and filling up on Quality Street and After Eights. I also like the excuse for big hugs on a cold day, and mistletoe hanging in unexpected places.' She slid a sideways glance at Noel. 'There are lots of good things about Christmas.'

Noel sighed. Despite what she'd said about respecting his wishes, he was sure she was making a play for converting him. But she was nice, really nice. It made him feel bad about the partial lie he'd told her about the reason for Jay not being able to learn tricks, in terms of Matt being overprotective. The core of the truth was that because of who Matt was, he wouldn't want Jasper attracting any attention. He was all about keeping his kids out of the spotlight, not thrusting them into it.

'Noel?' Holly waved a hand in front of his face.

'Hmm? Sorry I was thinking about something.' He zoned back in. 'What did you say?'

'That there are lots of good things about Christmas.'

'Oh yeah, hugs and mistletoe.' He paused, a sudden image of kissing her under a bunch of small white berries and green leaves springing into his head. He shifted in his seat, wishing for looser jeans. 'I suppose it might have some compensations.' He agreed slowly, looking at her intently and raising an eyebrow.

Holly blushed, then shook her head. 'I—I'm going to have to go,' she jumped off her stool. 'Thank you for the hot chocolate, Noel,' she gave him a tight, polite smile but turned a megawatt grin on Jasper, so he was in no doubt whose company she'd preferred, 'it was lovely meeting you. I really hope I see you tomorrow. If not, have a great Christmas.' She held a hand out to the boy and they shook solemnly. 'Take care,' she backed away, and ran out the door.

And with that she was gone, Noel staring after her bewildered, with a *goodbye, thanks for everything,* dying on his lips.

***

Holly skidded to a grinding halt on the ice, much less graceful than her usual style. So they were back then. She'd spent half the day hoping Jasper and Noel would return so she could spend more time with the boy and get him started on some basic spins if his dad okayed it, and the other half dreading them showing up. She'd made an idiot of herself yesterday running out so abruptly, but the look Noel had given her had been unnerving in intensity. The last time a guy had looked at her that way it had ended in heartbreak. Hers.

Still, they were heading over, so she'd better suck it up and be polite.

She'd just have to ignore the flutter of excitement mixed with nerves in the pit of her stomach.

'Jasper! It's so cool to see you again,' she crouched down on her skates, tucking her hands into her armpits to keep them warm. It was colder today than the previous day, but she didn't like wearing gloves, it didn't feel right. She'd always skated bare-handed. 'I wondered where you'd got to yesterday.'

'Hi, Holly,' Jasper touched her shoulder shyly, 'Daddy said you can show me some things later today, if he can come and watch.'

'Excellent. I'm on split shift today because I'm working the club night tonight though. Do you know when he might come down?'

'He said around five or six,' Noel addressed the top of her head, and she craned her neck to gaze up at him. 'And it took a lot of convincing for Matt to say yes, and come down. A lot.'

He was wearing a hat pulled down over his dark hair again, but his coat looked thinner – it might be thermal – and he wasn't as bundled up, his blue jeans baggier than the black ones had been. He'd followed her advice about less restrictive clothing then. But he still looked far too good, far too appealing.

'That might work. You and Jasper managed it then.'

'Yes, and hi again,' he smiled down at her. 'I also managed to convince Jasper to cut me a break after our drinks yesterday. Which is why you didn't see us afterwards.'

'Hi again to you too,' she rose slowly, watching as Jasper started skating rings around them. 'So how did you manage that?'

Noel eyed the boy warily, extending his arms slightly to balance. 'I asked nicely and made him an offer he couldn't refuse.'

'Did it by any chance include a certain fast food chain?' she teased, thinking of her sister's favourite bribe for her sons.

'I couldn't possibly comment,' he shot back, 'except to say that I used all the charm and patience at my disposal—'

She pulled a face.

'Hey!' Noel protested, 'I know I was a bit grouchy about the whole Christmas thing, but—'

''Ncle Noel bought me a Happy Meal yesterday, Holly,' the boy trilled as he slid past.

She laughed at the look of consternation on Noel's face. 'Busted!'

He burst into laughter. 'Oh well, it was worth a shot! Anyway, I think Matt should make it, he's been working pretty hard the last few days, so he kind of promised Jasper he'd be here. If you can show the kid a few things, I'd appreciate it …' he went quiet, a funny expression stealing over his face, 'And I'm sorry if anything I said yesterday made you feel awkward—'

'Oh, not at all,' she said quickly, 'why would you think that?'

'Just the way you left so suddenly.'

'I didn't want to be late back from my break, that's all. I love this job.' Nice save, Holly.

'Clearly,' he paused, 'still, would you mind sparing us a few minutes of your break later on? Jasper is keen to have a look around the rest of Somerset House and although I know the layout of the four main wings and the new one, I probably can't make it come to life for him like you can.'

Holly frowned, biting her lip. It was an innocent enough request, and she didn't have an issue giving up part of her break or spending time with Jasper, it was his godfather she wasn't sure about spending more time with. Noel made her feel so unsettled. She'd almost called one of her best friends, Carly, to talk it through last night. But what would she have said? *I met a guy but he's closed off and sensible and hates Christmas and I don't want to get involved with anyone anyway.* What a waste of breath that would have been.

'Don't worry,' Noel dismissed, turning his focus on Jasper. 'It was just an idea.' His body language and tone said casual, but a red tinge started creeping up the back of his neck between his collar and hat.

'No, it's okay,' she scrambled for an excuse, feeling bad for hesitating. And after all, what could it hurt? 'I'd be happy to do it, it's just I'm not that qualified. I don't really know about any of the art stuff in the North Wing, or the history of the place. I only really know parts of the South and East Wings. But I could walk you around those and show you my favourite things if you want. I was thinking about timings too. I could be free in an hour or so?'

'Great,' he beamed at her, and it was such an open, happy expression compared to the scowls of yesterday he looked like a different guy.

'Okaayyy,' she said slowly, 'I'll tell you when. In the meantime, do you need any help?'

'No, thanks, I'm still not interested in learning to skate. But I am wearing plasters and extra thick socks. I've got blisters the size of the London Eye,' he joked.

'Poor baby,' she replied before she could censor herself. 'I'm thinking that may be a slight exaggeration though.' *Stop flirting. He's not your type, remember. You've got other more important things to be focusing on.*

'It's possible. So, what about you? Don't you get blisters, skating around all day?'

'I was a professional figure-skater, my heels are rock solid.' Wow, that sounded so attractive.

'You were?' he looked confused.

'I told Jasper yesterday. Weren't you listening?'

'Obviously not,' he said sheepishly, 'sorry. So what were you, regional?'

'International, medal-winning,' she enjoyed seeing the shock on his face, 'I had sponsorship deals and everything.' Now it sounded like she was showing off, when all she was doing was stating facts.

'You did? I don't remember you.'

'It was a few years ago,' she glanced down at the ice, digging a toe-pick into it, a nervous habit from her childhood, 'and if you didn't follow the sport, it's not surprising you wouldn't know who I was.'

'Is it classified as a sport? I always thought it was just dancing,' he spun a finger round in a circle, 'on ice.'

'Figure-skating takes stamina, athleticism and agility, not to mention being fearless,' she flared, old sensitivities rising, 'it was the first winter sport included in the Olympics in the early 1900's. Have you ever had the ice whistling past your head while doing a death spiral? Until you've tried it, don't tell me it's not a sport.'

'Hey, I didn't mean to cause offence,' Noel held up both hands, 'I'm really sorry. Genuinely. I just don't know about this kind of stuff. It's ignorance, nothing else.'

Holly took a deep breath, seeing the sincerity in his chestnut brown eyes. 'I'm sorry for snapping. I'm just so used to some people not getting it …'

'That's okay. We all have our things, the ones that catch us on the raw, like me and Christmas. But I have nothing but respect for skaters in terms of the danger involved; when I've caught it in passing on TV the sight of people being twirled and thrown around in the air, and those razor sharp skates skimming past people's ears …' he shuddered. 'The health and safety side of me goes on full alert. There must be an incredible amount of injuries every year.'

'Oh, loads,' she agreed, 'in terms of minor ones; banged knees, scraped skin, sprained ankles and wrists. Fortunately there aren't that many serious ones, involving heads and backs. But then, it's not always the major ones you have to worry about.' She dug her toe-pick deeper into the ice, working a dent into it.

'Is that what happened to you?' Noel asked softly. 'I assume you don't figure-skate professionally any more.'

She frowned.

'You said was, in the past tense.'

'I'd rather not talk about it, but in short, yes that's what happened. It doesn't matter though,' she forced a smile, 'I have other plans now.'

'Good for you.'

'Yes.'

There was a silence as they gazed at each other.

'I'd better-' Noel broke eye contact and scanned the ice for Jasper. 'Where's he gone?' he muttered.

'Yes, I need to,' Holly caught a sharp glance from a manager who was walking past with a stack of pale blue SKATE flyers, 'get back to work.' How had she neglected her duties for so long? 'Do you see him?'

'Yes,' Noel huffed with relief, 'he's weaving around that group over there.' He pointed to the other side of the rink. 'Stay there Jay, I'm coming!' he yelled, then raised an eyebrow at Holly. 'Thank god I didn't lose him. That would be awful.'

'Yes, losing people is pretty brutal,' she agreed, sure that they were talking about more than a four year old boy going walkabout when a darkness settled over Noel's face.

29

'Anyway,' he turned and picked his way carefully over to the plastic wall, starting to pull himself around the edge of the rink towards Jasper, 'I'll see you later.'

'See you later,' Holly echoed, as Noel stop-started away, his broad-shouldered, long-legged body somehow looking forlorn. She had a mad urge to skate after him and hug him, though they hardly knew each other.

Weird. Unexpected. Scary.

'So, you've been in the Fortnum's Lodge in the West Wing, and you know there are shops in the Christmas Arcade too?' Holly turned to Noel as he and Jasper trailed along behind her.

'Yes,' Noel nodded, hooking a quick hand into the hood of Jasper's coat as he made to dance off somewhere. 'We had a quick look as we left yesterday.'

''Ncle Noel bought me some sweets, and Daddy told him off,' Jasper ratted him out.

'He did not tell me off, cheeky, he just said they would make you hyper!'

'And?' Holly looked at Noel, eyes shining with amusement. He wondered how he'd ever thought of her as an ice princess. She was one of the most engaging people he'd ever met.

He mumbled something under his breath.

'Pardon?' she leaned closer and he inhaled her perfume, something fresh and sexy.

'I said, it took me over an hour to get him to bed last night.'

She let out a giggle. 'Hilarious.'

'Yeah, right. So come on, show us around.'

'No problem,' the look she gave him quite plainly said *you lost that one,* but she let it slide. 'As I said, I don't know much, but Somerset House was established as a charity in 1997 as an arts and culture hub to enhance the education of the general public. It's also meant to maintain the historic buildings. Apparently they're of English national heritage interest. The public programme includes open air films, festivals and art exhibitions, but other than that I can't tell you any more. You'd have to come back for a guided tour for that.' She smiled over her shoulder at him, gesturing to one of several sets of double pale grey doors of the South Wing facing the rink. 'But I'll tell you about my favourite bits, like Rizzoli's bookshop. It's got illustrated subject books and gorgeous home-made cards, pads and other stationery. In here.' She led them into a lovely shop with white walls, shelves and displays of books, puzzles, notepads, pens and knitted Christmas toys laid out on antique wooden tables, decorated with red berry wreaths, seasonal prints and posters. The shop was arranged in a series of connected rooms, and they were in there for five long minutes, Noel browsing at the same time as trying to stop Jasper from touching the merchandise and asking for everything. Several times he let out exasperated breaths, and caught Holly holding back smiles.

'I know a little girl who will like this.' He showed Holly an embroidered journal, with something about dreaming, planning and doing on the spine. 'Do you mind?' he jerked his chin at Jasper.

'No, that's fine. I'll take him along the corridor into the main lobby of this wing. Just use the door over there,' she gestured opposite the till, 'rather than the one back out into the courtyard. Turn right.'

'Thanks,' he nodded. For an instant he wondered if he should trust Holly with his godson but when she smiled down at the little boy and squeezed his shoulder, he relaxed. He was just being paranoid.

A few minutes later he found them relaxing in matching curved black leather chairs, exactly where Holly had said they'd be. 'This is another favourite spot.' She explained, smiling lazily up at him. 'I mean, there are some great places to eat in here, like Tom's Kitchen, and Fernandez and Wells in the East Wing, where they do mean mince pies and hot dogs, but I like sitting here and people watching. Seeing their faces. And this is pretty cool,' she pointed her thumb at the wall behind her head, where there was

31

a painting in an alcove, something grey and orange with antlers on top. He stepped closer to read the writing next to it, absently resting his hand on her shoulder. She fidgeted under his touch as he read the quote from T*he Lion, The Witch and The Wardrobe* out loud, about the Snow Queen and it always being winter but never Christmas.

'A bit like you'd have it,' Holly jumped up, shuffling a few feet away and catching hold of Jasper's sleeve as he leapt out of his seat, 'imagine that.'

'Wrong actually,' Noel smiled wryly, 'I'd have it always summer and never Christmas.'

'Silly me, of course you would,' she let go of Jasper and swung away, heading for a pair of doors that lead outside, but on the opposite side of the building to the courtyard. 'Right,' she called, 'time for one last thing before I have to get back to work.' She threw open the right-hand door with an unintended bang, 'Oops! Every time,' and headed outside and down a flight of wide stone stairs. Throwing her arms out, she spun around as Noel and Jasper reached the bottom. 'The River Terrace,' she said, sounding content, 'with a view of the London Eye and Westminster.' She indicated the busy Thames, length of the stone terrace and rows of chairs and tables set out along it. 'I'm coming back here in the summer. I might not get on with the sun, but can you imagine how heavenly it will be when it's nice weather and people can sit out here enjoying it?' Her eyes lit up further. 'I wonder if they have weddings here. What a venue.'

'Woah, slow down, we've only just met,' Noel said playfully, though he immediately regretted his words when she uncomfortably checked her watch and avoided eye contact.

'I'd better go,' she murmured.

'I was joking, you don't have to run away.' Noel wandered over to her, resting his elbows on the stone balustrade and studying the grey-green depths of the river. Jasper was only a short distance away, running in circles with his arms outstretched, so it was easy to keep an eye on him.

Holly blew out a long breath, 'Sorry. I know you were.'

'Been burnt by a guy with commitment issues?'

'My ex-fiancé,' she stared over at the capsules on the London Eye. 'About the same time I found out I wouldn't be able to skate professionally again, he cut and run. We were too young to be engaged really, but still,' her eyebrows folded together, 'it was crappy of him and I loved him so it hurt, a lot.' She sighed. 'How about you? Been burnt by someone at Christmas, or was it a bereavement?'

Somehow the fact she wasn't looking at him made the question easier to answer. And while he didn't usually offload his baggage on people, she'd shared her angst, so it only felt fair to do the same in return. 'Both,' he admitted grimly, 'my long-term girlfriend and I broke up on Christmas Day two years ago, and it's also the anniversary of my mum's death. I was eight years old when she died.'

Checking Jasper's location over Noel's shoulder, Holly laid a hand on his arm. 'I'm sorry,' she said sympathetically, 'that's utterly awful and sad, on both counts.'

Turning to make direct eye contact, he was horrified to see pity in her eyes and the softness of her expression.

'Don't feel sorry for me!' He shook her hand away. 'I'm fine. I got over it a long time ago.'

'The way you hate Christmas says something different,' she pointed out, hurt shining in her eyes.

'It's not about that, I told you I just don't like or agree with all the commercial rubbish and pressure.' He could feel his teeth gritting, but he wasn't sure how to stop the anger building.

She went to answer, but instead flew past him to yank Jasper down off the wall he'd been trying to climb, a ten foot drop to the street below his likely destination. 'Jasper, no!'

'Jay! You're a liability. Honestly.' He eased the boy out of Holly's arms and unclenched his jaw. 'Thanks. I'd better get him inside before he causes more trouble. And thank you for showing us around. We enjoyed it. I'll catch you later.' Slinging the boy over his shoulder, he took the stairs into Somerset House two at a time without looking back at Holly.

Aware he'd left her standing there, open mouth and wide eyed.

'That was incredible, Jasper.' The dark haired man patted his son on the back after watching him perform a few spins. Holly had spent only an hour showing them to him at the end of her first shift. 'Thank you so much,' Jasper's dad turned to her, 'I really appreciate it.' He grinned charmingly, forest green eyes twinkling.

'No problem,' she said faintly.

'Come on, Jasper,' he turned to his son, 'let's go do a few laps around the rink.'

Holly stared after them. She'd known Jasper would pick the skating up quickly, but what was flooring her, what was making her heart squeeze up her chest and into her throat, was who his father was.

She turned accusing eyes on Noel where he was lounging against the other side of plastic wall, and skated over to him. '*Matt Reilly* is Jasper's dad? *Matt Reilly* is your best friend?'

'One of my best friends.' He corrected, straightening and plunging his hands into his coat pockets. 'But uh,' he cast his eyes up as if the darkening indigo sky contained all sorts of interesting things, 'yes.'

'Matt Reilly. *The* Matt Reilly. Mega-famous, mega-rich music producer. The guy in all the magazines—'

'Yes, all right, I get it.' He dropped his gaze back to hers. 'He's got the wow factor.' His jaw clenched, 'And you think I should have told you, but if I had, security precautions would have clicked in because Matt's so overprotective and I wanted Jasper to have normality, just for a few days, while his nanny is away. You wait and see, as soon as Matt thinks people are clocking who he is, he'll take Jasper and vanish.'

34

Holly watched Matt and Jasper skate around the rink, arms down by their sides. 'Still …'

'Be cross if you want, but I was thinking of Jasper. Like I said earlier, it took a lot of persuasion for me to be able to bring Jasper back and let you work with him. Matt seriously dislikes anything drawing attention to his kids.'

'I—I guess I can't judge. You know him better than I do. And I suppose you were keeping it from me for the right reasons. Still, I wished you'd told me, you can trust me—'

'We hardly know each other,' Noel stepped back, voice cold, 'I've had people I know and trust far more than you let me down.'

Direct hit. It was a good thing she wasn't seriously interested in him, or that one may have hurt. The sharp sensation in her side was a stitch. Just a stitch.

His eyes flickered over the top of her head. 'As predicted,' he nodded at Matt, who was beckoning to Jasper to hurry up as a couple of people started to notice them, 'time to go.'

'Noel, wait—'

'Yes?' he bit, face hard.

There were so many things she could say but Matt was bearing down on them fast, and Noel looked so unwelcoming she doubted he'd listen anyway. 'Nothing, you'd better go. Take care then.' She spun away quickly.

She didn't wish him a Merry Christmas, there was no point. Besides, there was work to do.

'Bye,' he said to her back, and there was a tone to his voice that hinted he wanted to say more. But when she checked over shoulder, he was already striding away with Matt, both their heads down, Jasper between them. That was it then. He was gone.

Making her way into the skate entrance building she stomped off to staff quarters to have a rest and something to eat before getting ready for the club night.

Her eyes stung and she knew moral support was needed. Pulling her phone out, she tapped the screen. 'Carly? It's me. Fancy coming clubbing with a difference tonight?'

Noel leaned up against the rink wall by the oversized Christmas tree, hands stuffed in his pockets for warmth, face burrowed in the depths of his navy scarf. He must be mad, standing in the freezing cold like this.

He hadn't planned to be here. Originally he was supposed to be at home, like he usually was on Christmas Eve, drinking beer, eating a take-away and watching unashamedly non-Christmassy TV. Then Matt had persuaded him to spend a few hours with him and the kids, and this year for some reason Noel had softened and agreed. But as he'd stared blankly at the crackling flames and logs in Matt's fireplace, he'd known he couldn't leave it like that with Holly. So unfinished. He hadn't thanked her properly for everything she'd done for Jasper, or – even as he thought it, he realised how true it was – told her how much he'd enjoyed her company. He'd got up from his chair and found Matt in the kitchen.

'Look, Matt, I need to—'

'Don't tell me. You've changed your mind and are heading home to hibernate,' his friend joked as he made coffee using the space-age looking machine. It probably cost more than Noel earned in a month.

'No. But I am heading out for a while.'

'You going back for the girl? I saw the way you looked at her.'

He thought about denying it but settled on a shrug. 'She's nice. And I just need to clear the air, that's all.'

'Right. Still flying the *no complications* flag then?'

He avoided an answer, because he wasn't sure he knew it himself. 'I hardly think you're one to talk, mate.' He smiled to take the sting out of it, 'I'll see you a bit later.'

Matt threw a bunch of keys across the kitchen. 'Take the P1, and park in my usual space at the hotel.'

'Thanks.' Noel caught the keys and pocketed them. Matt drove an environmentally friendly Prius but had a few other cars and had insured him and Stephen on them all a long time ago. The P1 was Noel's favourite; sleek, sexy, low to the ground and fast.

Stephen charged in, shrugging into his jacket. 'I'm coming too,' he insisted. 'I want to have a look at the hot blonde totty who's taught Jasper all these tricks. Maybe she can teach me a few things.'

'That's not what I said about her,' Matt protested.

Noel threw Stephen a dirty look. 'I don't think so.' He ground out. 'She's far too nice for you.'

'Come on,' Stephen spread his hands, 'I'm not that bad am I? I wine and dine the ladies.'

Silence greeted his comment. They all knew that while he was good at romancing women initially, he was not good at anything that came after that. Like returning their calls, being honest with them or telling them when the relationship was over.

'Thanks.' Stephen sighed heavily, green eyes mocking. 'Can I come if I promise to behave?'

Noel blew out a breath. 'If I say no, are you going to turn up at Somerset House anyway?'

'Of course.'

'You might as well get a ride with me then.'

'So where is she then?' Stephen asked now, jumping up to sit on the plastic wall, ignoring the dirty look he got from a passing member of staff. He seemed unaffected by the cold, leather jacket open over a white open necked shirt.

'I don't know,' Noel scowled as the DJ started a club anthem up, lights starting to spin across the ice.

He looked around, unable to see her in the heaving crowds of skaters and spectators. And then he did.

Wow.

Jasper had asked Noel to help hang the Christmas stockings above the fireplace the night before, but as Holly skated gracefully onto the ice, and Noel caught sight of an expanse of long, lean thigh encased in black tights below a short, twirly figure-skating dress it was a different type of stocking he was thinking of. Black

37

sheer stockings that ended as lacy hold-ups on upper thighs, leaving inches of bare skin sexily bare below lacy black knickers … he gulped. *Shit*. He had the hots for Holly. Pity he'd blown it by acting like such a cold bastard earlier.

He watched as she helped someone up off the ice, and then checking she had enough room, went into a series of spins and jumps to the beat of a remixed Ellie Goulding track. Some kind of diamanté studding on her skates flashed and caught the lights and the way she moved her body was stunning. She had control and precision but a flair in the flick of her arms. The way she went so low down to the ice with one leg bent in front of her and the other extended behind, in what he now knew was called a drag – he'd googled figure-skating while at Matt's – was almost artistic. And at the same time, sexy as hell.

Stephen let out a loud whistle and looked at Noel. 'That's her, isn't it?' His grin was wide and knowing. 'She's gorgeous. Looks like an ice princess.' He dismounted and turned to scope Holly out some more, slapping Noel on the shoulder. 'If you don't, I will.'

'Don't you fucking dare,' he shot, returning Stephen's slap on the back with a gratifying *oof* from the younger man. He was shocked at how possessive he felt over Holly.

'Doing your principled bit, are you?' Stephen raised one eyebrow, looking taken aback. 'Fine. But don't try and pretend it's all about being noble. You want her too.'

Noel opened and closed his mouth a few times, but couldn't actually deny it. He did want her, and he really liked her. He just hadn't acknowledged it until now. She'd definitely managed to creep under his defences.

'I knew it,' Stephen crowed. 'Never mind, I'll find someone else. I always do.' He smiled arrogantly. Studying Noel's face under the strobes. 'So, what are you going to do about it?'

'No idea, Stephen. Not a clue.'

Carly slithered out onto the ice. It was the only way Holly could

38

think to describe it because her friend inevitably spent more time on her hands and knees, or bum, or spread-eagled on her stomach with her arms pulled in tight to her body to protect them, than upright.

Anyone else who was so bad at skating would look silly, but Carly was one of those girls who was effortlessly graceful and stylish. She made a pair of jeans and plain top look haute couture and Holly had never seen anyone look as devastating in a skirt, slim Bambi legs attracting the attention of every guy around.

'So what do you think?' Holly asked, gripping her friend's arm to steady her.

'Of?' Carly tossed her long black hair away from her face, pale skin looking Snow White-ish in the club lights.

'Of Noel.' She'd spotted him half an hour earlier, but was unsure whether to go and talk to him, and if she did, what she would say. Did he even warrant five minutes of her time after the way he'd spoken to her?

'Do you like him?' Carly challenged.

'I don't know,' Holly moaned. 'I didn't think so, and he was off with me earlier, but there's something about him. Sometimes he's pretty cool. Oh, I don't know. I don't even want a boyfriend so I don't know why I'm bothered.'

Her friend pursed her lips thoughtfully, running assessing hazel eyes over Noel, who was in animated conversation with a younger guy. 'He's kind of hot,' she grinned, 'but not your usual type.'

'Not in looks, no. But maybe my usual type is overrated?' Holly frowned. 'Never mind, this is making my head hurt. Come on, let's skate.'

'You know I can't skate,' Carly laughed, 'that's a really bad suggestion.'

'Yes, but you can stand still and concentrate on the dancing bit. We both know you can shake that booty.'

Carly grinned, 'Yep, we do. And yes, I can.'

Noel clutched a cup of non-alcoholic punch, watching Holly twirl around the rink. Her friend had gone home, and so had Stephen, thank god. The crowds had started drifting away and the music had been turned down once it hit ten. Club night was finishing early given it was Christmas Eve and the place was closed the next day. Holly was still on the ice though, eyes closed blissfully as she skated around. It was easy to see how much she loved it, how she got lost in the flow.

Then something went wrong. Her right knee seemed to lock and then fold. She turned white, wobbling and starting to go over, but just saved herself from falling by sinking down onto the ice on her bum. She clutched her knee, face contorted.

'Holly!' Noel ran over the ice in his trainers. Reaching her, he knelt down and ran careful hands over her leg, first-aid training kicking in. 'Where does it hurt? Is this better, or worse? Do you feel sick? Did you hit your head on the way down?'

She squirmed as he ran hot hands up and down her leg.

'No, I didn't hit my head. I'm fine, just in pain. It's the old injury. I've just overdone it. Noel,' she stilled his hands by laying hers on top of them. 'I just need to get home.'

She inhaled through her nose and blew out through her mouth, fighting to control the pain. Wincing, 'Mum is going to have a field day. She's been telling me not to skate so much. Fantastic.'

'If you're in a lot of pain you should go to A&E.'

She looked aghast. 'No way, not on Christmas Eve. Are you kidding? Scrub that, are you mad? It'll be heaving. I'm not waiting around for hours surrounded by drunks. I just need to get home and take an anti-inflammatory.'

'I really think that—'

'Noel.' Her blue eyes, when he looked into them, were calm. 'I've been here before. I know what I need; go home, medicate, and rest my knee. It'll be better in a few days' time.'

'I'll take you home then. I'm parked up just around the corner.'

'Haven't you been drinking?'

'Nothing alcoholic.'

'Right. But,' she pushed off the ice, wincing, 'I can probably tube it. I live in Wembley.'

'I'm driving you home,' he stated as he wrapped an arm around her waist and lifted her up, 'just accept it.'

She threaded an arm around his neck, staring up at him. Her cheeks reddened. 'Only if you're sure.'

'I am,' he nodded, picking his way carefully across the rink.

Holly hissed and muttered at regular intervals at his slow progress, but he ignored her and concentrated on getting off the ice safely. Once on the grey lino flooring, he sat her down and gingerly removed her skates, kneeling at her feet. 'All done.' He murmured, looking up at her.

'I – I, y – yes,' she stuttered, gazing down at him. Her pupils dilated in her ice-chip blue eyes, creamy skin darkening with a blush that swept up from her chest and into her face.

He felt his own temperature rise in response, and shifted uncomfortably. At least his jeans weren't as tight today. 'Are you all right? In much pain?'

Her expression cleared and she frowned. 'No. Yes. Can we please get on with it?' she asked thinly. 'The sooner we're on the road, the sooner I'll be at home with my prescribed drugs.'

Following her additional instructions, he found a manager drifting about starting to lock up, explained the situation and got Holly's belongings from her locker. He smiled. Who'd have thought that for once it was her being a grouch, instead of him?

To Holly's mortification, Noel insisted on carrying her to the car. She hid her face against his chest, just inside the collar of his coat. The streets were still busy, and it was difficult to ignore the wolf whistles and catcalls from party-goers, caused by both the way he was holding her and the amount of leg she had on show in her tiny figure-skating dress.

Even so, there was a pang of regret when he set her down

41

in the underground hotel car park next to some kind of black low-slung super-car. He'd smelt amazing, and in the end being held by him hadn't exactly been a sacrifice. The way he helped her into the expensive car, carefully sliding her injured knee in, then taking his coat off and tucking it under her leg to elevate it, really touched her.

'How are you feeling?' Noel asked, staring into her eyes. 'Ready to go?'

She nodded but was quiet on the way home other than giving him directions. The pain in her knee worsened with every movement of the car, even though he was driving sensibly, and she closed her eyes, nausea rolling across her in heavy waves. She did *not* want to throw up in a car like this; the damage would probably cause tens of thousands.

'It's snowing.' He remarked into the silence.

'Really?' her eyes fluttered open but she felt too ill to be enthusiastic.

'You really must be suffering,' he mused, 'if you can't even raise a smile for a white Christmas.'

'Tell me again later, after I've taken my painkillers.'

'Will do.' A silence, 'Holly?'

'Yeurgh?'

'Tell me your home address. You've been dozing for the last two minutes and we must be getting close.'

'Kay,' she murmured, clocking distantly that she sounded a bit like Jasper. Reciting the address, she let her head fall back against the chair in the cosy darkness, concentrating on not being sick.

Thirty seconds later, or at least that's what it felt like, although her watch said over five minutes had passed, she was back in Noel's arms, cold flakes of snow kissing her face.

He leaned on the doorbell, waiting several moments before pressing his elbow on it again.

She mumbled under her breath.

'What was that?'

'Said you still smell amazing!'

He laughed oddly. 'Pain has a strange effect on you by the look of things. Ah, um, hi!' he exclaimed as the door swung open. Light and noise, including seasonal music, spilled out into the front garden. 'I believe she belongs to you? She hurt her knee at the rink.'

'I ruddy knew it!' An exasperated voice said over her head. 'She never listens to me. She's so bloody stubborn.'

'Muuum,' Holly grimaced, and snuggled closer to Noel and comfort, and away from the fierce warmth emanating from the centrally heated terrace house which was making her feel sicker. 'Please, not now.'

'I can't think where she gets her stubbornness from,' another voice, this one amused, spoke over the top of her mum's.

'Hi, Dad,' her mouth curved.

Loud, rapid-fire barking joined in over the rabble and she waved a floppy hand in the air. 'Hi, Pudding. I love you too, but don't feel well, so please be quiet.'

Immediately the barking stopped.

Noel stood patiently as the large chocolate Labrador came out of the house, circled him and Holly three times, sniffed them both, gave Noel a half approving, half distrustful look then pranced into the house with his moist, dark brown nose in the air.

'He thinks he's a show pony, I swear.' Holly said, burrowing her face further into Noel's coat, making him smile.

'Come in, son,' Holly's dad ushered him into a narrow hallway, while his short, rounded wife made constant clucking sounds with her mouth, concern etched on her face. 'Second door on the right.' He told Noel. 'I'm Tom, by the way. We'll take her out to the back room, away from this rabble,' he explained as they went past a front room packed with milling people and loaded plates of food and bottles of drink lined up everywhere. 'She'll feel better after some cold water and fresh air. There are patio doors in there. She'll be fine, love,' he said, turning to his fretting wife,

43

'go and find her tablets.'

Noel caught sight of the dog standing in the doorway to the room Tom had indicated. *Hurry up for god's sakes*, his big brown eyes seemed to say, *we haven't got all night*. Noel nodded, readjusting Holly's weight and carrying her into the back room. Then he realised he'd taken instruction from a dog. He must be tired. Or going mad.

Tom was already ahead of them, throwing open the double patio doors so a fresh breeze swept through the room, bringing mini snow flurries in with it.

Noel settled Holly in the middle of one of the sofas facing the doors, with a pang of regret, sorry to have to put her down. She came to a little, when he guided her head down between her knees, complaining about the position hurting her leg.

'I know Holly, but the pain is making you feel sick and dizzy, so it's a good idea to get some blood pumping to your head.'

The Labrador seemed to agree with him, padding over and holding Holly's arm still when she tried to move by gripping the fabric of her sleeve gently between his front teeth.

'Here you go.' Holly's mum bustled in, holding out two sugar-coated tablets and a glass of iced water to Noel.

He stared at her.

'She seems to listen to you, so you can do the honours,' she bossed, dropping the tablets into his hand.

He studied them, then looked at the dog, who was watching him expectantly. Okay then. 'All right. But I'm going to give her a few more minutes like this first.'

Holly's mum nodded and sat down on the edge of the sofa cushion beside her daughter, lifting her long hair off her neck to help cool her down.

'I'm Tina by the way,' she said. 'She always reacts to bad pain like this, ever since she was small.'

'I see. I'm Noel. Pleased to meet you.'

'How do you know our Holly?' she asked, flicking a glance at her husband, who was standing in the open doorway with his face lifted to the falling snow.

Noel fidgeted under Tina's scrutiny, then the dog's, who was next to his knee, practically sat on his feet. Honestly, who'd have thought an animal's face could be so expressive.

'Customer. Friend. I—' he shifted in his seat, 'I'm not sure yet,' he said honestly.

She nodded, looking entirely comfortable with his non-answer.

He cast his eyes around the room, hoping for a change of topic. 'I'm sorry, but can I just ask … what's with all the—?' Pointing at ruined wooden table legs, holes in the arms of the suite, upholstery hanging out, a large chunk of plaster missing from the far wall, like a little dip. 'Did you get burgled or something?'

Tina let out a long, pealing laugh, joined by a deep guffaw from her husband. 'No. That's all Pudding's doing. Labs eat a lot, and some of them eat everything. He's one of those, or he was when he was a puppy. He should know better by now.' She remarked disapprovingly, looking at the dog.

Pudding at least had the grace to look shamefaced, getting up and leaving the room but, Noel noticed, still with a slight air of disdain and a dainty picking up of the front legs.

'Holly.' He turned back to her. 'Holly.' She lifted her head and clear blue eyes met his. 'Feeling a bit better?'

She nodded, 'Leg still hurts like a bugger though.' But normal colour was starting to seep into her face. 'Tablets please,' she said, hand held out.

Within twenty minutes of taking the meds, and sitting quietly whilst sipping the water, Holly was feeling almost human, or so she said. 'I don't feel sick or dizzy any more. My knee is much better,' she assured him, 'a dull throb rather than shrieking agony.'

Her eyes widened when he stood up.

'Good.' He stated, 'Then I should go.'

'Why?' her bottom lip stuck out sexily. Did she want him to stay?

'It's after eleven,' Noel said, 'getting on for midnight.' He started along the hallway and they all followed him, Holly with her arm around her dad's shoulder at her insistence. 'It's almost Christmas.' He continued. 'I can't intrude.'

'You can't go back out in this weather on Christmas Eve after bringing our girl home. Stay with us, have some fun.' Tina grabbed his hand, smiling up at him.

'Come on Noel,' Tom said, 'I think you'll enjoy it. Our way of saying thanks.'

'What kind of fun?'

Holly, standing beside him, looked awkward.

He groaned inside, having reached the front room, over-whelmed by the sheer Christmassyness (was that a word?) of it all, including a pine tree rammed with a clashing assortment of baubles and miles of gold tinsel, shiny foil and paper chains hanging down the walls, a nativity scene, candles lit around the room, letting off the scent of berries. Festive cards were strung across the ceiling on coloured threads, making him feel like he was enmeshed in a giant spider's web. Panic kindled and began to catch fire. His breath twisted in his throat, hands clenching. Could he do this? He wasn't the family Christmas type.

'Christmas themed games?' he asked shakily.

'No!' Holly's mum gave him an appalled expression. 'Sod that. Drinking games!' Shuffling over to a cupboard, she pulled open a door to reveal shelves packed with no end of snacks, bottles, packs of cards and tea towels, like an overstuffed sock draw, and yanked out a garment covered in turquoise sequins.

'This is the drinking jacket. Put it on love,' she didn't give him much of a choice, shoving his arms into it. She ran her hands over his broad shoulders. 'Nice fit,' she said approvingly.

Holly clutched her head with her hands. 'Oh, Mum!'

Noel hid a smile. Holly looked adorable. Exasperated, but adorable.

'Don't worry, handsome,' Tina put her hands on her hips, 'if you drink too much we'll stuff you in a cab. Or there's a spare room you can stop in.'

'That's really kind but like I said, I can't intrude on you, with tomorrow being what it is.'

'Nonsense, we have guests all the time,' she marched over to a table and picked up a bottle of whiskey.

Sorry, Holly mouthed at him. 'Mum, Noel probably has other plans.'

As she said it, giving him an out, something strange happened. The panic started receding.

'Pffttt, if that was the case he'd be there already. You listen to your old mum. He wants to stay. You're going to have to be careful though love,' she told Holly, 'after taking those tablets. Don't go trying to be drinking champion like you usually do.'

Holly rolled her eyes. Great, now Noel was probably going to think she had a problem with alcohol.

'Are you staying, Noel?' Tina peered up at him. 'It'll give you a chance to relax. You look too uptight for a youngster.' She pinched his cheek and patted it, turning away, assuming she'd convinced him. 'Right everyone,' clapping her hands to get people's attention, 'let's get started. Form the circle.' Obediently, people stopped their conversations. Someone switched off the TV, and they all lowered themselves to sit down cross-legged on the floor, even an old lady with pink tinted hair who looked about a hundred, who rubbed her hands gleefully. 'Bring out the port!'

Holly signalled frantically behind her Mum's back, 'Go now, quickly,' she whispered, 'escape while you can.'

'I don't know,' he drawled, 'it kind of sounds like fun.' It did. Plus there was still the matter of the sheer black tights and flirty black dress. He wasn't ready to give that up yet. And Matt probably wasn't expecting him to come back now anyway, it was too late, but he could easily text his friend to let him know where he was.

'But … I really didn't think it would be your thing. You don't like Christmas.'

'It's not Christmas yet, and it's just a drinking game. It would

47

also be rude to leave when your Mum is so obviously keen for me to stay.'

'Huh, if you're not careful she'll have us married off by New Year,' she muttered.

'What?' he dipped his head toward her.

'What?' she echoed innocently.

'Come on you two,' Tina called across the room, 'I've made space for you to sit together,' Holly let out an audible groan at her mum's match-making, 'and we need Noel to start it off. He's wearing the drinking jacket.'

'Okay, stay.' She looked up at him, and he fought a mad urge to stroke her hair. 'I'm warning you though,' she said, looking serious, blue eyes wide, 'about my Aunt, the one in the dark blue twin set. She uses the mistletoe.' She pointed to a sprig above the kitchen door. 'Don't let her catch you under it.'

'I'll be careful,' he said solemnly, taking her hand and leading her across the room. Tensing, she looked down at their joined hands. He let go quickly. Maybe he had it wrong, perhaps she didn't want him there and she'd only stopped him leaving out of gratitude for helping her. Settling on the floor, Noel ignored the thought, slowly relaxing as Tina explained the rules of the game, a version of Fizz Buzz, where any number divisible by three was replaced by fizz and any number divisible by five replaced by buzz, and players took it in turns round the circle to say a number, fizz or buzz, counting upwards from one to a hundred.

At the beginning of each round everyone had one drink. Players only had three seconds per turn.

'Three seconds? Is that it?' he turned to Holly, who was biting the inside of her cheeks.

'You were the one who decided to stay,' she shrugged, eyes twinkling.

'So where does the drinking jacket come in then?' he asked.

'Every time one of us gets it wrong, you have to have a drink. Every time you get it wrong, you nominate someone else to have a drink. After the first round of one hundred, you pass the jacket to someone else.'

'Wait,' he said suspiciously, 'if I have to drink every time someone gets it wrong, the odds are against me. Aren't I going to get drunk pretty quickly?'

Holly's dad smiled sloppily, raising his glass of whiskey in a toast. Noel realised they'd all been drinking for a while, it was just that his appearance with their daughter had sobered her parents up rapidly.

'I'm going to regret this aren't I?' Noel asked Holly mournfully.

'Shut up and have your first drink,' she ordered, fanning her face and standing up to scramble out of her tights, before sinking down again. 'That's better. I was getting hot.'

'You're telling me,' he said under his breath, eyeing the generous length of bare legs on display, and casually readjusting his jeans. 'Okay,' he said, 'let's start then. Cheers,' holding his shot glass aloft then throwing back the contents.

'Wait!' Holly said, grabbing hold of his arm. 'Mum forgot to tell you, when you nominate someone to have a drink, you can include Pudding too.'

'What?' staring at her, amazed. 'What were in those tablets I gave you?'

'He likes the taste of straight coke,' she ignored his dig, 'so we let him join in.'

On cue, the chocolate Lab appeared next to Noel, eye-balling him fiercely.

Noel had never known any family quite like them. 'All right, fine,' he put his hands up, palms out like he was being held up. 'This is getting more surreal by the minute.'

Holly laid her head on his shoulder, gazing up at him and fluttering her eyelashes. 'But it's also getting more fun, right?'

Grinning, he nodded. 'Right.'

Two in the morning found them sitting outside on a frozen wooden bench, an inch of snow crunching underfoot, giving the night a fairytale feeling. Despite her mum's protestations, Holly had proved herself Champion again, and was giggly as a consequence. After Fizz, Buzz they'd drunk creamy Baileys over ice, played monopoly, Pictionary and charades, and at one point Holly had laughed so hard that rum and coke had shot out of her nose. She'd put on a funny Christmas jumper as they'd left the back room, and now she shivered, huddling into his side.

'It's a shame about the jumper,' he remarked, studying it, praying his eyes didn't cross.

'Yeah, I'm sorry I had to ruin your fun by reminding you of what day it is,' she hiccupped.

'It's not that. I was just sad to see the sexy dress covered up.'

'Oh.' Her eyes brightened, 'Oh, do you like it? I designed it.'

'You did?'

'Yeah,' she paused, eyes sliding closed, then jerking upright. 'After the injury, when they said my knee wasn't healing right, that it would never be the same again and I couldn't skate professionally any more … well, it was bad. For a while at least.'

'So what did you do?' he wrapped an arm around her shoulders for warmth.

'Felt sorry for myself then realised I had to make other plans. So I studied design at college and decided to set my own company up designing and selling figure-skating dresses. It's something I know about, what's comfortable and what isn't, what emphasises and what distracts.' She raced straight on into her next thought. 'Noel?'

'Yes?'

'You don't like Christmas because your mum died at this time of year, and you broke up with your ex, and I get those are horrible associations to have, but you must have had some nice Christmases growing up?'

'My mum did love it, and the ones I can remember with her were … really special.' He drew in a deep breath. 'My grandparents raised me, and loved me, but they weren't very warm people, and were deeply religious, so it was all about the Christian tradition, and symbolism, not the kind of Christmas a kid who'd just lost his mum needed. They passed away a few years ago, six months apart.'

'It must have been hard,' she took a sip from the beer she'd brought out. 'But can't you start creating Christmases that you enjoy?' she suggested in a soft voice. 'After all, it's not about the time of year really is it, why you don't enjoy it? It's about that relationship, those people. The memories. So you should try and separate it out in your head. Spend some time with your family, just for the enjoyment of being with them, and don't worry about the whole exchanging presents thing.'

'I don't have any left.' His arm tightened, and he picked up her hand, tracing a pattern over the knuckles.

'You have your friends,' she replied, breath audibly hitching, squirming on the bench. 'Family is whatever you want it to be, whatever that might look like. Sometimes you choose them, it's not always who you're stuck with through blood.' She laughed. 'And maybe you should be glad, I mean look at my lot! They're pretty overwhelming.'

'Well, your aunt did pin me up against the fridge and tell me the mistletoe was pointing in our direction earlier.'

'Nooo,' she shook her head from side to side, blinking slowly.

'And they are pretty overwhelming. But I like it. And you're part of that. You overwhelm me.' Sod *no complications*, and not risking his heart. He had to get to know this positive, bright, energetic girl better. It might not be part of the plan, but it was the only thing that made sense.

'Say again?' Holly sat bolt upright, gazing at him. 'In what way?'

'In a good way.' Sliding his hands around her waist, he hauled her in close, watching her watching him.

An endless silence grew, and she leaned in to him. 'What is it?'

'You're worried about what happened with your ex-fiancé, and about needing to focus on your business.' He summarised, despite the fogginess of alcohol in his head. He wanted to get this right.

'I—yes.'

'But I'm not here to hurt you.'

'Okay.' Running a hand up over his broad shoulders, she stroked his stubbly cheek.

'Okay.'

'So?' she nudged.

'So?'

'Are you going to kiss me, or what?' she blurted.

'Oh, that. All right then. But we might have to conduct a risk assessment,' he joked. 'After all, kissing in the snow could be a dangerous activity, or if there's too much heat—'

'Ha ha,' she murmured, and solved everything by kissing him.

He was gratified when she wrapped her arms around his shoulders and clung on, moaning when he lifted her up and sat her on his lap. He ran a hand up her bare thigh, then broke away from her luscious pink mouth, framing her face with gentle hands.

'Merry Christmas, Holly.'

'I thought you didn't like Christmas,' she said breathlessly, twirling shaky fingers through his dark hair.

'Still don't,' he said bluntly. 'I still think it's stressful, expensive and driven by retailers.'

'You do?' she looked disappointed.

'I don't think I'll ever like it, but I do like you, so I'll consider not hiding in my man-cave.'

'Yeah?'

'Yes.' Resting his forehead against hers, chest to chest, the button of his coat caught her jumper, starting up an electronic, jangly *Silent Night*.

They both roared with laughter, their cold breath forming clouds between them.

'There's something I should probably tell you,' Holly admitted.

'What? Another ex? A child? A horrible disease that will cause hideous boils?'

'Nope. Just that I hate summer.'

Noel smirked, 'Wow, what a pair. Well, how do you feel about spring? Is spring all right?'

'Spring is good,' she grinned, 'I guess during certain times of the year we'll just have to distract each other.'

'I can definitely see certain activities being distracting enough to keep me happy.' He kissed her, hard and fast, and when he lifted his head she looked dazed.

'Wow,' she breathed.

'Yes,' he agreed. Squeezing her tight, he nodded. 'You know, you were right.'

'Right about what?'

He grinned. 'The unexpected things can be the best parts.'

'They can,' she nodded, blue eyes sparkling. 'Hey, what are you doing?' She yelped as he dug his phone out of his pocket and she almost slid off his lap into the snow. 'You're not texting or calling someone now?'

'I am,' he arranged her on his lap and looped his arm around her, holding on tight. 'I'm going to text Matt and thank him.'

'What for?' she rested her head against his broad chest, snuggling in.

'For making me take Jasper Skating at Somerset House.'

New Year at The Ritz

'Oh, balls!' Frankie Taylor stared at the mirror in dismay. She touched a hand to the back of her neck, where she *used* to have hair, and glared at her hairdresser in their shared reflection.

'You don't like it?' Davey asked, freezing with comb and scissors in mid-air against the backdrop of the heavy chrome and red leather salon. 'You said you wanted something different, a fresh start.'

'Yes, I wanted a change, because everyone keeps on at me to move on, and a new haircut is easier than bowing to pressure and getting a boyfriend.' She yanked on the ends of her glossy black hair, which were now only a few inches from her scalp, rather than shoulder length. 'By something different, I didn't mean half-bald!' The amount of hair on the floor was truly disturbing. 'So much for treating myself to a nice post-Christmas present,' she muttered.

'Oh, love … I really thought you wanted something radical and besides, I've always thought short hair would suit you.' Putting scissors and comb down, he gently extracted her fingers from the newly blunt-cut locks and shaped the side-fringe across her forehead. 'It shows off those gorgeous almond-shaped violet eyes to perfection. And look at those cheekbones! You look a bit like Frankie from The Saturdays.'

'So now I share my name *and* a haircut with her.' She stroked her exposed neck, feeling oddly naked with nothing covering her nape or tops of her ears. 'I'm going to be freezing – it's midwinter!' Shaking her head, she watched the strands fall back into place. 'Okay, I guess it's not that bad,' she conceded. She wouldn't look so pale with make-up on. It'd hardly been worth applying any today, given she lived three doors down from the hairdressers above a kebab shop and was off work until 5 January.

'No?' Davey heaved a relieved sigh.

'No. And you're right, it really shows off that stone I've lost since the break-up,' she said self-mockingly. 'Plus, we can hardly stick it back on, can we?' Wrinkling her nose, 'So what's the point in being upset?' She'd learnt the hard way there were some things you had to let go, some things you couldn't control.

'You said it,' he drawled, picking up the scissors again.

'Hold it! You're not taking any more off are you?'

'Just neatening up, my love,' he assured, sticking his tongue out at her. 'Relax.'

'I'll be relaxed,' she grumbled, 'if (a) you don't scalp me (b) Dad doesn't ring every five minutes to check on me (c) my friends stop insisting it's time to find a new man and give up plastering my profile all over dating sites, and (d) when my boss stops giving me funny looks because she thinks being single is unnatural.' She paused as Davey used the hair-dryer to get rid of the stray bits of hair that inevitably got into everything, picking up the conversation once he'd switched it off. She met his amused blue eyes in the mirror, 'I've only been single for just over a year which really isn't that long, and I'm happy being selfish for now, doing what suits me, thanks very much.'

'Hmmm.' Davey whipped off the cape he'd covered her jeans and jumper with and spun her around in the chair. 'The problem with that, my lovely, is it would be really easy to stay like that for too long. Don't get used to it, or you'll never want to be with anyone ag—'

'Pfftt!' she interrupted, sitting up straight and raising an eyebrow. 'You're just saying that because you move from one relationship to another with the speed Superman flies at. Being alone isn't what you do.'

Grabbing her by a belt loop, he yanked her from the chair. 'Hey, watch it!' She giggled as he spun her around the shop. He grinned naughtily, 'I could be alone if I wanted to. I just don't want to. And if you're comparing me to HC's Superman, I'll take that compliment gladly.' He released her, arms dropping.

'Oh god,' she groaned, 'you are so obsessed with Henry Cavill!'

'Don't try and pretend *you're* not.'

'I—oh, okay, I won't. That black hair, those baby blue eyes,' they both let out a sigh of appreciation, 'he's so hot it's obscene.'

'That bit on the ship in The Tudors …' Davey's face took on a dreamy, faraway expression. 'No wonder it was difficult for you to break up with Christian. I mean, he does bear a passing resemblance to Lord HC. Hey, d'you remember that time I called in at The Superflat,' his name for the multi-million pound apartment on the Thames she and Christian had shared, 'and he was getting out of the shower? All he had on was that teeny, tiny towel—'

'Oi! Snap out of it,' she clicked her fingers in front of his glazed eyes. 'We're not going there, okay? It's over.'

'Sorry.' Grabbing her cropped, battered leather jacket from a hanger, he helped her into it. 'In all seriousness though,' he turned her to face him, looking uncharacteristically solemn, 'everyone needs love. It's a fact of life. It's biology.'

'Whatever,' she shrugged, straightening the collar of his patterned shirt, 'personally I think it's just sex. *That's* life. *That's* biology. Speaking of which, where are we going out on New Year's Eve?'

'Not sure yet. There's The Crown and Roses,' he mentioned their local, and she groaned, 'or maybe something in the city. I did hear about this party—'

'Oh no, what are you going to get me into?'

'I've got to find out the details, so you'll see. Now, get lost.' Giving her a hug and a kiss on the cheek, he propelled her toward the door. 'Enjoy your trip home. See you in a couple of days.'

She stopped in the doorway. 'What about the money for the haircut?'

'You want to pay me for scalping you?' he joked.

'Or making me look like a super-model?' she answered hopefully.

He pulled a face. 'You know I love you, but no. Anyway, call it a late Christmas prezzie and if anyone asks who gave you such a divine style, point them in my direction. And don't forget what I said. Everyone needs love.'

'I'll hurl them in your direction, never mind point them,' she retorted, and was rewarded with a playful smack on the bum as she skipped out the door.

The conversation with Davey was spinning through her head as Frankie walked into her pokey flat at midnight a few days later. Dumping her rucksack in the hallway, she picked up a thick pile of post which included a ridiculous amount of takeaway menus.

The train journey from Southampton to London hadn't been too bad, considering the time of year. It was the tube ride from Waterloo that'd been a royal pain in the arse. She'd left it really late to head back but had wanted to maximise her time with her dad. There wasn't enough money to make it home very often. And now he was alone, it was even more important to spend as much time with him as possible. He was the only parent she had left.

Everyone needs love. Davey's words resounded in her head.

He might be right – but there was more than romantic love in the world. Love for friends, love for family. Which reminded her; pulling her phone from her pocket, she tapped out a quick text to her dad.

Home safe, thanks for a lovely couple of days. Will come down & see you again as soon as I can. F xx

Traipsing into her lounge, she groaned. 'Oh, bloody hell!'

She'd left a window open while she'd been gone. The scent of frying food was forever escaping from a vent on front of the kebab shop below and wafting into her flat. Now the place stank of meaty kebab, raw onions, crisp jalapeno peppers and oily chips. Nice. Flinging her coat off, and chucking the post on the sofa, she slammed the window and picked up one of the numerous cans of air freshener crowding the low bookcase, spraying it so heavily around the room it sent her into a coughing fit. Crouching down, she turned on the plug-in air freshener and cast her eyes over the damp, peeling ceiling, before giving up and storming out of the lounge.

Was she ever going to climb out of this hole?

No, it was too late for that kind of thinking. She had her health, an okay job in a department store, a loving father and good friends. And right now, thank god—she rubbed her temples tiredly while stumbling into her tiny bedroom—she also had a comfortable bed, one of the few luxuries she'd budgeted for when taking up the tenancy.

Falling face down onto the duvet, she kicked off her ankle boots and let sleep claim her.

Frankie felt much chirpier the next morning. It might have had something to do with the massive lie-in until gone eleven, the bucketful of milky coffee she'd drunk and the hot water she'd managed to coax out of the decrepit boiler for a steamy shower. Or it might be that for the first time since her trip to the salon, she'd managed to tame her hair into something resembling an actual style. Alternatively it could be that she finally fit back into her black jeans, the ones she'd had before meeting Christian. Teaming them with the fashionable soft peach jumper her dad had bought her for Christmas, she felt comfy but a little glam too.

Whatever it was that explained her good mood, she felt better than she had in weeks. Not quite ready for 2015, but getting there.

Curling up on the sofa, she picked up the pile of post.

Sifting through it, she rolled her eyes. Takeaway leaflet, fast food menu, ironing services, window cleaning. Bill, bill, bill, and what a shocker, bill. Then another b—hang on. She gazed at the plain white envelope, her name written in bold script on the front, no stamp, no postmark, meaning it'd been hand-delivered.

Open on 31 December was inscribed in the top left hand corner. Not Davey's hand-writing, or anybody else's she knew for that matter. Weird. But it *was* New Year's Eve, so she ripped into the envelope, apprehension and excitement mixing in her belly.

Pulling out an A4 sheet of paper, she breathed in deeply and frowned. She recognised the smell; her favourite perfume. Anyone who knew her knew that she wasn't the pink flowers and hearts type, so plain stationery and her favourite scent was a good compromise. But was it also a little creepy? They knew where she lived, and what perfume she wore. Stalker alert?

Unfolding the note, her eyes widened. No, *I'm watching you, I long to stroke your hair while you sleep* stalker type of message. It looked like a rhyme, or a puzzle.

A New Year's surprise, the path to your heart,
Main Knightsbridge station, that's where you start.
Follow the clues across London, see where they lead,
this object meets the need for speed.
Look in the window, see it revolve,
the road to the next clue you will then solve.

? x

p.s. Set off at 4.00 p.m – and try not to be late!

Reading the letter a second and then a third time, she rested her head against the back of the sofa, blowing out a long breath. It was cool and scary and intriguing all at the same time. Someone had gone to quite a bit of trouble for her. She itched to know who was behind it and what the end game was. But she wasn't sure. The path to her heart? She wasn't sure she had one left after her mum, and Christian, and had told Davey only a few days ago she wasn't interested in having a boyfriend at the moment. So was there any point in doing this, this game, whatever it was? Wouldn't it be better to stick to her plans, go out partying with Davey and the rest of the gang, instead of short-changing some poor bugger by turning up and saying *thanks for all the effort, but no thanks.*

No, she wouldn't go. It was the best thing.

Tapping her fingers on her knees, she sat up and studied the bookcase stuffed with sci-fi books, overflowing wall shelves stacked with photography magazines, the scarred wooden coffee table positioned on a rich, multi-coloured Indian rug brought back from the post-uni travelling she was still struggling to pay off. Her eyes lingered on the wooden family of elephants lined up on the floor by the TV, walking in a row, trunks holding tails to link them together. She didn't have much but it was hers, and she wasn't ready to share it with anyone.

Standing up, she strode across the room and stuffed the mystery letter in between two ancient, dog-eared Isaac Asimov books she and her dad had discovered on a stall in a musty indoor market one day, when she'd been about twelve. If she pulled one of the paperbacks off the shelf and opened it the smell would take her back to her childhood; to overflowing bookcases and Sunday afternoons spent wandering around car-boot sales and markets, a cheap and cheerful way of feeding her parents' reading addiction.

Slinking back to the sofa, she threw herself down and picked up the TV remote, flicking restlessly through the channels. She'd just veg out until it was time to get ready for the New Year festivities, whatever they might be. Davey hadn't messaged yet, but he would. He always came through with a plan.

She put the remote down and checked her phone. No messages. Nothing interesting on Twitter. Not much doing on Facebook, apart from various posts about how excited people were about their New Years' Eve plans. She sighed, picking up the remote again and eventually settling on an Eastenders omnibus. By the looks of it, someone was dead. It was probably another dramatic shooting. She liked the programme, the writing could be brilliant, but she had to have the appetite for it otherwise it was a bit depressing.

Her gaze was drawn to the shelf where she'd hidden the letter. What was that first clue referring to? Need for speed. Road. Some sort of transport then. *No*. Her decision was made. She was not going on some mad scavenger hunt. Today she was relaxing, given how tired she'd felt recently and how her ribs had been aching. It would be criminal not to make the most of being one of the lucky few people in the store with the whole Christmas and New Year period off. At interview she'd asked for her pre-booked holiday to be honoured if she was offered a job. At the time of applying, the role had been a symbol of independence, perhaps even rebellion. But after the break-up it had quickly become a necessity, a way to pay the rent.

So she would definitely *not* think about the fact she was supposed to be in Bali right now. Must not dwell on the idea of lying on a sun-drenched beach in a designer bikini, with a warm breeze stirring the tropical palm trees and a chilled cocktail in her hand. It was fine. She didn't need any of that stuff. She could lie on the sofa in her warm flat – thanks to hitting the radiator with a spanner a few times to crank it into life – and please herself. Relax. Chill. Revive.

Perfect.

Three hours later and she was seriously bored. She'd read a photography mag, got out her favourite old-style Nikon camera and cleaned the lenses and painted her nails in seasonal gold glitter varnish. She'd also tweezed her eyebrows, sorted out her wardrobe and even resorted to scrubbing the bathroom for entertainment.

Her phone pinged and she snatched it up.

Hey love, the city party has fallen through and after a vote we're going to the C&R. See you there at 8ish, don't forget there's a tenner charge on the door. Will save you a seat if you're late!

D x

She groaned. She loved going to the local with her friends but was there practically every week, so it was hardly somewhere special to celebrate the New Year. Although she guessed beggars couldn't be choosers and all that. It wasn't like she had any better offers.

Her eyes strayed to the Isaac Asimov books, or rather, what was hidden between them. She could see what it was all about, couldn't she, and be back to the pub for eight? It was only just past four now. If she left soon she could fit it in.

She stood up. Sat down. Bit her lip. But how involved was this going to be, and who was behind it? What did they want, or expect from her? No, maybe it was better not to poke the bear.

Opening the text from Davey, she re-read it. Perhaps she should phone him, ask his advice? She knew his response would be go for it though, follow the clues. *Everyone needs love.*

Tapping her hands on her knees, she stared at the walls. She needed to talk to someone level-headed, sensible. Someone lovely who would advise what was best for her, not get swept away in romantic notions. She'd consider phoning Zoe, one of her best friends from uni, but Zoe was in the States at the moment so the call would cost a fortune. Besides, she was completely loved up with Greg, engaged to be married, so she was hardly going to be objective about the whole thing. She was as worried about Frankie's single status as everyone else. If she was over in the UK now, she'd be one of the *let's put Frankie on every dating website going* brigade. What was so wrong with being single, though? She was barely past her mid-twenties, and had loads of time to settle down if she wanted to.

The other option was Rayne, another uni friend, the third part of the triangle she and Zoe formed. Vivacious and a little rebellious, Rayne was fantastic for a night out, but Frankie hardly ever saw her nowadays. Journalism was consuming her friend at the moment; she always seemed to be chasing down a story. Personally, Frankie thought it was all about getting over her first love, Adam, but had never said that to her. Rayne could be pretty forthright, if not scary. *That* was definitely a conversation to be had over several bottles of wine.

So, who to call? What was that saying; the old ones are the best? Yep, that was it. She picked up her mobile, going to the favourites menu.

'Kate, it's me. Have you got a minute?' Her childhood friend might be happily in love with her long-term boyfriend, a strapping South African, but was still fab at offering clear, non-soppy advice.

'Sure, Hun,' Kate's warm tones filled her ear, and Frankie could picture her sparkling eyes, shoulder length chestnut hair and massive grin so clearly it was like they were sat next to each other. 'I've just taken the dogs for a walk,' Kate said. 'Hang on while I sort them out.'

Frankie waited, listening to the sounds of her friend talking soothingly to her two beloved dogs, finger clicking, doors opening and closing, footsteps padding nearer, rustling and then a sigh. 'Okay, I'm back. What's up?'

'So, I've got a bit of a dilemma.' Putting her phone on speaker, Frankie propped it on the arm of the sofa and lay back against the purple patterned cushions. She pictured Kate in her comfy lounge, blue jeans on, with wellies, anoraks, leads and dog collars filling the long hallway.

'Go on.' Kate's voice filled the room.

Frankie closed her eyes, wishing her friend was here instead of in a small leafy village just outside Milton Keynes. 'I got home from seeing dad yesterday, and—'

'He still being a bit overprotective?'

'Yep. It's driving me mad.'

'Ah, bless. Well, you can see why, Hun. I mean, after your mum, then what happened to you—'

'It's been a tough year,' Frankie cleared her throat, 'anyway, I got this letter and it's a clue, I'm supposed to go to Knightsbridge—'

'What? Who's it from? Read it to me.'

Frankie grabbed the letter and did so, adding in the bit about lack of postmark and scented paper. 'So what do you think?'

'Well, it sounds cool, but who do you think is behind it?' Kate's voice was cautious and Frankie was reminded of their teenage years in Southampton, the mornings they'd sit in the back of Kate's mum's people carrier, Kate's younger brothers chattering away while the girls talked about school and boys and Kate's mum would add in dry, no-nonsense comments. They were fond memories and sometimes Frankie missed those years, when life had been simpler, though they hadn't known it back then. As teens, everything had felt intense and dramatic and like the world would implode if the boy they had a crush on didn't like them back or the Topshop dress they were after wasn't in stock, or if they got a C grade for an essay instead of an A.

'You still there?' Kate asked.

'Yes, sorry. I don't know who it is.' Frankie frowned, opening her eyes.

'Oh, come on! It'll be someone you know, it has to be. Delivered to your home address, your favourite perfume? And that *don't be late* comment.'

'What do you mean?'

'Come on Frankie, you're late for everything. Whoever sent it knows you.' Pausing. 'D'you think the letter could be from Christian?'

Frankie's short square gold nails dug into her palms. 'Unlikely. I haven't heard from him since we broke up. Even when I went to get my stuff once I was up to it, he wasn't around. He wasn't interested in seeing me. I think he took me ending it with him pretty badly. So I doubt it very much. Besides, he's in Bali at the moment.'

64

'Oh, yes. You missed out there on the holiday in paradise. But then again, money isn't everything.'

'Yes, that's what I keep telling myself.' Frankie muttered, scowling at the peeling ceiling above her head.

'What's that? Is everything okay?'

Yeah, just hunky-dory. I live in a rough part of London, have no money, a job I can barely tolerate, debts coming out of my ears, and will probably end up with severe pneumonia because of the insane damp climbing my walls. But apart from that, it's all good.

'Frankie?' Kate's voice was strained, 'You're worrying me.'

Self-pity is not attractive! Frankie gave herself a proverbial kick up the arse. *You have your health back, your independence and the freedom to make choices. More than some people have.* She made her voice breezy. 'Ignore me, everything is fine.'

'Okay. If you say so.' Kate said dubiously, but let Frankie off the hook. 'If it's not Christian, who else could it be?'

'I don't know. Davey?'

'I thought he was gay?'

'Oh, he totally is, but it could be his idea of a joke.' She sucked in her cheeks, considering the options. 'Or maybe a way to remind me romance isn't dead?'

'Sounds a bit mean to me. Or a bit extreme, sending you on what could be a wild chase across the city. Do you really think he'd do that?'

'I—hmmm, maybe not. I don't know. The hand-writing doesn't look like his though.' Her side was aching, so she repositioned the cushion behind her head and crossed her ankles, resting them on the opposite arm of the sofa.

'Any other likely suspects?' Kate quizzed.

'No, I—,' she hesitated.

'What?'

'There is a guy at work. But … no.'

'Who? And why not?'

'Zack. He started a few months ago. He's a sweetheart and we get on really well. But there isn't a spark, and I'm not sure if the letter is his style.' Shaking her head, 'Nah, I can't see it. We're just friends and I've not given him any reason to think otherwise. Besides, it's too soon.'

'Maybe, maybe not.' Kate replied, carrying on quickly before Frankie could object. 'Anyway, perhaps he'll surprise you, and spark isn't everything. Chemistry can grow over time. There are lots of other important things—'

'I know that from experience, remember? But like I said, it's unlikely.'

'Well, whoever it is, what's the risk?' Kate asked.

'What? The risk of following the clues?'

'Yes. Let's think it through. I suppose it could be a stalker,' she paused dramatically, 'or, dun-dun-dun, a serial killer.'

Frankie thought of one of her favourite films, *This Means War* and the main character's objection to internet dating, and grinned, 'Yes, I guess I could end up as some guy's skin suit.'

'That wouldn't be good.'

'No, it would put a serious cramp in my style,' she giggled, and Kate joined in.

'Seriously though,' Kate said softly, 'if the clues lead you to public places, you're fine, right? If they don't, you can always just cut your losses and go home.'

'So you think I should do this?' Frankie sat up, grabbing the remote and switching off the TV, side fringe swinging into her eyes. She blew it away impatiently.

'I'm not saying you have to, I'm just saying why not? It's kind of exciting.'

'What would you do?'

'I'd do it, as long as it was safe. But you already knew I'd say that. It's why you called me. You were torn. Part of you is really tempted. If you weren't, you wouldn't have bothered getting in touch, you would have just binned the letter.'

'What? I didn't-,' Frankie blew out a breath, eyes straying back

66

to the A4 sheet of paper lying open on the table. The bloody thing had been like a magnet since she'd first read it. 'Argh, I hate it when you're right. Okay. What's the harm? I don't have to commit to anything. And it's not as if I have anything else to do for the next few hours.'

'Yay,' Kate let out an uncharacteristic squeak, 'you're going on a romantic scavenger hunt. Amazing!'

Frankie made a dismissive sound. 'Shut up.'

Kate guffawed, 'Whatever! Listen, I'm around for the evening, call or text me after every clue. I want to know where you end up going, and who it is. Now go, you're late.'

'Shit.' It was gone twenty past four. 'Okay, speak later. Thank you! Love you!' Ending the call, she shoved the phone in her jeans pocket, grabbed the letter, yanked on her leather jacket and whirled out the door. She might as well get on with it. And Kate was right, she was late.

On the tube on the way to Knightsbridge, Davey's words spun in her head. *Everyone needs love.* It had never been so obvious after visiting her dad. She knew he worried about her, living in London, barely any disposable income to her name with Christian out of the picture, but *she* was more worried about *him*. He'd been quiet, grey.

'Missing Mum?' she'd asked softly as they'd sat in the front room of the pebble-dash semi-detached house she'd grown up in.

'Yes. It's worse today. This time of year.' He sighed. 'It's a time for families.'

Putting her patterned porcelain teacup down with a clink – her dad insisted on brewing a pot of tea the old-fashioned way, just as his wife had – she crossed over to his beige velour armchair. Squeezing his shoulder, 'I know it is. But that's why I'm here.'

He put his hand over hers, his skin dry and firm, but lined. She was an only child and they'd had her in their early forties after years of trying, so he was older than most of her friends' parents.

Gazing up at her, he smiled sadly. 'I love you Francesca, you know that. And there is no fiercer love than a parent has for a child, that's one thing me and your mum always agreed on, as you'll find out for yourself one day. But,' he continued, shifting his attention to the photo hanging above the mantelpiece, the three of them on her graduation day, both her parents' faces glowing with pride, no clue that a few short years later one of them would be gone, 'it's not the same. When you've had someone who's been your best friend for more years than you can count, who's always made you smile and laugh, battled through awful things with you … being alone after that, without them, well, it's …' he drifted off, still staring at the photo.

'Hard? I know, I get it. I miss her too.'

'No.' He denied, switching his attention to the gold watch Anna had bought him for his fiftieth, a rare extravagance. Tracing a shaking finger across the face. 'No,' he repeated, 'it's not hard. It's unbearable.'

'Dad?' Knowing her voice showed alarm, she rearranged her clinging black woollen dress and sank down to the floor. 'What do you mean? You're not going to do anything silly, are-'

Jerking his head up at the quiver in her voice, his eyes widened, face immediately clearing. 'What? No, I'm just having a bad day, that's all. Don't worry, I'm fine. The port is just getting to me. Stupid old bugger!'

She clambered up, knowing the best way to handle him, 'Well, I agree with the old and the bugger bit, but I'm not sure if you're stupid. You're too good at all your game shows and puzzles for that.'

'Very droll.' He spoke to her back as she drifted around the room.

She realigned Christmas cards from neighbours and relatives, straightened the scrappy red tinsel on the tree, punched the sofa cushions until she was satisfied they looked right. Their conversation had taken a turn down an alley she didn't want to walk down. Keep moving on, that's what she needed to do.

Yanking back the curtains, she squinted out the window. 'Neighbourhood kids behaving now? Things any better?' This area of Southampton wasn't particularly nice, but it was home. She would always have a soft spot for it, despite the rubbish tumbling along the pavements, the broken street-lights and some of the front gardens being filled with junk fit only for the tip. It had changed a lot since she was little, when she'd played games on the road with her friends and they'd felt safe staying out until after dark, even at seven or eight years old.

'Of course,' he pushed out of his chair and joined her, hand clutching the window frame. 'They're too scared of you after your last visit to try anything.'

She flushed. 'All I did was tell them to behave. And if it worked, it was worth it.'

'You turned the air blue! And your eyes flashed just like your mother's used to. You were lucky they didn't beat you up.'

'Well they shouldn't have tried to mess with my dad. Throwing missiles at the house is totally out of order. And now I live in a rough part of Landon,' she put on a thick east end accent, 'I got street smarts.' As his face clouded over, she drew the curtains rapidly. 'Come on, get your shoes on. Pub.'

'You think you can beat your old dad at darts?' he asked with a glint in his eye.

'Nope,' she said breezily as she wandered into the hallway to pull her ankle boots on. 'I *know* I can beat my old dad at darts.'

After he'd locked up as they'd meandered down the street arm in arm, he'd leant in close. 'One of them kids told me afterwards that you had respect.'

'I'm supposed to believe they respect me?' she made a *pfftt* sound. 'And why's that exactly?'

'He said you can swear better than they can.'

Dropping her head back, she let out a long, low laugh. 'Is that right?'

'Yes.' He squeezed her arm. 'You look like your mum when you laugh, you know. She had a lot of love to give.' He emphasised the last sentence.

69

'What's that supposed to mean?'

'Nothing.' He looked at her innocently, 'Absolutely nothing.'

***

As Frankie jumped off the tube and climbed up the stairs of Knightsbridge station, she recalled his words. She didn't think she had any love to give, not right now. Her mum's premature death had seen to that.

But apprehension and excitement nonetheless sizzled inside her as she reached street level. She sucked in a breath. Maybe she was crazy. Only the next few hours would tell. Unfurling the letter, she read the clue again, picking out the important sections. Need for speed, window, see it revolve, road. A car then, in a shop. Pulling out her phone she typed car dealers and Knightsbridge into Google maps. It was probably a bit of a cheat but she was late and a girl had to use any tools at her disposal. There were a few likely candidates, but the closest was McLaren. Turning right, she set off, striding past several tall posh buildings with big metal gates.

Coming to a halt outside a narrow shop front with floor to ceiling windows, she peered in. Sure enough, there was some kind of orange two-tone supercar revolving slowly in the window, all smooth lines and curves with laser effect lights. The massive round ceiling light above it, wider than the car itself, set the paintwork off perfectly.

It fit the bill in terms of the clue, but what did she do now? Go in and ask if anyone had left anything for her? She'd feel like an idiot if they said no. Then again, she could just move swiftly on to the next dealership. There was a Ferrari place down the other end of the road.

Hovering uncertainly, trying to make her mind up, she jerked when a guy in a sharp black suit opened the glass door and appeared next to her.

'Can I help you?' he smiled politely. 'We close soon, given what day it is.'

The *try not to be late* part of the clue flashed through her mind, as she smiled back.

There was a method to whoever's madness this was. 'Yes, sorry. I, that is, a friend sent me here,' no way was she admitting she had no idea who the person was, 'to pick something up. But I'm not sure what. I know that sounds stupid,' she finished lamely.

'Not at all, if you are who I think you are. Your name?'

'Frankie Taylor. Do you need to see some ID?'

He laughed, white teeth flashing. 'No, you're okay. Come in.' He pulled open the door, gesturing her ahead of him.

'Thanks.' She stepped into the sparkling chrome showroom, huge silver pillars supporting the low ceiling.

'No problem at all. If you don't mind waiting here a minute?'

'That's fine.' She glanced around, noticing another car slowly turning on the spot, this one gleaming white with black accessories.

'Why don't you have a go while I get your package?' he asked.

'A go?'

Sauntering over to the orange two-tone car, he ran his fingers around the edge of the door and pressed something. The door swooped upwards, a bit like the Batmobile.

'Wow!' she breathed. She wasn't really a car girl but it was gorgeously impressive.

'Have a seat. Watch out, it's quite low to the ground.'

'Are—are you sure?' She took a step towards it, eyes drawn to the button-filled grey interior.

'Of course.'

She frowned down at her stiletto boots. 'What if I damage it? How much is it worth?'

'Don't damage it,' he said mildly, 'be careful. It's a 650S,' he explained, 'so it's retailing for only two hundred and seventy five thousand.'

She stopped mid-climb into the low slung sports car. 'Only?'

'Well, there are a few other models but the most expensive, the P1, sells for over eight hundred thousand.'

'Eight—Jeez.' Christian had been loaded and owned a Lamborghini Huracán. It'd been worth less than two hundred thousand pounds and the value of it had made her squirm every time she'd got in it.

'Like I said, just be careful.' The man said, nodding, 'I'll only be a few minutes.'

Watching his departing back as he strode off the showroom floor, she lowered herself into the flashy car, mindful not to snag her heels on the carpet.

Resting her hands on the velvety textured steering wheel, she stared out of the low, wide windscreen unseeingly, thinking about a day trip she and Christian had gone on the previous summer.

***

He'd arranged to test drive an Alfa Romeo 8C Spider. He'd loved the look of the long nose and how close to the ground it was and wanted something for sunny weekends. On walking out of their flat wearing the required designer dress and high heels, she'd looked it over with interest.

'What do you think?' he'd asked, throwing his arms out, black hair gleaming in the July sunshine.

'It's quite pretty,' she answered, moving around the back and taking in the high red round lights, registration plate dead centre and double exhausts on both sides below. 'Looks a bit like a face,' she mused.

He raised an eyebrow. 'Somehow I don't think that was what they had in mind when they designed it,' he said drily.

She smiled, 'I'm just saying. So what are the double exhausts for?'

Opening the door for himself, he'd gestured for her to get in opposite. 'Come on, let's go. We have lunch plans.'

'We do?' The change of subject was so obviously a tactic to avoid answering the question. She didn't call him on it. It wouldn't be worth the sulky silence that would follow. Besides, she already knew Christian was more interested in how cars looked than what was under the bonnet or how they performed on the road. Maybe it was an apt reflection for his taste in women. They'd been together for three years but she sometimes wondered if he saw her, really *saw* her, or if he was more interested in how she looked on his arm.

'Yes. We're going to Tunbridge Wells.' He grinned, blue eyes twinkling and a dimple flashing in his cheek. 'Now come on, woman, get in. I'll show you a good time.' He leaned in and kissed her as she settled in the seat, stroking her face before helping her buckle up.

Her fears dissolved at the loving gesture and she shook her head. She didn't know what was with her at the moment, doubting him, doubting their relationship. They were fine. Everything was fine.

And it was fun, leaving the city and driving down country lanes, whizzing around bends and turns with the roof down, Frankie struggling to control her long black extensions, which kept flipping up around her face.

'Can I have a go?' she turned to him as they stopped at a crossroads.

'I don't think that's a good idea.'

'Why? I'm fully comped on my car, so we're covered if something happens.'

'No, you're okay,' he answered coolly, pulling away with a quiet roar.

'But it looks like fun! I want to see what it feels like-'

'I'll buy you any car you want to run around in,' he interjected, 'but you're not driving this.'

She laughed, 'Don't be silly. It's not even yours! Come on. Pull over.' She gave him a playful nudge with her elbow.

'No.'

'Come on!' she giggled.

'No!' he said sharply, shooting her a dark look. 'Leave it alone. This test drive is for me.'

'Okay, fine.' She edged away from him, gazing at the passing green, leafy countryside. Sometimes this unpleasant side of him came out. The *new money, offered life on a plate,* spoilt side. He'd grown up with rich parents who gave him everything without question.

But everyone had strengths and weaknesses, everyone had flaws. There were lots of things she loved about him. He could be fun, he made her smile, he spoiled her rotten – she didn't want for anything. He gave her a way of life most people would kill for. She didn't have to work, could have a dream wedding and be a stay-at-home mum when the time came, instead of having to put any children in nursery and trekking out to work all hours, the way her parents had done. They'd always struggled financially, looking worn out and overwhelmed, trying to give Frankie everything she needed. Because she'd been a much wanted baby, they'd treated like a precious gift, wanting the best for her, trying to protect her and keep her safe. She'd always pulled away from that, had been a tomboy more interested in climbing trees and riding her BMX with the boys than chattering with girls and playing with Barbie dolls. Strange that she'd ended up here with Christian, living a life that was like a Barbie and Ken set up.

She glanced over at him, studying his straight nose and tanned skin. He'd get over his sulk sooner or later, and after all, it wasn't a big deal; there would be other cars, other opportunities. He'd always been there for her when it counted, that's all that really mattered. Yes, everything was fine. So she squelched down the feeling of disquiet in her stomach.

***

Frankie shook her head, pulling herself from the past, running her hands along the soft steering wheel, taking in the various gadgets and gizmos on the dashboard. She smiled, the corner of her mouth crooking up on one side. This car was about as far away as you could get from the beaten up Fiat Zack had given her a lift home in a month or so before.

**

It'd been pouring with rain as she'd stopped in the front entrance of the department store, checking the Transport for London app on her iPhone for her journey home. 'Fantastic.' She groaned at the alert telling her there was a line closure, and looked out at the road. The pavement was glossy with rain and giant oily puddles gleamed under the streetlights.

'What's up?' Zack appeared next to her, peering out into the deluge. 'Oof, that's heavy.'

She shivered. 'Line closure. I'm going to have to take three different tubes to get home. And it's already seven.' They stayed open late on Thursday nights and she'd been down on the rota to cover Womenswear.

'I'll give you a lift.' He offered, tossing his keys in the air and catching them easily, open face relaxed and friendly.

'Are you sure? I thought you lived across the other side of the city.'

'I do,' he shrugged, 'but you'll get soaked on the other end, there's no sign of it letting up. It'll also take you ages. I've got no other plans tonight. Let me help.'

She glanced out at the rain again, heavier than before if possible, big fat drops striking the pavement. Switching her gaze back to him, she hesitated. 'Are you sure you don't mind?' The idea of sitting in a heated car was preferable to the idea of traipsing up and down tube station stairs and getting wet on the frigid walk home from the last stop, but she felt edgy, though unsure why.

It wasn't like she was afraid of him. Quite the opposite, he made her feel comfortable, safe.

'Frankie,' he shook his head gently, 'please don't turn into one of those girls who make easy things complicated. Let's make this easy. Just say yes.'

'Well, I wouldn't want to be one of those girls,' she flashed back lightly, 'okay, a lift would be appreciated, thank you. Where's the car?' She scanned the street.

'Ah, yes. The car. I should probably tell you she's not much to look at. But she does do what I need her to.'

'Is she mechanically sound?' Frankie asked.

'Absolutely,' Zack said, tucking his keys in his trouser pocket and zipping up his jacket.

'That's good enough for me then. Where is your car?'

'You stay here, I'll go and get her. No point in both of us getting wet. I won't be long.' Without waiting for a reply he dashed off into the rain.

'Ok-ay then.' Frankie rolled her eyes and did her coat up as a chilly wind swept into the entranceway. 'Brrr.'

Zack was back within minutes, pulling up as close as he could. He hadn't been kidding about his car. From what she could make out in the winter darkness, it was a weird beige shade and one of the wings didn't match colour with the rest of body. The aerial was bent off to one side, and there was a dent above one of the arches. But if it drove, she really didn't care.

She expected Zack to reach across and unlock the doors so she could climb in, but he got out instead, coming round to open the door for her.

'You're getting wet,' she said stupidly. 'You didn't have to do that.'

'I wanted to,' he replied, grinning, 'And Mum drummed good manners into me.'

He looked earnest and kind of cute, his blond hair darkened in the rain. 'Thank you then, I guess.'

'Get in then,' he smiled, 'we're both getting wet now.'

'Sorry!' Ducking down, she slid into the car and after checking she was settled, he slammed the door. Hard. So hard it shook the whole car.

'Sorry about that,' he laughed as he got in, closing his door a lot more gently. 'That door can be a bit of a pain. I wouldn't want it swinging open mid-journey.' He laughed again and she knew her eyes had widened. 'Don't look so worried, it probably won't.'

'Probably?' she squeaked.

'Ninety per-cent.' He see-sawed his hand, 'Eighty minimum.' He paused as there was a sudden gust of wind and the rain rattled on the roof. 'Anyway, you'll have a seatbelt on. Just in case.'

'Ha, ha.' She replied, knowing from the twinkle in his eye that he was joking.

'Speaking of,' he reached across her for the seatbelt tongue, pulling it across her body, 'this is a bit fiddly too.'

'Right,' she breathed, as he did the seatbelt up. He had a dimple near his cheekbone, higher up than the norm. It was sweet. She'd never noticed it before, although they spoke every morning in the staff room before their shift. His easy, laid back manner was a pleasant start to the working day.

He sat back and stared at her. 'Are you okay?'

'Yes, thanks. I'm just a bit tired.'

'Side hurting?' he asked sympathetically, putting the key in the ignition and turning it.

'A bit of a niggle,' she said, touched by the concern, 'I was stood up a lot today.' Most of the staff knew she'd sustained some kind of injury to her ribs the year before, and that sometimes she needed to take a break or find some painkillers. They didn't however know the details. Zack had never pressed her for them.

'Have you taken anything?' Music came on, and he fiddled with some buttons, getting the heater started.

'A couple of ibuprofen earlier,' she answered distractedly, 'this is Bastille.'

'Yes.' He nodded.

'I didn't know you liked them.'

'You said they were good so I bought the album to check them out. That's what friends do, right?' he cranked the heater up. 'They share their likes and dislikes, recommend stuff to each other.' She nodded in agreement. 'By the way,' he continued, 'how are you getting on with the book I leant you?'

'It's really great. I love it.'

'Good. Well, let me know when you've finished it and I'll recommend another.'

'Okay, and I'll bring some of those sci-fi books in that I was telling you about.'

'Sounds good.' He stared at her, hands on the steering wheel.

'All ready to go then?' she asked pointedly, shivering.

'I, uh, yeah, sorry.' Turning to face the windscreen, he shook his head, his hair brushing his jacket collar at the back.

They chattered away as he drove across town, comparing notes on favourite films and TV programmes, mock-arguing about whose line manager was going to explode soonest in the race for the best sales results, exchanging stories about their childhoods, her as an only child, him as one of four brothers.

'Oh my god, your poor mum!' she joked, tracing a snowflake shape into the condensation on her window that had built up from their shared breathing.

'Nah, it could have been worse,' Zack replied.

'How?' she glanced at him. '*Five* boys?'

'No,' he said with a completely straight face, 'it could have been four-'

'Girls!' she finished off, pretending to punch his arm. 'Oi!'

'Come on … Are girls not higher maintenance than boys?'

'You're at risk of sounding like a complete sexist. Luckily for you, I know you're joking!'

'Yeah, I am, but that doesn't mean I'm wrong,' he answered cheekily.

'Boys are just as bad as girls, but in different ways.' She sighed, pretending to be exasperated. Actually, she was having fun.

'Boys tend to be more adventurous I guess,' he mused. 'So tend to get hurt more.'

'Oh, I don't know about that. First exit off here,' she directed as they came to a roundabout. 'We're only five minutes away. I mean, I was quite adventurous,' she carried on with their conversation. 'I went and travelled the world for a year after finishing uni.'

'Oh, yeah?' His face lit up. 'So did I! Where did you go? I did Europe; France, Spain, Italy. Then some of Asia, finishing off in Australia.'

'Me too! I mean, no, I mostly did Thailand, but spent three months in Australia, at the end. Worked my way along the Gold Coast, had casual jobs in some bars and then picked grapes in a really beautiful vineyard. God, it was so great to feel the sun on my skin. The rainforest and waterfalls were sensational too.' She sighed longingly, 'I could have stayed there forever.'

'Yeah, I'm a sun worshipper too. I worked along the road from the Mount Tamborine Vineyard, at the Glow Worm Caves.'

'That place is amazing!' Frankie turned to face him, 'Wow, talk about a small world; that was the vineyard I was at. We could have met! I was there in 2011, how about you?'

'I was there in 2010. It *was* amazing, but a bloody expensive trip too. It was worth it, really once in a lifetime stuff, but I'm still paying it off now, four years later. Still, at least I only have a year left.'

'Yes! Exactly! Me too. About the expensive bit I mean.' She fell silent. She'd be repaying it for a lot longer, given when she'd been with Christian she'd barely made a dent in the debts. He'd offered to pay the loans off for her lots of times, but something in her had always balked. It'd felt too much, him paying for the fun she'd had before meeting him. Now she wished she'd taken him up on the offer.

'I always meant to go travelling again,' he shared, 'maybe I'll look into it towards the end of next year.'

'Yes,' she replied absently. 'Right here, please,' she directed him down a side road that cut through to the main high street with all its shops and bars.

'Thanks. Everything all right? You've gone quiet on me.'

Even though she was staring out of the window at the soaked streets, she could feel him looking at her. She bit her lip, wondering if her life would have gone in a different direction if she had been at the vineyard a year earlier, if she'd met Zack then, had come back to the UK with a good friend, someone who had shared experiences and shared money worries. She might not have met Christian, or if she had, might have thought twice about falling into a whirlwind relationship with him. Of course, she'd fallen out of it almost as quickly, and on bad days wondered if that had been a mistake.

'Frankie? You're worrying me. I'm not used to you not spouting some opinion or bit of gossip at me. Is everything okay?'

'Sorry.' She turned and smiled at him. 'I was just thinking. Anyway, my place is just down here on the right, just after that white van,' she pointed out a dodgy looking vehicle with a partially concealed number plate, orange twine hanging out the slightly open back door.

'All right,' he pulled over, 'here you go. I'll walk you up.'

'Er, no,' she grabbed her bag from the floor, opened the door, 'I'm only on the first floor. There's no need.' She jumped out. She wasn't a snob but she was embarrassed about where she lived, the back alleyway always full of stinky, old potato peelings and her cramped, damp flat smelling of fast food. She ducked her head back into the car, quivering as chilly rain dripped down inside her collar. 'Thanks so much, Zack, for the lift I mean. I really appreciate it. I'd invite you up but it really is getting late and I need to take a hot bath. My ribs are pretty uncomfortable.'

He relaxed back in his seat, tapped a hand idly on the steering wheel. 'Whatever you need,' he smiled gently. 'As long as you're not running away because you're traumatised by riding in my car.'

'Oh well, there is that as well,' she countered, 'but at least it was clean.'

'I do my best,' he said. 'Okay, well take care and have a nice evening.'

'Will do. See you at work tomorrow.'

'See you in the staff room,' he gave a friendly wave.

Slamming the door with a thud due to his earlier comments, she crossed around the back of the car, staring up at the shop sign *Starr's Kebabs*. Huh, there are no stars here, she thought. Zack's engine started behind her and she swung around to watch him pull away. As he went to drive off, a sudden thought occurred to her. She ran over to the car and knocked on the window.

Zack wound it down. 'What's up?'

'Random question.'

He looked amused, 'Fire away.'

'If something happened and I needed to drive your car, or if I wanted to, what would you say?'

'I can't imagine for a minute why you'd want to drive this crap heap,' he replied, 'but if you needed to drive it, and were insured, it wouldn't be a big deal. Why?'

'Nothing. That's what I thought. Night.' Frankie stepped back from the car, tucking her hands in her pockets. It really was bitter tonight.

'Right. Not sure about weird question,' he quipped, starting to roll up his window, 'more like weird girl! See you in the morning.'

'See you,' she whispered, watching his rear lights as he pulled away.

***

'Here you go, found it! It was buried in a colleague's in-tray in the office.' The McLaren salesman's voice sounded next to Frankie's ear through the car's open window.

81

She let out a little yelp, hand flying to her chest.

'Apologies,' he tacked on, helping her open the car door, 'I didn't mean to startle you.'

'No, it's okay,' she waited for the door to finish swooping up over her head and slid out sideways, a lot harder than it looked, as the car was so close to the ground. He offered her a helping hand and she accepted it gratefully, feeling like he was hoisting her up from a horizontal position. 'It was my fault,' she excused him, 'I wasn't paying attention.'

'You did look quite deep in thought,' he agreed, handing her an A4 manila envelope, which looked suspiciously bumpy.

'Thank you,' she ran her fingers over the envelope, wondering what was in it.

'No problem. Sorry for the delay.' He closed the car door smoothly and walked her over to shop front. He paused, manicured fingers wrapped around the door handle. 'You know, he was lucky. We're not open all the time, some days we only do private appointments.'

Intrigue fizzled in her belly, 'He? What did he look like?'

The man smiled politely, 'I don't think that's for me to say, but to be honest I don't think the young man who delivered the envelope is necessarily the one who arranged whatever this is, for you.'

'Why do you say that?'

'Well, by my estimation he looked about twelve.'

'Oh.' Now she was really confused. Christian didn't have any relatives or know anyone that age and neither did anyone else she knew. Was this all a part of some elaborate schoolboy prank then? Was she going to come out looking like a prize idiot? But what schoolboys wrote poems / clues like that? There was only one way to find out.

'Do you mind if I open this in here?' she asked the salesman, 'I probably need to go on somewhere else after this and it's quite dark outside, even with the street lights.' She checked out the window. It also looked freezing cold out there from the way people were rushing past, huddled in their coats and scarves, heads bowed against the wind.

'I can give you five minutes while I start locking up.'

'Thank you,' she said gratefully, ripping into the envelope as he walked away.

The bumps she'd felt turned out to be a handful of mini Bounty bars, her favourite chocolates. Smiling, she unwrapped one and stuck it in her mouth, savouring the rich milk chocolate alongside the crisp nuttiness of the coconut centre. She doubted anyone would go to all this trouble to poison her, and there were no signs of any serial killers so far.

This note was similar to the first.

You've found the next clue, you know what to do,
You don't have to go far, you won't need a car.
Footsteps only to this destination,
Opposite main Knightsbridge station.
Their range is extensive, but very expensive.
A flagship store; beauty, designer and more.

? x

P.s Hope the chocolates makes you smile.

P.p.s. Ask for Millie on the second floor.

Frankie hit the redial button on her phone, peering out along the road as the double tone rang in her ear. The clue was vague in one way—everything around here was pretty expensive, she was in Knightsbridge for heaven's sake—but she was pretty sure from the reference to flagship store where she was going next. One side of her tingled with anticipation at the thought. It was where she'd used to shop all the time, when she was with Christian. But, oh god, the other side of her thought, did that mean it was definitely him?

83

'Hi, it's me.' She said as Kate finally answered the phone.

'Hi, Hun.' Her friend sounded breathless. 'Sorry, I was out back with the dogs. How's it going?'

'Good, I think. I made it to the first place, a McLaren dealership and they had an envelope for me. Apparently it was delivered by some twelve year old kid, which is a bit strange.'

'That is odd. So what was in the envelope?'

'Another clue, and some mini Bounty bars.'

'Ooh. Nice.'

'Christian knows my favourite chocolates,' Frankie said flatly.

'Yes, but anyone who works with you knows that too. I bet you still eat them all the time. It's like your thing. It's a wonder you're not three foot wide.'

'Thanks. Helpful.'

'So, do you think it is Christian?'

'I thought it was unlikely but I am starting to wonder. I think I'm off to Harvey Nichols now, which is totally his style. And I can't imagine Davey or Zack being able to afford anything in there, so by a process of elimination … I don't know how I feel about it if it's him. We split up for a reason.'

'If it is him, he's gone to a lot of trouble to see you and you're there, so you might as well see it through. And it might not be him. Go to Harvey Nicks and give me a call when you're done there.'

'Okay, but for the record, I'm not sure about this.'

'Noted,' Kate laughed, 'now stop being such a big baby and get going. It sounds great to me; I'd loved to be treated to something expensive.'

'Noted in return,' she said drily, 'catch you later.' Ending the call, Frankie threw another thank you over her shoulder as she left the McLaren dealership, hoping she wasn't going to regret this.

'I'm supposed to ask for Millie?' Frankie spoke to the top of the girl's downturned head, hoping she was in the right place.

'That's me,' the girl said coolly, looking up. 'You must be Miss Taylor.'

'I am.'

'Welcome. I'll be your Personal Shopper today.' She smiled, green eyes steady, brown hair tucked neatly back into a low ponytail. 'I'm here to help you get ready. You are cutting it a little fine though Madam, we shut at six 'o' clock today.'

'Sorry. I'm always late. And Frankie's fine. Madam is far too formal.' She raised her eyebrows hopefully, 'I don't suppose you know what I'm getting ready for?'

The girl smiled politely, as if she handled questions like this every day. 'Your date. The Daniel Hersheshon Salon on the floor below us are going to do your hair and make-up, very quickly, and then I'll sort you out an outfit. Have you ever been to the salon before? Do you know it?'

'Yes.' In another lifetime she'd spent a lot of time there, having manicures, pedicures and regular blow dries. As much as it was nice to be treated, she wasn't sure how she felt about being that person again.

'Do you know who the date is with?' Frankie blurted. This was looking more and more like it had Christian stamped all over it. But he should be halfway across the world, and why make contact after all this time, and in this way?

The girl gave her a strange look at that one. 'You don't?'

'Erm, no,' she stumbled, 'I'm kind of on this scavenger hunt thing where I have to follow the clues and—

'Oh, that's so romantic!' Millie clasped her hands together, eyes sparkling, 'Like in a film. I am so jealous. You lucky thing!' She seemed to have completely forgotten herself and the composed professional she'd first presented as, but Frankie much preferred this version. 'Oh, wait until you see the dress, I can't wait to see your face. Come on, we need to hurry.' Gesturing her over to the lift, Millie beckoned Frankie to follow her.

'I don't suppose the name Christian means anything to you,' Frankie asked as they stepped in together and the lift descended soundlessly.

'No. It was a woman who made the appointment.'

'A woman?' Frankie frowned.

'Yes.'

This day just got stranger and stranger.

Half an hour later Frankie stepped back into the warm-toned, beige and brown Personal Shopping suite with Millie, stiletto heels of her ankle boots clicking on the marble floor.

'You look fantastic, Frankie,' Millie said, leading her into a separate dressing area.

'Thanks,' Frankie stopped and looked in a mirror as she entered the room.

The senior stylist in the salon had done something incredible with a hair dryer and texturising spray, creating a sexy, messed up look that said *just got out of bed after an orgasmic all-nighter*. The make-up technician had done her proud too and Frankie could hardly believe how flawless her skin was, how sculpted her cheekbones, her violet eyes defined and feline-like, a bit like Gemma Arterton in a magazine advert she'd recently seen.

'Do you like it?' Millie came up behind her.

'Yes.' Frankie breathed. The girl staring back was definitely her, but better. She might even venture, striking. She'd forgotten just how flattering luxury make-up was, in comparison to the stuff she'd been buying from the supermarket for the last year. She knew it was shallow, but she had missed this. Missed looking stylish and polished. Missed the superior products and designer names.

'It's a pity they didn't have time to do your nails,' Millie said, backing away and walking into an adjoining room, voice carrying through to Frankie, 'but what you have on will still work.' She came back in with a garment over her arm. 'Time for the dress.' Millie's eyes were shining and Frankie felt an instant of friendship with the personal shopper, like they were in this together.

'What are you so excited about?' Frankie asked. 'Oh.' The dress was gold, knee-length and strapless, with sequins and beading around the plunging sweetheart neckline. 'Wow.'

'Yes.' Millie giggled at her expression. 'I think I probably wore the same expression the first time I saw it. Difference is, you get to wear it. You are so lucky.' A tannoy announcement sounded above their head. 'Quick,' Millie urged, 'the store closes in ten minutes.'

'Oh, I'll be quick!' Frankie whipped her jumper over her head, stopping when she realised the kind of bra she had on wouldn't do.

'Sorry, I forgot.' Millie rushed back out and returned to fling a strapless bra and invisible underwear at Frankie. 'Hurry! Call me when you need zipping up, I'll be out there tidying,' she gestured to the reception area.

'Thank you.'

Five minutes later Frankie gazed at the mirror in awe, her expression twinned with Millie's, who'd come in to secure the zip, hooks and eyes running up the back of the dress.

'He got the fit exactly right.' The personal shopper said. 'He must know you really well.'

'Hmm,' Frankie made an indistinct sound. It was the most beautiful dress she'd ever seen and she felt like a princess, but the accurate sizing was more puzzling than ever. She'd lost a lot of weight since the break-up. Between the hospital stay, when she'd barely eaten through grieving for her mum and pain had driven away the need for food, and the change in lifestyle of having to budget constantly to afford to eat, she'd dropped at least two dress sizes. So how would Christian know what would fit her now?

Zack was the most likely candidate; they'd been messing around with a tape measure in one of the stock cupboards only the week before. But how on earth could he afford something like this, on his wages as a Merchandiser? And how would she feel if it was him, when they were only friends?

***

87

'Hey, weird girl!' Zack appeared next to Frankie in the open door. 'What's up?

'Shit!' She dropped the box she was holding with a clatter and the hangers spilled out onto the floor. 'Zack, you scared me.' Crouching down, she started picking them up, shoving them away.

'Sorry, I thought you heard me coming.' Stooping next to her, he took the hangers back out of the box and lined them up neatly before putting them back in. 'I *was* whistling.' He added, eyes twinkling.

She stood up and went over to one of the cupboards to find some skew tags, seeing as he had the hanger situation under control. 'Sorry,' she replied in a mock sniffy tone, 'I was too busy humming to hear you whistling.'

'Oh, I'm so sorry, Lady Frankie, is humming now a superior art form to whistling? Who do we send the memo to?' he teased.

'Human Resources, who else? Maybe it qualifies as part of a staff well-being initiative.'

'Well-being? Ha, ha. Where do you work?' Zack straightened, inserting the box back into its space on the shelf. 'Because it's definitely not here! Isn't it odd,' he mused, 'how pristine the shop floor is, how polished and neat the shopping areas, and then how tatty the back of house areas are? If only the customers got the behind the scenes experience.'

Frankie stopped in her tracks, having had the same thought a hundred times before, every time she'd stepped off the shop floor and into the staff room or one of the store cupboards. 'Yes,' she said softly, 'it is odd.' She smiled, 'Imagine if one day we didn't close a door properly and a customer saw the fourth floor corridor with all the mannequins and boxes of crap along it; a complete fire hazard. There'd be mayhem!' she joked.

He laughed, 'You are strange, weird girl.'

'Stop calling me that,' she exclaimed, setting the skew tags aside, and bending over to root through one of the cupboards. The flexible measuring tape in Womenswear was forever going missing and the sales manager had asked Frankie to search some spares out.

'Why?'

'Argh. What a mess!' Her hands tangled in the assortment of stuff shoved in the box by colleagues, measuring tapes and thick white parcel string and paperclips and tags. 'Because I'm not weird.' She spun around, hands extended to him. She pulled a pitiful face, 'Help me, please.'

'Oh, I don't know,' Zack came over to her and started unpicking string from around her thumb and forefinger. 'I mean, who else could imprison their hands just by going through a box?'

She stuck her tongue out at him in answer.

'And who else has got freaky alien eyes?' he quipped, grinning to take the sting out of any insult.

'Oi! What do you mean alien eyes?' she growled, pretending to glower at him.

'They're a really unusual colour,' he said, head bent over her hands as he tried to unwrap the requested measuring tape from around her wrist, and separate it from the string.

Frankie didn't answer, distracted by the space between his hair and collar, noticing a row of freckles along the back of his neck. It was hardly surprising how fair he was, but it was funny the things you saw when you stopped to look at people. She wondered if he had freckles in other places too. The thought shocked her into talking. 'They're a kind of deep violet,' she agreed. 'It is quite rare. Comes from my Mum's side of the family.' She stiffened.

'Yeah,' he lifted his head to gaze up at her, but didn't give any indication he'd picked up on her tension, 'for weeks after I started I thought you were wearing some of those fake party contact lenses you get. I even asked George,' one of their colleagues from Menswear, 'and he laughed at me. But the shape of your eyes is sort of different too, sort of cat-like.'

'You've been spending far too much time thinking about this,' she sniggered, pulling her hands away as he unravelled the last of the mess. 'Cheers.' She took a measuring tape off him and started wrapping it up and he took the other. 'Next you'll be telling me you've been trying to calculate my dress size too.'

'Which is?' he wiggled his eyebrows suggestively, holding the tape out to her and trying to wrap it around her waist.

'Get lost!' she squirmed away. 'A lady never shares that information.'

'Fair enough,' he smiled, 'not that it really matters.'

'God, you're not going to go all Bridget Jones on me, are you?'

'What, and tell you that I like you,' he batted his eyelashes and she realised just how long they were, 'just as you are? Nah, I'm hardly Colin Firth.'

She smirked, 'But you do watch rom coms.'

He shrugged his broad shoulders. 'Occasionally, but I'm man enough to take it. But we're just friends right?' he waited for her to nod, and dropped the rolled up measuring tape in her palm. 'And besides, I'm not really into any of that soppy stuff. I'd rather just tell a girl I like her and ask her out.'

'Okay. You don't have to act like I've accused you of being a mass murderer.'

He swiped a pair of scissors off the side, a fake manic gleam in his eyes as he advanced towards her. 'How do you know I'm not?'

'Eek! Please, don't hurt me,' she threw her arms up in front of her as she edged toward the door, 'please spare me. I'll do whatever you want. I'm too young to die!'

'Oh, all right then.' He threw the scissors aside. 'It's coffee time anyway. Do you want one?'

She giggled, dropping her arms, 'You'd make a crap serial killer, so easily distracted by caffeine. And, yes please.' He'd taken to making them fresh coffee in a cafetiere every morning and afternoon, a new brand with hints of vanilla. She loved it, and appreciated the effort. One of the girls from the Dior counter had grumbled the other day that he didn't make coffee for them.

'A sensible serial killer,' he argued, checking his watch, 'I think a caffeine hit would be pretty important. Get the blood pumping and the adrenalin spiking for all the running around I'd have to do, stalking big-breasted blondes down impossibly long corridors with thousands of doors.'

She laughed as they closed the cupboard behind them. 'Again, you've spent too much time thinking about this. I'm concerned that you haven't got any meaningful hobbies. Anyway, I'm just going to take these down to Womenswear,' she held up the tapes, 'so I'll meet you up there.'

'No problem, see you in the staff room in a minute.'

Frankie turned away, humming under her breath.

'Oh, Frankie?'

'Yes?' she spun around.

'The reason it wouldn't matter what your dress size is, is because it's about shape and proportions, not size. But given part of my job involves dressing dummies and working with clothes, I reckon you're probably,' he reeled off a set of figures that made her eyes widen because of their accuracy. 'I'm guessing from your face I'm close, but don't worry, I won't tell anyone, or else all the girls will want the same service.' He ducked and guffawed as a tape measure went sailing over his head.

She was smiling as she turned away, and still was a few minutes later.

***

'I said, here are the shoes that go with it,' Millie extended a pair of black stilettos to Frankie, and she got the sense it wasn't the first time the personal shopper had tried to hand them to her. 'We're going to get locked in, and you're going to be late.'

'Th-thanks.' Frankie shook her head, 'Sorry.' Slipping them on, she checked her reflection. 'Okay, good to go.' She hesitated, 'Do you know where I'm going next?'

'No,' Millie placed a black wrap around Frankie's shoulders

and handed her a matching handbag. 'All I know is there's a car waiting at the front entrance to take you to the next stop. Now, don't worry about your jacket and clothes, a courier will run them home to you tomorrow. I put your phone, money, keys and other things in the bag. Let's move.'

'Thank you. I feel like a celebrity with her own entourage,' Frankie admitted as they rode the lift down to the ground floor.

'Let's hope you're going somewhere fitting then,' Millie replied, leading her out to the entrance on Knightsbridge, signalling to a driver standing next to a silver limo. 'Just promise me you won't act like a diva.'

'I won't,' Frankie grinned as they both stared at the luxury car. 'Although it might be hard. Thank you for all your help,' she said, sashaying over to the car door the driver was holding open, and sliding in carefully in the tight dress.

'Just doing my job.' Millie stooped to peer in at her, shaking her head in disbelief at the ready poured glass of champagne Frankie was already holding in her hand. 'If you think it's appropriate, I'd love to know how you got on.'

Frankie took a sip of fizz, sneezing as the bubbles went up her nose, 'Of course I'll let you know,' she replied.

'Great. And if you could arrange for the limo to circle back and drop me home, even better,' Millie quipped.

Frankie nodded and winked, 'I'll do my best.'

As the car drew away from the kerb and the waving personal shopper, Frankie leaned forward to speak to the driver, 'Do you know where we're going?'

'Not far, Madam,' he replied, 'not far at all.'

A minute later they were pulling in beside Hyde Park Corner, Frankie having only drunk half of the glass of delicious champagne. 'We've only come about half a mile.' She peered out at the grey statues, arches and columns.

'Just under,' the driver said, eyes meeting hers in the mirror, 'but you wouldn't want to walk it in those shoes, would you?'

'I guess not,' she said wryly, looking down at the pin-sharp heels. 'So what now?'

He gestured her forward and she shuffled toward him. 'For you.' Handing her an envelope. 'I'll wait while you read it. You have to tell me where we're going.'

'Right.' She took another sip of champagne and set the flute aside. 'Here goes then.' The envelope was smaller than the others but with a bulkier object in one corner, so she opened it with care, unfurling the scented paper.

A world class hotel, with old world glamour,
A slice of pink heaven, refined not with clamour,
Louis sixteenth design, art easy on the eye,
Best dining rooms in Europe, that's FYI.
Bronze gilt and sumptuous chandeliers,
join me for dinner, it won't end in tears.

? x

P.s. wear these.

She tapped the envelope against her palm and a square jewellery box fell out. She flipped back the lid, holding her breath. A pair of twinkling diamond earrings nestled on the velvet pillow. This was too much. Getting her iPhone out, she did a google search and then texted Kate.

Hey, hope you're having a good NYE so far. Decked out in designer togs, with hair & make-up done. Heels, bag, expensive jewellery – the lot. Looks like it's Christian and I'm going to a famous hotel. Will catch up with you later, F xx

Frankie tucked her phone away, took a deep breath and let it out slowly. 'I know where we're going,' she announced to the driver.

'Where shall I take you Madam?' he raised an eyebrow.

'The Ritz, please. But can you circle the block a few times? I need a couple of minutes.'

'Of course,' he replied automatically.

'Thank you.' She said softly, sinking back against the seat, gazing out at Hyde Park Corner, where she and Zack had gone for a walk on their lunch break only a few weeks before.

***

Zack was leaning up against the inside of the impressive Wellington Arch, traffic streaming past them, roaring and beeping. His breath was puffing out in front of him in clouds. It was the coldest day so far, and personally Frankie would much rather be in the staff room warmly wrapped up, but Zack had convinced her to jump on a bus and get some fresh air. Well, as fresh as you could get in the middle of London.

'It's the anniversary, or close to it, isn't it?' he asked her, tucking his hands in his jacket pockets. 'You look sad today.'

Frankie nodded, wrapping her purple scarf tighter around her face. 'Mum died a year ago today,' she gulped. She'd told him about her mum's premature heart attack over lunch one day, when he'd picked up a health magazine and made a comment about an article in it. They'd had a debate over what caused heart attacks and how devastating the unexpected ones were for families and friends. A swift departure for people who were supposed to be around for a long time yet. 'I suppose I should be over it a bit more by now.' She sniffed, hunching her shoulders, hoping he wouldn't hug her. If he was sympathetic, she might cry. And she wasn't the crying sort.

'Rubbish,' he said bluntly, 'a year isn't that long, and everyone is different. People react differently,' thankfully he seemed to pick up on her body language, staying where he was against the arch, 'some people need routine, or a longer time to assimilate. Some need to take a break from work; others need the normality of getting up every day, having a purpose.' He gazed at her. 'Unfortunately death is something that everyone has to deal with at some point or another. No one is exempt.'

'It's part of life,' she mumbled, recalling the words Christian had thrown at her during their last argument.

'Yes. But it's a horrible, shitty part of life,' Zack expanded, 'probably one of the shittiest parts. You have to give yourself time, until one day it doesn't hurt so badly.'

'I guess. It's just that it was so sudden, so quick. One day she was there at the end of a phone, and we were planning a visit, and then … she was gone. I hadn't seen her in months.'

'Don't feel guilty,' he looked at her, dark blue eyes intense, 'I can see that's what you're doing. But she would have known you loved her. You were her daughter. You're still her daughter. You're here, and you remember her. That's what matters.'

'And my dad,' she agreed fiercely, 'Dad still loves her. He remembers her.'

'And loads of other people too, I can almost bet on it.'

'Yes.' Frankie nodded, gulping again, tears filling her eyes. She blinked. 'Do you mind if we change the subject?'

'Sure,' Zack nodded. 'But am I allowed to ask if you got hurt before or after she died?'

'It was a few weeks after,' she said, 'I was in an accident. I'd rather not talk about that either though. It happened, I got better, now I'm largely fine, apart from the odd bad day when I ache. I don't like thinking about it.'

'I understand,' Zack pushed away from the wall, 'Brr, that was freezing!' He offered her his arm, 'Take a five minute spin on this,' he said, 'and then we'll head back to work.'

She looped her arm through his companionably, 'Sounds like a plan. Thank you for listening to me, and not pushing.'

'Happy to, and it's not an issue. Just one thing though Frankie.'

She ground to a halt, knowing he was serious from his use of her first name. She'd almost started answering to *weird girl* recently. 'What's that?'

'Sometimes to go forward, you have to look back.'

***

Zack's words rang in her head as she walked up the stairs of The Ritz and through the gold revolving door, having received welcoming nods from the staff dressed in smart, gold buttoned uniforms and top hats. Was this going to be her chance to confront her past? Or was it going to be an opportunity to move forward? Who was waiting for her at dinner?

She bit her lip to hold back a gasp as she entered the reception area, thinking of the clue. It really was a slice of pink heaven, and she could totally understand why the interior architecture was so praised, with high vaulted ceilings and impressive bronze detailing and fine art hanging from or painted into every available space, glittering chandeliers and large vases of deep blood-red roses. It screamed refinement and luxury and old money. She'd never been here with Christian; he'd always preferred the more modern establishments. No matter what happened, she couldn't regret coming on this scavenger hunt. The destination was beautiful and definitely worth the journey.

She walked along the red and white patterned carpet. It was busy, lots of people milling around and seated in a lounge area with a piano, with guests walking along to the ornate dining room. Chatter filled the air, but it was still muted somehow, like everyone was too polite to speak or laugh too loudly.

'Miss Taylor?' A man in a tux appeared next to her.

She nodded, and he slipped the wrap from her shoulders. 'You're to come through to the Rivoli Bar please, while your table is prepared.'

She followed him as he lead her into an art deco ante-room equipped with a bar, all dark wooden wall panels inlaid with gold details, gold raised ceilings from which chandeliers hung, white and gold curtains gathered in at the centre with what looked like large gold coins with tassels hanging from them, black and white animal print chairs, smooth round yellow tables with glass candle holders, parquet floors with tasteful but modern block multi-coloured blue, gold, red and white rugs laid down on it.

'Here you are, Madam.' The waiter gestured to a table, his body blocking Frankie's view of the guest sat at it. For a moment, before he moved, she had an instant, crazy, confusing hope it might be Zack sat there.

'Oh. Hi.' She was disappointed to see Christian's dark-haired sex godlikeness lounging in the chair, looking as cool and collected as ever. He always looked good, super slick and super cool. Tonight he was wearing a white, open necked shirt under a suit jacket. But slick and cool wasn't always the preferable option. She was starting to realise she might like warm and quirky and nice instead.

'Don't look so pleased to see me.' Christian stood up and came round the table, kissing her on the cheek.

She edged away slightly as his aftershave hit her, the same one he'd worn when they were together. It brought back memories of frustration and sadness, feeling low and uncontrollably angry. And then, bitterly disappointed. 'Sorry, I'm just surprised, that's all. I wasn't sure it was you.'

He pulled her chair out for her and she sank into it with a murmured thanks. 'Why wouldn't it be?' he asked, sitting down across from her. 'And who else would be doing all this for you? Have you got a boyfriend or admirer I should know about?'

Surprise number two, he hadn't pulled a chair out for her in a long time. It was like he'd started forgetting his manners the last year or so they'd been together. But maybe that was as much her fault as his. She should have called him on it.

The waiter appeared next to them, handing them white and gold embossed cocktail menus. Frankie took hers with a smile, noticing that Christian uncharacteristically did the same. 'No admirer or boyfriend,' she smiled coolly, 'but I was told a young boy delivered the envelope to the dealership, and a woman booked the personal shopper at Harvey Nicks. The sizing of the dress was spot on too.'

'I called in a few favours,' he lifted one shoulder in a casual shrug, running a finger down the menu. 'Let's get a drink before we talk more.'

She bit her lip in annoyance but another minute of suspense wouldn't kill her. 'So,' she leaned forward once they'd ordered their cocktails, a Red Fruits Manhattan for her and a New York Sour for him, 'why am I here?'

'You look stunning,' he grabbed her hand, stroking her wrist, and she quivered. 'Absolutely gorgeous.'

'Thank you, the dress is beautiful, the shoes too.' She didn't want to seem ungrateful. She extracted her hand subtly.

'But you're not wearing the earrings.' He frowned.

'I didn't know what all this was, who they were from. They're too expensive, I felt uncomfortable. Now stop avoiding the question Christian, why am I here? And why aren't you in Bali?'

'I've missed you. I didn't want to go without you.'

'And you've waited an entire year to tell me that? Even though you wouldn't talk to me when I came to get my stuff? You couldn't have got in touch before? You had to wait and do all this?'

'I was hurt and shocked when you ended it. Flabbergasted, actually. But I'm telling you the truth, I have missed you.' His clear blue eyes shone with sincerity.

'That would probably be romantic,' Frankie said drily. 'If I didn't think, sorry, *know*, that you've probably had a series of women parade through the apartment since I left. Don't forget I knew all about your playboy reputation when we got together the first time,' she reminded him.

He looked at her, opened his mouth then closed it. She stared back steadily 'Come on, don't try and pretend you've been pining away without me, living a celibate lifestyle.'

He flushed, cheekbones going dark red, 'So I've dated. There have been other women—'

'A few I'm guessing.'

'But none like you,' he insisted.

'Oh, really?' She sat back in her chair as the waiter brought green olives, nuts and mini crackers to the table in a silver and white snack holder, swiftly followed by their cocktails. She took a sip of the tangy, crisp Manhattan and set it back down. 'How's that then?' she prompted him.

He put his cocktail down with a slight clink against the table. 'They were all kind of … plastic. Not real, like you. You've got opinions and values and a good sense of humour.'

'You found my opinions and values annoying when we were together. Sometimes you said I had too many.'

'I know, and I'm sorry. I was wrong,' he reached for her hand, and she let him hold it while he apologised. 'They agree with everything I say, everything I want. I thought it would be what I wanted, but it's boring.'

'You always picked women who were into vanity and society, until me,' she pointed out, 'if you've reverted to type, what else do you expect? To be honest I'm not sure I understand how we were together for three years. We're so different.' She lowered her voice, aware that a touristy-looking couple at the next table were trying to listen in. 'It doesn't make sense, and now that we've been apart—'

'You're wrong,' he said anxiously, clasping her hand tighter, 'And I've changed.'

'Have you? Even so, you weren't there for me when—'

'We were good together.' He whispered, 'I treated you like a princess. I was there for three years. I messed up once—'

'You bought me a lot.' She conceded, seeing real pain reflected in his eyes. 'You kept me safe and gave me a life of luxury. But I was a princess locked in a tower. I never saw my friends, barely went home to see my parents,' she closed her eyes briefly, 'something

I've regretted ever since. It had all become about you, the dinners and parties. That was okay for a while. At the beginning it was fun, living that kind of life, but ultimately … even without what happened, I was starting to feel trapped. That's why I went and got the job. You didn't listen to me, barely engaged in conversation, talked about your day but never asked about mine.'

He lifted his hand from hers, 'Most men are like that,' he excused, 'and maybe that was because all you really did was shop and lunch. How much was there to ask you about?'

'You wanted it that way!' she said furiously, forgetting where they were, throwing the rest of her cocktail back and then choking with the sting of alcohol. She cleared her throat. 'You wanted me to be available and on call all the time, wanted me to look good and dress right. That's why you didn't like me getting a job.' She took a calming breath, 'Yes, you bought me things but you were never thoughtful,' her mind settled on Zack driving her across town, and making her fresh coffee every day, and something in her stomach hitched, 'you never made me a fresh coffee, or cooked for me.'

'I didn't need to. I have people to do that.' He'd had specialist coffee delivered every morning by a high end catering company.

'Yes, but you could have done it anyway, to show you cared.'

'I do care,' he insisted, 'and I have changed. You can do whatever makes you happy.'

And perhaps he had changed. After all, the old Christian never would have organised a romantic scavenger hunt, never would have made the effort to put something so elaborate together, just for her.

'Come back,' he moved his chair closer, rested his arm against hers, stroking her cheekbone. Her pulse quickened. Oh, he was good. Sex had never been an issue, they'd always been compatible, she'd always found him attractive. He was a good looking guy.

'What do you mean?' she asked, shifting away.

'Come home, back to the flat. Quit that horrible retail job with the long hours and live with me. You can get another job that you like, or I can set you up in business. I can scale back my hours, we can do more together. Let me pay your debts off this time, so it's not hanging over you, and we can make a fresh start.'

The thought was incredible appealing.

No more money worries, no more damp flat. Someone who would look after her, who would offer her security, someone she knew, who she could fall back into a routine with.

It sounded like bliss, and she knew it would be crazy to consider turning him down.

But … But still, for all of that, she couldn't make her mouth form the words to accept it.

'What do I have to do to convince you?' he urged.

'I don't know,' she said slowly, honestly. 'I just can't see how I can move back in, how we can just pick it up as if nothing has happened. After a year, you just ride up on your white horse and solve everything?'

He let out a growl of frustration and signalled the tuxedoed barman for another cocktail.

She knew she complained about her job, but didn't everyone? And she wasn't *that* miserable. The thought of jacking it in was appealing though. She pressed her fingers down on the table, knowing Christian was waiting for an answer. If she quit her job, she would lose her independence again, and wouldn't see Zack, wouldn't get to have morning coffee or lunch with him or whinge when a nightmare customer made her want to bang her head against the wall and offer surrender.

She would miss that, she really would.

She would miss him.

Damn it.

'I know I wasn't that supportive when your mum died.' Christian muttered. 'And I am sorry about that.'

'Not *lost her*? You can actually say *died* now?' she demanded, alluding to their argument, the one right before the accident.

He at least had the grace to look ashamed. 'I made some mistakes.'

'You gave me three days and then bought me a four thousand pound handbag to '*cheer me up*' before telling me to pull myself together.'

She could still hear the echo of their conversation now, over a year down the line.

***

'You've lost your Mum,' Christian said, slinging his briefcase on the white sofa, 'I do understand that, and I know it's hard. But I really think that putting on something nice and wearing some make-up,' he gestured to her bare face and swollen red-rimmed eyes, 'will make you feel better. Besides, I've got that dinner tonight and need you with me. It'll be expected. In a few days' time I'll be losing you for a week to go and help your dad make the necessary arrangements. Come on,' he said, ignoring her gobsmacked silence, 'people lose other people all the time. It's part of life. It happens.'

She gaped, mouth open, unable to articulate any words.

'Well?'

'I didn't lose her Christian. We haven't gone shopping and got momentarily separated. She's dead. I will never see her again.' She spoke through clenched teeth, sobs rising up in her throat. 'Do you understand that? And yes, people die, but she wasn't supposed to go for years. When your parents get old you know you're going to have to deal with at some point but not when they're in their mid-sixties, and die of a massive, sudden heart attack.'

The argument had gone on for half an hour after that, until, exhausted and wracked with grief, she'd run out of their flat with no shoes or coat on, no handbag or belongings. Christian had pursued her, calling her name, but she'd been in such a state she'd sprinted across the road and into the path of a car. She remembered the impact, the feeling of pressure, the sound of crunching glass, the poor driver's alarmed face, but she didn't really remember any

102

pain. That came later, when she woke up in hospital to be told her leg was broken and she'd fractured three ribs on one side. Ribs that, as it turned out, never healed entirely right.

The recovery period in hospital gave her time apart from Christian. Hours of staring at light green walls, or gazing at mindless TV, reassessing her life. She hadn't meant to run out in front of the car, it hadn't been some death wish to join her mum, she'd just been careless and driven by loss. But the accident did give her space and distance. Enough of a breather that when Christian came to pick her up, she told him she wasn't going home with him, would never go home with him again. He'd let her down too badly and the last few weeks had changed her too much. She wasn't happy with him, with their life together.

***

'I am sorry,' he repeated, lifting his second cocktail and gesturing for her to do the same, 'really. Give me another chance. What do you say?'

'I'm sorry too. I know the way I broke up with you, how sudden it was, must have been hard. And what you've done today, the letters and hunt, are incredibly romantic. If you have genuinely changed, maybe—'

The sound of Christian's ring tone interrupted her answer, and several nearby customers gave him and Frankie dirty looks.

He glanced at the screen. 'I need to get this. Apologies, I'll be back in thirty seconds.'

She gaped after his departing back. Or he hadn't changed at all. Taking a sip of her cocktail she rooted around in her bag, finding a brief Ok, Good Luck x text from Kate. She selected another unopened message.

Hey, weird girl! Just to say Happy New Year, whatever you're

No matter what, Zack always made her smile. Could she say the same about Christian? But did she want, or need, either of them in her life? And if she did, in what role?

She drained her cocktail, feeling light-headed and a bit drunk, on top of the champagne in the limo earlier. Christian had been gone a lot longer than thirty seconds. What on earth was he doing? Signalling to the waiter to keep their table, she wandered out into the main lounge area, creeping up behind Christian as he sat in a winged chair, in animated conversation on the phone.

'Yes, it worked, she loved it, said it was really romantic. Yes, I'll send the bank transfer later tonight. I'll be recommending the service to my friends. Thank you.'

'You didn't organise this yourself?' Frankie's outraged voice made Christian jump and he fumbled his phone, dropping it on the floor.

Scrambling to pick it up, he turned around. 'Frankie, what are you doing out here?'

'Finding out that you haven't changed at all apparently,' she replied, crossing her arms over her chest. 'Same old Christian, throwing his money around. Whoever that was, they wrote all the clues, right? Picked everything out?'

'It's the thought that counts.'

'When you put the effort in yourself, not when you pay someone else to do it for you!' She could see from the look on his face that he just didn't get it. And she didn't think he ever would. 'Tell me what really happened. Why aren't you in Bali? It's not like you to give up a trip like that.' She stepped right into his space, eyeballing him. 'You may as well be honest. You've blown this anyway.'

'But what about the dress and the earrings? What about dinner? I've booked a table.'

'That's your problem, not mine.' A tingling feeling ran over her shoulders, like a weight she hadn't known she'd been bearing

104

had lifted away. 'I felt bad about ending things the way I did,' she shared, 'and I'm sorry if I hurt you and this is some odd *the one that got away* thing you're doing, but I've changed. And I don't think you're ever going to.'

Christian's face tightened. 'You didn't hurt me that badly, don't worry. My girlfriend and I broke up last week and I didn't care to go alone, that's all.'

'So you had a gap to fill?'

'No! I'm not that bad,' he softened, 'I—I got this wrong. I'm sorry.'

'All right then, take care.' Nodding, she spun on her heel.

'Frankie, wait, where are you going?'

She looked over her shoulder, 'I'm going to get the wrap and find somewhere I can get some air. Alone,' she emphasised. 'Then I'm going to spend the rest of New Year with my friends.' Smiling at the thought, 'I'll get the rest of the things returned to Harvey Nicks as soon as I can. Take care Christian, and good bye.'

'Stay,' he exclaimed, talking to her back. 'Have dinner, relax. It's on me.'

'No, thanks.'

He sighed heavily, 'You won't owe me anything, it's an apology. I miscalculated. I'm leaving, don't worry.'

She hesitated. Was she really going to turn dinner at The Ritz down out of principle?

'Please.' He walked past her, 'I'll let the waiter or someone know. Stay. Call a friend to join you. Try and have a happy new year, if I haven't ruined it for you.'

Softening – he wasn't all bad – she laid a hand on his arm. 'Fine, I'll stay. Thank you.'

Nodding briskly, he tucked his phone in his pocket and strode away. He didn't look back.

She decided to dine alone at a leisurely pace. It was a once in a lifetime opportunity, especially now Christian was gone for good. She also needed time to think things through without distraction, or conversation. No advice from Kate, or Davey – she texted him to say she'd join them later – no instinctive reaction about her single status. She ate a sumptuous three course meal that she was convinced ruined her taste buds for all other food, and reflected on the last year, and everything today had shown her.

Sometimes to go forward, you have to look back, Zack had said.

By the time she finished eating, the restaurant was nearly deserted. She went back into the Rivoli Bar and pulled out her phone.

I need to see you. Can you come & find me? F xx

She attached her location to the message using Googlemaps and sat down to wait.

Two hours later, she stood shivering on the roof terrace of The Ritz, overlooking Green Park and Westminster. Four large copper lion statues guarded the corners of the roof, and the London Eye was lit up with the night's festivities. Barges and boats floated on the Thames and music sounded on the air. She couldn't see the crowds of people down by the river, but she knew they were there.

'You look extraordinary Frankie.'

'Zack!' she swung around to look at him. 'You made it. Thanks for coming. And thank you for the compliment. But was there a *but* in there?'

'Yes. You look extraordinary, *but* not like you. I kind of prefer the tight jeans and off the shoulder tops with your stiletto boots. Like that time at the pub for Fiona's leaving do. It was sexy.'

'Really?' Hope flared, making her nerves jangle.

'Yes.' He made his way over to her.

'Do you think I'm sexy?' she demanded, stumbling closer to him. 'Are you drunk?'

'Nooo,' she may have ruined it by her eyes crossing at that precise moment, 'all right,' she held a thumb and finger up and squeezed them together, 'maybe a little bit.'

'Weird girl,' he sighed, 'what have you been doing to yourself? And why are you here?'

'So, I'm here because my ex set up this scavenger hunt thing where I had to follow these clues, and I got my hair and make-up up done at Harvey Nicks and they put this dress on me and then there was a limo ride here.' She blurted in a rush, and then took a breath. 'But I did not put on the earrings,' she said sternly. 'I had champagne, and cocktails, then a gorgeous red wine over dinner. I think there may have been cocktails after that,' she shrugged, 'I can't quite remember.'

'Sounds romantic, although I'm not quite sure I follow about the earrings. So where is he?'

'It would have been romantic, but he paid someone else to do it all.'

'Ah. Not so romantic after all.' He drifted nearer, rubbing her arms to keep her warm. 'So, what happened?'

'We talked, he told me he'd changed, wanted me to go back and live with him. He's stinking rich.'

'Which would have solved some of your problems,' he concluded, looking concerned.

'My financial ones, yes. But it wouldn't have solved the issue of being lonely. You ever been in a relationship where you feel completely alone?' she spoke carefully, trying hard not to slur her words.

'No. Sounds sad.'

'It is. It was.' She nodded solemnly, then nodded again to underline the point. Followed by a scowl, 'But he hasn't changed really and I was the back-up plan. I deserve better than that.'

'You do.'

'He can offer me the financial security my parents couldn't when I was growing up,' she'd figured that one out over dinner, 'but when Mum died, he couldn't deal with it.'

He glanced over her shoulder at Big Ben, wrapping his arms around her to keep her warm. 'You're freezing. It's coming up to midnight.' As if his words were magic, the clock tower's bells started tolling. 'You said no to him.' *Dong.*

Pulling back, rocking on her heels, she looked at him, puzzled. 'How do you know that?'

Dong. He shook his head, mumbling something under his breath. 'Because weird girl, you're here and he's not, and you texted me.'

'Oh, that makes sense.' *Dong.* 'Now I'm only lonely sometimes, because I'm busy and I have friends and family that make me feel loved. One of those friends is you.' *Dong.* 'You get me,' she hiccupped, 'I think.'

'I'd like to think so,' he said softly, taking his coat off and wrapping it around her shoulders, producing an umbrella from somewhere to shield her from the soft patter of rain that had just started. *Dong.* 'And I would also like to think,' his open, honest face had never looked so appealing, white teeth flashing as he grinned, 'that one day, when you're ready, we could be more than friends.'

Big Ben was still ringing out the countdown to midnight in the background but she blocked it out now. 'You like me like that?'

'I just drove across London on New Year's Eve, abandoning my friends and family to see you, and pulled up outside The Ritz in a beaten up Fiat. You should have seen the way the doormen looked at me. So what do you think? Yes, I like you. Have done since day one, when Simon introduced us.'

She shook her head, 'I don't even remember that meeting.'

'I know. You didn't see me. But maybe you will, one day.'

'And if that happened, what would I need to do, to show you I was ready?' she breathed.

'I don't know,' he shivered, 'kiss me?'

'Right,' she answered thoughtfully, as Big Ben finally struck twelve and hundreds, if not thousands, of people lining the Thames yelled out *Happy New Year* and started singing Auld Lang Syne. Above her head, Zack looked out across the rooftops at the London Eye as enormous white sparkles started rotating on it. 'Zack?' she stared up at him.

'Yes?' he switched his attention back to her.

Rising up on tiptoes she threw her arms around his neck, plastering her body along his, breasts pushed against his chest. 'Happy New Year,' she whispered.

As the sound of fireworks filled the air with whizzes and bangs and fizzes, she kissed him, mouth hot against his, eyes closed. After a brief hesitation he kissed her back, one arm tightening around her, the other still holding the umbrella. And it was amazing. And she saw. There was chemistry there, there was heat. Sometimes it took time to grow. She *saw* him, in the way she knew he saw her.

She saw how thoughtful and respectful and lovely he was to her, and how important that was. Much more important than whether he could put her up in a luxury pad by the Thames and shower her with gifts or not.

'Woah!' he pulled back, eyes slightly glazed, hair damp from the drizzle that had crept under the umbrella. 'What was that?' He seemed oblivious to the sparkling multi- coloured fireworks filling the London skyline, a dazzling array of greens and purples and oranges lighting up the darkness.

'A New Year kiss.' She said impatiently, rolling her eyes. She thought it was her who was tipsy, not him.

'What did it mean though?' He looked hopeful and scared at the same time. Some of his question was obscured by the deafening pops of fireworks but she understood him anyway.

'It means I'm ready,' she said, 'not ready for anything heavy, or quick. But ready to try.'

He pushed a strand of hair behind her ear, 'Are you sure? There's no rush.'

She stared up into his face, studied his freckles, the way his blond hair curled slightly on his collar, the face that got more attractive every time she looked at it. 'I am sure,' she nodded.

It might be the cocktails talking or it might be the closure with Christian, so she could stop wondering if she'd done the right thing. It might even be what was in the air with the dawning of 2015, a hint of promise, a dash of new beginnings, a pinch of hope.

Or it could just be that of all the people she'd had in her life over the last few months, he made her laugh the most. And that's what made her certain she was making the right decision.

'Come on,' she wriggled around so she could snuggle into his side, 'let's watch the fireworks. It would be a shame to waste them. The colour-bursts are stunning.'

'You're stunning,' he whispered in her ear.

She shivered, but not from the cold, slid him a sideways look and smiled slowly. 'Do you know what Zack?'

'What?' He hugged her closer, his body heat transferring to her.

'I know it might sound weird, seeing as I kind of came here on a date with my ex, but I'm really glad that I celebrated New Year and the start of 2015 at The Ritz.'

They both *ahhhed* as a starburst of white showered down towards them, illuminating their grinning faces.

'So am I, weird girl,' he agreed, squeezing her tight, 'so am I.'

Valentine's on Primrose Hill

Now

Leo Miller still wasn't sure how he'd ended up standing alone on Primrose Hill on the most romantic day of the year, both hoping and dreading his Valentine would show up. The girl he'd thought would be a friend but had turned out to be so much more. The girl he owed the truth to, instead of the version she thought she knew.

If she came.

He stood at the top of the panoramic park, the London skyline sandwiched between a bright blue sky and leafy trees. Rolling green grass flowed below him, intersected by numerous paths lined with Victorian-looking lamps. He could make out all the main landmarks in the distance, no longer needing the long, narrow metal plaque on the circular brow of the hill to read the city. He'd brought too many classes here over the last five years to show them the glorious sights of their capital. He knew this skyline off by heart.

Left to right was the spire of St Mark's Church, the high-rise, closely huddled towers of Canary Wharf, the dark curved outline of The Gherkin and lower, crouching St Paul's Cathedral, the soaring sharp-edged Shard. Further over was the pinnacle of the BT Tower (plumper at the top), the rounded upper half of the

London Eye wheel then over to Westminster and the Houses of Parliament, Crystal Palace Tower and smaller, tucked away on the edge, Westminster Cathedral.

Shoving his freezing hands into his coat pockets, he shivered in the crisp February sunshine. It was a beautiful Saturday, though cold, and gusts of wind shook the last of the leaves that had somehow survived autumn and winter from the trees. Hard to believe it would be spring soon. Happy, noisy families with push-chairs and plump, eager toddlers on reins panted their way up the concrete paths, and dog walkers rambled across the amazingly healthy green grass, some of them throwing tennis balls for their canine friends. A couple wandered past hand in hand, bundled up in scarves and woolly hats but not looking like they felt the frigid temperature at all, too wrapped up in each other. Cars zipped past, making their way in and out of Camden Town. At the bottom of the hill was Primrose Hill Bridge, spanning Regent's Canal. If she didn't come he'd walk down there, take a tube to Oxford Street and distract himself by trekking around the shops.

He checked his watch. Five to twelve. He'd asked to meet at noon, but had wanted to get here early.

As bitter as the weather was, he'd prepared a mini-hamper filled with champagne and gourmet foods, had thought they could sit on one of the benches and share a feast and the view, the backdrop they'd met against. It was probably a crazy idea given the near sub-zero temperatures but he'd thought it would be romantic and had limited the madness by also bringing a rucksack stuffed with two blankets, some hand warmers, and two bobble hats as well as panda ear-muffs for comedy value. He'd once joked he'd need to wear them to block out her constant chatter, a tongue-in-cheek comment given how hard it could be to get her to open up. Still, with time and patience, he'd got to know her over the past four weeks.

And when you dug under that shy, sometimes fragile exterior, once she forgot what had happened to her, how she now looked or

112

thought she looked, her smile could light up the whole park. You could see shades of the intelligent, outgoing girl she'd been before and would be again. Since that first meeting he'd known what she needed, apart from a friend. To see and believe that although she might never be the same person as before the accident, she'd become someone stronger and more capable because of what she'd been through. And that whatever she might think or feel, she was still attractive to the opposite sex; love wasn't something that was forever out of reach if she didn't want it to be. Hopefully he'd been showing her those things over the last month. What he hadn't realised until it was too late was that she'd been unwittingly showing him something along the way too. How to fall in love.

Shit. Double Shit.

He would never forgive himself if the challenge his friends had set for him – to find a date for Valentine's Day and finally get a love life – had ruined what little self-confidence she'd built, as well as their friendship. Because if being friends was the only thing he could have of her, he would accept it in a heartbeat.

Swivelling around, searching the numerous paths for her tall figure, he blew out a long, slow breath. He was the only single person here without a dog. On Valentine's Day. Talk about sad. Ironic too. All those years with no-one he'd wanted to spend it with, so wasn't bothered by covering for colleagues who wanted to leave early, and now there *was* someone, and the day cupid was famous for was actually on a weekend … and she wasn't here.

The question was, would she be? A few more minutes and he would know.

Before

Georgiana Dunn yelped as a wriggling weight landed on her chest, wrenching her from the foggy doze she'd been having cocooned in her duvet. Instinctively bringing both hands up to protect her face, her fingers encountered the scarring around what used to be her right eye. She flinched, placing her hands against the covers instead.

'Don't be silly,' she muttered to herself. 'You should be used to it by now.' It wasn't as if the damage could be forgotten during the day either because the itchy, annoying eye patch she wore dug lines into her forehead and cheekbone. It also did a crap job of covering the scar running from her cheekbone down towards her mouth.

Something sharp pressed into her shoulder and thudded on her stomach, driving the air from her lungs.

'Eurgh, oof' she grunted, pushing upwards against the duvet in search of escape. What had been a comfortable nest a moment before now felt like a hot, suffocating tomb. Flexing her legs, the muscle in her upper right thigh protested, the one under the wound that always felt hot and achy even though it'd been four months since the accident and should have healed completely by now.

Accident. Disaster. Trauma. That's what the doctors, nurses, surgeons and physiotherapists had taken turns calling it. To her it would always just be the worst day of her life. Who would have thought that someone else's unexpected heart attack at the wheel could change her world so radically?

Feet drumming against the mattress, lifting her head, her long plait somehow wrapped around her neck. She sucked in a panicky breath and with a grunt of effort managed to flip down the duvet, freeing herself from the hair noose at the same time.

'Thank God!' Her relieved exclamation muffled a thud somewhere near the end of the bed. Fresh air and sunlight hit her and she winced, turning toward the wall. Then she bolted upright, wondering what had been on top of her. She twisted her head back and forth to see as much as the bed as possible, but there was nothing there other than a rumpled purple throw.

'Good morning, darling,' her mum sang brightly.

'Jeez!' George jumped, hand clutching her chest as she swung her head around to a spot a few feet from her bed. 'You almost gave me a heart attack. Why are you on the floor? Praying for patience?' she joked, sweeping aside the covers and swinging her feet down to the

114

thick dark grey carpet. It reminded her of brewing storm clouds, the complete opposite of the sunny wooden laminate floor in her childhood bedroom, which they'd left two weeks before. However hesitant she'd been about moving initially, she had to admit that although she missed their old place, the en-suite bathroom here was fab because there was no need to stumble to the other end of the house in the middle of the night.

'Well? What are you doing?' George prompted her mum. 'It's not like you to be so quiet.' She smiled to take the edge off the comment.

'As much as I may soon have to pray for patience,' Stella said, sinking back on her knees, 'if you insist on staying in so much, no, that's not my current activity.' She fussed with some kind of round, quilted cushion. 'I was leaving you a gift.'

'Another one?' George sighed. 'Mum, you don't have to keep bringing me things. I'll be fine. I just need more time, that's all. It's sweet, but presents aren't going to miraculously cheer me up.' It made her feel cared for, but didn't change how she felt about herself. She didn't know if anything ever would. The new therapist kept telling her she needed more time, and to focus on the positives. She was trying her best, she really was, but it wasn't just the physical scars she had to contend with. There were emotional ones too.

'Mmmmm.' Stella made a non-committal sound and dropped her head to plump up the cushion.

George knew she'd hurt her mum, and bit her lip. Well, at least she hadn't shouted like in the weeks after first being released from hospital. Those had been dark days, and she'd been to some dark places. She'd just been so unbelievably angry all the time at the unfairness of it all. Some days that rage still surfaced, but she'd learned to get a better handle on her emotions, to stop striking out at those around her.

She smiled sadly. It wasn't that long ago she'd attended lectures and gone out shopping with friends to blow her student loan.

It was Saturday today. On a Saturday at uni she'd have studied in the library in the morning and worked in the bar from lunchtime onwards before dancing and drinking the night away in a club, tossing her hair over her shoulder before turning to see how many guys were checking her out.

That might be only a handful of months past, but in reality it felt like forever since she'd laughed and grinned and had fun like a normal twenty-one year old. But she wasn't normal any more, nothing was. The injury in her thigh made her limp when it was cold or rainy (which was most of the time given it was winter in Britain), her right eye was gone and her face was scarred.

She was slowly accepting that none of those things were insurmountable, that it could have been a lot worse, but a lot had changed. Now one of her most prized possessions, rather than her extensive clothes collection, was the large round spa-bath in the en-suite. She could hide her new, strange body under a layer of bubbles in a bath, rather than being confronted by her scars in a shower. Getting naked was definitely on her list of least favourite things to do these days. Still, at least a month ago she'd been able to take attending physio off the list. They'd said it was up to her now, and she'd been doing her daily stretching and muscle strengthening exercises like a good girl.

'Mum?' she said softly, focusing her thoughts, 'Please stop buying me things. You really don't need to.'

'But they can't hurt, can they?' Stella replied. There was something in her tone that made George wonder if it made her mum feel better to buy presents for her. 'Especially this one,' Stella added. Making a funny clucking noise under her breath, she lifted something and shifted nearer on her knees, before depositing it in her daughter's tartan pyjama-clad lap.

George peered down one-eyed at the warm, furry body wriggling around on her thighs. A yipping sound was directed at her face. She closed her eye, groaning. 'Please Mum, please say you didn't get me a guide dog after everything I said?' Leaning over, she carefully deposited the small black and white splotched puppy on the floor. It immediately rolled onto its back and started squirming around on the carpet, paws pumping blissfully in the air.

Stella smoothed her low ponytail down. 'Yes, he's yours,' she glanced down at the puppy. 'He could be useful to you, but—,'

'Yes, if I want to look like even more of a freak,' George replied in an undertone, watching as the animal abandoned its army manoeuvres and started chasing its tail, spinning in tireless circles.

'You're not a freak.' Her mum's cheeks went pink. 'And he's not a guide dog. They're usually different breeds, about a year old and fully trained. He's just a normal Springer Spaniel puppy because you made it clear you wouldn't accept a guide dog.' She smoothed her ponytail again. 'You can train him yourself. They're usually quick to learn, and enthusiastic. It'll give you something to do now you're on the road to recovery but not back at uni. Walking him will keep you fit and get some fresh air into you. Besides, he'll keep you company when I start my new teaching job next week. Spaniels like to be around people. They're social dogs.'

'I'm glad someone feels social.' George responded, but despite her best intentions found herself sinking down to the floor to stroke the puppy's downy neck. She smiled. Who could resist? Puppies were so cute. They had such big soulful eyes and little pink tongues. And a lot about her might have changed, but she could feel her heart melting already.

'I know you'd rather be left alone to hide away from the world.' Stella said. 'But it's not good for you.'

'Hang on. I've come a long way since those weeks when I was holed up in bed all day.' She switched to stroking the puppy's back, smiling when he turned to lick her hand. The arguments between them had been heated, especially since she'd refused to shower for days on end, or come out of her room to eat with her parents, or see friends or family. It'd taken her dad intervening and suggesting they move to London to make a fresh start to pull her out of herself. Normally taciturn and unwilling to get between his wife and daughter, it was like his daughter's crisis had finally given him words. 'I've been out since we moved here, Mum,' she defended, uncurling her legs to stretch her leg out, 'trying to learn the streets.'

'Twice,' Stella answered, 'barely qualifies.'

George flushed. So what if she mostly stayed in watching TV or, when she got bored of that, watching passers-by from the living room window? It was perfectly normal to look at people sweeping up and down the leafy London street or dashing to bus-stops, and wonder who they were and where they were going. Wasn't it? And it wasn't creepy at all that she had a favourite; a tall guy with shaggy brown hair who was always smiling, no matter what the time of day was, no matter what the horrible weather was doing. He looked nice. Open and relaxed. She wished she felt how he looked. It had been pretty embarrassing though when he'd glanced sideways one evening and caught her gawping. He'd grinned wickedly and she'd let out a squeak and slid to the floor under the window. From then on she hid behind the net curtains when she dared to people-watch.

'Once a week isn't enough, darling,' her mum interrupted her musings.

'It's hard. Everyone stares,' George admitted reluctantly. Initially she'd been scared of moving to London; scared at the thought of leaving everything and everyone she knew behind, at the familiar becoming unfamiliar, but in the end realised that being back home in her old life wasn't helping. That in a funny way, starting over might make things easier. But it was more difficult than she'd expected.

'I'm sure not everybody does. Besides, London is a very big place; there are a lot of faces in it with their own stories.'

'You're probably right. But it's still hard. Give me some credit for leaving the house, especially when you know how I feel about this,' George pointed to her face.

'All right, thank you for trying.' Her mum shook her head, 'But you're still a gorgeous girl Georgiana, and anyone of any value will see past the physical damage.'

George hugged her arms around her waist, staring at her unvarnished toenails. 'Whatever you say.'

There was a small tense silence before they both looked over at the puppy, who was now tugging on the edge of the duvet cover with a row of tiny, pointed teeth. His ears were pricked up and his tail was wagging. George smiled and switched her attention to her mum. 'I'm sorry this has all been so disruptive for you.'

Her mum sighed. 'Darling, don't apologise. Yes, we've both been cast back into roles we thought we'd left behind – you know I came to terms with you leaving home over two years ago, taking the promotion as Head of English, starting the OU course, but it's fine. Life throws things at you sometimes that you have to deal with, and we're dealing with it. I'm excited about my new job. Your dad got that transfer. Not a day goes by that I don't wish I'd made you leave straight after dinner that evening, or insisted you stay an extra night, anything to stop you being on that same strip of road with that poor lorry driver—,' her voice broke and she stifled a sob, 'but there's no use torturing ourselves with things that can't be changed.'

George bit her lip, tears scorching her eyes. She'd not once been able to cry for herself over the last few months, but somehow her mum's pain almost undid her. 'I know that, Mum. It'll be okay.'

'It will.' Stella nodded and pointed at the puppy, who'd managed to tear a small hole in the bedding through shaking his head and wiggling his body, splayed paws digging into the carpet. 'So he's staying. Enjoy him, have fun with him. But he's your responsibility, so promise you won't keep him in all the time.' She clambered to her feet, gazing down at her daughter, who'd slid back to rest against the side of the bed. 'You'll take him for walks, won't you?'

George rolled her eye. She knew when she was beaten. 'When I'm ready.'

'Georgiana …'

'Yes, okay, I will, I promise.'

'Good. I'm going to go and finish unpacking. You should try and do some of yours too. Your bedroom's a mess.' Stella raised an eyebrow pointedly and swept from the room, clicking the door quietly shut behind her.

George sat on the carpet, face burning. How did her mum still have the ability to make her feel like a child, when she'd been an adult for over three years? She felt seven years-old again, having just been told off for touching one of her mum's prized ornaments or getting sticky chocolate fingers all over her dad's extensive record collection. She'd planned to empty all the boxes and put everything away, it was just hard to summon the motivation or energy these days. Sighing, she swivelled her head around to find the puppy, and ran a hand down his back. His fur was so incredibly soft. He yipped and turned to look at her. 'Looks like we're stuck with each other,' she chuckled, 'but please, just give me a few more days before we venture out, okay?' She tapped him gently on the nose, 'A week would be perfect.'

She didn't get seven days, nowhere near.

Because she was feeding him the puppy took an immediate shine to her, following her around adoringly, getting under her feet and tripping her up more than once. Her bruises, despite the plush carpets, had actually multiplied since his appearance because he wasn't quick enough to get out of her way when she turned around. And without one eye, she had one hell of a blind spot. She smiled at her own joke. Maybe she was making progress.

'Mum, the puppy's going to kill me at this rate.' She complained over dinner on the Monday night after his arrival. 'I've fallen over him three times just this afternoon. And he yip-yaps at me every time I sit down. Can't you or Dad take him for a while so I can have a break? Or better still, take him for a walk?' she looked at her dad hopefully, noticing how he'd coordinated his glasses frames with his tie. 'Nice match today, Dad.'

'Sorry darling,' her mum said firmly as Warren opened his mouth. 'We're both working full-time now and are tired in the evening, whereas you're here all day. He loves you, just accept it. And stop trying to sweet-talk your dad into helping you.'

'The puppy doesn't love me,' George said drily, 'I feed him. There's a difference.'

'Not to dogs,' her dad replied, smoothing his thinning brown hair off his forehead. His blue eyes were amused behind his glasses.

'I guess not,' she agreed. She bet his socks were odd again. It was a peculiarity; every work day he dressed so carefully, coordinating his suits, ties, glasses and cufflinks, but for some reason he never wore a matching pair of socks. 'So what's it today? Green and blue? Purple and grey?'

Her dad shook his head.

'Wait.' George licked a finger and stuck it in the air, like she was testing the direction of the wind. 'One red, one blue?'

'Bingo,' he nodded.

Stella tutted, grabbing George's finger to get her attention. 'Stop trying to change the subject.' She looked at her daughter sternly. 'Have you walked him yet?'

George wiggled her finger out of her mum's grasp, pushing the plate of lasagne and garlic bread aside. 'No.'

'He's had all his jabs and is old enough. Springer Spaniels need plenty of exercise. Just don't let him off the lead until he knows the area better. We don't want him getting lost.'

'He's okay going out in the garden. Just give me a few more days.'

'The garden will do for some things,' her mum replied, 'but he needs to stay active. Dogs need to be walked, especially his breed. They're full of energy.'

'You're telling me,' George said, unable to believe how restless the puppy was during the day.

'If he gets bored he might get destructive,' her mum warned.

'Okay, I hear you.' She didn't want to admit that the two trips out she'd taken since the move here had made her so self-conscious she was dreading leaving the house again. 'Thanks for dinner.' As she slid her chair back to clear her plate and cutlery away there was a yelp. 'Oh, for heaven's sakes.' She turned in a circle and bent over, straightening up with the puppy in her arms. 'You silly thing.' She smoothed his paw with gentle fingers. 'I keep telling you, we're not stuck together. You can use your bed sometimes you know.'

She glanced up to find her parents watching her with bemused expressions. 'I'll take him out soon.' As soon as she was brave enough.

On Tuesday morning the puppy kept bringing her things. She was lying on her bed reading in her dressing gown when he appeared at her side, front paws up on the mattress with one of her socks in his mouth. He'd stolen it from the laundry basket. It was kind of sweet; his little furry face was so earnest and he seemed so proud of himself, that she took it from him and patted his head. Mistake. What followed was a systematic flow of belongings including more underwear and a pair of pyjamas from the laundry basket, a battered old teddy from a pile in the corner that she'd kept for sentimental value and some of her old uni textbooks. When he carried on with his task for the next half an hour she regretted the moment of weakness as she ended up buried under a pile of stuff.

'All right, quit it. Now it's just annoying.' She stood, sighing heavily as she looked at the bed and then around the room. Her mum was right, it was a tip. Ignoring her command to stop fetching, the puppy spun around in a circle searching for something else to grab. When he couldn't find anything, he started scrabbling at the wall. 'Okay, come on you.' After letting him out for a few minutes while she made herself a hot chocolate, she brought him back in, settled him on his bed with a doggy biscuit and had a quick bath. After dressing in black jeans and a navy hoody and tying her hair up in a knot, forgoing the eye patch as she was alone in the house, she started unpacking a stack of boxes from the corner of the room. It took her longer due to her injuries, but by the end of the morning there was a definite sense of achievement welling up inside her as her belongings were tucked away in various homes and there was a sense of order to the room. Buttons even cooperated, watching contentedly as she went back and forth, opening drawers and stacking books and DVDs on shelves. Making a quick cheese sandwich and taking it into the lounge, she stood eating it at the window, peeking round the edge of the net curtains. It was just after one o' clock. The woman two doors down would be getting back from nursery with her twin toddler girls soon and smiling guy might mooch along too. It wasn't every day but at least twice a week he walked past, then back again half an hour or so later. She assumed he worked locally and went home for lunch. Just as she was thinking it, he appeared, brown hair hanging in his eyes and hands tucked away in his coat pockets. Looking across the front wall at the house, he pulled one hand free and gave her a cheerful wave.

'Bugger!' she muttered. Caught out again. She wanted to hide but ducking away twice would be even more embarrassing than being busted in the first place so she gave him a feeble wave in return before oh so casually moving away to sit down on the sofa.

Buttons, lying on the rug in front of the TV, gave her a pointed look and rested his chin on his front paws.

'What?' she said defensively.

Pricking his ears up, he let his tongue loll out of his mouth. She swore he was laughing at her.

'Oh, shut up,' she retorted, picking up the remote.

She couldn't settle after that, and bored with TV, and reading, started to get cabin fever. Buttons was restless too, pacing up and down on the rug, whining, spinning in circles. Muttering a rude word, she put him out in the garden and scrubbed the marble-effect worktops in the kitchen, clenching her teeth, feeling tight and knotty.

She needed someone to talk to. Juliette had always been a good listener and supportive, a friend bound to her by a shared childhood. Going to her room she dug around in her knicker drawer for her mobile phone. She hadn't turned it on in weeks, since before the move. She'd wanted time to settle into the new house before contacting people. It was a surprise when the screen lit up and there were hundreds of pending messages on Whatsapp, numerous voicemails and texts and loads of alerts on Facebook.

As she dialled Juliette's number, she pictured her friend's girl-next-door beauty, the blue eyes and long brown hair. The ringtone sounded. She held her breath.

'Hi, it's me.'

'Oh my God! Hello stranger! It's so good to hear your voice. I thought you'd dropped off the side of the planet,' Juliette said, a smile in her voice.

'Not quite,' George answered quietly, 'but I made it to London okay.'

'I know, Hun.'

'You do?' George looked out of her ground floor window, narrowing her eyes. Where was he? After a moment she caught sight of a small shape zipping back and forth at the bottom of the garden.

'Your mum let me know. Hang on, I'm just going somewhere private.' The sound of movement and a door opening and closing filled the static space. 'Okay.'

'It wasn't you.' George said quickly, 'I wanted to get comfortable here before I got in touch with people. There was a lot of change going on.' She gulped, 'I feel guilty now. I'm sorry. I should have called sooner.'

'Don't worry.' Juliette laughed, 'And don't be silly. It's not as if we didn't see each other before you left. I'm always happy to be at the end of a phone. But I'd love to come and see you. I want to know what you've been up to.'

George laughed drily, thinking of the people-watching. 'Not much, believe me.'

'Right. No men on the horizon then?'

'No.' A picture of smiling guy flashed through her head. No chance. He wasn't her usual type, and she wasn't ready for anything right now. 'Definitely not.' She reiterated. 'That's the last thing on my mind.'

'Shame,' Juliette cleared her throat. 'So was there a reason you called today?'

'Mum bought me a puppy and he's driving me mad,' George blurted, before laughing at how ridiculous it sounded. When Juliette giggled too, George realised how good it was to feel genuine humour again.

'So what have you called him?' Juliette asked. 'And what's he doing to drive you barking, ha ha, pun fully intended?'

'Buttons.'

'How come?'

'Because when he's not tripping me over I think he's as cute as one.' She rabbited on, feeling a little like her old self again. *This.* She could do this. True friendship, the kind where you could pick up where you left off, as if no days had passed since you'd last spoken. 'He jumps up and spins around loads,' she explained, 'is always right on my heels and every time he wags his tail he knocks three things over. His worst habit though is that whenever I turn in his general direction, he launches himself at me. Literally. One minute I'm minding my own business, the next I'm spread-eagled with a smelly, panting puppy filling my mouth with fur.'

'Aww, I think he sounds cute,' Juliette chuckled. 'Come on, it's not that bad. He's a baby, he just needs to learn.'

'Now you sound like my mum,' George accused lightly, 'are you sure she didn't coach you for this conversation? She wants me to train him too.'

'Absolutely not,' Juliette replied, 'although if she'd called me for a coaching session, I'd have been hard pressed to say no. Your Mum is pretty impressive sometimes. Especially when it comes to you.'

'You mean full on. Like a steam roller. Or a high-speed runaway train.'

'She wants what's best for you,' Juliette said loyally. 'She loves you.'

'But she's so obstinate and—,' George stopped, feeling mean. Her mum was ridiculously stubborn at times, but you couldn't question her motives. 'Actually, you're right,' she agreed, focusing on her hands, which were gripping the windowsill. When had she bitten her fingernails down so much they were red and sore? She'd always taken such pride in her lovely oval nails.

'Of course I'm right. And she's got that stern teacher thing going on.' Juliette added. 'Remember that time she talked us through behaviour management strategies?'

'Do I ever.' George sniggered, 'We were like, what, twelve? You looked so bored. But the worst thing was, I found it really interesting.'

'I know. It wasn't long after that you started talking about wanting to be a teacher when we grew up.'

'Yeah, I'd forgotten that.' George smiled sadly, thinking about how much she'd loved her English degree and the planned PGCE - post-graduate certificate in education - her tutor had said he'd support her in the application for. She'd been so full of excitement and aspirations. It seemed she had a lot to be thankful to her mum for. Not that she could imagine pursuing her dream of being a teacher at the moment.

'Oh, crap.' Juliette muttered, 'I'm sorry, Hun, but I have to go. I'm late for a meeting. I got that promotion, and they kind of need the chair of the meeting present to go ahead with it. Oh, and next time we speak ask me about Jon.'

'You've got a new boyfriend, as well as the promotion? That's fantastic, well done! And yes, of course I want to hear all about him.'

Juliette had worked for a corporate bank since leaving college and had talked about climbing the career ladder whenever they went out for drinks. George gulped, feeling ashamed. She had no clue about what had been happening in her friend's life recently, whereas Juliette had always been there for her; hugging George after disagreements with her mum; comforting George when her first boyfriend dumped her; visiting George at uni once a month like clockwork to help drive away homesickness in the first few terms. Friendship was a two-sided coin and she wasn't pulling the weight her end.

'I'll let you go for now,' George said, 'but I'm calling you in the next few days so we can sort out you visiting one weekend.'

'Try and stop me. Phone me soon.'

'I will,' George answered fiercely.

'Fab. Oh, and Miss Dunn?'

'Yes?'

'Train that puppy, why don't you? I don't want him peeing all over me when I come visit.'

George laughed. 'Fair enough, will do. Take care.'

Staring out the window after ringing off, she hissed a swear word upon spotting Buttons happily digging a hole in the lawn. Her parents and Juliette were right. The dog needed training. Tucking her phone in her pocket to check the rest of the messages later, she went out to the garden, pulling the puppy out of the hole and dusting soil off his damp nose. 'No, Buttons! Naughty dog. You don't dig holes!' It might be her cousin's house that they were renting, and Matt was probably too loaded to care about a teensy hole at the bottom of the garden of the fourth property he owned, but her parents would care, and Buttons couldn't go around being so wilfully destructive.

The puppy sat down and tilted his head to gaze up at her. She knelt to look into his face, and saw a woeful expression staring back. Yapping, he looked over at the fence, looked at her, faced the fence again.

'Oh, for f—,' she bit back the obscenity, 'heaven's sakes. Okay. You win.'

They were waiting in the hallway when her mum came in from work, George holding Buttons on his lead, pink oval tongue panting and tail wagging frantically against the ceramic floor tiles.

'Everything okay, darling?' Stella asked, pausing in the act of shrugging out of her lilac winter coat, face alight with hope.

'I don't want to go alone,' George bit her lip, nerves churning her stomach in grotty, oily circles.

Her mum sucked in a breath, eyes growing wet. 'Primrose Hill is only five minutes away. I'll walk with you today. After that, you go on your own.'

'But—,'

'A guide dog may have given you the same freedom of movement as everyone else, but someone,' she emphasised, 'was dead set against it, so it's you and Buttons now. Come on,' Stella tugged her coat back on, re-buttoned and belted it, 'I'll write your father a note while you wrap up. It's cold outside.'

'It is January,' George replied as she pulled on a green anorak and yanked the fur-trimmed hood as far up as possible. She repositioned her eye patch then shook her head so her dark hair fell forward in waves to cover her face.

Turning around, her mum threw her a sharp look. 'I don't know how you're going to see anything like that. You need to pin your hair back and have your hood down so you've got maximum visibility.'

'Do you want me to leave the house or not?'

'Have it your way,' Stella shrugged, opening the door and gesturing her daughter to go first so she could lock up.

George hesitated, chewing her lip, hands going clammy. Before full blown anxiety could hit though, Buttons, sensing freedom, had pitched forward eagerly onto the front path, giving George no choice but to be tugged out of the house or fall over. 'Woah!' He was surprisingly strong for a twelve week old puppy, but she guessed that was what a mixture of desire and determination could do. Give you strength you didn't know you had.

'Are you all right?' her mum called, quickly locking the door and shoving the key in her pocket as she raced down the path to catch up with them.

'Yes,' George panted. 'Oi, Buttons!' she tugged on the lead to remind the puppy she was there. 'Slow down, and remember who's in charge.'

'Never let them get their head in front of your knee,' her mum advised, slipping a pair of gloves on. 'You need to lead, not the other way around.'

'Okay,' George said, pulling the dog up and making sure they were in line with each other.

The three of them stepped onto the pavement and turned right, Stella walking on her daughter's left so George was in the middle of the group, with Buttons nearer the wall.

Cars whizzed past and pedestrians stepped around them, George turning her head back and forth to look out for any obstacles. While she hoped no-one could see her face, her mum was right. Between the hood, her flowing hair and the eye patch, she could barely see. Inhaling sharply, she pushed the hood down, talking to her mum to take her mind off how scary this was for her. 'Where did you learn that?' she asked. 'About leading? We've never had a dog.'

'Internet,' Stella's hand hovered by her daughter's elbow as a red letter box came up on the right, but as if he knew something, Buttons walked around it, his shoulder against George's knee to steer her away from it.

'Clever doggy,' Stella exclaimed.

George glanced at her suspiciously, 'Are you sure he's not a guide dog? Or trained in some way?'

'Not as far as I know,' her mum replied. 'He's just got good instincts.'

'Hmmmm,' George agreed dubiously, lifting her head towards a street light. She had to admit it was refreshing being out and about, much more than she'd imagined. Nothing disastrous had happened and no-one was staring at her in the early evening darkness. Perhaps this wasn't so bad.

She regretted the thought a few minutes later when upon reaching Primrose Hill, Buttons got overexcited about the wide open green space and other dogs and tore off with George hanging onto his lead. She tripped over and smashed her knee on the concrete path. Wincing, she rolled over onto her bum, clutching her leg, the puppy's lead somehow still wrapped around her right hand.

'Stupid dog!' George gritted her teeth against the stinging pain, her jeans ripped open to reveal an oozing gash on her knee.

'Are you all right, darling?' her mum dropped into a crouch beside her, grabbing Buttons' lead. 'Here, I'll take him. How bad is it?' Stella's face was clenched and white.

'Just a cut and probably a bruise,' George got up carefully, not wanting her mum to worry, and was reaching for the puppy's lead when a guy came running over.

'Are you okay?' he panted. 'I saw you fall. Do you need any help?'

George automatically dropped her chin to her chest. 'I'm fine, thanks.' She got an impression of tousled brown hair before hiding her face. It was smiling guy. Shit, this was *so* embarrassing.

'*Fine* usually means exactly the opposite,' he answered drily, smiling at her.

George stepped towards her mum, yanking up her hood.

'You fell pretty heavily. It must have hurt,' he insisted. 'Can I help? I could give you a piggy-back or something. I don't live far from here.' The raised eyebrow and grin he gave her, which she caught from the corner of her eye, communicated that he knew she knew that. He recognised her.

'No, thanks. I'd rather walk,' she said curtly, turning away, cheeks burning. Fabulous. Caught gawking at him twice, and then she fell over in front of him too. And his concern just made it so much worse.

Her mum leaned in, speaking quietly. 'Are you sure you'll be all right to walk home, darling?'

'Yes,' she hissed. 'Please just—just get rid of him.' It came out louder than she'd intended, and she backed away, even more embarrassed, stumbling over her own feet. This was getting worse with every passing minute.

'I'm sorry,' she heard her mum say to him, 'my daughter was in an accident and now she finds it hard to talk to people.'

George sucked in a breath. *Go Mum, sharing all my secrets. Yay.*

'Thank you very much for the offer,' her mum added, 'but we'll manage.'

'Sure,' he agreed easily, 'I'll leave you to it then. It was nice to meet you both properly.'

Was it George's imagination or did he emphasise the word *properly*?

'Properly?' Stella picked up on the intonation too.

'I think we're quite local to each other. I've seen your daughter around.'

'Really?' Stella frowned, looking at George, questions in her eyes.

George stared down at her feet. *Thanks, smiling guy. Set the Spanish Inquisition on me, why don't you?*

'I see.' Stella murmured. 'It's nice to meet you too. And thank you again for coming over, it was very kind.'

'No problem. See you around.' Nodding, he walked off briskly towards the brow of the hill.

'What a nice young man,' Stella said pointedly, rejoining George and handing over Buttons' lead. 'Where did you meet each other?'

'We didn't.' George wrapped the lead around her right hand, shaking her head at the puppy, who was trying to dance away from them. She drew him towards her. Her knee was stinging like crazy. There'd been enough drama for one day.

'Oh,' Stella pulled a puzzled expression. 'Well, I think he likes you.'

'Don't be silly,' George swung away and started towards one of the park entrances. 'Come on, let's go home.'

Despite the fated first trip out, George walked Buttons the following day. Even with her nerve-tightening self-consciousness, she enjoyed stretching her legs and being out in public again. As long as she had her hair down and could pull her hood up if she felt the need to, the anxiety stayed at bay.

Over the course of the next week, she upped it to two walks a day; one in the morning and one in the evening, and she and Buttons fell into a rhythm, walking the same route every time. The puppy largely behaved himself and by the fourth day she was able to let him off his lead for short periods of time. By the sixth day he was coming back on recall, as long as she kept a supply of *Bonio's* in her pocket. Because it was damp and her thigh ached, she stuck to the lower, flatter paths around the base of the hill at first.

She kept wondering if she'd run into smiling guy, and wasn't sure what she'd do if she did, but never saw him. And instead of people-watching now, twitching the curtains, she spent her days in the house or back garden training Buttons.

'Come on,' she clicked her fingers at him on the Tuesday of the second week, and pointed to the top of the hill. 'Let's give it a go.' He turned to face the right way, barked once and set off up the path ahead of her, free from the lead. George followed with a wry grin. She could swear he was more person than canine. She wiped the back of her arm across her forehead as she panted up the hill. It was late morning and the sun had climbed in the sky, beaming its rays down. After days of driving rain, it was unseasonably mild. George was building up a light sweat under her long sleeved top and hoody, so she stopped and drew the top layer off, tying it around her waist, and adjusted her eye patch before setting off again. When she reached the brow of the hill, she inhaled deeply, swivelling her head from side to side to see the London skyline. It was amazing.

Dropping to her knees on the concrete circular area, she hugged the dog. 'Good boy,' she muttered into his fur. He licked her cheek in response in one long sandpapery rasp, then his body quivered and he lurched forward as the chattering of people filled the air.

George's fingers caught in his collar as she straightened up, trying to stop him running off. 'Stop!' she cried, but he was already moving and had too much momentum and speed. She couldn't pull him back or untwist her fingers. She was being yanked toward the edge of the concrete area, towards some kind of lip she had a nasty feeling she was going to trip over. With only one eye, her depth perception was skewed.

'Shit!' she squeaked, careening towards the edge.

A pair of warm hands grabbed her around the waist and lifted her slightly as she fell forward, her hand freeing at the last minute from the puppy's collar, and she tumbled down onto the cold grassy slope, her saviour next to her.

'Careful, you don't want to roll down the hill. You might never get a chance to tell me your name,' a deep, familiar voice joked.

'Bloody dog!' Flustered, George sat up and shot Buttons a filthy look while she gathered her composure.

'I think he was excited by the children,' smiling guy rolled closer and picked a leaf out of her wavy hair. 'Are you okay?'

Glancing over her left shoulder she saw a group of milling children and several stressed-looking adults trying to wrangle them into some kind of order. He was probably right. Buttons did seem to get excited by clusters of people, especially the type who might give him attention.

Turning back to her rescuer, she straightened her eye patch with trembling fingers. It had been a long time since she'd been so close to a guy. Close enough to feel the heat of his broad shoulder and a muscular thigh against hers. *Don't humiliate yourself.* 'Uh-huh,' she mumbled, pulling her hair forward around her face. It would probably be rude to pull her hood up mid-conversation. It would also be weird given how sunny it was. 'I mean, yes, thank you.'

'Good.' He leapt to his feet. 'Did you come to see the skyline?' he asked as if she hadn't just been embarrassed in front of goodness knew how many people.

'Not really,' she said awkwardly. If she talked to people they'd look at her. And if they did that … she ran a finger along the puckered skin of her scar.

Ignoring the gesture, he grabbed George's other hand, hauling

133

her up easily. 'Lark, Emily,' he called.

George twisted around and narrowed her eye. Two little heads popped up from among the group of children. The pair started to make their way over to them, one a blond boy of about eight who reminded George of the milky-bar kid, except with a white cane. He was smiling, totally at ease with the stick. The girl next to him was grinning, signing something with her hands at George's rescuer. Smiling guy signed something back, moving his mouth at the same time.

He turned back to George. 'Hi, I'm Leo.' He held out a large hand.

After a brief hesitation George took it. He'd just saved her from probable injury, so it would be rude not to shake his hand. 'Georgiana,' she whispered. What she didn't expect was the soothing heat of his palm, or how the texture of it against her own made something in her tummy quiver. Oh. A blush started to climb her throat. No, no, no.

'Nice name. Good to meet you.' He said as the children arrived next him and he directed them to stroke and make a fuss over Buttons, who'd panted over to George in search of a treat.

George drew a couple of biscuits out of her pocket and gave them to the black and white puppy as Leo crouched down and placed his hand on the boy's to show him where the animal was sat. Buttons obediently lay down and started crunching away at his snack while the kids petted him. He looked thrilled with the combination.

'So, are you getting out more nowadays?' Leo gazed up at her. 'Instead of drooling over me through your lounge window?'

It was so cheeky, a loud, 'You wish!' burst out.

He grinned and straightened up, several inches taller than her. 'Sorry, I couldn't resist.' A light breeze blew his tousled brown hair into bracken coloured eyes. 'Look, I'm a teacher at St. Michael's, one of the local schools. Why don't you tag along?' He turned to someone, and nodded before turning back. 'I'm going to do the skyline.' He looked down as the little girl abandoned lavishing attention on Buttons, and signed something at him. Nodding, he signed something back. 'I agree,' Leo said out loud. 'She says you're pretty,' he explained.

George shook her head automatically and drew her hair around her face. 'No,' she denied, gulping. 'I need to go.' Bending over to hide her anger and confusion, she clipped Buttons' lead onto his collar and started walking away. 'Bye,' she called over one shoulder.

'I'm sorry. We weren't trying to offend you,' Leo hollered. 'Stay for the skyline talk. You might enjoy it.'

'Not today,' she yelled, picking up the pace, breaking into a jog as she went down the hill. It was things like this that made her reluctant to go out.

She'd come too far to slide back into a black hole again, so she and Buttons carried on with their daily excursions. And the next time she saw Leo, on a walk she'd deliberately changed to late afternoon in order to try and avoid him (epic fail), the first thing he did was apologise.

'Hi, Georgiana,' he walked right up to her, touching her elbow as she stood halfway up the hill watching Buttons swoop across the grass in diagonal streaks chasing a bird, ears flapping.

She jerked her arm away from him.

'I'm sorry if I upset you the other day,' Leo said, dropping his hand and stepping back to give her space. 'I was just translating. I wasn't trying to hit on you. It's genuinely what Emily said.'

Well, that was clear. He hadn't been flirting with her. He was just being his pupil's mouthpiece.

'I thought it was Lark who was blind, not Emily,' she flung back, hurt. 'Didn't she see the state of this?' She pointed at her scar. Sucking in a shaky breath, she immediately felt awful for what she'd said about the children. 'Sorry.'

'Don't worry about it. You are pretty though,' he frowned.

'I don't need pity,' George blinked, thinking furiously of the

135

way she was going to get out of this conversation.

'No pity. I'm just being honest. It's the way I'm built. I'm also used to dealing with parents of children with special educational needs, where we have open conversations about their child's challenges and the support they require to maximise their opportunities. So I say what I think. I'm sorry if that upsets you.'

'Uh-huh.' She nodded, pulling her hair forward.

He grinned, 'Careful, I may have to get ear protectors or ear muffs to block out your constant chatter. I'm not sure I can stand it.'

Despite herself, George smiled.

'No, don't smile. The straight-faced look goes much better with the cool eye patch. Like a brooding, sexy, girl pirate.'

'Are you for real?' she blurted, looking around for Buttons. It might be a good idea to leave. Leo was either mocking her or flirting with her and she wasn't sure how to handle either.

'Buttons. Buttons!' Darkness was falling and she couldn't see him. She rattled the biscuit bag in her pocket and called the puppy again.

'Last time I checked, I was real,' Leo said, falling into step with her as she started up the hill, hoping for a better view from the top 'And don't get defensive. We're just chatting. I come here for a walk most evenings to unwind after work. So, you're here and I'm here. Hey, why don't we do the skyline this time?'

'Why?'

'Why not?'

George expelled a long sigh. Might as well get it over with, she got the feeling he would just keep asking every time he saw her otherwise. When she got to the top of the hill, Buttons was waiting for her expectantly; the expression on his face seeming to say *what took you so long*? Shaking her head at him, she gave him a chew and hooked him back onto the lead. Leo moved up beside her when she was done, turning her to face the City and slowly describing the different buildings from left to right. She did nothing but nod along as he spoke, conscious of the warmth of his arm against hers as he pointed things out, and the fresh scent of his aftershave. When he finished, she took a deep, shaky breath, staring at the view as twilight descended. 'Thanks.'

'My pleasure.'

After a few minutes of companionable silence, he spun around to study her profile. 'So, what's your story?'

She shrugged. She didn't want to talk about horrible things. She wanted to enjoy the beauty of the night, the lights of the city twinkling as the light of day faded.

'Do you ever say more than five words in one go?' he asked.

She shrugged again.

This time he laughed. 'Ok – ay. Well that's fine, I can do enough talking for both of us. I was born in Holborn to Cathy and Chris Miller on 10th March 1988.' The dry crisp tone was in the style of an old fashioned BBC presenter. 'A rather small baby, I shot up at the age of seven, when I discovered a hereto unknown brand of sweetcorn known as Green Giant, eating it every day with my greens, convinced I could make it to six foot five at least.' He glanced down wryly, 'and believe me, I was very disappointed when I stopped growing at seventeen and had only reached six foot one. I started walking and talking very early.' He grinned, getting into the swing of it. 'At my three year health visitor check, my Mum—'

'All right!' she shook her head. 'Stop, please. I'll tell you just to shut you up. I don't know why you want to know anyway.'

'Maybe I enjoy your company.'

She snorted.

'Or maybe it's because I've always had a weakness for surly, impatient brunettes with eye-patch complexes.'

She gaped and burst into giggles. She wasn't offended. In fact, he was really the only person who didn't ignore the scars and patch, or look away, or fumble conversations. He had the gall to joke about it. It made her slightly uncomfortable, but it was also honest and real.

'I was on my way back to uni on a Sunday evening in late

137

September. My car got hit by a lorry. The driver had a heart attack at the wheel.' She stared out at the distant skyline, describing the events of that horrific night in short, sharp sentences. She did not want to cry in public. 'He didn't make it, because of his heart ...' she gulped. 'It wasn't his fault.'

'Wow,' Leo stated. 'That really sucks.'

George let out a disbelieving laugh. 'Are you serious?'

'It's tragic and awful and unfair,' he said gently. 'But the only way I can think of to summarise it is, it sucks. I bet you've used some much stronger words.'

'In the beginning,' she shared, 'the f-word featured a lot, but lately I've been going with, *it blows.*'

'We've both been watching too many American TV shows,' he decided, shifting closer. 'Do you remember it? The accident?'

She took in a long, shaky breath, squaring her shoulders. 'I have flashbacks sometimes,' she whispered. She hadn't admitted that to anyone but her therapist, and hadn't wanted to burden her parents, but there was something about Leo, his easy manner and non-judgemental ways that made it easier. Perhaps it was the fact they barely knew each other, so had no emotional investment in one another that made it possible for her to share. 'I remember the dark motorway lit only by my headlights. The rain thrashing down against my windscreen so that I had my wipers on the highest speed.'

'Anything else?'

'No.' She winced. Time to go home.

'Nothing about the crash itself?'

'I-,' she hesitated, 'I can't.'

'But it might help.'

'Respect my feelings, okay?' she turned to leave.

'Of course,' he agreed easily. 'So are you still at uni?'

'Of course not.'

'Why?'

'I'm not ready.' She pointed to the patch again. 'Look at me.'

138

His eyes ran over her face as if he didn't see anything of concern. 'So, what do you do?'

'Nothing, at the moment.' She hugged her arms across her body.

'You know, Georgiana, if the kids I teach can have meaningful lives, then so can you. We don't think about their disabilities as limitations, we think of them as challenges and opportunities. We don't look at what they can't achieve. We consider everything they *can* achieve. You're no different.'

Her mouth dropped open. 'I have to go,' she said abruptly, feeling reprimanded. Tears were scorching the back of her eyes. 'Bye.' Tugging on Buttons' lead she walked briskly towards home, not giving Leo a chance to respond.

When George saw Leo ducking into the local corner shop a few days later, she didn't mean to stop. She definitely didn't mean to linger until he came out, but somehow her feet wouldn't move.

It was getting on for dinner time, and she'd just taken Buttons for a stroll on Primrose Hill. There'd not been a single trace of disappointment that Leo wasn't there. None at all. Why would she want to see him when she'd made such an idiot of herself, running off like that, just because he'd called her on something? She'd been cross with him for the rest of the night and some of the next morning, but once she'd cooled down, she could see he had a point. She was as physically recovered as she was ever going to be. So, what was she going to do now?

It was something she'd mused over as she strolled through the park, the lamps along the paths doing a good job of lighting the way. The fresh air had felt cleansing, healthy. She'd puffed her way up and down the hill but wasn't as tired as previous times. Her mum had been right; this was good for her. After an initial curious glance at her eye-patch and scar, most people looked away. They didn't gawp or stare. She was feeling better getting out of the house regularly. As a teenager she'd never been the type to loll around in her room reading books or watching TV. Instead she'd been with her friends in town or at the beach or watching scary films in a large gang around someone's house, sharing bottles of lemonade and tubes of Pringles. Her stomach growled at the thought and she wondered what Leo was buying. Just as she peered into the shop window, Buttons sniffing the door frame, he appeared, holding a blue carrier bag filled with a carton of milk and various bits she couldn't make out.

'Hello you. Stalking me again?' he grinned, stepping onto the pavement and zipping up his jacket. 'How's it going?'

'Errr,' she croaked, tongue tied.

'Nothing much to say again?' he teased.

Clearing her throat didn't help, and neither did swallowing. Bloody hell, now as well as everything else she was turning into a mute. Embarrassment flooded her.

'That's all right; we both know I can talk for England if required.'

His light brown eyes twinkled down at her. Another feeling, far scarier than embarrassment, tightened her fingers on Buttons' lead. Leo was cute. He really was. Not her usual type, pre-accident, but very appealing. Something was fluttering in her tummy in reaction.

She closed her eyes and gulped. Oh my god, what if he knew, and she made a fool of herself?

'Are you all right?' A large hand wrapped around her upper arm.

She opened her eyes to find him peering down into her face. He felt sorry for her, he was compassionate because of the amazing work he did with those children. She swept her hair forward over her patch and nodded. 'Uh-huh.'

'Not quite words yet this evening, but we have sound,' he jested. 'We're making progress. Come on, I'll walk you home.'

'I'm fine,' she managed. She didn't know how to do this anymore. The old George (once she decided she fancied a guy) would have launched a flirt offensive, finding excuses to bump into him, making sure she looked her best at all times, talking about fun plans and including him in them, dropping hints about spending some time alone together.

Now she had zip. No play at all. Not that she was in a place to pursue anything anyway. Plus why would he want to date someone like her, when he could have his pick of normal, unscarred girls?

'You're talking! How about this then? If we're heading in the same direction we'll do it at the same time until we have to go our separate ways.'

She blushed, feeling silly. 'Okay,' she murmured, and turned towards home. 'Buttons,' she commanded, pulling him away from the wall of the shop. After sniffing it and weeing on it for about the twentieth time, the puppy gave her a slightly haughty look and deigned to start walking. George shook her head and smiled wryly, looking down the street ahead for obstacles. Leo fell into step with her, and she inhaled sharply, catching a whiff of sexy, crisp aftershave, like she had the other night. He smelled gorgeous. She took another breath. They couldn't walk in silence for more than a minute without it being uncomfortable, and she wasn't sure if she'd be able to cope with another round of his dry as a TV presenter style narration. She also needed to work her way up to an apology for leaving so abruptly last time. If she didn't look at him it might be easier.

'What did you buy?' she asked huskily.

'Buy?'

'In the shop, apart from milk?' she asked, already kicking herself. Could she have thought of a topic any less boring? *Really?*

'I picked up a few things for the kids. Some glitter, glue, card, straws. Stuff we didn't have in the resource cupboard for some reason. My Teaching Assistant and I are going to help the children make Valentine's cards for their parents or carers.'

'Valentine's Day.' Dismay filled her. It was only two weeks away.

'Not my favourite day of the year,' Leo frowned. 'All those hearts and flowers everywhere. Although, it's not that I have anything against it per se, it's just that it's never been high on my priority list. I was too much of a geek as a teenager to do anything interesting with girls. I studied hard at uni, then the last few years I've been too career-oriented. That's why my friends—' he stopped talking, readjusting his jacket as he strolled along.

'What?'

'Make fun of me,' he finished quickly. 'My friends say I'm a sad old case.'

'Hardly old,' she quipped.

He laughed, throwing back his head so his dark hair touched his collar. 'No, just sad. Thanks a lot!'

She nodded, strangely satisfied that she'd made him laugh. For a moment she'd felt like her old self. Maybe she had some banter left after all. They turned the corner, making slow progress given that Buttons stopped at practically every wall, sniffing it and considering whether to provide it with urinary decoration or not. To be honest, it suited George fine. She could take her time to sweep her head back and forth to make sure the path was clear. It was nothing to do with enjoying Leo's company. Absolutely nothing.

'So, ah, are you looking forward to Valentine's Day?' Leo asked.

'No,' she said flatly. She was dreading it. How was she going to feel this year when no cards landed on her mat, when since the age of thirteen she'd always received a handful to clutch to her chest and squeal over with her friends? One of them, every single year, had always been from Eric, a next door neighbour one year above her in school, who'd always had a soft spot for her. At one point she'd feared that her mum was going to form a plot with Eric's mum to marry them off, but Stella had never pushed it, apparently getting that George didn't think of Eric in that way. He was sweet though, and she'd always enjoyed catching up with him.

'Why?'

She rolled her eyes. Well, her left eye. 'Really?'

'I get it. You've got so many guys lined up with offers that you don't want to pick one and traumatise the rest of them. That's very generous of you. You've got a big heart, Georgiana.'

Snorting laughter through her nose, not even caring how undignified it was, she nodded. 'Yes, that's what it is. I've decided to let the men of Great Britain off the hook this year. No more drunken messes in A&E as they drown their sorrows. It'll save the NHS a fortune.'

'Well done. I like your style.' They turned a corner, a pitter-patter of rain starting to fall on them, the drizzle highlighted under the street lights. 'Even if it is costing you a day of romance,' he remarked.

'I don't even know what real romance is,' she said, wrinkling her nose as her face and hair dampened with the rain. Trust her not to wear a hoody today. 'I mean, is it really giving someone flowers and going for a fancy dinner once a year because it's expected?'

'I don't know.' He turned his collar up. 'I suppose you find out when you're really in love.'

'Have you ever been in love?' she fired off, not liking the thought of him and other girls. *Woah, where did that come from?*

'No,' he said decisively.

'Not ever? How are you so sure?'

'Simple. Because I've never felt strongly enough about someone that I'd rather be with them instead of at work with the children. The pull has never been strong enough. The job, other than my family and friends, is the most important thing in my life. Actually, it's not a job, it's more of a vocation. It would have to take someone really special to compete with that. Does that sound selfish?'

'No. It sounds honest. You love those kids. And it's not selfish to know how you feel so clearly. I just hope that one day you find that special girl, and she helps you realise it's not a competition, it's a balance. It's not one thing or the other. Your love life and career can co-exist.' She thought about her parent's solid, happy marriage. 'As long as she respects its importance to you and you respect her aspirations in return.'

'Maybe.' He looked thoughtful, pushing his lower lip out. Shrugging, he nudged her shoulder with his, 'So what are you really doing on Valentine's Day?'

George chewed the inside of her mouth. Perhaps stay in all day

143

and watch the most unromantic films possible. Either all the *Die Hard* movies back to back, or the *Fast and Furious* series. Ice-cream could be on tap and she would pretend it wasn't happening. The thought of going out and being surrounded by soft-eyed couples, and bunches of roses, and heart- shaped signs and chocolate display stands really didn't appeal.

'Still in there?' Leo prompted, nudging her shoulder with his again, but harder than last time.

Unfortunately the nudge caught her by surprise and she stumbled, letting out a small yelp.

'Shit, sorry!' Grabbing her to stop her falling over, his strong arms wrapped around her upper body. She moaned and he let go immediately. 'Sorry. Again.' He backed away, hands up, staring intently at a passing car. Its windows were down despite the rain and the mellow notes of Passenger's *Let Her Go* drifted out.

'It's okay,' she wheezed, stunned at how unbelievably good it had felt to be held by him, made safe in his warmth, against his firm body. She hadn't wanted him to let go.

They came to her front wall and Buttons pawed at the gate.

'This is me.'

'I know,' Leo reached out and swept her hair away from her face. 'You should wear your hair back more. Anyway, I should say goodnight. The rain's getting heavier.'

'I guess,' she said gruffly, looking down as Buttons circled her, wrapping the lead round her legs.

'Buttons, bad idea,' Leo said, crouching down at George's feet and encouraging the puppy to run back around the other way to free her. For a moment her fingers itched to smooth his shaggy hair, to learn the shape of his head, and her hand rose in the air.

'So will I see you again?' Leo asked, stroking Buttons, who arched and wriggled with delight under his touch. 'It seems like you could do with a friend.'

Her hand dropped. She was a complete dreamer. Why would he want her as anything else than a friend?

He stood up, and she turned away to face the house, so he couldn't see her expression.

'Sure,' she said over her shoulder, 'I'll see you around.'

'Georgiana?'

'Yes?' she replied, voice small.

'It's a nice name,' he said awkwardly, like he'd changed what he was about to say.

'I've always wanted something more modern, rather than a name out of a Jane Austen novel. Mum's an English teacher,' she expanded. 'I usually go by George.'

'No, I don't like George for you. Too boyish. I'll call you by your full name.'

'Okay,' she said, shyly. 'Night.'

'Can I have your phone number?' he asked. 'There's something I'd like to send you.'

She tramped down the swell of hope in her chest. He wanted to be friends. She guessed it couldn't hurt to have a friend in London, and it would please her parents. It wasn't as if she was giving him a front door key and inviting him to use it whenever he wanted. To sneak into her bedroom, and crawl under the covers with her and—*No. That was never going to happen.*

She handed over her mobile so he could save his number into it, ringing himself to get her number. 'Done,' he said, sounding satisfied and tucking the phone into her coat pocket. 'I'll be in touch.'

'Okay, bye.' She stood on the pavement for a long time after he'd left, in spite of the droplets now pouring from the sky, staring blankly at the space he'd occupied.

She didn't know what the hell she was doing. She could get really badly hurt. But did it matter, when being around him felt so good?

After that evening, he sent her a message every day, sometimes two. The first was a film recommendation for *The Shawshank Redemption*, which she dubiously followed. She messaged him mid-afternoon straight after watching it, totally forgetting he would be in class. In her excitement she reeled the message straight off, not even agonising about whether to put a kiss at the end of it or not.

Leo, thanks so much for introducing me to such a brilliant film. It made me cry! Who'd think a story set mainly in a prison could prove that hope does spring eternal? :) :) G x

Glad you liked it, I'll send you more. I'm generally right about these things. Lol. L :)

Sometimes his messages were jokes, dirty or clean, and sometimes he sent an inspirational quote to brighten her day. Some messages contained a random question.

If you could live anywhere in the world, where would it be and why?

If money was no object, what would you do with your life?

When you were little, what did you want to be when you grew up? Did that ever change? Why?

What's the best thing that a friend has ever done for you?

The messages made her laugh, or think, and she didn't mind answering the questions. It was somehow easier over the phone rather than face to face. Her scars didn't matter, they just chatted and had fun and she looked forward to her phone pinging with incoming messages. His questions brought back happy memories of life before the accident.

When messages weren't from him she was disappointed, but she caught up with other people, slowly getting up to speed with their news and renewing friendships, starting to talk about when they might pay each other visits. For the first time in months, when her uni tutor emailed to ask how she was doing, she answered his email, telling him she was doing okay and missed uni. He sent a response asking her to consider coming back, that they could think of a way to cover what she'd missed. She didn't reply. In fairness she was closer to uni now that she was in London, but it was still too big a thing for her to contemplate.

One evening Leo asked a question that was too big to answer in a message, so she called him.

How did you end up moving to London? L x

'Uncle John, my Mum's older brother, called from Hong Kong one night,' she explained, sinking back against her pillows after asking him how his day had been. 'His son, my eldest cousin Matt, offered us the use of this house. It was the one he bought with his late wife, Helen. The lodgers moved out and he was going to rent it out again but thought of us.'

'He sounds like a good guy,' Leo's deep voice trickled into her ear, making her shiver.

'He is. The best thing about him is that even though he lives in a multi-million town house in Knightsbridge with four cars on the driveway and is a famous music producer to rival Simon Cowell – except without the high-waisted trousers, alarming amounts of chest hair and smug smirk – he isn't pretentious at all. He does however have an impressive set of straight white teeth.'

'Cosmetic dentistry?'

'No. I've been jealous of Matt's wide, flawless grin since I was seven and he was sixteen. I totally hero-worshipped him growing up.'

'So that's what a guy has to do to earn your adoration,' Leo joked. 'Straight white teeth added to Georgiana's ideal man list. Tick.'

'Ha-ha. No, actually my ideal man would have to make me laugh, support me and love me for who I am.'

'Utter crap,' Leo teased, 'he'd have to be a millionaire with a six-pack!'

147

'Nah, an eight-pack at a minimum, like Jason Derulo. You can see his abs on stage from miles away.'

'No, that's probably just his gold bling.' He paused. 'So, I've been meaning to ask you something.'

George's heart jumped in a double ka-boom in her chest. 'Hmmm?'

'Uh, how long can you stay?' He cleared his throat, 'London prices are extortionate, and it's a pretty nice house.'

'For as long as we want. We're family. The deal is that we keep it secure and do maintenance on it instead of paying rent. Matt doesn't have a mortgage or need the income. Dad insisted we'd pay bills though, Mum too. She finds it hard accepting help off Uncle John.'

'What about your family home?'

'My parents have rented it out to keep it as an investment, but we're not planning to move back any time soon. Why?'

'I just wondered. It was pretty radical moving from Somerset to London.'

'Yeah, and I was scared at first. I felt really threatened by such a big change.'

'So why did you agree?'

'I didn't want to disappoint Dad. I've already short-changed my parents in the biggest way possible. I'm not the daughter they had any more.' She whispered. 'I felt like I'd never live the life they'd hoped for me.'

'I don't think that's true at all,' he said huskily. 'There's no way you've short-changed them. And how do you feel now?'

'Well, I hadn't counted on Mum getting me Buttons, or falling in love with him. Or you. No—I don't mean that I'm in love with you,' she blustered. *Oh, shit.* 'I mean that I hadn't counted on meeting you. That we would talk so much, that you would bring me out of myself. That I could trust you.' Argh, she hadn't meant to say that either. God, this was excruciating. It was so bad. Her face was bright red, she was sweating. 'I'm going to have to go to bed soon.' She faked a yawn. 'I'm really tired.'

148

'It's okay. Relax.' He laughed. 'You are adorable sometimes. You sounded so mortified. I'm not that bad you know. A woman could fall for me.' He paused. 'If she tried very hard, had lots of patience and didn't mind that my job is pretty much my life.'

'Nah,' George covered her embarrassment with teasing, 'that's too big of an ask. You're way too annoying. But you sounded confident. Have you got some extremely easy-going girls ready for Valentine's Day or something?' It was painful to ask. She wanted to know and not know. But it was only three days away, and she would rather prepare herself now if he said he was going on a date.

'No, absolutely not.'

George was shocked at the amount of relief coursing through her. How had he become so important to her in a few short weeks? Maybe it was because they were so open and candid with each other. It felt intimate, and intimacy usually went hand in hand with romance. And friendship. Two out of the three wasn't bad, she supposed.

'Which reminds me, I want to ask you something. Will you meet me tomorrow night, at around six on Primrose Hill?'

'Yes, okay,' her pulse quickened. 'What's it about?'

'Just a friendly favour,' he answered casually.

George let out a breath, deflated. 'No probs. See you tomorrow.'

'Great. Oh, and by the way, I enjoy our chats and messages too,' he remarked. 'They make me laugh, and I look forward to them. Night.'

George clutched the phone in her damp palm after he'd rung off, wondering what that had all been about. She daren't get her hopes up. They were just friends.

Just over twenty hours later, she walked into the park, the Victorian lamps providing little spotlights along the paths. She automatically let Buttons off the lead and started wandering up the slope toward the brow of the hill.

Leo was waiting for her there, sitting on a bench overlooking the city. 'Hey, you. Had a good day?' Patting the seat next to him.

'Yeah, good thanks. I went shopping.' It hadn't been easy, and one or two of the shop assistants had been less than subtle with their staring, but she'd survived.

He grinned, 'That's great. Finally going to ditch the Goth wardrobe and wear some colour?' He'd teased her a few times about the dark clothing she always wore.

'Ta-dah!' Unbuttoning her coat she revealed a turquoise jumper.

'Argh! It burns.' He reeled back, pretending to be blinded.

She punched him in the arm and sat down, doing her coat back up. 'I know you've got a favour to ask me,' she took a breath and exhaled it slowly, 'but I wanted to ask you for one too.'

He looked almost relieved. 'Of course. You go first.'

'Are you sure?'

'Yes,' he watched as she knotted her fingers together. 'What is it?'

'I'm ready.'

'Ready for what?'

'To tell you what happened to me. My therapist suggested it, and I think she's right.'

'You're seeing a therapist?' he frowned.

She lifted her chin, willing her cheeks not to burn. 'Yes. There's no shame in it. Sometimes talking helps.'

'I'm not judging, I'm pleased for you. You've obviously been through a lot. I think you should talk about it. So, why now? Why not before?'

'I didn't know you well enough.'

'And?'

'I told you last night. Now I trust you.'

'Right,' he shifted in his seat, looked uncharacteristically edgy.

'What's wrong?'

'Nothing. Go on, please tell me.'

He picked up her hand, wrapping his warm fingers around her

cold ones. She tried not to squirm, tried to focus on the heat of his hand rather than the tingles it sent through her body.

'It made the regional papers.' With her free hand she reached into her pocket, drawing out a piece of newspaper that had been folded and refolded umpteen times. Her first counsellor had said it might help her, make it real at a time when all she'd done was try to deny her new reality. 'This is what my car looked like afterwards.'

He drew the scrap of paper from her clutching fingers, staring down at it, drawing in a sharp breath. 'Jesus, Georgiana! The state of your car … It's almost crushed.' He shook his head. 'It's a wonder you made it out alive.'

'How did you think I got to look like this?' she asked him, but there wasn't as much bitterness or anger as before. Thanks to him, her parents, her puppy and her friends.

He twisted his head to look at her, 'Don't do that. Don't. You're still beautiful. And even if you weren't, looks aren't everything.'

She clenched her teeth. Did he mean it or did he feel sorry for her? Was he just trying to comfort her because of how lovely he was? 'I don't feel beautiful. I feel … imperfect. Like all anyone will ever see is the eye-patch. Or the way I limp slightly when it rains.'

'No-one who cares about you will care about any of those things, and anyway, they make you who you are. And I think you're pretty cool.'

'You do?'

'Yep. You're not really bitter. Even though you make comments about your eye and the scar, you don't complain, not compared to how some people would. You could be depressed right now, with everything you've gone through, but you somehow pulled yourself out of it. You make me laugh. I check my phone in class for your messages, even though it could get me in trouble. My concentration is shot. That's never happened to me before. You don't take yourself – or me – too seriously, I like that.' He cleared his throat, threw his head to look up at the twinkling stars in the navy blanket of sky. 'Anyway, I think you have more to tell me,

151

so I'll shut up. What do you remember? How does it make you feel?' He waved the newspaper under her nose.

She gulped. The stuff he'd just said was positively overwhelming and she needed time to make sense of it but the article clenched in his fist was bringing it all back. 'I have nightmares about it,' she whispered, 'and I wake up sweaty. My favourite Rihanna album was playing on the stereo when my car got plastered along the barrier, and since the accident I haven't been able to listen to a single one of her songs without feeling sick.' She fell silent.

'What else?' Leo asked, pulling her closer to his side by their joined hands. Like always she was overwhelmed by the heat of his touch, the depth of his voice, the sexy crispness of his aftershave.

Her face creased up. 'I was minding my own business, driving along and picturing the bottle of red wine me and a flatmate were going to open when I got in. Then there was a violent smash as he rear-ended me. My Clio spun around like I was on a fairground Waltzer and there was an instant feeling like I was going to throw up. It was that go-fast, but slow down feeling everyone talks about.' She began to shake, reliving the horror. 'The lorry smashed into me again, sending me into the central barrier and the car flipped on its roof then back over again. I remember glass splintering around me, piercing into my body. There was the sound of metal grinding and screaming … or maybe that was me. Then absolute stillness. After a moment rain pounded my face because the windscreen and half the roof had come off. I couldn't look down because I was pinned to the headrest by something sticking into my head,' she touched her eye patch with her free hand. 'It hurt so much, so badly. Then there was this searing, horrendous pain lower down and I knew half the engine was in my lap. I wondered if that was it, if I was done.'

'Oh, Georgiana,' Leo murmured and let go of her hand. Wrapping both of his arms around her he hugged her tightly, like he was trying to absorb some of her pain.

Slowly, slowly her arms crept up and she let herself be held.

She leaned into him. There was nothing sexual in it at first. It was just comfort, compassion. She hadn't realised how much she'd needed it. But here with Leo, someone who'd been a virtual stranger only a few weeks before, here in this windy, cold London park, she finally wept. She pushed her face into his neck and let go, let him give her what she hadn't known she needed. She cried; tears of sadness, anger and loss trickling down her face. He held her close, stroking her back and murmuring soothing words, and she was no longer scared that the broken pieces of her couldn't be put back together. *This.* This was true romance. Not a card and flowers. Not chocolates and the movies. It was letting someone else see the most vulnerable part of you, and not being afraid that they would turn away or use it against you.

That's when she realised she was falling in love with him. But she wasn't ready for confessions yet.

'Thank God I blacked out then,' she whispered into the skin where his jaw met his neck, a light stubble coating it, salty from her tears. In answer his arms tightened fractionally. 'I didn't know anything until I woke up three days later, in desperate pain, confused and not understanding what had happened.' As the unbelievable devastation of that moment resurfaced she wept again, quietening when he moved his hand up to smooth her hair away from her face. 'Apparently, it took a team of paramedics and firemen half an hour to cut me out of the car,' she said shakily, 'and that first hour, the golden hour they call it, is so important, in terms of survival … I owe those staff my life. In fact,' she heaved a deep breath, feeling lighter after crying, and confiding in him, 'I'm going to go and see them, to say thank you. It feels … right. I can't drive but I could get the train or coach. I need to conquer doing both of those things at some point.'

'Yes, you do.' He smiled, putting some space between them so he could look down into her face, rubbing the tears from her left cheek. 'And it's great to hear you say that. But if you don't mind company, we'll go together. I'd like to thank them myself.'

'Why?'

'For saving you, silly. The world would be a sadder place without you in it. Why else?'

'I don't know.' There were two different ways to interpret his comment; as a loyal friend or a loving boyfriend. But he'd never even asked her on a date, so thinking about the second option would probably only lead to heartbreak hotel, and the last thing she needed was more pain.

After a few moments, she leant back and wiped her face, aware of how muscular his arms were and the rolling, tightening lust in her pelvis. 'Anyway, thank you for listening, and the hugs, but enough of that weepy stuff now. What did you want to ask me?' She eased away from him, unzipping her coat so she could cool down. His body heat was incredible.

He stared down at her, brown eyes intent. 'I wanted to know if you wanted to hang out on Saturday. We could meet here at noon?'

'That's Valentine's Day!' Shock and delight unwrapped a warm feeling in her chest. She hesitated. 'You seriously don't have anyone else you'd rather spend it with?'

'It would just be as friends,' his cheeks turned red. 'Like I said, this is just a friendly favour. No pressure.'

'Oh,' her stomach plummeted through the bench and hit the concrete floor underneath them with a thud. Her heart followed a close second. 'No, of course not,' she replied, praying her voice was steady, rolling her head back to gaze up at the rising moon. 'I'm not sure, Leo. I'd planned to stay in, well out of the way of all that soppy, romantic stuff. Can I let you know, or do I need to make a decision now, so you can sort out plan B?' She struggled to mask the jealousy that streaked through her at the thought.

'I can hang on,' he shrugged, 'and in the meantime I'll try not to be too overwhelmed by your enthusiasm. I might not be able to fit my head through my classroom door tomorrow.'

She laughed, 'I just don't know how I'm going to feel about it, on the day. Look, I've made progress, a few weeks ago it would have been an automatic no.'

'You have made progress,' he agreed. 'My work is almost done,' he rubbed his hands together, unfolding his long body from the bench.

'What do you mean?' she shot back suspiciously, standing up and rustling the biscuit bag to get Buttons' attention. 'This isn't the moment you tell me that Mum hired you to help me, is it? God that would be awful.' If that was the case, she might cry. Again.

'Don't be paranoid,' he answered, avoiding eye contact, 'there's nothing like that. I'd never met your Mum before that first day you fell over, I swear.'

But he still looked a bit shifty, transferring his weight from one foot to another.

'There's nothing you're not telling me?'

'Nothing you need to worry about,' he backed away. 'I have to go, I have books to mark.'

'You're not going to walk me home?' she said, confused.

'Do you need me to?' he stopped, jiggling his hands in his pockets.

'No.' *But I want you to*, she added silently in her head. 'Don't worry, go on. I have to find Buttons anyway.'

'You sure?' Leo walked backwards, like she was on fire and he was in danger of being burnt.

'Yeah. I'll let you know about Saturday. Go.'

'Thanks. I'll message you later to say good night,' he waved and spun away, jogging down the hill. 'And hopefully I'll see you at the weekend,' he yelled over his shoulder.

'Weird,' George muttered, turning her head back and forth and whistling for the puppy. 'What's his deal then, huh?' she scratched Buttons behind the ears when he screeched up to her, claws skidding on the ground. 'I suppose it will all become clear on Saturday, if I meet up with him.'

By the time she got home, she'd made her mind up. Even if it was just as friends, there was no-one else she'd rather spend

Valentine's Day with. Even so, the things he'd said to her, the way he'd held her, that couldn't just be a friends thing, could it? When he looked at her, smiled, laughed ... it felt like he didn't see the scars. They didn't matter. He'd called her beautiful.

L, okay, you're on. See you on Saturday. G x

Valentine's Day. Maybe it wouldn't be as dreadful as she'd thought it was going to be?

***

'What the f–,' George pushed away from the computer screen and stared at it disbelievingly. Her hands curled into fists and she felt room-spinningly ill. It couldn't be true. Leo wasn't like that. He was nice, and decent, and lovely and trustworthy. He couldn't have done it. She bent over the desk and peered at the Facebook status again.

Can't believe you've won the bet! Someone called Ewan had written on Leo's wall. *You actually have a date for Valentine's Day this year, you sad case! And I hope the G stands for gorgeous. Beers are on me on Sunday night, get ready to collect your reward.*

Underneath it someone else had commented, *I don't believe it, Miller has finally manned up and won something! How much did you have to pay the poor girl?*

'No.' She shook her head, and dropped into the chair, feeling winded. It was all a bet? He'd asked her to spend Saturday with him to win a stupid bet with his friends? She got up, and throwing herself down on the bed, let out a low moan. He didn't really like her. Of course he didn't. How could he, with her imperfections and fears? No, she was just someone handy to have around to fill the gap in their immature contest. Had he been laughing at her behind her back, with his mates, about how quickly she'd responded to his messages? At the way she'd laughed at his jokes? Burying her face further into the pillow, she bit down on the cotton pillow case. She'd opened up to him the other night, shared her worst memories with him, cried on him.

That made her sit up, filled with rage. How bloody dare he? How dare he pretend to be someone he wasn't? How could he take advantage of her vulnerability like that? What a pig. Striding back to the computer, she thudded a message out on the keyboard onto his Facebook page.

Looks like the joke is on you, Leo. I won't be helping you win any bet, I'm spending Saturday at home packing for uni. Three counties over isn't far away enough for me.

And btw Ewan, the G stands for grateful, which is what I feel towards you for helping me see what your friend is really like. And I'm way too expensive for him.

The message gave her a flashing moment of satisfaction before it dawned on her how publicly she was sharing her fury and humiliation. Leo had over 600 friends and two of them had already clicked to 'Like' her post. She paused, horrified, then went for the delete button, but before she could do anything, her message and the two left by Leo's friends had vanished. Immediately her phone started ringing. She wrenched it from her pocket and checked the screen. Leo. He knew. It was him who'd deleted the messages. She let it go to voicemail, tapping her hands on her thighs. He didn't deserve a chance to be heard. It was despicable. He rang five times before giving up, texting and Whatsapping the same message three times.

It's not what it looks like. It wasn't for a bet. I *promise.* **Let me explain. Meet me tomorrow please. And think about all our**

**conversations and messages. Think about what we mean to
each other. You'll know the truth. Xx**

Now

She had come.

Leo winced as Georgiana appeared on the left hand path, staring straight at him, expression as glacial as a winter snowstorm.

Happy Valentine's Day, he thought wryly.

Her long legs carried her to him in no time, but when he tried to put an arm around her in greeting, she shrugged away from his touch and strode over to the bench. She dropped onto it wordlessly and crossed her arms.

There was no Buttons with her today, and Leo didn't know if that was a good thing or not. 'Here,' he scrambled around in the rucksack and threw a blanket around her shoulders, snapping the hand warmer to activate it and handing it over. 'I don't want you freezing to death. It's a cold one.'

The murderous glare she gave him said it wasn't her health he should be worried about.

'So we're back to no words,' he muttered. 'Look, I'll get right to it. Just,' feeling like a stupid, flustered school boy he poured her a small flute of champagne and handed it to her, 'have this. I know you probably don't feel like celebrating, but it might help you relax.' He smiled hopefully, knees trembling. She meant too much to him to cock this up. She couldn't go back to uni with things not right between them.

Sniffing the champagne suspiciously to make a point, she took a sip and sneezed as the bubbles went up her nose.

'Right. I got that. You trusted me and now you don't think you can. So, I'll level with you. My friends did bet me to get a date for Valentine's Day.' He made sure to hold her one-blue-eyed stare as he said it, 'And I wanted to get them off my back for a bit, I'll admit it. I was fed up of some of the comments, like it wasn't okay to be single or that I hadn't met anyone yet, or that my career was the most important thing to me.' He saw a flicker of understanding in the eye not covered by the patch. 'So when I met you initially, I thought it could be the perfect solution. You obviously needed a friend and someone who could boost your confidence. I needed someone to hang out with today.'

'So I was a project?' she demanded, clutching the blanket tighter. 'You wanted to fix me.'

'No, of course you weren't a project. You're a person. An amazing, strong girl. And you didn't need fixing, you just needed to see yourself as whole again. I suppose with my job, I do help and support people and if that translated into our friendship, I'm sorry.' Closing his eyes, he pinched the bridge of his nose then opened them again. 'But I never saw you as just a bet. Or as someone to be pitied. I am so sorry. I promise you I didn't ask you here today so I could brag about it to my friends.' He slid a bunch of red roses from the bag, 'I don't suppose it's worth getting these out yet?'

She raised an eyebrow. 'You probably think they're romantic, but what I want from you, all I really want, is honesty.'

He ran a hand through his hair. 'I'm telling you the truth. There was nothing ever malicious about it. It was never for male pride, or to be one of the lads. I swear. You can ask anyone who knows me even one of those two pillocks on Facebook, who by the way were just taking the piss out of me.'

'I have had time to think … and maybe stalk you on Facebook a bit more,' she admitted, taking a sip of champagne.

Taking a deep breath. 'And?'

'There was nothing on there about girls, or anything too laddish. In fact it was pretty boring.'

He beamed. 'I told you.'

'I was furious,' she leaned forward, direct eye contact locked onto his, fingers clenched around the glass. 'Because of the way I feel about you. Seeing that message about a bet played into all my worst fears. That I wasn't enough for you, for any guy any more. That it would be just because guys felt sorry for me. That I wasn't worthy. But then,' she looked down at the bubbles rising to the surface of the bubbly, 'I read your message and lay on my bed and thought about the last few weeks. About, like you said, the conversations and things we've shared. About the way you pushed me to challenge myself, to think, to act. The support you gave me, the way you held me when I told you about the accident. I don't think you can fake all that. So I decided you deserved a chance to look me right in the face and confess the truth, the whole truth. So, here I am.' Setting aside the glass she took a deep breath, and clenched her teeth.

'What do you—?'

'Leo, stop talking.' She took hold of his hand and moved it to her thigh, so that his fingers could trace the scars through her jeans. 'I have muscle missing here, and ugly scars. I don't like looking at it when I take my clothes off.' She sucked in another deep breath, looking pale, and let go of his hand. He left it on her leg while she took a hair-band from her pocket and tied her hair back in a jaunty ponytail that showed off her amazing cheekbones. Focusing only on him, she reached round behind her head and slipped her eye-patch off. 'This is me. This is who I am now. Is this a face you could feel strongly enough about to spend time with every day?'

His lips tightened as he saw the scarring there, and knew she was testing him, but he didn't care. He was glad to have the chance to prove himself to her. Grabbing her face between his hands he brought her in close, resting his forehead against hers, unflinching. 'Without hesitation,' he said, and kissed her softly. 'You've taught me how to fall in love.' He felt a smile form on her lips and eased back. 'This is the bravest thing I've ever seen anyone do. You're the last person who deserves pity, and if you don't go back to uni soon, I'll personally drive you there myself and dump your arse there. You're going to be an incredible teacher.'

There were tears in her eyes when she nodded. 'I'm signed back up. I start back after Easter. People can look if they want to. After a while they'll get bored with it.'

'They'll just be checking out the hot pirate girl,' he grinned as she put the eye-patch back on, before he kissed her again. 'So am I forgiven? Do you believe it wasn't for a bet? That once I got to know you there was no way it could ever be a bet? I said friends only because I didn't want to push you into something—'

Wrapping her arms around him she squeezed hard, then threw her legs over his. 'I believe you. And what you just did—' she nodded her head, 'the way you saw me at my most vulnerable and didn't flinch. It was the most romantic thing anyone has ever done for me.' She groaned. 'God, that was so cheesy. Yuck!'

'Well, it is the most romantic day of the year.' He tugged gently on her ponytail. 'We might as well enjoy it, now we're here,' he pointed to the hamper at their feet. 'There's all sorts of cool stuff in there. Fancy sharing them?'

'Absolutely. But in a minute, when I've finished my bubbly and taken in the view.'

'Great,' he picked up the other flute and poured himself a glass. 'Cheers.'

As George rested her head on his shoulder, holding his hand underneath the blanket, Leo gazed out across the London skyline. It was the perfect way to spend Valentine's Day on Primrose Hill.

Cocktails in Chelsea

Thursday

Sofia Gold sighed as she stepped into the trendy bar on the King's Road. If she cared less about being polite, she'd be wearing her own clothes. Instead, she was tugging down the hem of the clinging, vibrant yellow designer dress Tori and Christie had wrestled her into and fighting the urge to pull the plunging neckline up a few inches closer to her chin.

While showing off tons of leg and cleavage wasn't her at all, she had to admit the yellow outfit didn't look *too* bad with her long golden hair, which Christie had made her straighten. It was just a shame she was being slowly crippled by towering four inch high heels. They might make her short legs look amazing, but the balls of her feet were already aching and they'd only left the girls' exclusive white-pillared, black-gated residence twenty minutes before.

Of course she liked partying, enjoyed going out and having a laugh. After all skating ramps and riding the waves on her beloved surfboard couldn't take up all of her spare time. She was also lucky enough to live in Bournemouth, and the coastal town had a great night life humming with stag and hen parties despite its reputation as the retirement capital of the south. The difference was, she usually went into town in tight jeans, mid-range heels at most and a cropped vest-top, not in outfits that felt designed to torture. Plus she drank at lively bars with the best, pulsing music and happiest, loudest crowd, not airy warehouse spaces with tons of lighting, exposed vintage-looking iron pipes and dark wooden floors packed with privileged and wealthy trust-funders.

But Tori and Christie were Mum's best friend's daughters and she'd promised to make an effort during this visit. If she offended them it'd be a giant dinosaur bone of contention with her mother for years. The idea of being on the wrong side of her mum was scarier than the thought of wearing the outfit for the evening.

'You look lovely, Sof,' Tori leaned close to whisper into her ear, 'but you would look better if you stopped pulling at the dress constantly. Just try and own it.'

'Thanks,' Sofia murmured.

It was good advice.

Except.

Except she felt awkward and out of place. It wasn't her scene. Everyone was on show, all the little circles of people air-kissing and studiously not watching each other while totally watching each other, there to be seen and talked about. What did she know about dressing in luxury brands and living it up with the glitterati in the capital? Nothing.

'Come on darling, don't stand there gawping.' Christie grabbed Sofia's elbow, wrenching her from her thoughts and steering her around a couple of smooth looking guys in casually stylish jacket and jeans combos. 'Let's order some champagne. Despite being on the French Riviera at the moment, Mummy was so pleased you agreed to come that we simply have to make the most of it. She'll be very upset if she thinks we're not looking after you,' Christie continued sharply, her narrowed blue eyes bright against her English rose complexion.

Sofia nodded, letting the other girl lead her to a high, round table with black stools set around it, glad to sit down and take the weight off her feet. Trying to ignore the way the tight dress rode up her thighs, she glanced across at the assorted wall-mounted optics behind the bronze-tiled bar, smiling slightly. She guessed it wasn't so bad here, because although hanging out with friends with cold beers on the beach was more her thing, she had a serious soft spot for cocktails. The colours, flavours and varieties were amazing and she loved watching barmen create dizzying concoctions. There was something ridiculously sexy about guys throwing and twirling bottles around in that confident, competent manner they had. Although that could be less to do with their skills and more to do with her long-time crush on Tom Cruise. The late 80's film *Cocktail*, though dated, was one of her older sister Isobel's favourites and they'd watched it a load of times as teens.

She studied the embossed ivory drinks menu. The booklet was thick, the cocktail list vast; champagne based, gin based, rum based, vodka based, whisky based, exotic, with a twist and traditional. She'd have preferred to stay in tonight after this morning's tiring, chilly coach trip to Victoria and the stuffy, harried tube journey from there to Chelsea, but the cocktails would definitely serve as compensation for having to leave the house

Running a polished oval nail down the list of vodka cocktails, she frowned, feeling like her hands belonged to someone else. The sisters had insisted she get her nails done and she'd agreed out of courtesy, and she had to admit the French manicure with the light pink overlay was kind of pretty. It wasn't a word she usually associated with herself. Not that she was complaining. She loved her life, the adrenaline thrill of all the outdoorsy stuff she was into, so if the result was that she came across as a bit of a tomboy and wasn't one of those glam girls that men chased, so what? It did however mean that tonight was her chance to be something different, so she should really just try and enjoy it. Once she was home, it was back to good old Sofia, hanging out with the guys she designed skate-parks with and her surfing buddies.

Anyway, what was the worst that could happen over the next few days of the Easter Bank Holiday weekend? She could take in a bit of lively, diverse springtime London - eat, drink and see the sights - and hopefully sneak off to watch a footie match. She'd heard Chelsea were playing a home game against Stoke City on Saturday afternoon at Stamford Bridge. She chewed her lip and looked over at the other two girls. It was no wonder she felt out of place here. Tori and Christie probably wouldn't be caught dead at a footie match full of chanting, sweaty, beery men and cheering women. Unless they sat with all the WAGs then they'd probably be right at home. Or maybe she was being too quick to judge. What did she really know about their lives nowadays? It'd been years since they'd spent any real time together.

She looked at the bar again. 'Shall I go and get the drinks?'

'Don't be silly,' Christie drawled, craning her head to look over Sofia's shoulder at someone. 'It's table service.'

'Its fine,' Sofia replied, smiling tightly, 'I'm not too sure what I fancy so I'll go and have a scope at the bar.'

'Scope?' Christie repeated, looking faintly horrified.

'Christie.' Tori chided in cultured tones, tucking an escaped strand of glossy chestnut hair behind a diamond-studded earlobe. 'Be nice.'

'Nice is so boring.' Christie flapped a hand dismissively at her younger sister.

Tori turned to Sofia, squeezing her upper arm. 'Ignore her. If you want to go to the bar, do. You may as well order us a bottle of Moet and give them Mummy's name while you're there. We have a tab here.'

'Okay, no probs,' Sofia nodded, sliding off the stool.

'Oh, Sofa?' Christie's voice cut through her. 'Please don't embarrass us.'

Sofia heard Tori gasp her sister's name. She closed her eyes, counting to five in her head as slowly as possible. *Remember Mum.* 'Yes, Christie,' she gritted, opening them again. 'I'll try.' *Really hard not to strangle you with your ice-blonde ponytail.*

Sofa. The childhood name she'd always hated. Whenever their

families got together - biannual short breaks at a fabulous holiday home in St Ives - she'd always felt like the fat girl because the sisters were both so effortlessly, elegantly slim. The nickname referred to the couple of extra pounds she'd carried until her mid-teens, later lost through swimming in the sea every morning, pier to pier from Boscombe to Bournemouth.

Clanking across the floorboards in her high heels, she let out a long, loud sigh as she reached the bar. Resting her elbows on the wooden surface, she leaned forward to study the bottles in orderly rows inside the glass, condensation-coated fridges.

'Careful,' a deep, mildly sarcastic voice rumbled in her ear, 'or you'll give them a show a few hours early.'

Turning scarlet as she realised the ruddy dress had crept up at the back, she straightened, whipped her head around and opened her mouth to respond. But there wasn't time to challenge the comment because its owner had already placed a tray of glasses on the bar and melted away. She caught a glimpse of a white shirt, tight black trousers and dark hair as she stared after him. She also clocked that he was tall. Very tall.

Sofia gulped. He'd been out of order, there was no doubt about it, but still, what he'd said, how much had people seen? Had she actually flashed her tiny pink knickers at the whole place? Fleeing to the toilets, she spent a few minutes trying out different poses in front of the full-length mirror before coming to the conclusion that although the dress was quite short, her knickers probably hadn't had an outing. 'Thank god.' She exhaled, running both hands under the cold tap to get rid of her momentary fluster.

Returning to the bar, she waved at the staff member who was stacking glasses on a shelf. 'A bottle of Moet please, and two glasses.' What was she doing? Why had her voice come out all cut-glass? It was like being here worked like osmosis, absorbing the traits of the people around her. Or maybe it was Christie's comment about embarrassing them. Yeah, perhaps it wouldn't hurt to be someone else for this visit. She grinned. High-society

Sofia, quaffing champagne and living the good life.

'Yes, of course.' The barman's smile was fleeting as he turned to glance at her, and the coolness in his eyes was baffling. It was the guy who'd made the comment about her dress. It was a shame he seemed off with her, because he was cute. Mega-tall and lean, thick messy black hair, light stubble and doe-like chestnut eyes under straight black brows. He looked intense and intelligent, a touch dorky ... and really, really appealing.

'Thank you.' She picked up a menu, enunciating her vowels, 'And I would like—'

'Let me guess,' he interjected, 'a champagne cocktail.'

'No, actually,' she lifted her chin and looked down her nose at him, his tone annoying her, 'I'll have a Sex on the Beach.' The choice was pretty apt, seeing as the beach was practically her second home.

There was the hint of a genuine smile on the barman's face but it disappeared swiftly as another thought seemed to occur to him. He muttered something under his breath. It didn't sound complimentary.

'Excuse me?' she demanded, putting her hands on her hips.

Little rich girl slumming it, Nathan thought, but offered a bland, 'Nothing,' in reply to the haughty blonde, before making a big deal of checking the various fridges. 'I'll just go out back to grab the champagne,' he called over his shoulder as he strode away.

He'd seen the way she looked at him, the hunger in her eyes. He was sick of rude, entitled women and this bloody place. As soon as he had enough money that was it, he was out of here. Perhaps it'd be different if he was on the other side of the bar, the one buying expensive drinks and being fawned over by beautiful girls, but he wasn't, and although female customers flirted with him every night, it was obvious they only saw him as someone who served them. Someone who wasn't worthy. Jesus, he was getting bitter. What was wrong with him?

He marched down a corridor and into one of the storerooms, grabbing the chilled champagne from the fridge and slumping back against its door. Blowing out a breath, he rubbed his eyes with shaking fingers. He was so bloody knackered from working all these insane hours. Sometimes he could hardly think or see straight. But it'd be worth it, to show everyone he could do it on his own, that he didn't need to rely on his cousin Matt to get ahead. Matt was a great guy and a famous music producer, but there was no reason Nathan needed his cousin's money or connections to open doors.

His thoughts circled back to the blonde he was holding the champagne bottle for. She looked pretty much like the other girls in here, all perfect hair, nails, face and expensive outfit, but there was something a bit different. Her body was slim but athletic, her stomach toned enough that abs were visible through the skin-tight dress, but she wasn't as thin and angular as some of the other women. Then there was the vulnerability in her massive green eyes and a slight softness around her mouth. Her full, sexy mouth.

His body reacted to that thought.

'No. No way. You don't want her.' She was the last sort he'd go for. He liked the nice, sincere, girl-next-door type. The kind he'd want to take home to his grandparents. Not that he was looking to do that at the moment. His business plans meant too much for him to get sidetracked by a relationship.

Or by an uppity but gorgeous girl on a night out with her friends.

No.

Pushing away from the fridge, he slammed out of the storeroom. *Just do your job Nathan.*

Where the heck is he? Sofia wondered. Mr Hot but Grumpy had been gone for ages. Was he treading the grapes to make the Moet himself?

'Madam.' He swept in behind the bar, bending over to get an ice bucket and giving her a delicious view at the same time.

Straightening up, he planted the frosted champagne bottle in the bucket and set it down in front of her with two slim flutes. 'Sorry to keep you waiting.'

The fact he barely glanced at her was irritating. Especially when her eyeballs had nearly fallen out of her head at what an awesome backside he had in his tight trousers. 'Yes,' she retorted, 'I had started to wonder if you'd flown to France to get it from the vineyard yourself.'

Raising an eyebrow, he opened his mouth to say something but then closed it again, staring at her silently with wide, brown eyes.

It made her realise how bitchy she'd sounded. 'Sorry,' she murmured, 'I was—,' pausing, she searched for an excuse, but there wasn't one she wanted to share with him. So, 'I'm sorry ....?' she simply said, making eye contact so he could see her sincerity and understand what she was asking.

'Nathan.' He supplied, surprise registering on his face before he stepped away. 'No problem. Right, let's get you that drink.'

'Sounds good. I do love cocktails. Don't you think you owe me something in return though?' she prompted, mimicking Tori's pronunciation. It wasn't hard, a game they'd played as children. One memorable, humid afternoon the sisters had encouraged her to walk around the attic playroom of their holiday home with a book on her head, reciting phrases from their elocution lessons for endless hours. Her neck had ached for days.

'Owe you something?' Nathan squinted, expression puzzled as he filled a large, curved cocktail glass with ice chips.

'That comment you made earlier about my dress? That was you, wasn't it?'

'Oh, yeah.' He shrugged, broad shoulders moving under the snug white shirt. 'Sorry.'

'Try not to sound too sincere.' She crossed her arms.

Putting the glass down on the bar with a clink, he stopped and stared at her. Nodding, 'Of course Milady,' he said mockingly. 'I thought trying to protect your dignity might be appreciated, but

169

apologies for any insult caused.' His eyes dropped to her low neckline. 'Besides, I can see now that I've got a front view that your dignity isn't really a priority.'

Her mouth dropped open and she looked down, realising her folded arms were pushing her boobs up so they were almost spilling over the edges of the yellow material. Dropping her arms, she stared at the bar top, cheeks burning and unsure what to say. Why was it that when it came to work, or travelling, or anything other than her love life, she was confident and bold, but when faced with a guy she found attractive, she fell to pieces? It didn't help that she didn't feel quite herself tonight, in the alien outfit and surroundings.

'Hey,' a long-fingered hand slid around her wrist and squeezed it gently before letting go. 'Sorry. That was harsh. Are you okay?'

Perfect. Now he felt sorry for her. *Suck it up Sofia, you're better than this.*

How would Christie handle the situation? Sofia might not like the girl much, but she was ultra-cool when it came to the dealing with the opposite sex. It was worth a go. Tilting her chin up, she smiled at him breezily, ignoring the tingle where he'd touched her skin. 'Of course I am.' She arched an eyebrow and flipped her trailing hair over one shoulder. 'Now, is that cocktail going to make an appearance this year, or not?'

Nathan nodded, sliding the ice-filled glass out of the way. 'Coming right up.' He took a metal cocktail shaker off a shelf and scooped some ice cubes into it as a shorter barman with slicked back hair and model-material chiselled features appeared. 'Hey, Quinn,' Nathan jokily threw an ice-cube at him, 'you've been gone ages. What's going on?'

'You know me, mate. They've been eating me alive.' Quinn grinned, selecting a tall pint glass from the side and filling it from one of the curved silver beer taps. He glanced at Sofia and then did a double take. 'Hi, there.'

She smiled. 'Hello, back.' He wasn't her type, was far too smooth, so there was no danger of him making her tongue-tied. It was also nice to be appreciated rather than mocked. She widened her smile, noticing Nathan scowl from the corner of her eye.

'Quinn, can you pass me the orange juice?' Nathan growled.

'Sure, here.' Without taking his eyes off Sofia he handed over a plastic beaker of juice from beneath the bar.

'Thanks,' Nathan replied, rolling his eyes at his colleague's obviousness as he poured the OJ into the cocktail shaker. 'Do you want to add a bit of a twist and have pineapple juice in it too?' he asked Sofia, adding a double measure of vodka to the shaker along with some cranberry juice, before pouring some Peach Schnapps in freehand, not bothering to measure it.

'Sure,' she agreed. 'I can be adventurous.'

'Really?' he drawled, sloshing in the pineapple juice from a jug.

'Yes!' She propped her chin on one hand to watch him work. 'You don't believe me?' She scrunched her feet up inside the high heels, toes starting to hurt from standing for so long.

'I guess I'm just surprised,' he pulled a mock shocked face. 'Girls like you usually like it straight up.'

'Girls like me?'

But he didn't answer, instead he started vigorously shaking the container full of mixture up and down, arm moving so fast it was just a blur.

She forgot what they'd been talking about as she gazed at him. His movements were easy and super-confident and her heart pounded, hands going clammy, mesmerised by the way he flipped the shaker over his shoulder and caught it underarm before spinning it in a circle on his fingertips, as if by magic. *Tom Cruise, you've got competition*. It was a shame Nathan seemed to have taken a dislike to her. He really was bloody sexy.

Slamming the container down, he grabbed the glass he'd put aside and threw the ice chips into the sink. 'Chills it,' he explained when she frowned.

She nodded slowly, mouth dry. 'Uh-huh.'

Straining the mixture into the glass, he twisted a slice of orange onto the rim, and then garnished the cocktail with a maraschino cherry. 'There you go,' his mouth quirked in a lopsided smile, 'worth waiting for; Sex on the Beach.'

Yes, please. Sofia thought hazily. Clearing her throat, she managed a croaky, 'T-thank you.'

Quinn sauntered up with a circular tray in his hand, sliding her drinks onto it. 'I'll carry this over for you.'

'I'm okay, thanks,' Sofia took a step away from the bar and stumbled. It was embarrassing how badly the heels were crippling her, she was usually quite tough. There was no point being an idiot about it though. 'I mean, that would be helpful, thank you.' Spinning around, she walked carefully across the room to Tori and Christie, a little part of her hoping that Nathan was watching. But when she glanced over her shoulder he had already turned his back on her.

The guy might be aggravating in some ways but he made mean cocktails, Sofia thought some time later, on drink number four and feeling a pleasant buzz. There was zero chance of waking up with a clear head in the morning.

'Are you ready to go on to the next place Sof?' Tori giggled, draining the last of her champagne and standing up, waving a hand at someone, tiny charms twinkling on a delicate gold link bracelet around her wrist.

'Sure, why not?' Sofia laughed then let out an unladylike snort. Uh-oh, she may be more drunk than she'd thought. She focused on Tori, deliberately not checking Nathan's whereabouts. She'd done her best to ignore him since earlier, but had basically failed. It was cringe-worthy; her gaze kept going back to the bar constantly like it was on an invisible string, yet he hadn't even glanced in her direction.

Not much had changed since school, she mused. Even then the boys barely seemed to notice her. Shaking off the *poor me*

172

thought, she slipped sideways off the stool without bothering to pull her hem down. It was that point in the evening when it had stopped mattering.

'Come on then, you two. Let's go.'

'Ooh, the nice girl can be bossy!' Christie remarked, rising to her feet gracefully and threading her arm through Tori's. 'Onwards and upwards then.'

Following her childhood friends out onto the street, Sofia fixed her eyes straight ahead. She wouldn't look back. She'd only exchanged half a dozen sentences with him and he didn't like her for some reason.

I don't care.

She told herself that through the next few hours of drinking and dancing, as well as when a group of posh boys latched onto their group and bought them all drinks. They were perfectly nice guys; but they weren't Nathan. None of them made her palms go clammy.

But you don't care, remember?

She repeated that under her breath on the way home in the taxi at four in the morning. And the next day, when she woke to sunlight pouring in through muslin curtains and groaned at the pounding in her head and her thick-tongued mouth, she almost believed it.

Friday evening

'Here, again?' Sofia asked in a high pitched voice, looking up at the sign above the door.

She'd hoped, after hours of exhausting shopping in Sloane Square and Kensington, with a stop-off for facials and a lazy champagne-fuelled lunch, they might stay in. That hope had died when, upon returning to the girls' home, they'd immediately started making dinner plans. Couldn't they at least have gone to a

173

different bar though after their delicious meal at Bluebird?'

'Sorry,' Tori gave her a gentle smile, nudging Sofia into the entrance. 'This is our favourite place. We always come here to start off the evening.'

Sofia pulled a face, 'Doesn't that get kind of boring?'

Tori paused and then frowned, looking serious, 'I've never thought about it.'

Shrugging, Sofia made her way into the bar, stomach churning at the thought of seeing Nathan again. She didn't know whether to dread it or look forward to it, but it might be nice to know what it was about her he had a problem wit. At least Christie had agreed to Sofia wearing a more modest outfit this evening; a black scoop-necked sleeveless top with a clingy, black and white skirt with a sexy split up one side. It still wasn't her, but it was at least closer than the yellow dress had been and she felt a bit more comfortable, despite the stupidly high heels gracing her feet.

'So, what do you fancy tonight?' she asked Christie and Tori as they slid onto stools at the same table as the night before. 'My shout.' They'd put themselves out to spend time with her. Even if the day hadn't been her kind of thing she could still show her appreciation by buying them a drink.

Tori leaned forward, smoothing her shiny brown hair back into its intricate bun, her flicked up black eye-liner making her blue eyes look darker. 'May I have a cocktail please, Sof?'

Christie raised an eyebrow. 'You're not having champagne?'

'No,' Tori gave Sofia a considering glance, 'I thought it might be fun to try something different.' She met her sister's stare then picked up a menu, flicking through the pages with long, bejewelled fingers. 'What should I have?'

'A Cosmo,' Sofia replied decisively. 'The sharpness of the cran-berry juice and the Vodka is perfectly balanced with the fruitiness of the lime juice and the orange Cointreau.'

'Sounds divine. Yes, please.'

'Champagne,' Christie simply muttered, surveying the room

for people she knew.

Sofia rolled her eyes, 'Okay.' *Your Majesty*, she murmured under her breath, turning to stroll to the bar. When she got there, no-one was manning it. She waited a few minutes, tapping her nails on the black marbled surface, wondering again if Nathan was working. Something sparked in her belly. Oh, boy. After another minute, she craned her neck, searching the room for bar staff. Nope. She may as well go to the Ladies then. Striding across the room and through an archway, she slowed at the corner of the corridor and found Nathan carrying stacked crates out of a door marked *Staff Only*.

He was in the white shirt and black trousers again but his sleeves were rolled up around his biceps, which were rounding with effort as he hefted the crates higher in his arms. As he swung around to pull the door shut with a couple of fingers she saw his back muscles move smoothly beneath the thin, close fitting shirt.

Yeah, he was tall and ropey, but built too. She wondered what the front view would be like, but naked. As her inner thigh muscles clenched in response and her mouth dried up, he twisted around and stumbled slightly. Without thinking she rushed forward and grabbed the top crate from him.

Stepping back, he placed the remaining ones on the floor and looked at her in surprise. 'You again.' He raised an eyebrow as she held her crate easily against her body, lithe arm muscles defined. 'And I didn't expect that. You've got good upper body strength and great balance on those things.' He nodded at her black stilettos.

'Yes I do.' The core strength came from all the sports activities she did. She bit her lip, silently rerunning his comment, hearing only the criticism, and realised how horrified Tori and Christie would be at what she was doing, especially in their designer gear. 'Gym.' She clipped out, mimicking Christie, before looking down at the scuffed, plastic red crate she still held. 'I suppose this isn't very ladylike.'

'I didn't mean it like that,' Nathan said quickly. 'Actually, it's kind of cool. I didn't think a girl like you would get her hands dirty.'

She smiled, some of the previous night's shyness dropping away. 'I suppose sometimes people surprise you, don't they?'

'Yeah,' he frowned, 'I guess they do.'

As he put his hands on his lean hips and gazed down into her eyes, she caught a hint of fresh, crisp aftershave. Yes, he was outrageously sexy, that was a definite. Her face started burning and her skin tingled, a sure sign she was getting turned on. Then self-preservation kicked back in. *Don't make an idiot of yourself.*

'Anyway, I must go.' Hastily, she crouched down and slotted the crate on top of the others, her thigh revealed by the high slit in the skirt. Standing up, she smoothed the skirt back into place. 'I was on my way to the bathroom.'

'Okay.' He looked amused as she edged away. 'See you out there.'

On returning to the bar a few minutes later however, it was Quinn in charge and she ordered drinks with a slight sense of relief, smiling at him gratefully. There was something about Nathan that made her feel so jittery. It was unnerving. Carrying a glass of champagne and two Cosmos over to her friends, she slid the tray onto the table. The sizeable drinks bill had made her swear under her breath and she'd handed her poor debit card over reluctantly, not sure she had enough money in the bank to cover it. Thankfully, the transaction had cleared, so she hadn't been left red-faced.

Christie reached for her champagne eagerly and threw most of it back, while her sister watched in bemusement. 'Thank you for the drink.' Tori picked the cocktail glass up and sipped from it delicately. 'Mmm, very nice. By the way, your phone rang while you were gone. I don't like to answer other people's phones though, so I left it in your bag.'

'Thanks.' Sofia undid the clasp of the clutch purse and checked the screen on her mobile. Isobel. 'It was my sister. Do you mind if I go outside and call her to make sure it's nothing important?'

'Of course.' Tori took another sip of her Cosmo.

'Cheers. I won't be long.' Leaping off the stool she walked over to the door while dialling her sister's number.

'Woah, watch out!' A strong pair of arms caught her around the waist as she bounced off a hard chest and nearly fell over.

'Sorry!' she exclaimed, 'I—Oh.' Looking up and up and up into big brown eyes, she squirmed, breath catching in her throat somewhere. Nathan again. God, his fingertips felt like they were burning holes in her top and through to her skin. She inhaled deeply. He smelled so good. It was totally unfair.

'This,' he tapped her smart phone, lifting one straight black eyebrow, 'isn't more important than your health and safety, surely?'

Trying to calm her zinging body, she forced the shyness away with an effort. 'I suppose it depends on the phone call,' she joked unevenly.

'What is it then? A national emergency?' he quizzed dryly. 'Contact from the Queen? Or maybe it's a playboy lounging around on a boat waiting for you somewhere?'

'Don't be silly,' she said in a playful tone, her nipples peaking inside her bra at his closeness. 'He wouldn't be on a *boat*.' She could do this. She could talk to him, it wasn't so hard.

'No? Is seasickness an issue for you, Princess?' His hands tightened on her waist.'I meant it wouldn't be a mere boat,' she prayed her voice wasn't shaking, 'he'd be on a super yacht, a Sunseeker, worth tens of millions. And he wouldn't be lounging; he'd be preparing a lobster dinner and warming up the hot tub on the upper deck for me.' She'd seen one like it moored up at Poole Quay once. It had been awesome. In fact she had a picture. Scrolling through the gallery on her phone she held it up to his face. 'Look at that. Nice, yes?'

He released her. 'Sure,' he said flatly, 'if you like that kind of thing.' Stepping away, he moved further into the bar, 'Catch you later.'

'I was—,' *only joking*. She finished silently. What was his deal? Stepping out onto the street, she slouched against the front of the building and closed her eyes. Her hormones were rocketing around like they were jet-fuelled. Talk about pure, instant lust.

There was a distinct chance that if he touched her again she'd jump him, whether he liked her or not. Not a great idea, and not like her at all.

'Issy.' She said when her sister answered the phone. 'Everything okay?'

'Everything's fine.' Her older sister laughed. 'I just wondered how you were getting on with Tori and Little Miss Queen of the World. They driving you mad yet?'

Sofia grinned. 'Not quite. You know Tori, she's actually quite nice. Christie's had a few moments though.'

'Have you told her where to go yet?'

She snorted. 'You know Mum will go ape if I argue with her.'

'Yes, but still don't let Her Majesty walk all over you. You're pretty straight up with your surfing buddies, you should just be the same with her. Unless you're scared of her that is,' she teased.

'Ha ha. Don't be silly. I'm just trying to keep the peace.'

'You're too nice, Sofia.'

'Now you sound like Christie.'

'Argh, no! Don't say things like that.' Isobel let out a pretend sob. 'So, any hot guys there?'

'Beautiful.' It just fell right out of her mouth. *Nathan.*

'Oh, yeah? Anyone in particular?'

She paused for an instant too long before answering. 'Erm—'

'That means yes. Tell me, tell me now,' Issy urged.

'Just a guy in the bar we go to.' She grimaced, going red. 'I don't think he likes me much though.'

'Knowing you, you're over-thinking it. So how hot is he? Oven warm? Summer's day sunshine? Or volcanic?'

'Hotter.'

'Wow. Hotter than Rob?'

'I—,' that was a hard one. She'd been mooning on and off over Rob for years, even though nothing had every happened between them romantically, and he'd once heartbreakingly told her he thought of her like a little sister.

'Please don't tell me you're still hung up on him?' Issy sounded exasperated.

'No, I'm not,' she answered instinctively, 'and this guy's much hotter. Tall, dark haired, gorgeous brown eyes, smart looking. All he needs is a pair of those trendy glasses and he'd be perfect.'

'Wow, the Rob-haze has finally lifted. Funny how the slightly geeky look is your thing these days, given what a total surf bum Rob was.'

'Yeah, funny.' Sofia echoed, while it dawned on her that she really didn't feel that way about Rob anymore. Her infatuation had become a comfortable habit, like wearing a favourite pair of joggers, but she couldn't feel that away about him if Nathan, a virtual stranger, inspired such a strong reaction. A tiny knot of tension unfurled in her chest, and she smiled, feeling lighter somehow.

'So … what are you going to do about it?' Issy demanded.

'Do? About what?'

'Duh, the hot guy.'

'Nothing.' Sofia stared at the leafy trees across the wide, busy King's Road, and then counted the black cabs going past, their paintwork gleaming under the street light opposite. Somewhere a horn blared and there was a shouted response.

Issy blew out a frustrated breath. 'I don't get you little sis. How can we be related? Live a little, get a sense of adventure.'

'Uh, hang on. I have a creative job which I travel for, I've tried most extreme sports and I spend most of my spare time throwing myself around ramps and into waves. What's not adventurous about that?'

'You know I wasn't talking about that stuff.' Issy paused. 'I meant you should try taking a few risks in your personal life. You don't really date. There's been no serious relationship in two years. You're twenty-three and in danger of turning into a lonely old cat-lady.'

'Hardly, I have loads of friends, and—,'

'You're in the city for the weekend,' Issy talked over her sister's protestations, 'and you've met a guy you want to do things to, so why not go for it?'

'Issy—,'

'No-one need ever know, other than you and him. As long as you're careful—'

'Isobel, stop. You might be my older sister, but please,' she dropped her voice to a whisper, '*please* don't give me the safe sex talk.'

'Fine. But just think about it. You might really enjoy it.'

'Okay, that's it,' Sofia said, 'now I'm putting the phone down. Take care, Sis.'

'Scaredy-cat.' Issy laughed, 'Fine. Love you, have fun.'

'Love you more. Bye.' Sofia answered automatically, but was frowning as she ended the call and wrapped her arms around herself. The April evening was getting chilly.

Was Issy right? Was she playing it safe, not giving men any time in her life? She was so used to being slotted neatly into the friend-zone by her male friends that maybe she'd stopped trying, because it was easier. After all, rejection wasn't a possibility if you didn't put yourself out there. The truth was, Rob had made her feel crap as a woman, and her last relationship had been a disappointment. Six months with the same guy and they'd had no fun together and nothing to talk about. He'd been shitty about her hobbies and didn't rate her career much either, so she'd packed it in when he suggested they take a break (translation: he'd started seeing someone else). She hadn't been sorry and there hadn't been anyone since.

What her sister said was true. Sofia had never been into casual sex. However, the thought of pinning a guy she could hardly take her eyes off – aka Nathan – up against a wall and doing naughty things to him was incredibly appealing.

But she wasn't confident or experienced enough, not when it came to guys, to do something like that. Traipsing back into the bar and feeling a little sad at the thought, she slung her purse on the table. 'Sorry I took so long.'

Tori looked up, cheeks flushed, 'That's all right. I ordered another Cosmo.'

Christie wasn't as gracious. 'You took forever. What were you doing, trying to resolve world peace?'

'That would be pretty much impossible with you around,' Sofia replied sweetly, before swinging away, 'I'll be back in a minute, I'm going to the Ladies.'

Leaving Christie gaping open-mouthed behind her, Sofia stalked across the room and down the corridor. She shouldn't have made that comment to Christie, but the girl was relentless. Careening off one wall, Sofia came to a halt. Nathan was sitting on a couple of stacked crates staring out of the open fire door a few feet away.

The look on his face was fierce and no doubt she should leave him to his own thoughts, but the words erupted anyway. 'Taking a break?' The sentence came out breathless as she stepped toward him. Which was how he left her as he swung his gaze to her and frowned, big dark eyes intense.

'Something like that,' he muttered.

'Okay.' Obviously not in the mood for chat then. Brushing past him, she tripped slightly, surprised at the intensity of the hot lust that scorched through her, along with the heat coming off his body. 'Sorry,' she mumbled, rushing to the toilets. Staring at her reflection in the round, bulb-lit mirror, she was shocked by her pink cheeks and sparkling eyes. God, if her work colleagues could see her now … Good old Sofia in the sexy, tight outfit, looking excited and on an adrenalin-high like she'd just surfed out of the biggest tube imaginable. They'd either wet themselves laughing and take the piss out of her, or ask who the heck she was.

She had to be careful around Nathan, it could lead to epic embarrassment otherwise.

Expecting him to be gone when she came out, her heart bump-bumped against her ribs when he was still sat in the same position, though this time with his head resting against the wall. Clicking toward him on the stilettos, her nose twitched at the gorgeous aftershave drifting off him. She moved closer, eyes fixed on the stubble under his jaw. She wasn't the type of girl to swoon, but he had her pretty close.

When he rolled his head forward and looked at her through slitted eyes, she realised she'd stopped right beside him.

'Can I help you with something?' he asked.

'No. I mean, yes, what time do you close tonight?' She really was getting the hang of this upper class accent. Except posh girls were probably subtle enough not to drool over guys, and her gaze had dropped to the open neck of his shirt, tracking the shadow of his perfect collarbone. She swallowed.

'Four in the morning.' His voice was iced-over Thames cold.

'I see. Thank you.'

'Anything else? Only I've got another five minutes of my break left.' He put his head back against the wall and shut his eyes again.

'No. Thank you.'

'Good.'

Go, now. Her brain ordered, but her feet refused to budge.

'I can feel you watching me.' A tiny smile tugged at his mouth.

'I'm going.' But still she didn't move. Her mouth fell open as she took in his broad shoulders, and the muscles of his long thighs in the fitted black trousers. Her breathing got quicker and sharper and she gulped, swaying closer. He smelled so good, looked so good.

Before she knew it she'd stepped between his legs, bent down and planted a kiss on him. Hooking her hands into his thick messy hair, she gently bit his bottom lip. For a brief, delicious moment he returned the kiss, head tilting further back, hands sliding around her hips. Then he pushed her away.

'What the hell are you doing?' Shooting up, he shoved his hands in his pockets.

'I—I'm sorry.' Oh shit, mortification 101. Why had she done that?

'You can't just kiss someone without their permission. I could

182

have a wife, a girlfriend, anything.'

'Bloody hell, have you?' she gasped, abandoning the posh accent.

'No as it happens, but that's not the point.' He said sharply, 'You think that because you're some rich Chelsea Princess you're entitled to do what you want?'

'Of course not.' She flung back, all traces of upper crust girl completely gone. This was *so bad*. 'Look, I'm sorry. I didn't mean to, honestly. And I'm not one of those rich girls, I'm just a normal girl from Bournemouth who's up here for the weekend. I'm nothing special at all.'

Why had she said that last bit? Talk about revealing.

Nathan looked confused. 'You what? You're not even from London? You lied?' he asked quietly. 'Put on the accent, and talked the talk?'

'I—I wasn't lying, I just wanted to fit in.' But that wasn't the whole truth was it? She'd wanted to be someone else, a girl who men looked at and wanted. 'Anyway,' she said defensively, 'what does it matter to you? Why do you care?'

'It doesn't matter.' His eyes narrowed. 'I'm only bothered because I don't like dishonesty. Or people pretending to be something they're not. And it's a bit weird. You must be in your twenties at least; you're not a little kid.'

She flinched. When it came to some things, like men, she may as well be a child. 'Well it must be nice to be so perfect,' a blush swept up over her face, tears scorching her eyes, 'you'll have to let me in on your secret one day. Until then, I'm sorry again for kissing you. It was a big mistake, obviously.'

His face softened, 'Sofia, wait—,'

Swinging around, she bolted, not even registering that he'd called her by name. She'd made a total arse of herself and embarrassment didn't even begin to cover it.

Pleading a headache with Tori and Christie, she insisted on leaving and they were too polite as hostesses not to accompany her back home, chatting about some summer ball while Sofia stared silently out of the cab window, unable to believe what a mess she'd made of things.

Her face was still burning with humiliation as she curled up in bed half an hour later, but not as much as her mouth was burning from that unbearably sexy moment when Nathan's tongue had met hers. She'd never been kissed like that before.

Saturday

Despite how the previous night had ended, Sofia had an amazing Saturday. After a late lie-in, Christie had departed the house, immaculately dressed for a prior commitment, leaving Tori and Sofia alone. Sofia, missing her daily swim in the sea, did twenty laps in the luxurious basement pool and went looking for Tori. She needed a distraction from last night's disastrous run-in with Nathan.

'Hi.' Sofia peeked around the side of Tori's bedroom door, expecting her to still be languishing in bed, but her friend was fully dressed in a tasteful white dress, frowning at the mirror while trying to clip her hair up.

'Morning Sof, did you sleep well?' she turned on the padded stool to look at her. 'Has your headache gone?'

'Headache? Oh,' Sofia blushed at the lie, 'um, yes thanks. I think I was just a bit knackered. I was wondering,' she mooched over to the bed and sat down on the edge, 'if you'd be up for a little adventure?'

Tori's eyes widened. 'What did you have in mind?'

'I kind of wanted to do the touristy thing; wander around Westminster, see Big Ben, take a ride on the London Eye, have lunch, maybe go to Borough Market.' There was nothing for it, the last bit of available credit on her Visa card was going to get hammered. 'What do you think? Are you up for it? I know it's not your usual style, but—'

'I'm in,' Tori interrupted, eyes lighting up.

'Really?'

'Yes, absolutely. Let me just finish doing my hair.'

'I think you should let it down.'

'All right,' Tori looked doubtful. 'Christie always says—,'

'It'll suit you better loose,' Sofia said firmly, 'Anyway, Christie's not here. You're getting changed too. That's way too dressy, have you got anything more casual?'

Tori shot up from her seat, shaking her hair out so that it fell in soft waves around her face. 'I've got a pair of somewhere,' she chewed her lip thoughtfully, 'and a cashmere sweater and some leather riding boots. Will that do?'

Sofia sighed, thinking of her own battered skinny jeans, comfy purple jumper and Converse trainers. 'Yes, that'll do.'

Their day went to plan and Sofia took more photos on her phone than she knew it could hold, laughing with Tori as the wind whipped their hair around their faces on the bank of the grey Thames and gasping at the astounding views of the city from a capsule at the top of the iconic London Eye. Cajoling Tori into sharing a mid-afternoon cream cake in a cafe near Borough Market, it also took pleasingly little effort to talk her into watching the Premiership game in a high-street pub. It was too late to get match tickets but they got a spot near the flat-screen TV, which was good enough for Sofia.

The atmosphere in the pub was good-natured and other customers threw comments at the screen when a player missed a goal, or moaned when Stoke City got a corner. Tori was a big hit with a group of Chelsea supporters at the next table over and the girls ended up sitting with the men during the second half. Tori even had some beer and, dizzy with daytime drinking, flipped beer mats with one of the men, a cute red-haired joker who kept taking the piss out of her for being posh. Sofia watched with a smile, joining in with the fun. At one point, Tori wiggled closed to Sofia, exhaling beery breath into her ear. 'I think I might like a bit of rough, Sof. What do you think?'

Sofia smirked, 'I think you're a bit drunk, but it's not such a bad idea.'

After the match, when the men had departed with hugs and waves, leaving a few of their numbers behind, Sofia leaned back in her chair. 'You know Tori, this is the most relaxed I've ever seen you.' There was a softness to her face that made her look gorgeous and carefree, and Sofia remembered the girl was actually a couple of years younger than her.

'It's the most relaxed I've ever been, I think. Thank you for such a fab day,' her friend replied, nodding. Pausing, she looked Sofia in the eye, swaying slightly. 'You didn't have a headache last night, did you? Or if you did, that wasn't why you wanted to leave. Something happened between you and that barman you kept staring at.'

Sofia grimaced. Had she been that obvious? Bugger. 'Well, I …'

Tori flapped her hand around, 'It's fine. Don't make up excuses. But you do know he came and asked us your name, when you were outside on the phone to your sister?'

'No …' She'd had no idea. But now she thought of it, hadn't he called her by name as she ran out?

'Yes.' Tori nodded. 'I think he liked you.'

'You do?' The memory of Nathan's kiss had resurfaced constantly during the day, no matter how much she tried to forget it.

'Yes. Come on,' the other girl pushed out of her chair, looking determined. 'Let's go home and get changed. We're going back to the bar.'

Sofia rose slowly, grabbing her jacket and shrugging into it. 'I don't know.' The thought was scary and exciting at the same time. Maybe she should listen to Tori though. She'd basically run away from Nathan, and maybe he'd have something else to say to her, once he wasn't so angry?

'We really need to go.' Tori tugged on her elbow.

'You think he liked me that much?' Sofia raised an eyebrow.

'I'm not sure. Maybe.' Tori tapped the expensive gold watch on her wrist, and held up her phone, which had a list of missed calls on the screen. 'But I've just realised it's almost eight o' clock. My sister is going to kill us.'

'You've changed.' Nathan looked her up and down as she strode over and hopped onto a stool at the bar.

'I'm not sure if that's a compliment or not, but this is more me.' She waved at the scarlet camisole top and form-fitting black jeans she was wearing, feeling good. Feeling herself, and more in control. She and Christie had wrangled over the outfit, but Sofia had stood her ground. The sisters weren't better than her, they were just different. Once Sofia had made that clear to Christie, and the other girl had realised she wasn't going to get her own way, she'd retreated in a huff. Sofia was sure she'd seen a hint of respect in her eyes though.

Nathan stared at her. 'You look … better.'

'Wow, don't knock a girl out with too many compliments.' She wasn't that used to flirting but at least being friends with a lot of guys had given her some banter.

'Sorry. I just know I can be quite overwhelming sometimes, when I'm on the charm offensive, so I try to hold back,' he teased, grinning. 'I like to give the girl a fair chance.'

She smiled, shifted her hips a little, watching with delight as his eyes tracked the movement. *So maybe he does like me, at least a little.* 'I appreciate your thoughtfulness. I guess I'm forgiven then? For the kiss, I mean, and for pretending to be someone else. I thought I should say sorry again.' She held her breath.

'Thanks, but there's no need.' Folding his arms on the bar, he dipped his head toward hers, face becoming serious. 'Look Sofia, I over-reacted, mostly because I'm exhausted, and tired of this place. I have got a bit of a thing about honesty too, but you obviously had your reasons for doing what you did, so I shouldn't have judged you so harshly. Despite the way I reacted yesterday, I do know I'm not perfect. You caught me by surprise, that's all.' He looked into her eyes, long lashes flickering. 'I've hardly been on my best behaviour, so I'm sorry too.'

'You are?' she asked croakily, breathing in his gorgeous, crisp scent.

'Yes. I don't understand why you were faking it, but—'

'It was just a bit of silliness,' she mumbled, 'I got carried away.'

'Well, don't get me wrong,' he gazed at her mouth, making her stomach swoop to the floor, 'you looked stunning, but I much prefer you like this.' He pointed at the bright top and golden, messy, rippling waves dropping almost to her waist, his brown eyes warming. 'Also,' he leaned even closer, 'to be honest it's a relief to find out that you're,' his voice dropped to a whisper, 'you know, *normal.*'

She laughed giddily, turning to look at Tori and Christie, who were watching her exchange with Nathan. 'They're normal,' she smiled, 'just not brought up in the same way as you or me.'

'I don't know,' he smiled crookedly, 'the blonde looks like she'd take me apart in a heartbeat.'

She giggled, wondering where on earth tomboyish Sofia had got to. She might not be experienced but she knew he was interested from the way he spoke to her, the expression on his face as he looked at her. There was a power in that knowledge and it made her feel exhilarated. It was fun. Was this what Isobel had been talking about? 'Christie has her moments,' she shared, 'but she's not that bad.'

'Hmm.' His eyes dropped back to her mouth. 'I'll take your word for it.'

'I guess you'll have to.' Her hands were trembling so she pressed them down on the bar.

'So, can I get you a drink?' Nathan unfolded his mega-tall body as Quinn sauntered up and put a tray full of empties on the side.

She felt ridiculously disappointed. 'I—champagne for Christie please, and Tori and I will have Mojito's tonight.'

'In the mood for something Cuban, huh?'

'I'm lucky to have visited Cuba a couple of years ago and it's amazing,' Sofia breathed, nodding enthusiastically, 'and I got addicted to Mojito's when I was over there. But it's the rest of it that's amazing; the history, the culture, music, salsa, the peeling colourful buildings, all the classic cars, the passion of the people. The variety is incredible.'

Nathan raised an eyebrow, 'Wow. So you want to go back?'

'Maybe one day. But there are loads of other places to see first. I'm planning on a cheapie trip to Jamaica next, the setting of one of my favourite films. Backpacking in Vietnam has been my favourite so far.'

He nodded seriously, 'I see. You don't stay still for long then?'

'I flat-share with three friends so that I can save up and go away a couple of times a year. I travel for work too, usually just in the UK, but we're slowly expanding into other parts of Europe, so I'm excited about the possibility of some longer distance trips.'

'You've really been bitten by the travel bug then,' he said with an odd twist to his lips.

'I guess,' Sofia agreed. 'But don't get me wrong, I love my home town too. Bournemouth is great.' And perhaps if she had her own space and someone lovely to share it with, she wouldn't feel the need to fling clothes in a bag and hit the road quite so often.

'Right. Well, er, I'll sort these drinks out for you and bring them over.' He turned away, reaching left and right for different glasses.

'Okay, thank you.' Disappointment hit her again, because she wanted to stand at the bar and drool as he worked his magic with the cocktails. But she could hardly tell him that.

Nathan's deep voice stopped her as she went to move away from the bar. 'Sofia?'

The way he said her name made her knickers ping.

'Yes?' She twisted to face him, licking her lips. Was he going to ask her out? Maybe see if he could have her number?

'These are on me.' He grabbed a cocktail shaker and wooden stirrer. 'For giving you a hard time.'

'Thanks.' She said lamely, before traipsing back to the table, feeling decidedly flat.

'I don't see what the attraction is.' Christie sniffed a few drinks later, checking the platinum watch on her wrist. 'He's *only* a barman.'

'What did you say?' Sofia fell back in her chair, staring at her.

'Isn't there a song about it? Working as a waiter in a cocktail bar?'

'It's waitress actually.' Sofia gritted, sitting forward. 'And so what?'

'I could never date or be with someone in the service industry. I'm just saying.'

'Christie.' Sofia sighed tiredly, standing up. 'Please don't say stuff like that. I'm sorry, but that's it.' She was done with being polite. 'I've put up with your rubbish because of our Mums but I'm done.' She grabbed her bag off the table, watching Christie's jaw drop. 'You're a snob, and I feel sorry for Tori, putting up with you day in and day out. I'm out of here.'

'Me too.' Tori said, jumping up. 'I have a date.'

'With who?' Christie demanded, spiking a look at Sofia before gazing her sister.

'With a man I met today,' a dimple flashed in Tori's cheek as she smiled, 'if you want to know. He seems interesting, and is very good looking. He went to the cinema with friends and just texted me. I've agreed to meet him in the West End.'

'Fine,' Christie snapped, scraping back her stool. 'But it's me who's leaving. And don't bother coming back to ours tonight,' she fumed at Sofia. 'I'll be locking the door. She frowned at her sister. 'We'll talk in the morning.' Whipping around, back straight with indignation, she stalked out.

Tori and Sofia looked at each other.

Sofia's mouth twitched. Tori bit her lip. Sofia smiled and couldn't help it getting wider.

'Did you see her face?' Tori choked.

'Yes.' Sofia started giggling, clutching her side. 'I love her, she's my sister, but—,' she erupted in full-out laughter, the tinkling sound drawing admiring glances from the crowd of men around them.

'She needs to have a bit more fun.'

'One hundred per cent.' Tori agreed, getting to her feet. 'I'd better go or I'll be late for my date.'

'Good luck.'

Tori paused, 'Thanks. You can probably come back to ours tonight, just give her a few hours to calm down. Anyway, I can make sure the door is unlocked for you. The only thing is, I don't know what time I'll get home.' Her face dropped, and she looked torn.

'Don't worry about it, I'll hang out here for a bit.' Sofia assured her. She didn't have the money in her account for even a budget hotel, and as predicted her credit card was now maxed up to the limit. But life had a way of working out.

'Are you sure?'

'It's fine. Shoo. Go, enjoy.' Sofia waved her towards the door.

Tori hesitated.

'Don't worry, I'll take care of her.' A deep voice said.

'Nathan. Where did you spring from?'

'Actually,' a crooked smile quirked up one corner of his mouth, and he slid his hands into his pockets, making the shirt pull tight across his shoulders, 'I've just been over there,' he nodded to a VIP booth a few feet away, 'for the last ten minutes.'

'Oh.' How much had he heard? Everything Christie had said? Cringe.

He raised an eyebrow at Tori. 'You go. Sofia's coming home with me.'

'She is?'

'I am?'

Both girls spoke at once.

'You need somewhere to be for a few hours by the sounds of it and your friend needs to go and meet this guy without feeling guilty for abandoning you. Right?'

'Yes,' Sofia replied. It was true. She wasn't sure Tori would leave if she declined Nathan's offer and she didn't want to ruin her friend's night. 'Okay, sounds good.'

'I'll leave you to it then?' Tori wiggled her eyebrows behind Nathan's back and winked. 'Call me later, Sof. Bye.'

Sofia nodded, 'Have fun.' She waited for Tori to leave before glancing up at Nathan. 'It's okay, she's gone now. It's Saturday night. Surely you need to work?'

'I wasn't saying it for show. You are coming home with me. And work-wise, Scott and Lee are in too and Quinn owes me a favour. Besides, it's gone eleven and getting quiet, people are moving on to other places.'

'Oh. Well, only if you're sure.'

'I am. Come on.'

She hesitated. She did need somewhere to be for a while, but … 'I don't even know your surname.'

'Black.'

She couldn't help it, she snorted. 'Nathan Black?'

'Yep.' He seemed mildly offended. 'What's wrong with it? I think it's a cool name.'

'It is a cool name.' She smiled wryly. 'And I'm Sofia Gold.'

'Oh.' He got it immediately. 'Black and Gold? You're kidding.'

'Like the song. I know. Ha ha.'

'So now you know my full name,' he undid a shirt button and her eyes widened, 'are you coming?'

Almost, she thought naughtily. She chewed her lip. She hardly knew him. On the other hand, he was kind, trustworthy and oh so delicious. Nothing was going to happen. Probably. She squirmed at the thought of something happening, at the funny feeling down low in her pelvis. What was it her sister had said, that she should take more risks in her personal life?

Taking the hand he held out towards her, she smiled up at him. 'Let's go.'

They stopped for coffee on the way back to his flat. It was part of his routine after work and he felt like it would be awkward if they headed straight back to his, like he was picking her up for a one-night stand. Which was definitely not the case. He liked her, but he didn't want to be presumptuous, especially when they lived in different cities.

'Do you actually like this place?' She wrinkled her nose as they stepped through the door, surveying the stark, over-lit cafe with its white walls, black and white tiled floors and wooden tables.

He looked around. 'I've never really thought about it. It's on the way home, and it's convenient, so I come here. I'm usually kind of zoned out, winding down after work. You hate it don't you? Do you want to look for somewhere else?' Checking his watch, 'I'm not sure how many cafes will be open around here at this time of night.'

'No, it's okay, don't worry,' she walked in ahead of him, choosing a table in the corner and slinging her jacket on the back of the chair. 'I'd hate to be accused of being high maintenance,' she smiled up at him playfully. 'It's just kind of soulless, that's all. I prefer a bit of colour.'

'What, like a high street coffee chain with comfortable maroon chairs and standard menus?' he teased her.

She mock shuddered, 'No, they're almost as bad. They're comfy, but they're all the same. You know exactly what you're going to get when you walk into one.'

Nathan sank down into the chair across from her, signalling to the young waitress across the room that they wanted to order. Looking back at Sofia, he raised an eyebrow. 'Some people like that consistency. That's the whole point; that the customer can expect the same standard of service if they go into a cafe at opposite ends of the country. When I open my own cocktail bar—,'

'Whoa,' her green eyes widened, 'when you do what?'

He flushed, used to his parents' criticism of the idea, and his friends asking him why he'd do that when he could use his degree and get a nine to five office job instead of risking every penny he had. 'I know it's not really contributing to society, it'll be hard work with long hours and there's every chance it could fail, but—,'

'Don't be ridiculous,' she squeaked, 'I think that's amazing. And never mind whether it contributes to society or not, if that's what makes you happy, owning your own place and serving cocktails, then you should do it. Who cares what other people think?'

'I—,' he could feel his mouth trying to form words but nothing came out. After a minute he croaked, 'Thank you.'

'For what?' she asked, looking puzzled.

'I don't think anyone has ever been so enthusiastic about it or immediately accepting of, the idea before.'

'Are you kidding? You've got to follow your dreams.' She waved a hand, 'Life is way too short.' She paused. 'Oh, my God. You are Brian Flanagan!'

'Brian who?'

'Brian Flanagan.' Her eyes sparkled with excitement. 'From *Cocktail*.'

He stared at her, aware he was grinning like a loony. There were some moments when she was like a little kid, full of the joy of life and as if she was unaware of how harsh it could sometimes be. It made a nice change to some of the cynical city girls he was used to who came into the bar.

The waitress arrived at the table before he could ask Sofia what she was on about, so it wasn't until after she'd taken their order for two coffees, with a wide grin at Nathan and a frowning glare at Sofia, that he leaned forward, forearm against hers on the narrow table.

'*Cocktail*?' he prompted.

She glanced down at where their arms were touching, and shivered slightly. 'One of the best films of the eighties,' she explained, looking into his eyes. 'Tom Cruise plays the main character, Brian, who leaves the army and moves to New York with a dream of owning his own bar. He works in different places to learn his skills and meets this guy he becomes friends with, but …' she smiled, 'well, you'll have to see for yourself one day.'

'Okay, I'll make a note to check it out, and see what you're so excited about. But, one of the best films of the eighties? You can't be an eighties kid, you're too young.'

'Twenty-three,' she answered, 'but my sister Isobel is three years older and started raiding our mum's extensive film collection as soon as she could and because Mum had a soft spot for eighties films, we grew up watching them.'

'Right. So what are your other favourites?'

Scrunching her face up, she made an hmmming noise, 'That's a hard one, but The Breakfast Club would have to be on the list.'

'Now that one I've seen. A classic coming-of-age film. That's a good one.'

'Wasn't it great how these kids who had nothing in common except for being in detention together somehow found common bonds?' she exclaimed. 'Genius.'

She stopped talking and sat back in her chair to let the waitress clink their coffees down in front of them. She smiled her thanks, but the girl ignored her, focusing completely on Nathan. It was a bit embarrassing. The girl always flirted with him but he seldom returned it. She looked about seventeen, and there was something vulnerable in her eyes. At twenty five he felt like he was too old for her. 'Thanks,' he murmured, pointedly shifting his arm closer to Sofia's again.

'Uh-oh,' Sofia teased once the girl was out of earshot, 'it looks like someone's got a crush.'

'Not me,' he said hastily, before wondering why he cared that much.

'I know that,' Sofia tutted, rolling her eyes at him.

'I have tried to give her the polite *thanks but I'm not interested* signals.'

'Sounds like you need a decoy girlfriend, to protect you,' she raised her eyebrows.

'Are you offering?' he shot back.

'Are you asking?'

An uneasy silence fell as they stared at each other, then she cleared her throat and took a sip of coffee. 'So anyway, you were saying about opening your own cocktail bar, off the back of consistency of service. You don't plan to only have the one place then?'

'I'll start off small with the flagship bar,' he stirred milk and sugar into his coffee, and tapped the spoon on the side of the mug before placing it on the table, 'but if it was successful, then yes, I plan to expand to a chain, even if it's only a few dotted around London city.'

'But you'd make every place look exactly the same?' she chewed her lip. 'Everyone has their preferences, but to me that's playing it safe, and might be boring. That's why I love travelling. No two places are exactly the same; you're going to have different experiences in every country or city you go to.' She leaned forward, 'I think you could have a chain of bars that were recognisably yours because of their branding without having to be identical throughout. There's a group of bar-restaurant lounges in Bournemouth that do it very successfully, and the service, food and setting are consistently excellent across all the sites. The decor of each one is different but the feel across all of them is the same.'

'Well, it's something to think about,' he mused. 'You're an opinionated little thing, aren't you?'

'Mouthy do you mean?' She took another sip of her drink, dropping her gaze to the table.

He hooked a finger under her chin and tilted it upwards. 'I like it,' he emphasised. 'It's nice to be with a girl who isn't always worried about saying the wrong thing or agreeing with me for the sake of it.'

'Oh, you'd never have to be worried about that with me,' she wrapped both hands around her coffee. 'I'm too used to arguing it out with some of the contractors at work who don't want to deal with me during the build process because I'm a girl.'

'Contractors? What do you do then?'

'I design and engineer skate parks.' She nodded, 'It's the perfect job for me. I've been skateboarding since I was six and started surfing at nine. Being on a board is as natural as breathing. That's why it drives me mad when some of the contractors won't listen or follow instruction. I probably know more about urban landscaping and CDM than all of them put together.'

'CDM?'

'You don't want to know, trust me.'

'Fair enough. It all sounds pretty cool though, and I admire you for the surfing and skating.' That would explain the defined stomach and toned arms. 'It takes a lot of skill, right?'

'If you're good at it, yes,' she grinned, 'bloody hurts if you don't concentrate though, especially the skating. I've lost track of how many times I've come off the board, but there are so many variables. If you're street skating, it can just take one crack in the pavement or an uneven paving slab or a pebble caught in a wheel and you're off, praying you fall into a wall rather than into the road. And if you're on ramps, if you miscalculate by a centimetre or start off wrong, you can be face-planting before you know it. I've had all sorts of scrapes, bruises and sprains in my time. In comparison, the sea can be a lot more forgiving, as long as it's not rough.'

'You got any scars?' Nathan drained the last of his coffee.

'Oh, loads,' she said casually.

'You sound fearless. And you don't seem bothered.'

'I don't even notice them anymore,' she shared, 'and besides I don't think of the injuries as a reminder of a bad fall or a landing, I think about the fantastic time I was having *before* it went wrong.'

'That's a positive way of looking at it.' He chewed the inside of his mouth thoughtfully. 'I guess you could look at a lot of things in life that way.'

She smiled, 'That's me.' Finishing her coffee, she put a hand to her mouth and yawned, before looking mortified. 'I'm so sorry, you're not boring me! It's just that we've been out late the last

197

few nights.'

'It's fine, don't worry. I'm tired too.' But he wasn't, not in the least, he felt wired and wide awake, not like how he usually felt at this time of night. Perhaps the waitress had made the coffee stronger today. Or maybe it was Sofia.

Standing up, he reached around and grabbed her jacket as she stumbled to her feet, eyelids looking heavy. He helped her thread both arms into the sleeves, using it as an excuse to free her long blonde hair from her collar and arrange it across her shoulders. It felt unbelievably soft in his hands and smelt like kiwi fruit.

'Anyway,' he stepped back and threw a fiver down on the table. 'Time to go.'

'Bloody British weather!' Nathan complained as he hustled Sofia through his front door twenty minutes later. 'Where the hell did all that rain come from?' Locking the door, he turned around to face her.

'April showers, remember?' She laughed, gazing around his small, cluttered lounge as she tied her hair, which had twisted into sodden ropes, into a knot. 'And I quite like the rain. Great to surf in. Very refreshing and invigorating.'

'If you say so.' He beckoned her further into the room, extracted her from her damp jacket and hung it up next to his on a hook on the back of the door.

'Tea?' When she nodded, he moved into the kitchen area in the corner of the lounge, switched the kettle on and popped teabags into two mugs. 'Sugar?'

'I could make that joke about being sweet enough,' she followed him over and rested against the counter next to him, 'but I take one spoon please.'

'Ha ha.' He stared at the mugs, looking oddly tense.

'Nathan? Are you okay?' she quizzed, staring at him.

He answered without looking at her. 'Yep, fine. I'd er, better get some towels for us.'

'Towels?'

'You're wet,' he pointed out, switching his attention to the wall.

'We both are. We got rained on.'

'Your top, Sofia.'

'My-?' she looked down. The scarlet fabric was clinging to her body and the lacy red bra underneath was clearly visible. 'Oh.' She pulled it away from her body, but almost didn't, just to see what he would do. She liked him. A lot. She liked the way he spoke to her, the way he looked at her, how gentlemanly he was in making her go first through doors, helping her in and out of her jacket and he'd also steadied her outside on the slippery paving slabs when she'd almost tripped over. Okay, so it was the twenty-first century and women could look after themselves, but it was still nice to find a guy who believed in some of the traditional values. He was also funny and ambitious and totally hot.

So she came very close to shuffling closer to him, taking a giant risk and asking him if he wanted to help her out of her top, but she wasn't quite brave enough and it wasn't fair, when he was clearly uncomfortable, and hanging back for a reason.

'You know,' he poured hot water into both mugs and stirred the teabags round, 'you should never feel the need to pretend to be someone you're not to fit in. I prefer you far more when you're being yourself. I mean, the way you stood up to your stuck-up friend back there, when she was saying those things about me, was amazing.'

Her face went hot, embarrassment at Christie's comments making the skin of her neck prickle. 'She was out of order, and I'd been really patient with her up until then. I couldn't not say anything. It wouldn't have been right.'

'Well, I appreciate it.' He cast her a sideways glance.

'It was nothing.' Her mouth dried up as their eyes met. She could feel the heat coming off his tall, wiry body despite the rain-spotted white shirt, and his crisp aftershave filled the small space between them. She lifted a hand off the side, seriously thinking

199

about grabbing a handful of shirt and yanking him in for another sexy kiss. A proper, long-lasting one this time.

'Anyway, towels.' He cleared his throat and she jumped. 'Sorry. I'll go and get some towels.'

'What? Ah, all right.' Her hand dropped to her side.

Scooping the teabags out of the mugs, he slopped some milk in jerkily and span away. 'Back in a minute. Make yourself comfortable. Stick the TV on or something.'

'All right,' she repeated. He'd practically run out of the room. Run away from her? The thought made her feel tired as she took her tea across the room with her and settled into a corner of the sofa, eyeing the black, mid-heeled, strappy boots she was wearing. She should take them off, but couldn't summon the motivation or energy. Maybe he wasn't interested after all, and was just being nice. If that was the case, she should remember it and not humiliate herself again by making another move on him.

She studied the stuffed bookshelves and pictures on the blue walls, photos of Nathan with various people in a range of poses and places, some of them family by the resemblance around their eyes and mouth. A guy in one of them looked vaguely familiar, black hair curling at his nape, nose crooked like it had been broken, eyes squinting into the sun. She knew him from somewhere but couldn't immediately place him.

'So, I've made a decision,' Nathan sauntered back in, looking a little more relaxed, and handed her a small navy towel. He rubbed a matching one along the back of his neck to catch some stray droplets from his black hair, which was going wavy.

'Which is?' Sofia asked, untangling her hair from the knot and dabbing it with the towel.

He avoided her inquisitive gaze, moving over to the unit to grab his tea. 'It's late.'

Bolting up, 'You want me to go.' She felt deflated, wanting to spend more time with him.

'No.' He looked surprised at her words. 'I think you should stay.

It's almost one in the morning; it'll take ages to get a cab, especially because it's a bank holiday weekend so the clubs are busier, and you don't even know if you can get in if you do get back there. You take my bed. I'll sleep on the couch.'

'Ri-ght.' She said slowly, spinning the word out. 'Makes sense to stop here I suppose.' Clearly he didn't want her in his bed with him.

'Good.' His massive smile as he sat down on the other end of the sofa made her insides flip over and do a loop-the-loop.

'Yes, except, you in your bed, me on here,' she added.

'No way, you're the—'

'Woman?' she flashed. 'Don't be so sexist. I've slept on far worse. Kipped in sleeping bags at festivals, slept on the beach on a ratty towel in Thailand. I insist. I'm not putting you out. I'm smaller than you too, I can fit on this,' she gestured to the tatty but comfy three seater they were on and raked her gaze up and down his body, which turned out to be a mistake, because all the moisture left her mouth, 'and you can't.' She ended huskily, glancing down so he couldn't read her face.

'Actually,' he said mildly, 'I was going to say you're the guest but if you feel that strongly about it, fine. I'll take the bed.'

'Oh.' Now she felt silly. And doubly deflated as it could have been the perfect in for him to suggest they share his bed.

'I'll get you some stuff,' he said, getting up and leaving the room.

Once he was gone she dropped her head into her hands and groaned. What was she doing? And how was she going to cope with sleeping in the next room, only a few metres away from him?

'I hope these are okay?'

She glanced up and sucked in a breath. He'd quickly changed into loose grey jogging bottoms and a white t-shirt that hung off his broad shoulders and suited his tall, rangy body perfectly. Oh, wow.

He looked sheepish as he came towards her with a bundle of things.

'What is it? Why have you got that expression on your face?' she asked as he handed it all over. Trying to distract her hormones from his proximity, she studied the small pile of belongings. 'New toothbrush. Great, thanks. Towel. Check. T-shirt, Brazil, World Cup; I like your style. And—Oh.' A pair of tight jockey shorts. His underwear. That he usually wore against his—

Gulp.

'I thought you might prefer to borrow a pair rather than wander around in your- er, knickers.' He stated, voice rough as his eyes dropped and ran over her black-denim covered hips before lifting back to her face. A muscle in his jaw jumped while he waited for her answer.

Something in her warmed, but she could be reading this all wrong. 'Yes, thanks.' She replied, setting everything down on the sofa and sitting next to it, deliberately crossing her legs and leaning over to take off the boots, aware he was staring. 'My feet are almost beyond repair after the last few nights,' she grumbled, fumbling with the straps.

'Here, let me.' He cleared his throat and crouched in front of her, pulling her foot onto his taut thigh so he could deal with the tiny buckles.

She squirmed as he bent his neck in concentration, his head practically in her lap, so close she could feel his hot breath through the fabric of her jeans. It would be so easy to lift his chin with her hand and kiss him.

'Cheers,' she squeaked. Then tried to joke her way out of it. 'I could get used to guys kneeling at my feet.'

'I'm sure they'd be more than happy to.' He bantered back, Bambi eyes gazing into hers as he slipped off the first boot and swapped her feet over.

The breath stopped in her throat.

He took off the second boot and set it aside, gazing at her. It took a huge effort, watching Nathan's pupils dilate, not to fantasise she was falling into them, and correspondingly *not* to lean forward and kiss him. To see if she could fall further. To avoid temptation and making an idiot of herself, she sat back. As if on connecting

202

threads, Nathan followed, moving so he was kneeling up with his waist between her open knees.

And he kissed her.

She jerked, eyes drifting shut, arms wrapping around his broad shoulders as her mouth opened. She pulled him in tight, fingers moving up into his thick hair as he ran his hands up into hers, holding the back of her head as he kissed her passionately. When he nipped her bottom lip she moaned into his mouth. His chest rubbed against hers, his hips pressing against that sweet spot. It felt so incredibly good. Completely different to how it had been with her last boyfriend, who'd only ever gotten her lukewarm at best. Nathan already had her scorching hot, just with a kiss.

'Mmm.' She arched her back, tugging him closer.

And then he was pushing away. 'We don't have to do anything. I don't want you to think I'm taking advantage. I offered you somewhere to stay.'

He seemed totally unaffected by the kiss, apart from a slightly reddened mouth and ruffled hair from where she'd clutched at it.

'No. I mean, yes.' Her lack of experience swamped her. Maybe he'd only kissed her because she was there? He couldn't be that into her if he found it so easy to stay in control, while she was practically panting. 'I—I'll go to sleep then.' She faked a yawn. 'Night, Nathan. Thanks for everything.'

'Oh, yeah. Night.' He untangled his legs from hers, getting to his feet. 'I—uh.'

'Yes?' she asked hopefully, standing.

'Sleep well. See you in the morning.'

'Uh-huh.' Swallowing away the lump in her throat, she made herself respond. 'You too.'

Was that it?

He found her in the kitchen area half an hour later just as she was stretching up to grab a glass from one of the cupboards.

'Can't sleep?'

She paused, the football shirt riding up over the back of her shorts, before returning to a flat-footed position. 'Nope.'

'Here,' he reached past her for a glass and put it down in front of her. 'And me neither,' he continued, referring to his question about sleep. 'Any particular reason?'

'Don't think so,' she shook her head. Praying he couldn't hear the tremor in her voice. The one that screamed how impossibly sexually frustrated she was. The one that said, *if you ask, you can take me now.*

'This is stupid,' he muttered, stepping up behind her and sliding a burning hand onto her shoulder. She swore every ridge of his fingerprints was imprinting on her skin through the cotton top.

'Why?' she asked shakily. 'Because if you're going to start going on again about me taking the bed—'

'It's stupid because we want to be in bed together.' He nudged her forward, trapping her between the unit and his body, his front against her back.

She could feel his erection against her bum, and his hard chest against her shoulder blades and nearly moaned the words, 'We do?'

He went still. 'Don't we?'

She folded back against him, knees weak. Be *brave. Take a risk. You do in everything else that matters.* She sucked in a breath. 'I do,' she muttered, putting her hands behind her back so she could run her nails up his thighs.

He hissed out a breath. 'Me too. So much. Come here.' He swept his hands around her front and up under the shirt, cradling her bare breasts, tweaking her nipples with careful, deliberate fingers.

She gasped and pushed back against him, muscles and nerves between her legs clenching.

'Do you want me to stop?' he dropped his head to nibble her earlobe, his fingers playing and teasing.

'Don't be so bloody stupid.' She blurted. Shit, that had hardly been sexy. 'Sorry, what I meant was—,'

He chuckled in her ear, 'You are brilliant, Sofia. You make me laugh, in a good way. Just say what you think, I like it.'

'Okay,' she gulped, 'in that case, if you stop I might have to take a contract out on your life.' It felt incredible being touched and held by him. Better than any clever skateboard trick or good surfing day.

'I wouldn't want to be hunted down by trained killers,' he breathed into her ear and she could hear the smile in his voice, 'so I guess I'll have to obey.' One hand slipped down inside the waistband of the shorts and her hands curled around the edge of the kitchen unit as his fingertips drew circles on her hip and drifted to her flat lower belly.

'Oh, thank god,' she whispered and he laughed in a low quiet way that made her insides squish. Both of his hands returned to breasts. 'Sorry I haven't got much.'

'You've got a tight, sexy body and I love it.'

'You do?' She always worried she was a bit too taut, too boyish.

'It's lovely. You're lovely.' He ran his hands down her sides and traced a forefinger along the bottom edge of the shorts, over her trembling thigh.

She squirmed.

He kissed her neck and tilted her slightly, moving his hand up and then down inside the front of shorts but this time his index finger dipped lower, using just the right amount of pressure in just the right way in exactly the right place. Sofia moaned, knees shaking and going to mush, grateful his hard body was supporting hers, or she'd be a hot mess on the floor right now. It was so delicious. He was so delicious, and sexy and confident as he kept touching her. She could feel how turned on he was and there was a gathering urgency between her thighs and deep internal muscles were clenching and sparking and getting hotter and hotter as he kept moving his fingers. She twisted her hips and gasped, hands gripping the unit so tight they were almost numb and her eyes were clenching shut and then she let out an, 'O-oh-oh God,' and waves of pleasure and release flowed over and through her.

He rested his forehead against the back of her head and took a deep, unsteady breath. 'Come on.' He said urgently, stepping away, 'I'm taking you to bed.'

Whirling around to look at him, his intense dark eyes and messed up hair and glazed expression, she took a step and almost folded. He laughed and whisked her up easily, throwing her over his shoulder and racing to his room. All she got was a hazy impression of a double bed and white walls before he threw her down on the pillows and yanked the shirt off her, pressing open-mouthed kisses onto every bit of exposed skin, his big, warm hands everywhere while she laughed breathlessly and pulled his top off, pushing his shorts off, gasping at the outrageous perfection of his lean, toned body and wrapping herself around him so that a few blistering, panting, exciting minutes later there was no telling where he ended or she started and the real world – where she was tomboyish, overlooked Sofia – didn't exist.

Sunday

When Sofia woke up in the morning next to Nathan, she didn't feel guilty, ashamed or awkward, she felt liberated. She'd taken the risk Issy had talked about and it had paid off. Nathan was so lovely, the way he'd cuddled her close after the astounding sex and asked if she was okay – to which she'd replied with a giggle and resounding *yes* – all she could think was, *that was incredible*.

As she lay in bed in the dawn light, snug under his duvet and wondering if she should get up or jump him again, he rolled over and grabbed her and they had blurry, glorious, morning sex. It was better than the night before. Hotter, sweeter. Almost as good was that when she peeked out from the corner of the duvet an hour later, he was standing next to the bed wearing nothing but jockey shorts and a pair of black framed glasses, with a huge cup of coffee in one hand, and an Easter Egg in the other.

'Morning.' He murmured, hair sticking up in tufts, sinking down onto the bed and handing her the hot drink and the chocolate. 'Happy Easter.'

He might just be the perfect man. 'Hi,' shifting to sit upright with the covers anchored under her armpits, she shook her tangled waves back from her face. 'Thank you. Happy Easter to you too. Did you have a stock of them?' She nodded at the box in her hand, the purple bunny looking delighted to be featured on it.

'I pulled some clothes on and ran down to the corner shop,' he smiled.

'Thanks, that's sweet.' She paused and stared at him. 'I love those glasses on you.'

He touched a hand to them self-consciously. 'Thanks,' he cleared his throat.

'They suit you.' Her lips parted as her gaze dropped to his chest. He was so gorgeous. And she'd had him. And yes, there was a sense of pride in that and she was pleased that she'd taken a chance and it had worked out, but it was more than that. She wanted to spend more time with him. To see if really liking him could turn into something else. But he was in London and she was in Bournemouth and this was probably only a one-time thing. He came across as genuine, but the bottom line was that he was a handsome barman and for all she knew, might bring girls back here all the time. Which probably meant that once she was done with her coffee she'd be on her way, doing the walk of shame.

'Drink up,' he instructed, then shocked her by adding, 'we're having a shower together and then, unless you've got a burning need to see your friends, I'm taking you around some of my favourite places in London.'

'Oh.'

'What is it?'

'Nothing, it's just not what I was expecting.'

He frowned, looking unsure. 'Right. Well, if you don't want to I can get you back to Chelsea—,'

'No! I want to,' she grinned, rallying. 'I'd love to, if you're up for it. And if you don't mind lending me a clean top.'

'No problem.' He tucked a strand of hair behind her ear, making her shiver, then got up and started rifling through his wardrobe, before tugging her into a hot shower.

It took them an hour to leave the flat.

They had a lazy day full of laughter and intense conversations and kisses, walking Tower Bridge while playing a silly game of *animal, vegetable or mineral,* strolling hand in hand along Oxford Street and popping in and out of shops before dropping down to Piccadilly Circus to share a tasty meal at Jamie's pop-up diner.

When Nathan took her back to Toni and Christie's that evening, Sofia knew it had been one of the most brilliant days of her life. He was so easy to be with, and she could be herself with him. It was a shame it had to end, and she felt a weird mix of happy and sad at the same time.

'Night.' He grabbed her around the waist and kissed her soundly. Wiggling in his arms, she sank back against the tall, white garden wall of the gated residence she was to spend her last night in London in. God knew what the girls were going to say when she walked in there after nearly twenty-hour hours of being AWOL. Although, at least she'd texted Tori to let her know she was safe and not to worry.

'Night.' She smiled. 'Thanks for such a great day.' *Keep it light Sofia.*

'Yes. I was thinking …' He trailed off, gazing down at her.

'Ye-es?' She bit the inside of her cheeks. Was he going to ask for her number? Suggest they stay in touch? But just because she'd had a fantastic time, it didn't mean he had. Or that he was in a position to offer her anything. It had hung between them all day, what might or might not happen between them after today, but neither of them had said anything, and now it felt too scary to ask him outright. The girl who wasn't confident when it came to men had made an unwelcome return.

'Nothing.' He stated.

'Okay,' she eased back out of his arms. It was time to say goodbye. 'I should go in then. Good night and take care of yourself Nathan. Good luck with everything.' Kissing him quickly she pressed the intercom on the wall and announced herself, waiting for the automatic gate to swing open. Needing the moment to be over. Gutted because the sexiest, loveliest guy she'd ever met, who seemed to enjoy her company and who she loved spending time with and who she had the most incredible chemistry with, was about to walk away.

No. That wasn't good enough. She'd learnt something from this. Despite her interests and profession, and that in the past she'd been overlooked as a tomboy, she *was* a normal girl worthy of a guy's attention. Added to which, this particular guy had made her feel special and wanted all day. That had to mean something. She just needed to grow a pair, when it came to her love life. *Just do it, Sof.*

She spun around, 'Nathan, I'd really like it if—,'

'I don't think so,' Nathan said at the same time, grabbing her gently around the shoulders. 'Sorry, what were you going to say?' he looked down at her intently, black hair ruffling in the evening breeze.

Scooping in a deep breath, 'I want to see you again,' she spilled. 'What were you going to say?'

His mouth quirked in the crooked smile she liked so much. 'I was going to ask for your number, Princess.'

'Yay!' She launched herself at him and kissed him soundly, as he swung her off her feet.

'I take it that's a yes,' he grinned when they broke apart, panting slightly.

'Hell, yes,' she said fiercely, before grabbing his mobile from his pocket and tapping her number into it. 'And if you don't call me, remember I know where you work, and where you live.' Her eyes twinkled with mischief.

'Don't worry, I'll definitely be calling you,' grabbing her front pockets he hauled her in for another long, steamy, delicious kiss.

'And maybe I can come visit you in Bournemouth at some point, maybe check out those bar-restaurants you were talking about?'

'That sounds like a plan.'

He swept her hair back from her face, ran his forefinger across her full bottom lip, making it tingle. 'Great. I've always fancied a trip to the seaside. And what about you? Are you up for trips to London, as well as overseas?'

'Absolutely.' She craned her head back to look into his intelligent, Bambi brown eyes. 'Yeah.'

'Yeah?' He hugged her closer.

Running her hands up his arms, she tightened her grip on him. 'Yes. A girl could definitely get used to cocktails in Chelsea.'

Strawberries at Wimbledon

'Hey, isn't that Adam?' Lily elbowed Rayne, pointing down a packed Henman Hill next to No.1 Court and the Aorangi Pavilion, her blonde curls glinting in the mid-morning sunshine.

Rayne dropped the cooler bag with a thud and the wine bottle inside rattled against the specially bought plastic glasses. 'Huh? No, it can't be.' She gulped. 'He's working abroad.' Or he had been the last time she'd checked on LinkedIn six months ago. The trick was not to look at his profile too often.

Lily shielded her eyes with one hand, squinting across the sea of heads, shoulders and multi-coloured blankets. 'Really? It looked like him.' Standing on tiptoes, she peered into the expectant crowd, who were watching the introductory Wimbledon coverage on the big screen. 'Damn, he's gone.'

'I'm sure it's not him.' Rayne replied firmly, to make it true. 'What did you even see? The back of his head?'

'No, the side of his face. He had stubble and I know Adam never did, and his hair was different too, but still—' Lily turned, noticing her friend's expression. 'Maybe I was wrong.' She back-tracked hastily. 'It could have been anyone.'

'Yeah.' Rayne picked the bag up, curling her fingers tightly around the woven fabric strap, and forced a smile to her face. Just because Lily's announcement had caught her off guard, it didn't

211

have to spoil their day during the opening week of Wimbledon. It was just she'd never imagined seeing Adam again. She thought of him as a match that had been played and lost. In the past, with no chance of a replay.

Anyway, it didn't matter. Today was about fun and friendship, about being British and making the most of whatever summer they'd have. It was about tennis whites, yellow balls, lawn courts, fruity Pimms, sunshine and laughter. It was definitely not about men. Especially ones that belonged to her uni days, and being young and stupid.

'I know we constantly complain it's wet and windy,' Lily fanned her letterbox-red face with the latest copy of *Cosmo* a few hours later, 'and moan about not having proper summers, but is it me or is it too hot?'

'There's no such thing, it's just you,' Rayne grinned, basking on her back on the navy picnic blanket, arms cushioning her head. 'You're a complete wimp.'

They'd decided to relax on the manicured grass until it was time to go down to the Centre Court for the Men's Singles qualifying rounds. She still couldn't believe they'd managed to score tickets. Mind you, they had joined 'The Queue,' at eight the previous evening and spent an uncomfortable night in sleeping bags in a tiny pop-up tent. Just as the sun was rising, a steward had woken them and told them to pack up, stow their belongings in the left luggage facilities and go through the queuing card system. The broken night's sleep had been totally worth it for the ticket and an interesting life experience, even if she did now feel a bit grubby and jaded.

'Gee, thanks.' Lily stuck her tongue out in response to Rayne's wimp comment. 'I just don't get it, though,' she went on, giving her friend a mock dirty look, 'here I am, blonde and feeling like I'm about to bake alive and you're lying there with thick black hair, with blue eyes so dark they're almost navy, looking as cool as a block of ice.'

'What can I say?' Rayne replied cheerfully. 'I have many talents. Plus it also helps that I'm not wearing as much as you.' She nodded at Lily's pale peach sundress with capped sleeves, which perfectly suited her Amanda Seyfried fair looks. People were always telling Lily she bore a strong resemblance to the American actress from the Mama Mia! movie.

'Well, just because I'm not a complete exhibitionist, unlike some.' Lily pointed at the floaty red vest top lying discarded between them.

'I'd hardly call a bra and cut-off shorts exhibitionist.' Rayne replied lightly, aware Lily was teasing. 'I didn't realise it was going to be this hot either, and come on, a bra doesn't really show off any more than a bikini, does it?' She gestured to the turquoise lace encasing her modest chest. 'And it's not as if there's much to see.'

She was actually hotter than she was letting on. It had to be in the high twenties, and she'd heard someone's radio predicting that it would hit thirty degrees before the day was out. She could well believe it. A line of damp was creeping along her nape. The backs of her knees were coated with crescent-moons of sweat. Dew was pooling behind the tiny gold bar threaded through her belly button, and there was pink through her eyelids when she closed them because the sun was so bright. But she wouldn't tell Lily any of that, it was too much fun winding her up.

'Whatever,' Lily gulped some chilled water from a plastic bottle then flicked some on Rayne, making her jump. 'You just don't care, do you?'

'Not nowadays,' she laughed. 'Thank you, hippy, new-age parents.' They'd been loving and kind but unconventional, and although she'd rebelled against that in her early teens, since they'd been gone she'd drawn strength from their example and her unusual upbringing. She made her own choices in life, and as an adult had learned to worry less about what other people thought of her and place more importance on what she thought of herself.

Part of that was being comfortable in her own skin.

Lily lay down on the blanket, twisting her long hair up in a knot away from her slender neck. 'You must still miss them.'

Rayne nodded decisively, picturing her parents singing along to The Beatles in the cramped kitchen of the caravan they all called home, or gazing at the rolling sea off the ragged Cornish coastline, arms linked, her mum's head resting on her dad's shoulder. 'Always. I regret the fact they're not here every single day. But I think they'd be proud of me.' She frowned. 'At least, I hope so.'

Lily sat up, staring down at her. 'Of course they would. Come on Rayne, it's not like you to doubt yourself. You've done well. You've got a job you adore and a nice flat, plus a great car.' Referring to her sporty black Mini Cooper S, with the Union Jack on the roof. 'Not to mention your awesome friends,' she grinned

'Thanks, Lily. Yeah, I guess you're pretty cool.' She deadpanned, though at the same time, she couldn't help but think that the one thing her parents had instilled in her was that you didn't hurt the ones you loved.

And she was guilty of hurting the one person she'd loved the most apart from them.

She'd met Adam a few weeks past the one year anniversary of her parents' untimely death, while still knee-deep in grief. He'd been unlucky enough to come between her and the exit route as she'd stumbled from her half-unpacked room in halls on her first day at Loughborough University, seeking fresh air followed by the student bar.

'Hey, easy!' He steadied her as she ran into him, almost taking them both out.

'S-sorry,' she choked, glancing up.

His face softened at the smudges of black mascara under her eyes. 'Are you okay?'

'Dunno. Yes. No,' she scrubbed her face with her sleeve. 'Not your problem.' She made for the exit but his arms tightened around her.

'Are you sure that's a good idea?' he asked, glancing down at her outfit and then out of the window. Burnished red, orange and yellow leaves whipped in circles around the base of trees bearing naked, spindly branches. October had brought in autumn with a vengeance to the Midlands. 'You'll freeze out there.'

'Don't care. The alcohol will help.' Fighting her way out of his arms she stepped back, noticing his eyes flicker over her long, bare legs in the short skirt she wore. He wasn't her type, way too preppy looking in his ironed jeans and white jumper looking like he was about to go play cricket, but familiar habits were hard to shake. She put a hand on one hip and pushed her bottom lip out.

He frowned, pale blue eyes unreadable, and ignored the opening. 'Well, you can't carry on like that every day. For one thing you'll ruin your liver, and for the other, are you here to study or party?'

'Both,' she muttered, crossing her arms over her chest in the low cut top. Who was he, the fun police? Or maybe more like the traditional type of father who was supposed to keep you on the straight and narrow, locking you in your room and away from boys until you were at least thirty. Not that she'd had any experience of parenting like that; her dad hadn't instilled many rules and her mum believed in giving children choices. She'd loved them to bits, but sometimes she'd craved a structure, the certainty of a routine, a house they could call their own. It didn't matter now anyway, they were gone. She had to make a life for herself without them. Her eyes welled up. Shit, this was embarrassing. She wasn't a crier, never had been.

The guy stared down at her, before taking hold of her elbow. 'Come on, I'm making you a cup of tea.' He started off down the grey-carpeted hallway, towing her along behind him.

She snorted. Tea? As if that would solve anything. Still, she was so surprised by his take-charge attitude that she let him lead her into the communal kitchen and push her down into a plastic purple chair. Watching him move easily around the space, flicking the kettle on and rooting around the modern white cupboards for mugs, she realised he was the most self-assured guy she'd ever met. The most gentlemanly too – some boys would welcome the opportunity to try and get her drunk.

'How old are you?' she demanded, swinging back on the chair, balancing on its back legs.

'You'll break your neck doing that. Eighteen.' He threw her a teasing look as he placed teabags into two mismatched mugs. 'And I'm Adam by the way. Just in case you were wondering.'

'I wasn't wondering,' she said airily, swinging on the chair again deliberately. 'I'm nineteen.' She tacked on as an afterthought. Unable to face university straight after her parents' tragic motorway crash, she'd deferred for a year. It'd felt like the right thing at the time but now she wondered if it had been wrong. She'd squandered the last twelve months of her life, immersed in drinking, loud music and late night hook-ups. None of which had made her feel any better. If anything they'd made her feel worse.

'Nineteen?' Adam smirked, as he pulled a carton of milk from the fridge. 'That's an unusual name. Do you come from some weird sci-fi island lab where they only assign you numbers?'

'Ha ha, very funny,' she drawled as he went back over to the unit and rested up against it, facing her. She narrowed her eyes. 'You're very—'

'Confident?' he inserted, giving her a proper, wide smile this time.

It made his blue eyes light up, and she was shocked at the tiny tingle in her lower belly, one she hadn't felt in ages. Her encounters over the last year had felt detached and meaningless. Perhaps a way to distract herself? A counsellor would have a field day with her, she was sure. Not that she planned to speak to one any time soon.

Her physical reaction to him annoyed her. 'Bossy. Sensible.' She snapped, slamming the front chair legs back onto the floor. 'A bit arrogant too.'

'Wow, thanks. I'm glad I offered to make you a tea now.' He

216

turned away. 'Sugar?'

'Three.'

'What? You'll rot your teeth.' But he spooned the sugar in, added milk to both teas then returned the carton to the fridge. Lining the sugar and teabag pots up exactly as they had been, he grabbed a blue cloth off the side and wiped down the counter precisely as if any speck of dirt or spillage would be an insult.

'Whatever.' She felt bad for her comments but it was better not to apologise. Maybe he'd think she was a massive bitch and steer clear in future. The last thing she wanted was to like someone; that might lead to caring and caring could lead to pain. She was trying to deal with an indecent amount of that already, not go looking for more.

'Tell me about it.' He turned and placed the two mugs with steam curling off them onto the beige laminate table.

'Tell you about what?' She pulled her sleeves down over her hands and curled her fingers inside.

He sank down into the chair opposite, staring at her, pale eyes unblinking. 'About whoever or whatever it is you've lost.'

'I don't know what you mean.'

'I recognise the look,' he said. 'Just talk to me.'

'No.' She answered belligerently, but slid the tea towards her. She wasn't sure if she wanted to go back to her room yet. It would mean too much time alone. Too much time to think.

'You can. And maybe you need to.'

'Is this where you give me a talk about how it's good to share?' she retorted. 'Throw psycho-babble at me, tell me I'll feel better for talking about it and time healing all wounds and-'

'No,' he interrupted, his voice mild. 'This is where I offer you an out, a way of getting through *this* moment.'

He talked like he was old, like he'd seen too much of life already. She wondered what his story was. *You don't care, remember?* Opening her mouth, she closed it again, wondering if she looked like a goldfish tipped out of its bowl, gasping for water, suffocating.

217

But she barely knew him, and if she started bawling again she was afraid she wouldn't stop.

'I'm fine.' She set her jaw, teeth clenched.

He looked at her for a long, silent moment and she didn't think he'd drop it, but then he shrugged and took a sip of tea. 'Okay. Whatever you want.' His expression was full of understanding. 'Right, we've established you're not called nineteen. So, what is your name?'

She hesitated, noticing a poster of the *Arctic Monkeys* taped up on the far wall, the right-hand corner loose and drooping over. She'd gone to one of their début world tour concerts a few years before. It'd been amazing, her blood thrumming with the bass of the music, heart pumping madly, grinning so widely that after half an hour her cheeks ached. Her parents had been amused by how she'd raved on about it for days, smiling at her indulgently as she babbled on, her mum leaving their latest album on her fold out bed as a random gift. That was … *before*.

And now here she was, in the *after*. Without them. Completely alone, apart from her grandparents, who were on a world cruise, distancing themselves from her behaviour.

'So?' Adam's voice jolted her.

'Huh?'

'Do you have a name?'

'I, I—' she couldn't breathe, couldn't gulp the grief away. It wasn't fair. She wanted her dad here, to heave the boxes around and help her unpack. She wanted her mum here, to hug her and murmur words of reassurance, to soothe her nerves about starting uni. There were so many things that would happen in her life that her parents should be here for, but never would be. What had she ever done to deserve losing them? She had to leave. The emotions were too close, the urge to cry on this stranger's shoulder too strong. 'Ask me another time,' she choked, 'I've gotta go.' She shot up from the chair. 'Catch you later.' Spinning around, she sprinted down the hallway.

Adam didn't say anything. He just let her go.

Rayne relaxed in the green chair on Centre Court, the plastic warm beneath her bare thighs in the denim cut-offs, revelling in the early afternoon sun burning high in the cloudless sky. The ball kids were shading themselves under striped Wimbledon Championship umbrellas on the side of the court and the stands were rammed, no seats unoccupied, anticipation of the forthcoming match creating a noisy buzz and ripples of energy. The crowd wore an assortment of outfits, some in casual shorts and t-shirts, others in posh dresses and beribboned sun hats. The smart ones had brought water with them and purchased red cushions to sit on. Wimbledon veterans obviously. Not like her, a Wimbledon virgin. The word made her smile. Virgin. Like Adam, when they'd met. Until one very memorable night.

'What are you smiling about?' Lily asked, raising an eyebrow.

'Nothing!' Rayne wrinkled her nose. 'Was I?'

'Yes. Were you thinking about Adam?'

Guilty. 'No! Why would you say that?' She tucked her black shoulder-length bob behind her ears.

'You've got that dreamy faraway look you always wore when you were together. I've never seen you like it with anyone else, or since.'

'Pfftt! Whatever.'

'Just saying. Plus, I know you're busy and I go on about this a lot, but you really should think about getting a love life.'

'Please. Don't go there.' Rayne turned her attention to two teenage ball girls walking onto the white-lined grass. 'Did you know around two hundred and fifty ball girls and boys help out during Wimbledon?' If she didn't make direct eye contact with Lily, maybe she'd drop the subject. 'Or that what we call Henman Hill is actually Aorangi Terrace? And why do you suppose Murray Mount isn't as popular as Henman Hill as a name?'

'Henman Hill has a better ring to it, I guess.' Lily ignored the deflection. 'Come on, Rayne. I've seen that look in your eye recently,

219

as well as that hunched shoulder thing you do. You've been biting your nails too. You need sex, and soon.'

'Have not! And do not,' she denied, sliding her nearly-nibbled-down-to-the-knuckle fingers under her bum. Lily had come a long way since the uni days, she never would have made those types of remarks so openly back then, wouldn't have had the confidence. But gradually Rayne, Frankie and Zoe had brought her out of her shell. It was a shame she didn't see Frankie much now, even though she lived in London as well, and that Zoe was abroad. She missed the girls. But at least she still had Lily, who was a work colleague as well as a friend, even if she was being annoyingly and unusually blunt today.

Lily's eyes flickered down at Rayne's hidden hands and she raised an eyebrow in amusement. 'Thousands would believe you. I don't. How long has it been?'

'Doesn't matter.' Rayne tried out her best *back off* look. It didn't work.

'You don't usually mind talking about this stuff, so it must be a while. Everyone needs it. It's natural, normal. Like wine, chocolate, shoes,' she wiggled both fair eyebrows. 'You know, all of life's essentials. Speaking of which,' reaching under the chair she produced the punnet of strawberries and fresh cream she'd bought earlier, and held them out, 'here you go. Fresh from Kent.'

'Thanks.' Freeing her hands and picking a ripe, red strawberry up Rayne twisted off the green stalk. 'Okay, I forgive you. Thanks for the lecture, Mum. So, what are you suggesting I should do about my non-existent love life, *if* I was interested in having one?'

Lily pursed her lips. 'Well, you could always go out to a bar, have a few drinks, and meet a hot, willing guy.'

'As much as I'm amused you of all people would advocate that I go trawling in bars, I'm fine thanks.'

'Why? What's the problem, if it suits you—'

'And you're safe. I know. But *you* don't do it.'

'I'm not you.' Lily flushed at the look Rayne gave her and

concentrated on rooting around for the fattest strawberry. 'Sorry, I—I mean … argh.' She looked up. 'Yes, I only believe in sex in committed relationships. But at least I date.'

'I don't have an issue with dating. I'm just not bothered at the moment, that's all.' Rayne was aware her voice had a defensive tone to it as she rolled a small, firm strawberry between her fingers. 'And it's not like I've never had a hook-up before. I've been with guys since—' for some reason, Adam's name stuck in her throat. 'The problem is that when I think about it, I want relationship sex.' She sighed. 'But without the relationship.'

Lily frowned. 'Explain.' She dipped her strawberry into lashings of cream and dropped it in her lip-glossed mouth.

'I'm not after a serious relationship right now. Sex without strings would suit me, but,' she sighed, 'the sex isn't usually that great. They don't know what I like, and vice versa. They don't know me, there's no connection, no cuddling afterwards. It's just physical.' She held up a hand. 'Before you say it, I *know* that's the whole point of no strings sex; the physical without the emotion or affection. But if the sex isn't that good, if I don't get that much out of it, what's the point?'

'Right. Hmmm … not complicated at all then.' Her friend sat back, plucked up another plump strawberry and chewed it slowly, expression thoughtful.

'I know,' Rayne groaned, stifling a laugh. 'I'm not hard to please, am I?' She rolled another strawberry in the cream and ate it, lush fruitiness and smooth sweetness coating her tongue as she closed her eyes and tilted her face to the sun's glorious heat.

There was an announcement over the speakers that the match was about to start and a few good natured, excited cheers erupted among the spectators. People started returning to their seats, the general volume increasing as the commentator said something about it being a beautiful day for a match.

Lily said something, but Rayne didn't catch it, opening her eyes and leaning closer. 'What was that?'

'I … *something* … *something* … perfect!' Lily beamed, looking pleased with herself.

'Huh? What is?' Lily's lips moved again but Rayne still didn't hear. 'Say what?'

'You need to have sex with an ex!' Lily exclaimed, just as the crowd around them fell silent. 'Oh.'

A few sniggers and titters sounded, and a lady in a straw hat with a white ribbon wrapped around it turned and raised one perfectly plucked eyebrow at them. Two rows down, a group of guys sporting *We did Wimbledon* t-shirts looked over and let out a round of good-natured *wahey's!*

'Oops. Oh, God.' Lily went scarlet, closing her eyes and leaning forward to bury her face in her knees.

Rayne choked on laughter, holding her side. 'Good one, Lil.'

'Stop it!' Lily hissed, sitting up and fanning her face with one hand.

'S-sorry.' Rayne sniggered.

'I was just trying to help.'

'I know. Sorry. Great timing though; now everyone's going to think I'm desperate.' Her wry smile took any sting out of the words. 'Not that I care.'

'Of course not. You never do.' The red in Lily's cheeks started fading to a pretty rose pink. 'I do think my suggestion's worth considering though. If you sleep with someone you already know you're compatible with, you'd have a good time. Plus you'd be comfortable because they've seen it all before *and* you wouldn't fall for them because you'd know all the reasons it wouldn't work, because of the break-up. See? Sex with an ex,' she finished triumphantly. 'The idea rocks.'

'Thanks for sharing your logic with me, but really I have no intention of going there.'

'Why not?' A sickeningly familiar, deep voice quipped right behind them. 'I agree with Lily. Sounds like a great idea to me.'

Something in her midriff plummeted to the floor through the

soles of her feet. Time slid sideways and she nearly did the same out of her seat.

Oh, shit.

She turned her head slowly. 'Adam.'

'Hello, Ray,' he grinned, using the nickname he'd adopted after they'd started sleeping together. 'How are you? It's been ages.'

How long had he been sat there? 'Yes. Four years, nearly five.' Fab, now it looked like she'd been counting. Which she hadn't. 'Good thanks,' she gulped, unable to believe it was really him, within touching distance, and how different but the same he looked. So grown up, with shorter brown hair, much broader shoulders and laughter lines scrunching up the corners of his pale blue eyes. Was it just the baking sun making her hot and dizzy? 'You?' she squeaked uncharacteristically, ignoring the smirk on Lily's face. A few deep breaths helped secure some sanity.

'Excellent.' He nodded at the court as the players came on wearing their whites, the English guy wearing a sweatband round his forehead, the Spanish contender looking cool and unaffected by the high temperature. 'We should catch up after the match.' Adam's voice lowered and he touched her shoulder briefly, fingertips burning her bare skin. His glance swept past her. 'Lily.' He nodded and smiled. 'Everything okay with you?'

Lily craned her head around and returned his smile, eyes warm. They'd always got on well at uni. 'Good thanks, Adam. Hello,' she added to his companion, her smile growing.

'Sorry.' Adam gestured to the younger, strawberry-blond guy beside him. 'This is Flynn, my intern.'

Rayne was surprised by his use of the word. Intern was so American and Adam had always been so British. Maybe travelling abroad had changed him. And intern for what? Not that she cared.

'Hi,' Flynn waved slightly, a dimple flashing, staring admiringly at Lily's English Rose beauty.

Adam and Rayne exchanged a bemused look. At uni they'd protected Lily together. There'd always been men trailing around

223

after her, and she'd been pretty naïve about some of their motives. More than once, while Rayne had chatted to Lily about being careful and not falling for guys too easily, Adam had taken those guys aside and warned them to treat Lily well. To only pursue her if their intentions didn't involve bedding and then dumping her. He was old-fashioned like that. Gallant. She'd always loved that about him. It was unusual for an eighteen year old guy, but a product of his upbringing. An upbringing that'd come between them more than once.

'It's starting.' Adam gazed at her, and whispered huskily, as one of the Umpires' signalled first serve and the crowd edged forward on their seats with an expectant hush.

'It is.' Rayne turned to face forward. She didn't like the fact it felt like they were talking about more than the battle to be played out on the striped lawn.

It had never been a battle with Adam, except for their last few weeks together. The majority of their relationship had been easy, playful and happy. So, so happy.

He'd turned up at her room a few days after they'd met, two mugs of tea in his hands, holding one out when she answered.

'Hey, Nineteen. I thought you might drink this one? Three sugars, right?'

She stepped back and leaned against the door, amused. 'You mean it's not the same one you made the other day?'

'Well … I can't deny I didn't consider trying it, after the way you ran out on me, but on balance I figured that giving you food poisoning from off milk wouldn't be very clever.'

'No?'

'No,' he said solemnly, 'this set of halls isn't that big and since I've noticed I'm the only one you've really talked to, I thought they'd easily trace the crime back to me.'

'Really?' She grinned and took the mug off him, surprised at how much better she'd felt the past few days. She'd been immersing herself in classes, making friends with a lovely but quiet fellow classmate called Lily and sharing a quick coffee with some louder but equally nice girls – Frankie and Zoe – who were studying different degrees but in the same halls. Getting a decent night's sleep for the first time in months and drinking less alcohol was also helping. 'Thanks.' She wrapped her hands around the mug, nodding for him to come into the narrow room. 'That's the only reason you wouldn't force-feed me old tea? Because of the fear of getting caught?'

'Yes. That's the only reason.' His eyes met hers then fell away, and he sat down in the flimsy black chair on wheels that sat in front of her desk. 'I guess you haven't got any coasters,' grabbing a spare piece of paper, he put his tea on it beside her laptop. 'Great job unpacking by the way,' he arched an eyebrow, looking at the two boxes with clothes, make-up and other stuff spilling out of them stacked up against the bare wall. It made the room feel impossibly cramped. There was a restrained energy about the way he studied her belongings that made her think he was itching to get up and start sorting it all out, but was too polite to.

She shrugged one shoulder, setting her mug down on the floor. 'It'll get done when it gets done. And you're wrong, you know,' she said, sinking down on the edge of her messy bed, loose vest top riding up her stomach as she stretched. She'd not long woken up. Her first lecture didn't start until after lunchtime.

'About what?' his gaze flickered over her legs in the tiny pyjama shorts she wore, her knees no more than six inches from his.

'You're not the only one I've spoken to. Lily and I have been hanging out quite a lot.'

'Lily?'

She rolled her eyes at his puzzled look. 'Come on, don't act as if you haven't noticed her. The daintily gorgeous blonde three doors up.'

'Oh, her.' He grinned. 'She's very pretty and seems sweet, but she's not my type.'

'Is that so?' she drawled, scooting back across the covers so she could lean against the wall. The plaster was cool against her back, but it felt good to have something solid to lean against. For too long she'd felt like she was falling through air.

'She's too much like some of the girls back home,' he replied solemnly. 'Wholesome. Well-bred.' He wrinkled his nose. 'It would be like fancying my little sister, Belinda.'

She laughed, 'I see. But still, what's wrong with wholesome and well-bred?' She paused, 'God, I don't think I've ever actually heard someone use that phrase in real life. Who are you, the Lord of the Manor or something?'

A shadow chased its way across his face but he shook his head and smiled easily. 'Not quite. You can blame my mum. She's very well spoken. Likes to host lots of social events, work tirelessly for deserving causes and generally hold everyone around her up to very high standards.'

'Sounds like a heap of fun,' she mused, matching his determinedly light tone. 'So where are you from?' she asked curiously, leaning forward over the edge of the bed to grab her tea, aware as she sat up and his eyes flickered from her top back to her face she'd flashed him accidentally. She suppressed a smile, fighting to keep a straight face. Maybe he wasn't that much of a gentleman. Or maybe he thought she was hot too. That would be interesting. Even though she'd decided the other day she should stay away, there was something about him she found endearing and attractive. The flutters in her belly made it feel like she was starting an exciting, new game. 'And what is your type?'

'Buckinghamshire. And I'll let you know when I find it.'

'Right.' Not her, then. She took a mouthful of scalding tea, his last comment not just taking a few points off her but throwing her out of the whole match.

'So,' he stretched his arms behind his head, muscles bunching under his jumper, 'now that you've decided I'm not trying to poison you,' he nodded at the mug as she took another warming gulp, 'and you've let me sit in your room, do I get to know your name?'

She let out a long suffering sigh, shaking her head in pretend sorrow. 'It's all take, take, take with you men isn't it? You bring me tea and immediately want something in return. You want to know all my secrets.'

'I'm starting to think your name's a national secret,' he retorted, 'what's the matter, are you ashamed of it or something?' Dropping his arms he sat forward in the chair, eyes sparkling. 'Is it really embarrassing? What is it? Come on, it can't be that bad, as long as it's not … Griselda?' he guessed.

She shook her head solemnly. 'Nope.'

'Gertrude? Ermintrude? No, I'm not sure that's even a name.'

'Neither of those, and actually, I think she was the talking cow off *The Magic Roundabout*,' she laughed.

'Oh, that was a bit before my time.'

'My parents still had a video recorder when I was growing up, and that was one of the box sets.'

'Right.' He frowned. 'I give up then. Quasimodo?'

She spluttered tea over her quilt, setting the mug down on the carpet and clutching her side as she giggled. When she recovered, she wiped her eyes. 'Oh, thanks a lot! So, that's what you think of me!'

'You left me no choice.' He sat up straight. 'So? Give up the goods.'

'All right, I guess you worked hard enough for it. I'm Rayne.' Her eyes met his, searching for mockery, but his gaze was direct and open.

'Short for Rainbow?' he asked.

'No. Rain, like the stuff that falls from the sky, except with an E and a Y.'

'You're a poet and didn't know it,' he joked.

'Funny.' She paused. 'My parents were pretty unconventional. I guess I'm just lucky it wasn't something worse.'

'I like it,' he said, turning to pick up his mug, 'it's unusual.'

As his long fingers hooked round the handle, she noticed it was white with a round, yellow smiley face on the side. It reflected his personality. He was so … nice. Maybe nice was what she needed? *No*. She picked her tea up again and focused on their conversation. 'I hated it growing up.' She admitted, feeling a bit disloyal. 'All the kids made fun of me for having a weird name and hippy parents. Mum used to pick me up from every school I attended in tasselled, patchwork dresses and Dad wore these awful waistcoats with tiny bells on.' She shook her head fondly. 'So stereotypical. But I loved them.' She fell silent, nose tingling with the threat of tears. Loved. Love. Will love and miss forever.

'Loved? Past tense?' Adam said. Sucking a deep breath in through his nose, he blew it out through his mouth. 'So it was them you were upset about the other day? They died.' He nodded. 'It's all right. You don't have to answer if you don't want to. I know what it's like to have lost a parent.'

She dipped her head to acknowledge he was right, waiting silently for him to expand.

'My father. It's …' he gazed at the walls she hadn't hung posters up on yet, 'brutal, wrenching. But to have lost both is unimaginable, I'm really sorry.'

She gulped. 'I'm sorry too, about your dad,' she whispered, but couldn't manage anything else.

'So, why rain?' he cleared his throat. 'Doesn't that have negative connotations?'

'God, you really are so well-spoken!' she replied. When he shrugged at her comment, and waited, she understood he was trying to distract her, and was grateful. 'Mum liked it,' she answered, mouth curving, 'she said that everything felt cleaner after it rained. Like the dirt had been washed away. Besides, they were both really into nature, the cycle of life. And rain is good for living things.' As she finished the sugary tea, she felt stronger somehow, more resilient for talking about them and not dissolving into a damp mess.

'I see. That makes sense. So what are you studying? And why

uni?' His pale eyes were intent as he leaned forward, his knees only a couple of inches from hers now. 'Wouldn't that have been too conventional for them? Too establishment?'

Ignoring the whiff of intriguing, expensive aftershave, she put the mug on the floor. 'Communication and Media Studies; the sandwich degree. I want to be a journalist. They always encouraged me to make my own choices, even ones they wouldn't have made for me, or themselves.' She paused. 'It's funny, if I stick this degree out I think it'll be the longest I've ever been in one place. We were always moving around, travelling the UK and abroad in the caravan, my parents picking up odd jobs here and there, following the latest good cause.'

'You lived in a caravan? That's different.' But he didn't look mildly disgusted like some people did, he looked intrigued. 'It must have been amazing, travelling, having that freedom. That they supported what you wanted for yourself too.' Something dark flitted across his face again but he covered it up by draining his tea in one long, steady glug.

'It is. I mean, was. It was great they supported my choices, and I got to see some fantastic parts of the world, but I hated being the new girl every time I changed school, and we argued sometimes, when I wanted to stay put. I found it hard. They always did their best for me, it was just t-that-' she stumbled, feeling guilty for questioning their decisions when they weren't here to defend themselves. Clearing her throat, she tossed her hair over her shoulder, putting the focus back on him. 'Anyway, what are you studying?'

'Economics and Business Management.'

'Are you enjoying it? Is it interesting so far?'

His face tightened. 'It's necessary.'

It was a strange thing to say. 'What do you mean necessary?'

He waved the comment off. 'So are you like them at all? Your parents I mean.'

He obviously didn't want to talk to her about it, and given how he'd let her run off a few days ago, it only seemed fair that she respected his feelings about this. 'Am I like them? I—' she sighed and shivered. There was a draft coming in from somewhere and suddenly she felt like a total idiot, sitting around wearing practically nothing in the narrow, ice-box dorm room. Squinting at the packing boxes, she tried to remember which one had her winter clothes in. A sensible girl would have a dressing gown given the time of the year. For the last twelve months though, she'd been anything but.

'Here.' Adam whipped his jumper off to reveal a pair of surprisingly broad shoulders in a branded polo top, his light brown hair a little too long at the back, brushing his collar. He threw the jumper at her and although a piece of her wanted to say, *no that's okay thanks, I don't need it*, she couldn't be bothered. And it would be plain weird if she got into bed to warm up with him sat there. He might think she was inviting him to join her, which she wouldn't be, given the earlier message that she wasn't his type.

So she just mumbled a quick thank you as she fought her way into the jumper and pulled it down. Her knees trembled at being wrapped up in his gorgeous smell. *Sort yourself out, you silly mare.*

'My pleasure,' he replied. 'So?'

'Honest answer?'

'Yep.'

'The irony is that I spent until I was eighteen fighting it,' she admitted. 'I didn't want to be like them. I studied hard, didn't drink or party, took part in every extra-curricular activity I could, dressed sensibly, refused to go to the rallies. I basically did nothing people might think was rebellious or alternative. Then they died, and I …'

'You what?'

'Ever heard the phrase *good girl gone bad*?'

He grinned. 'Sounds exciting. How bad?'

'Piercings, tattoos, drinks, parties, dropped out of society for a while.'

'Do I get to ask where?'

'Ask me again another time and maybe I'll show you the naughtier ones. You can see the PG rated for now.' Pulling back her long, thick black hair, she pointed at the stud in her helix and the silver hoop in the upper ear cartilage.

'I meant where you went when you dropped out of sight.'

'Oh.' Damn. If she'd been the sort to blush, that would have been the moment. He definitely *didn't* fancy her.

'So, is the good girl back, or is the bad girl still running things?' He looked around her room again, eyes scanning the dog-eared pile of books on the floor and the plastic bag that had notepads, pens, rulers and paperclips spilling out of it. He was probably thinking that for a girl she didn't own much. He'd be right; they'd never really had any money, and she'd got used to travelling light.

His fingers drummed the chair either side of his thighs as he gazed at the unpacked boxes again. It gave her the chance to study him, the smooth clean-shaven jaw, his neat ears and slight bump on the bridge of his nose. He wasn't her normal type but there was something about him that was quietly sexy. Was it wrong to feel deflated that he hadn't pushed to see the other piercings and her tattoos? *No. Forget that.*

'Actually, I think I'm both. But I may need to keep the bad girl in check a bit more.' Saying it solidified it in her mind. Now she was here, she had to buckle down. Her parents may not have believed in further education and traditional career paths, but they'd supported her dreams and ambitions. Because they loved her. Her grandparents did too, despite their disappointment in her. Remembering she was loved might get her through until it stopped hurting less.

'I don't know, I wouldn't be too well behaved.' He replied, looking almost sad. 'Sometimes I wonder if it's overrated.'

'You say that, but you don't know the things I've been up to over the past year.' Her mouth pulled down. It wasn't in her nature to regret, but in unravelling, she'd nearly unravelled completely. Thank god drugs had felt a step too far.

'No regrets.' He declared, standing and scooping both mugs up carefully. 'I think you were just trying to keep them alive.'

'What do you mean?'

'Perhaps by being more like them?'

She pursed her lips, and tugged the jumper down over her knees. She hadn't thought of the last twelve months in that way before. She had just been lost in a fog of grief and hadn't known how to cope with it. 'Maybe, but they didn't drink heavily or sl—' for some reason she didn't want him to think badly of her. 'Sleep on people's sofa's.' She finished lamely, instead of *sleep with random strangers*.

'Doesn't sound too bad to me.' He stared out through the double-glazed window before checking his watch. 'Bugger, I've got to go. I'm going to be late for a lecture. I'll find you later.' Swinging around, he strode to the door.

'Adam, wait.'

'What is it?' He looked at her over his shoulder, fingers curled round the door handle.

'Your jumper.' She knelt up on the bed to whip it off over her head.

'It's fine. Keep it as long as you want. Actually, just keep it,' he smiled and winked. 'Looks better on you anyway.'

'I can't just have it. It looks,' she rubbed her cheek against the soft fabric of the shoulder, 'and feels, expensive.'

'Oh, it is.' He said carelessly, tugging the door open, 'But don't let that bother you. I've got loads like it. Mum has me drowning in upmarket wool.'

'I can't just take it from you, Adam.'

'Why? You've already given me something.'

'Huh?' she scrambled off the bed as he stepped into the hallway, sticking her head out of her room to shout after him as he jogged away. 'What are you on about?'

There was a smile in the reply he threw over his shoulder, his deep voice echoing along the corridor, bouncing off the walls like a tennis ball on a clay court, until it ricocheted into her. 'Your name.'

'So, what's with the Cleopatra haircut, Ray? I liked it long.' Adam rolled up next to her as she stood in the queue for drinks following a close, bated-breath tennis match. 'And the knuckle-dusters?'

It'd taken a tie-break in the penultimate set followed by a two-point lead in the last set to get to a clear winner. The whole time, she'd been mega-aware of Adam behind her, occasionally leaning forward at tense moments, his breath warm on her neck, making her whole body tingle. At one point she'd thrown him a dirty look, thinking crossly that he was doing it on purpose, but he'd seemed oblivious to the effect he was having on her stupid hormones. It had almost ruined the tennis for her. It was nearly impossible to concentrate on the thwack of the racquets, the thunk and bounce of the yellow ball, the athleticism and stamina of the players as they sprinted back and forth grunting with effort, with Adam so close.

'Cleopatra?' She touched the ends of her sharp bob, brushed the blunt fringe out of her eyes. 'Nothing. I fancied a change, needed something more grown up.' Wiggling her long fingers, which sported a selection of colourful cocktail rings, she gave him a pretend scowl. 'And they're hardly knuckle-dusters, just decoration. Anyway, what about you? What's with the semi-thuggish look?' She gestured to his brown hair, which was shorter at the sides and no longer brushed his collar at the back, the day old stubble and the edge of a tattoo that circled his defined bicep, peeping out from beneath his white t-shirt sleeve. He reminded her a bit of the actor Tom Hardy. Gorgeous but a bad boy. Not the Adam she was used to.

'Haven't lost the spunky attitude I see.' He answered back, grinning, throwing his serve. 'God, I used to love the way you stood up to my mum.'

She chose not to answer directly. No way was she going there. There were too many old scars.

And damn it. Why did he have to be even hotter than when they'd been together? He'd been a twenty year old boy when they'd split, always with an old head on his shoulders, but he was definitely a man now. A broad-shouldered, muscle ripped man with clear blue eyes that still had the ability to make her feel like the only girl in the world.

Effing hell, stop it Rayne. Too many years have passed, you've made a new life for yourself, and so has he.

Shuffling forward in line, she pretended to study the menu while she thought of a suitably bland answer. In truth, she'd already made her choice. She was at Wimbledon, and it was sunny. It'd be rude not to have a refreshing, tangy Pimms. 'I wouldn't be me if I didn't speak my mind would I?' She lobbed lightly back at last.

'I guess not,' he returned.

'You though, you've changed.' The upper class look had all but disappeared. 'No-one would know from looking at you, that you come from money. Shit,' shaking her head, 'sorry, that sounded like an insult. What I meant was, you always used to be so—'

'Boring?'

'No! Posh. Well-dressed. Articulate.' Sensible. Nice. Maybe too nice in hindsight? Not enough of a risk-taker for her? He'd been her home, her centre for two years. She'd always felt guilty after he'd left. Like she'd used him somehow. If that was the case, it hadn't been intentional.

'Wow, sexy,' he drawled.

'I always thought so,' she mumbled under her breath.

'What?'

'Nothing.'

'Okay.' Adam shifted in line, flexing his shoulders.

As he moved, she caught a whiff of his aftershave. Not the same one as when they'd been together – this was different, with darker undertones – but it was still just as fresh and appealing. Basically, him all over.

'So, there's a lot to catch up on,' he said casually. 'What have you been doing with yourself?'

'Left uni with a First,' she rattled out, stepping forward another place, 'got a junior reporter job at the regional paper I did my

234

industrial placement at, moved to a national after a year, did well there and I'm a news journalist in the City now.'

'You don't sound very enthusiastic. It's everything you wanted, right?'

'It is.' She smiled briefly, not wanting to talk about it. It had always felt like their relationship had been sacrificed for her career. The right choice at the time, but it felt uncomfortable, even now. Out of all the people she'd known in her life, Adam was the one who deserved to be let down the least. 'I just don't really want to talk shop today.' She was super-aware of his muscular arm tight against hers, the zing of excitement shooting through her, the warm breeze blowing her hair against her cheeks. 'Lily says I'm a workaholic, and she's right. So when I get time off, I like to relax. Switch off.'

'What? Come on! There's no way you've changed that much. Are you really telling me you're not working on a story?' He raised an eyebrow, gesturing around them with his arms. 'At uni that busy brain of yours was always whirring away on some idea, or failing that you were working on a blog post.'

Sticking her tongue out at him, she laughed. 'Fine. If I could get an exclusive interview with one of the British players, even though I don't work on the sports desk, my editor would love me.'

'I knew it!' he chuckled, white teeth flashing.

She flicked him playfully on the shoulder. 'All right, you win that one.' Then inhaled sharply, glancing away. She was flirting. *Stop it*. She must be mad. But it felt so delicious, and was so much fun.

'So, what else?' he quizzed. 'Are your grandparents okay? And as for the rest, I already know you don't have a boyfriend,' he teased.

Thanks, Lily for airing your views on Centre Court. She side-stepped the subject of her love life, and no way was she going to ask about his. She didn't want to know. But she had to keep the conversational ball in play. 'Gramps and Gran are fine. Getting older, but in good health.' Her dad's parents. Her mum had never known hers. 'I see them about once a month or so. They always liked you. I'll tell them you said hi.'

'Do that. I liked them too.' He smiled down at her.

'They liked you because you brought me back to them.'

'Oh, I don't know.' He gave a one shouldered shrug. 'You would have made it up with them eventually.'

'Yes, but it was you who talked me into bridging the gap sooner rather than later. I think they're still hurt even now that I chose to sleep on strangers sofas for that year before uni, rather than living with them. But it just didn't feel right. It was too hard being with people who reminded me of Dad, when I missed him and Mum so much.'

'I think they understood more than you realised,' he replied, taking a step forward and guiding her along with a hand on her elbow. 'They lost a child, even if he was an adult. And I didn't want you to have any regrets, after what happened with my father.'

She shivered at the white-hot zing of his touch, and subtly inched away, 'I know.' But she couldn't stop the sympathy and care for him washing over her like an echo. Touching his arm in a comforting gesture, 'Does it feel any better now?' she asked.

He nodded jerkily, 'It's faded. It's been a long time. But still, there are so many things I wish we'd had a chance to talk about. If I'd have known he was going to have a critical heart attack so young, I would have done things differently, you know?'

She smiled up at him. 'I do.' It had always been this way with him, so easy to share her feelings and innermost thoughts. But it was too dangerous to do that now. She had to step back. Wrinkling her nose, she asked, 'so, how's your mum?' Who had disliked her intensely.

He laughed, 'You haven't got any better at your poker face, I always knew what you were thinking. She's fine thanks, about the same, except now she runs *Parsons* permanently,' the family's exceptionally profitable luxury-food company, 'with Dad's old business partner, Richard.'

'That makes sense, with you out of the country.' Emotion

bubbled up in her chest as she remembered one of their last arguments as a couple, the memory of the anguish and anger pressing down on her lungs.

'Let's not talk about it now, all right?' He craned his neck to study the drinks menu written up on the blackboard.

'No problem.' She took a deep breath and cleared her throat. 'By the way, do you think it's the universe playing tricks or just coincidence that you ended up sat behind me, after all this time?'

'I got my tickets via ballot.' He looked uncomfortable, shifting from one foot to another. 'It's great to see you though.'

'I'm surprised you're actually talking to me.' She confessed. Oh balls to it; she might as well say what she was thinking. Plus there was a burning curiosity that longed to know what he thought of her. 'I always imagined you hated me, after the way things ended and you left.' And that he'd never got in touch with her, not once.

He stared down at her, eyes cooling, and a pulse fluttered in his jaw. He curved his mouth into something resembling a smile. 'It was a long time ago. And, it would be ridiculous for me to hold it against you nearly five years later, right?'

'I guess.' A wash of relief spread through her, although she was equally disappointed that he'd got over it so well, when she still had so many regrets.

'What can I get you?' The barman gazed down at them expectantly. She'd not even noticed they'd reached the front of the queue, so caught up in her conversation with Adam. *Uh-oh. Big uh-oh.* Men never distracted her.

'Er. Um. I, can I have –?' *Come on Rayne, pull it together. Deep breath. Act like you're on a job, chasing a story. Professional, calm, competent.* 'Two Pimms' please.' She ordered. 'Adam, what can I get you and Flynn?'

'If you're sure, we'll have a beer each.' He nodded. 'Thanks.'

He obviously still remembered it was best not to argue with her about that kind of stuff. How she'd always insisted on going halves, paying her way, even though he'd always had loads more money than her. 'Two beers, as well,' she finished, shoving both hands into her shorts' pockets, looking away from him and feeling awkward. Nerves were tumbling in her tummy, her palms were damp and the sun was burning the back of her neck. It was too weird, being with him again. He was familiar and at the same time a stranger. Coming up to five years was a long time, and uni felt like forever ago. How could you miss someone and not realise it until you saw them again?

'Hey. You okay?' A gentle finger lifted her chin, pale eyes gazing into hers.

'Yes.' She smiled too brightly, casually moving her head away. 'Fine, thanks. Hot and looking forward to that drink.'

'Fair enough. As long as you're sure.'

'I am. What could possibly be wrong?' she replied lightly, knowing it was a dangerous question.

Luckily Adam chose not to reply, stepping back out of her way so she could pay the barman. After they'd loaded up with the drinks in plastic cups, they headed back towards Henman Hill, where Flynn and Lily had relocated their stuff.

'Lovely day.' Rayne mumbled as they walked through the streaming crowds, matching footsteps. He was six foot two but she was tall, over five foot ten with a long stride. She sighed, mentally kicking herself. How inane could you get, talking about the weather?

'It is.' He stopped, giving her a cheeky look, eyes twinkling. 'I've been thinking.'

Uh-oh. It was an expression she'd learnt to recognise after they'd moved into a shared student flat together in their second year. He used it when he was up to something. But on the older Adam, who had those ridiculously broad shoulders, dark, delicious-looking stubble and crinkles around his eyes, it was no longer cute.

It was overwhelmingly sexy.

'Yes?' she croaked, halting next to him. The Pimms sloshed

238

over the rim of the cup, sprigs of mint and pieces of strawberry, orange and cucumber knocking together. Bringing her hand up, she licked her sticky fingers.

He watched, eyes darkening. 'I could do you a favour.'

'Oh, yeah?'

'Are you coming tomorrow? Do you have tickets?'

'I wasn't planning to. We were in the queue overnight to get tickets for today and I have loads of work on at the moment so was only allowed to take the one day off. My editor's riding me for three stories I'm working on and I'm pitching another to her in two days' time. Why?' she cocked her head.

'I have some VIP tickets, and can get you in tomorrow.' He sipped his beer, foam coating his top lip.

It made her want to wipe it off. Or lick it off. A familiar tingle started in her belly and between her thighs. Her hands tightened around the plastic cups and more Pimms spilt over the side.

'Hey, careful with that,' he joked, stepping back out of the danger zone.

'Why would you offer me tickets for tomorrow?' she quizzed, trying to work out his plan, now oblivious of the noisy press of people shuffling around them.

'I could get you interviews with some of the players if you wanted me to.'

'You could?' Excitement pitched her voice high and she stepped towards him. 'That would be amazing! I could definitely clear the day to do that. How?'

He smiled softly. 'Through a mixture of family connections, *Parsons* being one of the Wimbledon sponsors, my marketing expertise and calling in a few favours. Interested?'

'Of course I bloody am! Marketing expertise? What do you mean? Did you get into it in the end then? I thought you'd been abroad doing charity work?' She flushed. Balls, now he'd know she'd been keeping tabs on him. 'I mean …' she trailed off, 'I remember how interested you were in the marketing stuff when

I was doing the related modules for my degree. You kept nicking my course books.'

'Guilty.' He studied her face as he admitted, 'I'm involved in running *Parsons* now. But instead of heading it up like Mum wanted me to, I do the national marketing.'

'*You do*?' She couldn't have been more surprised than if he'd turned up in whites and blithely announced he was going to be a contender at Wimbledon. 'How the *hell* did that end up happening?'

'It was part of the deal. I'm involved with the family business, but doing something that I like rather than having to run the whole thing and getting bogged down in the financials.' Despite his reticence of a few minutes before, he now seemed at ease talking about it, maybe because they weren't stood in a queue of people. 'And when Mum and Richard want to retire, his son Rafe will take over. Bel works for *Parsons* too, just doing admin at the moment, but she's learning quickly.'

She shook her head disbelievingly. 'Belinda is working with your mum? Your sister was always so ...'

'Rebellious? Spoilt? Lazy?'

Rayne smiled at his matter of fact delivery. 'Well, I admit she could be difficult, but it's just how much she seemed to dislike your mum, and the idea of *Parsons*. Almost as much as you did. It's a huge turnaround.'

'She's changed.' Adam nodded. 'I have too. Yes, I used to dread the idea of *Parsons*, but I'm actually enjoying it. Besides, I haven't decided if it's temporary or permanent yet. I'll have to see what happens.'

'You're enjoying it because it's on your terms,' she breathed, worried by the flutter of disappointment she felt that he might not be staying. 'Well, good for you.' She rallied, 'So, you're back home?' He'd always hated the family house, saying he'd felt suffocated there, despite the rolling open fields and fresh air. She'd always thought that it was more about the people than the house.

'No. I live in Islington. I don't need to be in Buckinghamshire to do the job. Email and conference calls more than work. I have a home office, and can step out the door any time I want to hear the traffic or see friends.'

'Wow,' she whistled, 'Islington. Nice. Doesn't your mum mind? She always preferred you close.'

'It's true she only originally agreed to uni in the Midlands because Loughborough was one of the best,' he acknowledged, 'and was very clear that I was expected to come home afterwards. But lately she's accepted that London is where I've chosen to be.'

'She has?'

'Yes, on the basis that it's better than halfway across the world.'

Rayne laughed, starting to walk again. 'You were always a good strategic thinker, Adam.' She shook her head as he meandered beside her. 'I'm glad it's worked out for you.'

'Speaking of which, we've strayed off court a bit. This is about something working out for you. Shall I set those interviews up? We can meet outside St. Mary's Gate at eight tomorrow morning.'

'If you're sure you can manage it, that would be really brilliant, but why are you doing this? Especially after the way we broke up. Do-' she looked at him out of the corner of her eye, took a breath and blurted, 'are you after something in return?'

He stopped dead, looking exasperated. 'I hope that mind of yours isn't going down seedy little avenues. I told you, I'm not bitter about the break up. We're fine.' But his lips looked pale at the edges, like they used to when he argued with his mum. 'And, I don't want anything from you, other than you agreeing to have lunch with me tomorrow so we can do some more catching up. But you don't have to feel obliged. It's only if you want to. If you don't, that's cool,' he took a sip of his beer, the condensation dripping off the bottom of the cup in the fierce late afternoon sunshine, 'and you can just owe me a professional favour. Maybe you could ask your editor to do a spread on *Parsons*, or at least interview Mum?'

She stared at him, narrowing her eyes at his easy, sincere expression. Interviews with some players would be a massive boost to her career; they could even make the front or back page if juicy or interesting enough. Plus, one little lunch with Adam couldn't hurt, could it? It was a no-brainer. 'No problem. Oh my god, this is incredible. Thank you so much.' She skipped ahead, and then twirled around to face him, nearly causing the man strolling up behind her to drop his drinks. 'Lunch sounds good and I'm happy to talk to the lifestyle editor about *Parsons* too. I'm sure they'll be thrilled to do something, given how well known the brand is. Can you get Lily entry for tomorrow too? We work for the same paper. She could do the photos.'

'Sure. You look like a kid at Christmas,' he ribbed, 'all flushed cheeks and wide, eager eyes. Come on, we should get the drinks back to Lily and Flynn before you spill them all and we have to go back to the bar.'

Rayne looked down at the cups, then at Adam. The mention of Christmas made her think of their first one together, of the tense atmosphere at his mum's and how closed off he'd become, a different boy than the one she'd started to fall in love with. She remembered how keen he was to get back to halls, how they'd secluded themselves away in her room together, away from the world. The breach with her grandparents hadn't been healed at that point, so there'd been nowhere else they had to be. Eating and drinking, watching DVD's and having sweaty, astounding sex, they'd barely left her bed for a week. It had probably been the best seven days of her life.

Something sharp clenched in her chest and she gulped. 'Okay.' She started walking again, suddenly eager to rejoin Lily and get away from being alone with her ex.

Except when she got back to Lily and Flynn, who were sitting on the crowded grassy hill filled with spectators lolling in the sunshine, they were huddled together on the picnic blanket looking cosy. The look her friend threw her said, *please don't make me leave too quickly.*

'I guess you're stuck with me a bit longer,' Adam said, sinking down on the grass and handing Flynn his beer.

'Here you go.' Rayne sank down next to him and passed Lily's drink over, smiling in amusement despite her discomfort. She really could have done with some space from Adam, needing time to settle herself.

'Thank you.' Lily's cheeks pinkened at the look Rayne was giving her. 'Oh, don't forget—'

'The gin.' Rooting around in the picnic bag, Rayne produced two miniatures and poured one into each of their drinks.

'Steady girls.' Flynn laughed. 'Daytime drinking in the sun and all that.'

'Believe me Flynn, you don't have to worry,' Adam stated, 'these two can really handle their drink.'

'Oi!' Rayne smacked his bicep lightly.

'Ow!' He clutched his arm, pulling a wounded face.

She rolled her eyes and shook her head.

'We don't usually drink in the day,' Lily said solemnly, looking innocent. 'We're too busy working. But we promised ourselves a free pass today. And you've got to have a shot of gin in Pimms.' She smiled. 'It's a classic. Here, try a bit.' Offering the drink to Flynn, she pursed her lips and watched him take a sip, fluttering her blonde eyelashes.

Rayne groaned and this time it was Adam who rolled his eyes. 'She hasn't changed much, has she?' he whispered in her ear, his bare hair-roughened knee brushing hers in the black deck shorts he wore.

She shivered. 'No. Still a heartbreaker.'

He muttered something that sounded suspiciously like her not being the only one, but when she asked him to repeat himself, he instead plunged into telling Flynn a funny story about a house party he, Rayne and Lily had gone to at uni that ended with a rubber blow-up sheep and a supermarket trolley.

A while later, as the drinks started running out, he leaned closer. 'By the way, I'm single,' he murmured. 'Just in case you were wondering.' Echoing the words he'd used when they'd first met.

It brought a bittersweet lump to her throat. 'I wasn't,' she immediately fired back. 'Thanks for the update though.'

But as Rayne stared at his profile, at the barely there bump on the bridge of his nose, she knew she'd lied. His was a face she'd loved looking at once upon a time. Her hand dropped to the necklace around her neck, a finger tracing the delicate gold chain, glad the treasures that hung from it nestled in the hollow between her breasts, hidden safely against her heart.

'Morning ladies,' Adam smiled as he strolled up to them outside the Wimbledon complex the next morning. 'Are you ready? How are your heads?'

Lily clutched her temples and groaned, pawing through her bulky camera bag for sunglasses and a bottle of energy drink.

It was another sunny day, and likely to be a scorcher again later on. Rayne almost felt sorry for Lily, except she was going to enjoy teasing her about her hangover too much. Plus, hung over or not, her petite friend still looked sickeningly beautiful in a pale yellow dress, making Rayne feel boyish and tall by comparison in the beige city shorts and casual white shirt she'd picked. Still, at least she'd slung on wedge multi-coloured sandals and a bulky statement necklace on the way out the door.

'Rayne?' Adam turned to her, sucking on his bottom lip.

She adjusted the satchel handbag on her shoulder, pasting her professional face on. It had been so lovely to spend time with him yesterday, but so simultaneously heart breaking – like she'd lost her best friend then found him again, only to have to say another goodbye – that she was determined to keep her distance. 'Fine, thanks. I got home last night, took a cold shower to sober up, and once you'd texted me the names of the players we could interview, I did my research and got my questions ready.'

'Great. Is Lils going to be okay though?' he asked as Lily produced a Mars bar and started nibbling on it, white-faced. 'Are you sure she'll be able to focus the camera?'

'Hey!' Lily scowled at him before wincing. 'I'm right here, and I'm not that bad. Besides,' she said sheepishly, 'it's got all the bells and whistles on it, including auto focus.'

'Thank god for that,' Adam grinned, gesturing for them to follow him over to a steward, who waved them through the entrance after checking his clipboard.

As they walked into the grounds and down Henman Hill, Rayne looked out across the concrete paths, low leafy buildings with their dark green branded Wimbledon signs, kiosks and neat hedges. It was like a mini village and she'd expected it to be messy, covered in litter and debris from yesterday's teeming crowds, given the relatively early hour, but it was pristine.

'They clean it up at night,' Adam said, reading her mind, 'sometimes it takes them until one in the morning.'

'I'm not surprised, with capacity for over 38,000 spectators,' Rayne responded, descending the stairs carefully in her high heels. It gave her an excuse to avoid looking at him, which made it easier to ignore how sexy he looked in a pair of tight jeans and a navy polo top. The outfit was the closest she'd seen him to his old self, but the effect was ruined by the tattoo on his bicep and the fact he hadn't shaved again.

'You've been doing your research,' he grinned, leading her and Lily into the No. 1 Court building.

Rayne followed, trying hard not to stare at his bum, keeping her eyes on the line of his shoulders instead. She wasn't sure how much better that made it, given how broad they were 'You know me,' she said, 'I like to be prepared.' It was the one thing they'd had in common. How seriously they'd taken their studies, although for entirely different reasons. Her out of passion, him out of duty.

'Oh, thank god,' Lily muttered faintly behind her, letting out a small groan of relief as they stepped into the shade.

Adam chuckled. 'Poor Lily. Don't worry; I'll make sure they supply you with plenty of iced water.' He glanced over his shoulder at them both, as he led them up a set of carpeted stairs. 'The Press Officer suggested you interview the players in the Membership Suite, is that okay?'

'Wherever suits is fine,' Rayne raced up the stairs behind him, trying to keep up, 'I'd interview someone in a toilet cubicle if that's what it took to get the story. Correction, I *have* interviewed someone in a toilet cubicle to get a story.'

He chuckled as he took her into a reception area with dark wooden floors and a couple of smart beige sofas up against the wall, walking straight through into the suite. 'I'd love to hear about that sometime, but I think you'll prefer this place a bit more.'

'Well, anything would be an improvement on—' she stepped into the room, and let out a low whistle. 'Oh. Wow.'

'Do you two have to walk so quickly with those giraffe legs you both have?' Lily complained as she wobbled up behind them, sunglasses pushed back on her head. 'What are you doing?' she squinted at Rayne, before turning to face the room. 'Hmmm. Right. Nice.'

'Yep, that would be one description.' Rayne answered, taking in the floor to ceiling windows along one side of the long space, the muted light brown carpet, circular white table clothed tables with posh flower centre-pieces, the white, brown and beige chairs and tasteful red light shades, with a modern bar accented with lime green stools crowning the end of the room.

'The light's great for the photos,' Lily turned her face towards the windows, squinting slightly. 'It's a lovely setting. I was going to set an area up for the pics but I think I'll just take them of you with each player at the table. Go for that relaxed look, but in tasteful surroundings. Our lifestyle section might be able to use some too. I might take some extra photos of the bar area and

246

table settings. Maybe I'll move this table further over there ...'
Lily wandered off muttering under her breath.

'She's still got that distracted fairy thing going on then,' Adam
grasped Rayne's elbow to move her further into the room as a PR
girl arrived, followed by a member of the restaurant staff.

Rayne sniggered, remembering how he'd christened Lily that
one night when she'd gotten distracted by something, lost them
for two hours and then called them to come find her. It'd taken
half an hour to track her down at a random cafe bar a few roads
away. 'She only goes off into her own world occasionally.' Watching
her friend talking to herself, completely oblivious to the fact she'd
just stepped right in the way of the PR girl, who shook her head
and skirted around Lily in a circle. 'I think the dregs of alcohol
coursing through her bloodstream are the problem today.' She
glanced down at Adam's hand still holding her arm, pulling their
bodies close together, his heat warming her side. 'Adam?' Lifting
her head, she found him watching her intensely and forgot to
breathe. Was it always going to be like this with him and never
the same with anyone else? The question was enough to jolt some
common sense into her, providing the motivation to step away.

'Rayne—'

'Anyway,' she stalked over to a table by the window and started
rooting through her bag, cutting across whatever he'd been about
to say, 'I'd better get on with it.' Yanking a tiny hand-held voice
recorder out, she slammed it down on the table and whipped out
her notes. 'I'll see you at lunch,' she said evenly, hunting for a pen
in one of the side pockets.

He appeared beside her, running a hand around the back of
his neck. 'Is everything okay, Ray? I didn't mean to ...'

'I'm fine. Just busy,' she replied tightly, immediately feeling like
an ungrateful cow, given he was doing her a championship sized
favour. But she could apologise at lunch. Right now she needed to
focus on the job in hand, not the man whose heart she'd broken
as a boy. These interviews could send her career stellar.

247

'No problem,' he answered mildly, no doubt remembering it was best to leave her when she was like this. 'I'll see you downstairs at one.'

She didn't answer, checking her mobile phone for any urgent calls, aware of Lily giving Adam an absent wave as he strode out the door.

Thank god she'd have a chance to regroup and have a few hours without him. She was sure lunch would be fine, as long as she didn't touch him. Or look at him.

Besides which, Lily would be there to play chaperone. So there was absolutely nothing to worry about.

'Oh, my god, that was amazing,' Lily squealed as she and Rayne walked out of No. 1 Court into the heaving mass of spectators

'I have to admit, it was pretty brilliant,' Rayne agreed, stretching her back out. Although she'd gone to Wimbledon the day before for the life experience rather than as a die-hard tennis fan, it had definitely been a thrill to spend the morning talking to some of the world's best tennis players. Every interview had gone well, and one of the players had told her something she was almost certain was an exclusive. Her editor was going to love her to bits.

'I got some great photos, I'm really happy with them.' Lily was almost hopping on the spot.

'Good.' Rayne chuckled. 'I thought you were hungover?'

'Not anymore. How do I look?' She'd snuck off to the toilets just before the last interview and come back wearing dusky pink lipstick, with newly brushed, shiny hair and smelling suspiciously of her trademark floral perfume.

'Beautiful, as always. But Lils, why are you tarting yourself up for me and Adam?' Rayne asked, and then froze. Oh god, Lily didn't fancy Adam now did she? They'd always just been friends at uni, and Rayne had never worried about them together in that way, despite Lily once joking about it. She dipped her head, panic slamming into her. If Lily's feelings were changing, what was she going to do? And what if Adam looked at Lily differently after so many years apart? But surely her friend wouldn't do that to her, she was too loyal. God, this was awful. He wasn't hers, but would she be able to stand it if he—

'I'm not, you daft mare,' Lily nudged her with an elbow. 'I'm meeting Flynn for lunch before we carry on with this afternoon's interviews.'

Rayne jerked her head up. 'What? Aren't you coming to lunch with us?'

'No. You and Adam have catching up to do, and air to clear. I'm going to leave you to it, and let a gorgeous brunette take me to lunch instead.'

'Like the one who asked for your number upstairs?'

'That was very flattering,' Lily blushed, flicking a look over Rayne's shoulder, 'but I told her I liked men.'

'What's this?' A deep voice asked.

'Lily got propositioned by the PR girl,' Rayne told Adam as he appeared beside them.

'Wow, Lils, you've still got it,' Adam winked.

'Well, two of the male players asked Rayne to dinner and a third slipped her his personal number,' Lily blurted.

'I'm not surprised,' Adam said, crossing his arms over his broad chest. 'And what did you do?' He turned to ask her, cocking his head.

'I thanked two of them politely but declined, and I gave the other back his number and told him maybe he should stick to his wife. I don't mess around with married men.'

Adam nodded. 'Good girl. Now, shall we go to lunch? I'm starving.' He took her hand. 'Flynn will be here in a minute Lils, he's just parking the car. Rayne and I are walking.'

'We are? And good girl?' Rayne repeated as he started guiding her across the complex on the opposite side from St Mary's Gate. 'Good girl? And what's it got to do with you? Bloody hell, Adam,' she grumbled, 'you used to be bossy, but now you're practically high-handed.'

'Calm down, Ray.' He tightened his grip on her fingers as she tried to steal them back. 'I was only joking. You can do what you want.' He flashed a grin at her as they exited out of gate seven onto Church Road with its white painted houses, cars roaring past. Somewhere a dog let out two sharp barks, and the smell of BBQ drifted by on the air. 'Although obviously I was pleased that you decided not take them up on their offers.'

'Why?' Sucking in a breath, she both hoped and dreaded that he'd say he wanted to ask her out himself. It was unlikely, given what she'd done to him, but if he did, what the hell would she do? Obviously she fancied him like mad, and some of the residual feelings were there – he was still kind and generous, funny and gentlemanly – but they hadn't been able to make it work before, and he'd said his job might only be temporary. He was still not ready to put down roots, and that was the one thing she'd always craved, needed and fought for. The one thing that had driven them apart all those years ago.

You couldn't go back, surely? Too much time, and life, had filled the intervening gap.

'Relax,' he soothed, 'don't look so worried. It's just that sports players have a reputation, don't they? Travelling the world, bags of money, sponsorship deals, women throwing themselves at them … I wouldn't want you to get hurt, that's all.'

'Oh. Right.' Relief was the emotion bouncing through her. She was sure it was. Which was why it was weird that, instead of tugging her hand away as they walked onto the High Street and entered the infamous Dog and Fox pub with its tennis rackets on the walls, her fingers curled around his, heat sparking through them.

Adam pulled out his phone as it beeped and checked the screen. 'Sorry, I know it's really rude, but I need to get this. It's an urgent work thing.'

'Go for it,' she said as she found a table outside and he moved to stand on the pavement to take the call.

Rayne was glad of the respite, sinking her head onto her hands. She just had to get through this lunch. They'd finish catching up, she'd apologise for her earlier bitchiness, thank him profusely for the generous favour he'd done her setting up today's interviews and say goodbye. Then she could work on forgetting that she'd ever run into him again. What it had made her think. How it had made her feel. Simple.

After Adam returned to the table and their meals were served, they filled the spaces in between eating bites of food with idle chatter about other uni friends, their favourite places in London and some of the places he'd visited abroad.

When he was done, Adam pushed his plate away and stared at her meaningfully, pale eyes direct. 'So.'

'So?' she put down her forkful of salad. It had always been the same; he would wolf his meal down and be finished when she was only halfway through her own.

'We never had closure, did we Ray? It ended too abruptly.'

She stared at him, surprised he'd brought it up, but couldn't deny what he said. He was right. 'I guess not,' she agreed slowly. 'But I thought you were okay about it all. Yesterday, you said that-'

'I needed to spend more time with you to work out how I felt and to gauge how you feel.' There was a watchful quality in the way he looked at her, but he stayed slouched in his seat, fingers idly playing with a serviette.

'And how do you think I feel?' she challenged as she picked up her drink, careful to keep her voice steady.

'I think you feel the same as me. I think we need closure.'

'Right.' She raised an eyebrow. 'And how do you suggest we get that, Adam?'

'Sex.'

'Sex.' She spluttered out some ginger beer, and made a hasty grab for some serviettes from the centre of the table, wiping her face and swiping at a few drops on the table. *Smooth, Rayne. Very smooth.* Looking up at his amused face. 'Oh, ha ha. Good one.'

'Who says I'm joking?' He straightened his face. 'Yeah, I think we should have sex. One night. A hot, sweaty way to wrap things up between us properly.'

'What? It's been years. We've not seen each other since the break-up.' *No. Don't even think about it. And definitely DON'T imagine it. It's outrageous. Silly. And far too tempting. But above all really, really silly.* 'I can't sleep with you just like that. Are you nuts?'

'No, and we wouldn't get much sleep.' His voice was deep and his expression made her rebellious hormones jump, hop and skip around in excitement. 'But seriously, why not? We're both single. You can't deny we had amazing sex, even if we were young and relatively inexperienced. And even if you thought I was boring.'

'I never said that! Where's this coming from? It's the second time you've mentioned it.'

'The way you used to look at me sometimes.' He ran a hand through his light brown hair, sitting up straight, his bunched arm muscles stretching his top. 'I also overheard you talking to Zoe on the phone once, when we lived together. *Sometimes I wonder if he's too nice.*'

'Too nice for me, I meant.' Sod it, as they were doing this, she might as well be honest. Sighing, 'Translated as, too good for me.'

'What?' he looked stunned. 'I didn't know you felt that way, and *I* never thought that.'

'We both know your mum did!' It was funny how old wounds that you'd thought had long knitted over could still hurt. How clear the recollection of the way his mum Tamara used to look down her nose at her was. Because she was parentless and hadn't come from a respectable family. Because she was planning to have a career rather than be satisfied with life as a society wife. Because she didn't wear the same things or talk the same way as the girls in Tamara's social circles did.

'Mum's a complete snob. No-one and nothing will ever be good enough for her. Although she has mellowed a bit while I've been away. But still,' he grasped her fingers, 'I'm sorry. I knew you never felt comfortable at the house, and obviously you and Mum didn't get along, but I didn't know it bothered you that much.'

She looked down at their linked hands, his palm hot and sending prickles of heat over her skin. 'I guess she hit a nerve. You know I had an unconventional childhood and we didn't have much money, but the latter was mostly because my parents didn't set much stock in material things. But it still hurt that I wasn't good enough for her.' Tilting her face up to gaze at him squarely. 'I suppose I always thought the fact I loved you and wanted the best for you should be enough.'

He nodded. 'It should have been, but maybe Mum's ideas of what was best for me, and your ideas were too different and she felt threatened. Then again, it's always been about her, and what everyone else will think, rather than what will make her children happy. The only future she could contemplate was me finishing my degree, coming home and being MD of *Parsons* for the rest of my life.'

'Which was the only future you *couldn't* contemplate at the end. I know.' She stroked his fingers reassuringly, trying not to let the sexual tension distract her. 'I probably should have said something. I nearly did, so many times, but I didn't want to put you under any pressure when your mum already was. I didn't want you to feel like I was tugging you in the other direction.'

'Asking me to choose between you and my family,' he finished the thought.

'Exactly.' It was tragic; he'd always understood her so well. The only one who ever had.

Leaning over the table, he stroked her cheekbone, blue eyes capturing hers. 'Thank you, Rayne. I appreciate the way you supported me.'

It got to her, him acknowledging what she'd tried to do, the way he touched her and used her full name. Something inside her started thawing; a tiny, tight, balled up knot of pain she hadn't realised still remained. 'Thank you.'

'Do you feel better?' he asked.

'Yes,' she replied on a shuddering breath, mixed emotions tumbling through her. Regret, sadness, hope, affection. Could things have been different if they'd talked more about the important things? But she'd made the decision she felt was right for her at the time, and although she'd lost him as a result, she still couldn't help feeling that she would have been miserable if she'd chosen to do what he asked of her.

'Me too,' he stated, a sad smile curling his lips.

As cathartic as it was, she needed to back off, to process how she felt about their conversation. She was also still reeling from his outrageous *let's have sex as closure* proposition and all the tingling but naughty possibilities it held.

'I need to finish lunch,' she cleared her throat. 'We need to get back soon.' Gently disentangling their fingers, she picked up her fork.

'Fair enough. I'll settle the bill.'

'You don't need to do that,' she made a grab for her bag, 'you've done enough. I was going to pay as a small thank you, though it's nowhere near enough.'

'I asked you to lunch, so it's my treat.'

'No, I really want to,' she slid her purse out.

'How long are you willing to keep arguing about this?' Adam folded his arms over his chest.

'As long as it takes for me to win, knowing I've got to be back for my next interview in twenty minutes, so it'll probably be a lot less painful if you just give in,' she eyeballed him.

Chuckling, he threw up his hands. 'Fine, you stubborn woman, if it means that much to you.'

'Thanks. Here's the cash, you run in and sort it out while I finish eating,' she replied cheekily.

Rolling his eyes he stood up. 'Some things never change,' drifted over his shoulder as he stepped inside the white and pale green frontage of the pub.

'But a lot of things do,' she muttered under her breath, swallowing the last few mouthfuls and standing up so she'd be ready when he came back.

'So, have you come up with a convincing reason yet?' Adam asked as they turned off the High Street and sauntered down a teeming Church Road on their way back to the Wimbledon complex.

'What for?'

'For you and me not to have sex.'

She gulped at the tremor that ran through her, at the thought of them getting naked and rolling around, but pulled a mildly offended expression. 'That's a bit arrogant isn't it? You think I've been sat around for the last few years waiting for you to look me up and make me that offer?'

'No.' He looked hurt, but annoyed too. 'Of course not.'

'Sorry. That was mean.' Sighing, she increased her pace. 'I just don't think it's a good idea, Adam. You can't go back. *We* can't go back.'

'I'm not trying to. Sometimes sex is just sex. Remember what Lily said about sex with an ex? It's perfect. And don't forget about the closure.'

She bit her lip. God, it had been so long since she'd been with anyone, and the sex between them had been pretty incredible. All her good girl instincts screamed *no*. All her bad girl needs shouted *yes*. The good girl won out. He wasn't just any ex. He was the one she thought she'd spend her life with. 'I don't think so. But thanks anyway, and it has been nice to see you.'

He sucked on his top lip, then took a step back. 'Okay, whatever you say. No problem,' he raised his hands in a casual, *I give up* pose. 'Come on, let's get you back to those interviews.'

As he loped ahead of her she stared at his back, unsure of whether to be relieved or annoyed that he'd let the idea of them having sex drop so easily.

'Thank you for everything, Adam, I really appreciate it.' Four hours later the interviews were all wrapped up and she had a hell of a lot of typing up to get home to. 'I forgot to say at lunch that I'm sorry for being off with you earlier this morning.'

'It's been a pleasure, and don't worry about it,' Adam smiled, tucking his hands into his jeans pockets. How there was space for them she didn't know. They were that tight.

'I mean it though. Really, today has been fantastic,' she patted her bag, which held her notes and the voice recorder. She squeezed her handbag strap. It was a weird feeling. One part of her wanted to run away as fast as she could, to put this behind her because it had brought up so many buried, conflicting feelings. That was her sensible side, her head. The other part was desperate not to say goodbye to him, faltering at the idea of letting him go, because she'd loved spending time with him and wanted it to carry on. That was her romantic side, her heart. She'd let her head rule what happened between them last time.

Sucking in a breath, she looked over his shoulder as Lily said goodbye to Flynn with a kiss on each cheek and started making her way over them. 'I think your intern is waiting for you.'

'Right. Yeah, I should go.' Adam answered, a deep breath expanding his chest. 'I think we're going to meet up with some people.'

'Have fun.' She bit her lip, gazing into his striking eyes. They were the bluest she'd ever seen outside of the movies. 'Take care of yourself, Adam. It really has been good to see you. You seem more relaxed than you used to be. You seem … happier. I'm glad.'

'Thanks. You too, you seem more settled. Which is what you always wanted.' He blew out a long, slow breath, a funny twist to his lips. 'Look Ray, you know I'm renting that place in Islington.' Yanking her close, he slowly tucked something into the back pocket of her shorts. For a trembling, breathtaking moment his hard, warm chest brushed against her boobs and the fresh scent of his aftershave filled her nose. 'My business card. My mobile number's on it. I'm back in the UK for at least a few months. Stay in touch, or if you change your mind about … us, call me. I promise I'd hold you afterwards.'

He let her go and spun away before she could reply, jogging over to his car without a backward glance as she stared after him, mouth hanging open.

'You okay Rayne?' Lily skipped up, face glowing. 'Flynn is so sweet and handsome.'

'That's nice Lil,' she replied absently, watching as Adam jumped into a curvy hatchback that looked like a 4x4 but was too compact.

'It's a BMW i3,' Lily said, turning to watch as they left, pointing at the black bonnet and silver panelling. 'It's electric. Makes sense that Adam would have an eco-friendly car with the work he's been doing overseas.'

Rayne stared at her friend in amazement. 'How the hell do you know what type of car it is? Apart from mine, all you usually know is that they have a body, four wheels and a steering wheel.'

Lily grinned, 'Flynn told me. Adam's bought him one to use for work too, but in black and orange.'

'Right.'

'So, it must have been weird seeing Adam again?' Lily studied her friend's face. 'There didn't seem to be any hard feelings?'

'Yes. No.' She answered in order, pointing to the car park. They started strolling towards her Mini. 'No hard feelings and he's not bitter. In some ways he's still the same guy; nice, kind and funny … but with a bit of an edge. He was always confident, but now he seems really comfortable in his own skin and not as tense as he was sometimes. It's in the way that he talks, and acts.'

Lily snorted, 'Er, yes, and not to mention the fact he's about a hundred times hotter than he used to be! He was always good looking in a boy-next-door kind of way, but you've got to admit he's grown up to be absolutely drop-dead. And did you see those arms? They're ridiculous.'

'Mmmm. I did. I really did.' Rayne shook her head to clear the buzzing hormones bouncing around her system. 'All right Lily, we should control ourselves. I'm not blind and yes, he is unbelievably sexy, but he's changed in other ways too.'

'Do tell?' Lily shook her rippling blonde waves off her face.

'He made me an offer I don't think the old Adam would have.'

'What was that?'

'He said we should spend the night together. For closure.' She explained as she unlocked her car.

'Wow,' Lily had crossed to the other side of the car, but stopped to look across the bonnet at Rayne in amazement. 'And you said what?'

'A lot of things actually. But it boiled down to thanks, but no thanks.'

'You're an idiot. What about my sex with an ex plan?' Lily pouted as she swung into the passenger seat.

Rayne got into the driver's side, slinging her bag onto the back seat. 'I never signed up to that. And as much as I can see the upside, I'm just not sure. There's too much baggage.'

'Still, I told you all the reasons it's perfect, after what you said—'

'Some things end because they need to. Because it's right. So starting them again doesn't make sense.' Still, she would never forget their first time, when they had really begun …

After the day she exchanged her name for a jumper, Adam made her a cup of tea every day. No matter what time she got up, there was always a knock on the door and a mug of tea ready at the end of an extended hand, usually accompanied by a warm smile and a cheery *good morning*. Initially she couldn't work out how he timed it so perfectly, until Lily let drop one afternoon that he'd photocopied her class schedule, and knew that Rayne always got up half an hour before class began, given she didn't eat breakfast and was a speed demon in the shower.

Life fell into an easy pattern of hanging out together in their spare time over the next couple of months, sometimes with Lily but often without as she tended to spend time in her room alone.

They got on well in spite of, or maybe because of, their differences; their upbringings, their family situations, their financial positions. He was articulate and upbeat where she could sometimes be withdrawn and bolshy. He had a wealthy, overbearing, upper class family with a pile in the country, while her grandparents had a tiny, well-loved terraced house on the edge of Richmond. They found each other's childhoods fascinating and spent hours talking about their patchworks of memories.

It was unthreatening and normal and Rayne quickly realised that she valued Adam's friendship in a way she hadn't anticipated. They talked about books and films, went to parties together, studied textbooks and compared essays in the library. He gave no sign they were anything but friends, slinging his arm around her shoulder companionably, agreeing with her when she pointed out good-looking guys, sometimes to try and needle him, though it never worked.

At first it didn't bother her. She didn't want him to be into her anyway. But the more time they spent together, the more she appreciated how lovely and genuine he was. How much fun they had together. How good he made her feel about herself. How every day the grief over her parents burned a little less brightly. Because of him.

A few weeks before uni was due to close sessions for the Christmas holidays, Rayne was in her room with Lily, finally taping posters up and making the place feel a little more homely with scatter cushions, cup mats (largely to satisfy Adam's needs) and candles. It'd taken her that long to believe she was actually staying.

'Rayne?' Lily looked down at her friend as she stood on the bed holding up a corner of an *Arctic Monkeys* poster.

'Yep?' Rayne tore off a strip of sellotape and handed it to her.

'Don't yell at me but …'

'What?'

'I was just wondering …' she continued hesitantly as she ran her fingers over the tape to make sure it was properly stuck to the wall.

'What is it Lils?'

Lily turned to face her. 'Why aren't you and Adam a couple, given that you're always in each other's pockets and get on so well?'

Rayne dropped the tape on the bed and went over to the window, laughing oddly as she stared out the window. Even to her own ears it sounded off key and high pitched. 'Don't be silly, we don't feel that way about each other.'

'Really?' Lily stepped down off the bed and came over to study the grassed courtyard below them that her friend seemed so interested in. 'Because the way you look at him sometimes, the way your face glows like you've got a light bulb inside you that only he has the switch for, makes me think you like him as more than a friend.' Her voice was soft, 'I know it would be scary for you, that you're worried about getting close to people, but you're friends with both Adam and I already, plus Frankie and Zoe, so would it really be such a leap to imagine him as a boyfriend?'

'Yes. And even if that wasn't the situation, he's been pretty clear that I'm not his type.'

Lily laughed, 'I think you're wrong.' Pausing, she looked at Rayne pointedly and did a very brave thing. 'But if you're really sure you're just friends, do you think Adam might be interested in dating *me*?'

'W-what?' Rayne spluttered, 'You can't. I mean, I didn't think you liked him like that. You never said anything—' panic and dread filled her at the thought of Lily and Adam together. Scrub that, at the thought of Adam being with any other girl. What would she do without him? There hadn't been a day in the last eight weeks they hadn't spent time together. He made her smile every morning and her tummy did that weird flipping thing whenever she caught sight of him. She wanted to be near him, and hear his deep voice say her name and tease her.

And in that moment, she knew. It was scary how territorial she felt. Oh, crap.

She did like him. She really liked him. The thought of losing him to someone else was far scarier than the idea of taking a chance on a relationship with him.

If Lily was right, and he felt that way about her too.

'Shit.' Rayne put a hand to her chest. 'Look, Lily, the truth is-'

Lily raised both eyebrows meaningfully and waited for Rayne to catch up.

'Oh, you're good,' Rayne backed up and grabbed a pillow off her bed. 'You're really good.'

Lily held her hands up, instinctively moving sideways as a pillow sailed past her head. 'You said you wouldn't yell!'

'I'm not,' Rayne smiled, 'but I thought you deserved at least that.' Crossing over to her friend, she gave her a quick squeeze of gratitude.

'What are you going to do about Adam?' Lily asked as she climbed back onto the bed to resume her taping duties.

'I'm not sure. I don't want to ruin our friendship, but at the same time I do want to jump him. I need to think about it.'

'Well, don't take too long,' Lily tossed her hair over her shoulder, 'or someone else might snap him up.'

'I won't,' Rayne murmured, looking across at the jumper he'd given her, which was hanging off the back of her computer chair. It was just about her favourite piece of clothing in the world.

Every day after that the urge to tell him how she felt got stronger, only matched by the quivering nerves and knee-knocking outright fear that doing so would be the wrong thing, and completely mess things up between them.

Studying in Adam's tiny room in halls one night a week later, Rayne fidgeted, feeling edgy and restless. It'd been a tiring day full of lectures and she was mad with longing to kiss him. She glanced around at the perfectly aligned Big Bang Theory posters stuck up on the walls, at the symmetrically arranged pads, pens and books on his narrow desk. Studied the CD player with a precisely stacked pile of CDs beside it.

'Have you ever considered you might be a bit OCD?' she blurted.

He went still on the bed, gripping a pencil between his rigid fingers, shoulders tensing.

'Sorry. Sorry.' Jumping up from the floor, she sank down on the blue quilt cover beside him and touched his arm. 'Forget I said that.' He'd been so good to her and now she'd hit him with this.

His jaw clenched. He breathed in, put the notepad down.

'It's just I worry sometimes. You can get a bit uptight.'

His eyes were cool. The first time he'd looked at her like that. 'You think I'm uptight?'

'No! I just noticed that when you're stressed you tidy, and arrange things. You're very particular. And I've never seen this room messy.' She tried for a joke, 'Which for a boy-'

'Being neat is a crime now?' he interrupted. 'You sound like my dad used to. And Mum always said to leave it to our cleaner, that I should spend more time worrying about more important things than the state of my room.'

'No. Sorry.'

He didn't seem to hear. 'Maybe I don't think there's anything wrong with being tidy.'

'Adam-' she tried to interrupt but he was in full flow.

'Maybe taking charge is a good thing—'

'Adam, stop-'

'Perhaps knowing where everything is and being in control—'

'Adam.' She leaned in and kissed him. It started off as a way to shut him up and melt the tension away from his scowling face, but when she pressed her lips to his, slid her hands into his thick, soft brown hair where it met his collar, the feelings she had for him took over. It felt amazing.

She was just getting into it when he pulled away. Put space between them on the duvet, staring at the opposite wall. He gulped and looked uncomfortable. Clearly he did just see her as a friend. Lily was wrong; Rayne really wasn't his type after all. God, this was awful, mortifying. Her face started to heat up, and an itchy feeling started spreading across her chest. 'I know I'm not pretty.' She closed her eyes and spoke into the silence. Saying it before he could might make it hurt less.

'No, you're not.'

Her eyes sprang open. 'You don't have to agree with me that quickly!'

He ignored the comment, shifting on the duvet to look at her. 'You're not girl-next-door pretty.'

'Okay, thanks Adam, I get it,' she bit. She started to unfold her long legs from the bed, planning on a quick getaway.

'But you are striking.' He said seriously, grabbing her arm to make her sit. 'And very attractive. Strikingly attractive. I'd be happy with that.'

'Well thanks for trying to bolster the old ego.' Glowing but smarting as well. What if she wanted to be girl-next-door pretty? 'Really kind.' But her ego was kind of destroyed seeing as he'd just rejected her. 'Obviously not attractive enough for you.' She sat back, crossed her arms, trying not to show how gutted she was. How was she going to face him tomorrow? This was sooo bad.

'God, it's not that!' he said, expression incredulous. 'I like you. I think you're amazing. I love that you're spirited, bright and ambitious. I really love the fact that you're not like the other girls back home; you've lived such a free life, travelling with your parents, and are so much more worldly than them, with an incredibly open mind. None of the other girls have excited me the way you do. I wanted to be your friend first, and get to know you. I didn't want to scare you off – and most of all, I don't want to take advantage. You're still grieving.'

Relief almost knocked her out. Was that what it was? He was being sweet, gallant Adam? 'Yes, I am grieving. Yes, the thought of falling for you scares me shitless. But you wouldn't be taking advantage. This is what I want. But, if you want to go that way,' she grinned widely, wrenched off her top, revealing a black lacy bra, and his eyes nearly popped out of his head, 'take advantage of me. Take total and utter advantage.' Leaping up, she undid her skirt and let it fall to the carpet. Knelt down over his lap on the bed, straddling him. 'All night. Starting tonight. Now. I want you to.' She kissed him hard, slipped her tongue into his mouth. Bit his lower lip. Moved back to look into his pale blue eyes. 'Or are you too much of a nice boy to accept a girl's invitation?'

He laughed once, hoarsely, searching her eyes for something. Apparently finding it, he yanked her closer by grabbing her hips, making her gasp. 'No.' He replied in a deep voice. 'You only have to ask once.'

'Really? I thought you'd put up more of a fight—'

His hands slid down to her bum, fingertips creeping beneath the edge of her knickers. 'Shut up, Rayne.'

And she obeyed for several hours, while he demonstrated in his narrow, student bed exactly how well nice, considerate, generous boys accepted invitations. It was only afterwards he told her it had been his first time. She wouldn't have known it from the things he'd done to her.

'You've got that look on your face again.'

'What look?' Rayne shook her head, and frowned at her friend.

'The Adam look.'

'Shut it, you.' Rayne growled.

'Fine. But you do realise we've been sat here stationary for the last five minutes while you've been gazing at nothing through the windscreen? A girl could get old waiting for you to start the engine.'

'Sorry. Home then.' She paused, drumming her fingers on the steering wheel, purple gemmed cocktail ring catching the sunlight.

'You don't sound sure.'

'Do you mind if we go and have a drink somewhere? I'm not in the mood for home yet.'

'That's not like you. You're usually dying to get back and work on a story.'

'I know.' For some reason the thought of returning to an empty flat was depressing. 'I'll have you dropped off at home by seven, okay?'

'Sure,' Lily started climbing out of the car. 'Let's leave the Mini here and walk up the road. It's still warm and there are a few places on the High Street. Although I guess you know that from your indecent proposal lunch with Adam.'

'Ha ha, very good,' Rayne replied before diving back into the car to grab her bag. 'Let's go.' She spoke as she re-emerged, locking the car and putting her keys away.

The pavements were still surprisingly crowded as they walked up the road. They swerved the Dog and Fox on account of the massive gaggle of men out front who appeared to have been drinking since dawn with no intention of stopping. Their volume was ear-splitting, they stank of beer and they appeared to be rating women as they walked past. When one of them shouted 'Nine,' at Lily and another shouted 'Eight,' at Rayne, Lily ducked her head down. Rayne stuck her middle finger up at them as they strolled past. Neanderthals.

Agreeing on a posh bar just up the road, they settled at a table on the wooden decked sun terrace out back, surrounded by pink and purple flowers in pots.

'What do you want to drink?' Lily stood up.

'Just a coke please.'

'Coke! I thought you were going to have at least one. You'd be okay on a small glass of wine, surely?'

'Probably, but I'd rather not take the chance with my licence. I'd miss driving my baby too much. Besides, I kind of feel like I need a clear head at the moment. You go for it though. Enjoy.'

'You can't be responsible all the time, you know,' Lily wagged a hand at her. 'You've got to live a little once in a while. All you do is work, work, work.' She turned to go into the pub and let out a squeal. 'Ooh, look, there's Flynn!' She simultaneously smoothed her hair and adjusted the bodice of her dress. 'I'm going to go and say hi.'

'You only saw him half an hour ago, Lils. Maybe you shouldn't seem too keen?'

Lily gave her an exasperated look. 'You know I don't play those sorts of games. If I like someone, I like someone.'

'I understand that. And I don't play games either, but there's such a thing as being too available.' One of the reasons Lily seemed to regularly get her heart stamped on.

'Better than not being available at all. Oh, Adam's with him. Are you coming over?'

'Nope, I'm happy here thanks.' The memory of how he'd pressed in to tuck his business card into her back pocket still made her go hot and tingly. She wasn't sure she could trust herself around him.

Lily shrugged. 'Okey-dokey. I'll be back in five.'

'Have fun.' Rayne smiled, tipping her face back and closing her eyes to make the most of the evening sunshine. Which was relaxing for all of thirty seconds before she started thinking that it was silly not to have gone in with Lily. What was she trying to prove? Adam might think she was being weird, or was upset about something for staying out here and being anti-social.

With a sigh, she heaved herself out of the chair and stepped inside. It took a moment for her eyes to adjust to the dimmer interior. When they did, it was to see Adam leaning up against the bar, surrounded by a random group of people, with some brunette girl hanging off his arm. Standing and watching him laugh down at her, Rayne was aware of stinging jealousy creeping along every nerve ending, anger blasting through her. She wanted to race up and yell at the redhead. *Get your hands off him!*

Except he wasn't hers and he was single so he could do whatever he bloody wanted. It was funny, over the years the knowledge that he was out there somewhere, getting on with his life, perhaps in a long-term relationship, hadn't bothered her that much. On the occasions he'd fluttered through her head, she'd hoped he was happy, had found someone to be happy with. It hadn't been her back then, at uni, when they were both still practically children.

She hadn't been ready for him and the life he wanted. It was only fair therefore that he would have moved on. Meaning she had absolutely no right to feel jealousy or longing when faced with him now, with another woman.

But, seeing him, spending time with him again, had changed everything. He wasn't some faded, ghost-of-boyfriend-past out in the world, he was *here* and *real*, and still lovely … as well as hotter than ever. She was super aware of him, of her physical reaction, her skin tingling, feeling breathless, a throbbing between her thighs. She couldn't stop staring at his lean hips in the tight jeans, her eyes creeping upwards to focus on the bicep that bulged in his arm when he lifted the glass to drain his drink. As he slipped out of the girl's grasp and turned to the barman, he still had the best arse she'd ever seen on a guy. Her mouth dropped open at the taut curve of it.

Maybe the jagged jealousy was also because of his offer, the awareness that she could be rolling around naked with him if she wanted to, having a great time, and the thought of him doing it with the brunette instead gave her a sick feeling.

Lily had said sex with an ex would be perfect.

Adam had agreed.

She wanted him. It would give them closure.

Her feelings were all over the place, but maybe one hot night of unbelievable sex would crystallize them and she could deal with them, whatever that might look like. He was probably leaving in a few months so the chances of running into him again would be reduced. Or maybe it wouldn't be as good as she remembered between them and that would help get rid of the nostalgic gooey feelings.

Lily said she was responsible all the time, and needed to live a little. Maybe she was right, maybe Rayne needed to let the bad girl – the one she'd been in that lost year before uni – out of her cage for a while. At least she'd be safe doing that with Adam. No matter how many years had trickled past, she still trusted him implicitly not to do anything to consciously hurt her.

And if it's a choice between her or me, I know which one is preferable. Squashing down every good girl instinct she had, shutting down all sensible thoughts, she marched straight up to Adam and tapped him on the shoulder.

Swinging around, he grinned. 'Hello, you. I didn't think I'd see you again so soon.'

Rising on tiptoes she planted a whopper of a kiss on him, pulling him close by the back pockets of his jeans.

It was scorching hot and intense. As his hands slid up into her hair without hesitation and he kissed her back, the years fell away and she was back in halls again, kissing the boy she loved. Except he was an even better kisser now, nibbling on her lower lip, tongue seeking hers sensuously. Rubbing herself against him she made a soft *mmmm,* totally forgetting they were in public.

There was a distant huffing sound before a pair of noisy heels clicked away. Presumably the brunette stalking off.

When they came up for air she simply looked at him and said. 'Yes. Now.'

Grabbing her hand he spun around to Flynn, Lily and a few other stragglers. 'Sorry guys, we've got somewhere to be.'

Lily gaped at Rayne, eyes round. Slowly an approving twinkle filtered into them and she winked. 'It's okay, I'll get a taxi home.' She offered, 'Or Flynn can give me a lift home?'

'Sure,' Flynn agreed eagerly. 'I was designated driver tonight anyway, so I haven't been drinking.'

'Fine. No funny business though.' Adam joked.

Lily punched him in the arm, blushing. 'Ha ha. We're not in halls any more, Adam. I can take care of myself.'

Flynn nodded at Adam. 'I'll get her home safe.'

Rayne leaned in and gave Lily a hug and kiss on the cheek. 'Thanks, speak tomorrow.'

'Definitely.' Lily whispered, 'And remember my plan. Great sex, no emotions.'

'Of course.' Pulling back and trying for a look that said *I'm not stupid!*

'Come on,' Adam tugged on a belt loop at the back of her shorts.

'Yes.' She turned back to him, grabbed his hand, palm sliding against hers. Her fingers tightened and she watched his pale blue eyes start to burn. 'I'm ready.'

'A hot tub? Really? Wow.' Rayne swept out onto the decking at the back of the luxury flat after a long car journey across town. Adam had offered to call a cab but Rayne preferred to have her own transport, and needed her zippy little car for work the next day. How the hell she was going to type today's stories up, she didn't know. Possibly with a mega-early start and hiding from her editor until they were done. Right at this moment, she couldn't quite bring herself to care. Unprecedented for her. Men never came above her work.

'Nice, huh?' he mused.

'Impressive.' She studied the massive tub as he hefted the lid off and pressed a few buttons on the side.

'I can afford it.' He shrugged, as lime green lights came on and the water started to bubble gently. 'Want to take a dip? It'll only take a few minutes to heat up.' His eyes darkened. 'We never did make use of the jacuzzi at Lily's parents place.'

'That's right, we didn't.'

She could remember that Friday evening so clearly, staying at the exclusive Kensington house while Lily's mum and dad were in the Caribbean. She and Adam were down from Loughborough so he could attend an interview for the work placement as part of his degree. She'd already secured her own forty week placement at a regional newspaper based on the outskirts of Surrey, commutable from her grandparents' house. It would be strange living with them, especially after living in a small flat with Adam for a year, but it made financial sense, and they were willing for Adam to move in too if he could get a placement in London or surrounds.

He'd been striking out so far and his mood had darkened over the course of the previous two days. Rayne knew he was starting to get desperate. The problem was, his mum had called him home for a few weeks due to some emergency issue at *Parsons* and he'd all but missed the window for applications, and assistance from the uni to help him get a placement. Therefore a lot of the placements had been filled. She'd had a sneaking suspicion Tamara might have done it on purpose.

He'd returned that evening wearing his best suit, looking very mature and respectable for a twenty year old. She'd leapt out of the six-man jacuzzi in a tiny black bikini, slightly sozzled on white wine, eager to know how he'd got on. Hurling herself at him, she looped her arms around the back of his neck, boobs squashed against his hard chest. 'What happened? What happened? Did they love you? They must have loved you.'

He pushed her away, gesturing to his suit jacket. 'What are you doing? Look at the state of this thing.' He held the expensive material away from his body between finger and thumb, frowning. 'You've probably ruined it.'

Her face dropped. She hated it when he was like this, so stiff and formal. When he was stressed, the neat-freak thing was worse. 'Most guys would be thrilled to have their hot girlfriends greeting them in a wet bikini,' she accused, half teasing, half angry.

'Maybe I'm not most guys.' He threw her a look.

Disdain? Disappointment? It was the way his mum looked at her on their rare visits to his family home. The thing was, she could almost ignore it from Tamara. But not from Adam.

He ran a hand through his hair. 'Sorry.'

'I know,' she sighed, her lazy, relaxing afternoon dropping away. 'So,' she stepped back, wrapping her arms around her suddenly chilly skin, 'how did it go?'

'Fine.' He replied flatly. 'I'm going to go and change out of these damp clothes and have a shower.' His mouth turned down, jaw tight.

Sympathy coursed through her. This wasn't him, not really. He was usually only like this when his mum talked about his future at *Parsons* or made pointed comments about daughters of friends they'd seen at social events, and what a good match they'd be for him.

Most of the time he was her caring, kind boyfriend. Relaxed, playful and supportive.

Reminding herself of that she forced a cheerful smile. 'Wanna join me in the jacuzzi instead of taking a shower?'

'We'll see.' His lips squeezed together.

Which meant no, when he was in this mood. It was best to leave him to it until he'd worked through whatever was bugging him. Was it ridiculous that she wanted to cry? She'd been so excited for him about the interview, and about a whole weekend away together in a nice house once the interviews were over, the sights of London to be explored together.

So she tried again, in case he was willing to share. 'Do you want to talk about it?'

'No. I don't.' He raised his voice, making her jump. 'Just leave me alone, okay?'

Turning away, 'Okay,' she muttered, standing up and climbing out of the tub. Grabbing a towelling robe off the side, she wrestled her way into it, the fabric catching on her wet skin. 'I'll turn the jacuzzi off.'

'I can't do this.' Adam's voice froze her in position.

'Can't do what?'

'I can't go on pretending that I'm happy. That I'm okay with this being my life.'

'What do you mean, Adam?' she asked tremulously, eyes tearing up and fear closing her throat.

'I'm miserable,' he ran his hands through his hair, clutching handfuls in his palms as if to pull it out.

'With me?' she whispered, feeling like he'd punched her. Winded.

Unable to breath.

'What? God no, of course not!' Crossing the patio he hugged her tight, then pushed her away so she could see his face. 'I hate the degree. I'm bored out of my brain and can't stand the thought of another two years studying something I have zero interest in and couldn't care less about. Mum is putting pressure on me to work at *Parsons* for my placement if uni will let me. Meaning I'd be home for a year.' He yanked the knot in his tie down and wrenched the whole thing over his head. Turning his back on her he stalked into the lounge. Unfreezing, she ran after him, needing to understand what he was saying.

'And?' she sank down beside him where he was sat on the sofa hunched forward, arms hanging between his legs.

'I can't do this. I can't go back. I'm not ready. I feel suffocated just at the thought.' He undid a button on his shirt and took both of her hands in his, clutching so hard she could barely feel her fingers. 'And I've realised that I don't ever want to go back. Not now, and not in two years time. I need to see the world. I need to see some of the things that you've seen. See the sun set in the Sahara, watch the Northern Lights swirl up and fill the sky.' His eyes, that had been so anxious and dull, started filling with excitement. 'I'm dropping out, Ray. I'm not going to live the life Mum wants me to. I'm going to live the life I want to. Maybe it's selfish but I can't sacrifice my whole life, my chance of happiness to make her happy. She can find someone else to run it. I don't want it, or deserve it, feeling like I do. Dad would have understood. We weren't close just before he died, there was too much going on with Mum and the business, but when I was younger he talked about regret sometimes. He had many, and taking over the business young was one of them.'

'What are you saying Adam? If you're dropping out of uni, what does that mean? What do you mean, see the world?' There was a tumbling, roaring feeling inside her head, and she felt dizzy.

'I want to go abroad and work for a charity. I've been looking into it—'

'You have? You didn't say anything.' Because he'd already started to pull away from her? 'You want me to wait for you? How long for?'

'I wasn't sure … I was just exploring my options, but after today … after the interview I called the charity I've been discussing this with, and they'd be pleased to have me. I could leave in the next few weeks. I'm sure this is what I want to do. It wouldn't be fair for me to ask you to wait that long, particularly as I don't know how long I'm going for. Come with me, Ray. We'll spend two years, maybe three, travelling overseas, volunteering or working for good causes. I still have part of the trust fund I accessed when I was eighteen—'

'What?' she gulped. 'But what about my degree? I'm going to start my placement in a few months. I worked really hard to get it. Then my final year … What are you asking me to do? Give up my dream for yours?'

He stared at her like he'd never seen her before. 'You can defer for a year or two. Or get a placement abroad. We'll work something out. You could get some international experience.'

Jerking her hands away from his, she got up, stumbling backwards over the long robe. 'But it's all set up. And I don't want to defer. I want to work at that paper and then finish my degree before moving here permanently. I've moved around my whole life, Adam, you know that. The last two years, being in one place, it's the happiest I've ever been. I need roots, I need certainty.' Her voice was rising, choked with tears. 'I can't believe you're asking this of me, just dropping it on me. I can't believe you would ask that I abandon everything I've worked so hard for—'

He sprang up, 'I can't believe you won't come with me, or even consider it. I thought it was us, you and me together. Please, Ray. Come with me. You love me, I know you do.'

'It's not about that. Of course I love you, but in the same way you feel suffocated by the thought of *Parsons*, I feel suffocated by the thought of being rootless for however many years it takes to satisfy this need, this travel bug, in you.' Wrapping her arms around her waist. 'It wouldn't feel like an adventure Adam, like it would for you, it would feel like,' groping for the right words, 'a prison sentence.'

'You won't even think about it?' his voice was filled with disbelief. 'Talk to your grandparents and the university, maybe speak to the paper and see if they'd be willing to hold the position for a while?'

He looked torn and she ached to go to him and tell him what he wanted to hear, soothe him with her touch but her feet wouldn't move. 'No, because that's not what I want. I'm sorry.' She couldn't believe that twenty minutes ago they'd been in love and planning a future together, and now with this bombshell, they were talking about the unthinkable. The end of them.

Tears started rolling down her face, accompanied by big, fat sobs. 'Are you really sure about this?' she cried. 'You can't quit uni and tell your mum you're saying no to the family business, and then find a job here in the city?'

He shook his head, face pale, blue irises glassy. 'No. I need to get away. I need freedom.' His tone hardened. 'So you have to make a choice, Ray. It's me. Or your career. You can't have both. What are you going to do?'

Rayne faltered. She thought about the nights they'd spent together, curled up in bed, his arms holding her close. The way he made love to her, like he couldn't get enough and never would. The wonderful support he'd given her over the last two years in dealing with her grief. The laughter, and late nights, and friendship they'd shared. She didn't want to give that up, was not sure if she could bear to. But then she thought about dropping out of uni, of calling the paper and telling them she wouldn't be starting in October, of travelling the world like she had when she was younger. Never staying in one place more than three months at a time, leaving new friends behind each time, having no proper home.

She couldn't do it again. She had too much here that she wanted.

Looking at him helplessly, she shook her head in despair.

'I guess I have my answer then,' he answered grimly, marching from the room and reappearing no more than thirty seconds later with his bag half unzipped with clothes spilling out of it.

Rayne bolted up from her spot on the sofa. 'Please, Adam, wait.'

'You've made your decision.' He threw open the door.

She grabbed his arm and tugged him back by the shirt sleeve. 'Just wait, let's sleep on it—'

'I've been living a lie for two years, I can't do it a minute longer.'

'But you're asking me to sacrifice my happiness for yours,' she flung back at him furiously, 'so how are you any better than your mum?'

His jaw clenched and he stumbled out of the house, gazing up at her from the gravel driveway for what would turn out to be the last time in nearly five years. 'Maybe I'm not any better than her.' Hoisting his bag on his shoulder, he backed away before twisting around and breaking into a run.

He left her there alone, staring after him, her heart breaking into tiny pieces in her chest.

They stared across the hot tub at each other, in their shared recollection of that night.

'You made me feel horrible.' She said softly. 'You put me on the spot and gave me an impossible choice.'

'I know.' He ran a hand through his hair. 'I'm so sorry. The only thing I can say is that I was young, and felt trapped and desperate. I should have spoken to you sooner. About how awful I was feeling and what I was thinking of doing. I should have given you more time, but there was this little voice in my head overruling everything else. *Run away, run away, run away.* I was scared that if I didn't leave straight away, Mum would somehow convince me to stay.'

Tucking her hair behind her ears for something to do, because there was no way she was prepared for a conversation this heavy.

'That's the problem with relationships when you're young, isn't it?' she sighed. 'There's too much chance of miscommunication, you're not mature enough to deal with the big things.'

'Maybe. Or maybe we just wanted different things back then. The time wasn't right for us.' Adam glanced away, tapping a few buttons on the hot tub, so that jets of water shot out. 'I must admit that I was angry with you for a long time. But after a while I understood the choice you made. Because apart from that argument, we'd always got on, we complemented each other. We were happy, right?'

'We didn't see eye to eye all the time. We always argued about the housework.' She said lightly, recalling the year in the shared flat, the bickering followed by the frantic make up sex. This was too hard. It brought up too many bittersweet regrets and what-ifs. If she wasn't careful she might dissolve into tears the way she'd used to after her parents died. She didn't do that nowadays. This was still grief though, only a different kind.

'You were lazy,' he replied to her comment, but the corner of his mouth quirked up.

'Maybe,' she conceded, 'but you were too far the other way. Everything had to be tidied and cleaned the instant it was used.'

'I couldn't relax with it messy.' He strode past her into the kitchen, opening the fridge and bending over to take something out. 'I'm not as bad anymore.' His disembodied voice floated toward her where she stood on the decking, admiring his lovely bum.

'N-no?' she fanned her face, glad he wasn't able to see her reaction.

'No.' He straightened up, a bottle of frosty champagne dangling from his fingers. 'I can leave a bit of a mess nowadays.'

'Really?' she raised an eyebrow.

'Yes!' he replied straight-faced, grabbing two flutes and a metal wine cooler from overhead cupboards. Then, gazing across at her, he broke into a wide grin. 'For a few hours at least.'

'Ha ha. Well, I'm better too. When you live alone you soon learn no-one is going to pick up after you. Anyway ...' Swinging around, she trailed her fingers through the hot, churning water. Enough of the yesterdays, it was time to enjoy the here and now. 'How about this dip you promised me?'

'Right away, Miss.'

She felt him come up behind her, heard a clatter as he put everything down. Shivered when he pressed a soft kiss on the back of her neck. Let out a quiet moan when he rubbed his whiskery stubble along her bare shoulder.

'I just thought of something.' She said in a strangled voice. 'I don't have a bikini with me. I'll have to go in, in my underwear.'

'Or you could go in naked.' He whispered wickedly in her ear, hands sliding down over her hips, a firm finger travelling beneath her shirt to gently stroke her belly button piercing.

She gulped at the spark of his touch and tried to think clearly. If she took everything off, the treasure on her necklace would be revealed. 'Won't your neighbours see?'

'It's a pretty private balcony,' he gestured to the side, 'only one other property overlooks it. And I don't think they're in. It'll be fine.'

'Hang on, I'm not doing it alone!' Knowing he'd never in a million years join her.

'I wouldn't dream of letting you.'

Spinning around, 'You'll go in starkers too?'

'Yes. Why not?'

She stared at him in amazement. 'God, what happened to you?'

He shrugged. 'When you've cliff jumped nude in Thailand on a new moon with a beach full of people watching you, sitting in a hot tub on your balcony isn't such a big deal.'

'How—' she gaped.

'A dare,' he anticipated her question. 'From a very good friend, who taught me a lot about life and how to chill out.' There was a flicker of pain in his pale eyes but it faded as he looked her up and down challengingly. 'Anyway, get your kit off.'

'Fine.' She hastily undid the necklace and stuffed it in her pocket. 'Don't want it to get damaged,' she explained. Whipping off her top, she wiggled out of her shorts, kicking them aside. This was it. All or nothing. So what if she was more than four years older since the last time he'd seen her naked? He'd always loved her body, and though she was curvier now, if you were attracted to someone it was the whole package you liked. An extra inch here or a dimple there didn't matter.

He gulped, stepping back so he could see more of her in the matching red bra and knickers. 'Wow. You look amazing.'

'Thanks.' Trying not to beam at the compliment but failing miserably.

'My turn.' Undoing his shirt to reveal the most defined pecs and the most ridiculous set of abs she'd ever seen.

'You-' her voice deserted her. How embarrassing. 'You look great too. I mean, more than great.' Ryan Gosling eat your heart out. 'You obviously go to the gym.'

'Nah.' He unzipped his jeans and pushed them down his thighs. She gazed open-mouth as his back muscles rippled. She didn't know they could do that. 'I prefer to be outside,' he explained as he straightened up and stepped closer, 'I run a lot, do press ups and sit ups, mainly in Regents' Park. I love being outside.'

'That's miles away!'

'Just over three. Doesn't take too long if you run it.'

'You never used to be outdoorsy.' She sighed as his fingers trailed along her collarbone and came to rest at the back of her neck, tunnelling into her shoulder-length hair. It felt so damn good, like coming home at the end of a trip to where you belonged.

'I became a bit of a sun worshipper while I worked abroad. I love the feeling of sunshine on my face, seeing waves of heat rise in the distance, watching a beautiful orange-red sunrise.'

'You must be bummed to be back in Blighty then.' Why did

they keep talking? Surely they should have got down to it by now, should be rolling around on the floor getting messy and sweaty? No point in sex with an ex if you never got to the sex part.

'It has its compensations.' He kissed her, bit her bottom lip, then moved his face a breath away, his fingers massaging her scalp, sending tingles down her entire body. 'And it was time for me to come home. Time for me to settle, at least for a while.'

'Uh-huh. Good.' Her brain function was quickly disappearing with his fingers working their magic. Eyes sliding shut, she squirmed closer and tucked shaking fingertips into the waistband of his jockey shorts. His skin was burning hot, and smooth. 'Adam?'

'Yeah?' He cleared his throat, his other hand tracing a circle on her lower back, before sliding into the top of her knickers.

'Do you think we can hit the hot tub later?' Pushing her bra clad boobs against his solid chest.

He groaned, squeezing her bum and pressing his hips against hers, so her hands were trapped between their bodies. 'What have you got in mind?' he demanded hoarsely.

A burning, pleasurable ache started spreading outwards from her pelvis, clenching her inner thigh muscles, tightening her nipples. 'Kitchen. Now.'

'Yes. Definitely.' He picked her up with flattering speed, arm muscles flexing. Wordlessly she wrapped her legs and arms around him as he strode into the apartment. 'Sod the tub, and the champagne.' He gritted his teeth as he set her down on a kitchen unit and sank down to his knees to start kissing the inside of her thigh. 'They can wait.'

She moaned and grabbed his hair as his mouth travelled higher, his stubble scraping her sensitive skin.

It took three hours and two attempts before they made it into the tub. The whole bottle of champagne was consumed at a leisurely pace … and neither of them wore a stitch of clothing.

Lifting her head from Adam's ridged stomach, Rayne started sitting up. Dawn light filtered in through the blinds. It was going to be another sunny day. Despite that, and the incredible night they'd had, she felt dark inside, sad. She'd totally missed the point of Lily's plan. Sex with Adam, without emotions? Yeah, right. All the old feelings had boomeranged on her. The joy of being with him, the person who'd been her world for over two years. The easy pleasure she took in his company and the way he made her body sing like no-one else had ever been able to.

'Where are you going, Ray?' He tugged her back down to lie across his chest.

She studied him from under her lashes, the nickname and him lying back against the pillows flooding memories back. Other times and places they'd lain in bed together, talking and laughing. 'I figured it was time for me to leave.' She murmured. 'We got our closure, right?'

'You think so?' he asked roughly.

She pulled away, grabbing a duck-down pillow and holding it to her front. 'I thought it would help. This. But it hasn't.' She paused. 'It was great though. The sex I mean,' she finished lamely, wishing she could vanish into a convenient cave somewhere right about now.

'I know, to both.' He sat up, raking a hand through his ruffled brown hair.

The sheet fell to his waist and even with the serious turn of their conversation her gaze flitted over his gorgeous body. 'Are you angry with me? For back then? For now?' This was horrible, the gnawing guilt returning to bite her.

He took in her expression, and sighed. 'Honestly? Maybe I was still holding on to some resentment that you didn't love me enough to come with me, back then. But talking to you about this stuff, and hearing you say last night how hard it was for you when I dropped it on you ... I was like my mum, I was selfish to a degree. And before you say it, you probably could have been a bit more flexible too, but I pretty much blind-sided you. So I do understand. 'Now, I don't feel anything other than regret that our timing was off.'

'I see.' At his words more of the tiny, balled up knots of tension and pain she'd felt at lunch the day before unfurled, but it didn't go altogether. Their timing had been off then, and it was still off now. He'd said he was only staying for a few months. He still wasn't ready to settle down. And while she wasn't actively looking for a serious relationship, she couldn't do this again, couldn't be with him only to lose him when he went off to see the world again. That hadn't changed for her. She still needed a place to call home, she still wasn't ready to give up her life for him. History did repeat itself after all.

Leaping off the bed, she started toward the door in search of her clothes which were scattered around his flat.

'Where are you going?'

'I have to go to work.'

'You're leaving? Just like that?' He bounced up off the bed, completely naked.

'It's for the best. Nothing's really changed. I'm settled in London, you're likely to go off somewhere again.' Scuttling out of the room she made a beeline for the kitchen, where she found her red lacy knickers on the floor and the matching bra hanging from a cupboard handle. Scrambling around, she was at least in her underwear by the time he came storming out of his bedroom in his jockey shorts.

'So, that's it? How the hell is this closure?'

'I don't know what to tell you, Adam, apart from the fact that you're wrong about something.'

'And that would be?' Putting his hand on his hips.

'You said I didn't love you enough to go with you. You're wrong. I did love you enough. I love – loved,' she fumbled the words, 'you enough that I didn't want you to be unhappy. If you'd have stayed you would have been miserable, you said it yourself. If I came with you, I would have been miserable, you would have known it and it would have dragged you down and ruined your adventure. The best thing was to break up and let us both move on, doing what we needed to do back then.'

'Move on? I was miserable for months out there. I was helping build villages and they gave me an award for being the quickest worker. Heaving bricks around and mixing cement until I ached all over so that I could fall into bed every night exhausted, was the only thing that helped me survive.' He stopped and ran a hand around the back of his neck. 'Thank you for saying it, but I can't believe you suffered the same.'

'I did.' Shaking her head. 'I adored you.'

'Really?' He stared at her, waiting for her to say more.

'Yes. Here, if you don't believe me …' She was committed now, she may as well own up. She owed him the truth. Maybe this would give him the closure he needed, even if it didn't bring her the same peace. Going over to the sofa, where they'd brought their clothes in from outside in the early hours of the morning, she dug around in her shorts pocket. Padding over to him, she placed her gold necklace in his open palm, watching him expectantly.

He frowned down at it. 'Your parents' Claddagh rings. And …'

'The ring you bought me for our first anniversary, that we always joked was a pseudo engagement ring.'

'You kept it.'

'Yes.'

'And you wear it every day,' he mused, running his fingers over the jewellery.

'Uh-huh.' Tears were welling up.

'I always thought you'd never agree to marry me. That's why I never asked. If I'd asked when I wanted to, it would have been about two weeks after we met,' he admitted.

'Wow,' she gulped, touched. 'What made you think I wouldn't have married you eventually, if you hadn't decided to go abroad?'

'Your parents never married, so I thought that like them, you didn't believe in all that.'

'We were too young to think about it back then. If my parents were still here now, they'd probably want me either barefoot and pregnant or campaigning for justice in some way, but ultimately they'd respect my decisions.'

He squeezed her fingers lightly. 'What are your feelings? Do you want to be barefoot and pregnant at some point? Will you settle down?'

'Not yet, no. But yes, one day. I'm really enjoying my career, I'm only just coming up twenty-six and I've not met anyone I'd even consider having kids with. But someday I'll get married and start a family.'

'Interesting.' He lifted a hand, hooked her hair behind her ear, stroked her cheekbone.

She gulped. 'What's interesting?'

'Considering what you've just said, I've got a proposition for you.'

The breath left her lungs. 'What's that?'

'I'm sticking around, Ray. I haven't got any plans to go abroad again, other than the occasional holiday. I said that it might only be temporary because I didn't want to scare you off. I was trying to keep things light-hearted. But I'm here to stay, to settle down in the UK. In fact,' he reached around her and pulled some paperwork from a drawer, 'one of my jobs this weekend is looking for a property to buy.'

'You are?' she gazed at him, afraid to hope. 'It is?'

'Yes. So, how would you feel about having sex with someone who's no longer an ex?'

'You want to try again?' She squeaked, heart thudding. 'Even though you agreed with me that you can't go back?'

Picking her up against his chest, he ambled to the sofa, stopping to kiss her tenderly a few times on the way. Sitting down with her on his lap, he hugged her against him and rested his forehead against hers. 'Going forward seems like a plan to me.' He kissed her again, inched back to meet her gaze. 'We've both grown up.

We'll talk more this time and make decisions together, instead of getting distracted by fun and sex.'

Her mouth curved slowly. 'Well, I wouldn't be too hasty …'

Throwing his head back, he laughed loud and low, making her stomach do that swoopy-turny thing.

'Seriously,' she grabbed his face between her hands, 'why would you risk it? Are you really sure?'

'I am.'

'How? Why?'

'Because,' he placed his long, magic-making fingers over hers, 'I knew I had to try again, when I realised I was still in love with you.'

'When did you realise that?' She grinned, the sound of him saying it heavenly, as crazy as it was after so many years apart.

'Isn't it obvious?' he grinned back. 'After I'd begged the couple sat behind you to swap tickets with me, while you were eating strawberries at Wimbledon.'

Picnics in Hyde Park

1

Matt Reilly is a complete, unbelievable bastard and I'm going to make him pay, Zoe Harper vowed as she pounded the gold lion-head knocker against the door of his exclusive Knightsbridge residence.

When there was no response, she switched to thumping the glossy black wood with the side of her fist.

Thud. Thud. Thud.

Answer. The. Door.

Utter fury was squeezing her chest so tight it felt like her ribs were suffocating her lungs and a horrible pressure was building behind her eyeballs, the sure sign of a tension headache.

Where the hell was he? She stepped back to gaze up at the impressive facade of the town house, which had to be at least four storeys tall including the basement area below her. The top two floors were exposed brickwork but the ground and lower floors were painted white, decorated with manicured window boxes. The property screamed refined wealth, as did the beautiful leafy communal garden area in the middle of the square. He must have paid extra for the property, which sat back from the road slightly. It was one of the only houses with off-road parking.

She turned to look at the gravel driveway. Someone had to be in, there were three cars parked up; a garish, canary-yellow convertible sports model, a sexy low-slung black supercar and a more modest silver Prius hybrid.

Thudding the door again, there was still no answer.

If she was some kick-ass action movie heroine she could bust the door down, flatten whichever of the selfish idiots was inside (although both at the same time would be preferable) and just be done with it. But at five foot seven, as well as pounds lighter than she'd been in years, she hardly looked or felt the part. Still, if there was anything guaranteed to bring out her fighting side it was protecting her younger sister Melody. She was her only proper family left apart from their Great Aunt Ruth, who'd always been distant and had all the affection of a watermelon.

What it came down to was that anyone who hurt Melody deserved justice. But she didn't really believe in violence, and ruining her beautiful nails with their miniature stars and stripes design on every tip didn't appeal either. The manicure was a present from her ex-boss Liberty, named after the statue of. It was something to remember New York by, a city she'd come to love. But better not to think about that, or what else she'd loved and lost.

Where the heck was Mr. High and Mighty Reilly, or for that matter, his younger brother Stephen? Surely they had enough staff to answer the bloody door for them. A girl could die of heatstroke out here. The midday sun was ferocious and prickling heat along the back of her neck. It was sure to be scarlet by dinner time.

Thud. Thud. Thud.

Her hand was never going to be the same again. Then she'd be suing the sods for personal injury as well as emotional trauma for Melody. Her sibling had been crying so hard at Jemima's flat in multicultural, packed Holloway that Zoe hadn't been able to get the full story on arrival from Heathrow. There'd just been a lot of mumbling and sobbing around swollen red eyes and handfuls of soggy tissues. Still, what she'd figured out had been enough to instantly trigger her big sister reflexes. The stale, stuffy black cab had made for a nightmare journey across London but the sunlight glinting off the windows had matched her heated, murderous thoughts perfectly. She'd avoided direct eye contact with the chatty driver, jaw clenched as she replayed the fragments of her sister's story in her head.

Fell in love with Stephen … Matt ended it, fired me … kicked me out without notice … never see the kids again … looked after them for three years!

How dare he? It was bloody outrageous and unbelievably unfair. How could anyone be so uncaring that they'd do someone who trusted them out of a relationship, job, home and salary all on the same day? So here she was outside of his posh, rich-guy's, *I'm so fabulous* home, fully intending to grab her sister's belongings as well as telling Matt Reilly exactly what she thought of a guy who'd treat a naïve twenty-two year old like dirt. If she could grab his brother by the scruff of the neck at the same time and give him a good shake for helping break her sister's heart, she'd do that too. He had a lot of explaining to do as to why he wasn't answering Mel's calls.

Bloody men. They were a faithless lot at the best of times, the reason she'd left the States after five long years. But her sister's boss had reached new levels of bastardom, if that was even a word.

Part of her wished that when confronted, Matt might admit he'd made a terrible mistake, beg forgiveness, tell Melody that of course she was good enough for his brother, and ask her to come back to them. But the text that had just pinged on her mobile meant the idea was a non-starter.

> **Appreciate the support Sis, but**
> **please don't cause a scene and**
> **DON'T try and get my job back.**
> **I'm never going back there.**
> **M x**

Zoe didn't really want her sister anywhere near them anyway. Still, an apology from Matt, an opportunity for Melody to say goodbye to the kids properly, pick up her belongings and be offered some kind of compensation for the notice pay she was surely entitled to would be something. Along with some explanation as to why Stephen had gone AWOL and seemed to be letting Matt make all the decisions. Perhaps he didn't feel able to stand up to him? Or maybe he was intimidated by his older brother's success.

According to the tabloids, Stephen was abroad a lot of the time, a playboy who basically partied and shopped his way around Europe with the family money. Why her sister had fallen for him she couldn't understand. At thirty, Matt was older by seven years, a famous music producer who was hardly ever out of the press, despite his attempts to evade the spotlight. Snapping pictures of his children was a rabid hobby for British journos and there were rumours of a new girlfriend every week, although you couldn't believe everything you read in the papers. She and Melody were close, despite the vast miles that'd been between them, and Melody had told her a lot about Matt's children via Skype and text messages but nothing about any of his personal relationships, respecting her boss's right to privacy. Not that she'd got any thanks for that loyalty and professionalism.

Zoe banged her fist on the wood one last time and to her satisfaction finally heard footsteps. The door was yanked open by a dark-haired guy in his twenties.

'Yes?' he drawled, stepping out into the sunlight, forcing her to move backwards down the three concrete stairs and onto the pavement.

Cocky green eyes ran over her flat black shoes, tight black jeans and the fashionable short-sleeved print top that hung off one shoulder. Having had no chance to change out of the clothes she'd travelled in, she felt rumpled, sticky and at a distinct disadvantage.

She couldn't afford to jump to any conclusions, but this guy had to be Stephen.

'Are you planning to say something today, or not?' he demanded, looking her up and down again, a bit too slowly for her liking.

Sucking in a deep breath, shudders of rage and adrenalin swirled with the giddy exhaustion of jet lag and noon heat, making her feel light-headed and dangerously out of control. Face scalding, she started shaking, hands bunching into fists around her over-sized bag. Ignoring the feeling, along with the urge to ask if he was done checking her out and start demanding what the hell he was playing at with her sister, she expelled the breath. If she lost it too soon it was game over; he'd likely slam the door in her face. Getting over the threshold was the important bit. *Then* she could tear strips off them both.

'Yes, sorry. Hello. Matthew Reilly?' It was Matt's house and it might seem weird if she asked for Stephen.

'God, no! Definitely not,' smirking, he turned his head to yell over his shoulder. 'Matt, there's some Katy Perry lookalike-wannabe here for an interview.' A pause. 'I'm off.' Shrugging when there was no reply, a strange expression flashed across his face. 'All right,' he hollered, 'see you when I'm back.' Reaching back inside the hallway, he grabbed a travel bag and hustled past her, leaving the front door yawning open behind him.

See you when I'm back?

'Wait—' she yelped, spinning around as his comment registered.

But the arrogant jerk ignored her, running down the steps and leaping into the yellow open-top car like some Dukes of Hazzard extra. Screeching away with a spin of tyres, gravel flew everywhere in an unholy rain of stones and he barely paused before roaring off towards the main Knightsbridge road. God knew how many people he was going to take out driving like that. Complete maniac.

Then his other words sunk into her sluggish, travel-addled brain. *Katy Perry lookalike-wannabe?* He was a cheeky bugger! She might have black hair and blue eyes but was no wannabe, wasn't here to audition for some tacky talent show, didn't care that Matthew Reilly was in the music business— Hang on, interview?

'That was my brother Stephen. I'm Matt.' A deep, terse voice said behind her.

291

She swung around to face the door, stumbling slightly. She needed to get out of this relentless sunshine, she was starting to feel pretty sick.

'Ready?'

'Ready?' she repeated, thinking. She'd missed her chance to have it out with Stephen for now, but it was this man stood in the shadows who was ultimately responsible for her sister's confused distress.

Keep calm, just breathe. She squinted, hardly able to make him out. The inside of the house was too dim and it was so bright outside, red dots blurring her vision.

'Look, I'm very busy. Are you here to interview for the nanny position or not? I haven't got any time to waste.'

He'd got rid of her sister only yesterday and was already trying to replace her.

At her dumbfounded silence, he began shutting the door. 'Okay then, goodbye.'

'I, uh— hang on! Sorry, of course I'm here for an interview,' she thought fast. 'There's just a slight problem.'

The breath hissed loudly from between his teeth. 'Which is?'

'I flew in from New York this morning and came straight from the airport, as you can see from my lack of a suitable outfit,' she gestured to her jeans, 'so I don't have my CV with me.'

'How did you hear about the job then?'

It was hardly surprising he was suspicious. 'A contact at the agency called me, knowing I was due back in the UK today,' she fibbed, hoping she was right. 'Zoe Harper, pleased to meet you.' She nodded briskly in greeting to avoid shaking his hand. 'I was added to the list at the last minute,' she finished the lie, 'haven't the agency emailed the updated schedule?' She prayed it was the same agency that'd placed Melody here originally, the one Zoe had also got the placement in America through.

A ringtone filled the hallway. Blowing out an exasperated breath, he prised a sleek mobile from his pocket and after checking the screen, cut the call off.

As he tucked the phone away, she chattered on. 'When this job was mentioned,' ironically one she was more than qualified for, 'I asked to be put forward, especially when it's working for you and this is such a lovely area to live in.' Sucking up to him felt wrong but if it gave her an in, it'd be worth it.

'My assistant is off sick, I haven't had time to mess around checking emails and my kids are due back in two hours,' he said in an irritated tone, 'so I'm sorry but—'

'But I've come all this way—'

His phone started ringing again and he swore, wrestling it back out of his pocket. 'Sorry.' After a quick glance at the screen, he answered. 'Matt Reilly,' he barked. 'Yes?'

She forced her lips into a polite smile while she waited. It wobbled when she realised he was talking to the recruitment agency.

'No, it's not good enough. I'm completely dissatisfied with the level of service I've received. You know I need a new nanny urgently. You sent someone else along, but— What? Oh, never mind, forget it.' He hung up, clenching the phone in his fist.

Jeez, was he this grumpy all the time? He must have been a joy for her sister to live with. Or maybe he was just having a bad day. If that was the case, it wasn't going to get any better with her arrival.

'That was about another no-show. Incredibly, the third today.' He paused, then shook his head, as if already regretting what he was about to say. 'I've only got this afternoon set aside for interviews, I suppose as you're here you may as well come in.' Gesturing her over the threshold. 'You can talk me through your experience and the agency can get me your details later if things go well,' he bit, slamming the front door behind them.

Gee thanks, don't do me any favours. She stuck her tongue out crossly at his back as her eyes adjusted to the light inside the house, then blanked her expression as he moved past her.

But he didn't stop, striding off down the wooden parquet

hallway so that she had to hurry after him. 'This way.'

She caught a flash of a staircase to her left and a dazzling though unlit chandelier overhead, but her focus was on following Matt. The scents of vanilla polish, flowers and some unnameable but appealing fresh male aftershave drifted over her as she caught up with him.

'I'm presuming the agency will have up-to-date references for you, along with an enhanced DBS clearance,' Matt threw open a door and lead her into a massive lounge filled with windows and light.

Zoe made a non-committal *mmmm* sound, taking in her surroundings. The parquet flooring continued straight through from the hallway, but apart from that everything was white; the ceiling, the walls, the fireplace that looked like it had never been used. On the far side of the room two French doors opened onto some kind of outdoor space, with matching conifers in square black pots sat outside them. There was very little furniture and no paintings on the walls. She walked over and sat on one of the shiny black sofas that faced each other across a blocky glass coffee table. Hiding a grimace, she slung her handbag down on the floor. It was so impersonal, more like a show-home than a real one. She hated it. It was way too pristine. How on earth did kids live here? Where was the personality, the clutter, the colour? Perhaps the children were kept in a cupboard under the stairs like Harry Potter, she thought unkindly, tongue in cheek.

She knew from her sister that Matt's daughter Aimee was seven years old, didn't talk much and was exceptionally bright, and that his son Jasper was nearly five and about to start school. Melody had described the little boy fondly but seeing her sister's sometimes strained face on the laptop screen and listening to funny stories about what he'd got up to, Zoe had concluded he was a bit of a handful.

'Anyone in there?' a gravelly voice broke into her thoughts.

Straightening, she lifted her chin and met Matt Reilly's gaze properly for the first time. 'I—' Oh.

Oh, man. The Americanism resounded in her head. Freezing, heart thudding, her mouth dropped open. Realising she must look like the village idiot, she shut it immediately, teeth clicking together. 'Yes. Sorry.'

'Good.' Leaning forward, he grabbed a notepad and silver embossed pen, and made a few notes on the paper.

She sucked her bottom lip into her mouth. She'd seen blurred photos of Matt in the press, but he was always ducking his head away or wearing sunglasses, so there'd never been an opportunity to see what he really looked like.

The reality was that he was outrageously, jaw-droppingly gorgeous.

He shared his brother's colouring, the green eyes and thick dark hair, but the similarity ended there. Stephen was tall and wiry, but with the long spread of his ridiculously muscular legs and the breadth of his shoulders Matt was far bigger and better built. In fact, he looked more like an international rugby player than some arty creative type who spent most days holed up in a dark studio.

And though she could understand why Melody found Stephen attractive, Matt was far more appealing. His face was leaner, rugged with stubble and with a fierce intelligence shining in his gaze under thick dark eyebrows. James Marsden chiselled cheekbones and a stern mouth might have given him a rugged male beauty were it not for the two tiny imperfections she'd always been a sucker for. A sinking feeling tugged at her tummy as she stared at a bump on the ridge of his nose, perhaps from a break, and a small, inch long scar that ran down into his top lip.

She'd had a thing about bad boys since a teenage crush on Harrison Ford in the *Indiana Jones* films, sparked by watching Christmas re-runs with Ruth. Their great aunt, who'd raised them since Mel was seven and Zoe was thirteen, loved adventure movies despite her appearance and stilted manner. Since then, the rebel characters in TV series and films had prolonged Zoe's obsession with bad boys. It was unfortunate for her, because Matt definitely looked like the kind of guy who'd ride up on a motorbike wearing leathers and whisk a girl away for a dirty, dangerous weekend. The sinfully tight blue jeans and black t-shirt clinging to his broad shoulders reinforced the image.

'Shall we get started?' he asked, frowning.

'Of course,' she straightened in her seat, trying to reassert her professionalism.

His phone pinged. 'For the love of—' putting the pad aside, he checked his mobile, reading something and scowling like it was telling him the end of the world was nigh. 'The sooner my assistant is better, the sooner my sanity will return,' he muttered absent-mindedly, touching the screen and typing a reply message.

The deadpan delivery was unwittingly amusing and made him seem less grumpy. Zoe couldn't help chuckling under her breath as she stared at him. A tingling awareness ran through her, a purely sexual heat beating between her legs and tightening her skin, raising bumps along it.

No. You detest him. He hurt Melody.

A pretty face and a toned body mean nothing.

Men aren't to be trusted.

Get over it.

It was easy to clamp a lid on her unruly hormones as she reminded herself of those facts. Plus the intense physical reaction was ridiculous and just too much. It had to be down to the jet lag and fury, as well as her spinning, conflicted emotions about coming home.

Then she sighed, studying him as he tapped away on the phone. Damn. One thing she didn't usually do was lie to herself and the truth was she'd never had such an overwhelming and immediate attraction to someone before. Fancied them, sure. Had flings, a few. Longer term boyfriends, yes ... which unhappily lead her thoughts to Greg. What an awful waste of five years he'd turned out to be.

Why didn't I see it coming? Why didn't I know?

Rage swamped her, despair pulling her down. She was obviously no judge of character where men were concerned. She'd virtually abandoned Melody to follow Greg across the ocean, and in return he'd betrayed her.

She straightened her shoulders, setting her jaw.

No. No man was ever going to come before her family again. She owed her sister more than that … and she owed the Reilly brothers revenge.

2

'I'm sorry,' Matt silenced his phone and placed it face down on the glass table. 'Today's been nightmarish,' he ran a hand distractedly through his hair, 'to say I'm short-staffed is an understatement.'

If part of the reason for his stress hadn't been down to him throwing her sister out on her arse, Zoe might have felt sorry for him. He looked genuinely pained. But it was his own stupid fault.

'That's okay,' she said politely, wondering how much of the interview to go through with before sharing the real reason for turning up on his doorstep. She felt like she needed to know more about him first. What if she started accusing him of what he'd done to Melody and he denied it all, or threw her out too? No, that wasn't good enough. She had to think about this strategically. It was just a shame that dragging tiredness and anger were befuddling her brain.

'Right, the phone is being ignored and I'm not going to answer the door if the bell goes,' he declared. 'Let's get on with this.' Leaning forward to grab the notepad again, the movement showed off strong chest muscles shifting under the cotton of his top.

Her eyes flew up, noticing the petal pattern in his forest green irises, and how focused his gaze was.

'So, tell me more about why you wanted the agency to send you over for this job in particular?' he asked, pen poised over the paper.

'Er … um,' she stuttered. It was an easy warm-up question, but her brain couldn't seem to come up with an answer. What the heck had she said earlier? She couldn't remember clearly, she'd been so intent on getting through the door.

'Well?' he raised both eyebrows.

Glancing out of one of the French doors, Zoe caught sight of a flowering indigo plant and a section of deck railing. It looked pretty out there, idyllic. Which nudged her memory. 'Like I said, it's a lovely place to live,' she mumbled.

'That's it?'

'Yeah,' she said lamely. God, this was awful. She was acting like a space cadet. *Get it together.*

Matt twisted his wrist and checked his battered but expensive looking watch. 'Are you sure you're actually here for an interview? To be frank, I'm really busy, so …' he started unfolding his tall body from the sofa.

It was enough to shake her from the fog. What was she doing? She was here for a reason, couldn't blow it. 'N-no,' she squeaked, and then cleared her throat before speaking with more confidence. 'I mean, no.'

Shooting up and stalking around the coffee table, he jerked her from the sofa by one elbow. 'Why the hell are you here then?'

She stumbled against him, letting out an *oof* as their bodies clashed awkwardly. Typically, his muscles were as solid and defined as they looked and her face bloomed pink as scorching sexual awareness ran through her, hardening her nipples. She glanced down quickly to check he couldn't see them through her top. Luckily he was more focused on other things, like drilling her for information. He didn't seem to notice how close they were or how tight his grip was.

'Are you with the press?' he demanded softly, the tone somehow scarier than if he'd shouted.

'No! Absolutely not! I'm not part of *that* lot.' She hoped her tone was suitably scathing and convincing, given that one of her best friends was a journalist. 'And can you let go of me please? That's way too tight.' The determined shake of her arm must have convinced him of something, even if it was only that she wouldn't put up with any high-handed crap.

He let go immediately. 'Sorry. I hope I didn't hurt you?'

To his credit he looked sincere. It was the perfect opportunity to make him feel bad, but he hadn't actually hurt her. Plus, if she went on the attack, it might make him defensive, which would get her nowhere. 'You didn't,' she shrugged, 'don't worry.'

'Good. So now you can explain yourself.' He crossed his arms across his chest, shoulders tense.

'Sure. Okay. When I said no, I only meant that no, I didn't want to leave. You were getting up and I thought you were going to say it was over before it had even begun. I don't usually perform this badly at interviews, I swear. I wasn't talking much because I'm jetlagged and feeling a bit funny from the sun.' She fanned herself to illustrate the point. Did she look as stupid and fake as she felt? But hey, she was committed now, and might as well go for it. 'I only landed a couple of hours ago, it's really hot outside and I burn easily. I mean look at this rubbish pale skin.' She pointed to her face. 'I may have a bit of heatstroke, but I feel better now I'm inside.' She mustered her best acting skills and smiled brightly. 'So perhaps you could offer me a glass of water and a minute to compose myself then we can start again? I'm not from the press, honestly.' It was easy to hold his gaze, given it was the truth.

There was a long pause as he stared at her. 'Fine,' he said, expression guarded. 'I suppose.'

'Really?'

'Yes. I know journalists. If you were one you would either come clean and bombard me with questions or maybe try to tempt me with something,' his eyes flickered over her body, 'in exchange for an exclusive story.'

Her spine stiffened and she smiled coldly. He was either deadly serious and an absolute pig, or was testing her.

'Luckily neither of those applies. Anyway, what would someone from the press want with you at the moment?'

'You really don't know?'

'Nope.'

Now she was fibbing, having read about a supposed broken engagement in a trashy celeb magazine on the seven hour flight home. The break-up was allegedly because his pop star fiancée had set up a cosy photo shoot with his kids without permission, prompting him to storm into a conference room to collect them, followed by hustling them out of the private entrance at the back of the hotel. As well as leaving with his children, he'd also apparently left with the massive diamond rock he'd proposed with six weeks before.

He shook his head. 'Never mind then. It doesn't matter.'

Was he embarrassed? Ashamed? Hurt? None of the above, surely. He didn't look particularly heartbroken.

'Hang on. I think it matters. If you gave me the job would I have to live with the papers breathing down my neck all the time? For instance, do your children get followed?'

'Getting a bit ahead of yourself based on your input so far, aren't you?' he asked dryly. 'Talking yourself into the job. A bit over confident, maybe?'

Arrogant was the unspoken word hanging in the air. From the glint in his eye, he wanted to see how she would react when provoked. But he wasn't going to see that side of her. At least, not yet.

'Over confident? No.' She shrugged. 'Over qualified? Maybe. I got a CACHE level three Diploma in Home-based Child Care when I left school before it was replaced with the QCF framework, and worked in a nursery for a few years. I progressed to a degree in Psychology with a view to specialising with children, but hated the job itself when I did my placement year at an independent school. So I left uni early, got a Paediatric First Aid award, did basic health and safety training, undertook a food hygiene certificate

301

and became a nanny. My plan tomorrow is to apply to get onto the OFSTED Childcare Register so I can care for under eight year olds …' She continued talking, reeling off her experience and skills, taking great pleasure in shutting him up. By the time she was done, his eyebrows were so high they'd almost disappeared into his dark hair.

'Now we're getting somewhere,' nodding his head, 'we'll get on with the set questions after I've got you that glass of water.' He loped away, long legs carrying him quickly to the door.

Her eyes dropped to his deliciously muscular butt and she twisted away, swearing. She was almost twenty-eight, not a teenager. She should not be susceptible to crushes on the latest bit of man-candy in the media.

Think of Melody. What do I do about the indefensible way he treated her?

Matt was so self-assured that Zoe doubted simply taking her sister's stuff and having a go at him would have the slightest affect, never mind making him feel bad enough to offer to make amends. Her hands curled into fists, picturing her sister's pale face and bloodshot eyes. According to Jemima, Melody had hardly spoken or eaten since rolling up on her friend's doorstep unexpectedly the previous day.

Matt walked back into the room and placed two blue glasses filled with sparkling water, ice and neat slices of lemon on the table. Zoe dropped onto the sofa and thanked him politely, hiding her churned up feelings behind a bland expression. As she sipped her drink, her hand was steady, a new determination burning a hole in her stomach. She wasn't sure how she was going to get even with him yet, but would ignore his physical appeal if it killed her.

'So,' she put her water down and clasped her hand together in her lap, 'what's the next question?'

For the following half hour, Zoe answered his competency-based questions calmly, talking about educational standards, setting up

302

routines, and how she handled behaviour management issues through shared partnership and agreed strategies with parents. She was candid with her professional opinion of what Matt's children needed based on their ages, following up with questions about their likes, hobbies and extra-curricular activities to show her interest. At times she accidentally slipped into enjoying the challenge of the interview and as much as she hated the idea of thinking anything positive about Matt, it was obvious from his probing questions that he was bright, sharp and knew what he wanted for his kids. She was shocked to feel genuinely interested in the job when Matt gave an approving smile to her last answer and asked if she had any questions of her own.

'I assume it's a live-in position?' she said after quizzing him about the hours, salary and next stages of the interview process.

'Yes, you'd have your own bedroom, bathroom and a small lounge area on the top floor.'

'Great. Could I see them please?'

'Not today,' he said brusquely.

No wonder. Melody's things were probably still in her bedroom and he'd be unable to explain why. Because, after all, not many people would voluntarily leave their stuff behind, and he'd hardly want to admit to slinging a previous employee out so quickly he'd not let them pack up their belongings.

'Okay, maybe next time, if I'm invited back.' Sliding forward on the sofa, she leaned toward him with her head tilted to indicate interest and encourage honesty. It was basic psychology. 'So, am I allowed to ask what happened to your last nanny?'

His lips tightened, a pulse beating in his stubbly jaw. 'I'd rather not discuss it,' he replied, shuffling his paperwork together on the table.

'It's important for me to know, given I'm applying to replace her,' she said, peering at him so he had to meet her gaze or appear rude. 'Did she leave for professional or personal reasons? Was she not happy here? What have you told the children? If I get the job I need to know what happened so I can be prepared for any questions your son or daughter might have about her going. They may be upset, or miss her. They could feel like she abandoned them. Particularly after what happened to your wife …' she trailed off as his expression turned grim and his knuckles turned white around the notepad. 'I'm sorry,' she said, meaning it. 'I didn't mean to upset you.' She might not like the guy but she wasn't a robot. There was genuine grief and regret on his face. One thing they had in common.

'Its fine,' he said in a taut voice, 'it's common knowledge. It's not as if my family has any right to privacy or anything.'

She sidestepped the bitterness in the remark, choosing not to get into the debate. It was his choice to have a career that put him in the spotlight, so it was for him to deal with the consequences. It was just a shame if it affected the kids. 'I appreciate it must have been difficult and I don't want to pry. I'm thinking purely of your children's welfare.'

'I understand that. And I suppose you might be right about needing to know what happened. But how do you know my last nanny was a woman?'

She nearly lost her nerve but wouldn't give in that easily, holding his gaze. 'Statistically, the number of women in the field compared to the number of men makes it more likely your nanny was female.' Pushing a strand of black hair behind her ear, she watched his deep green eyes flicker along her collarbone before returning to her face. That was interesting. 'Seriously, I know I'd have to meet Aimee and Jasper and pass all the clearances and checks, but if you offer me the job I'd quite like to know what happened to the last employee in it.' Forcing a nervous laugh. 'She's not buried under the patio or anything is she? Or chained up in the basement? What's the big mystery?'

His smile was fleeting. 'No mystery, just simply not pleasant. She, ah,' he picked over his words, 'did something I didn't agree with that meant she was no longer suitable to be my children's nanny. It turned out she wasn't the person I thought she was. It was disappointing,' he shrugged one shoulder casually as if he didn't care, but there was something in the set of his chin that suggested otherwise, 'but these things happen, and I need to replace her urgently. Does that tell you enough?'

'I guess so,' she replied through stiff lips, longing to jump up and yell at him. 'Thanks for sharing.' He really was an absolute bastard. It felt like every muscle in her face was clenching, but she breathed in and out deeply, striving to keep calm. Since when was falling in love such a crime that it meant you were unfit to look after children? And he could have said anything, taken the diplomatic line and said his nanny had left for personal reasons. Instead he was suggesting Melody had let him down, when the truth was that it was the other way around. Especially after all the time, energy and passion her sister had devoted to his children, who she'd grown to genuinely care about.

Zoe could hardly believe it. He clearly had zero conscience. Was it the industry he worked in that made him think he could treat people this way, or did the nature of the industry happen to support an arrogance that had already existed before he'd made it big? She resisted the urge to bounce out of her seat, grab his precious bloody paperwork and whack him around the head with it repeatedly, very hard and with great satisfaction. Fury didn't even begin to cover it. Bloody, bloody men.

'So, what about you?' he asked, looking at her expectantly.

'Sorry?'

'Why have you just left your job after five years and come back to the UK? You must have liked it over there to stay that long? You still sound very British but I noticed you use American slang quite a bit.'

'I guess it's normal to pick things up when you're living and breathing it every day,' she said shortly. 'And in answer to your question, personal reasons, including to be with my family again.'

'Fair enough,' he stood up. 'Right, I think we're done here.

Thank you for your time.'

'Can I have another glass of water before I go please?' She needed a minute to think, as well as rein her anger in.

'Sure,' he checked his watch, 'but it'll have to be quick. The next candidate will be here any minute.'

'That's fine. Thanks.'

He nodded and picked up the glasses, leaving her alone. Springing off the sofa she strode across the room and flung open the nearest French door, propping herself up against the frame. Her heart beat a rapid *ga-doom, ga-doom, ga-doom* in her chest, pumping adrenalin around her body. What a bastard Matt was.

The scent of freshly cut grass filled her nose and normally the heady smell of British summer would be a lovely distraction, a balm to the last few years of homesickness. Not today. Her fingers clenched around each other, knuckles tight.

Then as if her system had used the last of its energy up with the hot blast of anger, belated jet lag hit hard again. A drowning wave of languor washed over her, making her eyes go gritty and heavy. Just like that, she couldn't wait to get out of this house and away from the whole sorry mess. God, she was weary. Curling up in a ball and sinking into a deep slumber suddenly held massive appeal. She hadn't slept properly for almost two weeks before leaving New York. There'd been too much to do, wrapping up her life and returning to her old one. The nights staring dry-eyed at the ceiling hadn't helped either. Somewhere inside her there was a healthy need to grieve and cry, but she hadn't been able to manage it before leaving the States.

It had been a mistake coming here, a knee-jerk reaction. Would it be better if she simply left? Went back to Melody and helped her put her life back together, while doing the same for herself? But then she heard Matt moving around the kitchen, whistling along to a pop track currently in the UK download chart, perhaps one that he'd produced. He sounded so happy, so unconcerned. It was completely unfair. Why should he be acting as if life was peachy when he'd practically ruined her sister's?

She went to shut the door and her head jerked as she spotted a wooden bench tucked away in a corner of the manicured lawn, not far from a sturdy apple tree and rose-beds resplendent with pearl-white blooms. Her gaze zoomed in on a scrap of fabric draped over the seat. It was a rich mulberry colour. Melody's cardigan, one Zoe had bought in Bloomingdale's and paid to have shipped back to the UK for her last birthday. Next to it was a book, left open face down to keep the page. The spine would be permanently creased by now. They'd always argued about Melody's inability to treat books with respect. Then it dawned that her baby sister had been ejected so quickly she'd not even been able to grab her things from the garden and she shook with regenerated rage, adrenalin boiling up and smothering her exhaustion.

It was time to give Matt, a guy too similar to Greg for comfort, what he deserved. He needed to feel humiliation and hurt on every level. She was sick of men who thought they could treat women like that, tossing them aside when they were done. It wasn't right and it stung. It ripped apart your self-esteem so you were left wondering, *what's wrong with me? Why aren't I good enough?* It ripped apart your heart so you thought, *I never want to go through this again.*

Matt Reilly would pay, and not only for making her sister jobless, homeless and breaking her heart with the help of his brother, but for all the other women he'd hurt in the past. She'd read the articles. Sure, you couldn't take everything you read in the tabloids as a given, but there had to be a grain of truth in them. If only a fraction of the hearts he'd reportedly broken since becoming a widower three years ago were true, the line of devastated women would stretch from London to Brighton and back again.

But how was she going to do it?

Then there was that sweet, magical moment when inspiration hit. As Matt swept back in and she turned to him, smoothing her hands down over her top, she saw an appreciative glint in his eyes, quickly hidden. Put that together with his near paranoia about

307

the press and his desperation for privacy and she knew exactly what to do.

This was going to be so goddamn satisfying … if she could pull it off.

3

'I don't know about this, Sis,' Melody twisted a piece of long, dark blonde hair around her nail-bitten finger, frowning. Lowering her voice so customers nearby couldn't overhear, she leaned forward. 'Aren't you worried it might backfire?'

Zoe stared at her sister's pale, hollow-eyed face. 'I don't see how it can,' she replied, putting her mug of latte down on the sticky table. They'd met at a cafe near Jemima's flat in Holloway, given that part of the plan relied on Matt and Stephen not finding out they were related. 'The risk is all his,' she added, sliding the coffee aside so she could grasp her sister's chilly hands. 'And don't you think he deserves it? Don't you think it will do him good to be humiliated and confused, the way you've been? I mean, you still don't even know why, do you? Not properly. All Matt said to you that day was that you weren't suitable for his brother or to look after his kids and had to leave immediately. There was no conversation, no chance for you to ask why. He just threw you out.' Melody had told Zoe more about it a few days earlier. About the way that one day she'd been a girl in love, part of Matt and Stephen's family unit, and the next she'd been out in the cold with barely any explanation. 'But you said that Matt seemed okay about you and Stephen seeing each other before then? You'd been together a few months?'

'Yes.' Melody gnawed her bottom lip, dark brown eyes looking bruised. 'He was. I just don't get it. Why the change of heart? And why wasn't I good enough? Because we're not rich? He never seemed like a snob to me.' She gulped. 'I thought he liked me.'

'I don't know. It doesn't make sense.' Zoe paused. 'Unless he thought you and Stephen were just casual, and then when it started getting serious he wasn't happy? You said that you and Matt always got on well though. Why wouldn't he just talk to you about any concerns he had?'

Melody's eyes brimmed. 'No idea. Yes, we did get on well, he was more like a big brother than an employer sometimes.'

Zoe sighed, her sister's naivety paining her. 'Oh, Mel. You should never confuse professional and personal relationships. That way can only lead to hurt.'

'Pardon?' Melody stared at her, dazed eyes clearing.

'You should always keep a personal distance from the people you work for. You know that.'

'Don't start lecturing me. You don't know what it was like.' Melody flashed, yanking her slim hands away. 'I was with the family for three years. It's a bit late to wade in and start pulling your big sister act just because it's suddenly convenient!'

'Right,' Zoe murmured through dry lips, throat aching. Ouch. Direct hit.

'I'm sorry,' Melody gasped immediately, 'I didn't mean it. You know I didn't. I'm just such a mess …' she dropped her head into her hands, shoulders heaving, 'and I'm so angry.'

'I know. Don't worry.' Melody was normally the gentlest person in the world. Zoe scooted her chair around the table to get closer, the legs scraping on the tiled floor. Placing a hand on her little sister's back, she waited quietly, giving her time.

If she'd been there for Melody, maybe none of this would have happened. Mel wouldn't have gone looking for the guidance and friendship from her boss that she should have been getting from her big sister. Even though they'd texted and Skyped a lot, it hadn't been the same, living on opposite sides of the ocean. Zoe might blame Matt and Stephen for her sister's heartbreak, but part of the responsibility rested on her shoulders too.

The look on Matt's face when he talked about Melody letting him down flashed across her mind and as much as she wanted to dismiss it, or think he'd been lying, there'd been something there. Something he was unsure of or puzzled about. It would do no good to tell Melody what Matt had said because it might upset her. But perhaps her plan could serve two purposes; not just revenge, but finding out just what the heck had happened.

She stroked her sister's back soothingly. 'I know you're worried about my plan, and don't really agree with it but maybe if I can find out *why*, it will give you closure?' She nodded at Melody's raw, tear-filled eyes. 'I take it that Stephen still isn't taking your calls or answering your messages?' Thinking of his travel bag and *see you when I get back* holler to his brother. 'I suppose he could be abroad. Perhaps he's having problems with his phone.'

Melody shook her head, a lone tear running down her cheek. 'I don't think so, and he can more than afford the roaming charges. I just don't get it. Everything was fine. We were happy. And I just can't understand the way Matt acted— Oh, Zoe, I don't know what to do-oo …'

The last word ended on a wail and reignited the hot, rolling rage and fiercely protective instincts in Zoe. She sucked her bottom lip into her mouth, rubbing her sister's back more firmly, wanting to scrub away the hurt. 'I'm sorry. I didn't mean to upset you. But Matt hasn't been in touch to check how you are either. I mean, you could be living on a park bench somewhere for all he knows. It's disgusting. I really think he needs to be taught a lesson.' She looked into her sister's face, jaw set, thinking of the added insult of a few days before, when she'd gone to Matt's house. 'Let me do this for you, Mel,' she said fiercely. 'Let me get answers and teach them they can't behave this way. That you can't ignore people and pretend you've done nothing wrong. It'll be fine, I promise.'

Melody sighed heavily, running a finger over some spilt grains of sugar. 'Okay,' she whispered.

'Good. It's the only thing that makes sense.' Zoe paused. 'Also, I know that Jemima is happy to have you,' she broached, 'but sleeping on her couch is less than ideal. What do you think about me calling Ruth and seeing if you could stay with her for a while? You always got on well together, right? I'm sure she still has the guest room set up ready. It might give you some distance. Fifty miles might not be very far, but it's not on Matt's doorstep either. One of the worst things about a break up is running into the person, or the possibility you're going to. If Stephen gets back soon, you'll have two people who upset you to avoid. I don't want you to think I want shot of you,' she added, 'because I can't wait for us to spend some quality time together after I've been away so long. I'm just thinking of what's best for you right now.'

Melody sniffed. 'It would be good to have some space, and be somewhere familiar. I know it never seemed like home to you, and Ruth isn't the huggy sort, but I feel safe there.' She nodded. 'Can you call her please? If you can do it without arguing that is. I'm going to splash some cold water on my face.' Pushing her chair back, she grabbed her bag and hitched her chin up, trying to be brave.

Zoe watched her go. Poor thing. Sucking in a deep breath she dialled her Aunt's number, dreading the conversation. 'It's me,' she said when Ruth answered with a curt hello.

'Oh. You are still in the land of the living then.'

'I did text you from the airport the other day.'

'Messaging relatives is no substitute for a good old fashioned phone call,' Ruth said in a sniffy tone. 'I expected you to follow the text up with a call. I knew you'd be jetlagged but surely you could have—'

'I've had my hands full,' she cut across her Aunt's accusation, picturing her grey hair in its no-nonsense bun and the pursed lips, shoulders bolt-straight, her dark eyes cool and unforgiving. When in this mood, the result was stilted accusations Zoe didn't have the time and energy for today. Obviously she still wasn't forgiven for what had happened before her departure for the States, despite the birthday and Christmas cards she'd always sent, accompanied by luxury gifts. However, now was not the time to try and sort it out. That didn't mean she shouldn't be conciliatory. 'I'm sorry, you're right, I should have called. The thing is, Matt's fired Melody and kicked her out, and Stephen's gone AWOL.'

'What? What on earth do you mean? What happened? The absolute brutes.'

'I'm not sure yet.' Zoe didn't know whether to be grateful or sad that her Aunt would jump so easily to her sister's defence, when if it had been her the first thing Ruth would have asked was *what did you do*? 'I'm trying to sort it out,' no way was she telling Ruth the details of what she was up to, 'but in the meantime I think it would be good for Melody if she came home for a while. We've talked about it and it's what she wants, if you'll have her.'

'Of course I will. The guest room is made up for when she visits during the holidays. Put her on the first train you can and let me know when she'll be arriving. I'll pick her up from the station. She can stay as long as she likes.'

'Okay, thank you,' Zoe said, relieved. At least that was one less thing to worry about. There might be a lot of muddy ground between her and Ruth, but Melody's well-being was always a given. 'I'll text you. I'm aiming to get her on the train this afternoon if I can manage it.'

'Right. And what are you going to be doing in the meantime?'

'I'll be trying to work out what's gone on, and see if the situation can be retrieved.' She had to talk in the language that Ruth understood.

'You do that. Keep me updated, will you? If you need me to speak with either of the swines let me know. I don't know enough about Stephen to comment, however it's odd about Matthew, I didn't think he was like that. He always seemed so nice. I met him a few times when I came into London for lunch with your sister.'

'That's what Melody thought too,' Zoe replied. 'I'll be in touch. Bye.' She hung up, sitting back in her chair. Formidable was not the word for her aunt. She almost felt like setting her on Matt because it was what he deserved, but that wouldn't get them anywhere. She was convinced that direct confrontation wasn't the route to take. Staring down at the greasy table top, she frowned, anxiety coiling in her stomach. Was it always going to be this way between her and Ruth? Was there ever going to be a time that they could come to some understanding? Or when Ruth would tell her why she'd always been the odd one out in their little patched together family?

When Melody returned a minute later, Zoe forced a smile. 'Good news,' she said. 'You can go to Ruth's as soon as this afternoon if you want. We can grab your things from Jemima's and get you on the train in no time.' She thought longingly of the coarse sandy beaches of Southend-on-Sea. Pictured the world's longest pleasure pier, the row of multi-painted beach huts, the rides and roller coaster of Adventure Island on the Western Esplanade. Could almost taste the salt that carried on the sea breeze and always tangled her hair. While Ruth's house with its dark shadows, locked rooms and no-nonsense air had never felt like home, she loved the seaside town she'd spent most of her teens in.

'That would be good,' Melody murmured. 'I do think I need to get away and the sooner the better.' She closed her eyes then opened them again, looking horrified. 'I haven't even asked about you, Sis. Are you doing okay? Funny that we're both going through break-ups at the same time.'

'I'll be fine.' Zoe grabbed her bag from under the table and started rooting through her purse. 'At least I know what happened,' she muttered, head down. The memory of that last night with Greg flashed in front of her eyes. 'Besides, I've got other things to concentrate on. I'll be checking out of the bed and breakfast in a couple of days' time and moving in with Matt.'

Melody shook her head. 'That's the part of the plan that makes me nervous.'

'Why?' Zoe frowned at her sister as she threw a ten pound note down on the table. At least that was one thing; she was returning to the UK with money in the bank, courtesy of her ex-fiancé and their cancelled plans. 'You think he might rumble me straight away?'

'No. It's more that while he has a tendency to be closed off from the children, and really distracted, he's a nice guy. Kind of charming actually. I never saw him that way but lots of women—'

'Not such a nice guy that it stopped him from doing what he did to you,' she interrupted, 'and that's all I'm interested in. Don't worry, I won't fall for the act.' Thinking of Greg, something in her chest twisted. 'There's no chance.'

Later on, when they said goodbye as Melody boarded the train, her shoulders slumped like a puppy that had been kicked one too many times, a new determination burned through Zoe. The sooner this was done, the sooner Melody might be able to move on with her life, and come back to London, where the two of them belonged side by side together again. Sisters.

Huffing out a breath, Zoe slung another huge canvas bag on the bed, a trickle of sweat snaking down her back. She bit her lower lip, pulling out her phone to re-read her sister's text from that morning.

> **All settled and Ruth is**
> **looking after me. I'm still**
> **not sure about this Sis.**
> **But if you're going to do**
> **it, please be careful. M xx**

Melody was obviously worried so Zoe had done her best to reassure her.

> **I'll be fine.**

Can't wait to see the
look on Matt's face when
it all comes together.
Then on to Stephen! xx

It probably was a kind of madness, moving in with a guy she
detested. But it was part of the plan. Besides, if she wasn't meant to
do this, why would the universe have co-operated quite so nicely?
When the agency had called the day following the interview to
tell her Matt wanted her to go back and meet the kids, it'd felt
like cosmic rebalancing, like it was meant to be. Not that she was
superstitious. But the agency—Exclusive London Nannies—had
been happy to re-register her, delighted to make money from the
placement. Once Liberty had supplied a glowing reference and Zoe
had registered with the online DBS service, her enhanced disclosure
and barring clearance available within days, with her certificate
of good conduct on its way from America, it had been too easy
to meet Aimee and Jasper. To convince Matt of her suitability to
be his nanny. Of course it had helped that Melody had been able
to give her some inside tips about the family.

Surprisingly, the children weren't the spoilt brats she'd expected.
Maybe that was down to her sister's influence over the last few years.
They did however have a few issues that Melody hadn't articulated.

Number one was that they were crying out for their dad's
love, the net result being that Aimee was so incredibly shy she
was virtually mute, finding it hard to hold eye contact and hesitant about speaking, while Jasper's behaviour was so demanding
and energy levels so high he was on the verge of hyperactivity.
Zoe couldn't help feeling Jasper was attention seeking, trying to
establish communication with his only parent.

Number two was they were bored out of their skulls and weren't
engaging with the activities Matt had chosen for them.

She'd seen it all within an hour; interacting with the three of
them, noticing Matt's distracted and distant manner, the way the

316

light went out of his kids' eyes whenever he glanced at his phone, or gazed off into space with a faraway look, or scribbled something on a notepad he kept in his back pocket. They weren't a happy, cohesive family unit. Not at all.

She could do a lot of good for these kids. It was a shame she was only here for a few weeks to get revenge, which she'd started referring to as *Plan Nannygate* in her head. Nothing over the past week had made her feel like Matt didn't deserve it. What she hadn't mentioned to her sister in the cafe was what had happened during her brief third visit, just after accepting the job.

Finally allowed to see her living quarters, she had been horrified to find Melody's things shoved into black bin liners and left carelessly in a pile in one of the upstairs hallways, the contents overflowing and getting trodden on every time Jasper ran past. Which he invariably did, as his default speed setting appeared to be supersonic. The lack of respect for her sister's stuff had her fuming, never mind the health and safety hazard to the kids if they tripped over the bags.

'This is really dangerous,' she'd raised an eyebrow at Matt. 'You must have storage space. It needs to be put away.'

'Dangerous?' he'd answered her without lifting his head, typing something into his iPad.

'For your children. They could fall over the bags and down the stairs?' She pointed out exasperated, before realising she had to watch her tone. She couldn't be bolshy. He was about to become her boss and she wanted to earn his trust, so she had to play nice. 'I'm just concerned. I have a duty of care towards them, remember?' Like he did as their parent.

He swiped the tablet screen to lock it and looked up, shaking his head as if bringing himself back to planet earth. 'You're right. Sorry. I hadn't even noticed. I'll get our cleaner Roberta to move them tomorrow.'

'Or we could do it now?' she suggested, not giving him much chance to disagree, scooping up two bags and running downstairs.

'Where shall we put them?' her voice echoed up the spiral white staircase.

A loud, resigned sigh sounded on the landing above her. She bit the inside of her cheeks to stop from smiling as she heard the rustle of plastic bags, followed a moment later by the beat of approaching footsteps. It was satisfying knowing she'd annoyed him, just a little bit.

'There's a double garage, and I only use one of them when Stephen's away because I always have one car on the drive. We can put these in the empty side.'

'Is it clean and dry?' she prompted. 'We wouldn't want it all getting ruined. I'm guessing your old nanny might come back for them at some point?' The last was uttered through gritted teeth. *Sweetness and light Zoe*, she reminded herself.

He looked troubled by the thought. 'It's possible,' he turned around, 'garage is this way.' After twenty minutes of traipsing up and down, everything was safely stowed away and Zoe felt like she'd scored a victory. The garage was easily accessible from both the front and side of the house, so at some point she'd make plans with Melody to collect her stuff with Ruth. Or perhaps she'd smuggle it out a bit at a time, she mused, like illegal contraband.

The fact that, as well as failing to check on her sister's welfare, Matt also had no respect for her belongings reinforced Zoe's feeling that he didn't give a crap. Well, she thought grimly, he needed to be taught to care.

So here she was, in the enemy's house surrounded by her clothes, shoes and other belongings. The original idea had been to sling a few suitcases in the car and live out of them, but she'd realised it would look suspicious if she brought hardly anything with her after accepting a permanent position. So she'd called the storage company and asked them to deliver some of the boxes shipped over from New York and phoned Rayne, who'd been letting Zoe use the loft in her attic flat for some of her old stuff, pre-America.

'It's so great to see you,' Rayne had hugged her earlier, before stepping back to study her appraisingly. 'I know coming back to Blighty now isn't what you'd planned,' she paused as they looked bleakly at each other, knowing what *had* been planned, 'but I'm still glad you're here. I'm not that pleased to see how skinny you are though, Zo.' Squeezing her friend's narrow waist. 'Tell me the truth, how are you doing?' She swept her black fringe out of her eyes, Cleopatra sharp bob falling back around her face, multiple cocktail rings glinting in the early morning sun.

'It's good to see you too.' Zoe smiled tightly. 'And, yeah, okay,' her throat closed up, and she realised she'd barely thought about her own heartbreak because of dealing with the fallout of her sister's. Maybe that made it easier. 'You know what it's like after a break up. The weight falls off, doesn't it? Best diet around,' she joked weakly.

'Hmm. Well, just don't lose too much will you? I don't want to let that bastard make you ill. I still can't believe he—'

'Can we not talk about it?' Zoe touched Rayne's arm. 'Another time, all right?' She wasn't ready to deal with the implosion of her life yet.

'Sure,' her friend looked worried but nodded, turning to gaze up at Matt's house. 'Wow, it's really something. You've landed on your feet haven't you? I know you're here for less than savoury reasons, but still.'

'Thanks.' Zoe replied dryly. If there was one thing you could count on, it was Rayne being honest to the point of bluntness. *Less than savoury.* Her plan wasn't going to cover her in glory, but it was justifiable in the circumstances. 'You're going to help me, right?'

Rayne hesitated. 'If you're sure this is what he deserves, and you're not going to get hurt.'

'I'm one hundred per cent sure,' Zoe said firmly. 'This is what I need to do. I mean,' she said hastily, 'what Melody needs me to do.'

'All right then, I'm in,' Rayne nodded, 'you know you've always got my support. If he's as much of a bastard as you say he is, let's go for it. When the time is right, I'll put you in touch with some of the celebrity reporters I know.'

'Thanks.' Zoe moved the conversation on. 'And what about you and Adam? How's it going?' The question choked her a bit. It was hard being newly single when the rest of the world seemed to be coupled up, but she couldn't begrudge her friend's happiness. Rayne had run into her uni ex-boyfriend at Wimbledon a few weeks before and after nearly five years apart they'd ended up giving it another go.

'Amazing so far,' Rayne grinned, practically glowing, 'the way it was back then, but even better. He's still lovely, and *so* much hotter too. You remember he had that preppy handsome look going on at uni? Well he's got a few rough edges now, cut his hair, got a tattoo and he's much more relaxed. You'd love him. But not too much,' she teased.

'I do like bad boys,' Zoe mused, wondering how the heck she'd ever ended up with Greg, who was polished Kennedy-American uptight, 'but I draw the line at body art.'

'Fair enough, each to their own,' Rayne smiled easily. 'Adam would like to see you again. We've been going on double dates with Lily and his intern Flynn, but it would be nice to get more of the old gang back together.'

'Sounds great, how about we do something in a few weeks' time, once this is over,' Zoe gestured at the property behind them, 'and I'm settled somewhere else?'

'Cool, but if you end up needing to escape the madness with a girlie night out sooner, let me know. We can try and get your sister involved; Adam has plenty of spare rooms in his place in Islington she could stop in. We might be able to convince Frankie to put Zack down for a minute and join us too. It would be good to get the dark trinity together again.'

Zoe laughed at Rayne's description of how madly in love their other best friend was with her boyfriend, and the name Adam had given the three of them at uni because they all had black hair. 'Yeah, thanks. I will. I don't really feel like going out at the

320

moment though.'

'Fine, but don't lock yourself away for too long.' Rayne ordered. 'You need to keep busy, not mope over that deaf, blind and dumb idiot, which he totally is to do what he did as well as letting you go so easily. Besides, I don't want you turning into some sad old spinster who's going to get chewed on by her cats. Especially as you're such an oldie.' Referring to the fact Zoe was two years older than her.

'Gee, thanks for the sympathy.' Zoe stuck out her tongue, playing along, knowing Rayne was trying to cheer her up. 'I'll let you know when I'm ready to leave the fortress of solitude,' she smiled, 'but nothing too wild, for gawd's sakes.'

'Nooo,' Rayne said, backing away, holding her fingers out in front of her in a cross sign, 'she's turned American on us! Quick, call the Queen!'

'Ha ha. I probably have picked up some bad habits. I was over there for long enough. You can be in charge of my conversion back to British citizen if you want.'

'It's a plan.' Rayne saluted, clicking her heels together. 'I'd better run. I've got a story to finish and a meeting with my editor. Sorry I can't help you move your crap upstairs,' she finished cheekily, her turquoise blouse bringing out her navy blue eyes, which flashed with humour.

'Sod off, it's not crap!' Zoe replied automatically, reverting back to their uni days. 'And it's fine. You're a star for getting it down from your loft and dropping it over. Thanks so much.' Zoe leaned in for a quick hug before shooing Rayne away. 'Go. Speak soon.' She shook her head as her friend roared away in her sporty black Mini, a Union Jack design on its roof. The girl certainly had personality.

God, she'd missed her. Had missed all her friends. She'd given so much up when she'd moved to the States. Pretty much everything in fact. And all she had to show for it was a bare left hand, a few extra laughter lines and a dress she'd never wear hanging in her closet.

By the time she'd heaved all the boxes and bags up to her top floor living quarters, she was hot, sweaty and swearing. She was also grateful her new boss and his kids weren't around to see what a complete mess she was; damp dark hair coming loose from its high ponytail and sticking to her slippery face, denim shorts creased and the straps of her dust-smudged white vest top falling off her shoulders. It was a scorchingly hot day and although the lower floors of the house were cool and spacious, the upper floor was carpeted, more compact and suffered from heat rising upwards. Throwing open the skylight windows hadn't helped much, there was no wind outside to offer any relief.

Thankfully Matt wasn't due back for hours as he was holed up in his studio with some new talent he'd discovered and both kids were visiting with their grandma, his late wife's mum. It was his way of giving her time to settle in, which she should be grateful for, but instead of abandoning her maybe he could have stuck around to see if she could do with a hand?

She shook her head. It wasn't his job to help her move in. Why on earth should he? Looking at all the stuff spread out over the length and breadth of the bedroom, a mixture of old and new, cases and boxes of clothes, shoes and her beloved books, knowing there were more in the lounge area, she blew out another long breath. It was strange to think that this set of rooms had been her sister's home for three years. She felt uncomfortable, like an impostor. It was going to take hours to unpack too. Mind you, there was no bookcase so her books could stay packed away for now, which would save some time.

As she opened the first crate from America and a long black and white Marc Jacobs gown slithered to the floor, her addiction to clothes caught hold and she forgot how uncomfortable she was. Leaping up, she unpacked everything else in delight, rediscovering old friends from before she'd left, including the ancient Alaia chain-link leather sandals she'd saved up a month for when living at Ruth's. Haphazardly laying clothes, shoes, belts and handbags across the bed and every available surface, she stroked them lovingly, holding the soft, luxurious fabrics against her face. God, she adored all this, and given enough money would shop every single day. New York had been a revelation. She'd fallen in love with the stores as much as the loud, straight-talking people. She'd also been lucky that even though Liberty had been bossy and occasionally unreasonable about her children, she was generous and had fallen into the habit of gifting her collections to Zoe after every season. She was going to sorely miss that perk of the job, along with her charges Ava and Grace, and a hundred other tiny little things she'd come to love about NY.

As well as the life she'd had planned. One that Greg had robbed her of with his stupid, selfish behaviour.

All of a sudden it flowed over her.

Bastard! How could he *do* that to her? After everything they'd been to each other … Friends, lovers, partners. But clearly she'd been fooling herself, because if that was really the case, he could never have done what he'd done. For god's sakes, it was the oldest story in the book, sleeping with someone else. Couldn't he have at least been a bit original? Or ducked out of their relationship if he wasn't happy? She wanted to punch him, yell at him, tell him all the ways she'd like to make him suffer, how much she hated what he'd done, how three and a half thousand miles between them would never ever be enough.

She ground her teeth. Watching him hurt would give her satisfaction, definitely. But she wasn't sure it would make her feel any better, and there was no way she was going to give up her dignity by losing control. Sometimes all a girl had left was her pride, along with her instinct for survival. The best thing was to cut him off completely, forget he even existed, until she could speak to him without having a total meltdown.

Picking up a hot pink, strapless dress she'd worn to a party not long before leaving for New York, she shook her head. What *had* she been thinking? She couldn't imagine wearing it again. Her mum, if still alive, would have probably told her to put it in the bin or give it away, that once things became useless, you should just get rid of them. But Zoe was feeling sentimental, so she tucked the dress into the back of the massive built-in wardrobe in her new bedroom and hung up a beautiful sequinned blue top. Spying her favourite black Manolo Blahniks she slipped them on, mood instantly lifting. She'd saved up her bonuses to buy them and they were totally impractical, but boy, did they make her feel great.

Grabbing a cropped jacket she'd once worn to a rock concert, she stroked it before hanging it up, smiling at the memories of the blaring music and sweaty, jumping crowd. Unpacking her old things, marvelling over them and remembering the girl she used to be, along with the good times in New York, might be the closest she'd been to happiness in a while.

That, and the thought of Matt's face when he was plastered all over the weekend papers, his precious privacy blown sky high. There might be a confidentiality clause in her contract, but she had absolutely no fear of breaching it. He'd hardly want the publicity of a big court case, and she would do whatever it took to do right by her sister.

4

Matt crashed his car keys into a bowl on the expensive white sideboard, kicking the heavy black front door shut behind him.

He hissed out a swear word. The studio had been a nightmare. For some unknown reason the singer with the incredibly rich, adaptable voice who'd seemed so passionate, enthusiastic and energetic when he'd offered her a contract after weeks of sound tests and negotiations with her agent had today been listless and disinterested. It was like working with a different person. He could only hope the chance he'd taken on her wasn't going to backfire. The fact it might frustrated him, made irritation burn inside. She had it in her to be amazing, world-class. So what the hell had happened to change her so radically? To make her avoid his gaze and mutter that she was fine, when she quite clearly wasn't? He would never get women. Why did they always *do* that? Not that he'd been thinking of her as a woman, despite her fragile blonde beauty. He only saw her as a gifted artist. The talent was always off limits, at least in his code of practice.

He pulled a hand through his dark hair, itching for a cool, calming shower and a strong black coffee before going to his office and dealing with the tedious mass of emails he was behind with because his assistant Sadie was still recovering from her procedure. He supposed he should do the polite thing and find his new nanny first though. Say hello, ask if she needed anything.

Taking the two sets of spiral staircases in large leaps, up from the ground floor and past his and the kids' rooms on the first floor, he strode down the top floor corridor and swung into the doorway of Zoe's living space. Not in the white and beige lounge area. She must be in the bedroom. If the door was closed he'd knock, but it was open, so he walked straight in, impatient to get it over with.

The greeting he'd planned died on his lips, breath unexpectedly clogging in his throat. There was a knee-jerk response in his lower body, his jeans going uncomfortably tight.

Bloody hell.

Of all the beautiful women he'd worked with over the years—the singers and divas with their glamorous designer outfits and fashionable haircuts, manicures and pedicures, their gym-perfect toned bodies and fake tans—she was by far the sexiest he'd ever seen.

Sitting on the plush blue bedroom carpet, she was leaning against the ivory wall-paper, head tipped back as she gulped thirstily from a can of coke. Her creamy skin was flushed and her shapely but slightly too slim bare legs were on display, stunningly shown off by a pair of ultra-high black heels and some nearly non-existent cut-offs. A white vest-top outlined generous breasts and a tiny waist, the plain top a contrast against her black hair, dark brows and lashes.

Tamara Drewe eat your heart out, he thought, recalling the scene in the film where the intrepid journalist had made an all too memorable picture striding through a Dorset country field in tiny denim shorts.

When interviewing Zoe, of course he'd noticed she was attractive. Okay, striking, with a lovely face and athletic body. But he was surrounded by good-looking women most of the time. For a start, his recording artists were almost always easy on the eye. Not fair maybe that looks should be as important as talent, but the paying public invariably preferred something appealing to look at with the music. It was part of why Taylor, Rihanna and

Rita had done so well.

He'd never had a problem keeping his hands off his artists, never had an issue keeping the relationships strictly professional. When Helen had been alive, he'd believed in being faithful and sticking to his marriage vows, even if, as it turned out, she hadn't felt the same. Since she'd been gone, he'd had two small children to worry about, a successful business to keep afloat and an income to bring in if he wasn't going to rely on the family inheritance the way his brother did. Was it any wonder he'd avoided getting close to women over the last few years? The complete opposite to what the press thought, the flames of publicity fanned by his PR Officer to give him and his clients maximum exposure.

Whatever, Zoe had been the best candidate for the job by far and it had been an easy and pragmatic decision to offer her the post. He'd had no expectation that moving her in would be an issue, but now wasn't so sure. She was absolutely gorgeous, though a little on the thin side; her upper arms were a bit too defined and the slight ridges of her ribs were visible through the top. Nonetheless in this outfit she had an earthy sexiness that was going to make it hard for him to be around her without being in physical discomfort.

The thought brought back his earlier irritation. The last thing he needed was a complication, especially after everything that had happened with his last nanny. Getting involved with Zoe would be inappropriate. She was an employee. Look what had happened with Melody and Stephen, how that had turned out. Thinking about it brought on new waves of anger and disappointment. He'd thought Melody was such a sweet girl. So caring, so selfless. *Wrong.*

Frustration edged his voice as he stepped further into Zoe's bedroom. 'What's going on? I didn't realise you were moving your worldly possessions in. It's like a jumble sale in here!'

Zoe looked up at him, then at the devastation around the room, flushing. 'Oh. Well, I'm not finished yet, and wasn't expecting you back so soon.'

'Obviously.'

Jumping to her feet, rocking on the high heels, her black hair trailing down her back in its loose ponytail, her eyes flashed. *Great, the view's even better up close. Focus on talking Matt, look her in the eyes, not anywhere else. Definitely do not drop your gaze to those eye-popping breasts.*

'I didn't realise there was a limit on the number of items I was allowed when I took the job,' she said defensively, tucking her hands in her shorts pockets. 'Sorry, did I miss something in the contract?'

'No, of course not. Don't be silly—' he clicked his teeth together, seeing from her scowling face how well the comment had gone down. *Deep breath, try again.* Maybe if he didn't look into those massive baby blues he'd be okay, so he stared at her collarbone instead. 'I'm sorry, what I meant to say is, no. There's no limit. I was just, er, it's just that—' his gaze dropped a few inches, and he frowned, fighting an overwhelming urge to grab her and bury his face in her cleavage. *You're acting like a schoolboy, sad and needy. Get a grip.*

'Just that what?' she crossed her arms.

Shit, it just made the cleavage thing worse. *Eyes up.*

'I was just a bit surprised by the mess,' he muttered. 'I'm not in that great a mood either. My version of a bad day at the office. I shouldn't have taken it out on you though, so I apologise. I'm sure you'll have it all put away soon.'

'Yeah,' she hitched her chin up a few centimetres but didn't look very confident. 'I hope so.' Giving him an uncertain smile. 'What time are the kids back again?'

'Just under two hours. Let me help,' he said instinctively. Why had he done that? He'd never offered to help Melody in that way. He also had loads to do. The cold shower, the emails, phone calls to return. This was a bad idea, a stupid one. He should leave her to it. Instead, to his surprise, he stepped further into the bedroom.

A funny feeling swirled in Zoe's stomach as Matt came closer. He lifted a hand, rubbing a long finger over the scar that ran into his top lip. If it were anyone else she might have thought he was nervous, but he was so confident she knew that couldn't be it.

'Thanks for the offer, but I'll be fine.' She edged away, aware of his body heat and how big he was, towering over her. 'You don't want to help unpack a load of clothes and shoes, surely? I hardly think that it's part of your job description as my boss.'

He shrugged muscular shoulders in the clinging grey t-shirt he wore so ridiculously well.

'I want you to feel at home here,' he wandered around the room with an easy grace for such a tall, well-built guy. 'If you do, the kids will feel it. So whatever it takes. Where do you want me to start?' Frowning, and looking at the tottering piles of shoes in three different parts of the room. 'I take it you've seen there's shelving for shoes? Although,' he glanced at her, 'I'm not sure you'll fit them all in.' He bent over and plucked up a patent red stiletto, letting it dangle from one finger, raising one eyebrow.

She blushed and bit her bottom lip. The shoe looked tiny in his hands. It was a strangely personal feeling as he ran assessing fingers over the curve of the arch and turned the heel over. He might as well be delving into her lingerie drawer. Something about the confident way he handled the shoe sent a ping of lust zipping through her pelvis. Plus he smelled incredible and looked sexily rumpled with his hair in tufts, presumably from where he'd raked through it with stress, and she couldn't help noticing again the way his t-shirt stretched over his well-defined chest.

She was mortified to realise as he looked over that she was staring.

What? No, no, no! Stop salivating over him. He's a pig, remember? Remember why you're here.

'So, is this it or is there still more to come?'

His question threw her, given the battle she was fighting against rebellious hormones and the need to hang onto some brain power.

'No, that's it. Anyway, does it matter?' she asked, clearing her throat when realising how breathy she sounded. 'Because you've said I've no limit on the amount of stuff I can have, I mean.'

'It'll matter if this only scratches the surface and we end up with a house so full we can't move,' he grinned disarmingly. Then he looked down at the shoe. 'You've got expensive tastes, haven't you? Got a rich guy secreted in the States somewhere who keeps you in the good stuff?'

'Sorry, but that's not really any of your business, Matt,' she said stiffly. He was only joking but the comments hurt. Yes, she'd had a guy in the States, but contrary to what he might think she couldn't be bought by pretty things, wouldn't be blinded by them.

Temper flared in his eyes at her tone, but he didn't respond straight away, instead gathering up the matching red shoe and disappearing into the cupboard, presumably to put the pair in the rack. 'Fair enough,' he said casually as he came back out, picking up a silk top from a pile on the side, 'as long you're not going to have some guy turning up out of the blue.' He glanced at the king-sized bed behind her, and something in his expression tumbled her stomach, along with the way he was running his fingers absent-mindedly over the lace of the top's neckline. 'I don't allow sleepovers in this house. That *is* in your contract.'

She turned to stare at the bed. Her eyes closed on a rush of heat, her skin prickling with awareness and she suddenly felt tongue-tied. *Get it together. Anyone would think you were a teenage girl alone in your room with a boy for the first time.* As much as she was aware of his astonishing hotness in her weaker moments, she wouldn't act on it, mainly because of the whole Plan Nannygate and not liking him thing, but also because she wasn't ready for anything after Greg's betrayal. But back to the issue at hand, his comment on overnight guests. 'That won't be a problem.' She met his gaze. 'I'm single, and happy to stay that way.' But she mustn't be too adamant about it. At some point she needed to try and build a relationship between them, or at least the appearance of one. Which meant humour, trust, affection. Yuck.

'Great! Good.' He looked completely wrong-footed by the words flying out of his mouth. 'I mean, that's easier for everyone. I just don't like the thought of strange men wandering around my house with the children here—'

'No. One strange man is more than enough,' she joked, crossing the room and easing the silky top from his hand, raising her eyebrows. 'Could you please kindly stop feeling up my pyjamas?'

His eyes shot to hers, then down at the fabric. 'Oh. I, ah … sorry, I thought that it was a top. That you wear out, I mean. I-I'd better go, I have a lot of work to do.'

'You're not going to stay and help after all?' She couldn't resist teasing him, seeing his discomfort.

'I think its best you sort it out,' he started backing toward the door. 'If you can get the room straight and then get changed into something more suitable before Jasper and Aimee get home, that would be appreciated.'

She frowned. 'Something more suitable?'

He took a few more steps back. 'You're the other responsible adult in this house at the moment and need to set a good example. I'd rather not be confronted by my seven year-old daughter trying to wear shorts that go up to—' he paused before nodding at her bare legs, 'well, you know what I mean.'

Turning, he headed off downstairs before she could respond, leaving her standing in the messy room, face turning a slow bright red. Lovely. He'd just practically accused her of looking like a prostitute. What an ass. So much for Melody saying he could be kind of charming. Although he hadn't been doing too badly at first. Maybe Melody was right. Maybe this was a mistake.

She had to get out of here, get some fresh air, figure out what she was doing. She wasn't officially on duty until the morning, but had planned on spending some time with the children before their bedtime. So she'd unpack, shower and change into something Mr Clothing Police might approve of, see Aimee and Jasper for half an hour, and then she was escaping for the evening.

Matt was sitting at the breakfast counter in tight blue Levi's and a navy t-shirt watching the news when Zoe sloped into the kitchen early the next morning.

She murmured a quick greeting and looked around the room, admiring again the luxurious black and silver flecked marble counter tops, chrome equipment and spotlights set against the white walls and cabinets. Moving behind Matt to fiddle with the coffee machine, she placed a porcelain cup under the spout, frowning at the variety of buttons and levers. It looked more like a dashboard from a spaceship than something for making hot drinks. If she got desperate enough she'd ask him for help, but she'd give it a darned good try on her own first.

She poked at a black button, waiting for the chrome machine to do something. The orange ON light was lit up, and there was steam coming from somewhere, but nothing happened. Come on, she needed coffee.

They'd not spoken since Matt's comment about her shorts the previous day. He'd been in his office and she'd been with Aimee and Jasper in their playroom after they'd come back from his mother-in-law's and once they'd gone to bed she'd headed out, mooching around a few still open shops before trekking down towards Sloane Square and along Chelsea Bridge Road to take a walk beside the sluggish River Thames. The evening was balmy and bright, cars rushing past with beeps of horns, stressed commuters and cheerful locals streaming past her on the way to their next destination. She'd always loved London at this time of year. The sounds and smells of summer and the sense of endless possibilities. After her stroll she'd gone to see a late night comedy at the cinema.

She'd felt better and calmer on returning to Matt's. As much as he'd embarrassed her, reflecting on his behaviour she'd realised it was unintentional rather than trying to piss her off. Also, for the plan to work she had to get Matt on side. Which meant not sending waves of palpable dislike his way every time he moved or spoke. So the only sensible thing was to temporarily put aside what

332

he'd done to Melody and concentrate on being nice and becoming part of the household. She also didn't want to live in a house filled with tension. It wouldn't be good for any of them, least of all the kids. They mustn't be hurt by all this. It wouldn't be fair.

Muttering under her breath, she stabbed at a different button on the machine.

'Here, let me.' The deep voice sounded behind her and she jumped, the top of her head thunking his chin. His teeth clicked and a long, muscular arm grabbed the counter beside her waist, clutching it for support.

'Shit!' She span around, dismayed to see Matt's eyes clenched shut, face white, a trickle of blood running down his chin. 'I mean— argh! God, I'm so sorry. You took me completely by surprise.' She took hold of his arm, scared he was about to topple over. Breathing in his aftershave and noticing how hot his body was really shouldn't have been possible at that moment but somehow she managed both. Damn it.

'Uh-huh,' he groaned.

'Here. Sit down,' she ordered, guiding him back to his stool and pushing his head between his knees with a firm hand on the back of his warm neck. 'Stay there a minute.'

He didn't reply, staying put, so she edged away to get him a glass of iced water from the dispenser on the front of the big American style fridge and grab a piece of padded kitchen roll from the side, which she dampened. 'Here you go,' she held them out under his nose and after hesitating, he lifted his head slightly, grabbed the tissue and dabbed his mouth with it, followed by taking a few careful sips of water.

'I'm so sorry,' she repeated again, wincing. 'It was a complete accident.'

Making a deep *hmmming* sound of acknowledgement, he stared at the floor in silence for a minute, taking slow deep breaths.

As Zoe hovered next to him, she tried to take some satisfaction in his pain—after all, she'd regularly fantasised about punching him since her return to the UK—but totally failed. She hadn't meant to hurt him and the guy was so pale he looked bloodless. It wasn't funny what a sorry sight he was. 'Are you okay?'

Straightening up, he rubbed his jaw, poked a gentle finger in his mouth to check his tongue, and ran assessing fingers under his stubbly chin. 'I think so.'

Zoe sucked in her cheeks, expecting to be bawled out for being clumsy. Greg would have been furious with her for the lack of care. He'd also never been good at dealing with pain. In contrast, Matt had sucked it up and been a man about it.

Shaking his head and dabbing his mouth with the kitchen roll again, he smiled gingerly. 'I think I saw stars. And I definitely bit my tongue.' A pause. 'That is the last time I'm offering to help a woman make coffee.'

She was so surprised she burst out laughing. 'Sorry, again. I was zoned out thinking about something. You made me jump.'

'Clearly. Who would have thought you could jump so high though?'

'I know, like I was on springs.' She chuckled before turning serious. 'But are you sure you're okay? You might bruise under your chin. Your tongue will be sore for a few days too.'

'It's just a little cut. I'm sure I can cope. If there's a visible mark under my chin I'll make something up. I wouldn't want the world thinking my nanny could take me …' he trailed off, an odd look in his green eyes. 'In a fight I mean.'

'No,' she cleared her throat, stepping away as a tingling flush ran up and down her body. 'Obviously.' Spinning around, she went back to the fridge, opening it and sticking her head inside to cool down. 'Maybe I'll just have an orange juice. Safer for both of us that way.'

'No, I'll do you a coffee,' he replied, slowly getting up. 'You just stay over there where you can't injure me, and make toast or cereal or something.'

'Seems fair.' Emerging from the fridge she took two pieces of bread from the bread bin on the counter and put them in the toaster, pushing the button down and watching the elements glow red. The only reason her face was still warm was from the heat of the toaster. It was not about the thought of 'taking' Matt.

'So,' he looked over his coffee cup once she was settled across from him with her breakfast. 'Any injuries at your end?' Nodding at her head.

'A bit of a sore spot, but I think I came off better than you.'

'You might be right.' He grinned, but not too widely, wiggling his jaw. 'Look, I wanted to talk to you before the kids get up.' He slid a quick look at the digital clock on the front of the high-tech oven. 'They usually are now. It's past seven.'

'I'll establish a routine with them, but they both seemed tired and a bit out of sorts last night so I thought I'd let them sleep in this morning.'

'That's fine. It's the start of the summer holidays after all. As long as they're back in their routine for September—'

'They will be, no problem.'

'Good.' He pulled a face. 'Thinking about it, they do come back from my mother-in-law's a bit ratty sometimes.'

'Why do you think that is?'

'I … I've never really thought about it.' He stared into space for a moment. 'I suppose … it might be that she's not the warmest person in the world.'

'Yeah, I know someone like that,' she mused, thinking of Ruth. 'Or maybe their gran reminds them of their mum?' she suggested softly, off the back of a comment Jasper had made the previous evening. He'd said Gran had the same curly hair as Mummy, he knew it from photos at her house. There were no pictures of Mummy at home, Daddy didn't like them.

Watching Matt struggle with her suggestion, she was worried. A parent who knew their kids would instinctively know what was going on. Why was he so out of touch with them?

'I don't think so,' he said at last.

Feeling he was wrong, she also knew now was not the time to push. It was too soon. She'd barely been here five minutes and he was unlikely to trust her opinion yet about something so sensitive and personal. 'Okay.' Watching the news on the flat screen TV built into one of the walls, she chewed some toast and drank some of the delicious coffee. Gulping, she studied him. 'So, you wanted to talk to me about something?'

'Oh, yes. I wanted to say sorry for the comment about your shorts yesterday.' He looked down into his coffee cup. 'It was clumsy.'

'Thank you. I understand they might have been a bit skimpy, but—'

'But I could have been a bit more diplomatic,' he interrupted, flicking his gaze to her face. 'I sounded like a pompous git.'

Her mouth swung open, and she laughed. He wasn't at all what she'd been expecting. 'Well, I wouldn't have said that.'

'Well I can. I apologise. I just don't know how to talk to women anymore.' It was the last thing she'd have predicted him sharing and he looked embarrassed. 'I didn't mean to say that.'

'Obviously. After all, what about your reputation as a serial dater in the papers? And your last nanny was a woman, you must have talked to her?'

He scowled. 'You shouldn't believe everything you read. Besides, Melody was different. I wasn't—' he clenched his teeth. 'Never mind.'

'What were you going to say?' Was he about to open up, give her an inkling of what the hell had caused him to fire Melody and kick her out?

'Nothing. It doesn't matter. Next subject.' He drained his cup.

'If it's something I need to know, something that could affect the children—'

'It's not,' he said tightly, before making a visible effort to breathe in and out to calm himself. 'There was something else too, Zoe.'

'Oh?' Obviously she needed to let the subject of Melody drop, but it was weird how stressed he looked about the whole thing. 'Go on.'

'I'm um— not sure what time you got in last night but I really need you to be dedicated to the job, not coming in and out at all hours, dragging yourself around exhausted. Especially not smelling of alcohol.' His mouth tightened, the scar cutting into his upper lip turning white. 'Aimee and Jasper need stability and a responsible adult. I'm not unreasonable, you have a right to a life outside of work, it just has to be appropriate and come further down the list of priorities. My kids come first. Do you understand?'

She nodded, feeling a bit like a child who'd been told off for staying out to play too long, but she could see his point; she'd got in pretty late and was here to do a job. Plus how could she argue when he was looking out for his children? All she'd ever want from any parent was that they be child-centred and put their children's best interests first.

'Yes, absolutely,' she nodded, 'I want the best for them too.' Hopping down from her stool she stacked her plate and cup in the dishwasher, before straightening up to look at him. 'Just so you know, I wasn't out drinking. I went for a walk and saw a film. I like going out and having fun occasionally but that's it. I'm not a party girl.' Hangovers and looking after children were not a good combination. She'd learnt that the hard way when she'd worked at the nursery in her late teens. Coming into work hungover, dealing with the noise and demands of young children had been like slow-roasted torture and she'd ended up in tears before lunchtime. 'Is there anything else?'

His eyes raked over her beige safari shorts, a respectable mid-thigh length today, the floaty white vest top, chunky necklace and lace-up sandals.

'Yes,' he met her gaze. 'I can't let you leave the house like that.'

'Pardon?' Her eyes widened. He couldn't think this outfit was too revealing?

'The other nannies dress a certain way.' He ran a hand around

337

the back of his neck, seeming awkward with the direction of the conversation. 'I'm afraid that's not it.'

'I was planning on taking the kids out somewhere, spending some quality time with them. I'm not going to a fashion show.' No one loved clothes more than her but you had to dress for the activity.

'I appreciate that,' he rose from the stool and strolled over to her, 'but the thing is that I need you to fit in with my lifestyle, not the other way around. That outfit,' he looked down at her shorts, 'is too casual if you're going out. You're bound to bump into some of the kids' friends and their nannies or parents. I wouldn't want either of my children feeling …'

'What?' she questioned lightly, trying not to take it personally. 'Embarrassed to be seen with me?'

'Not embarrassed! But you won't fit in. I'm saying this for your benefit as well as theirs. Think of it like wearing a uniform. There's a certain way you're expected to look for this job. You must have come across that before.'

The truth was, she had. Liberty had expected Zoe to be immaculately groomed in well-cut clothes to fit into the society she lived in and she'd done it happily. But she hadn't really thought it through when she'd put her clothes on this morning, because her professional head wasn't on in the way it usually was, given she was here to get even, not make a living. She had to take more care. 'So what kind of thing do I need to wear?' she asked lightly, gazing past him out the window at the bright sunlight filling the manicured garden. 'Given it's not even half seven and already twenty degrees out? It's supposed to be another hot one today.'

'I don't know really. I think Melody wore a lot of dresses, but I never took proper notice. Just something smarter I guess.' To his credit he looked genuinely flummoxed.

She let out an exasperated sigh. 'Right, that's helpful.' Not. 'I'll go and change.' Marching out, she made for the top floor. At least he'd been more tactful than he'd been yesterday. They were making progress.

It was confirmed as she ran up the stairs, when he had the grace to yell, 'Thank you, Zoe!'

It made her smile, despite the fact everything inside her said it was wrong to.

5

She was downstairs again half an hour later, this time accompanied by Jasper and Aimee. After putting up with five minutes of moaning and groaning when she'd tried to get them up—aware of what they were like in the morning from Melody—she'd resorted to motivating them with a little competition. *Zoe's Ten Minute Challenge* had worked like a dream with Ava and Grace and it had worked a treat with Matt's children too. The added opportunity of picking a place of their choice to go had acted as a wonderful incentive for them to get washed and dressed with teeth brushed within the allocated time.

Aimee had narrowly won the contest which had triggered a tantrum from Jasper. Zoe had felt distinctively unimpressed and worried about a child of school age reacting like a toddler, and after telling him she'd be in the other room, had waited him out, pulling his door halfway closed while she helped Aimee pack a rucksack. The girl had looked at her a few times, mouth opening to say something but had shut it again each time.

'I give him two minutes,' Zoe had whispered out the side of her mouth.

Aimee smiled, as if to say, *in your dreams.*

He was done in just under. It wasn't long, yet he hollered pretty loudly and she was half expecting Matt to come thundering up

340

the stairs to demand what was going on, but he didn't appear.

Seeing Jasper's feet approach from the corner of her eye, she'd stood up, passing the rucksack to Aimee. 'Ready to go downstairs?'

The girl nodded, her auburn ponytail bobbing, blue eyes wide and looking impressed, possibly by Zoe's prediction about the length of Jasper's tantrum being right.

Jasper inched forward. 'Can I come too?' he hiccuped, rubbing at his green eyes, so much like Matt's.

Zoe wasn't fooled for a second; if they were real tears she'd put on trousers and call herself Bob.

'I suppose so,' she replied briskly, 'if you're ready?'

He pursed his lips like he was considering his options, then tucked his hands in his pockets, small dark head bobbing. 'Yes.'

'It was sort of silly behaviour, wasn't it?' she remarked conversationally as they wandered down the stairs, Aimee trailing behind them. 'After all, you can't always win. You'll just have to try really hard next time to be even faster. And I heard that you're a big boy. Your dad told me you're starting school soon and your birthday is not long after.'

'Yes!' his eyes brightened. 'In forty sleeps time on the second of September I go to school. It was forty, Melody helped me count before she went,' his little face clouded over, 'and I've been counting by myself but I'm not sure I'm right … and my birthday is on the third day of September. I'll be five,' he finished proudly.

Zoe gulped hard, upset for him and her sister that Mel wasn't going to be here to see him start school, or for his birthday. But she said nothing. It would do no good to upset him further and it wouldn't be fair to quiz a four year-old about adult decisions. 'Well then, you need to have a big think about what you might do at school if you lose a game, because if you get cross like that the teacher will probably make you sit on your own and the other kids might not want to play with you. I bet you want to make friends, don't you?' she affirmed by nodding.

'Yes,' he agreed seriously.

341

'So you have to find ways to not be cross. It's okay not to win everything, all right? As long as you try your best that's all that matters. If you feel angry about something, tell me and we can work out how to make you feel better. I know some really cool counting games. Can you do that for me? Will you let me know?'

'Uh-huh. That would be super cool. Holly might like to play those games with us.'

'Holly?' Her face froze, and she stopped on the spiral staircase. Who the heck was Holly? Had Matt moved on to someone new already? He'd only supposedly split with the pop star ex-fiancée just over a week ago. No wonder the kids were confused and insecure if he paraded an endless stream of women through their lives. Why wouldn't he have told her about a girlfriend? As their nanny, she needed to know these things. Every person in his life was part of his children's world, a role model or an influence.

'She's 'Cle Noel's girlfwiend.' Jasper lisped as he stared up at her.

Zoe had noticed that one of his two front teeth was not quite fully grown and occasionally affected his speech, but knew it would improve as the tooth grew. 'I thought the only uncle you have is Stephen?' she said. 'Did your mummy have a brother?'

'No, don't think so,' Jasper looked puzzled, glancing over his shoulder at his sister, who shook her head.

'So who's Noel then?' she asked gently, switching her gaze between both children.

'Daddy's friend,' Jasper replied, 'and my g- g …' He screwed his face up, rounded cheeks puffing out. 'My g- something. Can't remember. But Holly is really, really, really good at ice skating,' he said excitedly, 'just like me, we can both skate backwards but she can do spins but I can't yet and she has long yellow hair and blue eyes and white skin and her teeth sparkle and she makes 'Ncle Noel smile even though he hates Chwistmas and can be really gwumpy,' he finished on a gasp of breath.

'Wow!' Zoe grinned, 'Holly sounds amazing! Noel is a lucky guy.'

As Jasper nodded eagerly at her summation, Aimee leaned into

342

Zoe's side and whispered softly in her ear. 'Godfather.'

'Ah. Thank you Aimee,' she turned her head and murmured back in a low key tone, trying not to look too triumphant that the girl had actually spoken to her. Neither should she get a big head. Aimee had probably only supplied the information through frustration at her brother's inability to remember Noel's role in their lives.

When she looked at Aimee and saw her downturned face and pink cheeks, she knew it'd been right not to make a fuss. Starting down the stairs again, she watched to make sure Jasper didn't trip over his own feet.

'So, I bet you'll be extra quick tonight when you get ready for bed, Jasper. Do you think you might be able to beat your sister then?'

'I'll try my best!'

'Good boy.' Another victory, he'd taken something on board. 'Same goes for you,' she said casually at Aimee over one shoulder, 'anything you need, just ask.'

Aimee didn't reply, but her expression when Zoe flicked a look at her was quietly grateful.

Zoe felt strangely nervous on reaching the ground floor. Matt had given the impression the other nannies dressed smartly, but she had no idea what they wore in Knightsbridge, so had gone ultra-smart. Was she over-egging it in her grey knee length skirt and matching nipped-in jacket? She probably looked like she was off to the city for an interview. Plus she was going to fry in it. Her body temperature was already climbing.

She gestured the children to go in front of her. 'Come on, time to say good morning to your dad.'

Aimee turned around, pale red brows drawing together.

'But we can't go in and see Daddy in the morning,' Jasper piped up, 'we're not allowed into his office. He finds us to say hello and goodbye when he leaves for work if he can.'

'Sometimes,' Aimee supplied in a barely audible voice, staring at her feet.

What? Melody had said he could be closed off from the children, but she hadn't expected that they weren't allowed to see him in the morning. 'I'm sure he'll want to see you now that you're up,' she said blandly. 'Don't worry, come on.'

Jasper took a step forward then stopped again and Zoe's feet tangled with his. 'Whoa!' She grabbed him and steadied them both.

'Melody never let us into Daddy's office,' he insisted.

Unluckily for your dad, I'm not Melody. She thought inwardly. *I'm far more stubborn for a start.*

'I understand that,' she said, holding his anxious gaze, 'but I do things differently and I think your dad will want to say hello to you.' She squeezed his shoulder. 'Come on.'

Aimee raised an eyebrow and Zoe could read in her clear blue eyes that she thought their new nanny was making a mistake, but given Jasper had changed his mind and was now racing ahead, she shrugged and followed her little brother to the office door.

Zoe reached above their heads and knocked on it twice firmly, feeling sweat forming in the small of her back. It was so darned hot already. This suit was going to kill her. When there was no answer, she knocked again. After a minute, she lost patience and reached around Jasper's head, grabbing the door handle and nudging the kids into the room.

Matt spun around in the ergonomic office chair, a scowl on his incredibly good looking face, the desk behind him a chaos of paper, pens, Post-It notes and gadgets.

'Yep, what is it?' he turned back to the Mac screen.

'Aimee and Jasper wanted to say good morning.'

'Sorry. I'm busy.' He tapped a few buttons and rubbed the back of his neck.

'I'm sure you can spare a minute.' She kept her tone light.

'Not really.' He replied vaguely, moving the wireless mouse around. 'I'm in the middle of something.'

She gritted her teeth. What the heck was the matter with him?

344

Where was the kind, light-hearted guy from earlier in the kitchen?

'They're not sure you'll find them to say goodbye before you leave,' she explained in a gentle voice for the children's sakes, 'which I understand happens sometimes?'

As she said it, Aimee dropped her gaze to study the floor and Jasper started jiggling up and down on the spot.

'Hmmm?' Matt tapped some keys again.

'Matt? Matt!'

'Yes?' He looked at her over his shoulder, eyes distant.

Maybe he wasn't being rude, he was just caught up in what he was doing. She chose to give him the benefit of the doubt. 'I know you're not saying you don't have time to say good morning to Aimee and Jasper,' she stared at him meaningfully, 'and I'm sure that if you need uninterrupted work time you'll go to the office.' She let that giant hint sit there. 'It's fine if you don't want to speak to me about that other thing now,' she said softly, giving him a way to make this quick, 'so this will only take a moment. Kids, go and say morning to your dad. Give him a big squeezy hug.'

Jasper stared uncertainly from his big sister to his dad and back to Zoe, who immediately saw the tension in both children's shoulders. Looking across the room she saw an equal tension in the set of Matt's arms, and the way his jaw was clenched.

What was going on here? They never hugged? Zoe was utterly shocked, looking at her boss's closed expression. What kind of family was this, so shut off from one another? And why hadn't Melody told her how bad things were? They were young children for God's sakes. They needed warmth, love and affection to build their self-worth, to feel secure and happy. Self-esteem was crucial to their development and the people they would become.

'No. I mean, we don't usually …' Matt started saying, trailing off as Zoe shook her head slightly then nodded at Aimee to show him how his daughter's chin was tucked tight against her chest, fingers twisting nervously in the hem of her top. She gestured with a small wave at Jasper, bopping up and down, green eyes wide.

345

Don't push your children away, can't you see what you're doing to them? Zoe tried to communicate what she was thinking to Matt, looking at him with begging but determined eyes. Her tone was firm. 'We'll be out of your hair as soon as it's done. Just a minute, I promise.'

Staring from one child to another, he tapped his fingers on his knee, shoulders hunched over. Zoe could see the pained indecision on his face, but after a brief hesitation while he studied Aimee's pose, he conceded with a curt nod, face twisting with something she couldn't peg.

Full of relief, Zoe smiled brightly at Matt and his mouth swung open, looking surprised. Bending over she peered up into Aimee's face. 'Go on,' she encouraged. 'Your dad's ready for his hug now.'

Aimee frowned.

'He is. Come on, look at him. Get to it!'

The girl gave Zoe a look of pure disbelief but cocked her head around her to look at her dad. He crooked his fingers at her, jaw flexing again.

Aimee bit her lip and threw her a look. *If this goes wrong, it's on you.*

Zoe smiled bravely. *Fair enough.*

Shrugging her thin shoulders, Aimee wandered towards her dad, throwing a quick glance at her little brother, who was watching the action with interest, still jiggling away. Matt flushed as his daughter approached him, face still rigid, but moved forward in his chair, normally graceful movements strangely uncoordinated.

They wrapped their arms around each other hesitantly, and it was one of the most awkward hugs Zoe had ever seen, but then something in Matt seemed to unravel and he relaxed, muscular arms tightening around Aimee, eyes closing. He rested his head against her auburn hair, swallowing hard, and then opened his eyes and arms, inviting his son into their little circle.

Jasper sprang across the room like he'd been waiting for years, hurling himself at his dad and sister, his small face full of innocent joy as he snuggled into them. Matt scooped them tighter against his broad chest, closing his eyes again and Zoe melted a little as she saw his love for his kids. Why he wasn't usually affectionate with them she didn't know. He was a natural once he loosened up. And why she found him so extraordinarily sexy holding his children, her knickers melting along with her heart, she couldn't work out. She fanned herself. It was getting hotter inside and outside.

Maybe it was a biological thing programmed in by evolution, the sight of a big, capable tough man protecting his children triggering a need to make more. It might explain why the famous Athena poster of a bare-chested man holding a tiny baby had sold so many millions of copies. God only knew, but whatever it was, she didn't like the tender feelings racing through her. It was totally and utterly wrong. She started backing toward the door, intent on escape and happy to leave them to their private family moment. Maybe she'd splash her face with cold water to cool down.

'Kids,' Matt said huskily as he opened his eyes and saw her exit attempt, 'can you go into the kitchen and sit at the table? Zoe will be there in a minute.' He released them, standing up. 'Close the door on your way out please.'

Oh, crap.

Both children smiled widely at her as they left the room, and Zoe smiled back with pleasure for them but a sinking feeling in her stomach. As soon as the door shut she stepped forward, needing to take control of the situation. Waiting to be bawled out was awful. 'I'm sorry if I ambushed you, but I had no idea that's the way things were,' she was aware her voice was both apologetic and defiant, 'and really you can't expect me to let you reject your children by not hugging them and they're bound to want to see you in the mornings, they're kids, they need to know you love them. Also how would you feel if you didn't see them and then something happened to one of them, you'd regret it and—'

'Whoa! Slow down, Zoe! Wait a minute.' Matt held up his

hands, walking toward her, forest green eyes searching her face. He shook his head and blew out a long, slow breath, gathering his thoughts. 'Look, I wasn't pleased at the interruption when you first came in, I'll admit. When I'm disturbed I find it really hard to get back into whatever I'm working on and sometimes I have to start again, which seems to take twice as long. I guess it comes with being creative. I get so immersed I lose track of myself and what's going on around me, and then when I'm yanked out of that place I find it jarring. I know that can be difficult for other people to understand,' he stated. 'I'll also admit that I don't like feeling slightly bullied by you and your steely, *don't mess with me* eyes … I mean, at one point I was scared you were going to kill me if I didn't hug the kids,' he chuckled, 'but I can see that you were in a tough position. You weren't to know that we're not really the hugging types,' he trailed off, looking uncertain. 'When you forced me look at Aimee and I saw … what I saw, well, you were right to insist. But you don't get to tell me how to raise my children, and there will be some things I won't give in to,' he emphasised.

'It was the right thing to do, and I don't regret it,' she defended, 'but if you feel bullied, I'm sorry. I also accept that you're their dad and should know what's best for them.' Except that for years he'd given them little physical affection and appeared to have kept them at the periphery of his attention. She also knew from Jasper's chatter at bedtime the night before, that Matt had signed them up for hobbies they detested, like horse-riding, draughts and fencing. So at the moment, she needed convincing that he had their best interests at heart.

'Why do I feel like there's an unspoken criticism in there some-where?' he asked dryly, rubbing a hand through his messy dark hair.

She shrugged, letting him fill the silence. Sometimes you had to let other people do the talking, to realise things for themselves.

'Look. I love my kids, and I spend a lot of time protecting them,' he stated. 'Not everyone shows their love in the same overt way. Everyone's different. But believe me, I work hard to provide for them and be a positive role model,' he sucked in his cheeks, 'I just hadn't realised how much the lack of affection has affected them. Melody, my last nanny, never said anything about it and she was with us for three years,' he frowned.

No way was she going to criticise her sister, even if she was wondering the same as Matt. 'Perhaps she shouldn't have had to. In any case, as you said, everyone's different. Maybe she didn't feel able to bring it up with you. You can be a bit … erm, never mind,' she raced on when he raised both eyebrows, 'I'm just more confident than some people. So, when and why did you stop hugging them?' She gazed at him, wanting to know the story despite the fact that she shouldn't care.

'I'm really intrigued as to what I'm a bit of, but won't hold you to it,' Matt's stern mouth quirked up on one side, before his face turned grim. 'I don't want to talk about it though Zoe, if you don't mind. However, I'll make more of an effort going forward.' His expression was written with guilt. 'They both looked so happy.'

'Well, that's good, and as long as I'm not in trouble—'

'Don't speak too soon,' he replied. 'What exactly are you trying to prove with that?' Pointing at her jacket.

'Nothing,' she hitched her chin up, doing her best to pretend she wasn't incredibly hot and wanted nothing more than to rip the stupid suit off. 'You said I wouldn't fit in, that I needed to dress the part so as not to embarrass the children. So I got changed into something smarter, like you said.'

He shook his head, looking impatient. 'Not a suit! And I told you it wasn't about embarrassing us. Now go and change.'

She shook her head, even as sweat broke out on her face. He hadn't even said please.

His mobile started ringing on the desk. Stalking across the office he grabbed it and pressed the end-call button. 'Shit! I've got that meeting soon. Sadie, please come back, all is forgiven.' He cast both eyes up at the ceiling and joined his hands together in mock prayer. 'I'm not sure how much more of this I can cope with,' he said to Zoe. 'I'm so used to Sadie organising me. I don't know whether I'm coming and going, and all I want to do is get back into the studio. I just hope she recovers soon and that the hamper I sent helps … But anyway,' walking back over to Zoe, he threw her a hard look, 'I'm sorry, but I haven't got time for this. We both know you're being a little ridiculous. Please go and change.'

'I'm fine.' He was right, but she'd look silly backing down just like that and she didn't like being bossed around. It made her wonder if this is what he'd been like with Melody the day he threw her out. Her fingers curled into her palms. She couldn't forget what a bastard he'd been to her sister, even if he did seem to have some redeeming qualities, like wanting to be a good person for his children, and being nice to sick staff and having a sense of humour. *Stop it.* 'Really,' she insisted, 'I'm fine.'

'But you won't be, with the predicted temperature today. I can't believe you're serious. You'll bake if you leave the house.' He glanced down at his watch, swore and moved away from her to start grabbing things off his desk, throwing his iPad, notepad and a sheaf of paperwork into a messenger bag before looping it across his chest.

'It's not that hot,' she answered.

'It will be,' he shot back, stalking back over to her. 'Come on,' he stepped closer, eyes narrowing. 'Look how overheated you got at our interview; ready to fall over from standing on the doorstep too long. You'll make yourself ill, and then where will my kids be? Take it off.' Reaching out, he curled a big hand around the jacket collar and tugged her closer.

She froze, smelling his aftershave, far too close to his broad, muscular chest, her body flashing with heat, but not because of the weather this time. She mustn't sway towards him. Couldn't ask him to put his fingers down inside her collar, to run them over the tops of her boobs, to—

'Is this wool?' he asked in disbelief, testing the material between two fingers.

'Er—' she pulled a face. 'It might be.'

'It's the middle of summer. You're completely insane,' he joked. 'Right, that's it. Take it off. I don't want to get done at tribunal for not ensuring the health and well-being of my employees.'

'No!' She might have given in at that point but quite apart from sticking to her guns, there was a really good reason she didn't want to remove the jacket in front of him.

'Yes!' he insisted. To her shock, he started unbuttoning it, and she wrestled with him, trying to bat him away.

'Matt, don't!' *Oh shit,* she thought fleetingly. 'I said don—'

Unfortunately the jacket only had four buttons, his fingers made mega-quick work of them and she stepped back at the same time as he undid the last one.

The jacket flew open, revealing her pale, round breasts encased in a red lacy bra.

'Bloody hell!' His breath whooshed out, eyes all but popping out of his head as he took in her cleavage. 'You're not wearing a top!'

'Thank you Captain Obvious, I didn't know that,' she muttered, yanking the jacket back together, doing it up with fumbling fingers, face burning as he spun around to give her some privacy. This was so embarrassing, and would probably forever be known as either jacket-gate or bra-gate. Why it had to happen in front of Matt of all people, she didn't know. It was just her luck. 'Sorry,' she thought of how her sarcastic Captain Obvious comment must have sounded, 'I didn't mean to be rude.'

'That's fine. I'm sorry too. I-I just meant … Bloody hell,' he repeated. 'Why?'

'It is too hot,' she grimaced. Now the outfit choice looked really stupid. 'And I didn't think it would matter that I had nothing on underneath. You can turn around now,' she said. When he obeyed, it was like he couldn't quite bring himself to look at her, fixing his eyes on a spot on the wall over her left shoulder. She gazed up at him, seeing the nonplussed expression on his face. For some reason her mouth quirked up on one side. They must have looked like complete idiots during their little struggle, her trying to keep the jacket on, him trying to get her out of it. 'I wasn't planning on taking the jacket off,' she explained, 'and I didn't foresee a madman coming along and trying to wrestle me out of it,' she finished drily.

'No,' he conceded, dropping his eyes to her face, 'I don't suppose you did.' For a moment he looked solemn, but then his mouth curved, a spark of warmth in his eyes.

Their gazes connected. There was a silence.

'It was like a comedy sketch or something,' he choked out. 'Your face! I've never seen anyone look so panicked!'

She couldn't help it, grinning back. 'Well, you can understand why now.' She gave into laughter, holding her side. 'We must have looked pretty ridiculous. I mean, imagine if the kids had seen us,' she snorted.

'They'd think that we've lost it,' he agreed, laughing. 'Not a great example to set for them.'

Oh, bugger. The kids. She'd forgotten all about them. It'd never happened to her before. In her other jobs she hadn't ever neglected her professional responsibilities. 'Oh, God, they're alone in the kitchen. I should go.'

'Yes,' Matt crossed back to his desk, looking puzzled, 'me too. That's right, I have work to do, a meeting to go to.' He rammed his phone into his jeans pocket, hunting around in the mess of music sheets and other random items. 'Keys ... keys. Argh ... bloody things.'

Zoe stood by the door, watching as he cast various papers and a spare tablet around. 'Um, Matt.'

'Hmmm?' He picked up an expandable file, shook it, put it back down. Picked up a mug of all things, as if the keys would be hiding in it or under it somehow.

'Don't you put your car keys in the bowl by the door?' she asked, raising an eyebrow.

'The bowl,' his head came up and he glanced over at her, face clearing. 'Yeah, you're right, I always do. I can't think why I forgot—' his green eyes flickered over her chest. 'I've got to go,'

352

he blurted, racing past her out of the office. 'See you this evening. Bye kids.' She heard him yell, followed by the slam of the door and the quiet purr of the Prius rapidly fading into the distance.

Shaking her head at his odd departure, Zoe walked into the kitchen to find Jasper standing by the fridge, face covered in strawberry jam, slices of bread, utensils and bowls littering the floor and work surfaces.

'I got hungry,' Jasper explained woefully, staring up at her with an expression on his face that said *please don't tell me off.*

Aimee was completely oblivious, head stuck in a thick book of fairytales with line drawings on the cover.

'That's okay,' ruffling Jasper's hair, Zoe lead him over to the sink and started wiping his hands and face with a damp cloth, 'it was my fault. I took too long with your dad.' She blushed as she thought of all the things they could have done if they'd had more time. If when he'd opened her jacket he'd sunk to his knees and buried his face in her cleavage and—

No. Remember why you're here.

There was no doubt about it, Matt was hot, but her sister came first, she wasn't letting her down again. Plus, no good came of getting involved on the rebound. 'Next time come and get me, okay?' she asked the little boy, shaking her head as she found a clump of red jam in the hair behind his ear. 'When you want jam, remember it's supposed to go on something, Jasper. Like toast. Not the floor, or yourself,' she smiled.

'Yes, Zoe,' he nodded.

'Great. Now how about giving me a hand clearing up this mess?' Stooping over, she picked up a bowl and two spoons.

'Do I have to?' he whined. 'Melody wouldn't have made me.'

She loved her sister, but had she been half asleep on the job or something? At seven and nearly five, these children were old enough to know the difference between right and wrong, and to be clearing up after themselves. Just because their dad was super-rich and super-successful, it didn't mean they couldn't learn some traditional values and personal responsibility. She must ask Matt about it, and talk to Mel too.

'It would be great if you could,' she said to Jasper casually. 'But if you're worried I can pick up more things faster than you …'

'No, you can't!'

'Can!' Wiggling her eyebrows.

'Can't.' He giggled, racing over to grab a couple of forks off the side and bring them to her.

'Good boy,' she nodded approvingly scooping up slices of bread, and randomly, a bottle opener. They were definitely not being left alone in the kitchen again, until they were better trained. 'Everything that's been on the floor will need to go in a pile in the sink so I can wash them up.'

'Ok-ay,' Jasper sang cheerfully, clattering a mixing bowl and wooden spoon into the sink, along with a broken egg.

God only knew what he'd been trying to make.

'So, what would you like for breakfast kids? And where do you want to go today? Aimee's choice remember, because she got ready the quickest. Aimee?'

At the sound of her name, the girl's head jerked up, wearing the same look of fierce concentration as her dad when he was immersed in something. It was sweet.

'What do you want for breakfast? And where would you like me to take the two of you?'

Aimee bit her lip, squinting. 'Pancakes please. And …' she paused, started to say something then seemed to change her mind, 'um, the library?' she finished instead.

Jasper let out a little groan behind her. 'The library? Bo-ring.'

'It's Aimee's decision, Jasper,' she said firmly, while wondering how the heck she was going to keep him occupied in such a quiet, contained environment. 'Come on, books are fun. We'll find some good ones for you too, okay? I'm sure there's a nice children's corner,' praying wholeheartedly it was true. 'Aimee,' she asked hesitantly, 'how would you feel about going to the park on the way home? Just for ten minutes or so? The nearest one is Hyde Park, right?'

Aimee nodded, then shook her head. 'I don't want to. Maybe another day.'

'Are you sure? I thought it was a nice one, though I've never been. It's not far at all, and it's lovely and sunny today.'

But the girl shook her head resolutely with her lower lip sticking out and returned her attention to her book.

Ordinarily Zoe would go over to her, ask what was going on, but Jasper was tugging at her jacket insistently and it was obvious Aimee wasn't ready to open up. There was no point in pressing too hard; it had taken two visits and as many days to get Aimee to even speak to her in half sentences.

'No problem,' she said matter-of-factly, 'we can always find some games to play in the back garden.' She turned to Jasper, seeing Aimee pull a relieved face from the corner of her eye. 'So Mister, pancakes?'

'Yay! Pancakes! Pancakes!' Jasper started jumping up and down.

'Okay. If you calm down you can help me make them.' He really was a bundle of energy.

'Yay!' He bounded over to her, grabbing hold of her hand. 'Super cool! I want you to stay, Zoe.'

Aww, bless. 'That's lovely Jasper. Because I'm letting you help me make pancakes?'

'Because you're nice,' he decided solemnly.

'Oh. Thank you.' She gulped, his remark both warming and worrying her. They were good kids at heart, they just needed boundaries and the right kind of attention-slash-authority. But what she hadn't thought through properly when embarking on *Plan Nannygate* was that the kids might get attached to her.

'What about you, Aimee?' she asked gently. 'Are you happy with me being here?'

The girl looked up with a distracted air, and nodded once.

'Do you think I'm nice too?'

355

'Uh-huh.' She focused back on her book, turning the page. Zoe thought she was done, but just as she went to turn away Aimee spoke again. 'You got Daddy to hug us. It's been forever.'

Zoe bit the inside of her cheek, insanely sad for the kids. The plan was for revenge, but while she was here, there was no harm in trying to make things better for them as a family, for the good of the children. Was there?

6

It was a harried trip to graceful Mayfair library, during which Jasper caused near mayhem. Running around the ends of stacks, he pulled books off shelves and talked in the loudest voice possible despite stern glances from a staff member. Zoe used every behaviour management tool she could think of, along with repeated shushing, but eventually had to take him for a time-out, letting Aimee know she'd be out front for a few minutes.

They sat on the stone steps of the entrance while Jasper calmed down, his Ben 10 baseball cap pulled down low over his eyes, feet tapping on the pavement. She relaxed in the balmy sunlight, reading a leaflet picked up from the foyer about the weddings they performed in one of the two ceremony rooms. From the pictures, the venue looked romantic and intimate. Zoe could think of few nicer places to get married; surrounded by books in a nineteenth century building with the beautiful Mount Street Gardens next door, perfect for taking photos.

It was a far cry from the wedding she and Greg had planned at the *St. Regis* on Manhattan Island, which was as glamorously luxurious as it was hideously expensive. Greg had made his money on the stock markets and was more than happy showing his wealth off. She had insisted on contributing to the cost of the wedding but wondered now how comfortable she would have been on her own wedding day in such rich surroundings, when at heart she was an orphan from the British seaside. She also wondered how comfortable she would have been moving in with him permanently, subject to his world twenty-four-seven. Still, if they'd loved each other enough then it wouldn't have mattered. They'd have made it work.

Shrugging the thought off, she reminded Jasper of the need to behave and lead him inside by the hand with a firm grip. In sharp contrast to her brother, Aimee was in heaven in the library. Walking purposefully between shelves, she ran her fingers along scripted spines and stroked glossy covers. When she stuffed her rucksack full with the maximum amount of books she could borrow, checked in by a librarian who knew her by name, Zoe was surprised to see a copy of *To Kill a Mockingbird* go in. It was advanced reading for a girl her age.

As they walked home along wide Park Lane which guarded the eastern boundary of lovely Hyde Park—Zoe looking longingly at the green spaces and trees she could see across the road—down to Hyde Park Corner and along Knightsbridge, Aimee walked with her nose stuck in the Harper Lee classic. Zoe was tempted to tell her not to, especially with how busy the streets were with teeming crowds of tourists snapping away with cameras, shoppers swinging branded bags filled with new summer wardrobes and countless black cabs zipping past. It would be hypocritical though. She'd read books in the street right into her teens, skilfully learning to step around lamp posts and avoid people, and still recalled the guilty pleasure of every possible stolen reading moment. Heck, if she could get away with it now, she would. So she held Jasper's hand and settled for placing a guiding hand on Aimee's shoulder as the girl traipsed along.

When they got home, Aimee shut herself away in her room without a word and Zoe decided to leave her to it. She could hardly complain that one of her two new charges loved reading and was happiest when expanding her mind and vocabulary. In that way, she was a dream. On the other hand, she could do with learning a few more social skills. It wouldn't do her good being too insular.

For a few hours Zoe and Jasper painted and coloured-in while sitting up on stools at the kitchen units, newspapers spread out to protect the expensive marble, aprons on to protect their clothes. Zoe opened the window to let in some fresh air, and turned the radio on so that pop music created a white noise in the background. Occasionally the buzz of a lawn mower drifted in, punctuated by a child's laugh or call. There must be other kids in the neighbourhood, and Zoe wondered if Jasper or Aimee were friends with any of them.

Just before noon the beeping of horns and high-pitched two-note tone of a siren sounded, getting ever closer. Jasper jumped at the noise, arm freezing in place, paintbrush clutched in his sturdy fingers. Somewhere above their heads, a thud sounded.

'Everything all right?' Zoe frowned at the ceiling, and put a hand on Jasper's back.

Turning his head, he stared at her with solemn green eyes. 'Don't like sirens,' he answered in a tight voice, trembles rippling through him. 'Mummy went when sirens came.'

'Oh.' There were some residual memories of the accident then, even though he'd been so young. 'Well, there's nothing to be worried about now, okay? We're here, your sister is upstairs with her book, and your dad is safely at work. Besides, ambulances go to help people, right? They nee-naw like that to move cars out the way so they can get to people in trouble as quickly as possible. Everything is okay,' she soothed, stroking his back until the sirens faded away. 'See? They've gone.'

With a nod, he dipped his brush in the blue paint and started outlining swirling clouds. Zoe gazed down at his ruffled hair, marvelling at how freely he'd shared his fears with her, so soon after she'd arrived in his life. Still, that was kids for you, especially younger ones. They were open books. They barely had filters at this age and blurted out pretty much everything they thought.

'Stay there for a minute, all right? Just keep painting. I need to check on your sister.' Thinking of the thudding noise. Racing upstairs, she knocked on Aimee's door, pushing it open gently when there was no reply. 'Everything good up here?' she asked, hoping Jasper didn't get into too much mischief while she was gone. She stared at Aimee's downturned head, nose only a few inches from the page. 'I thought I heard something hit the deck,' Zoe said, 'was it in here?' There was no answer, just a slight tightening of the little girl's pink lips. 'Oh well, I must have imagined it then,' she added lightly, 'never mind. I'll leave you to it. Lunch is in a bit, by the way.' Aimee's gaze flickered upwards and she nodded once, but Zoe could see that her eyes were suspiciously bright. Maybe Jasper wasn't the only one affected by sirens. 'If you need anything, we're in the kitchen.' She backed out of the room, leaving the girl alone with her thoughts. When she was ready to talk about it, she would.

Zoe wandered down the spiral stairs, hand clutching the curved white rail. She could still remember the horror she'd felt when Mel had told her over Skype, brown eyes tear-filled, that both children had been in the car crash that killed their mum. Mel had only arrived with the family a few days before, and Matt had been battling along without help for three months before hiring a nanny. It had been a difficult time for all of them and Zoe knew that her sister, who could be emotionally fragile at times, had found it hard to deal with their grief. Slowly however, she knew things had gotten better. Or thought they had.

When she sloped back into the kitchen, heart weighed down with the sad thoughts, Zoe halted, mouth opening. 'Jasper,' she breathed, fighting not to laugh, 'what did you do?'

Grinning proudly, he pointed to his face, which was painted a bright shade of blue, save for a crooked, naked stripe down the middle over his nose. 'I'm Braveheart. It's one of daddy's favourite films. He won't let me watch it but 'Ncle Stephen lets me sneak peeks sometimes. This is what they do when they fight.'

'It is.' Shaking her head, she tried to be serious but sniggered

360

instead. He looked so earnest, and more like a haphazard smurf than a warrior. The fact he'd managed to miss his hair was a minor miracle. 'But that kind of paint is for paper, not for faces,' she pointed out. 'If you want to do this again, please let me know and we'll buy some proper face paints.' Reaching for her phone from one of the shelves, she held it out in front of her. 'Can I take a picture?'

'Yep! To show Daddy!'

'That's a great idea,' she said, deftly pressing two buttons and taking a selection of photos. 'We won't tell him you didn't ask permission, but I'll send him a picture if you promise that next time you will.'

He nodded decisively, blue dripping off his chin and plunking onto his plastic red apron. 'Deal.'

Grinning, she sent Matt a picture via WhatsApp, with the caption *Your son has the same movie tastes as you.* 'Right, done.' A reply wasn't necessarily something she expected, but a minute later a smiley face icon and *Lol, that's my boy* comment pinged her mobile. Smiling, she tucked her phone away and dampened some kitchen roll, standing Jasper at the sink to wash his face off.

After cleaning him up, they made fresh bread for lunch. At the end of the bread-making session, Jasper had managed to get little white-flour finger marks over himself, Zoe and most surfaces in the kitchen. With a chuckle Zoe wiped the sides down and they got the kitchen roll back out, turning the radio up and bopping around while they got clean again, before setting up a picnic in the garden. This time Jasper helped her without complaint.

When Zoe called Aimee for lunch, it took a full ten minutes to coax her from her bedroom at the same time as trying to keep an eye on Jasper, who was banging something about in his jam-packed room across the hall.

'Aimee,' she resorted to quiet authority after nice requests and cajoling had failed, 'you can't starve, and I'll be more than happy to discuss your favourite books with you or let you carry on reading after lunch, but if you don't come downstairs and eat with us before all the food gets swarmed by ants, I'm going to have to withdraw a privilege.' The girl looked at her with wide eyes, waiting to see what she'd do. Zoe knew it was a test. So she let out a big sigh, shaking her head sorrowfully. 'I would really, really hate to have to take one of your books away, because I understand how much you love them. I'm a big reader too,' she confessed. 'There's nothing better than getting lost in another world and making new friends. But you have to live in the real world sometimes, okay?' Throwing the door open wider, gesturing to the staircase. 'Come on. You can have a quick bite then sit in the shade and read some more, or you can have a longer lunch and we can talk books while your brother plays on his swing set. The choice is yours.'

Giving kids options seemed to help. It worked with adults too. But sometimes when you gave someone enough room to make a choice, they ran away from you instead of staying close, as you'd hoped. If you love someone set them free. That was the saying, wasn't it? If they loved you, they'd fly back of their own accord. But what happened when they didn't? In her experience it was heartbreak that could send you hurtling into the wrong man's arms. Heartbreak that could divide a family already poles apart. Because would she have fallen for Greg and moved to the States if she hadn't been so heavily on the rebound from her first love, Henry? And surely Greg was the wrong man for her after what he'd done? She gulped down the lump in her throat and breathed through the ache in her chest. It didn't matter. The break up with Henry was distant, hellish history. The only reason she was thinking of it now was because she was in that precarious state again, everything she'd known and planned wrenched away from her without warning. But she would get over that, and Greg too, in time. As soon as the anger was no longer a living, breathing thing inside her.

Smiling approvingly as Aimee trudged past into the hallway clutching her book, Zoe called for Jasper and they made their way down to the tartan blanket in the garden, her heartache fading away. After a lunch of bread, ham, cheese and fruit that dried out and quickly turned brown in the baking sun, and a few minutes to loll around and digest their food, she and Jasper set about playing a game of *tag*. It was almost unbearably hot. Running around the garden and dodging each other's footsteps, Zoe was glad she'd changed out of her suit after breakfast, exchanging it for a lemon sorbet coloured sundress with a cut-out hole at the back.

Aimee refused to join in with their game, resting against the bottom of the apple tree with her book instead. Every so often though, Zoe caught her watching them play, flicking her eyes back to the page whenever Zoe lifted her head. She wasn't sure why the girl was so reluctant to take part. Was it that she didn't like playing or that she didn't know how to? Melody must have played with the kids. She would have to call her sister on the quiet in the next few days and have a chat. She was starting to wonder if Melody leaving was having more of an impact on the kids than she'd first thought. Maybe Aimee was hanging back because she didn't trust that Zoe would be around for long? She wasn't wrong, Zoe thought, flushing with a pang of guilt. She didn't want to hurt anyone. It was only Matt's pride and self-important ego that she wanted to damage. He had to learn that actions had consequences.

She gradually slowed to let Jasper catch her, 'Okay, okay.' She held her hands up in mock surrender. 'You win!'

Jasper laughed delightedly. 'Got you!' he yelled, ploughing into her.

'Well done, you're very fast … for someone with such short legs,' she quipped, laughing as he stuck his tongue out at her.

He went quiet and looked up into her face, green eyes wide. 'Thank you for playing with me, Zoe,' he said, and then his mood flipped. 'Daddy doesn't weally play with us anymore,' he lisped, bottom lip trembling, a quaver in his little voice. He wrapped his arms around her waist and buried his head against her stomach.

As she looked down and stroked his dark head, glad not to

have to abide by the more rigid child protection rules of a nursery that restricted physical contact, she felt an unexpected and overwhelming pang of emotion. Jasper was hard work, but adorable too. The realisation wasn't good for her peace of mind, given she'd only just arrived here and it might take weeks to set her plan in motion.

Surely she was just feeling vulnerable after her break up with Greg? He'd hurt her, badly. She was bound to be a soppy mess.

'It's okay,' she said, hugging him briefly before easing away. 'You can always talk to me about things like this. Thank you for telling me. Your daddy is really busy but he loves you, always remember that.'

She crouched down in front of him so that she could look him in the eye. Casting a quick glance at Aimee, she saw the girl had finally put her book down but was peeling bark intently from the apple tree whilst pretending not to listen.

Zoe brought her gaze back to Jasper's and straightened his black and green Ben 10 t-shirt. She knew that Matt probably preferred them in designer stuff but it was what Jasper had chosen that morning so she would side with him if it came to it.

'I'll see if I can get your daddy to start playing with you a bit more. How about I ask him to slot some Jasper time into his diary?' A reassuring smile at Aimee. 'I'll also do the same for your big sister. Perhaps the three of you can get some time together every week, maybe have dinner out somewhere too. Would you like that?'

'Yes!' Jasper punched the air in reply to her proposal.

She didn't normally like setting expectations without first having discussed these things with parents, but she would find some way to convince Matt that his children needed some quality time with him. After all, he wasn't unreasonable; when he'd understood what was going on this morning, he'd done the right thing. She only hoped he would this time too.

Realising that Aimee had left the tree and was edging closer, casually picking flowers to disguise her interest in their conversation,

Zoe suppressed a grin.

'Zoe?' Jasper said brightly.

'Yes?'

He looked up at her thoughtfully, sucking his lower lip into his mouth, which she knew all too well was a habit he was already learning from her. Kids were like sponges at this age. They picked things up so easily. 'Can you come out with us to dinner too, Zoe? Please? Please, please, please?'

Her eyebrows pleated as she contemplated how to answer. It was important the three of them have time together as the family unit they should be. She wasn't a part of that, she was just doing a job and not even properly. They needed to learn to function as a family without her so that if, she mentally adjusted that to *when,* she left it wouldn't all fall apart. Added to which, it would be mortifying if Matt thought she was trying to wangle some kind of date-night via the kids. Plus, for her plan to work and be convincing, it all had to come from him.

'I don't think so, Jasper,' she answered in a soft voice, careful not to reject him, 'but thank you for the thought, it's very sweet. You'll spend lots of time with me without your dad around, so your time with him should be your special time, just the three of you. Anyway,' time for a change of mood she decided, 'you've got me now, and I think I know two children who might need to run round the garden some more, or be tickled!'

Swinging round, she lunged at Jasper with a pretend growl and on the rest of the spin lurched toward Aimee, who skipped out of arms' reach with a squeak.

Within minutes they had her pinned down on the perfectly manicured but somewhat prickly lawn, the smell of flowers and freshly cut grass filling her nose. She sneezed, the bright sun beating down on her head and shoulders. A bee buzzed somewhere and a breeze blew the leaves of the tree above their heads, pretty shadows dappling the lawn around them. Jasper laughingly pulled up short bunches of grass and threw them on her as she sat up, the blades tangling in her hair and going down the top of her dress. Aimee let out a series of uncharacteristic giggles as she saw what a mess her nanny was in. Somewhere in the distance a car beeped.

Throwing her head back and laughing like one of the evil geniuses in the programmes that according to Mel, Jasper was occasionally allowed to watch—*mwah-ha-ha*—Zoe jumped up to go after him, and was rewarded with a cackle of glee from Aimee, who stuck more grass down the back of Zoe's dress through the cut-out hole. 'You little troublemakers!' She ran after Jasper, grabbing him and lobster-pinching his waist to tickle him.

'Stop! Stop,' Jasper howled, giggling as he squirmed away, 'I'm going to wee myself!'

Aimee and Zoe shared a look and burst into fresh laughter. Zoe released Jasper and sank down onto the grass and Aimee copied, clutching her stomach. When Zoe rolled over onto her back, Jasper bundled on top of her, his sweaty, compact little weight half-crushing her. A wave of nausea hit her square in the tummy. Ignoring the sick feeling because they were all having such good fun and it was the most that Aimee had come out of her shell so far, Zoe wrestled the little boy onto the lawn, tickling him this time by squeezing his chubby knees.

Another wave of nausea swept over her as she sat up, touching a quick hand to her hot cheeks and moist upper lip. She didn't feel so good. She'd done a thorough job of protecting the kids from the sun, slapping sun cream on them, keeping them well watered and in the shade, but had obviously not done such a great job on herself. The kids giggled as she sat on the ground recovering, the sound making her smile despite the way her stomach rolled over in a sick flip. Yuck.

A shadow appeared over her and she arched her back to peer upwards, hand shielding her eyes from the sun. 'Matt.'

'What's going on out here?' he asked, hands on hips. 'I could hear the noise from out on the driveway!'

He'd returned early to work from home and catch up on some emails in Sadie's absence, but had been drawn outside by the sound of the kids' screeches of hilarity. They both quietened as he looked from them to his new nanny. She was certainly making herself at home, he thought. Walking through the house he'd noticed the paintings hung up to dry with pegs and string, paint pots and brushes drying on the draining board, the fragrant loaf of fresh bread resting on the kitchen unit and the sweet smell of pancakes, presumably from breakfast.

He couldn't remember the last time he'd heard his children being so noisy. Melody had spent most of her time trying to tame them into nice, quiet, obedient kids. Not that it had always been successful with Jasper, he mused. But he'd appreciated her efforts. He couldn't think properly when there was clamour going on around him, it made it almost impossible to work. Yet Zoe seemed almost determined to undo whatever Mel had done and make his kids as loud and distracting as possible.

Still, as he gazed down into their beaming little faces, he noticed that they also appeared happier than they had in a long time. The photo that Zoe had sent him of Jasper covered in blue paint had been hilarious. His mouth quirked, shoulders relaxing. As much as what had happened with Melody pained him, perhaps the change would be good for all of them. Even him, set in his ways. Zoe didn't seem afraid to challenge him, and although it was a bit irritating to have to explain himself, she also appeared to know what she was talking about, her bold confidence about children that she hardly knew somehow comforting. Hopefully she would stick around for a while. He'd just have to make sure he didn't let Stephen anywhere near her. It was probably just as well his younger brother was yachting on the Med to get over what Melody had done. Stephen had his own brand of arrogant charm (he'd once referred to himself as similar to Spencer out of *Made in Chelsea*) and it drove a lot of women crazy. Matt didn't want to lose another nanny because of his brother's love life. He grimaced at the thought of Stephen with Zoe, a pang of annoyance shooting through him. She'd said she was single, and bagging a young, rich playboy might appeal. That had certainly been the case with his last nanny.

His gaze dropped to his new one, where she still sat at his feet. 'Are you all right?' he asked abruptly, taking in her pale yellow sun dress, the top half filled with mouth wateringly generous curves that made his palms itch to touch them. Even in the studio, a place that was sacrosanct, he hadn't been able to get the sight of her stood in her red, lacy bra out of his head. He jerked his eyes upwards, away from her creamy cleavage. Her tangled blue-black hair was peppered with bits of grass and her cheeks were flushed with heat. She looked like she'd been for a tumble in a country field. His groin immediately tightened at the image that filled his mind. Her beneath him naked on a bed of grass, her breasts rosy and round in the sunlight—

'Y-yes,' she said, dazedly pushing her hair back from her face, cutting across his frustratingly inappropriate thoughts.

He frowned, taking in the slightly unfocused look in her eyes and the dewy hint of sweat on her face.

'You don't look it. You look as if you're suffering from the heat. If you're in this state, what on earth have you done to the kids?'

She pushed herself up hastily. 'Now wait just a minute! I—' too hastily as it turned out, because she swayed and stumbled forward into his unprepared arms.

He caught her against him with a surprised grunt, his muscular arms tightening around her as he looked down into her flustered face and then lower to her rounded cleavage, spying blades of grass tucked down there that he suddenly, desperately wanted to get rid of with his teeth, with his tongue—

He cursed as his body hardened even more and she must have noticed because she thrust herself away from him.

'Can you watch the kids please?' she said huskily as she turned to jog toward the house, 'I'm sorry, I—' she planted a hand across her mouth, 'I think I'm going to be sick!'

She ran off and left him, looking from her departing back to Aimee and Jasper in astonishment. He wasn't every woman's cup of tea—he could be distracted, tetchy and knew he kept people out of reach, plus he was her boss—but it wasn't often that he made grown women throw up.

Almost two hours later, after a long cooling bath and a power nap to ease away the worst of her mild heatstroke, Zoe came downstairs to tidy the kitchen and start prepping dinner. She met Matt coming out of his office.

'Hi.' He gestured at her loose pastel pink t-shirt and baggy white shorts. 'Feeling better?'

'Yes, thanks.' She peered around him, concerned. 'Where are the kids?'

'They're fine,' he replied. 'Sadie popped round to see me as she's feeling a little more human, so they're in there with her,' he hitched his thumb over his shoulder, 'playing hangman and chase the monkey.' He raised an eyebrow as she opened her mouth. 'It's okay, they've known her for years, and she was happy to help. Besides, what she's got isn't catching. It's a gynaecological … thing.'

'Oh, right,' she murmured, moving on quickly. 'Well, I'm sorry she had to look after them. I'm not usually unreliable but I felt pretty ill. This is the hottest summer I can remember for a while and I keep forgetting to apply sun cream and stay in the shade. New York was stifling in the summer, so we always retreated into the nearest air-conned building. I'll be more careful in future.'

'Don't worry,' Matt said, shifting nearer and touching her elbow, 'as long as you're better now, and don't make a habit of it.' He frowned as she jerked her arm away. 'Sorry. I was going to come and knock on your door to see how you were doing, but I thought it was better to leave you to it.'

'It was. Thank you.'

'I hope I didn't make you uncomfortable,' he said gruffly, 'out in the garden.'

'Uncomfortable?' she frowned. No. Not uncomfortable, just supremely conscious of his hard, muscular body despite battling rolling nausea.

'When I caught you, you backed away pretty quickly. I wasn't coming on to you, I promise. Jesus, that sounded so cheesy and sort of insulting.' He puffed out a breath and tried again. 'What I mean is, you work for me and I'm not really dating at the moment, haven't since Helen died and—'

'Wait. What? You said this morning I shouldn't believe everything I read in the papers, but you're seriously telling me that you haven't dated any of the women you've been seen with? What about your fiancée, the pop star?'

'We were never engaged. She just liked costume jewellery, and wearing the ring was good PR, according to my publicist,' he explained, a frustrated expression crossing his face. 'But me storming out of the hotel with the kids was true enough. Though how the press got tipped off for that one, I don't know. As for the dating,' he shifted from one foot to another, rubbing the small dark bruise under his chin from earlier in the morning, 'it's a fluid term, isn't it?'

She stared at him. 'Oh?'

'Well, what I mean is, I date occasionally,' his face started to burn a slow, deep pink, 'I just don't have significant relationships. So you don't have to worry about Aimee and Jasper, I don't bring women home with me, I just—'

'Stop, please,' she interrupted in a pained voice, holding a hand up, palm out. 'Wow, you really don't know how to talk to women anymore,' she sighed. 'Look, its fine Matt, don't worry about it, I get that you were just trying to help in the garden. I didn't read anything into it.' Talk about awkward. Though it would have been the perfect opportunity to learn more about his love life if she was going to get close enough for her plan to work, there was a strange reluctance inside her to pursue the conversation. She bit her lip, staring at the frayed collar of his t-shirt. 'So, um, how long has Sadie been here? Did she arrive right after I went up?' It was oddly disappointing that he could have played with his children but had instead got his assistant on the job.

'Don't leap to conclusions,' he shook his head. 'And definitely don't scowl at me like that. I've been playing with them for the last half hour too. I didn't have much of a choice, given your second-hand directive.'

'Huh? Sorry, what do you mean?' She squinted at him.

Matt tapped his chin with a long finger, as if he was pondering one of life's great mysteries. 'Let me see. How did Jasper so delicately put it? *Zoe says you have to spend more time with us.* Tell me, do you normally use children to try and manipulate men?'

Her mouth dropped open and her face flushed at the accusation. 'No!' Still, although she hadn't used the exact words Jasper had, the message was close enough. Bugger, she'd wanted to talk to Matt first. He had a cheek though. He of all people was in no position to judge someone else's behaviour after what he'd done to her sister, tearing her life apart without a backward glance. 'No,' she repeated defensively. 'Absolutely not, I only—'

The office door opened behind him.

'S-sorry.' Aimee stopped, picking up on the tension.

'That's okay,' Zoe replied in a soothing voice, talking to the girl and studiously avoiding Matt's gaze. 'Were you after something, Aimee?'

'Jasper asked about dinner.'

'I'm just on my way to sort it out. Can you tell him it'll be about half an hour please?' She turned to Matt as his daughter nodded and went back into his office. 'We can talk about this later. I don't want the children to overhear. Will Sadie be staying for dinner?' she asked in a neutral tone, studying the skirting board to keep her cool.

'Why would she?' Matt asked, confused.

'Um, because it's the polite thing to do, especially as she's just

371

been playing with your kids?'

'Oh, right,' it was like the thought was alien, had never occurred to him. 'I don't think so. She never has before. I should think she wants to get home to rest anyway.'

'Are you going to ask?'

He raised both eyebrows. 'I guess I am now.' Stepping around Zoe, 'Sadie,' he called, 'can you come out a minute please?'

The door opened and an attractive fox-faced brunette stuck her head into the hallway, 'Yes, Matt?'

'This is my new nanny Zoe,' he gestured. 'Zoe, this is Sadie.' He gave the women a moment to exchange polite nods. 'Sadie, Zoe wants to know if you're staying for dinner?'

'Matt!' Zoe muttered, shaking her head.

'Matt, you're a sod!' Sadie scolded, a dimple flashing in her left cheek, dark eyebrows arching. 'I need a break from the rabble for a while, but thank you for asking, Zoe. Matt never would have. He finds it hard to observe social niceties and talk to normal people, especially when he's working with a new artist.'

'Hey, I'm stood right here,' Matt protested, folding his arms.

'I know,' Sadie said impishly, ducking back into the room, 'that's the best time to talk about someone.' Her voice floated out into the hallway, full of mirth. 'You've got me for twenty more minutes. Then I'm escaping.' The door swung shut and she said something else, causing the children to chortle.

'I like her,' Zoe said as Matt turned to face her.

'Huh, I wonder why,' he remarked drily. 'Now you'll both gang up on me,' he said with a mournful expression.

'Oh, you poor baby,' she rebutted in mock sympathy, still so used to the banter of her relationship with Greg that she forgot who she was talking to. God, she'd better not be flirting with Matt, it didn't bear thinking about. 'Right, I need to get on.' Twisting away she started toward the kitchen. He trailed along behind her. 'Aren't you going to go back into your office?' Zoe said in a hopeful voice, his footsteps echoing hers.

'Nope,' he replied, 'we need to talk.'

The weight of his gaze on her back tingled a warning along her spine. She thought of the comment he'd levelled at her about manipulating men through children.

This should be fun.

7

'You're cross with me,' she pre-empted Matt as he rested against one of the marble countertops with a scowl. Reaching up to take Jasper's paintings down from their pegs, she tested them with careful fingers to check they were dry. 'However, if Jasper had given me time to talk to you first,' she continued, 'I would have explained that what I'd said to the kids was that I would *ask* you if you could spend some quality time with each of them, with some time as a whole family too.' Setting the paintings aside she put her hands on her hips. 'I don't do things through the children Matt, that's not my style. I approach things with parents directly, and prefer to work in partnership with them so we have common goals.' She nodded. 'Jasper was right though, I do feel that way. Living in the same house is one thing, but actually talking to each other and sharing your lives is another.'

'I appreciate your professional opinion,' he answered tersely, 'but we sit together in the lounge some evenings.'

'You sitting playing on your iPad, with Jasper on another and Aimee scrunched up on the other side of the room reading with her back to you both isn't what I'm talking about. You need to do some activities together, have a chance to connect, find some shared passions. You don't put them to bed, you barely see them in the morning, and you don't talk much,' recalling what Jasper had told her as they'd strolled along Park Lane. 'Look, I'm not having a go,' she held her hands out in front of her, 'I'm just trying to do my best for them, based on what I see,' she chose her words carefully, 'and what I see already is that they're great kids but could be happier. They also have some things to work through—'

He straightened away from the worktop, shoulders taut. 'What do you mean?'

'An ambulance went past today and Jasper got a bit upset. He mentioned something about his mum?'

'They saw the accident,' stumbling over the word, 'happen.' He tightened his lips and the scar running into the top one turned white.

'I know,' she said quickly, stepping closer. Trying to ignore how sexy the scar made him look. Bad boys, eat your heart out.

'How?' he frowned, black eyebrows pulling down. 'How do you know?'

Shit. She thought fast. 'It was in the kids' development folders that your last nanny left,' she blurted, 'and from what Jasper said it wasn't hard to put it together.'

'I see.' His mouth relaxed a little. 'I didn't realise it still bothered him.'

'I'm not sure,' she said hesitantly, 'but I think Aimee may be struggling with it too.'

'It is? I didn't realise. It was three years ago. They were so young.' He closed his eyes. 'She never said. Neither did Melody.'

'It might be that she found it difficult,' she answered, thinking of her sister's gentle nature, how she probably wouldn't have wanted to upset him. 'And your daughter's not exactly the world's greatest talker, is she? I mean, she'd rather escape into a book than talk to people. She's a bit like you in that way.'

Matt opened his eyelids, blinked, green gaze settling on her intently. 'In what way?'

'Like you said this morning, when you're working on something you get lost in it. She has the same focus.'

'I suppose. It's funny,' he mused, gazing out the window at the apple tree, 'Aimee always reminds me so much of Helen.'

'Maybe in looks, but she has a lot of you in her, personality wise. It's the nature versus nurture debate, isn't it? Genetics versus environment. Jasper is the spitting image of you though, lucky thing. He's going to be a heartbreaker,' she said unthinkingly.

'I'll take that as my first compliment,' his mouth edged up on one side.

'Pardon?' Realising what she'd said. Bugger. 'Oh. Sorry, I didn't—'

'It's fine,' Matt chuckled, 'relax. It's a relief to hear something nice from you.'

'Am I horrible to you then?' she said, alarmed.

'No. Just insistent about some things.' He nodded, 'As long as you're doing your best for my children though, I'll find a way to cope.' There was the smallest hint of seriousness in his ironic drawl.

'Good. So, anyway,' she hurried on, 'Aimee's social skills need to develop but otherwise her concentration is a good thing. I'm sure she's reading well above her age group. Have the school ever been in touch?'

'I don't know, Melody always handled that side of things.'

She pulled a face. Hadn't he even been interested? Why did this guy have so little buy-in to his children's lives? He did seem to love them in his own way, but the lack of engagement was puzzling.

'Before you say it, I work long hours and Melody was the expert, not me.'

'Whatever you say,' she shrugged, struggling to keep the disbelief from her voice. These were his kids. His to love, his responsibility. 'I'll take another look at the development folders and phone the school at the start of the term. I'd like to know what milestones they're setting for Aimee. She needs to be appropriately challenged or she'll get bored.'

'Fine by me. I was impressed by her hangman skills,' he added, 'in fact, she almost thrashed me.' He looked surprised. 'She's got a great vocabulary.'

'It's all the reading.' Zoe blew a breath out, sensing the conversation was calming down. 'So, what do you think about spending more time with the children? I understand your work commitments and it's great you have a hard work ethic, but can you spare one evening a week with each of them, with a morning or afternoon at weekends together? Proper time to talk and touch base would be really valuable for you as a family.' She smiled, 'Before you know it, they'll be teenagers and all you'll get will be grunts from Jasper and flouncing about from Aimee after she's applied a ton of foundation and taken endless selfies.'

'Don't scare me! I'm barely coping with them at this age,' he joked. 'I'll see what I can do, will talk to Sadie about my schedule once she's back at work.'

For a moment she thought he was still joking, but when it became apparent he wasn't her fingers curled into fists. He was an adult, so he should make time for his kids in his own goddamn schedule. They should be his top priority. She held her tongue though. It was a start and if she went at him too hard he would only retreat. 'Okay, sounds good.'

'So, um, should I be worried that an alarming amount of my son's paintings feature aliens having gun-fights, complete with spatters of blood?' he asked, picking up the pile of pictures and resting back against the counter as he flicked through them.

'No. I don't think it's anything to be concerned about. It's not unusual to be into gory stuff at his age. Besides, he's a big Ben 10 fan so it's hardly surprising.' Going over to the fridge she started pulling courgettes, onions and tomatoes out of the bottom drawer.

'Oh yeah,' he looked vague, 'Ben 10, that's right.'

'The boy with the watch? He's a hero and turns into different aliens?' Really, did this guy occupy another planet? She slammed the fridge door shut, rinsing the courgettes and tomatoes under running water over the sink. Yanking an expensive copper frying pan and a matching saucepan from a low cupboard, she filled the saucepan with water and set it on the hob to start heating, throwing in a pinch of salt.

'Yeah, that's right. Jasper's got a duvet cover and clock in his room,' Matt supplied. 'Melody bought them for him. For a birthday I think.'

Zoe kept her face straight as she set the food down on the chopping board, hiding her frustration. 'Do you ever take him out to buy stuff yourself?' She made sure her tone was curious rather than accusatory. 'Have you ever sat and watched an episode with him?'

'Not really.' Matt put the paintings aside. 'Shopping isn't really my thing. Neither are cartoons.'

She drew a knife from the knife block and held it up to the light to check it was sharp. 'When you have kids,' she said wryly, 'sometimes you have to do things you don't like. You should watch the programme with him sometime, it's quite good fun, and it would give you something to start talking about.' She started slicing the courgettes into small chunks.

'I don't need a cartoon to help me talk to my kids,' he crossed his arms over his broad chest.

'Oh?' she raised an eyebrow. 'What do you talk about then?'

He sucked in his cheeks, looking unsure. After a moment, 'Fencing. Horse-riding. Dra—'

'Draughts?' She finished for him. 'Thrilling stuff. I wasn't sure draughts were still played this century. You do know they don't enjoy those activities, don't you? Aimee doesn't mind the horse riding but Jasper finds it scary, they're both bored to tears by draughts and they could take or leave fencing.'

'Really? Melody picked them out. I asked what the kids should be doing and she spoke to some of the other nannies and suggested those.'

Maybe they were activities the children should be doing with their lifestyle. Yet Jasper had told her how he and Aimee felt about them, and if he'd told her then why not Melody? If Melody knew, why wouldn't she have spoken to Matt? He wasn't that unapproachable. 'You do live in Knightsbridge, I suppose,' she excused. 'It's a pretty affluent area and some of the kids go on to attend Independent schools. I'm guessing the nannies are very competitive about their charges, and those activities aren't necessarily wrong. I just feel they're wrong for your children.'

Matt watched as she slid the cut up courgette aside and started chopping the tomatoes. 'What do you think they should be doing instead?' he quizzed.

'Ask them.'

'Pardon?'

'Ask them. They'll tell you. Then it's up to you as their dad to make a decision as to what's practical and appropriate.'

A pulse beat in his jaw. 'Okay, I will.'

'Good.' Concentrating on not squirting tomato juice everywhere, she cut the tomatoes up with single-minded purpose, aware her shoulders were so tense they were near her earlobes. She must talk to her sister ASAP about what had been going on in this house and she had to wake Matt up before he missed the whole of Jasper's and Aimee's childhoods. Not that she owed it to him, it was the kids she was thinking of.

There was a dragged out, tense silence. Matt released a heavy sigh.

She flicked a glance at him as he pulled up a stool at the breakfast bar and sat down, the jeans tightening around his muscular thighs.

Rubbing his scar. 'I know what it must look like,' he muttered, looking troubled.

'What's that?' Moving the tomatoes aside with the flat of her knife, she started peeling the onion, hoping it wasn't too strong.

'I was much more of a hands-on dad once. When they were little. It's been complicated since Helen died.'

'Uh-huh.'

He tried again, 'I work really long hours.'

'Uh-huh.'

'I had to earn a living—'

'Uh-huh,' her voice climbed higher.

'Melody was here to look after them.'

'Uh-huh.' Picking the knife up and chopping the onion in half in one smooth motion.

He scowled. 'What does uh-huh mean?'

'Nothing,' she shrugged, turning half the onion on its side, glancing over her shoulder to see if the water was boiling yet.

'Argh, I hate it when women do that. Say one thing but mean another. Just like when you use the word fine, but are plainly not. The new singer I signed has been like that recently, all withdrawn and non-committal but still insisting she's okay.'

'Well, men are from Mars, women are from Venus,' she shrugged again, cutting the onion into neat lines.

'Just tell me, Zoe please. Say what you're thinking.'

'You won't like it.'

His expression was determined. 'Even so, I want to know. Although you're being pretty presumptuous for someone who hardly knows me, I promise not to take offence or fire you.'

She laughed bitterly, thinking of Melody, chopping the onion harder, the knife hitting the heavy wooden chopping board beneath with unnecessary force. 'You'd be lucky,' she breathed. 'Fine. What I think is that all those things you listed are excuses, not reasons.'

'What?' he shot off the stool, the legs scraping along the floor.

'You asked,' she reminded him, 'so here's what I think. You work for yourself so you could set your own hours and it's common knowledge that you have family money, so you could use that rather than driving yourself into the ground making a living. Melody was your nanny, employed to help care for your children, not to raise them for you.' She held his eyes, gaze direct. 'Those aren't the real reasons you're not involved in your children's lives.'

'What is the real reason then?'

'You need to figure that out for yourself.'

'Oh, for God's sake don't talk in riddles,' he glowered.

She stopped, surprised, and set down the knife. 'I'm not. I'm just not certain myself. As you said, I don't know you that well. I'm sure if you take some time to think about it and are honest with yourself though, it'll come to you. It's important for your family.'

Her concession appeared to deflate the worst of his anger and he sat back down, looking a mixture of thoughtful and annoyed. Hesitantly, she picked up the knife and resumed cutting up the onion, eyes starting to water with the fumes.

Matt pulled one of Jasper's paintings towards him, tracing a long finger over a self-portrait stick-figure that his son had topped with a shock of black hair, one hand holding a giant grey laser gun. 'This is Jasper,' he muttered, 'this is Aimee,' pointing to a red-haired figure in a barred cell, a taller one with long black hair next to it, 'and this must be you. And he's either locked you up or is trying to save you, but where am I?'

Zoe shifted from one foot to another uncomfortably. That's exactly what she'd asked Jasper earlier. 'He said you were at work. And he's trying to save us because you're too busy making cool music.'

'I see,' he cleared his throat, putting the painting aside and staring into space for a moment. 'Well,' he shook his head, 'I can't say it wasn't painful to hear what you think of my parenting skills and you're treading a fine line with some of your comments, but I said I wouldn't take offence, so thanks for the honesty. I'll give it some thought. That doesn't mean you're right though.' She didn't reply, letting him have that one. After a moment he sprang up, appearing restless. 'I need a cup of coffee. You?'

'Please, if you don't mind.'

'White, one sugar, right?'

She titled her head as tears blurred her vision. 'Yes, as long as you don't poison it.'

'It's tempting but I'll hold back this time,' he teased. 'So, the little girls you looked after in the States,' switching the subject as he clanked cups and turned knobs on the chrome coffee machine, 'what were their names?'

'Ava and Grace.'

'Seriously? Were their parents into classic movies or something?'

'You've got it.' She put the knife aside, arranging the pieces of onion into a pile.

'If they'd had a third, do you think they would have called her Marilyn, as in Monroe?'

Zoe chuckled, thinking of Liberty's extrovert ways. 'Probably.'

'Do you miss them?' The machine made a few hissing noises and started producing steaming black coffee. Matt moved the mugs along the spouts, topping them up with hot milk as he looked at her questioningly.

Zoe thought about the day she'd had playing with Jasper and coaxing Aimee out of her shell. There was something about children's innocent joy that lifted the spirits. She was exhausted, couldn't sleep and had no appetite and the anger, humiliation, hurt and disappointment over her ex-fiancé was raw, running a constant circle of questions in her mind as to why she hadn't been good enough. Somehow though, Matt's kids were getting her through, keeping her too busy to brood or mope. Rather than longing for Greg, New York and the girls, she was coping. It was like this job had been waiting for her just at the perfect time. She shrugged the thought off. It hadn't been, she was here by default. This was her sister's life really, she mustn't forget it, or the plan. 'Do I miss them? A bit.' She'd been fond of Ava and Grace, but had never bonded with them in the way she was already bonding with Aimee and Jasper. Perhaps it was because Liberty had always been there in the background making demands, whereas these kids were motherless. 'Not as much as I thought I would,' she mused. 'Still, its early days.'

Matt spooned sugar into both coffees and set hers down in front of her, resuming his position on the bar stool.

'What about New York? Do you miss the city? You must have had friends there? You said you were single but there must have been someone at some point?'

'Thanks for the coffee,' she gestured to the mug. 'Honestly? I'm not sure it's been long enough to miss anything properly. Yes, I had friends. Yes, there was someone. That's over though.' Tears blurred her eyes again. 'Definitely over.'

A hand reached over and curled around her wrist. 'I'm sorry, I didn't mean to upset you.'

Freezing, she took a breath. 'You didn't,' easing her arm away, she sniffed, 'it's the onions.'

'Oh,' he murmured. 'Well, now I feel like an idiot.'

She laughed, 'You said it.'

'Oi!' Sipping his coffee, he watched as she spun around, poured some olive oil into the frying pan and put it on the hob. Studying the now boiling water, she rooted through one of the units and pulled out a bag of pasta, emptying three quarters of its contents into the saucepan. 'Do you like cooking?' he asked.

'It's all right. I prefer it when there aren't kids running around under my feet. Makes it more relaxing. I love my job and being a nanny though,' she tacked on quickly.

'Don't worry, I know what you meant.' He paused as he heard his name called. 'Excuse me, I think that's Sadie on her way out. Back in a minute.'

As soon as he was gone, Zoe dropped her head and sucked in great gulps of oxygen. What the hell was she doing? She wasn't supposed to be bonding with the guy, or helping him out, she was supposed to be getting revenge. Her phone beeped and she raised her head, grabbing it off the side and checking the screen.

Hi, Sis. How's
it going? Found out
anything yet?
M x

Yes, as it happened. A fractured family. Things that didn't make sense, given how nice Matt could be some of the time. But replying to her sister by text wasn't going to do it. After the kids were in bed, they'd talk.

**I'll call you
this evening.
Around 8? Z x**

'Sadie was flagging,' Matt said as he walked back into the kitchen, 'she said to say bye.'

Flustered by Matt almost catching her texting Mel, Zoe threw her mobile into the corner, where it span in a lazy circle. 'Okay.'

Matt raised an eyebrow at the action. 'Everything all right?'

'Yes,' moving over to the chopping board, she heaved it over to the cooker, clumsily tossing the veg into the frying pan and seasoning it. 'What are the kids doing?'

'I've put them in their playroom with the TV on. I didn't think dinner would be long.'

'It won't,' she grimaced at him as he sat down to finish his coffee, 'but is there anything in there that Jasper can cause mischief with? Felt-tip pens, crayons, paints?'

'No, plus I put Ben 10 on for him, as Aimee's sat in the corner chair reading.'

'Again,' Zoe smiled. '*To Kill a Mockingbird* is holding her riveted today.'

'It's a great book. Prejudice, justice, love, hate. The nature of the human heart.'

She stared at him, 'Yes. I like it too.'

'Don't look at me like that. Music is my passion, but I enjoy reading books. I read *To Kill a Mockingbird* as a teenager for school and I still read occasionally.'

'Have you ever talked to Aimee about it? The books you enjoy?'

He paused, 'No, I don't think I have.'

'You should,' she suggested, planting the seed. 'I read as much as possible,' she stirred the vegetables, 'anything I can lay my hands on. Have you read anything good lately?'

'Harlan Coben is pretty good. Noel and I swap his books sometimes.'

'Ah, yes the famous Uncle Noel.'

'Have the kids been talking about him?' Matt drained his mug.

'Yes,' wandering across the room, she picked her coffee up and wrapped her hands around it, 'and about Holly.'

'Noel's my best friend. They're a nice couple.'

'I gathered that from Jasper's chatter.'

'He does talk a lot.' He leaned in, whispering conspiratorially, 'It makes my head hurt sometimes.'

Leaning closer to him across the breakfast bar, she whispered back, 'I get why.' Seeing the sudden spark of something in his deep green eyes, she straightened. Clearing her throat, she wiped the sides down, placed the chopping board next to the sink and prodded the pasta with a wooden spoon. 'So, uh, Sadie.' She pictured the brunette and didn't like the squiggle of discomfort in her belly. 'She's very attractive. Is she married?' She could have kicked herself for asking such an irrelevant and possibly sexist question. Why did she care?

'No.' He wandered across the room and leaned around her to put his mug in the sink, making her ultra-aware of his height and the breadth of his shoulders. She inhaled sharply as she saw muscles shifting under his navy t-shirt.

The room seemed to be getting smaller. She tugged at her top. Was it getting hot in here? It must be cooking over a hot stove that was responsible.

'She has a boyfriend,' he said. 'They're trying for a baby. The procedure she had was to remove some cysts. I'd appreciate you not saying anything about it though, especially to her. She's quite sensitive about it and it's very personal.'

'Poor her. Of course. Thanks for telling me.'

'You're both my employees, and I can trust you right?'

Holding his gaze was incredibly hard because the last thing he should do was trust her, but she managed it, and nodded. Silence stretched between them. He looked tired, slight bags under his eyes. Most men would look awful but for Matt it just added to his bad boy air. The hush between them continued and she felt as if they were in a bubble, well away from the real world. It was just the two of them.

She wrenched her eyes away from his and saw his chest expand, heard the soft whoosh of his breath as he exhaled. She could hear the murmur of the TV in the room above them and through the open kitchen window she could make out someone's radio, tuned to an old Blues station. A stupor crept over her, his body heat wrapping around her. Swaying, she leaned closer, closer …

'Zoe,' his low voice made her jump.

Stepping back, she shook her head, pulling herself from the daze with an effort. 'Yes?' She should be with her sister in Southend-On-Sea, she thought. Not stuck in the lifeless high-tech kitchen of a big house in Knightsbridge with a man who both annoyed and excited her.

'Is something burning?'

'Oh, crap,' whirling around, she stirred the veg, which had started breaking down into a saucy tomatoey mess and turned the heat down on the pasta, 'I mean, oops. So, um,' her voice sounded unfamiliar and croaky, 'I know it's possibly very un-PC of me to ask but how old is Sadie?' She stirred the sauce, the fragrance of onions and herbs wafting from the pan.

'It's probably indiscreet of me to tell you, but I don't think she'd mind,' he offered, 'forty-two.'

'Really?' she whipped around, spoon in hand, spattering sauce across his t-shirt.

He jumped back, swearing. 'Argh, that's hot!'

'Oops, sorry,' she choked, biting her lip.

His eyes narrowed under his black eyebrows, the break in his nose highlighted by the angle his head was tilted at.

'Yeah, you look it,' he answered drily. He gave her such a look of reproach she couldn't help but burst out laughing before flinging a wet cloth at him from beside the sink. He caught it in mid-air, 'Thanks.'

'I am sorry,' she repeated as he wiped the front of his top down, her mouth going dry as the damp spots made the cotton cling to his chest. What would he look like shirtless? She wondered, feeling uncomfortably hot. 'I was just surprised,' she explained as he threw the cloth into the sink. 'I would have put Sadie in her early thirties at the most.'

'Yeah, so surprised you pelted food at me,' his mouth quirking in amusement, he pulled the top away from his body, unknowingly exposing a patch of hair roughened chest. 'I'll have to tell her. She'll be pleased, no, thrilled.'

'She definitely looks a lot younger than she is.' She gulped down the huge lump in her throat and turned back to the sauce, stirring it round in lazy circles, perhaps trying to hypnotise herself into not staring at him. Turning away, she got another pan and went over to the sink, filling it with cold water. She liked to plunge the pasta in fresh water once it was done.

'That's good,' Matt said, 'because her boyfriend is a lot younger than her. Yeah, good old Sadie went and got herself a toy boy.'

She was so astonished at his laughing admiration that she twirled around holding the pan against her stomach and a huge wave of water crested over and spilt down her top.

'Urgh,' she squeaked, ramming the pan onto the kitchen unit and jumping back.

Matt clutched his side and chortled as she stretched the cotton away from her body so it couldn't cling to her bra. The wet t-shirt look was not a good one to sport in polite society. She pulled a face at him.

'Sorry,' he said around a wide grin, 'sorry. Sadie and I have known each other so many years I'm used to joking around like that. But it might have sounded odd the way I put it. You have to admit though, it was quite funny. I've never seen anyone move so fast. You also thought it was amusing when you got me,' he said as she grabbed a kitchen roll and ripped off pieces, ineffectually dabbing at her soaked top.

'It's not quite the same, is it?' she grumbled as water dripped onto her bare toes.

'Okay,' he held his hands up, 'I'll give you that. You go dry off and change and I'll mop up and serve dinner.'

'Are you sure?'

'Yes, I'm sure I can manage to drain some pasta and put food on plates.' His eyes dropped to her chest before resolutely forcing them upwards. 'Shall we eat together at the table in the dining room?'

'Actually, I prefer the kitchen,' she said, starting to blush at the way he was looking at her, 'it's cosier.' She studied the marble and chrome equipment surrounding them. 'Well, by contrast to the dining room it is anyway.'

'What's wrong with the dining room?'

'It's the same as the lounge,' she blurted.

'What's wrong with the lounge?' he demanded.

'It's so,' she shuddered, 'bleurgh.'

Putting his hands on his lean hips, smiling slightly. 'What's bleurgh?'

'White, pristine, cold. It reminds me a bit of my aunt's house. Homes should be warm, cosy and comfortable.'

'I see.' Matt looked bemused. 'I didn't appreciate that you were an interior designer as well as a nanny.'

'I'm not— oh. Ha-ha.' She flushed, 'Sorry, I shouldn't be criticising your home. I'll go and change. I'll send the kids down to help set the table while I'm up there.'

'They're going to do what now?'

'They're more than old enough, Matt, don't look so astounded,' backing away, she hustled towards the door. 'Oh, by the way, there's parmesan on the side too.'

Dashing up the stairs, she called for Aimee to please put her book down and Jasper to turn the TV off so they could go and help their dad because he was going to join them for dinner. Her tone brooked no argument. Fleeing to the top floor, she slammed into her room and sank down onto the edge of the bed, curling her toes into the blue carpet. What had she gotten herself into?

It didn't get any better later that night after she'd tucked the kids up in bed and called Melody. After the niceties were done and she'd consoled her sister that of course only crying three or four times a day was better than crying every hour, she got straight to the point.

'What's going on, Mel?'

'Pardon?' her sister asked warily.

'The kids, Matt. It's all wrong.'

'Wrong? What do you mean, wrong?'

'The way they are together.' Zoe rolled onto her side, hugging a cushion. 'There's no quality time, they're doing activities they don't like, Aimee's so introverted she's nearly a hermit, Jasper's bouncing off the walls trying to get his dad's attention. When I sent the kids into him this morning and told them to hug him goodbye—'

'You did what?' Melody exclaimed, sounding horrified.

'I didn't know, did I? It's normal for kids to say hello to their parents and have some affection from them. I didn't think I was doing anything outrageous.' Chewing her lip. 'Did you uh, ever challenge him with it?'

'Challenge him?' Melody said. 'You don't challenge your boss. You do what they tell you to do.'

Zoe sighed, remembering this had been Melody's first real job since leaving college. 'It's okay to raise things with them though, to make recommendations and provide advice. It's part of what we're paid for. Ultimately what the parents say goes, unless we've got safeguarding concerns in which case we refer it on to social services, but that doesn't mean you shouldn't try.'

'I did say something once or twice when I first started but

389

Matt wasn't interested. So I left it alone. Besides, I didn't think it was that wrong. Some families just aren't that demonstrative, are they? I mean, Aunt Ruth isn't a big one for hugs, but our childhood was okay.'

'Maybe you were happy, but I wasn't. Is that what you want for Matt's kids?' Zoe said sharply, sitting up on the bed and throwing the cushion aside. 'Nights lying awake wondering if they're loved or not? Waiting for praise and attention but never getting it? Feeling lonely and alone?'

'Wait a minute, I care about those children!' Her sister spoke fiercely in a voice that Zoe hardly recognised. 'And it probably doesn't help that you and Ruth have never agreed on much, does it? Also you have to remember that not everyone is like you, Zo. We don't all have your confidence, like Dad's.'

It was true enough, and perhaps Melody and Ruth got on better because Melody was content to follow orders, happy not to ask questions or want to share her opinions. Unlike her. Zoe knew she was lucky to have inherited or learnt the confidence Mel was talking about from their father, a trait that ran through her like the words imprinted down the centre of the sticky seaside rock they'd eaten as children. 'Still, you could have—'

'You've been there a couple of days.' Melody's voice was low and tight. 'I was there for three years. When I agreed to this plan I didn't think you were going to wade in and start judging me. I did my best given how inexperienced I was when I got there.' Dropping to a whisper. 'I thought what I was doing was right.'

Zoe gulped at the defeat in her sister's voice, feeling awful. 'I'm sorry, sis. I didn't mean to upset you. The last thing you need at the moment is me having a go. I'm just a bit shocked at the set up here, that's all. Listen, it's not beyond repair and it's really not that bad. You've done a good job with them and I genuinely think they're missing you.'

'They are?' Melody's voice was thick with tears.

'Yes,' Zoe said firmly. 'No matter what else happens, if there's any way at all I can arrange for you to see them, or say goodbye, I will. But sis, why didn't you tell me? I know it was difficult with me in New York, but I would have talked it through with you. I'd always be happy to give you advice. We Skyped regularly, but you never once said anything about the way things are here.'

'Like I said, I thought it was normal. Besides, it's hard enough to live in your big sister's shadow without having to run to her for help. The only reason I became ...' she trailed off.

'Became what?'

'Nothing,' she murmured, and Zoe could picture her little sister twisting a lock of dark blonde hair around her finger, dark eyes huge in her pale face, 'it doesn't matter.' Melody cleared her throat. 'Sorry, I have to go. Ruth's calling me for dinner. Speak soon.'

She rang off abruptly, leaving Zoe staring at the phone open mouthed. It wasn't like Melody to end a call like that. Not with her anyway. She hadn't even asked how the plan was going or whether she'd found out anything from Matt, or about Stephen's whereabouts. Also, Ruth always served dinner at seven o'clock on the dot, one of her regimental rules, so Mel should have eaten over an hour ago. Zoe picked the cushion up again, hugging it to her, thinking about her sister's comment about living in her shadow. What had she been about to say? The only reason she'd become what?

Her phone beeped and she picked it up eagerly, thinking it would be a message from Mel to say sorry or send her love, but to her shock it was a text from Greg.

I miss you Zoe.
We need to talk.
Call me.
All my love, Greg x

She stared at it, black rage climbing up inside her throat. He had a damn nerve. He missed her? He loved her? He could go f—

She hurled the phone onto the bed before leaping up and marching into the bathroom. Twisting the taps on violently, she started running a bath, accidentally throwing nearly a whole tub of bath salt in with shaking hands.

If you loved someone you didn't cheat on them and humiliate them in front of the whole of New York society. If you loved someone you treated them with honesty, trust and respect. If you loved someone you didn't ask them to marry you and plan a wedding with them, only to wreck it all two weeks before you tied the knot. And if you were going to miss someone, you'd better make bloody sure you were okay with letting them go in the first place.

Zoe sighed as she stared down at the whirling, swirling bubbles in the water. What the heck was going on with everyone around her?

8

As the dog days of July melted into August, Zoe and the children built a routine together. Breakfast and showers when they got up, greeting Matt before he went to work, an activity or outing in the morning, some quiet time at home over lunch followed by another outing or activities in the afternoon. Most nights she got them involved in making dinner, mashing potatoes up in a bowl with butter or folding pastry for a pie. They got used to setting and clearing the table with her every night in exchange for a scoop of ice-cream and a topping of their choice which they ate enthusiastically while she loaded the dishwasher.

Jasper wasn't that keen on her rule about there being no TV for an hour before bedtime, or when she insisted he have a warm bath filled with lavender oil to help him get sleepy every evening, and neither was he a big fan of reading together in his room before lights-out. However, after four nights of complaining and Zoe compromising by reading his favourite Ben 10 annual, he gave in with a faintly resigned air, accepting that she wasn't going to change her mind. By the end of the week he was looking more rested in the mornings, and was a little more settled in the day.

Aimee was interacting more often and loved that Zoe put half an hour aside every day for them to talk about books and pore over the small library in the girl's room while Jasper played a fun but educational game on his iPad. They had great fun talking about their favourite stories, and discussing why characters did things and felt the way they did. Zoe made sure to give Aimee lots of praise when she said something particularly insightful, impressed with her almost adult-like perceptions.

She didn't get much of a chance to push *Plan Nannygate* forward because she hardly saw Matt apart from for a few short minutes in the morning. It was probably just as well for her piece of mind, because every time she was near him the breath hitched in her lungs and warmth tingled over her skin. The broken nose, lip scar, broad shoulders and deep green eyes made her a goner every time. It was unfair for one man to be so scandalously sexy.

Thank God that although he was spending more time at home than she'd originally anticipated, leaving by eight every day and returning just before lunch time, he immediately hid himself away in what she discovered was a soundproof recording studio in the basement. He would often stay there until the early hours of the morning and never joined them for meals. However, a few times she caught him in the kitchen making a coffee and a sandwich. Watching the kids play in the garden, there'd be an expression on his face she couldn't place. It was somewhere between longing and fear, she thought, but wasn't sure.

They did make some progress because on two occasions he popped up from the studio to say goodnight to the children, giving them quick hugs before loping off, while she stood in the hallway to give them some privacy. Each time, he disappeared before she could speak to him. If she'd had something urgent to talk to him about she would have followed him down to the basement and insisted they catch up, but there was little to say at the moment so she left him to it. She didn't want to do anything to make him suspicious, and appearing for idle chats when she knew he was so busy would surely make him wonder if she was after something.

One balmy day Zoe and the children joined some other nannies and their charges in Green Park, with its tall trees, rolling lawns and deckchairs.

'You lucky thing. Matt Reilly!' Beth, a blonde haired girl who worked for a family in Belgravia, sighed dreamily. 'He's so gorgeous. Are you getting on with him okay? His last nanny Melody never said much about him.' Her blue eyes widened. 'Well?'

She reminded Zoe of a golden retriever, all high-energy and bouncing enthusiasm. 'Fine,' Zoe said in a non-committal tone. 'Nice.' She raised her hand and shielded her eyes from the sunshine to check on Jasper, pleased to see him racing over the grass playing a good natured game of football with the little tow-headed boy Beth cared for.

'Seriously?' Monica exclaimed. 'That's all you have to say?' A brunette with yellowish eyes who worked for a single mum entrepreneur in Chelsea, she was definitely the leader of the group with her expansive arm gestures and strident voice.

'I didn't even see the job advertised,' Phoebe remarked softly. A tiny Asian nanny who looked after a six month baby girl for a family in Knightsbridge, she was dressed neatly in a lilac dress with a high collar, her feet tucked under her while she rocked the shiny, expensive pushchair beside her back and forth.

Zoe liked her immediately. There was something calming about her gentle manner. 'I got it through an agency,' she explained to Phoebe, smiling politely.

'Has he got another girlfriend yet?' Beth quizzed.

Zoe glanced over at Aimee to avoid their expectant stares, seeing the girl lying on her belly in the shade of a tree, nose stuck in a book, beribboned straw hat protecting her fair skin. She'd finished *To Kill a Mockingbird* the previous week with a sad but satisfied expression, and had moved onto *Great Expectations*.

'So?' Monica prompted.

One of the core parts of being a nanny was discretion and confidentiality and while that might not be the case once her plan was achieved, for now she couldn't afford to say anything indiscreet that would give Matt a justifiable reason to fire her.

'Come on, spill,' Beth said, 'we won't tell anyone, it'll just be between us. The nanny code and all that.'

'Nanny code?' Zoe angled her face to the sun's belting rays, glad she'd remembered to apply sun cream.

'We gossip amongst ourselves, but never to anyone outside the group.'

'I see.' Zoe felt uneasy about the use of the word gossip, but didn't want to spend the whole afternoon getting hounded, or face being excluded by them for being snotty. Maybe she could tell them something that wouldn't be an issue if it got back to Matt. Sitting up, she checked on Jasper again, watching with a smile as he tipped his Ben 10 cap further back to see the football better, face stripy with neon-pink sun block. 'Well, in that case, Matt seems nice. He loves his kids, and works a lot. I don't think he's that interested in a relationship at the moment though. He's working on a big project.' The last thing Matt or the kids needed was all the nannies in the area bowling up on the doorstep on some kind of manhunt. She was shocked at the protective instinct that ran through her at the thought.

'Oh,' Beth looked disappointed. 'I've heard he's nice, though a bit work mad, which is why what I heard about what he did to Melody doesn't make sense. She always said good things about him.'

'In what way doesn't it make sense?' Zoe asked, struggling to keep her voice level instead of achingly curious.

'You know about it?'

'I know that she left in a bit of a rush, Matt told me that, but not much else.'

'I don't want to worry you, especially if you're getting on well, but supposedly he fired her without notice and threw her out the same day,' Monica said bluntly, 'apparently she did something really awful. But that doesn't seem like her. She was so sweet and kind. Great with the kids too,' glancing at Aimee, who was still reading, 'it's so strange.'

'Do you know what she's supposed to have done?'

'No, just something bad.'

'Where did you hear that from? Matt?' Zoe asked.

'No, he keeps himself to himself, and I've never heard that he's said a bad word about anyone.' Monica frowned, 'I can't remember, a friend of someone who knows his brother, I think. Everyone was talking about it a few weeks ago.'

'Please,' Beth shuddered, blue eyes glinting, 'let's not ruin the afternoon by talking about Stephen.'

Phoebe glanced over at her, pushing a black wing of hair behind one ear. 'Are you okay?' she asked her friend quietly.

'Yep,' Beth sighed.

Zoe raised both eyebrows, 'What's this about Stephen?'

Monica looked to Beth, who sighed and rolled her eyes. 'Go on then.'

'Melody was lovely, but she had lousy taste in men,' Monica stated.

'You didn't like Stephen?' Zoe asked, keeping her voice steady. It would be interesting to hear what they thought of her sister's ex.

'He's immature, spoilt, and a serial dater. He's been with half of London, including three quarters of the local nannies. Beth was one of them,' she nodded at the blonde, who pulled a face to indicate her own stupidity, 'unfortunately he's not that great at finishing one thing before starting the next.'

'He really sucked me in,' Beth muttered, staring down at the tartan red blanket they were all sharing, 'I thought he liked me. I should have known better when I was never allowed around the house to meet Matt, and when he only came to mine late at night.'

'Of course he liked you,' Monica squeezed her knee, 'why wouldn't he? Remember, you're too good for him.'

'I was a booty call and you know it. I just didn't realise it at the time.'

Monica put an arm around her shoulders. 'You're not the first girl to fall for it. Come on, you'll be okay.' She hesitated, and grimaced, 'I've got to admit though, Stephen's different with

Melody. Kind of softer, and from the way he looks at her he seems to really care. They do look quite loved up. Sorry,' she told Beth.

'Don't worry about me. I'm over it.' The opposite was quite clearly the case, but no-one said so.

Zoe wondered if the sense she'd got that Beth may be interested in Matt was anything to do with making Stephen jealous. Making a play for your ex booty-call's brother was sure to get the booty-call's attention.

'Anyway, she's welcome to him,' Beth added, 'I hope he's being useful and comforting her somewhere.'

'He's not,' Zoe said absently as she watched Phoebe get up and lift a beautiful little girl dressed in pink lace from the pushchair. 'He's gone abroad and she's gone home.'

'Really?' Monica's eyes widened. 'She's got an aunt over on the coast hasn't she? And how did you know they're not together?'

'A sister too,' Phoebe chipped in, looking at Zoe over the baby's head, 'although I think she's in America somewhere?'

Zoe's drew her focus back to the group, realising what she'd said. Bugger, she hadn't meant to blurt that out about her sister. And now they were asking questions about Mel's family. This was getting too close for comfort. A warning claxon sounded in her head. *Divert, divert.* Fighting a mad urge to scoop up the kids and run, she forced herself to stay seated and appear relaxed. 'Matt must have mentioned it,' she answered, waving a hand at a fly that dive-bombed her face.

'So they've broken up?' Beth asked, leaning forward. Monica flashed her a look. 'Not that I care,' the blonde added lamely.

'Not sure,' Zoe answered, 'it doesn't really affect me so I haven't asked.' She was such a big fat liar. 'Anyway,' time to change the subject before she landed herself in trouble, 'enough of that. Let's talk about something more interesting.' Something that would get them talking. 'So, how does a girl go about finding eligible men around here?'

Phoebe blinked at her as she placed the teat of a bottle into the baby's searching pink mouth and Monica stopped in the act of lifting a drink from a cooler by her side.

Beth looked at her like she was crazy. 'Um, I can't imagine why you need to ask. You're living with one of the most eligible men in London!'

Zoe stopped at the entrance of Hyde Park next to the cute, white pillared Alexandra Lodge. The traffic along Kensington Road flowed behind them, red double-deckers roaring past at regular intervals, motorbikes darting between slowed cars with high-pitched purrs. Clutching Jasper's hand and a picnic hamper, she looked at Aimee's down bent head anxiously. The little girl had told her the previous night that if Zoe really, really wanted to visit Hyde Park, they could go the next day. However, she'd been staring at her bookshelves and her tone had been hesitant as they'd sat side by side on the small pink sofa in her bedroom.

'Is that what you want Aimee?' Zoe had asked, surprised the girl had raised it when she herself hadn't mentioned going for a while.

'I think I want to try.' Aimee nodded. 'I want to do it for you too, because you've never been.' Gazing into space, 'I think you'll like it there. It's pretty.'

'Well, that's nice of you. I appreciate you doing that for me. But what do you mean, you want to try?'

Aimee tilted her head so she could meet Zoe's quizzical expression. 'It's been a long time. Daddy only took us once and Melody never took us because I told her it upset me.'

'Won't it upset you now?'

'Maybe,' she looked serious, eyebrows lowering over her blue eyes. Her voice dropped to a whisper, 'But I miss her.'

Zoe was confused. 'You miss Melody?'

'No. Yes. I miss Melody but I was talking about Mummy.'

Zoe edged away a bit so she could turn to face the girl, tucking one leg under the other on the sofa. 'You want to go to Hyde Park because you miss Mummy?'

'Yes. We used to go there. All four of us. Me, Mummy, Daddy and Jasper. We used to have picnics, Jasper was really little and we used to laugh.' A shadow crossed her face. 'There's a piece of her there.'

'A piece of her?' Now she was completely flummoxed.

'I'll show you when we get there.'

Zoe smiled. 'All right. Would you like me to pack a picnic?'

Aimee looked torn. A bit happy, a bit sad. 'Can I tell you in the morning?'

'Of course you can,' she laid a hand on the girl's arm, 'that's fine. Right, shall we read something?'

Her face cleared, 'Yes, please.'

Now Zoe wasn't sure if going into the royal park was such a good idea. Aimee had been unusually quiet this morning, playing Connect-4 with minimal enthusiasm and staring off into space at odd moments.

Jasper tugged on her hand. 'Come on, I want to splash in the water.'

Whatever was troubling his sister he didn't seem bothered by it. All morning it had been, water this and water that and did Zoe have his swim shorts and was there a towel and could he take a ball with him?

'Ready?' Zoe asked Aimee.

The girl sucked in a breath and rolled her shoulders back, like she was bracing herself. 'Yes.'

'Good,' Zoe led them over to the big tourist information sign and the map setting out the park and immediate surroundings with red circular tube signs dotting the edges. A large light green rectangle marked out the boundaries of the park, darker green indicating trees and bushes, beige lines carving out paths, buildings in browns and greys neatly labelled, the Serpentine a long blue curving body of water that cut diagonally from top left near the fountains, to bottom right near the Queen Caroline Memorial. Immediately next to the entrance they were standing at were the

400

pavilion, a bowling green and junior tennis courts.

'What are you doing, Zoe?' Jasper asked, pulling on her hand again. 'Come on, I want to play.'

'Looking at the map.'

'I know the way,' Aimee dipped her head, watching with big eyes as a smiling couple walked past them holding hands.

'Even after three years?' Zoe asked, moving the picnic hamper from her hand to further up her arm, crooking it against her body.

'We came every Sunday, even in the winter,' Aimee explained. 'We just wrapped up, that's all.'

'Great, come on then. Aimee, you lead the way.'

Zoe followed the girl in through the open black wrought-iron gates, scores of trees lining both sides of the drive.

'We have to go and see the Princess.' Aimee pointed forward and off to the right.

'The Princess?'

'Mummy said she was beautiful and kind,' Aimee replied solemnly, 'and liked to help children and people who were sick.'

'I see.' She wasn't sure what the girl was on about but it was bound to become clear soon. Strolling along the pavement while Jasper bopped up and down at the end of her arm, which made it feel like her shoulder was about to pop out of its socket, she dodged the numerous other visitors to the park, handbag swinging against her hip. The crowds were made up of both locals and international visitors; groups of teenagers in black garb, chattering families from exotic places driving pushchairs with other children racing along beside them, teenage girls in barely-there outfits, mature couples with walking sticks but purposeful strides, a fair Norwegian-looking pair with the woman almost as tall as the man, an expensive camera hanging around her neck from a Nikon strap. Most people were in shorts and t-shirts, with a lot of the women in colourful summer dresses, due to the weather. It was another bright, sweltering day and the heat of the sun on the back of Zoe's neck was like a presence pushing her to the ground. She felt like she wanted to take a nap and it was only just gone noon.

She adjusted the hamper on her left arm, already regretting the amount of food she'd packed because the straw basket seemed to get heavier by the minute, the twisted handle leaving marks on the inside of her arm. It also made it difficult because she didn't have a free hand for Aimee. At seven, the girl was a little old to hold hands but Zoe still preferred to have one spare in case anything went wrong. Still, there were no cars to look out for; it was more about keeping track of both kids in the steady procession of people.

'We go down there,' Aimee pointed to a path that branched right, the tennis courts on one side before being hidden behind a row of leafy trees, and a thick thatch of bushes on the other. They walked along the path for a few moments before skirting left around the bushes.

Zoe smiled. 'Wow, this is nice.'

In front of them was a space encircled by a dark green metal-railed fence with loops and arches along the top. Inside the fence was bright emerald grass, graceful trees and children playing and splashing happily in a stone fountain set into the ground in a large circle, with a raised lip. The water sparkled and glinted in the sunlight creating diamond reflections on the surface and the sky above it was an endless, deep blue. 'This is where the princess is?' she looked down at Aimee.

'It's a fountain for the princess, because she liked children.'

'Ah, I see.' Now it was starting to make sense. It must be the memorial fountain created and built to honour Princess Di. Zoe gestured to the nearest gate. 'Shall we go in?'

Jasper gave her a gappy grin and Aimee smiled slightly, moving ahead to hold it open for her.

'Thanks, Aimee.' Zoe hoisted the picnic hamper higher, releasing Jasper's hand and following them both in. 'Pick somewhere to sit,' she encouraged.

Aimee gestured to a spot over on the far side closest to the Serpentine and some kind of statute, but not so far from the fountain that Zoe wouldn't be able to keep a safe eye on them from a sitting position. 'Okay, off you go.'

Cheering, Jasper tore across the space, looping around the side of the fountain and coming to a halt on the spot his sister had picked. Jumping up and down, he grasped the bottom of his t-shirt and wrenched it over his head. Zoe was laughing by the time she and Aimee joined him, shaking her head wryly. 'Hang on, hang on. Don't you want to eat first? Aren't you hungry?'

'Nope,' Jasper jerked his head from side to side. 'I want to play.'

'What about you, Aimee? What do you want to do?' Zoe asked, setting the hamper down with a sigh of relief and flexing her arm. Letting her handbag slide to the floor, she gazed expectantly at the girl.

'I'll sit down for a minute,' Aimee decided, sinking to the grass and arranging the skirt of her cotton dress neatly across her knees, 'I'm not hungry yet.'

'All right. Are you okay to stay here and keep an eye on our things while I take Jasper to the water?' Not having been before, she needed to know how deep it was.

Jasper hopped from one foot to another. 'Come on, Zoe. Pleeeeeease.'

Aimee nodded, biting her lip.

Zoe held a hand up. 'Hang on a minute, Jasper.' Hunkering down, Zoe looked into Aimee's eyes. 'Are you sure you're okay with this?'

'Yes,' she whispered, eyes confused. 'I just want to sit down for a while. It's nice to be here again though.'

'I'm glad. We'll only be a few minutes.' Standing up, Zoe kicked her flip flops off and grabbed Jasper's hand. 'Right then, you. We don't need to put any sun cream on because we did it before leaving the house, but if you get your upper half really wet, we'll have to put some more on, okay?' The coconut scent still clung to her hands.

'Uh-huh,' he agreed, tugging her along.

Zoe laughed at his eagerness and they broke into a jog. Stepping over the raised lip of the fountain and jumping into the water, Zoe sucked in a breath. It was clean and fresh but frigging freezing, her toes immediately numbing and a line of ice lapping against her calves.

'Jeez,' she breathed. 'It's a bit cold isn't it?'

Jasper scrunched his face up and broke away. 'Don't care,' bending down he scooped up a handful of water and threw it in the air.

'Nooo,' Zoe squeaked, stepping back as the droplets rained down on her. 'Urgh.' She stopped, turning her face to the sun and feeling the slight breeze drying the water on her skin. 'Actually, that's quite refreshing,' she smiled at Jasper. Peering back over her shoulder to check Aimee was all right, the girl waved at her reassuringly, looking less troubled than before. That was good. She faced Jasper again, who was now running back and forth through the water, churning up waves on either side of his legs. 'Guess what?' she asked, squatting to plunge both hands into the water as the boy paused to look at her.

'What?'

'Water fight!' Flipping both hands up, she sent a shower of water over him, soaking one side of his shorts.

'Hey!' Chortling, he danced out of the way. 'I'm not in my swimmers!'

'Doesn't matter,' she grinned, pleased to see him have fun, 'you can change into them later and we can put those to dry on the fence like other people have, while we have lunch.'

'Cool.' Jasper grinned in return, and sent a cascade of water over her with a light kick, plastering her short, white summer dress to one thigh.

He backed away as she growled and pounced towards him with dripping hands.

They played for a few minutes, chasing each other, careful not to slip and fall in the fountain, hooting and splashing around. Zoe glanced at Aimee a few times to make sure she was okay, and on each occasion the girl was either watching them with a tiny smile or gazing out along the Serpentine.

Three screaming children ran past Zoe and Jasper, two boys and a girl yelling at each other to stop but continually spraying each other with water, before turning and scampering back past. 'Play with us,' one of the boys slowed, arching an eyebrow at Jasper and curling his hand into a *come here* gesture. He looked about seven or eight but had the confidence of an older child.

Jasper swivelled his head to look at Zoe. 'Sure,' she agreed, sitting down on the granite lip of the fountain and stretching her legs out in front of her. 'Go.' Her lips curved as she watched Jasper join in with the group, instantly flicking water at the girl, who also looked a few years older. The other boys gave a cheer and joined in and Zoe wondered if the girl was going to hightail it or start crying but instead she charged at them, guffawing and lifting her legs in ever higher kicks that sent water spraying in all directions.

Zoe rested back on her arms and studied the circle of the fountain as Jasper played happily. Wider at some points and narrower at others, one section of water was tranquil and on the opposite side the walls curved and tiny waterfalls cascaded over small steps or jets of water bubbled up in the stream. The space in the middle of the fountain was grassy, though some paths ran along the inner edge and one intersected the middle, and a few trees dotted around provided some shade from the relentless sunshine. *Princess Diana* was engraved into one of the fountain walls just above the surface of the water. Scores of kids were mucking around, leaping in and out of the fountain, scampering down the mini-waterfall, sitting in the water and swirling their hands through it, some in swimming costumes and others in vest and knickers. Children's laughter and shrieks floated on the air and somewhere a mother called out that lunch was ready. Soft grass cushioned Zoe's hands, and the meaty smell of sausages drifted past from a nearby family who were unwrapping onion-filled hot dogs from crinkled foil. It was noisy but lovely and Zoe exhaled, relaxing a notch at a time. She was suddenly glad she'd returned to the UK.

Her stomach growled as the tangy scent of mustard from the hot dogs filled her nostrils. Five more minutes and she'd tell Jasper it was time for lunch. Tilting her head to the left, she cast an eye at the spot where Aimee was sitting and was shocked to see the hamper and her bag abandoned on the grass, the girl nowhere in sight.

Shooting up, Zoe gulped, scanning the grassy area. Fear lurched in her stomach. Where the heck was Aimee? She should be there, sat down. Oh my god, what if she'd lost her? What if she'd wandered off and couldn't find her way back or someone had taken her? She'd only looked away for thirty seconds. This couldn't be happening. Tendrils of anxiety wrapped themselves around her ribs, squeezing tight. Eyes focusing on the area inside the grass, she examined each group of people in turn, trying to see if a little red-haired girl with narrow shoulders was among them. Nothing. Shifting her attention to the fountain, she looked all the way around it frantically, searching among the cavorting children for Aimee, while making sure she knew exactly where Jasper was. Nothing, again.

Lifting her hands, she cupped them around her mouth and shouted Aimee's name, projecting her voice across the grass. She would never forgive herself if something happened to the girl, and neither would Matt or Jasper. 'Aimee!' she repeated in a bellow, mentally starting to plan her next steps. Grab Jasper, get her bag, alert a member of staff, call the police, call Matt—

A flash of red just outside the metal fence caught her eye. She squinted, breath stuttering in her throat. Was it …? 'Aimee!' The person moved in response, and then a small hand lifted and waved. Oh, thank god. She was so relieved she almost cried, but held back. She didn't want to scare the girl. Jogging over to Jasper, she motioned for him to come out of the water. 'Sorry, Jasper. It's time for lunch and we need to go and get your sister.' She checked to make sure the girl was still in the same spot. 'Come on. Now, please.'

'But I want to play some more.' The boy waded through the water, legs stiff, expression pleading.

'You'll have a chance to play some more after lunch, okay? Right now I need you to come with me.' She smiled gratefully when he heaved a sigh and gave his newfound friends a double-shouldered shrug, as if to say *what can you do*?

'See you later,' he waved to them.

'Thank you,' she said, as she helped him out of the fountain. Hurrying past their belongings with Jasper traipsing along behind her, she opened the gate nearest the banks of the Serpentine and urged Jasper to follow her over to his sister. The girl was standing next to a statue of a stork or some kind of bird with its neck arched over, beak resting against its wing. Made out of a greeney-blue marble, the statute was graceful and communicated a sense of peace. Set into the plinth at its base was a silver coin slot, encouraging people to donate to the park and education centre. Radiating from that were loops of end to end metal plaques encircling the statue in long looping lines set into the ground. They were filled with inscriptions. Some had a simple name, others a longer message with dates.

'You worried me, Aimee,' Zoe clasped the girl's shoulder in a light grip, keeping her tone non-confrontational. 'I didn't know where you were. We agreed you would stay by our stuff, remember?'

'Sorry. I didn't mean to scare you.' The girl didn't lift her head, staring intently at something on the ground.

'That's all right. Just don't do it again please.' Letting go of Aimee's shoulder, Zoe put a hand on her own chest, echoes of the piercing fear bouncing back on her. 'It's important that I always know where you and your brother are. I have to make sure that nothing bad happens to you.'

'Because you're our nanny and you'd get in trouble?' Jasper questioned, cuddling into her side and looking up at her with big green eyes, so much like his dad's. 'Or 'cause you like us?'

Returning his trusting gaze, something in the region of Zoe's heart squeezed and then flipped over. She didn't give a toss if she got in trouble, she realised. It was about keeping them safe, wanting to protect them from all the bad things in the world. She never wanted to see them hurt, or sad.

Oh no, she was falling utterly in love with Matt's kids. This was not supposed to happen. It never had before.

'A bit of both,' she choked out, hugging him close. 'But anyway,' breathing in deeply for composure, 'that's not the point. You both need to stay near me. Got it?'

'Yes,' Jasper replied in a piping voice as his sister mumbled her own agreement.

'Good. What are you looking at, Aimee?' Zoe narrowed her eyes at the floor.

'Mummy,' Aimee pointed to a tiny metal plate in a ribbon of them. *Helen Reilly. Gone Too Soon. 04-06-12.*

Zoe could make out the sheen of tears in Aimee's eyes.

A piece of mummy, the girl had said. She supposed that to a child who'd lost a parent at four years old that must be what the engraved memorial plate seemed like.

'Ahhh,' Zoe nodded. 'That's nice.' Yet the idea that Matt had been sweet and sensitive enough to remember his wife in this way, in a place they'd been happy as a family, a place that was close enough to home that his children could visit it if they wanted to, jarred with the image of him firing and throwing Mel out. It didn't fit. She had to make it a priority to try and find out more about what'd happened between Stephen, Melody and Matt.

'What's nice?' Jasper tugged on her dress. 'And where's Mummy?'

Seeing the panicked expression on Aimee's face, Zoe motioned to the plaque. 'There's a little rectangle of metal there with your Mum's name on it. It's a way of remembering her.'

'Oh.' Jasper glanced at it quickly, but it obviously meant nothing to him as he turned to watch the other children playing in the Princess Di fountain. He was possibly too young to understand the significance of it. Neither did he ask what the numbers were. Zoe assumed they were the day Helen had passed away, yet didn't memorials usually have the dates of someone's lifespan on them, to celebrate the life they'd lead, rather than focusing on the day they'd lost it? Also, where was the usual wording about being a wonderful wife and loving mother?

The plaque raised all sorts of questions Zoe shouldn't want the answers to.

'Are you ready for lunch now, Aimee?' she queried. 'We can come back afterwards if you want.'

The girl lifted her head and scrubbed both hands over her damp cheeks. Something tugged in Zoe's chest again.

'It's all right,' Aimee met Zoe's gaze directly, 'I feel better. It was nice to see her. I told her things in my head. I'll eat lunch and then I'll play in the water with Jasper, while you sit down and rest,' she finished solemnly. 'But can we come here again? Maybe we can come back on Sundays, like we used to before?'

'Maybe.' Zoe gritted her teeth to stop from bursting into tears, the bittersweet comments taking her back to a time when she'd been caught in that awkward age between child and adult and had lost both parents at once. She'd been the bigger sister too, like Aimee. Memories flashed past. Melody's smaller hand slipping into hers as they stood in Ruth's shadowed porch, waiting to start their new lives. The lemony smell of her mum's hair and then the absence of it. The deep timbre of her dad's voice as he told them all a lame joke. The sticky, tangy multi-coloured Opal Fruits (she'd never get used to calling them Starbursts) her parents used to pass to them in the back of the Fiat on long car journeys. She swallowed down the aching lump in her throat. Her life seemed to be a catastrophe of losses of some sort or another. Her parents, Henry, and now Greg. No. She was getting maudlin. That wasn't who she was. 'Right then,' she said brightly, 'lunch.'

Swinging around, she put her back to the Serpentine Bridge curving over the water and the people enjoying the sun, pedalling

409

lazily in blue pedalo boats.

Grasping both children's hands she took them back into the memorial fountain grounds, unfurled the blanket from the hamper, and brusquely set up their picnic. The question of what to do about the attachment she was forming to the children would have to wait.

Half an hour later, Zoe lounged on her front on the blanket, chin propped on her hand as she watched the kids play in the water. Replete after a generous lunch of sandwiches, chicken, crusty sausage rolls, fresh fruit, cheese, mini scotch eggs, coleslaw, potato salad, crisps and juice, she felt a drowsy contentment stealing over her. She'd have to be careful not to fall asleep with the sun's warm rays pulsing down on her head. It was so lovely to lie here and watch Aimee playing with her brother. It was even better when she went one step further by talking to the girl who Jasper had been splashing earlier on, the two other boys rushing over to join in with the conversation.

When her eyelids drifted shut and her chin slid off her palm, she forced herself to sit up to stay awake. Grabbing her mini laptop from her handbag, she opened the lid and created a new Word file, glancing up to check the kids were playing nicely. Pausing, she sucked her bottom lip into her mouth before starting to type.

The Truth About Matt Reilly

It's well known that infamous London-based music producer Matt Reilly is fiercely private and camera shy. He never gives interviews to the press, and seems uncomfortable at public events, preferring the focus to be on his artists. In an exclusive story, the girl who was his nanny for X months shares a kiss and tell story about his love life, his relationship with his two children and his ruthless work ethic.

Stopping, Zoe went back and deleted the part about the kids.

410

It didn't feel right to talk about them. What could she say about his love life from what she knew so far?

Claiming not to have dated anyone seriously since the tragic death of his wife three years ago, Matt told his nanny that most of the women who accompanied him to social functions were friends or fellow celebrities seeking publicity, agreed via his PR Officer. However, we can exclusively reveal that he did in fact have arrangements for sexual-

Zoe paused again, a sick feeling swirling in her stomach. This felt wrong. Hearing her phone ping with a message, she hit the *Save As* button and named the file *Nannygate* before shutting down the laptop and shoving it in her bag. Retrieving her mobile at the same time, she cast a quick look at the kids before opening the text. Surprised it was from Matt, who hardly every contacted her during the day, she stood up and moved closer to where the kids were frolicking in the fountain.

**Hi, just wondered
when you'll be
back? May join
you for dinner. M.**

She was insanely pleased. He hadn't joined them for a meal since the day Sadie had dropped round. The flutter of excitement she felt at the thought of them all sitting down together was for the children, and only them. She wasn't bothered personally, of course not. Wasn't looking forward to the prospect of hearing about his day, seeing his face light up when he talked about his latest project or turned to listen to Jasper's chatter, like he had when he'd tucked them up the other evening.

**That would be lovely.
The kids will be happy.**

411

We're having a picnic
in Hyde Park atm. Back
around 4 p.m. Dinner
about 6 p.m. That ok? Z.

She could see the message had been delivered and he'd read it, so was puzzled when there was no immediate reply. Going over to sit down on the lip of the fountain but out of reach from getting sprayed, she watched Aimee and Jasper play with their friends and tried to relax in the sunshine over the next half hour. It proved to be impossible because worry nagged at her stomach. Checking her phone repeatedly for a return text, she chewed her lip. It could be that he was just busy, but he'd read the message so why not take a moment to send one back? What was going on? She didn't like the feeling she'd done something to upset him. Worse was feeling that way when it shouldn't matter. She should want to upset him after treating Melody so horribly. Increasingly though she couldn't square the person Matt seemed to be with the person she'd thought he was from his actions towards Mel. Mind you, she acknowledged bitterly, she was hardly the best judge of character. For five years Greg had fooled her into believing he was one thing, when he'd turned out to be another.

Finally she sent another message, unable to push away the squiggle of discomfort at Matt's lack of response.

Everything ok?
Will those timings
work for you? Z.

A message pinged back a few minutes later.

Yes, fine.
See you later.

There wasn't even a sign off. The message was either brief or cold, depending on which way you looked at it. Checking the messages she'd written it dawned on her. How could she have been so dense? *We haven't been in three years.* Aimee had told her. *We used to go – me, Mummy, Daddy and Jasper.*

She'd casually dropped into a text that they were having a picnic in Hyde Park as if it had no significance. But of course it might upset him that she was with the kids in a place he'd come with Helen as a family and that the mention of it could cause him pain. God, maybe she should have checked that he was all right with her bringing the kids here. It hadn't occurred to her, she was just so pleased that Aimee was continuing to open up and had thought it was a good step forward for her. Bugger, she'd have to try and speak to Matt before dinner. To apologise for her lack of sensitivity.

When her phone received another text, she hoped it might be her boss adding a polite sign off. But it was Greg again, with a message very much like the other three she'd received over the last few weeks.

Zoe, this is silly.
Call me please.
Lots of Love, G x

She stabbed at the phone to close the message. He was having a laugh. She was silly? No, he was crazy to think for one minute that she would want anything to do with him. Besides, if he was that bothered about talking to her, he'd call directly, not hide behind a text. Not that she wanted to talk to him. But when it came to serious issues, texts were for cowards. She'd been unable to believe it when one of her American friends, a nanny who looked after the four boys a few doors down, had been dumped by text. What kind of person did that? When had it become acceptable to ditch someone you'd been intimate with, in love with even, in truncated written form? If you had something important to discuss with someone, you picked up the phone, or spoke to them face to face.

Zoe sighed, shaking her head again. Hypocritical or what? She'd been avoiding it, but there were a few things she and her Aunt had to say to one another. It couldn't go on like this, especially now they were living in the same country. Even if what she'd done before leaving for the States had been for the right reasons, she'd hurt her aunt and needed to make amends. Especially if she was ever going to have the relationship she wanted to with her sister again. The three of them—Mel, Ruth and herself—might not be perfect but together they formed a lop-sided triangle. At the moment, she was the weak link.

Hitting the contacts list and call button before she could think too much about it, she held her breath as the phone rang, standing and wading through the chilly water while watching the kids. Jasper was giggling joyously as he zigzagged back and forth across the fountain in a game of chase with his sister and their new friends and Aimee had a rare, wide smile on her face.

'Yes, hello?'

'Hi, Aunt Ruth. It's me.'

'Oh, hello.'

'I thought I'd call and see how you are, and if you and Melody are getting on okay?'

'We're fine,' her aunt's voice was as frigid as the water Zoe was standing in.

She took a deep breath, pressing on. 'Good. How's Melody doing? I spoke with her the week before last and have sent her some messages but she's not really been in touch, so—'

'I'm not sure what you said to her, but she was ever so upset,' Ruth cut across her.

'Oh. Was she? We had a bit of a disagreement, it's true, but I hadn't realised I'd upset her this much.' That explained her sister's minimal contact. 'I apologised at the time. Can I talk to her?'

There was a pause. 'She's not here at the moment. She's gone down to the pier to meet an old school friend.'

'Anyone I'd know?'

'I don't think so, with you two being so many years apart in age.'

Zoe stared at the azure sky, praying for patience. No matter what she did, in her aunt's eyes it was wrong. Why did it have to be so difficult? 'Fine. I'll try her mobile then.'

'I wouldn't bother. She's left it here on the sideboard.'

Zoe wondered if that was a fabrication and was half tempted to ring her sister to prove her aunt wrong, but the point-scoring games between them had to stop. 'Okay,' she said reasonably. 'I'll try her later. In the meantime, I thought it might be good for us to talk. The next day off I have, I'd like to come and see you.'

'You would?' Her aunt sounded taken aback. 'Why?'

'We have things to discuss. I'd like to clear the air. I know you don't agree with what I did, but you shouldn't take it personally. It wasn't a criticism of your care, I just wanted—'

'You're right,' Ruth interrupted, 'you need to come visit. This conversation is hardly one to be done by phone. I have things to say too.'

Zoe winced. Of course she did. What a lovely discussion that was sure to be. 'I'll let you know when I can come.'

'I'll wait to hear from you. In the meantime, are you getting any further on with finding out what on earth happened? Your sister still hasn't heard from Stephen.'

'Not really,' Zoe admitted, feeling like a failure. Thinking back to the afternoon in Green Park with her fellow nannies. 'Other than Melody is supposed to have done something pretty unforgivable, though I don't know what.'

'Tosh!' Ruth exclaimed. 'I don't believe it. You need to keep digging.'

'I know. I will,' Zoe promised. Staring at Aimee and Jasper having such a great time together, she gulped. Siblings should always be there for each other, no matter what. 'Take care, Aunt Ruth. Bye.' Ending the call, her shoulders slumped. How did she do right by her sister, while also doing right by Matt's children? If she hurt him, she hurt them.

415

9

'Matt, I'm sorry,' Zoe said as soon as he loped up the stairs from the studio and into the kitchen later on that evening. 'I didn't even think to ask if it was okay to take them to Hyde Park.'

Not answering, he acknowledged her apology with a curt nod. Striding over to the sink he turned the tap on with a jerk, grabbing a posh blue glass from one of the cupboards. She stared at his broad shoulders outlined in a thin white t-shirt, the shifting muscles of his back visible through the light fabric. Gulping, she leaned over and checked the homemade lasagne through the orange-lit glass on the front of the oven, peering in at the cheese bubbling nicely on the surface of the pasta.

Thank goodness he'd come up before she'd served dinner. It gave them the chance to talk alone while the children listened to what Jasper referred to as *Daddy's Music* in the enormous white lounge. The last time she'd put her head in, they'd been bopping around the room to the latest pop track by one of the cutting-edge girl groups signed to Matt's label. Throwing their arms in the air and shaking their heads, they'd danced with no inhibitions and no self-consciousness. Zoe had grinned with amazement at seeing Aimee express herself so freely, remembering the little girl of a few weeks before who was only interested in reading. Jasper had catapulted himself onto one of the white sofas and was bouncing up and down on it with sweet abandon. Wondering if she should tell him to stop, she decided the furniture must be mega-expensive and should therefore be strong enough to cope.

Straightening now, she spun around to find Matt right in front of her, only a few inches between them. 'Oh, hi.' She fumbled with the tea towel in her hands. 'Wow, you moved quietly. Look—'

'Melody never took them,' he butted in, 'so I've never had to deal with how it might feel.'

'I completely understand. Next time anything like that happens, and I think it could be a sensitive issue for you because of Helen, I'll check with you. Melody probably didn't take them because she didn't want to upset them. Aimee wanted to go though, so I thought we should try.'

He expelled a breath. 'I'm not angry, Zoe. I was just upset earlier. I find it hard.'

'Yes,' she said in a soft voice, understanding his grief, 'I get that. I lost both my parents when I was in my early teens and when I went back to our old house a couple of years later it was one of the most challenging moments of my life. Thinking of the happy times and memories of my parents only highlighted that I'd never have new memories to make with them. Seeing another family living where we used to, a bike I didn't recognise propped against the porch, the eaves painted beige whereas Mum had painted them an ice-lolly orange, a strange tabby cat licking its paws in the garden …' Pausing, she swallowed past the enormous lump in her throat. 'I think that was the first time I truly started to accept that they really weren't coming back.'

'I'm sorry,' he said in a deep voice, eyes compassionate. 'That must have been tough, losing both of them at once.' Touching her arm, he shifted closer, and she had nowhere to go, crowded against the oven.

'Thank you,' she replied, gazing into his forest green eyes, noting again the pretty petal pattern within the irises. 'The reason I mention it is so you know I appreciate what you're going through and how you must feel about the thought of going back there.' She raced on, determined to stick to the subject and not get distracted by the tingles of warmth spreading through her body. 'But the kids enjoyed it, Matt. Jasper didn't seem to remember it much, but Aimee talked about a lot of happy times when you went as a family.' He stepped back and put his hands on his lean hips, dropping his head. Zoe sped on, needing to get it all out before he closed down again. 'She showed me the plaque you commissioned. It was a lovely thought. I think having it in a beautiful park rather than visiting a gravestone might help Aimee deal with missing her mum. It did her the world of good. They want to go back again. Maybe you can take them once a week or something? Even if you don't have time for them to play in the fountain each time, I still think it would be a nice idea to—'

'Zoe, don't. Stop, please.' Matt lifted his head and she was so stunned by the depth of pain in his face that she sucked in a sharp breath. He shuddered. 'I can't.'

'I understand you must miss her and it would make you sad. But it might be good for you as well as the kids.'

'Yes, that's it, I miss her and it would be very sad.' Matt repeated almost robotically.

She frowned. It wasn't the response she'd expected, or at least, not the delivery of it. 'Can you just give it some thought?' she murmured. 'I think it would mean a lot to them. If you want, I can take them until you're ready to?'

He stared at her so long that she raised a hand to her face to make sure there was nothing on it, wiping her cheeks. Nope, no crumbs, no food.

'You would do that?' he asked at last.

'Yes. I care about them.'

His mouth curved, eyes crinkling. 'Yeah, I can see that.' Nodding, 'I'd appreciate it. Thanks. I'll go and get the kids to set the table.' He swung back around to face her, 'Oh, remind me at dinner I've got something to give you.'

418

'You have? What is it?' she asked, clutching the tea towel. 'I love surprises. Well,' she crinkled her nose, 'good ones anyway.'

'It was going to be a surprise, but I'm rubbish at keeping them. My face can't lie. Hopefully it's a good one. I thought you might like your own car.'

Her eyes widened. 'Really? I mean, I'm happy to walk and Jasper loves going on the bus, but that would be great. It'd be nice to take the kids somewhere a bit further afield.'

'It's no problem. Just be warned, it's not very flash.'

'Hey, I'll take anything I'm given.' She grinned at the thought of taking the kids on an adventure. About to turn away to see to dinner, she was totally shocked when Matt suddenly scooped her up in a quick hug. Her toes barely scraped the floor and she clung onto his shoulders with a squeak, scorching awareness shimmering down her spine as the heat of his toned chest warmed her boobs. 'Matt?'

'God, you're great. Thank you so much,' he said into her neck.

'That's fine,' she choked, staring up at him as he released her and stepped back.

'Sorry, that wasn't very appropriate, was it?' He looked sheepish. 'Bosses don't usually go around hugging employees. It's just that you've made such a difference to the kids already. I'm really grateful. Melody was nice to the children and they got on well,' a flicker of uncertainty crossed his dark features, 'but you've arrived and straight away seen everything so clearly, everything that the kids needed that I couldn't recognise. Even though we've had some difficult conversations that must've been as uncomfortable for you as they were for me, it's all been to make my kids happier. And they are.'

Zoe gulped, feeling both flattered and guilty. 'I'm just doing my job.'

He waved a hand. 'It's more than that,' he dismissed. 'But anyway, I won't embarrass either of us any longer. You get dinner sorted and I'll get Aimee and Jasper.'

She nodded, mouth hanging open as he loped from the room. She could still feel his body imprinted on hers.

'I don't believe it!' Zoe hissed her annoyance through gritted teeth. She'd walked out of the house, Jasper and Aimee ahead of her, ready to drive them down to Longleat Safari Park and Matt's Prius was blocking her in on the gravel drive.

Again.

For the fourth time in a week. Arghh. What was wrong with the guy?

She'd been so touched when he handed her a set of car keys at dinner the day she'd gone to Hyde Park, guiding her and the children out the front of the house to reveal a smart white BMW 1 Series Sports Hatch. 'Nothing flashy?' she'd said, raising an eyebrow and stroking a hand along the bonnet.

Shrugging both shoulders, 'Not in the same league as my McLaren,' he pointed at the sexy black supercar on the driveway.

She laughed. 'No, but I expected a cheap little run-around or another Prius.'

'I don't do cheap, not anymore.'

'What do you mean?'

He ran a hand over Aimee's red hair absently as she stood in front of him. The little girl rested back against her dad, a tiny smile on her lips, like an adorable kitten basking in the sun. 'When I was younger the first car I bought myself was a second-hand Ford Escort,' he pulled a face, 'it was snot green. You could see me coming for miles. Mum hated it, said it brought the whole neighbourhood down. She's terribly upper class,' he mocked.

Her laughter pealed out as she propped both elbows on top of the car, watching Jasper as he started running round the Prius and BMW in loop-the-loops, arms out like an aeroplane with accompanying sound effects. 'Really? Why didn't your parents buy you a car?'

'They offered, I refused. I wanted to earn my own money and

buy my own things. I'd seen too many spoilt rich boys at school and didn't want to turn into one.'

'I see. What about your brother? Did he feel the same?' She was pretty sure she knew the answer.

His mouth turned down. 'I hoped I'd been a good role model, but no, he doesn't work. He has a trust fund. He bought that yellow monstrosity with part of it.'

'You don't seem that keen about his choice of cars, or lifestyle,' she blurted, before adding, 'sorry.'

Jasper scuttled past, increasing the volume of the roaring engine sound.

Matt dropped his hand to his daughter's shoulder, eyes narrowing as he nodded his head. 'No, it's okay. The truth is, I wish he wasn't so heavily reliant on the family money and that he'd find something worth doing with his time. He always seems so restless, although he travels, socialises and shops a lot.'

'Is that where he is now?' she asked in a careful voice. 'Travelling?'

'Yes, on our yacht in the Med. The poor guy's been through a rough time,' he explained, 'a girl broke his heart.'

'She did?' her voice came out high pitched and weird. What the hell was he talking about? It was Stephen who'd broken Melody's heart, not the other way around.

His eyes narrowed further and he focused on her flushed face. 'Yes. It's the first and only time I've ever seen it happen. Usually he's commitment-free, but Melody seemed to change him. I thought he was settling down.'

'Melody?' She bent at the waist and caught Jasper automatically as he stumbled and almost went over on the gravel. 'There you go.' She righted him and sent him on his way with a pat on the back.

Spinning around, Jasper glared at both adults. 'I like 'Ncle Stephen,' he piped, 'he's fun.'

'I like Uncle Stephen too,' Matt replied, 'and yes, he's fun but we both know he can be a bit of a handful too. Like you, right?' he teased.

421

Jasper stuck his tongue out with a grin.

As he resumed his flying game, Zoe gazed at Matt. 'Melody, as in your last nanny?' Her heart was pump-pump-pumping in her chest, knowing she was getting closer to the truth.

'Yes,' he looked grim.

'That must have been complicated, your nanny slee—' flickering her eyes at Aimee, 'I mean dating your brother.'

'It wasn't ideal, I'll admit. I thought it might get messy, but when they came and talked to me about it, I felt reassured. I was fine with it as long as it didn't affect the kids. My parents might not have felt the same because they're self-confessed snobs, but I just want my brother to be happy. Besides, I liked Melody until …' He looked down at Aimee at the same time as she looked up. Seeing her features creased in a question seemed to jolt him.

'Until?' Zoe prompted. If he was telling the truth, he'd had no objection to his brother having a relationship with Melody. So what had changed?

He stepped back and stuck his hands in his pockets. 'It doesn't matter,' he muttered, looking panicky. 'It's all over and done with now. It's also probably not something we should be discussing in front of the kids.'

Bugger, he'd been about to spill. She mustn't spook him. 'Maybe not,' she agreed. 'Anyway,' she clapped her hands, 'thank you for my Bimmer. It looks great.'

He relaxed, 'I considered a Prius, but wanted to get you something with a little more energy and power. I thought this would suit you. It's yours for as long as you're with us.'

'Thank you,' she twisted away to open up the boot so that he wouldn't see her wince. How long she might be there for was an increasingly troubling issue in her mind. 'This isn't a bad space,' she talked to the carpet lining the boot rather than Matt. Needing a minute to steady herself.

'It's insured and ready to go. I hope you enjoy it.' Crossing to the back of the car, he came and stopped beside her, touching her

422

arm gently. He waited until she lifted her head. 'Please be careful with my children, Zoe. I'm putting a lot of trust in you. To be honest, I'm very nervous about it. I asked Melody once if she wanted a car, but she didn't have a license. You can imagine how I feel, given the accident, which as you know …' Halting, his eyes rested on Aimee, who was observing them both with pained eyes. 'You know what I'm saying,' he finished gruffly.

'I know.' Zoe nodded reassuringly. 'I'll drive sensibly, I promise. I had to get used to driving in America and it's pretty hectic on the roads over there, so I have plenty of experience. I always got Grace and Ava safely from A to B.'

'Thank you, that's a relief to hear. Now why don't you take it for a spin? I'll stay here with the kids.'

'Are you sure?' How sweet, giving her a chance to enjoy her new car.

'I'd rather you get used to it without Jasper chatting away at you from the back seat.'

'Oh. Thanks.' Not so sweet then, merely practical.

Since then she'd used the BMW, or tried to, almost every day despite the London traffic and everything being basically within walking distance. She loved how smooth and responsive it was, the high gloss interior effortlessly modern and cool.

However, Matt constantly blocking her in was driving her insane. How he managed it she didn't know, but the total disregard it showed and the level of inconvenience wound her up. He was here all the time too, he never seemed to go into the City any more.

The first time he'd blocked her in, she'd gone to his office and very politely asked him to move his car.

'Sorry, haven't got time,' he'd grunted over his shoulder, not even turning from his Mac screen to look at her.

'Please, Matt?'

'I said, I haven't got time,' he ground out, yanking a hand through his hair. His desk was even more chaotic than usual, balled up pieces of paper littering the floor and discordant music playing

423

on the Mac. 'Do you mind leaving me to it? I'm in the middle of something. I'm sure you can walk if you want to go out.'

Just as quickly she was dismissed from his thoughts. It was a replay of his behaviour on the day he'd interviewed her and she wondered if Sadie's continued absence for an extra two weeks was taking its toll on him. It wasn't often he was snappy, but when he was, he was a pro.

In the interest of keeping the peace and because both Jasper and Aimee had been standing in the hallway behind her, she'd backed out. 'No probs, sorry to disturb you.' Smiling easily as if it wasn't a problem, she'd motioned to the children to follow her. 'Come on, your dad can't move the car at the moment, we'll walk down to the park instead, or do you want to take the bus somewhere?'

When it came to the parking situation, he just wasn't thinking, she decided, and he was incredibly stressed and busy. But now that it'd happened two other times with similar results and she'd geared the children's expectations up for a day trip, she'd had enough. No matter what he tried to say or do today, he was moving his damned car.

Leaving the children waiting patiently in the front hallway with promises of seeing monkeys if they didn't behave like ones while she was gone, she hurried down the basement stairs and rapped on the studio door.

Nothing. No answer.

She swore under her breath and knocked again.

Silence.

Curling her hand into a fist, she used the side of it to bang, bang, bang on the door.

Still nothing.

A flash of memory shook her, the action reminding her of knocking on the door of Matt's home nearly a month ago. If she'd known then what she would end up doing in the name of revenge, how much it was costing her when she was falling a little more in love with Matt's kids every day, would she have carried

424

on knocking or walked away?

She wasn't sure any more.

Sick of waiting for an answer that might never come, she grabbed the door handle and thrust the door open, almost falling into the room.

Matt swung around in a chair set in front of a darkened large plate window, his hands on a massive soundboard filled with buttons and sliding switches. 'When people don't answer the door,' he hit a switch to cut the music, a nerve ticking in his jaw, eyes flashing, 'it's usually because they don't want to be disturbed.'

'When people don't answer the door,' she shot back 'and when they speak to people the way you just spoke to me, it's because they're rude and ignorant.'

'Pardon?' He jerked out of his seat, the chair shooting back and hitting the desk with a heavy bang that made her jump.

Replaying what she'd said to him, she crossed her arms over her chest. The air con set into the low ceiling sent goose bumps over her skin and she fleetingly regretted the belly-grazing white vest top she wore with an Indian patterned ankle-length summer skirt. 'Crap. I'm sorry, Matt,' she shivered, 'I didn't mean that the way it came out, but if we're too noisy for you or you don't want to be disturbed, then maybe you should go and work in your off-site premises? I also understand that you're under pressure at the moment but the only reason I keep disturbing you during the day is because you keep parking the Prius across the driveway and blocking me in. All I'm asking for is a little consideration ...' she trailed off at the expression in his green eyes, noticing the dark stubble edging his jaw, much thicker than usual. 'What's the matter?' she asked.

'Why do you care?' he demanded irritably.

Taking a step back, her spine hit the doorframe and she winced. Had he found out who she was related to, and why she was here? Was that why he seemed so cross? But if that was the case surely he would just come out with it.

'I care about anything that affects the children,' she replied, 'which includes you. Unfortunately.'

'Unfortunately?' he glowered. 'Oh, that's charming.'

'Well, I'm sorry but you're not being very nice at the moment.'

He went to answer, paused, closed his eyes and took a deep breath. 'You're right. I'm not. I'm sorry.' He went quiet again, jaw clenching and unclenching as he inhaled and exhaled.

Zoe regarded his still pose, wondering if he was trying out some new-age Zen exercise. He looked pale, with crescent shadows under his eyes like he wasn't getting much sleep. With his broken nose and the scar above his lip, he was more bad boy and dangerous than ever. It was a look that worked entirely too well for him, and which caused an entirely unwanted reaction inside her. Knees feeling floaty, a familiar tingle of lust pinged between her thighs, heat sweeping in a slow burn through her body. Her hands curled into fists, nails biting into her palms. She was glad the door was propping her up and pinning her to reality because she desperately wanted to launch across the room and kiss him until it hurt them both. Wanted to have the kind of hot, angry sex that came with making up after an argument. The biting, clawing, sweaty kind that left you breathless, satisfied and purged of frustration. It was wrong to want it with him, but she couldn't control her thoughts, and her body was as traitorous as her imagination.

She moved forward to stand under the air con, hoping the stream of cold air would cool her raging hormones. 'Maybe you need to slow down, take a break?' she suggested into the taut silence. 'Sometimes when you're too close to something it makes it harder to see clearly. Feeling wound up can also make you less productive. I take it work isn't going well?'

Opening his eyes and letting out a harsh laugh, he returned to his seat, stretching out his long muscular legs and staring at the ceiling. 'You could say that. But it's not just that.'

'Do you want to talk about it?'

'Not really.'

There was another drawn out silence, the bristling kind that set her nerves on edge.

'Right, fine,' she said finally, frustration edging her voice as she thought about the eager children upstairs waiting for their fun day out, 'still, having stuff on your mind doesn't stop you parking considerately. If you're not going to talk to me, Matt, can you at least just come and move your bloody car?'

At his continued silence, she shook her head, swung around and thundered up the stairs.

The exasperation in Zoe's tone as she blazed from the room made it clear to Matt that she was mightily pissed off. He couldn't really blame her; she had every reason to be. He knew he'd been rude lately, as well as distracted. He was trying to do as she'd asked by joining them for dinner and tucking the kids up in bed a few times a week but kept slipping back into bad habits. He had a natural tendency to withdraw into himself when he was working, and had to stop himself from resenting every small interruption and biting people's heads off when they needed something.

It didn't help that the new female vocalist he was working with was still completely off-piste both vocally and emotionally. There was no way they were going to meet the deadline he'd set to cut her debut album if things carried on like this. The delay frustrated the hell out of him, made him twitchy and anxious. Something about the girl's fragile manner told him they needed to keep the momentum going or it might never happen. And she was capable of platinum albums and sell-out tours, he knew it.

He'd already started popping antacids like sweets and at times could feel himself shaking with sleep deprivation, catching only a few hours rest a night.

It also didn't help that Stephen had gone AWOL, not answering the satellite phone or radio aboard their yacht, which had last been reported as anchored up in a rocky Corfu port. There was probably nothing to worry about, it was in character for his brother to fall out of touch for days or weeks at a time, but Matt couldn't help feeling uneasy anyway. He'd give it a few more days then start contacting Stephen's international friends and likely places he'd moor up, before approaching the appropriate coastguards if necessary.

There was something else nagging at him too. Talking to Zoe about Melody had made him wonder once again if his old nanny was all right. He'd felt like a bit of a bastard firing and then chucking her out, but after what Stephen had told him, he'd had no choice and tried to comfort himself that he was one hundred per cent justified in his actions. She was just lucky he hadn't done worse. Still, it didn't stop him feeling a sense of responsibility towards her and hoping she wasn't living in a cardboard box somewhere. On the other hand, girls like her always landed on their feet.

As for Zoe, she was one of his biggest problems at the moment, and a definite contributor to his bad mood. She worried at him like a nippy terrier with a bone, insisting he do things differently for the children, challenging him to be a better dad, but what he'd said the other day when he hugged her was true. She was making the children happy and he couldn't fault her for that. The problem was, the living situation was making him ratty. He could think of little else but her. His concentration was shot. The way she smiled with that lovely pink mouth, the shine of her glossy black hair, the warmth of her voice when she spoke to the kids, her big baby blues when she fronted up to him, the compassion in her face when she mentioned Helen, the incredible body underneath clothes that he ached to rip off … It was distracting and unnerving and his physical frustration was spilling over into everything else, amplifying his shitty behaviour. Which included being a royal pain in the arse towards Zoe. Take the car thing. Would it really be so difficult to park at a different angle, or move the cars around when he got home? He sat up, blinking. Was blocking her in a way of keeping her close, or annoying her so she'd confront him? Had he subconsciously been trying to get her attention?

No, that was ridiculous. He wasn't interested in getting involved. His late wife had taught him that emotions tied you down, restricted your choices. Put you at someone else's mercy. Three years after her death Helen still had a hold on him and he didn't know how to break free. There was no chance he was interested in falling under another woman's spell.

One side of him longed for Zoe to quit just so he could have his peace of mind back. The other side wanted her to stay and share her good heart and generous spirit with him and his children. To continue teaching them to be more loving and open than he was capable of nowadays. To show them that independence and individuality should be encouraged, just like he did with his artists, nurturing and helping them to grow as people. He frowned. If he could do it for them, why wasn't he doing the same for his children? That wasn't right. What was holding him back? Fear, or the ever present black guilt? Zoe had said he should think about why he'd distanced himself from Aimee and Jasper, and he wasn't quite there yet, but like a window blind being raised to let in the daylight, Matt suddenly knew what he had to do. Grabbing his phone off the side, he flew up the stairs after Zoe.

As she reached the top of the basement stairs and arrived in the ground floor hallway, Zoe was muttering under her breath at Matt's stubborn behaviour. The children stood up from their spot on the bottom of the spiral staircase.

'Can we go on safari now please, Zoe?' Jasper asked excitedly, skipping up and down on the spot. 'I weally want to see the monkeys.'

An automatic grumble about 'your dad' sprung to her lips but she held it back. It wasn't fair to involve them in her and Matt's bickering. God, they were like an old married couple.

Where had *that* come from?

Nope. No way. Imagine being tied to a bloke who was light-hearted and funny one minute, and distant and infuriating the next. Talk about unsettling. Or exciting, a little voice whispered. She shook her head firmly to dispel the silly thoughts. It was just hormones, with Matt being such fabulous eye candy. Any woman passing him in the street would take in the height, the built body and that roughly hewn face and think the same.

Aimee interrupted her inner ramblings, tucking a stray bit of red hair into her ponytail where it had slipped free. 'Daddy won't move his car, will he?' she asked softly, eyes full of disappointment. 'I bet he's too busy.'

Damn him. Both children had been looking forward to this so much. She played the logistics in her head. A bus or taxi to the station, a train journey to Wiltshire, a taxi on the other end. It might be expensive but Matt was rich enough to bear the cost. That wouldn't make up for the increased travel time though, and it was already gone nine in the morning. Going by train rather than car was going to cost them a couple of hours at least, cutting into the day she'd planned.

She noticed Jasper's eyes welling up and realised she hadn't answered Aimee's question.

Her back went ramrod straight and a wave of irritation swept over her. No. This wasn't happening. She wasn't letting Matt upset his children because he was having problems at work and whatever else it was he'd alluded to.

'Don't worry,' she told them, pawing through the bowl on the side table to locate Matt's Prius keys and stuffing them in her bag, 'we're going to Longleat. If he hasn't got time to move his car we can do it for him, or use it ourselves. He can always drive the P1 if he needs to go out.'

She grabbed her bag and the picnic hamper she'd packed early that morning before the temperature had started climbing. Running a critical eye over the kids, who were both dressed in baggy light t-shirts and shorts, she cocked her head. 'Did you both put sun cream on after you washed, like I asked?'

'Yes,' Aimee said, 'and I helped Jasper with his, and put the bottle in the hamper like you said to. Our hats are in my back-pack.' Turning around to indicate the '*I Love Books*' bag perched on her shoulder.

'Thank you, good girl. Right, let's go.'

Throwing open the door she ambled down the front stairs onto the driveway, the gravel crunching under her Greek style sandals. The Prius opened with keyless entry when she touched her hand to door handle, detecting that the fob was in her bag. Cars sure were smart things nowadays. Sometimes smarter than people? she wondered.

'Daddy won't like this,' Aimee told her.

'Oh, well, I'm sure there are lots of things that he—' she broke off. It wasn't fair to badmouth Matt to the children. It wasn't professional of her or helpful to their self-esteem. She was better than this. She smiled brightly, her black hair swinging in her face. Reaching up, she tied it into a knot at her nape. 'Aimee, it will be fine. Come on, get in.' She couldn't be bothered to mess around moving the cars, and would be covered for an accident through the fully comp car insurance Matt had taken out for her on the BMW.

Aimee shrugged her shoulders and clambered into the back whilst Zoe loaded up the boot and took Jasper around to the other side, buckling him into the booster seat while he chattered on about lions and hippos.

He turned to his big sister as Zoe slipped behind the wheel. 'Daddy is going to kill her,' he said in a matter of fact tone tinged with awe.

'Yes, she's very brave,' Aimee agreed.

Zoe looked over her shoulder and rolled her eyes at them play-fully, grabbing the door handle. Pulling on it, she met with resist-ance. 'Huh?' She switched her attention to her arm, and found Matt stood in the space between the car and the door, jamming it open.

'What do you think you're doing?' Matt demanded, a firm hand grabbing her upper arm and pulling her from the car.

'Ouch!' she yelped, unbalanced as he tugged on her arm again, sandals slipping on the gravel. She fell up against his solid chest, gripping his belt to remain upright. His lips brushed her earlobe, the touch making her body do funny, trembly things.

Her mouth opened in shock. 'Matt—' she squeaked as big masculine hands settled around her waist to steady her, their heat burning through the material of her top, a couple of fingers grazing her bare tummy.

He was strangely pale, his cheekbones standing out starkly. 'I said, what do you think you're doing?'

She tried to shake his hands off without success. 'What am *I* doing? I was just going to borrow your car. What are *you* doing? Are you crazy? Let go of me, please.'

He gritted his teeth and started answering but glanced at Aimee and Jasper in the back of the car. Jasper had unclipped himself and thrown himself across his sister's lap, little nose pressed up against the window so that he could watch the action.

'Aimee, can you take your brother into the house please? I need to talk to Zoe.'

His daughter nodded, exiting the car through the opposite door and leading her brother up the steps by the hand. 'But I want to go to Longleat,' Jasper's plaintive voice carried across the drive as he waved his free arm around expressively.

'Shhh,' Aimee murmured, pushing open the front door, 'let's go in and play. Just be patient.'

As soon as they were safely inside, Matt towed Zoe over to the front of the house near the garage doors. 'We don't need to stand in the middle of the driveway in plain sight for this conversation.'

When they stopped, Zoe took a step back at the look on his face. It wasn't just anger, it was fear and something else she couldn't read. Talk about an overreaction. 'Matt, what is it? I don't understand. You wouldn't move the Prius and I promised the kids I'd take them to Longleat so I didn't think there was any harm in using it. If I'd thought you'd mind I would have asked.'

His green eyes fixed like lasers on her confused face. He went whiter still and swayed, dropping to sit on the gravel like his legs could no longer hold him.

'Matt!' Zoe crouched down. What was going on here? 'You're scaring me.' Putting a hand on the back of his neck to check his temperature she saw it was warm to the touch, but not boiling. 'Are you ill? You don't feel that hot.' She sat down next to him, rearranging her skirt so the stones wouldn't cut into her legs.

'No.' Raising his head, he gazed at her. 'Please don't ever get into my car with my children when you're angry, Zoe,' he begged. 'I'm sorry. I didn't mean it. I won't block you in again.'

'Angry? What?' Whatever was going on here she needed to know. For all their sakes. He looked haunted. This was not possessiveness over his car or about proving a point about whose driveway it was. Her eyes were unwavering as they met his. 'I was annoyed, but I wasn't angry. I just wanted to fulfil my promise to the kids, but you're acting as if I'm committing some crime.' He flinched at her words, skin becoming paler if possible, and she felt another twisting pang of unwanted concern. 'Why did you react like that?' She squeezed his neck, knowing she should let go, stop touching him, but it was like a magnetic force was joining them together. She thought over the last few minutes. The kids, the car, his comments. 'Is this about what happened to Helen?' she queried calmly. 'Was she upset with you before she got in the car? Before the accident? I am so, so sorry if the situation reminded you of that, but I swear I would never drive in a temper, or hurt the kids. Whatever happened back then—'

'Please don't start telling me you understand how I feel,' Matt interjected, eyes bleak. 'You don't know a thing.'

'What you feel?' She lost her cool a little at that. Forgetting the barriers between them as employee and employer, too cross to care. 'Do you actually feel anything? You're so closed off sometimes. No wonder Aimee is so reserved.'

The statement fell into the silence between them like a dead weight, an albatross hanging around their necks.

433

'Excuse me?' his voice was hoarse, as if she'd caused him real injury.

'You know what I'm talking about,' she whispered. 'She's closed off Matt, just like you are.'

'Aimee's fine. There's nothing wrong with her,' he uttered, but his eyes were shadowed.

He had his head stuck in the sand if he believed what he was saying. She finally lifted her hand from his neck, craving the warmth of his skin straight away. 'There's being introverted and quiet, Matt, but that's not what this is. She's getting there, but it's still like she's afraid to show emotions sometimes. I'm not saying this to be horrible, I'm just trying to help.' She gazed at the eggshell blue sky, because it was easier than looking at his gorgeous but hurt face. 'Kids learn behaviours from the role models around them. They're sensitive creatures.' Turning back to him. 'Can't you see how much they need you? How much they want to be shown love? You need to show them that it's okay to feel, to have emotions. I'm not just saying this with my nanny hat on, I have personal experience.'

'I love my children, Zoe,' he answered, the passion in his voice clear, 'and I want the best for them. I would do anything for them, including leaving my comfort zone. So if you say I need to try harder then I will, but I have been trying, honestly. It's just not bloody easy, is it?' Frustration came through his husky voice. He cupped a hand around her jaw, his thumb stroking her cheek, and shuffled closer. 'And if I'm unfeeling, then why do I want to do this?'

Before she had time to answer he lowered his head and kissed her. It was tender with a hint of restrained need that drove her wild. Everything she'd imagined it would be and more. His lips shaped hers, tongue slipping into her mouth and sliding sexily against hers. She sighed, sinking into him and kissing him back, murmuring at how good and right it felt. Tingles flowed up and down her spine, boobs swelling and straining towards him, waiting for his touch. Her hands went to his broad shoulders, wanting to push him away, knowing in a dim corner of her mind it was the sensible thing to do and that it should feel weird kissing anyone but Greg. Instead, her fingers clung to his muscular neck and she edged closer to his tall, hot body.

With a rough sound he yanked her onto his lap, pulling his head back enough so that his teeth could nibble her bottom lip. The warm tingles turned into a full on fire, and she wiggled on his thighs, aware of his hardness against her. Lust throbbed between her thighs and if he'd suggested in that moment they go upstairs and get naked, she'd have agreed in a heartbeat.

This was Matt. It was wrong, and God knew she had reason to dislike him, but there was something about him that kept drawing her back, sucking her in, and he was so outrageously sexy her hormones took over. She tipped her head back and his hands curled around her narrow waist, hauling her nearer.

Her hands climbed from his shoulders to the back of his head and into his hair, grasping handfuls of it to hold him tight. She kissed him back with everything she had, completely absorbed in him. She could smell fresh, spicy male scent rising from his stubble coated neck, could feel the thick silkiness of his hair beneath her palms, the rasp of his tongue against hers.

It was incredibly hot, searing and absorbing. The best kiss she'd ever experienced.

And just as abruptly as it had started, it ended.

Matt suddenly tore his mouth from hers. 'Shit!' he said dazedly. 'We're in broad daylight. If we got photographed now, necking like a pair of teenagers …' he shook his head. Depositing her carefully on the gravel, he scrambled to his feet, hauling her up with one hand. He put his hands on his hips, chest rising and falling rapidly. His eyes flickered over her generous breasts, clearly peaked beneath the thin cotton of her top. She blushed, struggling to come back to reality, praying her knees would hold her up.

Dark colour ran along his cheekbones. 'I'm sorry, Zoe. I shouldn't have done that. Look, take the Prius, and have a great day with the kids.' He smiled but it didn't reach his eyes. 'I need to get back to work.'

'Matt—' she stepped towards him.

'I'll send the kids out to you.' Turning on his heel, he took the concrete stairs two at a time, leaving her standing in the middle of the driveway. Wondering what had just happened between them and what it meant.

10

Zoe cupped her hands around her mouth. 'Aimee! Jasper! You've had your extra ten minutes,' on top of the twenty they'd begged for previously, so reluctant to leave the fun behind and head back to London, 'it's time to go home now! They're closing for the night. If you're not careful you'll get locked in with the spiders and snakes!'

Smiling, she watched Aimee grab her brother's arm and start towing him to the entrance of the kids Adventure Castle area where Zoe waited on a bench, basking in the balmy evening sunshine. Jasper looked longingly over his shoulder then gave in, trudging as slowly as humanly possible back to his nanny.

Getting her phone out, she texted Matt a quick message.

**Hi. Stayed longer
than planned.
Just leaving.
Back around 8
if traffic's good.
Z.**

She didn't necessarily expect an answer. The previous two texts she'd sent had received no reply. The first had been to let him know they'd reached their destination safely, and the second at lunchtime was to ask how he was and say the kids were having a great time. Tempted to put a *P.S. we need to talk* at the end of the last one, she was glad she hadn't bothered when he'd not acknowledged either message. Besides, some conversations definitely needed to be face to face.

'Okay?' she asked Jasper and Aimee as they walked up to her. 'Do either of you need the toilet, or are you ready to rock and roll?'

Jasper looked confused, but Aimee got it. 'I'm fine. Do you need a wee, Jasper, or can we leave?'

'Oh. No, I'm okay. We can go.' Looking over his shoulder again regretfully.

'Come on, then.' She set off for the car through the main courtyard with various closed food stalls, making sure the children followed. 'Maybe we can come again, another time?'

'Yay!' Double yells of glee greeted her question, and she grinned.

They'd had an amazing day at Longleat but it had also been tiring packing so much in, especially with the beating sun so high in the cloudless sky, sweat dripping down their backs and prickly heat making their arms and legs itch. Despite wearing excessive amounts of sun cream and hats, Aimee's nose was looking distinctly pink and Zoe felt a little frazzled. It was gone six and she was looking forward to getting the drive home over and done with, and tucking the kids into bed. As it was they'd stayed longer than planned and were going to have to stop off for a fast food dinner on the M3 motorway services somewhere.

It had been worth it though, Zoe thought once they'd loaded the car up and were on their way up the wide, sedate tree-lined road, heading away from the stately elegance of Longleat House. The kids had loved driving around the Safari Park and seeing the animals in the wide grassy spaces and shadowy forests, winding up their windows to ensure they had no unwelcome visitors for the first and last sections. Their favourite was the monkey enclosure with its '*roof surfing zone*' where the monkeys ran up and leapt onto cars, clambering over them, peering in through the windows and rubbing their rude bits up against the windshields to Jasper's hysterical delight and Aimee's wrinkle-nosed disgust. Pulling off aerials and number plates with a self-satisfied air they passed them to one another to play with and hitched rides on car roofs. Thankfully they'd not managed to pull anything valuable off Matt's car. At the gate a teenage girl with a white stick made sure that park visitors *'took no extra monkeys home other than the ones they'd arrived with'*, a sign that amused Aimee no end.

They saw enormous rhinos, dun-coloured camels, graceful giraffes and bright pink flamingos. They fed deer through rolled down windows with cups of dusty food, laughing with glee at their tickling rasping tongues and butting heads. They drove through the leafy forest enclosures that housed the lions, tigers and wolves with locked doors and wide eyes at seeing such magnificent animals up close. No activity or enclosure was left unvisited. The gorilla on his solitary island in the middle of the lake with TV for company, seen on the boat trip in Jungle Kingdom, sea lions coming up to the boat and clapping for the fish thrown in by uniformed staff members. Walking through penguins and standing in the enclosure with them, Jasper chortling when one pooed on Aimee's foot, her face filled with revulsion until Zoe handed her a wipe to clean up. Then there was the winding maze which Zoe solved in a few short minutes, taking the children's hands and giggling as they raced through high hedge walls. The air in the Butterfly House was heavy and humid, multi-coloured tiny wings flapping gently past them and from there they went into the tarantula and snake handling area that Jasper revelled in, but which made the girls shudder. They wandered around the newly opened exhibit of dinosaur statues complete with sounds, before walking through beautiful gardens packed with flowers and heart-shaped shrubbery.

The children even enjoyed the grand luxuriant interiors of Longleat House itself, the three of them dressing up in fur-trimmed cloaks and crowns, pretending to be royalty as they swept through the large rooms with rich tapestries and elegant French furniture.

The flat manicured lawns and fountains outside were just as pretty and provided a good place to rest and enjoy the ice lollies and fizzy drinks Zoe treated them to, though she knew she was probably going to pay for it when it came to bedtime. She'd just craved a day of innocent, childish fun for them. A special day they might remember when they were older, the way she still remembered and treasured a day trip to a theme park with her parents and sister when she was ten.

Sitting down with a glass of wine later on was something she was relishing the thought of, Zoe mused as she joined the M3, leaving plenty of space for a lumbering lorry to roar past. It was Friday today so in theory her day off tomorrow. Whether Matt remembered that or not was another matter. So far on weekends, while she curled up on the sofa in her lounge with a series of thrillers she was reading, he'd tended to drift in and out of the house looking sheepish, or arrange for the kids to have play dates with their grandmother or Noel and Holly. Zoe really hoped that Matt wasn't going to do the same again tomorrow given her conversation with him this morning about the need to show the kids affection.

As for the incredible kiss they'd shared, it had niggled away at her all day, like a label on a piece of clothing that scratches your neck and drives you half mad until you have no choice but to cut it off.

One part of her was mortified it'd happened, that it had been so bloody enjoyable, and—this was the worst bit—that she wanted it to happen again. That part told her to forget the plan, pack her bags and get out. That she was edging into dangerous territory like the lion enclosure earlier and should run now before she got torn apart and devoured.

The other part of her said to stop overreacting, that it had meant nothing, and Matt himself had said it shouldn't have happened. To stop being so damned wet and just get on with things. The truth was, until she had it out with Matt, she wouldn't know what the

440

right thing to do was.

She probably needed some distance and time away from him and the kids after the last few weeks of intensity, so she'd arranged to see Ruth the next day and also sent texts to Rayne and Frankie to ask about a girly night out the following evening. Rayne had texted straight back stating that hell yeah, she was up for it and Adam was a big boy who could amuse himself for the night. Frankie had replied a few hours later, confirming she'd had a cancellation for a party she'd been due to take photos at so she would love to come, her boyfriend Zack offering to drop her off and pick her up. They'd agreed on dinner and drinks, and 'who knew what else' after that. Zoe was looking forward to having a proper catch up with her two best friends, and a bit of advice about her current living situation might not go amiss.

After that, she'd finally got hold of Melody on the phone to see if she would come to London for the night, having a job convincing her that a bit of fun would do her good. When Melody had been reluctant, Zoe had resorted to big sister bossiness and told Mel she was planning to visit Ruth the next day so could bring her back and would eject her sister from Ruth's sofa forcefully if necessary. And, she added, the two of them needed to talk alone and the drive from Southend back into the capital would give them the opportunity. After a lot of sighs, and *I'm not sure*'s, Melody had agreed.

It was gone half eight by the time Zoe pulled up in front of Matt's house, and by then she was seriously dragging and ready to end the day. Looking at the spot on the gravel driveway where she and Matt had sat and kissed, she shivered, flushing all over. Bugger, how was she going to keep it together when she actually faced him? Peering around the front door and listening for her boss as Jasper and Aimee clattered in ahead of her, she was relieved when it was quiet. A few minutes to settle herself would be good. Sloping into the hallway, she slid the Prius keys into the bowl Matt usually kept them in, and set the picnic hamper on the floor.

The door of Matt's office flew open and he stuck his head out. Zoe had to hold back a laugh because it reminded her of the inquisitive meerkats they'd seen earlier at Longleat.

'How was your day?' he asked them all. 'What did you get up to?'

She groaned, shaking her head. That was a mistake; the kids would be talking for hours. As their excited chatter and descriptions filled the high ceilinged passage, Jasper doing his habitual hopping on the spot, Zoe picked up the basket again. 'I'll just go and empty this out in the kitchen.'

'Hang on kids. Everything okay, Zoe?' Matt caught her arm as she passed him.

Fixing her gaze on his left ear and ignoring the tingle where their skin touched, she forced a smile. 'Yes, fine. They've been really well behaved. It's been a long day, that's all.'

'All right. Well, you do that and I'll take them upstairs to start getting ready for bed.'

'Oh, Matt, that would be great, thanks. I'll be up in five.'

'No problem. It's getting late and I don't expect you to be on duty at this time of night,' he joked.

She stared at him. He was so calm and collected, whereas she was a bag of nerves thinking about their kiss. He'd been telling the truth; it really had meant nothing. She should be happy and relieved, but instead she felt flat. Jerking her arm from under his hand, 'I won't be long.'

He looked puzzled. 'Okay. Right kids,' he clapped his hands, 'upstairs.' He motioned them ahead of him. 'So what was your favourite part of the day?' she heard him ask as they disappeared up to the first floor together.

Her shoulders slumped as she emptied the picnic hamper, dividing the contents between the recycling and food waste bins, and the fridge. What on earth was wrong with her, that she should find Matt's carefree attitude upsetting? The best case scenario was that they forget the kiss ever happened, and she finished what she'd started here.

Telling herself to grow up and get over it, once she was done she made her way upstairs, amused to find Matt stood in the hallway between the children's rooms with a lost expression on his face. Trying to convince them to settle down, change into PJ's and brush their teeth, he turned to her with his hands out, *what do I do now?*

'Need some help?' she raised an eyebrow, taking pity on him.

Yes, please, he mouthed.

'Right, you two,' pitching her voice higher to get their attention, she held direct eye contact with each of them for a few seconds. 'We've had a brilliant day, but now it's time for bed. If you want to do something like that again, you need to show us that you'll behave once back home. Let's go. Hurry up. Who can win Zoe's night time challenge?'

Matt tilted his head questioningly.

'It's a task and reward system,' she explained, gesturing at Jasper and pointing at her watch. 'They get to do something of their choice the following day, or pick a treat.'

'Ah, I see. Genius.'

'I'd reserve judgement until we see how well it works, or doesn't work, tonight,' Zoe chuckled, some of her earlier awkwardness fading away. If he could act like nothing had happened between them, so could she.

As predicted, it was a nightmare getting the kids into bed. While she was wiped, they were energised, excited and continued to rattle on about their day. Aimee was quicker to settle with a promise that she could read an extra chapter of her book at bedtime the following night, but Jasper tried every trick under the sun to delay. A toilet trip, needing to tell Daddy something really important that couldn't possible wait until the next morning, another wee, a water to drink, he was too hot then too cold and his bed was too lumpy.

In the end Zoe promised to take him out shopping for a sticker chart the following Monday, explaining that if he could get a gold star at least four days in a week he could pick an item out of her special prize box. Unknown to him, and Matt as yet, she was also going to remove all the gadgets and gizmos from his room and put them in the playroom. He needed fresh air and intellectual challenges, not an overload of consoles and tablets. The promise of reward for good behaviour might help prevent any temper tantrums about the limited technology time.

Matt watched with interest while she talked to both children, and then hugged them goodnight once she had. Zoe was pleased to see the cuddling was starting to look and feel more natural.

When the two of them finally closed the kid's doors and stood in the hallway, Matt leaned back against the wall, pretending to mop his brow. 'Phew, that was hard work. I don't know how you do it.'

'It's my job,' she quipped, 'and it's usually quicker than that.' She slumped against the opposite wall, exhausted. 'They were over-excited from our mini-adventure. I'd hoped they'd be tired out by the time we got back, but ...' she shrugged feelingly.

'Fancy a glass of wine in the garden then?'

She hesitated. 'I'm pretty tired.'

'We need to talk, don't we? Plus, you get a lie-in tomorrow.'

Studying his open expression, she couldn't see how to reasonably refuse without looking petty or like she was upset with him. Besides, a glass of wine outside had already been in her plans. 'Yes. Okay, a wine would be lovely, thanks.' With her eyes on his broad back, she followed him down the spiral staircase.

They were soon settled on matching wooden sun loungers on the decking overlooking the large green lawn and abundant apple tree ripe with fruit. The white rose bed was in full bloom, lending a quaint English beauty to the hidden garden in the heart of London. Vibrant turquoise and mauve flowers in pots surrounded Matt and Zoe, their delicate floral scent filling the air. A dewy glass of white wine sat on a low table between the loungers for her, with a condensation covered beer for him. The air was still warm so there was no need for the cardigan she'd left hanging over the deck railing that morning after her daily dawn coffee. Although they

444

were only a few streets away from the main Knightsbridge Road, there was surprisingly little traffic to be heard, as if a strange hush had fallen over the city.

'Thank you for giving them such a fantastic day.' Matt leaned over to pick up his pint and took a few deep gulps, eyes on her the whole time.

She wiggled on the lounger cushion self-consciously. 'No problem.'

'They seemed really happy. You must have had fun.' He looked wistful.

'I've got some nice photos on my phone if you want to take a look. Yeah, it was a nice treat for them, but it really doesn't take that much to keep kids happy,' she rubbed the bridge of her nose, 'just some time and attention. If there's a fun activity thrown in, even better.'

He rolled his eyes, 'Yeah, yeah,' he teased, 'I get it. I need to spend time with them. Which is why you'll be pleased to hear I've cleared my diary and am spending the day with them tomorrow. I was thinking of taking them to the Harry Potter studio tour.'

'Matt, that's brilliant. I'm so pleased.'

'Actually, I was wondering if you wanted to join us?' he said casually. 'I know it's your day off, but—'

'Sorry, I can't,' she avoided his gaze by leaning forward to pick up her white wine. The curved glass was cool and smooth against her fingertips. She was tempted to say yes to Matt, but spending down-time with them all as a family wasn't going to help her see things any more clearly. Besides, she had a commitment to keep. It was time to finally sort things out with her aunt, if that was possible. Five years was too long a time for the divide between them not to have been bridged. 'I've made arrangements to see my—' she paused, realising it wasn't a good idea to mention Ruth by name in case Melody ever had, 'a friend tomorrow. I'm also going out tomorrow night. But thank you. It sounds like fun. It's probably just as well you get a chance to bond with them alone,'

445

she added, taking a big gulp of wine, 'if I was there I'd probably wade in all the time.'

'A friend, huh?' For a moment he looked like he was going to ask more. Instead he added, 'As for wading in, it wouldn't bother me.'

'But the children need to see you as an authority figure too,' she answered. Deflecting any further conversation. 'Nice wine by the way, what is it?'

'Pinot Noir,' he supplied, looking disappointed. 'Anyway, if you don't want to come tomorrow that's fine. Another time maybe.'

'Maybe,' glugging some more wine back, Zoe exhaled, letting the edgy notes of a Jessie J song spin her away for a moment, tapping her free hand on her thigh. Matt had put the radio on and opened the kitchen window so they had background music and Zoe could already feel relaxation beginning to seep into her muscles. Her eyelids were becoming heavy with wine and a hectic day in the sun with the kids. She rested back in the lounger, tipping her face to the wide, azure sky over the tops of neighbouring houses and trees. It was gone nine o'clock but was still light, with no trace of twilight. However, the blue of the sky was softer and vaguer than it had been that afternoon and the ferocious heat of the sun's rays had abated.

Matt seemed content to listen to the music and stare off into the garden, pint glass balanced on his knee and tense shoulders unwinding an inch at a time.

The silence stretched out, but it was comfortable.

Zoe released a long, low sigh. For the first time since leaving New York, she felt really and truly content. It hadn't been that long since the break-up but the five years with Greg were already hazy, like they'd been part of somebody else's life. It was surprising how quickly you could adjust to change if you had to. She was also surprised to realise it was a life she wasn't necessarily that sad to have left behind. Though thinking she was happy at the time, she was starting to wonder if working in America and marrying Greg would have been settling, rather than truly living. There had been no grand passion between them like in the movies, and she was starting to question if she'd really loved him. The shape and sound of her ex was already dissipating, the idea of him like a mirage rippling in the distance.

The pain and embarrassment of his betrayal was still there, niggling away under her skin like a splinter, but the fury had lessened and relief was starting to creep in. Yes, maybe she'd had a lucky escape. If he'd cheated on her a few weeks before their wedding, then why not once they were married or later, when there were children on the way? When confronted, Greg hadn't been able to articulate why it had happened. And if he didn't know why, what would stop him doing it again?

She glanced across at Matt, his black hair striking against his light grey t-shirt, the fabric pulling taut across his chest and shoulders. This was her life now, her normality. Her boss, his kids, the luxury home, summer in London.

But it was all a daydream, or a nightmare, depending on how you looked at it.

She shook her head. These weren't the kind of thoughts to have in front of him. He might see the truth written on her face. 'You always have music on,' she murmured. 'When you're not producing it, you're listening to it.'

'Music's in my soul, it takes me to another place. I just love closing my eyes and letting the running beat and notes wash over me, or energise me. It can make me laugh, or smile or get me,' he put a fist to his chest, 'right here. It's powerful stuff.'

'I feel that way about reading,' she confided, drinking her wine, the liquid cool and crisp on her tongue with a faint echo of peaches and lemon. 'I can travel to different times or lands and live inside someone else's head rather than my own.' She chuckled, 'No wonder Aimee and I get on so well.'

'Yes, I noticed. I also noticed loads of boxes of books in your room. How come you haven't unpacked them?'

'There's no bookcase to fit them all in, and I've got a bit of a thing about them needing to be arranged in orderly rows, according to genre and then within that alphabetically.'

'Yeah, you're very neat. You tidy up as you go along, your stuff is always folded, you don't leave things lying around the house. In that way you're the complete opposite to Melody, who always left a trail of mess in her wake.'

She nodded and kept her mouth shut to stop from blurting out that Mel had been the same when they'd been kids. It was the only thing she and Ruth had ever disagreed about, their aunt constantly having to remind her youngest niece to pick up after herself. While Ruth thought Melody had got better, in truth it was that Zoe had covered for her, sweeping along behind her putting things away and sorting her laundry.

'My office must horrify you then,' Matt remarked, 'the overflowing bin and all the paperwork. It's not usually that bad, but without Sadie it's got a bit out of control.'

'Yep,' she quipped, 'stepping into your office traumatises me, which is why I don't come in that often. I also don't want to encounter the grumpy troll who lives in there sometimes.'

Throwing back his head he unloosed a husky laugh that made her smile and set a flock of butterflies free in her tummy. 'Sorry about that,' he replied, 'I know I can be a bit of a grump at times. I don't mean to be, I just get caught up in what I'm doing. But I'm getting better, right?'

'A little. But you could spend a bit less time down in your man cave, Matt. It would be nice for us to see you more often.'

'It's not a man cave,' he said with a straight face but a twinkle in his eye, 'it's a studio, and very important work goes on there, I'll have you know.'

Waving a hand, 'It's in the basement, it's dark, you have a mini-fridge in there full of drinks and snacks, and no-one else is allowed in. It's a man cave.' She studied his lean face, the chiselled cheekbones and slash of dark eyebrows. 'Was it always music for you? Did you ever want to do anything else?'

'No, it was always music. That was always the dream,' he spoke with absolute certainty. 'It was the only thing that really made me happy when I was young. I couldn't stand the stilted atmosphere at home during the holidays. My parents are good people—both retired senior government officials and currently travelling the world on Mum's family money—but they're both very reserved. There wasn't much warmth or fun growing up. Stephen and I were sent to boarding school when we were old enough, because our parents travelled a lot for work or sometimes had overseas postings. I used to escape to my room to listen to music when I came home between term times.' One side of his mouth quirked up. 'And when all the other boys at boarding school were playing tennis or learning the violin, I was up in my dorm listening to techno and teaching myself to play the guitar and electric keyboard.'

Her laughter pealed out into the evening air. 'Techno? You don't strike me as that kind of guy. Most of your acts are Pop, or R 'n' B, aren't they?'

'Yes, they are. But I listened, and still do, to all sorts of music. Dance, Pop, Jazz, Blues, Rap, R 'n' B, Opera. Every type of music is inspiring in a different way. Every type of music means something to the person listening.'

'And every piece of music tells a story.'

'Yes,' he grinned so widely she was almost blinded by his straight white teeth, 'exactly.'

'You play instruments, that's so cool. I'd love to be talented in that way. I always wanted to learn something but never got round to it.'

'Actually, I play on some of the tracks I produce but don't put my name to them.'

'Why not?'

'I don't want to be known for being a musician, or have the focus on me. I want to help other people tell their stories. I love working with artists or bands, helping the finished song emerge from the raw ideas and melodies. Mixing the sound until the

449

magic comes out.'

'But what about telling your own story?' she shifted around on her side to face him, propping her right arm along the back of the lounger, glass clutched in her left hand.

'Nah, that would be boring,' he said dismissively. 'No one would be interested.'

'I am,' she blurted before she could think better of it, the wine making her feel mellow and a teensy bit reckless. 'Go on.'

'There's not much to tell.' Taking a contemplative gulp of beer, he wiped some white froth off his top lip. 'There's not that much to add about my childhood and teens.'

'Oh, come on. There has to be. At least about your teens. What about girls, and parties, and hanging out with mates? And if your parents were posted overseas you must have got the opportunity to travel when you visited them?'

'Not really.' He looked uncomfortable, rubbing his lip scar. 'I guess there's no harm in telling you. After all, you are subject to that confidentiality clause.'

'Uh-huh,' she murmured, thinking of the article she'd started about him on her laptop. A squirming sensation wriggled along her spine and she prayed her face wouldn't go red.

'Well, to be honest,' Matt explained, 'they didn't send for us that often. I remember a few airports and an embassy, but really I stayed at boarding school most of the time. To be honest, I was happier alone with my music. Of course I went to parties—I even DJ'd occasionally—and there were girlfriends, but again that was hard because of being at an all-boys school and not going home much. I was part of a crowd of boys, but I preferred to have a few quality friends rather than being Mr Popular. Nowadays I've always got one eye over my shoulder about my privacy, so it's simpler to keep a few people close, which is why there's only really Noel and Stephen. I met Noel when I was eighteen. We were in a house-share together in Wembley.'

'Wembley?'

'Yeah.' He chuckled. 'The roughest part. I was still on my *just because I'm a rich kid it doesn't mean I can't live a normal life* kick. My parents were horrified and would never come visit me there, but it was what I wanted. I had a pretty great time during those three years.'

'Good.' It was fascinating, this peek into the real Matt Reilly. She could understand why he was the insular, passionate, single-minded guy who spent hours alone in his studio, shut away from the real world. After all, he'd spent numerous, lonely years at a boarding school because the people who were supposed to love him the most—his parents—had sent him away for the sake of convenience. Unless that was unfair; maybe they'd wanted to give their sons the stability they couldn't because of their jobs. She realised Matt was looking at her expectantly. 'As for friends, there's nothing wrong with being selective about who you spend your time with,' she added. 'I'm the same.'

'Really?' he looked bemused.

'Yes.' She paused in the act of lifting her glass to her mouth. 'Why are you looking at me like that?'

Putting his pint down, he turned on his seat, mirroring her pose so he could talk to her face on. 'It's just that you're so confident, and warm. I imagined you with a wide circle of friends, the person in the centre of the crowd.'

Her cheeks heated. Although his comment had been delivered in a matter of fact tone, it sounded like a compliment and she felt like a flustered schoolgirl. 'Thanks, but not really. I was friends with a lot of the American nannies in the neighbourhood I lived in for my last job, but it was a loose kind of friendship created by geographic proximity and our jobs more than anything. I have two best friends,' three when you included Melody, who didn't seem to be her biggest fan at the moment, 'who live here in London. Frankie is lovely, just a really nice, considerate person. She works in retail and has her own freelance photography business, and is madly in love with her boyfriend Zack, who apparently is very

451

different to her last boyfriend. Not that I've met Zack yet,' she said with regret. 'Then there's Rayne.'

'Rayne? That's an unusual name.'

'Her parents were new-age. She's a real character. Independent, feisty, outspoken, not afraid to be different.'

'How so?'

'At uni she was the girl with the piercings and the skimpy, colourful clothes who did what she wanted and didn't care what people thought. She still is, to a degree. She has that amazing effortless sense of style that makes me feel boring in comparison, and says what she thinks. I love her individuality.'

'Oh, I don't think you're too shabby,' he mused, before straightening up and clearing his throat. 'I mean she uh, sounds like some of my artists. You said her parents *were* new-age?'

She kept her face blank but smiled inwardly at his awkwardness. There was something kind of endearing about his lack of smoothness when it came to women. 'They died in a motorway smash a year before she joined us at Loughborough University. It was something we had in common, losing both parents. Rayne, Frankie and I got on really well straight away, although I'm a couple of years older than them because I worked for a few years before taking my degree. Rayne's just got back together with her uni boyfriend after they bumped into each other at Wimbledon last month. He, Adam, used to call the three of us the Dark Trinity because we all have dark hair. There's also Lily,' she thought of the petite blonde who looked like the American actress Amanda Seyfried, 'but she's more reserved and was closer to Rayne.'

'They sound great.'

'They are. I've missed them a lot, so I can't wait to see them tomorrow night.'

'Ah, so that's who you're going out with.'

Was that relief on his face? If so, why? she wondered with a nervous jump in her stomach. 'Is there a problem?'

'No, I just thought you might be going on a date or something.

452

Not that it's any of my business.'

'I told you, there was someone and now there's not. But anyway, it would be too soon.' The fact she'd only split with her fiancé just over six weeks ago should be a factor, but nope, she grasped as she stared down into her empty wine glass, that wasn't it. The truth was that the idea of spending time with another guy seemed plain weird, especially after this morning's kiss. Shit, was she in a mess. Get back on track, fast. 'Back to you,' she said. 'You were talking about boarding school? What happened afterwards?'

He seemed taken aback by the change of topic, but nodded. 'I got some credible exam results but rather than study for A-levels with a view to going to Oxford or Cambridge as my parents expected, I came straight out of school. I took a music technology course, followed by a variety of music business, engineering and performance courses.' He smirked. 'My parents were mortified. It was far too creative and artsy for them.'

'Well it should be about what makes your kids happy, not what you expect for them. Children have to make their own way in life,' she raised her wineless glass in an imaginary toast, and realised she might be a bit tipsy. 'When I have children I'll keep them with me, rather than shipping them off to boarding school. I'm not denying that a better level of education or excelling at sports might be attractive, and it might be the done thing in certain social circles, but it just seems a bit cold. No offence to your parents. But you feel the same way, right?' she paused and he nodded. 'I'm so glad you're letting the kids go to a mainstream school, Matt. Aimee seems happy enough and at least Jasper will be able to see her on the playground if he's feeling a bit lost. It must have been the same for you and Stephen?'

'Not really,' he seemed sad. 'There are seven years between us, so we were in different dorms in school.' Something dark flitted across his face. 'We never really hung out. We got to know each other better when we got older. After Helen died he half moved in here. He stays in one of the spare rooms when he feels like it.

There's a flat in Chelsea but he's never there much. He's one of those people who doesn't like being alone.'

'Right.' Zoe tilted her head to one side. In that way Melody and Stephen were well-matched. Mel had always had a big circle of friends at school, and if she wasn't with them would sit in Zoe's room chatting away for hours, at times bugging the hell out of her older sister, who wanted to be left alone to read. Mel had never been at peace with her own company, so it must have been hard for her living here with Matt and the kids with Ruth a train journey away and only Jemima across town. Zoe knew she'd lost touch with a lot of her old school friends. 'Sorry, you were saying about doing all those music qualifications. What happened next?'

'Well, when I left college I managed to get a job as a glorified tea boy at a tiny music production company and also started putting ads out in local papers, looking for soloists or bands who might be interested in collaborating, or having some free production time from me. I worked my arse off trying to get up the ladder, and went without sleep for about two years while I went to obscure backstreet bars and smoke-filled gigs finding new talent to nurture and record music with, before setting up my own company on the side. There are different types of music producer, but I don't just do the creative bit producing the music and coaching the musicians and artists, I also have a wider role managing the budget, schedules, contracts and negotiations. Of course when my boss found out I'd created what one day might be a rival company they fired me, but by then I'd started to make a name for myself. Professionally speaking, the rest is history. I've worked with some amazing artists and have had some fairly big hits, probably more down to good luck and somehow being ahead of the market than anything else. I have put in a lot of blood, sweat and tears though. Especially tears,' he kidded.

She knew he was being modest by underplaying the platinum albums and worldwide successes as well some of his artists singing at the White House, but didn't want to make him uncomfortable by saying so. 'What about Helen? Where does she come in?'

'Helen.' He rolled the word around in his mouth like it had a bad taste. Looking away, he drank the rest of his pint in one smooth motion and slammed the glass down on the table between them.

She jumped at the sound.

'Sorry.'

'That's all right.'

'I'll get us a top up,' he grabbed their empties and climbed off the lounger, 'back in a minute.'

Watching him push through the doors into the lounge, she rubbed her forehead. The face he'd pulled at the mention of his late wife's name hadn't been one of grief. Her instincts told her it had been more like disappointment, guilt or anger. God, this was getting complicated.

He was back within thirty seconds with two fresh wine glasses and the Pinot Noir in a metal cooler. 'I thought we might as well finish it off. It's been a stressful week, and it's a nice evening.'

'Thanks.' It was probably a dangerous idea but she took the full glass he handed to her, and settled back against the cushion. 'If you don't want to talk about Helen, I'll understand, Matt.' She was such a liar, she was dying to know what the situation was.

'No, it's okay. You've made me realise over the past week that the kids are going to ask questions and want to know more, and I'm going to have to be ready for that. Though obviously what I tell them might be different to what I tell you.'

'Sure.'

'Okay, here goes.' He swallowed some wine, expression pensive. 'I met Helen in a bar when I was twenty-one. She was two years younger; beautiful, smart and outgoing. We wanted the same things, and she was ambitious for us as a couple, pushing me forward, initially handling my marketing and publicity. I'd had the company for two years at that point and was making pretty good money. Exciting things were happening. She loved that I had my own company and brand, and after four months we moved in together. I bought us a house near Primrose Hill and we got married.' He smiled briefly. 'We were happy. She loved shopping and the flash side of being married to a successful music producer; the parties, dressing up, having fun.' Two more gulps of wine went down. 'But then she got pregnant with Aimee and it's like a spark in her died. I feel awful and disloyal saying this, but she just didn't seem happy to be pregnant. After Aimee was born she was more interested in spending money and getting her figure back at the gym than bonding with our daughter.'

'She was quite young for a first child, and possibly overwhelmed. Could she have had post-natal depression?'

'It's possible,' he admitted, 'but she didn't seem low or anxious. It was more like she wasn't that bothered. Don't get me wrong, she was a good mum in some ways. I never worried about Aimee's safety with her, I just felt that she wasn't high up enough on Helen's priority list. After that, Helen lost interest in the business, and started resenting the amount of hours I had to put in at work. When she found out we were having Jasper she seemed uncertain at first but came round to the idea. The first year and a half after he was born were fine. We did things as a family, and I started to think things were getting better.'

'But?'

'She died soon afterwards,' he said, expression set. 'That's it.'

There was plainly more to it given his choice of wording, but he'd already opened up a lot and his face was set in hard lines. No wonder he felt torn about his wife's death if things had been difficult between them in the months leading up to it. She was mulling over whether to prod him about it a bit more when he leaned across the table and touched her arm, distracting her. Shivering at the tingle of heat his fingers produced, she squeezed her thighs together. She would not, absolutely not give into the urge to hurl herself into his lap, to sit across those rock hard thighs and offer her mouth to him.

'What about you?' he asked. 'I know about your education and

456

career path from the interview, you've told me about your parents and an aunt that made you feel unloved, but what about significant relationships? Have you ever been married?'

'Nearly,' she confessed, repositioning her arm so his hand dropped away from her skin. She couldn't think properly when he touched her. Holding her thumb and forefinger up a couple of millimetres apart, she squeezed them together so they almost touched. 'This close.'

'So what happened?' Swivelling around, he sat up on the side of the lounger so the table wasn't between them, leaning forward.

'He cheated. I found out two weeks before the wedding. I found *them*.' It slipped out and hung in the air between them like a mist.

'What? You're kidding,' he sounded shocked.

She puffed a raw breath out, turning her attention to the apple tree. Thinking of the picture Greg had made, twined naked around Shelly like it was the most natural thing in the world, eyes filling with panic when Zoe had burst into the room. What the hell was she thinking, telling Matt about it? It was humiliating, and stung. The wine was definitely getting to her. 'Unfortunately not,' she muttered, wishing the heavens would open and provide a distraction, but of course this was England; it only rained when you didn't want it to.

To her shock, Matt crawled over to sit on her lounger, his hip against her thigh, placing a finger under her chin so he could look into her face. 'Hey, are you okay?' His eyes were sympathetic, his breath warm on her cheek.

'Sure,' she squeaked. 'It's just that … everybody knew but me. And it was with one of the other nannies. Also, I still don't really know why, what it was about me that wasn't enough.' She was horrified when with an odd little pang in her chest tears welled up in her eyes. Oh, jeez. Not now, and not in front of him, not after almost two months of being unable to cry. It must be the wine, sun and tiredness.

'Come here.' Scooping her close, he pressed her face into his

457

neck, a searing hand rubbing her back in gentle circles. 'It's not about you, you're great. It was about him. There was something in him that meant he thought it was okay. But it's not. It's never okay to cheat,' he said fiercely, and she almost lifted her head to ask him if he'd had personal experience, but he carried on talking. 'As far as I'm concerned, he's a complete bloody idiot. Just let it out if you need to, Zoe. You're safe here. You can trust me.'

Everything in her rebelled at the idea of seeking comfort in his arms, for a multitude of reasons—Melody, the kids, he was her boss, it was embarrassing—but he was right, she did feel safe. Tears leaked out unbidden and he held her as she cried. They weren't the racking great sobs she'd expected, they were quieter tears that were more about sadness and regret and release. She snuggled into him, her hands grasping his waist. He moved a hand up to stroke her hair and the two of them stayed there for several minutes while she let the hurt, shame and disappointment go.

It was astonishing how much better she felt for it afterwards and she tightened her grip on Matt, feeling soft and gooey with gratitude towards him for being there, for his understanding. But slowly the gratitude slipped away and was replaced by something much more intense. She became aware of the burning heat of his body. The imprint of his long soothing fingers in her hair and on her back. His uneven breathing against her ear lobe. The tension in his thighs. The smell of his sexy aftershave, spicy and fresh, emanating from his neck.

Pushing her boobs against his chest, she could feel his heart thudding through his thin t-shirt.

He inhaled deeply. 'Zoe,' he said in a warning tone.

'Yes?' Lifting her head, she met his scorching gaze.

Moving his other hand up to her head, he used both thumbs to wipe the tracks of her tears from her cheeks. 'This isn't a good idea. This morning … we shouldn't have kissed.'

'I know,' she agreed, dropping her eyes to watch his mouth as he spoke.

'It's too complicated. You work for me. You're my kids' nanny, and they need you. I don't want to blow it for them.' He didn't mention Helen, but he didn't need to. It was clear that there were some feelings there he hadn't resolved.

Complicated? she thought. You have no idea.

'I understand,' she mumbled, in a corner of her mind knowing she should ease away, let go of him and get to bed. Run away from temptation. But that corner was wrapped in a fog of wine and lust and she couldn't. She didn't want to. Right this moment she wanted to be held by him, wrapped up in him.

Staring into his eyes, she trailed her hands from his waist all the way down his thighs, and then up again, feeling the taut strength under her fingers. He hissed out a breath and yanked her face to his, kissing her frantically, passionately, lips firm, their tongues tangling. He kissed her like he'd been holding back for an eternity, like he was desperate to have her and would fall apart if he didn't. A thrill of excitement buzzed along her veins. It thrummed through her blood and pumped through her heart, making it thud in her chest.

Suddenly his hands dropped to her hips and he grabbed her bum, swivelling on the lounger and scooping her forward so she was straddling him. She gasped, clutching handfuls of his dark hair and holding on as the kiss continued, his even teeth nibbling at her sensitive bottom lip, his fingers digging into her bum. She rocked her hips against him, feeling like she couldn't get close enough, that if they didn't get naked she'd explode. He groaned and dipped his mouth to her neck, blazing a trail of kisses down it, his teeth moving aside the strap of her top and bra together to bare her shoulder. Hoisting her up, he nuzzled his face down between her round, heaving breasts and turned his head to one side. Before she could work out what he was doing, her nipple was in his wet mouth and he was sucking on it in a rhythmic motion.

'Oh my god, Matt,' she choked. Thigh muscles clenching, pelvis scorching with heat, she bucked her hips against him, feeling his straining hardness rubbing against her clit.

Lifting his head slightly, his breath whispered over her naked skin, making her shiver. 'Do you like that?' he mumbled. 'I've been dreaming about doing this ever since I wrenched that stupid jacket off you in my office.'

'Yes! Don't stop. Harder,' she moaned, rocking her hips again as he went back to sucking her nipple. His erection pulsed against her in response, making judders of pleasure race through her. She was on fire, feverish, sweat breaking out over her skin. She twisted against him, pushing her hands down inside his t-shirt, raking her nails over his smooth, muscular shoulders then up to his hair, holding his mouth demandingly against her.

She couldn't believe how breathless and sizzling it was between them. It had never been like this before, she'd never ignited for any other man the way she did for Matt. When he switched his attention to her other nipple, making her moan again, she lowered herself slightly and ran questing fingers down over his toned stomach. When her hand landed on the zip of his jeans, and the bulge jutting up beneath it, he jerked and pulled away.

'Jesus, Zoe.' Grasping her hand, he brought it up and held it against his chest, easing back so there was some space between them. 'We have to stop.' He looked up at her, regret shadowing his eyes.

'Yes,' she whispered.

The evening air hit her bared breast, making the nipple stiffen even more, and with a groan he gently slid her bra and top back into place, before untangling her legs from his hips so they could sit side by side on the lounger.

'Wow,' he said, shifting uncomfortably and picking up her hand. 'That was … wow.'

'Yeah,' she said, dazed, turned on, confused and a little embarrassed. Not to mention guilty as hell. How was this helping her sister, or her peace of mind? She had a tough decision to make and having sex with Matt in his garden was not going to make it

460

any easier. Which was what would've happened if he hadn't pulled away. She closed her eyes, a blush creeping up her face.

'I'm sorry,' he murmured, tracing his thumb over her palm, which made her squirm. 'I really like you, you know I do, but …'

'It's okay.' Opening her eyes, she edged along the cushion and slid her hand from his. 'It was my fault,' she met his stare directly, 'you said not to, but I kissed you anyway. I get what you're saying, and agree. It is too complicated.' Shaking her head, thinking about the two kids upstairs she was totally besotted with. 'It was inappropriate and unprofessional. It won't happen again.'

'Hey,' turning so that his knee touched her thigh, causing tingles to run along her skin again, 'don't be like that. It was both of us, and we're only human. I'm just as bad. I'm your boss! You could sue me for sexual harassment.'

'Oh, hardly,' she blurted, 'more like the other way around.'

He chuckled, 'I think we were both as bad as each other, so shall we call it even?'

'I guess.' God, she was so sexually frustrated she was going to have to take the longest cold shower in the history of the world. A bucket or two of ice might be required as well.

'So, what are we going to do?' he asked, studying her face.

'I don't know.' She chewed her bottom lip, noticing the way his eyes tracked the movement. 'Be adults, and control ourselves?'

He hesitated. 'Okay, deal.' Standing up, he shoved his hands in his pockets and backed away. 'I, uh, should clear up.'

'Do you want some help?'

'No,' he rushed, 'I'll do it.' Clearing his throat, he shuffled sideways on the decking. As he came into her eye line, she realised why he seemed so uncomfortable.

'Oh,' she gulped, her mouthing going dry as she wrenched her eyes away from his bulging groin. 'I'll, uh, leave you to it then. Night.' Bounding up, she snatched up her half-full wine glass and lit out of there like a pack of wolves was nipping at her heels.

Racing through the house on light feet, she didn't stop until

461

she reached the top floor. Banging her glass down on the bedside unit, she hauled her top over her head, stripped her shorts, bra and knickers off, and walked into the massive double shower cubicle. Hitting the switch to start the water, she dropped the temperature to something so freezing it would probably cause frostbite.

Resting her forehead against the wall, she recalled Matt's confident hands on her body, his passionate kisses and the way he'd used his searching, clever mouth on her.

What the fuck was she doing?

11

Zoe's fingers clenched around the steering wheel as she swung the BMW onto her aunt's driveway. Nerves fluttered in her stomach. The whole way here she'd had the windows down and music turned up high, a summer hits dance album filling the car as the breeze fluttered her hair around her face. Usually she'd find the taste of freedom relaxing, but two of the tracks had been by artists of Matt's. There was just no getting away from him.

She'd hidden like a coward on the top floor this morning, making a coffee in her lounge area with the small pod-based drinks machine. Waiting until Matt and the kids had left the house, unable to bear facing him just yet. She had slept like crap and there were dark circles under her eyes when she'd been brushing her teeth in front of the mirror. There was no doubt about it, she looked and felt fragile and should definitely be in a stronger frame of mind for the conversation ahead. However, she kept her commitments, so here she was.

Grabbing her handbag and locking the car she smoothed down the navy dress with the flock of white birds dotting it and squared her shoulders. Gazing up at her aunt's imposing three floor house with the black railings leading up to the open porch, she traced uneasy eyes over the dark, old-fashioned dormer windows in the roof and the twin curved towers at either end of the property.

The place reminded her of the Bates Motel for some reason. There were other similar properties a few roads away that'd been converted into hotels or bed and breakfasts, but Ruth had always been steadfast that this was her home and she wasn't letting people traipse through it and certainly wasn't selling it to developers.

The front door swung open. 'Are you going to stand there all day, or were you planning to knock on the door at some point?' her aunt asked.

Zoe jumped, putting a hand to her chest. 'Jeez, you scared me.' Taking a deep breath and summoning all of her patience and courage, she walked forward and climbed the wooden stairs, stopping in front her. Ruth had aged over the past few years. Her pale skin looked sallow, new lines fanning out from her dark eyes. Zoe was shocked. The woman had always seemed so solid and unchanging. 'Hello, Aunt Ruth. It's good to see you.'

'Zoe.' She inclined her head and stepped back, holding the door open for her niece to pass. 'Come in.'

No response about it being nice to see her too, Zoe mused dryly as she ambled into the hallway and back into the past. Nothing had changed. The corridor was still dim, the skirting boards and high ceilings painted an immaculate but dull white, the carpet the same violent swirl of dark reds, the mahogany banister gleaming with polish. The scent of beeswax filled the air.

'Through to the front room,' Ruth directed behind her, and obediently Zoe swung to her left, pushing the glossed wooden door open and going into the lounge.

'Is Mel here?' she asked, taking a seat on the burgundy sofa and flickering her eyes over the glass fronted cabinet full of expensive china plates and Dresden figurines. Nothing had changed in here either.

'She's gone to London to see a friend,' the older woman said abruptly, 'Jemima, I think. Tea?'

Zoe's mouth dropped open. 'But she knew I was coming. I was supposed to be taking her back with me to London tonight.

We're going out to dinner with Rayne and Frankie. Why would she do that?' What the hell was going on with Mel at the moment? Was she avoiding her? The other day when they'd spoken on the phone her sister had been a little cooler than usual but for the most part Zoe thought Mel had forgiven her for the comments she'd made about Matt and the kids. After all, they'd only been made out of concern.

'I think she said she would text you about where to meet.'

'Right.' Zoe set her lips in a firm line.

'Don't be cross with her.' Ruth's face softened. 'She's going through a difficult time at the moment. The break up has caused her a lot of distress.'

What about my break up, Zoe wanted to scream. I was about to get married. But it wouldn't make any difference to her aunt, who'd always seemed immune to her eldest niece's feelings. Besides, Zoe wasn't as devastated about her break up as Melody seemed to be about hers. But after what the other nannies had said about Stephen and her only glimpse of him that first day on Matt's doorstep, Zoe wondered if Mel had also had a lucky escape.

'Zoe?' Ruth prompted, smoothing her hair back into its low grey bun, 'Tea?'

'Yes, please.' Sitting back as her aunt left the room, Zoe took in the familiar oppressive oil paintings on the walls, the lace doilies on the two round oak coffee tables, the same red carpet running in from the hallway. It was all very old-fashioned and proper. Very unsuited to the grieving but energetic and noisy girls who'd arrived on Ruth's doorstep one winter's day. The wind had blown so fiercely it'd made a whistling sound through the trees, sending rust brown leaves rushing into the hallway with Zoe and Melody as they'd stepped into their new guardian's home. Really, Zoe thought, the house had been as unsuitable for her and her sister as the girls had been for her aunt. Of course Ruth had done her best, but there must have been a reason why she had never gotten married or had children of her own. Still, it didn't explain why she'd always displayed a more tolerant and softer approach towards Melody than she had to Zoe. It was strange, and something Zoe had wondered about a lot of times over the years.

'Here you are.' Ruth had slipped back into the room while Zoe was lost in her thoughts. She placed a silver tray with a teapot, two cups on saucers, a jug of milk, a box of sugar and spoons down on the nearest table. Shortbread biscuits were arranged neatly on a small matching china plate. She sat down across from Zoe.

'Thank you. Why didn't you ever like me, Ruth?' she blurted. Bugger, that wasn't how she'd meant to start the conversation.

'I beg your pardon?' Ruth froze in the act of arranging her beige skirt across her knees.

'You know what I'm talking about,' Zoe said in a soft voice, deciding she may as well go with it now she'd started. 'I'm not referring to what happened in the year before I left, I know that upset you. This is about when Mel and I were growing up, when we were young. I'm not blaming you or looking for an apology or an argument. I just want to understand. Why did you treat us differently?'

'I thought we might do the polite chit-chat thing first, but apparently not,' Ruth tucked her skirt around her legs. 'So after five years, you're finally ready to have a conversation instead of arguing, or running away?'

Zoe felt her cheeks go red. Damn her fair skin. 'That's not fair.'

'Isn't it?' Her aunt's dark eyes were cool. 'All we did was argue.'

'Mostly when I was a teenager,' Zoe flashed, 'and it takes two to argue.'

To her surprise, Ruth let out a low laugh. 'It does. You're right. As for the running away, I'm not referring to when you were a teenager. I'm talking about America.'

'I didn't run away. I made a new life for myself.'

'It didn't have to be halfway across the world.' She raised a hand, palm out. 'Don't respond, just think.' Sighing. 'You haven't changed much, have you?'

466

'Neither have you.' Zoe shot back, before realising how childish she sounded. They couldn't ride this merry-go-round again. Something had to change. Surely things could be different now that they didn't have an ocean between them. Forcing herself to relax, 'I know I wasn't easy when I was younger,' she conceded. 'I answered back a lot.'

'You were stubborn and obstinate like your father.' There was something in her expression that made Zoe pause. A hint of pain, a tinge of regret. 'But maybe we are both older and wiser now and can talk like adults.'

'I'd like that.' Zoe twisted her fingers in the fabric of her dress. 'That doesn't sound like a good thing, what you said. I thought you liked Dad.'

Ruth sighed, looking troubled. It was the most human expression Zoe had ever seen on her aunt's face. Growing up, she'd been used to either cold disdain or stern anger. 'Do you want the truth?'

Zoe raised her chin, bracing herself for the blow. 'Yes.'

'All right.' Staring across the room at the china cabinet, the older woman set her shoulders. 'Do you know that when your mother and I were girls, we used to play with the figurines over there?'

'Yes, they were your mum's. Gran's.' Who had been a single mum when it was a mark of shame, and who'd died when Zoe was five. The only thing she remembered about her was a dark haired woman with a stony expression. 'They're worth a lot of money.'

'That's right,' Ruth nodded. 'I can still remember the way Susan used to take them out and sit on the floor running her fingers over them, holding them up to the light to study the curves and patterns.'

'Mum liked pretty things,' Zoe agreed, puzzled as to where the conversation was going. But it was the longest she and Ruth had ever talked without arguing so she let her aunt take the lead.

'I loved your mum a lot. She was my little sister.' It was a tiny smile, but it was there. Her eyes were misty. 'I looked after her. I enjoyed it. She was the only one I felt comfortable with. There

467

was only three years between us. We used to stay up late, talking for hours, sheets strung between our beds to make a den. We understood each other.'

'I feel the same way about Mel,' Zoe said, the thought of her sister taking a train to London rather than sharing a car with her piercing a small hole in her heart. As girls, they'd had a pink and yellow plastic Wendy house in the back garden of their parent's house. Inside were quilted blankets and a table complete with tea set. Zoe had always played in it with her little sister, even when Mel was six and Zoe was a teen and too old for such things. But it had been worth it to see Melody's toothy grin stretching her mouth wide, her outstretched hands holding out a brush and hair band for Zoe to plait her fair hair. She missed those girls, so full of happiness and hope.

'I know,' Ruth replied, leaning forward to pour the tea. 'It's the one thing you and I have always had in common. That we feel so strongly about taking care of our younger sisters. I've often thought it was the reason you became a nanny.'

Zoe frowned. 'I've never thought of it that way before. I've always loved kids so it was natural that I make a career of working with them. But I suppose it makes sense; I must have got my love of caring for children from somewhere. I'm not sure about Melody though.'

'Melody loves you and wants you to be proud of her.' She added milk and sugar to both cups while her niece tried to assimilate what she meant by that comment. 'You know,' she went on, 'I never loved anybody as much as I loved your mum. Although I'm talking about two entirely different kinds of love, it's part of the reason I never married. That, and the fact that I was petrified of being abandoned by a man, the way our father left our mother. The bastard.'

Zoe's fingers stilled. 'I've never heard you swear before.'

'Well, it's not a good example to set to children under your care. But I think you and Melody are old enough now that an occasional swear word won't matter. When I was a teenager you should have heard the words I used, until Mother washed my mouth out with soap. Your mum held my hand when I was sick afterwards.' She fixed her eyes back on Zoe. 'I was lost and resentful when Susan met your dad, but once I got to know him and saw how happy they were together, I was happy for her. We were still close, even after they moved in together and got married. I'm not sure you remember but I used to come round when you and Melody were small?' Zoe shook her head. 'Well, your mum and I used to sit in the postage-stamp sized back garden of the house on Sycamore Grove, drinking lemonade and chatting while you and Melody played in the paddling pool.'

'No, I don't remember that. So what happened?'

'Your dad got home one night and heard me make a remark he disliked. It wasn't meant that way but I was struggling to articulate a concern I had and he came in at the wrong time after a stressful day at work. We had a horrid argument,' Ruth shook her head, picking up her tea and staring into the milky brownness, 'it escalated rather badly and he ordered me out of the house. I tried to speak with him a number of times, and your mum tried too, but he wasn't willing to listen. Which is why I made the stubborn and obstinate remark about you. With your father it worked against me, but it can be a strength when you're defending the ones you love.' She drank some of her tea. 'For years your mum and I had to see each other in secret. She was worried it would upset your dad to know she'd seen me, and she loved him so much she didn't want to hurt him. It was very hard. As you and Melody got older she couldn't bring you along in case you told your dad. Which meant as you got older, Susan and I saw each other less and less, just talking on the phone when we could. Which is why you didn't know me that well when you had to come and live here.'

'It sounds awful,' Zoe sympathised, not wanting to contemplate the idea of she and Mel not being able to be part of each other's lives, or having their time together limited. She felt sorry for her aunt, being isolated from the one person she'd cared for more than anyone else. Lifting her tea, she drank a few mouthfuls. 'What was the argument with Dad about? What did you say?'

'They were planning to have another baby. I was worried, and suggested they should wait.'

'They were?' Zoe gaped. 'And why were you worried?'

'She had such an awful, dangerous birth with Melody I was worried it was too much of a risk to have another baby. The doctors told her it wasn't a good idea. Your dad thought I was trying to interfere, to make your mum's decision for her. He was worried she would be swayed by me instead of talking to him about it, who of course was the person she should make that decision with. I wasn't trying to influence or persuade her, I was simply expressing a concern. I thought they should wait a bit longer. Melody was only one at the time.'

'But you were just looking out for her!' Zoe said, trying to reconcile the man her aunt was describing with the laughing, easy going dad she remembered.

Ruth shrugged, tightening her grip on the fine china. 'It doesn't matter now. What matters is that for the last few years of my sister's life I didn't have the relationship with her that I'd had before. And I blamed your father. I also blamed him for your mother's death.'

'What?' Zoe placed her cup on the saucer with trembling hands. 'But it was an accident, right?' She closed her eyes, fearing her aunt was about to rip her world all apart. That she was going to say her dad had been driving recklessly, or worse, drink driving. That it was his fault his daughters had been orphaned. She'd asked for the truth though, and would have to face it.

'Yes,' Ruth said, and Zoe's eyes sprang open. 'Yes, it was an accident. There was no fault found against your father. Except that the day they died he'd turned up here, having found out she'd come to see me because of something you said. He made her leave. I tried to apologise again, explain my comment from all those years before, but he was too angry at your mum for

470

lying about where she was going to listen to me. The last time I saw her, she was looking at me through the window, mouthing that she'd call me later.' Her face creased up with grief. 'If only he hadn't made her leave. If only they had stayed and had a cup of tea and talked it through.'

'Something I said?' Zoe screwed her face up, trying to remember the traumatic day her parents had died. She'd been thirteen, Melody seven. She'd been in year eight at school, and on the school newspaper. Staying behind to work in the library with other pupils on the second issue, she'd returned home just after five to find her mum gone and her dad sitting at the kitchen table with a newspaper.

'Good day at school?' he asked as she shrugged out of her navy school blazer and went over to the fridge for a glass of milk. 'Let me guess,' his blue eyes crinkled and he pushed a hand through his black hair as she looked over her shoulder at him, 'you learnt loads and got another grade A?'

'Ha-ha,' she answered, shutting the fridge and turning around. 'But yeah, pretty much. Where's Mel?'

'At Mrs Briar's until half past.' The lady two doors down who picked her sister up from primary school three times a week so her mum could work at an upmarket clothes shop in town. 'Do you know where your mum is? I called the shop and they said she left at four today.'

'I overheard her talking on the phone last night when you were in the bath,' she replied carelessly, sitting across from him and wiping a hand across her mouth to get rid of any milk moustache. She tightened her high ponytail where it had started slipping out. 'I think she was going to visit a friend.'

'Oh?' he pushed the newspaper aside and there was a tension to his body language Zoe didn't understand.

'What's the matter?' she asked as he stood up, reaching for his car keys off the kitchen counter. 'Are you angry?'

'Of course not,' he reassured, although a vein was standing

471

out on his forehead, 'your mum's allowed to have friends. I don't suppose you know which one it was?'

Zoe stood up, sensing something was wrong. 'No, I didn't get a name, but there was something about meeting at the beach where they used to go?'

'Right,' he rammed the chair into place at the table. 'Zoe, can you go and get Melody in ten minutes or so? I'm going to go and see if your mum needs a lift home. We won't be long. Just watch TV or something, okay?' he ruffled her hair as he went past.

She squirmed and moved away. 'Dad, I've told you not do that. I'm not a kid anymore.'

'You'll always be my kid,' he dropped a kiss on her head, striding for the door. 'Love you, Zo.'

'That was the last time I saw him,' Zoe told her aunt as they sat together. 'I waited for two hours before I started to get worried, but Melody started getting upset and I didn't know what to do. That's when I went back to Mrs Briar's and she called the police and we were told that …' She brought a hand to her mouth, biting her knuckles as she remembered the two policemen turning up on their neighbour's doorstep, their faces solemn and drawn. Her stomach churned, eyes growing moist. 'If I'd have known that telling him that would lead to … Oh, God.'

'You couldn't have known what would happen, Zoe. You were a child. It wasn't your fault. I knew that, but it didn't stop me resenting you,' she admitted, looking ashamed, 'especially when you look so much like your dad, and have his confidence and stubborn streak. I was so angry with him.' Shaking her head. 'As for Melody—'

'She looks so much like Mum,' Zoe finished, 'it was natural that you'd want to be with her.'

'But it was wrong of me to treat you differently, Zoe. You're both Susan's daughters. She loved you equally, so I should have too.' She came over to sit with her niece. 'I'm sorry. I was wrong.'

'Thank you. I-I really appreciate you saying that, and explaining

472

this all to me even though it must have been so painful.' Heaving out a shuddering breath. 'I'm sorry too. For trying to get Melody to leave you in that last year before I left for the States. Just because I wasn't happy here, it doesn't mean Mel wasn't. I assumed she'd want to live with me. I said some unforgivable things to you.' She gripped her aunt's hand, trying to communicate how much she regretted her words and actions, 'I never should have asked her to choose between us. You looked after us after our parents died and I'm grateful for that. You were never cruel or hurtful, you put a roof over our heads and fed us. You just weren't warm and loving the way I needed you to be. I guess what it came down to was that you weren't Mum and Dad.' Ruth nodded, eyes looking suspiciously damp. 'I also shouldn't have threatened to try and get custody of her from you.' Zoe shook her head, hardly believing her cheek. 'It was stupid. She was sixteen for God's sake, nearly an adult, and I wasn't even in my mid-twenties. It was just that I was madly in love with Henry and caught up in the fairytale, with the idea of the three of us being a happy family. When Melody said she was staying with you and Henry broke up with me, I could hardly cope. I was lost. I guess that's why when I met Greg a few weeks later, he bowled me over. I was on the rebound.' As she said it, she knew it was the absolute truth. The sense of relief she'd felt about the break up the night before doubled.

'He swept you off your feet,' Ruth agreed, 'the rich American promising you the world.'

'I could be a nanny anywhere,' Zoe said, 'America was as good as any place, especially as he could pull strings for my visa. But maybe you're right, maybe I ran away.' She surprised both of them by clattering her cup down on the table and hugging her aunt. Ruth stiffened but didn't pull away, her slight frame trembling in Zoe's arms. 'Five years.' Zoe murmured, sitting back. 'It's a long time. But I'm home now. We could try and get to know each other properly if you want to? I know it'll take some time.'

'Yes, that would be nice,' Ruth wiped something from her eye, blinking hard. 'I've never been an affectionate type of person, Zoe. Probably because Mother was so cold. But you girls are the only family I have, so I'll try to unbend a little.' Standing up, she tried for a smile, the expression looking odd on her face. 'Shall we go for a walk down by the beach? There will be a lot of tourists out because the weather's so pleasant, but it would be nice to get some fresh air. We could have an ice-cream, if you like.'

Zoe pushed off the sofa, feeling clean and light, as if a weight she hadn't known she'd been carrying had been lifted. 'Like when we used to go down on Sunday afternoons, and skip stones?' She paused, remembering the day she'd managed five skips in a row. Ruth had let her have a double scoop and dripping chocolate sauce on her Mr Whippy from the ice-cream van as a reward. Of course Melody had wanted the same as her older sister, so Ruth had bought her one, but Zoe hadn't minded. Maybe her teenage years with her aunt hadn't been all bad.

'Yes.' Ruth stood up. 'So, young lady. I know you're living in London and trying to figure out what happened to your sister with those Reilly boys, but apart from that, what's your plan? What's next for you?'

Zoe gulped, her mind drifting to Melody, Matt and the kids. 'I don't know, Aunt Ruth. I really don't.'

Zoe smiled as she heard the children clatter into the hallway, the front door slamming behind them.

'Hang on,' she heard Matt yell as they thundered upstairs, 'Zoe might be busy doing something.'

'Zoe's not doing anything,' she called, making her way carefully downstairs to the first floor in her red stilettos. 'How was your day?' Holding her arms open so that kids could give her a hug.

Aimee and Jasper raced forward and cuddled into her, babbling about Harry Potter and Hagrid, Diagon Alley and Butter Beer, which daddy had hated and Jasper had loved, and Aimee had said tasted like sick.

'You look pretty, Zoe.' Aimee said, leaning back and looking up into Zoe's face.

'Thank you.' Zoe nodded. 'So do you,' tweaking her nose, she pointed at Aimee's fashionable nautical jumpsuit.

'You look like Snow White,' Jasper bounced up and down on the spot.

'I do?' Zoe cast a look down at her short black and red kimono style dress. She'd bought it that afternoon on Oxford Street after returning from Ruth's, feeling like a changed person and wanting the wardrobe to go with it. It was funny how one meaningful, cathartic conversation could make you see things in an entirely different light. 'Well, apparently Japanese styles are trending this summer. But I thought Snow White wore a nice flowing princess dress.' Thinking of the famous Disney animated film.

'Not in the version with Chris Hemsworth as the Huntsman,' Matt said, stepping into the hallway. 'But I think Jasper is referring to the black hair, fair skin and blue eyes.' Dipping his head, 'And, wow by the way.'

'Thanks.' She blushed at the appreciative look on his face, glad she'd decided to keep her make-up simple because the dress was so bold, choosing to line her eyes with black kohl and slick on some red lipstick. 'I'm going to have to get going actually. Come on kids, let's go downstairs and you can see me off.'

'But we've only just said hello,' Jasper protested.

'I'm only going out for the night, and you can see me tomorrow as long as you don't wake me too early. Maybe your dad will let you have a movie night. That way he can relax for a bit before you go to bed. I'm sure you tired him out today.'

Matt looked at her gratefully before switching his attention to the children. 'That's a fantastic idea. You can pick something you both like, and I might call for pizza and even let you have some popcorn. Why don't you go and have a look at the DVD's, so Zoe can get going?'

'Okay,' Aimee nodded at her brother, and they both released

their nanny and ran for the stairs. 'Come on.'

As they disappeared, Matt turned to Zoe and offered her an arm. 'Those heels are pretty high and the carpet's pretty deep. Do you need a hand down the stairs?'

'I should be all right, thanks.' It was thoughtful of him, and she loved a guy who knew how to be a gentleman, but keeping some space between them was necessary at the moment. Otherwise she might be tempted to jump him. He was looking particularly gorgeous in a pair of jeans and a black open necked shirt. His green eyes looked amazing, practically glowing against the darkness of the top. 'Oh.' She looked down at her shoes nestling in the fluffy beige carpet. 'Unless you want me to take them off? Sorry, I should have thought. If it helps, they're new, so they're clean.'

'Don't be silly. I don't care about that.'

'Well, I'm sure I can manage one flight of stairs.' She strode towards him, but as she reached the top step her ankle turned. Stumbling forward, she let out a squeak of alarm, but his arm was already under hers, holding her upright.

'Whoa! I've got you.'

'Thank you.' Her heart was racing at the prospect of a headlong tumble down the stairs. 'Seems like I overestimated myself,' she said with a twist of her lips. Bloody hell, it was typical. Just because she'd insisted she was fine, this had to happen.

'Or underestimated the shoes,' Matt replied, fighting back a smile.

'Oh, shut up,' she grumbled good naturedly. 'You were right, okay?'

'I always am,' he quipped.

They walked down slowly, their shoulders rubbing and their thighs occasionally brushing.

She gulped, heat rising up her chest and into her cheeks. Why did she have to be so ultra-aware of him? It was like every cell in her body was straining towards every cell in his, wanting to mesh and create sparks.

'That really is a stunning dress,' he said as they arrived in the hallway. Pointing at the slit, where her bare thigh was peeking out. 'Particularly that bit.'

His eyes rose to stare into hers, and she couldn't look away. He was still holding her arm, his fingers sending tingles down into her hands, which curled into fists. She could feel the scorching heat of his body only a few inches from hers, and forced herself to breathe normally. Panting would be so lame.

'I'm a bit worried about you going out like that actually,' Matt confided.

'What do you mean?'

'Well, it would be easy for some handsome, rich guy to swoop you up, looking like that.'

'And? What's the problem with that?' she raised an eyebrow.

'Well, before you know it he'd be wining and dining you, taking you out for fancy meals and inviting you to his private yacht for a holiday in the Maldives, and then you'd be swanning off to be put up in his penthouse flat by the Thames.' He looked mournful, but she could see a teasing glint in his eye. 'The kids would be devastated.'

'They would?' She daren't ask him how he'd feel, that was far too dangerous. 'You got all that from one dress?'

'I did.' He shook his head, the scent of his sexy aftershave weaving into the tiny space between them. 'It's easy for the imagination to run wild when we're talking about a dress like that.'

'The dress apologises for any offence it causes,' she laughed, 'but it's staying on and I'm going out. Don't worry, I'll be good. I'm not after hooking up with any millionaires any time soon.' *At least, none that live outside this house*, a sneaky shocking voice whispered in her head.

'Fair enough. It's just that I heard Henry Cavill hangs around these parts.' His fingers traced down her arm and she shivered in reaction. 'Please promise you'll look after yourself though?'

'I'll be with friends, don't worry.' Whether Melody was going to be there was still an unknown. Earlier on she'd texted the name of the restaurant they'd be at with the ETA, and all she'd got back in response was an '*okay, thanks.*' She had to sort things out with her sister. With that promise in mind, she managed to step back from Matt. 'I should go.'

'Do you want me to give you a lift, or come and pick you up?'

'That's kind, but not part of the terms and conditions of my contract,' she answered, deliberately reminding him she was his employee. She had to use anything she could to create a barrier between them while she got her head together. 'Besides, you need to feed the children soon and you'd have to get them out of bed later to come and get me, and that's not fair to them. I'm also planning to have a few glasses of wine tonight and I'm not sure I'd want you to see me in that state, or vice versa,' she joked.

'All right, but at least use the black cab company I have on retainer.'

'You don't have limos or a corporate car hire firm taking you places when you don't want to drive?'

'I don't like to attract attention, and I'll definitely do that if I go everywhere in flash cars. I like the anonymity of black cabs.'

'What about the McLaren P1?' she said, 'A high performance supercar is hardly subtle is it?'

'That's different. I love that car. Besides, good sense can't win out all the time, can it? Anyway, I have an account with the cab firm. Put the fare under my name. Call it a perk, but I just want to make sure you get back safely, no matter what time it is. They'll look after you. Here,' he dug his wallet out of his pocket and handed her a business card.

She stroked the glossy, embossed card, 'Thanks. I'm getting the bus there but I'll take advantage on the way back.'

'No problem.' He smirked, 'I don't expect to have to hold your hair back for you when you get in though. If you come home drunk and feeling ill, you're on your own.'

'Have you done that for many women?' she wrinkled her nose.

'Only Helen, she had the worst morning sickness when she was pregnant with both the children. She used to spend at least two hours every morning slumped on the bathroom floor. I used to get her ginger biscuits and provide damp flannels. Sometimes I'd sit in there with her and read *Vogue* to take her mind off things.'

'That's sweet.' When she'd been unwell with Greg he'd swerved away sharply, like a London bike rider around an open car door. He wouldn't see her again until she was better. *I just wanna give you space to get better baby,* he'd say, looking concerned. But maybe the concern had all been for himself. It was the only real reason she could think of why she'd had to rely on the other nannies to bring her soup and other provisions when ill.

'I don't know about sweet,' Matt said. 'It was just right. I was half to blame for her being in that state.' He frowned. 'I hadn't thought about that for a while.'

'I'm sorry. I didn't mean to bring back painful memories for you.'

'No, it's fine. I brought it up. And they weren't all painful.' He added in an odd voice, like it had only just occurred to him.

'Daddy, we've chosen a film now!' Jasper's voice echoed along the hallway. 'We're hungry too.'

Matt jumped. 'I shouldn't keep you, Zoe. You'll be late. Have fun tonight. You deserve it, you've worked hard.'

'Thanks, I plan to.' Grabbing her clutch purse off the side from where she'd left it earlier, she flung open the door.

'Aren't you taking a jacket or anything?' Matt asked, following her out.

'No, Dad,' she rolled her eyes. 'It's August, Matt. It's warm. I'll be fine.'

'If you say so,' he raked one last look over her outfit, 'just make sure the dress behaves itself.'

'I will,' she giggled, shaking her head. Swinging around, she picked her way carefully down the concrete steps and over the gravel driveway. Turning back to wave at him, a thought occurred to her. 'Oh, by the way, Jasper birthday's coming up in less than two weeks, isn't it? What have you got planned?'

A look of horror crossed Matt's face, dark eyebrows drawing together. 'Oh, shit. Nothing. Melody usually plans his parties. Jesus,' he threw a quick glance over his shoulder to check the hallway. Scrubbing his hands through his hair, he muttered. 'Oh, this is bad. Really bad. I am a bad parent.'

He appeared so guilty she didn't have the heart to agree. 'You're not a bad parent, it's just slipped your mind because you've been so busy. Don't worry. We'll sort something out.'

'We?'

'If you want me to help I will, but you have to be involved this time.'

He nodded. 'Sounds fair.'

'We can sit down and discuss it tomorrow, but not until the afternoon. I'll be sleeping in.'

'Deal. Have a nice night. Remember what I said about those millionaires. We've only just found you. My kids aren't ready to lose you.'

Nodding, she made for the pavement, striding as quickly as she could away from the house and its owner. Tears stood out in her eyes. She wasn't ready to lose them either. Any of them. When, she wondered, had it started becoming more about that than about getting justice and the truth for Melody. Was she once again failing her sister?

12

Clattering off the red double-decker bus in her matching stilettos, Zoe made her way through the cobblestoned alleyway into Soho, heading for the trendy bar-restaurant Rayne had chosen. Tonight she was just a twenty-something girl on the town, she'd decided on the way. She needed to have some fun. Life had been far too serious and stressful recently. The air was balmy, the summer night was young, London was pulsing and she was about to spend time with some of her most favourite people in the world.

As she approached the entrance to the bar, an orange neon sign hanging above the doorway, a group of middle-aged men in suits spilled out into the street. A few raucous laughs echoed between them, and a few 'good evenings' were tossed her way, along with a 'Wahey, nice dress love'. The comment made her think of Matt. *Stop it.* 'Thanks, lads,' she grinned.

Most of the group moved past her, but one guy with blonde hair and a shading of stubble stopped and held the door open, leering admiringly as her thigh slipped out of the dress as she stepped forward. Rolling her eyes at how blatant he was, she thanked him and slipped past into the bar, a low hum of conversation and pumping background music filling the space. The man took her eye-roll with good humour, acknowledging it with a nod. She shook her head. Didn't men realise how obvious they were, and that largely speaking, it wasn't a turn on? She smiled wryly. Typical English blokes.

But his cocky demeanour made her realise it was good to be home, good to be back in the UK. As much as she'd enjoyed the experience of living in another country and how great living in sprawling, thrilling New York had been, being in London and visiting Southend had shown her something. While she'd been wholly committed to staying in the States with Greg, this was where her heart was. It's where it would always be. And two of the best reasons for that were somewhere in this room. She hoped that the third would decide to turn up tonight as well. She missed her sister. Returning to the UK, Zoe had hoped they would spend time together, but instead all they'd done was spend it apart.

Her eyes swept over the heavy slab of glass that was the bar, balanced on two black pillars with blue up-lighters beneath it. Plush black sofas were set against designer blue and black printed wallpaper and islands of chest-high round tables and stools filled the room. The restaurant was off to the side and Rayne had texted to say she'd booked a table for half past seven. They'd agreed on drinks first, and she couldn't wait until she had a cocktail in her hand.

First she spotted Rayne waving madly at her from one of the tables with glasses dotted on it, chunky cocktail rings flashing on her long fingers. Then Frankie turned and beamed at her, sweeping her jaw length black hair behind her neat ears. With a massive sigh of relief, Zoe saw Melody occupying a third stool at the table, a small sad smile on her face.

Dashing across the dark wooden floor towards them, Zoe threw her handbag down and grabbed Melody in a fierce hug. 'I didn't think you'd come. Why didn't you stick around for me to bring you back, like we agreed? Are you still cross with me?'

Melody eased away, 'I didn't want to sit around waiting for you. I wanted to see Jemima. No, I'm not cross with you. We're okay.' But her eyes didn't meet Zoe's for long, and she untangled herself to reach for her wine.

'Hey, you,' Rayne exclaimed, brushing her blunt fringe out of her eyes and wrapping her arms around Zoe. 'It's fab to see you. You look incredible. You've managed to put a bit of weight on, I see.'

Zoe laughed, 'Just come right out and say it, Rayne. Are you trying to tell me I look fat?' Putting her hands on her hips.

'Noooo, of course not. It's just that the last time I saw you, you were far too skinny. I could almost see your ribs. You're looking much healthier now. It suits you. You look a lot better than I expected actually, under the circumstances.'

'Gee, thanks. You really don't hold back do you? You look fantastic too by the way.' She admired Rayne's gorgeous sapphire cutaway dress, swatches of fabric cut out on both sides of the waist to reveal silky bronzed skin.

'Aww, thanks. And you know I love you, sweetie,' Rayne pinched Zoe's cheeks playfully. 'We also know each other well enough that I can say what I think.'

'Except you do it with everyone,' Frankie said, giving Rayne a teasing look and standing up. 'Let her go. It's my turn.' Scooping Zoe into a hug, she whispered in her ear, 'It's so nice to see you.'

'You too,' Zoe smiled as they broke apart. 'I'm loving the hair.'

Frankie pulled a face, unusual violet-coloured eyes amused. 'It's taken about eight months for it to get to a length I'm happy with. My friend Davey is a hair dresser and he cut it really short just after Christmas. While I was panicking about the amount of hair on the floor, he was telling me not to worry because it made me look like Frankie from *The Saturdays*.'

'It looked cool,' Rayne said, hopping onto her stool and crossing her legs. 'Stop moaning. Besides, Zack liked it, didn't he?'

Frankie stuck her tongue out at her friend, jumping onto her own stool and pointing to the fourth one for Zoe. 'Zack's a love-sick idiot,' she smirked, 'he'd like me even if Davey had shaved all my hair off.'

'I don't think Zack's the only lovesick idiot,' Zoe noted as she climbed carefully onto her stool, mindful of her short dress, 'you look the prettiest I've ever seen you.' She gestured at her friend's clear glowing skin, taking in the tight black jeans, high heeled boots and this season's neon yellow top. 'I guess ditching the rich guy for the sweetheart has worked out for you, huh?'

'It has. Although there was a year's break in between them. I have to admit, I used to hate being stuck in a cramped, damp flat above a kebab shop, but I don't really care anymore because I've got Zack. Speaking of which …'

'What?' Zoe could see Frankie was desperate to share some news. 'Go on, just spit it out.'

'Ooh, what have you been hiding, you sneaky thing?' Rayne leaned forward eagerly, elbows on the table.

'Zack and I are moving in together!' Frankie grinned, eyes sparkling.

'That's amazing! Congratulations,' Zoe screeched, drawing the attention of the next table over. Oops. She slid down in her seat, lowering her voice. 'I mean, congratulations, I'm really happy for you.'

'That's ace, Franks,' Rayne toasted her friend. 'Spill the details then.'

'Well, we've both given notice on our tenancy agreements and we're getting a new place together in Richmond. We'll be renting to start with but our plan is to save up for a deposit for our own place.' She grinned wider. 'God, I can't wait to wake up next to Zack every day.'

'Bleurgh.' Rayne stuck her finger down her throat, pretending to be sick. 'Come on, I've just been reunited with my first love after almost five years and even I'm not being that soppy.'

'Oh, come on. We all know it's just a matter of time before Adam proposes,' Frankie picked up a cocktail napkin and threw it at Rayne, who laughed and ducked out the way.

'Hey, we've not even been back together two months.'

'You wore his ring through most of uni,' Frankie pointed out, 'don't deny that it's been round your neck for the last few years,' she pointed at the chain dangling between Rayne's boobs, something nestling in between them.

'Damn it, caught out.' Rayne stuck her tongue out at Frankie and tossed the napkin back at her.

'Behave, you two,' Zoe mock scolded, easing back into the warm friendship that had been there since their uni days. She was aware of Melody sitting silently to her right, watching them mess around. Her dark eyes looked too big for her thin face.

'I'm so sorry,' Frankie said suddenly, looking at the sisters. 'Here we are babbling on about our relationships, when you two have just gone through break ups.' She put a hand to her mouth, eyes full of guilt. 'We're such bad friends.'

'Shit,' Rayne said, 'you're right. That was bad. Sorry.'

'Don't be silly,' Zoe reached across the table and touched Frankie's arm, smiling at them both. 'Just because our love lives have imploded, it doesn't mean we begrudge you your happiness. Does it Mel?'

'Of course not,' Melody murmured, but there was a hollowness to her words that was worrying.

'Besides, I had a lucky escape. I'm not into guys that cheat. Do it once and I'm done with them.' Her jaw clenched as she thought of Greg. 'Anyway,' shaking the annoyance away, 'thanks for coming guys.' She slid a hand under the table to squeeze Melody's cold fingers, which were clamped together in her lap. 'I can't wait to catch up and have some fun.'

'Well, we'll definitely be doing that tonight.' Rayne poured Zoe an excessively large glass of wine from the metal cooler in the centre of the table, coloured metal bangles jangling around her wrist. 'We started without you, so you need to catch up,' Rayne ordered when Zoe pulled a *steady on* face. 'You too, Melody,' topping the younger woman's glass up with a generous splash of Pinot Grigio.

'I agree,' Frankie piped up.

'I guess we have no choice,' Zoe replied, trying to involve her sister in the conversation, 'after all, who are we to argue with a big-time city journalist and a talented freelance photographer?' Taking a sip of wine, rolling the sweet, crisp floral taste on her tongue, she looked expectantly at Melody. 'Come on sis, relax.'

With a nod, Melody took a sip of wine. 'I'll try.'

Zoe looked at Rayne and Frankie. 'So apart from both of you being ridiculously loved up, what else is new?'

She listened as Rayne launched into an amusing anecdote about some players she and Lily had interviewed at Wimbledon, and nodded in all the right places, but her head was tilted towards Mel, noticing how the black top and skinny blue jeans she wore hung off her slight frame. She gave her sister's hand another reassuring squeeze. No matter what, she would make sure Melody got the closure she needed.

It was half an hour before the conversation came around to Zoe, by which time they were into their second bottle of wine and had ordered their first round of cocktails. A Pimms for Rayne, who'd got the taste for it at Wimbledon; a Manhattan for Frankie, who'd had one on New Year's Eve at The Ritz, the night she'd been choosing between two men, and a Cosmo for Zoe, her favourite New York tipple. Melody stuck with wine, insistent she was feeling tipsy enough already. It was true her eyes were starting to cross slightly, and Zoe wondered when the last time was that her sister had eaten properly. She circled a hand around Melody's wrist, her middle finger and thumb touching. That wasn't good.

But at least Melody was talking now. It had taken twenty minutes but she was finally mellowing and joining in, laughing with the girls about the time she'd come to Loughborough to visit Zoe. She'd been sixteen, with Zoe twenty-two and fiercely overprotective. Melody had been a big hit with the guys in the dorm, and Zoe had spent the whole weekend scowling at them all and reminding them in firm tones that Mel was barely legal.

'I was so embarrassed,' Melody laughed. 'I wasn't sure I was ever going to forgive you,' shaking her head at Zoe.

'Hey, I was just doing my big sister duties,' she held up both hands.

'I'm not sure they're supposed to extend that far,' Mel answered lightly, but there was something in her tone that suggested she wasn't talking about what had happened almost six years before.

'To be honest,' Frankie picked up on the tension, trying to defuse it, 'I just kept expecting Zoe to walk out of her room wearing a black suit, like a bouncer's outfit.'

'Believe me, I thought about it.'

'Right. Enough of that.' Rayne raised one perfectly arched dark eyebrow. 'My curiosity is killing me. Tell all—how are you getting on living with The Bastard?' Her eyes were aglow with interest.

'What's this?' Frankie asked, straightening on her stool 'I think I've missed something. I know that Melody's boss fired her and kicked her out for no reason, and his younger brother who you were dating,' she nodded sympathetically at Melody, 'has gone AWOL, but what's this about living with a bastard?'

'Zoe's moved in with Melody's boss to find out what really happened, and get revenge for Melody,' Rayne lowered her voice as a waitress sauntered past holding a tray of drinks aloft, 'by selling a kiss and tell story about Matt to the tabloids. He'll hate it, has massive privacy issues. Zoe's going to use my contacts.'

'Really?' Frankie swivelled her head to Zoe, mouth open. 'That seems a bit extreme. Does he deserve it?' She looked at Melody then back to Zoe. 'Is he a bastard, Zo?'

'Um ...' Zoe used the pretext of taking a large slug of wine as an opportunity to gather her thoughts. How could she answer that without giving away how uncertain she was feeling about everything? That no, she didn't think Matt was a bastard. 'Well ...' But if that was the case, it made her a sister either a liar or there was something seriously screwy going on, which she hadn't got to the bottom of yet.

She gazed at her sister, whose attention was on a napkin she was turning in circles on the table. She couldn't back out of the plan now, could she? Otherwise it would mean that she was choosing a man over Melody again. The way she'd chosen to go with Greg to America rather than facing her sister and aunt to make amends. Leaving her family behind rather than staying and dealing with her heartbreak like other people did, one day at a time. Melody had been so upset when she'd left the UK. It had taken months to get her to contact Zoe with any regularity. She couldn't blame her. After all, she had abandoned her. 'That is ... Yes, he's a bit of a bastard.' She stuttered as she said it, blaming the alcohol, which was making her feel fuzzy headed.

Melody lifted her head, looking surprised.

'Wow, that was totally convincing,' Rayne drawled, 'not. Now tell us the truth.'

Zoe opened her mouth, wanting to try again, to say Matt was rude, sarcastic, ignorant, and arrogant. That he really was a bastard. That he had taken pleasure in Melody's downfall. But it wouldn't be true. He could be distant and a little rude with it, and he'd shut himself off from his children for far too long, but he was a good guy. Except for what he'd done to her sister. That still didn't make sense. She felt like she had two puzzle pieces that should match up, that were roughly the right size and shape, but when she laid them down next to each other, they wouldn't fit together.

Anxiety churned in her stomach, her fingers clenching round the stalk of her wine glass. She looked at her sister, who deserved so much better. 'I ... I can't.' She gulped. 'I'm sorry Melody. After what he did to you, I know you must hate him—'

'Why are you apologising?' her sister asked, lifting her head to meet her eyes. 'I told you he wasn't a bastard. I've thought about it a lot, I've done nothing else with Stephen shutting me out. I'm not sleeping and I'm never hungry. I can't get over him when I don't know why it's over. But Matt must have thought he had a good reason for doing what he did. It's the only thing that makes sense.'

'He does,' Zoe acknowledged, thinking of the way she'd circled around the subject with him, and what the other nannies have said, 'I just don't know what. But I get the impression it's really bad. Are you sure you don't know what it could be? It's not about you and Stephen seeing each other, you were right about that.'

'No,' Melody said in disbelief, a spark of anger kindling in her eyes, 'I have no idea whatsoever. What's happening here? Do you believe them over me now, is that what this is? I never did anything to hurt Matt, the children or Stephen. You're going to take Matt's side?'

'What? No. No!' Zoe hissed, putting her hand on Mel's arm to stop her as she tried to get up. 'Don't. I'm not saying that. I just wondered if there was anything that could have created confusion, or where wires might have got crossed. There are no sides here. I'm trying Mel, I am. I just can't get any clarity. Every time I try to talk to Matt about it, he shuts down. And I don't know where Stephen is, other than sailing on the yacht ...' she trailed off as something Matt had said struck her.

'What is it?' Melody sank back down onto her stool, face draining of colour. 'What? Is it another girl?' she flinched.

'No. It was weird. Matt said you broke Stephen's heart and he'd gone away to get over it. But obviously it was the other way around.' She hesitated, unsure whether this would help or not, 'I also spoke to the other nannies. The way they told it, he was devoted to you. You'd reformed him. He was a bit of a player by all accounts.'

'He was. It took him six months to convince me to date him because I'd heard of his reputation. I was also wary of getting involved, with him being Matt's brother. But eventually he won me over and it was just me. At least, as far as I know.' Melody ran shaking hands through her hair, pressing her fingers against her temples. Frankie and Rayne kept quiet, watching the sisters with concern. 'I don't get it.' Mel said, bewildered. 'It was going so well. We'd arranged to meet by the Statute of Eros in Piccadilly for lunch and he just didn't turn up. I called and called but got no answer, so I went back to Matt's. Stephen wasn't there, and neither was

Matt. The kids were at a friend's, so I sat in the garden to read a book, and that's where I was when Matt confronted me. I've never seen him look so furious. He wouldn't talk, wouldn't explain. He just wanted me gone. There was this look on his face, like he was disappointed with me but was holding back. It wasn't like him. I'd never seen that side of him before.' Mel finished, trembling. 'But he definitely wasn't enjoying it. He looked hurt. That's why I say he's not a bastard. You should know that, Zoe, living with him.'

Zoe got up, wrapping an arm around Melody's shoulders. 'Yes. I do know that. He's really kind of,' pausing, her face softened, 'nice.' It was a completely inadequate word to describe the passionate, funny, intense guy that Matt was, but she couldn't let on how she really felt about him and the kids. 'Things are getting better between him and the children too,' she tacked on unthinkingly, trying to give her sister something positive to hold onto.

'Meaning you're doing a good job of cleaning up the mess I made,' Melody muttered, jerking out of Zoe's arms, tears winding their way down her cheeks.

'Mel, don't be like that. I didn't mean it that way, I swear.' Taking her sister's face between her hands. 'I said sorry. I thought we were okay. I'm not saying you got it wrong. We're just different.'

'You mean you're better.'

'No!' Zoe released her and stepped back from the accusation, left ankle twisting in her stiletto.

'Come on, Melody,' Rayne interjected, 'your sister would never think that, let alone say it. She loves you.'

'I know you're angry with Stephen,' Zoe put a hand to her chest, feeling something tearing inside, 'but I don't want to argue with you. I did it for you, going to live with Matt, and—'

'I never wanted you to. I never asked you too,' Melody burst out, the effects of alcohol glazing her eyes and making her cheeks ruddy.

'What?' Zoe murmured, aware of people around them starting to whisper at the commotion. This wasn't the evening she'd planned.

Melody subsided in her seat, as if letting the confession out had deflated her. 'I agreed because you so obviously wanted to do it, whatever I was going to say or not say. You're stubborn, Zoe.' An expression of despair crossed her face. 'You were determined and had this idea in your head that they had to pay. Oh, you were angry at them with good reason and I appreciated you wanting to defend me,' her voice dropped, 'but I think it was Greg you were really angry with.'

'What?' Zoe gawped at her, clambering back onto her stool and draining her wine glass. She winced at the pain in her ankle, eyes welling with tears. 'That's not fair. How can you say that? I was doing it for you.' She felt like grabbing her clutch bag and running away from her sister's words, and was giving it serious thought when Frankie touched her on the shoulder in a comforting gesture. It grounded her, gave her strength. She thought about this morning's conversation with Ruth, one that felt like a million years ago. She'd run away before and would not do the same again, no matter how much it hurt.

'I'll admit I want to know why,' Melody's voice was determined, 'but I never wanted you to splash him across the papers. You're just so used to coming in and making decisions … my big sister taking charge.'

'It's what you needed after Mum and Dad died,' Zoe defended.

'But we had Ruth to be the adult, and I don't need you to make my decisions for me, Zo,' Melody's voice was kinder now, 'not anymore. Believe it or not, I've grown up while you were away.'

'Yes, I can see that,' Zoe blinked, Mel's face a blur. 'I'm sorry I missed it.' Holding back a sob, she grabbed her sister's hand. 'I'm sorry.'

Melody's face softened. 'Don't be, you were just trying to protect me. And don't be sorry for going to America. Whatever Ruth says and you might feel, I wasn't angry with you. I just missed you and I was sixteen so I was more interested in hanging out with my friends than sitting in front of a computer to talk to my older sister. Teenagers are like that. They're the centre of their own universe.'

'Really? You mean that?' Zoe asked, the knot in her stomach starting to unravel.

'Yes. Please, stop torturing yourself. Don't feel guilty. You're back now.' Taking a deep breath. 'But respect me, Zo. Let me try and sort my own life out. I know I look a mess,' she held a hand up at them all when they opened their mouths, 'please, don't even try for the empty platitudes. I look awful and I feel shocking. But I'll get there. I had a resilient older sister who showed me how to survive.' Curling her other hand tighter around Zoe's. 'This whole thing has given me time to think. I'm done being a nanny. I wasn't passionate about it, and you were right about Matt. I should have tried harder. The children in our care deserve better. I only became a nanny because you did.'

Zoe nodded, thinking of what Ruth had said. 'I'm sorry if you felt pressured.'

'I didn't, I just wanted to be like you.'

'That's a compliment,' Rayne joked as the tension at the table started to unfurl and drift away, 'though why she'd want to be like you is a total mystery.'

'Oi,' Zoe protested, wiping her eyes on a napkin. She felt exhausted after a day of revelations. 'So, what now?' she asked, clenching her jaw as Melody chuckled and Frankie smiled. They didn't understand the enormity of the question. Without a reason to stay with Matt and the kids, she'd have to leave. She would be anchorless, like a severed buoy adrift on the River Thames. The thought of leaving them caused a physical pain to arrow through her.

'Zoe, are you actually asking me what I want?' Melody teased, holding her hand to chest and feigning a heart attack.

In that twinkle of a moment, Zoe could see that Mel was going to be all right. 'Hey, I'm not that bad.' A pause, 'But yes, what do you want?'

'I don't want you to put Matt in the tabloids. It wouldn't be fair to him or the kids.'

'Oh, Mel, I'm really glad you said that,' Zoe huffed out a massive rush of relief, shoulders shaking, 'because I can't do it. I wasn't sure how to tell you, but it wouldn't be right. It's been eating away at me. I've felt so uncomfortable. I couldn't bear the thought of hurting the kids.' *Liar*, a little voice whispered in her head, *it was about Matt too*. 'But I didn't want to let you down.' Dropping her face into her hands, she took a moment to gather herself, thinking back to how she'd felt on arriving at Jemima's from Heathrow to find her sister so devastated. The sun beating down on her head and burning the back of her neck, rage and adrenalin charging around her body. 'You're right,' she whispered, looking up, 'the *Nannygate* plan was fuelled by my fury at Greg for cheating on me and deceiving me, for making me feel shitty and worthless. I got off the plane angry and when I found out what happened to you, it made me a hundred times angrier. I transferred that to Matt and Stephen. I did.'

Pausing as a waiter arrived and served their drinks, she smiled politely without registering how cute he was. She downed the pink citrusy Cosmo in one go, coughing as she slammed her glass down.

Frankie took a sip of Manhattan, pulling a face and looking unsure as to whether she liked it or not. 'Don't be too tough on yourself, Zoe,' she remarked, 'you were heartbroken.'

'I thought I was,' Zoe corrected her, reaching across and robbing a sip of Rayne's tangy Pimms.

'Steady on,' Rayne laughed, 'or you'll be under the table before dinner.'

'Nothing wrong with that,' she quipped.

Frankie waited until the chuckles had subsided, then cocked her head at Zoe. 'You're not heartbroken?'

'I expected to be, I was incredibly hurt and it was a huge shock, but when I look back, it wasn't right. You know, sometimes it's not until you have some distance from a situation that you can see it for what it is. I thought I loved him, but it wasn't the kind of love you should build a marriage on. And when he contacts me now—'

'What?' Rayne slapped her hand down on the table. 'He's had the cheek to get in touch? I hope it's to apologise.'

'He's said he's sorry and loves me, and wants to talk.'

'And?' Frankie asked, as Melody put a clammy hand on Zoe's arm.

'I have no interest in talking to him. I don't miss him, and nothing he says would change things. The thought of being near him makes my skin crawl. I'm still really angry with him, but there's absolutely no temptation to hear him out or go back to him. He would never be the same person to me again, not after what he did. Besides, I don't want to go back to the States. Now that I've been home I know this is where I belong.'

'Good,' Rayne exclaimed. 'I'm glad to hear it.'

The four of them smiled across the table at each other, all with suspiciously moist eyes.

'I'm happy to hear that too.' Melody tightened her hold on Zoe's arm, leaning in. 'You asked me what I want, sis. Well I've got one thing back that I wanted. You. Do you want to know what else I want?' Her voice was slurred, the alcohol sweet on her breath. 'I'd like to know the truth. So with Stephen still gone, do you think you could stand to be in the house for a few more weeks? Could you try one more time to get to the bottom of what I'm supposed to have done?'

'Sure.' Zoe threw an arm around her sister's shoulder, heart pumping. As much as she was relieved to be going home to Matt's tonight, there was also a piece of her that was petrified of getting in any deeper. 'Anything.'

'Thank you,' Melody rested her forehead against Zoe's and they sat there for a moment, making peace.

'Enough of the drama now girls,' Rayne tapped short burgundy nails on the table, 'we've done our Oprah section, established our female solidarity,' she teased to lighten the mood. 'Now to have some fun.' Grinning as the sisters straightened in their chairs, she looked at them expectantly, 'So, is he hot?'

'Who?'

'Marvellous Matt,' she said, tongue-in-cheek. 'He looks pretty fit in the papers, on the rare occasion he gets papped. Is he?'

'Yes,' Melody answered.

'No,' Zoe denied.

They spoke simultaneously and Zoe shot a frown at her sister for the affirmative answer. Melody returned her look with a level gaze and a raised eyebrow, some of the spark returning. *Oh come on,* her expression seemed to say.

Zoe's cheeks went red and she pretended a keen interest in the stocky blond barman who was shaking cocktails for a couple at the bar.

Rayne swept her gaze from one sister to the other, a smile quirking the side of her mouth up. 'Er, what are you two not telling us? You don't think he's attractive, Zo?'

'I guess he's quite good looking,' she said casually.

'Quite?' Melody arched both fair eyebrows. 'Sis, you are either in denial or blind. I never liked him that way, but even I can admit he's gorgeous. I mean he's got that scar above his lip and his nose is a bit crooked where it's been broken. He's also a bit old-' she stopped as Rayne snorted.

'He's only thirty,' Rayne said, amused.

'Well, I'm twenty-two, but as it happens I was going to say he's a bit older than me. He's also too serious. Stephen is twenty-three, so closer to me in age. We had more in common. Or at least, I thought we did.' A shadow passed over her face. 'Anyway, Matt's just a friend—or was—and my ex-boss, but he has these lovely green eyes and great cheekbones. Actually, Zo, I'm surprised you'd say he's only quite good looking. I would have thought he'd be right up your street. You always liked bad boys. Matt fits that description almost perfectly. He's tall and broad shouldered too.'

'Not really,' Zoe mumbled evasively, still pretending a fascination

495

with the barman, desperate for her face not to go any redder.

'What are you on about?' Melody demanded, clutching Zoe's arm.

'Huh? Nothing,' Zoe turned to face her sister and friends.

'Oh my God, you like him,' Rayne said in a slow voice.

'I—ah, no I don't.'

'Zoe?' Melody peered into her face. 'Do you like Matt? Because if you do, maybe it's not such a good idea for you to—'

'I don't.' Zoe stared into her sister's deep brown eyes. 'I don't.' It was an easy fib. What she felt for Matt was far more complicated than like.

'Right. Enough of that,' Rayne summoned the waiter and Melody let go of her sister, 'more cocktails, followed by dinner. Anyone fancy a dance later?'

Zoe rolled her neck, feeling the tension in her shoulders. 'Oh, yes,' she smiled, 'I'm up for that.'

'Oh, God,' Zoe clutched her head. 'Have they gone yet? I think I'm dying. Their voices were going right through me.'

Matt chuckled. 'You're safe. They're playing in the fountain. I can keep an eye on them. You rest up.' He looked down at her with amusement as she readjusted her big black sunglasses and lay back on the grass. 'You know that if this was a working day for you, I'd have to seriously consider firing you?' he mocked, tugging down the peak of the baseball cap he'd worn to conceal his identity.

'It's because it's not a working day for me that I saw fit to get myself into this state.' She groaned as Hyde Park span around her, the cobalt sky sitting at an odd angle, the grass beneath her feeling like it was tilted at forty five degrees, instead of flat. 'And you know that because it's a day off for me, that's why you have to keep an eye on them? Don't try and act like you're doing me a favour, Matthew.'

He laughed at her use of his full name and lay down beside her on his front, chin propped on his hand so he could watch

Aimee and Jasper splashing in the water. 'Like the favour I did you when you stumbled out of the black cab at four this morning and needed help making it up the stairs?'

She covered her face with shaking hands. 'Oh, please don't remind me,' she moaned. 'Sorry about that. But I told you, it was because I'd been dancing in heels for five hours and was crippled.'

'It had nothing to do with the massive vats of alcohol you'd consumed?'

'No,' she whimpered. Just the word alcohol gave her flashbacks to the drunken, loud meal that had followed the cathartic conversation with her sister, the hazy, laughing bar crawl and the banging club they'd ended up in. Somehow she'd acquired a penis helium balloon from a hen party and Rayne had given away all her bangles to random strangers. It had been one of those nights that had been planned as fairly low key but that'd ended up as unexpectedly fabulous. Her mouth curled at the memory of tequila shots. They'd seemed like a good idea at the time. 'Urgh.'

'What's wrong?' Matt asked, touching her arm.

'It hurts to smile,' she complained. 'And why is it so bloody sunny? It's making me feel sick.' Pulling her loose ankle-length patterned dress away from her body, she flapped a hand at the scorching sun, 'Go 'way.'

'God, you stink!' Matt fanned a hand over her face.

'Gee, thanks a lot.'

'Of alcohol. It's drifting out of your pores. Do you feel better for it though? Are you glad you had a night out with the girls? What about the dress, did it behave? You weren't in any fit state when you came home to tell me if you ran into any millionaires.'

'No millionaires and the dress behaved impeccably.' She swallowed away a wave of nausea, the sound of a nearby radio playing an R 'n' B tune driving spikes through her head. 'Let's not talk about feeling better at the moment. Ask me again on Wednesday, which is probably when this hangover will last until.'

He shook his head, 'You're really feeling sorry for yourself, aren't you?' He sat up. 'Here,' rooting through the straw picnic hamper he'd brought along, he handed her a bottle of icy water and started unwrapping a sausage sandwich from crisp foil.

'That's really kind, thanks,' pushing herself slowly onto her elbows, she took the water off him and unscrewed the top, tentatively drinking some, 'but I can't stand the thought of that at the moment.' She pointed to the sandwich, which was wafting meaty, tomatoey smells in her direction.

'Okay, but you might just want to try. When I used to have a hangover the only thing that worked for me was eating my way through it.'

'Not right now thanks. Has it been a long time since you had one?' she asked, flopping back down onto the grass and squinting at him. He was the most relaxed she'd ever seen him in a pair of deck shorts and a white t-shirt, his face missing that usual tense, set expression he had when he was working.

'About three years.'

The amount of time his wife had been dead. 'Oh.'

'Anyway,' he glanced over at the fountain, smiling as he saw Jasper chasing Aimee, flinging bucketfuls of water at her, 'we were going to talk about Jasper's birthday. Do you still feel up to it?'

'It's why I came isn't it? Although,' she pressed her fingers against her forehead, trying to massage the pain away, 'I'm not sure whether all of my brain cells are intact today, and those that are left have probably been pickled.'

'So you're saying it might be an improvement then?' Matt kidded.

'Hey!' Zoe rolled onto her side to face him and punched him on the shoulder, immediately regretting it when her stomach lurched. 'Oh, Jeez.'

Matt grabbed hold of her wrist, smiling down into her eyes, 'I'm pretty sure you're not supposed to physically assault your employer.'

'It's a good thing I'm off duty today then.'

'It is. Are you okay? You've gone a shade of white I'm not sure

I've ever seen.'

Zoe breathed in and out deliberately, sweat breaking out on her forehead, another current of nausea making her bare her teeth. 'I think so.' Please, do not let me throw up in public, she thought. Still, it didn't stop her being aware that they were lying on the grass facing each other, her boobs only inches from his chest, their legs nearly entwined, his fingers stroking the inside of her wrist. A prickle of heat grew at the bottom of her spine and was echoed in her pelvis, expanding outwards along her nerve endings. She had a desperate urge to snuggle into him, to curl up against his warmth and ask him to stroke her hair. God, she was such a sap when she was hung over.

'Lie down,' he ordered, 'you can rest while we chat about Jasper's birthday and I'll make notes on my phone.' Waiting until she rearranged herself on the grass, an arm thrown over her forehead. 'So, what sort of thing do you think he'll want? Should we try and rent out a hotel or restaurant do you think?'

'He's going to be five, Matt,' she murmured, 'he doesn't need anything fancy. You don't like him and Aimee being exposed to publicity because of your fame, so why do something a typical celebrity would? You could take him and friends out to an activity-based party, or better yet, why don't you have a party at yours and book some entertainment?'

'Really? I suppose it would be nice for us to do normal.'

'It's definitely worth considering. Personally I think Jasper would love having his friends over and would appreciate you being there and just being his dad for the day. Besides, there's less than two week to go now. All the function spaces are going to be booked out, especially as its summer.' She sucked in her cheeks. 'Why not make it a themed party?'

'What theme?'

Lowering her sunglasses, she stared at him over the top of them.

'Oh,' he tutted at himself, 'Ben 10?'

'I'd say so.'

'What about food? Shall I get the caterers in?'

'If you're going for normality, we do it ourselves. We could do a finger buffet, this is a bunch of four and five year olds we're talking about after all, or we could—'

'What about a BBQ?' he interrupted eagerly. 'I'm not bad at those.'

'What is it about men, meat and fire?' she rolled her eyes and then groaned as the action sent fresh barbs of pain through her head. Why had she drunk so much? 'Yep,' she exhaled, 'I think that would work. Most kids like burgers and hot dogs, but we'll have to include vegetarian and gluten-free options.'

'It's a bloody minefield,' Matt commented, typing furiously on his mobile phone.

'I just hope enough kids are free to come,' Zoe frowned, 'with it being bank holiday on the Monday, people might be away for the weekend.'

'Do you know what?' Matt paused. 'If we're going to do it, let's go large. We'll invite loads of people, not just Jasper's friends but their nannies and parents too plus my friends and family. You should invite Rayne and Frankie as well, I'd love to meet them.'

'Why?' She tensed. What if one of them let something slip accidentally?

'Why not? If you're going to be with us for a while your friends should feel comfortable visiting. I know it's my son's birthday, but it would be a nice event for them to come to if there are a variety of people there. Right,' Matt went on, oblivious to Zoe's expression behind her sunglasses at his comment about staying for a while, 'let's talk about the guest list and the kind of entertainment Jasper might like …'

They spent the next twenty minutes discussing ideas and arrangements for the party until with a feigned sob of distress, Zoe begged Matt to save what they'd done and leave it alone. 'We'll divvy up the tasks tomorrow at breakfast,' she said, 'but please, let's have a quiet half hour now.'

'Aww, is it time for a nap?'

'Not quite, but my brain is grinding to a halt,' she admitted.

'Fair enough. I do appreciate you doing this on your day off you know, and for helping me. Thanks.'

'Thank you for making the effort to come to Hyde Park with the kids,' she said, 'I know it wasn't easy but they're really enjoying it. I think it'll make a difference to you all.'

'I think so too. You were right, and I'm glad you got me to consider it. I have to admit,' Matt sat up, removing his baseball cap and scrubbing his hand through his thick black hair, 'it's not been as bad as I thought. Walking in was hard, I'm surprised I didn't cut off the circulation to Aimee's hand, but once I got past the first five minutes and faced the memories,' he sucked in a deep breath, 'it got easier. It probably helped that I had you to make fun of,' he said with a straight face, putting the hat back on. 'It's been great entertainment.'

She sat up, sticking her tongue out at him and reaching for the hamper. 'Whatever. Come on, let's get the kids over and get stuck into this picnic.'

'You're okay to eat now?'

'I should probably try, you're right. And if I'm not,' she said tongue in cheek, 'I guess you and kids will just have to carry me home.'

13

It had been a good week, Zoe mused as she sat at the breakfast bar the following Saturday morning. She and Matt had barely had any time alone, but he'd eaten with them most nights and there had been an easy banter around the kitchen table as the kids chatted about what they'd got up to that day. For the most part, she'd been doing her share of secretly organising Jasper's party around looking after them. Sending Ben 10 invites out, following up with whispered phone calls to apologise for the short notice and checking if people could come, sorting out decorations and ringing around children's entertainers had kept her more than busy. The last task had proved to be a fruitless one because as predicted everyone was already booked for the peak summer season. Matt had suggested asking one of his world famous acts to come along and perform a mini-concert in the garden but Zoe vetoed the idea; it would be absolute mayhem with security and sound requirements and hardly up Jasper's street. He'd agreed, so they'd had to come up with some creative alternatives, usually discussed over text during the day so there was no danger of the kids overhearing.

Matt had started writing out a food list, thinking about a birthday present and enlisting friends to help out with the BBQ. On Friday they were going to traipse around a supermarket together to get the food and drinks while Sadie watched the kids. She was back at work part-time phasing her duties and hours up and had offered to watch Aimee and Jasper for a few hours. It wasn't really in her job description, but she was so insistent that Matt agreed. Zoe thought she was probably trying to get some practice in looking after kids, if she and her boyfriend were about to start actively trying for a baby.

Matt had pulled a face at the idea of a food shop, telling Zoe they could just get it delivered from a luxury food supplier he used, but she'd teased him that if he wanted normality for his kids, he should try normal too. Besides, it was part of the fun.

'Look at this!' Marching into the kitchen, Matt flung a news-paper down in front of her.

'What's the matter?' she frowned.

'Check page fifteen, celebrity news.' His lips were compressed, the scar above his lip burning white.

Pushing her coffee away, she flicked through the paper until she came to the article he was on about. *Matt Reilly In Love Again?* screamed the bold headline.

'Oh.'

'They're bloody vultures! Why can't I ever have any privacy? I wore a hat for God's sake.' Spinning away from her, he moved around the kitchen slamming cupboard doors, clattering mugs around and flinging a metal teaspoon down on the side. 'Bloody hell.'

'It can't be that bad.'

'Read it.'

Zoe bent her head over the paper as he made a coffee. Bugger. A picture of her and Matt filled half the page. They were lying on a patch of grass facing each other, his head tilted towards hers, his hand holding her wrist. They looked cosy, as if oblivious to the world around them. It must have been taken the previous Sunday at Hyde Park when she'd punched him for saying she smelt of alcohol. There was a smile on his face as he gazed down at her. Luckily her back was to the camera so they couldn't identify her, or see how awful she'd looked that day. But it was still invasive and disrespectful, not to mention pretty damning. No one studying the picture would think they were looking at a boss-employee relationship. Although from what she could remember the conversation had been an innocent one.

She scanned the article, which alleged that, '*A mere five weeks since his broken engagement with his celebrity pop star ex-fiancée, Matt has been spotted snuggling up in Hyde Park with his children's pretty new nanny.*'

'Oh, shit,' she cringed, face burning. They'd identified her despite the sunglasses. Still, as she read on, she was relieved to see they didn't seem to know much about her other than she'd started working for Matt recently and was thought to have spent a spell of time working abroad. It would have been worse if they'd mentioned all the gory details about Greg, or worse still, revealed her family, meaning Matt would have found out about her relationship to Melody in a horribly public way. If they kept digging into her background and published a follow up, he still could. Oh, double, triple shit. Panic filled her, clammy fingers smudging the black print of the newspaper into the margin. She should come clean as soon as possible. At least if the truth came directly from her, she would have a chance to explain things from her perspective.

She carried on reading, dreading what was coming next. The female celebrity journalist went on to set out Matt's dizzy climb to fame and the death of his wife three years before. It was written in as spectacular fashion as possible, pulling out all the old speculation and rumours about Helen's death. Zoe winced at the details, at the pain it must have caused him to read it. Turning the page to read the last paragraph, she found it bookended by another picture, this one taken later on in the afternoon when they'd had a lazy wander along the banks of the winding Serpentine. Aimee and Jasper were in the middle with Matt and Zoe bracketing them, all of their hands linked together so they formed a chain. They looked like a happy family.

'We have it on good authority that Matt used to visit Hyde Park with his late wife Helen and their children,' the reporter finished, 'and he's never been pictured with another woman there since, so could wife number two be on the horizon for our favourite home-grown music producer?'

'Oh, for the love of—' she hissed. Talk about leaping to conclusions. 'Now they've got us getting married? How totally ridiculous. They've included a photo of the kids too,' she scowled at Matt, protective instincts for Aimee and Jasper kicking in, anger rising in her throat. 'That's not on.'

To her surprise, he said nothing about the marriage rumour.

'No. It's definitely not.' He banged his coffee mug down on the counter, steaming black coffee sloshing over the sides. 'I work so hard to protect them and now they're splashed right across the national papers! Printing any of it in the first place isn't on either. They didn't even ask my PR Officer for a quote. I'm really pissed off,' he gritted his teeth. 'Sorry,' he added as an afterthought.

'Don't worry about it. The kids are still in bed and I've already sworn once. I'll make it twice. I'm pissed off too.' It felt like an unbearable violation, making something public that was a private moment. It felt knotty and uncomfortable, the notion of all those people up and down the country reading the paper over breakfast, making judgements and jumping to conclusions about her and Matt.

Her face burned brighter, chest itching. She scrunched her eyes up in horror at what she'd been planning to do to him with *Nannygate*. A kiss and tell story would have been so much worse than this. What the hell had she been thinking? She was unbearably relieved she'd not gone through with it. It would have hurt him and potentially the kids, exposing them to all sorts of scrutiny and unwanted attention. It would have hurt her too. Her reputation would have been shot and she wasn't sure she would have ever been able to look herself in the mirror again. Also, how could anyone have ever trusted her after that? Even if the article had been printed anonymously, it wouldn't have taken much for people around them to put two and two together and disclose who she was.

'They're comparing me to Jude Law.' Matt rubbed the back of his neck as she opened her eyes. 'The whole scandal with his nanny.'

'Well, that's rubbish. It's completely different. Jude Law was engaged when he had an affair with his nanny. You're single.' She stared at him, swallowing hard. 'Unless there's something you haven't told me.'

'What? Of course not.' Putting his hands on his hips, 'Do you really think I would have kissed you if I was involved with someone else?'

She dropped her gaze to the silver flecked black marble. 'Some guys wouldn't have a problem with it. Besides, it shouldn't have happened.'

He strode over to her, tilting her chin up with his finger. 'Hey,' he said fiercely, 'I'm not like that. I'm not your ex-fiancé. I don't start one thing unless I've ended another. I swear.'

The comment echoed through her mind as she tried to ignore the sparkling sensation on her skin that his touch caused. She'd heard something like it before. Where had it been? She strained to remember who'd said it but it eluded her like a cloudy dandelion seed dancing on the wind just out of reach.

'But you're right,' he added, 'it shouldn't have happened. We've got to control ourselves.'

'Yes,' her mouth dried up as her eyes flickered over his tall solid frame, his muscular thighs and broad shoulders lovingly outlined in the habitual jeans and t-shirt he wore. She wished he hadn't said that. Telling her they shouldn't give in just made her want him more. The curse of forbidden fruit was that it tasted even better when you caved to temptation and took what you wanted.

Matt stepped back and walked across the kitchen to grab a damp cloth. 'You uh, don't know anything about it, do you?'

'Know anything about what?'

Crossing back to the breakfast bar, he moved the mug and wiped up the coffee he'd spilt. 'The article. You didn't tell anyone where we were going?'

'Are you accusing me of tipping off the press?' Her voice shook with suppressed anger. She knew nothing about it. Still, the fact it was so damned close to what she'd originally intended sent a sharp stab of guilt through her.

'No. I'm just asking if there's a possibility—'

She leapt off the stool, its feet scraping on the tiled floor like the screech of chalk on a blackboard. 'No, Matt. I didn't tell anyone where we were going.' Her conscience was clear on that. 'I had nothing to do with this, nothing,' she emphasised, sweeping around the counter and standing in front of him. 'I wouldn't do that to you or the kids. And it's not just you affected, is it?' She crossed her arms. 'I'm right there in those photos and they've named me. People are going to assume we're sleeping together, which hardly makes me look professional. We look like …' she was going to say *we're in love*, but held back. That wasn't the case and it would just embarrass them both saying it out loud. She ran her hands through her hair, thinking of what Mel and Ruth were going to say. 'God, my family are going to be asking me all sorts of questions. What a mess!'

He studied her face, breathing hard. After a moment he slowly exhaled. 'You're right. I'm sorry. You're caught up in this too; I'm afraid it's one of the risks of working for me.' He touched her arm, 'I didn't mean to suggest you were involved. Sorry. I do trust you.'

Nodding, she squirmed. But he shouldn't have trusted her. This was getting even more complicated. 'That's okay, I understand you're upset. It was probably a natural question to ask,' she edged away from him, returning to her stool and picking up her lukewarm coffee. 'So, why do you think they waited until today to publish the story? They've sat on it for almost a week.'

'I should think it's because there's a higher circulation on a Saturday,' Matt answered with a bitter twist to his lips.

'Right. And what are we going to do about the article? Will you be taking legal advice?'

His mouth quirked at her use of the word *we*, but he didn't comment on it. 'I've already spoken to my solicitor, although I already knew the drill. It's too late for an injunction as they've already run the story. We could consider taking formal action against them for libel, but we'd have to prove defamation and that would be hard to evidence definitively.'

'Sorry, you've lost me. What does that mean, in words of one syllable?'

'Defamation is when a false claim is made. Libel is proving that what's been printed has caused me or my reputation injury or exposed me to public ridicule. It would be almost impossible to prove we're not in a relationship, with you living here and ...'

'And what?'

He looked her square on, 'With me not being able to swear openly and truthfully that there's never been anything between us.'

'I see,' she murmured, her tummy dipping like she was back home in Southend on a rollercoaster, the sea breeze flapping her hair around her face at the speed of the ride.

'As for the libel,' he continued when she didn't say anything more, 'it would be hard to prove the story has caused injury to the kids simply by being photographed and as for injury to me that would be even harder. I'm single so it doesn't put an existing relationship at risk or make me look like a cheating bastard. I do look like a bit of a player though, moving on from my supposed ex to you within weeks. I don't want it to look as though I'm a serial dater.'

'What, when the truth is that you don't date at all? Does it really matter what other people think? The two most important people in your life,' she pointed to the ceiling, 'won't know anything of what's going on unless you tell them.'

'I know that, and you have a valid point, but I still don't want people to see me that way when it's not the truth. They had no right to print the story,' he seethed.

'No, they didn't, but I guess it's the price you pay for doing what you do. You love what you do, right?'

'Yes,' he nodded, 'absolutely. So I suppose it's worth it. Not everyone gets to do something they're passionate about for a living, do they?' He paused, calming down. 'I am lucky for that. I'd hate to be stuck in a job I hated. Life is too short.' He looked pensive. 'To answer your earlier question, after speaking with my solicitor and considering the options, unfortunately there's no point in pursuing a case. It'll simply draw more attention to us. As my solicitor pointed out, today's newspaper is tomorrow's chip paper. If I don't respond or retaliate hopefully they'll get bored and move on. As for looking like a serial dater, I'll just have to make sure I'm not seen with anyone else.'

At his words, the memory she'd been reaching for earlier arrived in a flash. She pictured outspoken Monica with the other nannies the day Zoe had joined them in Green Park. The other woman had been criticising Mel's lousy taste in men. '*He's immature and spoilt, and a serial dater …. unfortunately he's not that great at finishing one thing before starting the next.*'

'So that you don't look like a serial dater like your brother?' Zoe blurted in reply to his comment.

'Where did you hear that?'

She shrugged. 'The other nannies talk, Matt.'

'Of course. Well, the rumours are probably true, so I can't really be angry. The truth is,' he rested a hip against the kitchen counter, looking troubled, 'that I love my brother, but he's not got the best track record with women.'

'What about Melody, your last nanny? What was he like with her? You said she broke his heart?' Rising from her seat she crossed the room, emptying the dregs of her coffee in the sink and bending over to load the mug into the dishwasher.

'He was different with her; he seemed to really care. That was probably why he took what happened so hard and was in such

509

a mess when she left. It would explain why he felt the need to get away.'

Breathing in deeply, she clutched the edge of the dishwasher door. *But she didn't just leave. You made her go, and without telling her why.* Straightening up, she opened her mouth to ask him outright what had happened. She would tell him why she wanted to know and confess that she was Melody's sister. It was time to get it out in the open. Even though a piece of her didn't want the answer because it would mean she no longer had a reason to stay, at least she would have closure for Mel. Plus, she couldn't do this anymore. Anxiety was gnawing at her stomach all the time, a grey cloud of apprehension hovering over her shoulder. With the newspaper article added in, it felt a hundred times worse. 'Matt,' she said shakily, 'I—'

'Morning, Zoe,' Aimee skipped into the kitchen fully dressed, hair combed into a neat ponytail. 'Morning, Daddy.' Putting a book down on the breakfast bar, she walked around the counter and put her arms around his waist.

'Morning. Did you sleep okay?' Returning the hug, he looked down into her face as she pulled away.

'Yes, thanks.'

'What are you reading?'

'The first Harry Potter book. I really enjoyed the studio tour but realised I've only seen the films, so wanted to read the books too.'

'That's a great idea,' Zoe said, slipping past the two of them and heading for the door, ridiculously pleased to see the new ease of affection between father and child. 'Let me know how you get on. I'm off out for the day. Have a good one.'

'Were you saying something, Zoe?' Matt asked as Aimee clambered onto a stool.

'Nothing important. It doesn't matter.' There was no way she was having this conversation in front of Aimee, it would have to wait until another opportunity to speak with him alone came up.

'Doing anything nice today?'

'I'm going to a few galleries and lunch with—' she almost said *my sister*, but held back at the last moment. It would create questions she wasn't prepared to answer in front of his daughter. She paused, wanting to be honest with him about at least one thing. 'With someone I haven't spent quality time with in a while,' she finished, smiling sadly. 'You know there are those people you drift away from sometimes that if you spend a few hours with it'll be like you were never apart? Today I'm seeing one of those people.'

'I've never really experienced that. I've never had enough people in my life to drift away from.'

'That's sad, Daddy,' Aimee said seriously, in the act of picking up her book. 'You need more friends.'

Matt's face relaxed and he laughed. Zoe couldn't help but join in.

'Yep, I probably do,' he agreed, leaning across the breakfast bar to run a hand over her silky auburn hair. 'But as well as Noel and Stephen, I've got Zoe now too, right?'

'Yes,' Aimee beamed.

Zoe bit the inside of her cheeks. What'd happened to the boss-employee relationship? Since when had she become his friend? The problem was, she couldn't deny it. The last thing he felt like was her employer. 'I've gotta go,' she muttered, stepping backwards. 'Tell Jasper I said good morning when he gets out of bed.'

'Will do.' Matt picked up his coffee, the action stretching his top across his toned chest.

God, the man was so hot he was virtually on fire.

'Will you be home for dinner?' he asked as she turned to leave.

'I don't know. I may stay out late. Don't wait for me. In fact,' maybe time away from him would be a good idea and Ruth might be willing to put her up for one night now they were on better terms, 'I might not be back until the morning.'

'Right,' a nerve pulsed in his jaw, eyes narrowing. 'Well, you're an adult. It's your decision.'

Zoe pulled a puzzled face. Why was he being so weird about it? It was her day off tomorrow too.

He cleared his throat as Aimee gave him a look that echoed her nanny's. 'Never mind,' he said. 'Will you uh, be back in time to come to Hyde Park for a picnic with us tomorrow?'

'You want to do that? Even with …?' she gestured to the newspaper by his elbow.

Aimee cast an anxious look between them, 'Yes, Zoe, you've got to come. Pleeeeeease? Jasper will want you too as well.'

'I'm not going to let them stop me living my life,' Matt answered. 'The kids enjoy it, so that's the only thing I need to know. We'll just have to get better at disguises.'

'Disguises?' Aimee wrinkled her nose.

'I'll tell you about it later,' he squeezed his daughter's shoulder.

'Okay, if I stop out, I'll be back in time for the picnic,' Zoe agreed, not sure if it was the best idea. 'See you later.'

As she ran to her room to pack an overnight bag, the newspaper article weighed heavily on her mind. She thought about the softness in Matt's face as he gazed down at her in the main photo, and the other picture of them together with the kids, playing happy families. She thought about her reasons for coming here and the way she'd grown to care about Matt and his children. Then she thought about the fact she wasn't being honest with him and how the concept of leaving them caused her real, visceral pain and a sense of loss so acute it made her want to double over.

Physical disguises weren't the only type, she realised. There were emotional ones too; you could hide the truth from yourself as well as other people.

The next week passed in a flurry of activity which included taking the kids to the uniform shop to get ready for school. They were due to start on the Wednesday following Jasper's party, so she was in danger of running out of time. Matt was busy finishing a project in order to have Saturday off for the party, so Zoe took them alone. Nearly crying with pride when Jasper came out of the changing room looking both incredibly grown up while still just a baby, she sent Matt a photo of him in the grey trousers and red polo top with the emblem of the infant school on the chest. He was so impossibly cute in the outfit with his rounded cheeks and big green eyes.

> **Just look at how adorable your son is. Having a #proudnanny moment right now. Z :-)**

> **Sorry I couldn't be there, but having a #ProudDad moment too. Will ask him about it over dinner. M :-)**

> **p.s. don't cook tonight, will treat us to a take away.**

Aimee walked around the shop solemnly, picking out grey tights and gingham red hair bands to go with the white blouse, red jumper and grey skirt Zoe had already set aside with the help of a knowledgeable staff member. Remarking to her nanny that she was looking forward to going back to school to learn more, Aimee added pencils, a maths set and notebooks to the pile with a pleased expression that was utterly adorable.

How was she ever going to leave them? Zoe agonised.

Now it was the day of Jasper's birthday party and she wasn't any closer to an answer. There had been no chance to speak to Matt alone either. He'd been getting home excruciatingly late from his city studio, or they'd both been with the kids, or organising the party or he'd been down in the basement.

Stepping from the kitchen out onto the decking, Zoe peered up at the clear sky which was so bright it looked leached of colour, unlike the deep blue of the previous few days. The guests had started arriving half an hour before and the party was going well so far, pop music playing in the background from an iPod and speakers set up on the wooden table between the sun loungers, clusters of children and adults dotted around the emerald lawn laughing and chatting. The day had dawned warm and sunny, and it was beautiful BBQ weather. It was all just about perfect. The complete opposite to the crappy excuses she was making to herself about failing to come clean with Matt. The fact was she should have told him but hadn't. She didn't want to, wanted just a little more time. *I'll get them settled at school and then I'll sit down with Matt and tell him everything,* she promised herself.

It was no wonder she wasn't ready to let it all go yet. The latest picnic in Hyde Park the previous Sunday had been hilarious and they'd had the best fun together. Wearing matching baseball caps like an American family, Zoe and Aimee's hair tucked up inside theirs as part of their makeshift disguises, Matt had also bought them all silly eighties-style neon framed sunglasses and suggested they wear their most casual, grotty clothes. For Matt that meant a pair of discoloured grey deck shorts and a black t-shirt from college with a logo so faded it was indecipherable and a rip along the armpit seam. Zoe put on her denim shorts and a bright red baggy top that fell off one shoulder. She'd once worn it to paint a room, meaning there were streaks and splashes of ivory paint all over it. Jasper was in incredibly tight Ben 10 shorts and a t-shirt he'd grown out of the year previously but had insisted on keeping and Aimee had cheated by claiming she had no grotty clothes, wearing a pale pink dress with a belt that tied in a bow at the back.

They looked like the most mismatched group ever and Zoe had been aware of people giving them funny looks the whole afternoon. That hadn't been helped when Jasper jumped into the Serpentine from the pedalo he'd been on with his dad after deciding he was too hot. It had resulted in a damp, uncomfortable walk for him across to the modern kids' playground on the southern boundary of the park, which was Japanese in appearance with a climbing frame that looked like it was made from giant green and beige bamboo shoots. Once Jasper had dried out and the children had played, Matt had treated them all to ice-cream cones as they meandered home. Zoe had presumed Matt would be twitchy at the potential for the press to be camped out looking for them, but if he was it didn't show. On the contrary, he'd seemed to enjoy himself and at one point had slung a companionable arm around her shoulders, until with a sigh of regret and a hot twist in her stomach she'd eased away from the warmth of his body and fresh sexy scent of his aftershave. He'd been so relaxed that day she'd been able to convince him to invite Helen's mum to her grandson's birthday celebration after only a few minutes of persuasion.

Muttering that she was, 'impossibly stubborn,' Matt had rolled his eyes.

'Guilty!' Zoe had laughed, dancing away from him, holding Aimee's hand.

Padding along the decking in her jewel-encrusted sandals and down the stairs onto the grass, Zoe pushed the happy memories away to focus on Jasper's party. She was pleased at what they'd been able to achieve in just two weeks. Hanging from the apple tree was a bespoke Ben 10 Piñata full of goodies, the children taking turns with a solid plastic stick to batter it until sweets tumbled out at their feet. Frankie's boyfriend Zack was supervising the action, making sure that none of the kids got stick-happy or overzealous. He was good- looking in a pleasant way, his fair hair brushing his collar at the back and a dimple in one cheek that was higher than the norm adding a mischievousness to his face. He seemed like a sweet guy from what she'd seen so far. Frankie was laughingly supervising him in turn, clad in shorts and a long white button-down shirt, face tilted back as she giggled at something he said.

Zoe had decided that as much as she was worried about her friends letting something slip by accident, she trusted them and

515

needed their support. Having them here would help her feel less outnumbered by Matt's friends and family, along with the parents and nannies of Jasper's friends. The only people who were missing were Matt's parents. He'd told her they were on a cruise and not due back for another few weeks, but she wondered if they'd have come even if they were back from the Caribbean. Apart from the time they'd spoken about his childhood and their past relationships, Matt barely said a word about them.

Strolling down the garden, she fiddled with the Ben 10 plates, napkins and cups that were set up on a table against the garden fence, accompanied by endless rows of bottled fizzy pop and jugs of iced water and orange squash. A variety of sauces and pickles were lined up in jars near heaving bowls of deli-style coleslaw and potato salad, numerous containers of crisps and dips set out alongside them next to plates of ready-cut seedless burger baps and hot dog rolls. Matt's eyes had nearly popped out of his head at the amount of food they'd bought at the supermarket the previous day. Two trolleys had been needed to get it all back to the Prius, but Zoe had told him it was better to have too much than not enough, offering to go halves with him if he couldn't afford it. Matt had laughingly told her to shut up and get in the car.

She swept her eyes across the lawn. Set against the back fence was a bouncy castle that children were crawling, roly-polying and jumping in and out of at will, and a small ramp next to it with micro-scooters should any of the children be feeling particularly active or brave. Although it was anchored with ropes, Rayne was keeping a tally on how many kids were using the bouncy castle so that there was no danger of it tipping over. Her black bob and cocktail rings flashed in the sunlight as she counted them in and out with a stopwatch on her mobile phone. In her short Indian print dress, she was like an exotic colourful flower in a bed of plain English daisies, and Adam was hardly able to keep his eyes off her. Standing a few feet away to look after the kids using the ramp, his attention continually returned to his girlfriend. Zoe took in the tattoo on one of his brawny arms peeking out from a short-sleeved top, his short brown hair and the soft stubble covering his jaw. Rayne was right; he did look a bit like the actor Tom Hardy nowadays. Though from the giant hug he'd given Zoe on arrival and the soppy expression on his face now, he didn't have the hard-edged mob persona of Tom's most famous roles.

The massive double BBQ was in the far corner, manned by Matt and his best friend Noel, who'd she'd finally met when he'd arrived late morning to help set up. He was around the same height as Matt but with light brown hair, brown eyes and a friendly face. Zoe hadn't been able to see the grumpiness that Jasper had first talked about, but as she saw him concentrating on methodically turning sausages, his features settled into a fierce frown. Ahh, there it was. Equally she could see that Jasper had been right about Noel's girlfriend Holly. As the tall blonde walked gracefully towards the BBQ, her boyfriend glanced up. On seeing her he grinned, eyes lighting up. 'Come here, gorgeous,' he called.

'Whaddya want?' she asked playfully.

Pointing a finger at her, he mouthed *you*.

'Nah, I'm all right thanks,' she stuck her tongue out, 'I have other boys to look after.' Smiling cheekily she turned and made her way towards a group of children bouncing around on space hoppers, herding them away from the sumptuous white rose beds. Shaking his head as he watched her, Noel turned and made a remark to Matt, who smiled and clapped him on the back.

Matt was looking particularly gorgeous and summery in a pair of shorts and short-sleeved white shirt that showed off his black hair and forest green eyes. Zoe had spent the morning trying to avoid him so that she didn't do anything stupid. Every time she got near him her fingers twitched to undo his shirt buttons and her palms itched to smooth over his naked, hairy skin.

She'd spent over an hour hanging red, white and blue bunting along the fences to keep out of his way, followed by twisting tiny white fairy lights around the apple tree's branches and the decking rail in case the party went on into the evening. The overall effect of the garden was lovely, a mixture of British tea-party and sticky, good old fashioned fun for the children. Seeing that everything was under control for the moment and with the burgers, hot dogs and chicken on its way to being served, Zoe grabbed one of the red and white striped deckchairs she'd hired. Sinking down into it with a blissful moan, she smoothed the full skirt of her strapless watermelon coloured sundress over her knees. Getting up at half past five and running around like a mad thing ever since had been a mistake. She was knackered already and there were hours left to go. This might be her only chance to sit down for a while.

Rolling her head to the side, she watched Matt's tall, lean, dark-haired cousin Nathan for a moment. He was standing by a table full of assorted tumblers, glasses, drinks cartons and wide mouthed bottles. Shaking virgin cocktails and flipping plastic shakers over his shoulder and under his arm rapidly to entertain a group of children—mostly girls—he was mesmerising. They were all gawping in awe at his mixology skills. Among the five year olds sitting cross-legged on the lush lawn was a young petite blonde with rippling gold hair flowing down her back. Dressed in hip-hugging jeans and a red belly top, she looked just as impressed as the younger members of the audience but with an appreciative glint to her eye. Zoe assumed she was Nathan's girlfriend, Sofia. It was confirmed when he winked at her and she raised an eyebrow suggestively in response.

'Hi,' a guy with an open face and shaggy brown hair folded himself down into the deckchair next to Zoe.

'Hello,' she turned to him, wondering who he was. 'Sorry, it's been a bit hectic today, have we met?'

'Not yet,' he lifted a hand in easy greeting. 'I'm Leo.'

Zoe screwed up her face, trawling her memory.

'I'm Georgiana's boyfriend.' He pointed to a girl who was talking to Matt. Her brown hair was swept back in an intricate knot and she was wearing a black eye patch decorated with coloured gems.

518

There was a faint scar down one side of her face from her cheekbone to her pink mouth. It was a shame her skin was marred by it, but she was beautiful anyway.

'She's pretty,' Zoe observed, remembering something Aimee had said, 'and Matt's cousin, right?'

'That's the one,' Leo answered, his head tilting to track Georgiana's movements toward the bouncy castle. She walked with a slight limp, favouring her left leg, but didn't appear self-conscious about it. 'Matt and the kids seem happier,' he said, glancing back to Zoe. 'Correction, I mean happy. The last time I was here they hardly spent any time in the same room together and were pretty rigid with each other. I'm guessing you're the one to thank for the change.'

Zoe flushed. 'He wasn't doing such a bad job before I arrived. Neither was his last nanny.'

'It's nice of you to say that, as well as loyal, but I work with children with special educational needs,' he explained, 'so I'm very aware of behaviours and emotions. I told George after our last visit that something needed to change, but I didn't feel it was my place to say anything to Matt, not when I've only been part of the family for six months. They're not completely at ease with each other yet but they will be. You're getting them there, right? I've seen how you are with the kids, so positive but firm too. You're the same with Matt.'

'You got all that from the last half an hour?'

'Don't look so surprised. I can see that caring for other people is an instinct in you. It comes naturally. I wouldn't be surprised if you had a younger brother or sister. Am I right?'

'Yeah.' Shifting with discomfort at his probing, she toed her sandals off and curled her feet into the grass, the soft blades tickling her soles. 'You're very perceptive. Are you sure you're not a woman?' she said, trying to distract him from further questions, before colouring and wondering if he might be offended. 'Sorry.'

'It's cool. No, I'm definitely a man,' Leo grinned, 'and thank

519

god. Because I've met her,' he pointed at Georgiana, 'and she's the love of my life. Last Valentine's Day on Primrose Hill was the best day ever. I'd given her a reason not to trust me, although it was a misunderstanding really, but she came and found me anyway. We sat drinking champagne and eating a picnic overlooking the London skyline.'

'In February?' she gave a mock shiver.

'I brought blankets, hats and hand warmers too.'

'Oh, that's lovely,' Zoe blinked, 'so romantic and thoughtful. She's lucky to have you. Not a lot of guys these days know how to do old-fashioned romance.'

'No. I'm lucky to have her, and she makes me want to do those things for her, just to see the expression on her face. Plus, everyone's idea of romance is different, isn't it?' Pausing, he stared off into the distance as if recalling another memory, before shaking his hair out of his eyes. 'Anyway.'

'Anyway?'

'Matt's a good guy you know. Despite his issues.'

'Why are you telling me this? And what issues?' No way was she going to be the one to reveal anything first.

'I'm telling you because I think you should know, and as for issues, it's obvious he's still grieving.'

'Hmmm,' she made a non-committal sound as Matt flipped a sizzling burger and let out a shouting laugh when it landed on the grill and the BBQ smoke turned grey, wafting up into his face. He waved his hand over it, dispersing it jokingly towards Noel. 'Why do you think he's such a good guy?' she asked curiously. There was something about Leo that made her feel comfortable, even if some of the conversation was challenging. She got the sense he cared deeply about people. He also didn't seem to have any hidden agendas.

'He's the reason Georgiana and her parents could move to London for a fresh start after her accident. He owns a few properties and lets them stay in one rent-free. They insist on paying the bills of course, but he could still make a killing if he rented it out to someone else because of its location near Primrose Hill.'

'He's doing it because they're family,' she reflected. 'I guess it must be the house he bought when he and Helen got married.'

Leo jerked his head back, surprised. 'He's talked to you about her?'

'A bit. Sometimes. Her mum's here today. I thought it might be nice for all of them.'

'Wow, you're either a hypnotist or a miracle worker. As far as George is concerned, he doesn't talk to anyone about Helen and as far as I know he's never invited Cynthia into this house. The poor woman's not made it across the threshold in the last three years. Maybe he wants to keep it all separate in his head. You know he never lived here with Helen, don't you? He and the kids moved in a couple of months after she died.'

'Really? I hadn't realised. He never said.' She didn't suppose it had been relevant for Melody to mention either. She was oddly relieved. Helen had never been a presence here in this house because of the lack of photos and mementoes, but she'd still wondered a couple of times how Matt felt about going to bed in the room they'd shared. It had made her feel both sad for him but uncomfortable too, because of the tiny sting of jealousy.

'Well, he doesn't open up very often, does he? Most of the stuff I know is either from George or my own observations. What I want to know is how you managed to convince him to invite Cynthia?'

'I have no idea. Maybe he's just turning into a softie,' she murmured.

'Or maybe it's something else,' his gaze drifted over to Matt. 'I saw the newspaper article with the photos of you together.'

She groaned, thinking of Matt's reaction and the concerned, questioning phone calls she'd had to deal with from Ruth and Melody, her sister telling her in no uncertain terms to drop it and get out from under Matt's roof ASAP. It had taken more than twenty minutes to convince Mel that she could handle herself. 'It was awful,' Zoe answered Leo. 'He was so furious. I hate that they printed the photo of the kids and I also feel totally violated. The thought off all those people speculating that we're in a relationship, with me being his nanny,' shaking her head, 'gossiping and assuming that we're …'

'Assuming that you're in love,' he filled in dryly. 'Yeah, what a shocking idea.'

'What do you mean?' she asked in a high-pitched voice. She fanned her face, the sun's rays pounding down on their heads.

He dropped his voice. 'Well, it wouldn't be the worst thing in the world, Matt being loved up after so many years alone. You seem like a good person and you're great with the kids. I get that it's complicated with you working for him, but that shouldn't be a barrier if you really like each other. But please be careful with Aimee and Jasper; they've already lost too many people.' He unfolded himself from the deckchair, standing up and looking down at where she sat with her mouth agape. 'I'm sorry if I've been a bit blunt, Zoe. I hope I haven't upset you, especially when we don't know each other. I'm just looking out for Matt and the children. There are other reasons I'm grateful to him on George's behalf, so anything I can do to return the favour …' His mouth curved into a smile that could probably get anyone to forgive him anything. 'George often tells me I have a habit of saying exactly what I think, even when I shouldn't. It was nice to meet you. Hopefully we'll catch up again later.' He loped off before she had time to recover or reply, crossing the grass and sliding an arm around Georgiana's waist, dropping a kiss on her forehead when she turned to him.

Zoe clicked her mouth shut. Where had all that come from? Who had told him that she and Matt liked each other? She should probably be pissed off with him for being so outspoken when they were strangers, but there had been a complete lack of guile in his eyes that said he was only saying those things because he cared and thought it was the right thing to do. He seemed like a nice guy and there had been no trace of cockiness in his voice.

She sighed, thinking of his words. Shame and regret twisted together in her chest. Leo thought she was a good person, that she was great for Matt and the kids. On one level he might be right, somehow how they were making it work, the four of them. But on another level he was absolutely wrong. How was someone who had arrived in their lives with the sole intention of hurting Matt and then leaving, a good person?

It wasn't something she had time to fret over because as she started pushing herself from her seat, Cynthia sank down gracefully in the chair Leo had just vacated, a silk lilac high-collared dress making her look very Lady of the Manor.

'Good afternoon, Zoe. How are you?' She kept her eyes on her grandson, who was currently bouncing on a yellow space hopper, burbling in glee as he and his friends bumped each other playfully.

'Fine, thanks.' They'd met in passing a few times when the woman had come to drop the kids off and Zoe had thought her very polite, though a little reserved. 'And you?'

'I'm exceptionally well today. Thanks to you. It's so lovely to see Jasper enjoying himself, and Aimee too.' She pointed an elegant finger at the girl, who was launching herself into the bouncy castle under Rayne's watchful eye.

Zoe smiled. 'Matt and I organised the party together, I can't take all the credit.'

'The party is delightful, but I was talking about the fact that I'm here to see it in the first place. I suspect I owe that to you, and I'm very grateful.'

Zoe scrunched her fingers into the skirt of her green dress. Cynthia's comment was an echo of the last bit of her conversation with Leo, and it made her feel like a fraud. 'It's nothing. He was happy for you to be here,' she answered diplomatically, 'and it's nice for the kids.'

'Nonetheless,' Cynthia studied Zoe's averted face, 'in three years I have never been invited to any of the children's parties and neither have I been asked to come into the house. The only factor that is different about the equation is you. I'm not criticising Matthew, you understand. He's been wonderful in letting me maintain my relationship with Jasper and Aimee and he's happy for them to come and visit me, even if they find it a little raw.'

'Because you remind them of their mum?' Zoe guessed.

Cynthia dipped her head, 'I wasn't sure at first why they always seemed so unsettled with me. I thought I was too strict for them, or they didn't know me well enough. However, over time it's become apparent that the photographs of Helen in my home are the only ones they have access to, and that I'm the only one who talks to them about her.'

'I don't think it's deliberate on his behalf,' Zoe defended, relaxing her hands and looking at Cynthia, 'but I understand it's important for them and you to keep her memory alive. It's just very painful for him, I think.'

'There is no doubt he finds it hard, however—'

'Do you know that they've started visiting the memorial plaque in Hyde Park for her again?' She held a hand up, 'I'm sorry to interrupt, but I really think he's trying and you need to know that. The children talk to me about your daughter too sometimes, and when they do I encourage them to remember the happy times.'

'Yes, I was aware of the picnics in Hyde Park, I've seen the paper, the pictures of you all.' Her lips tightened.

'It's not his fault. We didn't know the press were there, and he definitely didn't want the kids splashed across the tabloids.' She paused, wondering whether to say the next bit or not, but feeling like Cynthia might need the reassurance. 'I'm not trying to replace Helen. I wanted him to start going to Hyde Park again because I feel the three of them need it. I'm just the nanny.' Even as the words poured from her lips, her face was tingling with a blush. Technically she *was* the nanny, but she'd never had a post that felt less like a job. She'd never had a post where she'd kissed her boss, or had come to care so much for her charges.

'I'm annoyed that the press are interfering,' Cynthia said crisply, 'but I don't blame him for the newspaper article. I suppose I could because by being his children they're automatically subject to that kind of interest, but I've seen how much he loves music, and how he's always tried to protect them from public scrutiny. At heart he is a good father.'

'He is.' Zoe watched as Matt starting serving burgers onto a large ceramic plate, movements fluid and face cheerful. When first arriving she'd been horrified at the disconnect between him and the kids, how much he distanced himself from them, but he had taken on board all the things she'd said, and what she'd seen recently was someone doing his best for his children, no matter what the personal cost to him. He genuinely loved them, she had no doubt about that, and Leo was right, they would get there. To a place they should be, where they were secure and comfortable in each other's company. The question was, would she be around when it happened?

'As for the other, no-one could ever replace my daughter, however Matthew does need to move on. Everybody does.' She paused. 'He blames himself, you know.'

'Sorry?' Zoe frowned.

'For Helen's death.' The pale blue eyes that lifted to Zoe's were haunted, grief etching lines into her face. 'It wasn't his fault though. My daughter was headstrong and made the decision to get into that car all by herself.' She put a hand to her chest, rubbing the spot over her heart. 'I've tried to talk to him about it, but he doesn't want to. He simply shuts me out.' She paused again, nodding to herself. 'I can't bring my daughter back, but I can make sure her children are happy, and they won't be unless he is. He deserves to be happy in his own right.'

'Of course,' Zoe agreed automatically. Why did people keep telling her these things today? It was like they were trying to give her their approval, or sell Matt to her as a catch. But he didn't want to be caught. He'd been very clear he wasn't looking for a relationship with anyone—let alone his kid's nanny. Her right hand rose to her chest, unconsciously mirroring Cynthia's pose, covering the same spot over her heart, trying to rub away the ache.

14

Lying back on the sun lounger with her legs curled under her, Zoe let out an exhausted but happy sigh. The food had been devoured under the baking sun, the children had played riotously for hours, the birthday cake's candles had been blown out by a puff-cheeked Jasper and most people had gone home around seven o'clock contentedly clutching party bags and extra chicken. Cynthia had offered at the last minute to have the children overnight and as it was Jasper's actual birthday a few days later rather than today, after a moment's hesitation Matt had agreed. Jasper and Aimee had seemed happy to go, the little boy's eyes starting to go heavy-lidded from the afternoon's excitement. He'd still been insistent on taking all his presents with him to unwrap however, so after some wrangling and Cynthia promising to make a list of the gifts and who had given them for Jasper to write thank you notes that had been agreed too. Zoe had chucked their things into bags while Matt had said goodbye to the last of the parents and nannies, and then they'd loaded Cynthia's car up together with the kids and their belongings, waving them off with matching expressions of relief. It had been a long day.

A few select friends and family members had stayed for some adult chill out time, and after picking at the buffet again and having more than a few alcoholic drinks, it had seemed like an exceptionally good idea to take turns on the bouncy castle, space hoppers and even the micro-scooters. Several people had fallen off various pieces of equipment, and general hilarity had ensued. It was hard to imagine they were all tax-paying adults, Matt had remarked, just before he'd slid sideways off the space hopper and onto the grass, causing hysterics. Now they were all sitting on the decking, the light fading as it ticked towards midnight, the evening winding down. Zoe had turned the fairy lights on and lit some citronella candles to keep the mosquitoes away. It was pretty and relaxing, and she stifled a yawn behind one hand, feeling mellow and trying not to think about how great it'd been to see Matt shrug off his responsibilities and take joy in some innocent though drunken fun.

'Here you go,' he handed her a glass of sparkling water and sat on the other lounger clutching a bottle of Mexican beer.

'Thanks.' She'd had more than enough alcohol, and had a sinking feeling a hangover was in her near future.

Across from Matt, Leo lounged in a deckchair, Georgiana sitting on a cushion at his feet so he could idly stroke her dark hair, which he'd unwound from its knot. Next to them, Nathan and Sofia were cosying up on the wooden bench they'd carried from the bottom of the garden, Nathan's arm resting around Sofia's shoulders and idly stroking her slim forearm. Holly and Noel had said they were leaving an hour before but were still reclining in deckchairs a few inches apart, their joined hands dangling in the space between them. Frankie and Zack were cuddling in a cushioned wicker two-person love seat that had been delivered that morning at Matt's request, and Rayne was sitting on Adam's lap on a wooden lawn chair, her arm curled around his neck, resting up against him as she sipped a tall glass of Pimms.

The couples all looked happy and in love and Zoe was pleased for them, but creeping jealousy coiled in her stomach anyway. She stole a look at Matt, wishing she had the right to sit on his lap like that, knowing at the same time that the thought was utterly crazy. Eyes stinging, she gazed at the fairy lights twisted around the decking rail until their bulbs had burnt dancing dots into her retinas.

'I swear to god I'm going to bruise,' Sofia muttered, rubbing her hip. 'We are such children.'

'Stop moaning woman,' Nathan said good-naturedly, 'a tumble off a micro-scooter is nothing. You do far worse to yourself when you come off your skateboard.'

'Or when you miscalculate with one of your cocktail shakers and it flies across the room at me,' she quipped back immediately, causing howls of laughter among the group.

'I'm surprised at you, Matt,' Georgiana tilted her head to look at her cousin when everyone had calmed down, uncovered blue eye twinkling, 'given you're the oldest by far and one of the hosts of this party, I thought you'd have been ordering us off the stuff, not taking the lead.'

'Hey, less of the old,' he exclaimed, 'I'm only thirty. And I know how to have fun, just like anyone else. Besides, my kids weren't around to see it, so I wasn't setting a bad example for them, was I?'

Zoe lifted her head, 'I think they'd have enjoyed seeing you like that actually. Although, probably not drunk.'

'You can be quiet,' Matt teased, 'you should have been keeping me on the straight and narrow as the other responsible adult in the house. But no,' he said mournfully, 'a few glasses of wine and the strict nanny persona goes completely out the window.'

'It probably went to the same place as your grumpy, serious *I'm a very important and dedicated music producer* guise,' she answered, raising one eyebrow.

'God, you are so cheeky sometimes,' he shot back, grinning and raising his glass, 'cheers to that.'

Rayne mumbled something into Adam's ear and then stumbled off his lap. 'Right, we're off, guys,' she said, 'it's been fab, but I'm whacked. It was lovely to meet you, Matt,' she gave him a brief hug and turned to Zoe, holding her arms out.

Zoe jumped off the lounger and swayed. 'Oops,' she giggled. 'Great to see you, speak soon.'

'Call me if you need anything,' Rayne whispered in her ear as they hugged, breath sweet with alcohol, 'and be careful.'

'Huh?' Zoe pulled back.

Rayne fluttered her eyelashes and patted Zoe's cheek. 'You know what I mean.' Her eyes flickered to Matt, who was shaking Adam's hand.

'Whatever,' Zoe tutted. 'Night, Rayne. Adam,' she wrapped her arms around him and squeezed, 'it's been lovely seeing you again.'

'Not quite like the uni days,' he grinned, 'but pretty close, huh? I remember the night with the trolleys …'

Zoe chuckled, before yawning again. 'Let's have that conversation another night.'

'Fair enough,' he released her and stepped back. 'Come on, you,' he turned to Rayne, 'let's get some fresh air and walk down to Hyde Park Corner to get a cab.'

She grabbed his arm, snuggling into his side, 'Good idea, lover.'

Their departure caused a flurry of activity and Zoe and Matt were soon waving everyone off, agreeing they'd do it again sometime.

Leo leaned back against the front door waiting while Georgiana and Matt said their goodbyes on the gravel driveway. He looked at Zoe, who was standing next to him on the top step. 'Was I out of line earlier?'

'Probably,' she said in a light tone, studying his face, 'but don't worry about it. It's done now and I bear no grudges.'

He smiled, 'You're cool. I like you, Zoe.'

'Why thank you, kind sir,' she did a mock curtsy but the effect was ruined when she tripped over her own feet and ended up clutching his arm for balance. 'I did *not* mean to do that.'

Shaking his head, he laughed. 'Not very elegant.'

'Everything okay?' Matt appeared next to them, a mild frown on his face as he took in Zoe's hand on Leo's arm.

'Fine. I nearly fell over,' she hiccupped, transferring her hand to Matt's forearm, 'I'm happy for you to prop me up instead.'

Matt's expression eased, 'No problem. Night, Leo.'

'Night, Matt. See you soon. Zoe,' he nodded, walking backwards down the stairs to join his girlfriend. Putting his arm around her waist, they wandered off, heads together as they talked, Georgiana limping slightly.

Matt escorted Zoe inside, locking the front door behind them. 'Have fun?'

'Yes,' she nodded solemnly, 'but I have a horrible feeling I'm going to pay for it in the morning.'

'Well, at least the kids aren't here first thing,' he said, 'we have the house to ourselves.'

'Yes.' Her mouth dried up as they stood in the shadows at the bottom of the stairs.

'What did you think of Leo?' Matt asked suddenly.

'He's a nice guy. A bit blunt, but nice.'

'It looked like he was flirting with you.' Shoving his hands in his pockets.

'What? Don't be silly!' She let out a disbelieving laugh. 'He absolutely adores your cousin. I can't imagine him doing that to her. We were just being friendly, there's nothing between us. If anything, he was encouraging me—'

'What?'

'Nothing,' she licked her lips.

'What was he encouraging, Zoe?' His voice was low.

'It doesn't matter.'

Matt took a step forward, hands sliding from his pockets. 'It does. Tell me.'

'No, it doesn't, because it's something you've already decided can't happen.' The remark slipped out, the wine fogging her common sense.

'Something—? Oh. Us?' Stepping nearer, he caged her in against the wall with his arms, body aligned to hers, green eyes starting to simmer.

'There is no us,' she breathed, gulping as she felt the heat of his skin. He was so big and strong and gorgeous, it was torture being this close to him and knowing she shouldn't get any closer.

'Maybe I was wrong. Maybe there is.' His eyes gleamed and he shifted nearer, dipping his head towards hers.

She groaned. 'You're drunk, Matt.'

'So?' Leaning in, he kissed her gently, sliding his tongue across her bottom lip and then nibbling it with his white, even teeth.

Sighing, she tilted her head back and opened her mouth, inviting him in. With a sound at the back of his throat, his kiss deepened, their tongues tangling. Their hands grabbed at each other and her fingers dug into his bum to haul his hips in against hers.

He jerked away, panting. 'Jesus, Zoe.'

'You'll regret it in the morning,' she whispered, staring at his mouth, watching it getting ready to form more words that were totally irrelevant because all she was listening to was what her body was telling her, which was to rip his clothes off and sink into him. Let him fill her, hold her and take her. Now. Hotly and desperately. Nothing else mattered. Her reasons for being here, her dishonesty, her need to tell him who she was and what she'd come to do, all faded. She was sick and tired of fighting the sexual spark between them. Tired of fighting her feelings for him. Tired of fighting herself. It was exhausting.

'I want you, Zoe. More than you can know,' he said hoarsely. 'And I'm pleasantly drunk, not hammered. So what if I regret it in the morning? All I care about is now.'

His comment was like a vat of iced water being tipped over her. If he'd have said he wouldn't regret it, that they could find a way to make things work, then she'd have launched herself at him again, kissed him until he begged her to stop. But he was agreeing he would regret it, and things were bad enough without adding extra dollops of guilt and shame to the mix.

'Then, goodnight.' With curled fists she slid out sideways from beneath his arms, and sprinted up the stairs as if the Ripper was on her heels along a cobbled London street.

'Zoe, wait,' Matt called after her.

But she ignored his words and flew up the two spiral staircases, not stopping until she'd slammed into her bedroom and was resting up against the door. Don't think about his kisses, *don't* think about his kisses, she commanded herself tipsily. So of course she thought about his kisses. Her hands fisted again and her heart pounded in her chest, lust scorching her face as she recalled how devastating and sexy those stolen moments had been.

Kicking off her sandals she flung them into a corner and wrenched the green dress over her head. Maybe a cold shower would help. It was what guys did when they were frustrated. God, was she frustrated. They had been so close, so close to … Yes, a cold shower. It might be the only alternative to going downstairs, pinning her boss down on the floor, peeling his clothes off and riding him until—

'Shit!' She was losing her mind. The sooner she could get into the shower the better. The sooner she could get out of this house the better. Turning as a knock sounded on the door, her mouth opened, 'Wai—' but the handle turned and Matt strode in before she could finish. Her hands flew up to cover her cleavage and she took a step backwards, the back of her knees hitting the bed. 'Matt, you're supposed to wait after knocking before coming in.'

'You're in your underwear,' he said stupidly, blinking as he took in her pale, creamy curves in the black strapless bra and shortie knickers.

'That's what happens when you take your clothes off,' she said breathlessly, rational thought fleeing at the way he was gazing at her so blatantly, so appreciatively, so hungrily. It had made her feel amazing and indescribably sexy, as if she was the most beautiful woman in the world. It was a heady feeling, but it was less about her ego and more about it feeling like he wanted her as much as she wanted him. It also put a serious dent in her willpower, making

533

it that much harder to resist the overpowering urge to give into the magnetizing chemistry between them. Their gazes clashed. Hot sexual awareness flashed between them, his eyes darkening, reading the message in hers. Her mouth went dry, her lips parted slightly and the oxygen in her lungs hitched.

He kicked the door shut deliberately, and with intent.

'What are you doing?' her voice shook.

'I won't regret it in the morning,' he grated. 'How the hell could I? Look at you.' Striding across the room, he grabbed her upper arms and hauled her against him. Her rounded breasts squashed against his muscular chest, her skin went hot all over in one massive wave and she felt the burn of his touch all the way down to her toes.

'Are you sure?' she stared up at him.

'Yes.' He started running searching, open mouthed kisses down her throat, and she gasped.

She should be scared. Emotionally this was the last thing she needed, it would make things so much more complicated than they already were. But physically, she'd never wanted a guy more. She'd never experienced a sexual curiosity like it, a hunger so strong. It wasn't fear that had made her voice shake. It was overwhelming excitement and the thought, *oh thank God, finally*.

His large hot hands swept down her back to her waist, his fingers settling and stroking the silken skin on her spine just above the line of her knickers. Her breath huffed out and her knees went to jelly, her heart pound, pound, pounding in her chest. 'Oh, Matt,' she moaned.

He gathered her closer, the muscles in his upper arms flexing and she made a weird squeaking sound as she felt the hard insistent nudge of his erection against her bare stomach. The muscles and nerve endings between her thighs quivered, her knickers dampening with lust. Her mouth dropped open as she tried to inhale, but it didn't work. She couldn't breathe properly. She was lost and taking him with her. All the way.

Throwing her arms around his neck she lifted her face to his, seeking his mouth, stealing tiny biting kisses as she rubbed up against him, twisting her hips. The next thing she knew he'd grabbed her around the waist and was throwing her back onto the bed as if she weighed nothing, following her down to lie on top of her. That action was like a spark lighting a firework and suddenly it was fast and frantic, his long muscular legs tangling restlessly with hers, the material of his shorts rubbing deliciously against the bare skin of her legs and feeling deliciously naughty. His hands held her face steady so that he could kiss her hungrily, insistently, his fingers in her hair.

He was so gorgeous, *this* was so gorgeous and so unbelievably hot, she thought dizzyingly. Arching her back, she tried to get even closer to him. He let go of her jaw to run blistering hands down her waist and over her flat tummy, then grabbed both thighs and wrapped her legs up around his hips so their pelvises aligned.

She rubbed against him as she felt his pulsing erection pressing against the material of her damp knickers, rocking her hips in greedy rhythm so that her clit rubbed along the rigid length of him. Grabbing the hem of his top she pulled it over his head so fast she was surprised that it didn't give him scorch marks. He drew back, panting slightly, his dark hair ruffled and sticking up in spikes. His dilated pupils were so large she could see only a rim of his green irises.

'You are so unbelievably sexy. I can't believe how hot it is between us,' he said huskily, before wriggling down to peel her bra away and feast on a swollen, hard nipple.

'Mmm,' she moaned, squirming and clutching his head to her breasts, encouraging him to suck harder and keep going. It felt like she'd waited forever, a lifetime to get naked with him, be with him. It felt right. Dangerously so. He unhooked her bra and tossed it away, taking her knickers off easily as she wriggled her hips to help him. The sweltering warmth between her thighs grew, her pelvic muscles twitching in eager little jumps, her nipples rubbing

535

deliciously against his hairy chest as he kissed her passionately.

He drew away for a moment to strip off the rest of his clothes and after a rustle of foil while he sorted out protection, his naked body met hers from top to toe. She moaned as his dark head dipped and licked around her nipple before sucking on it in a bold steady beat again, one that had her twisting back and forth and opening her thighs so he could settle between them.

'Now, Matt. Please. Now.'

He let out a muffled groan but carried on sucking her nipple while he inched his hips away and dropped a hand down between them to press a long finger against her, rubbing back and forth in a steady, relentless rhythm. Staggering heat gathered tighter in her pelvis, tingles shooting through her as he quickened the pace and moved his head from her breasts to her mouth. They were half kissing as she moved her hips demandingly against his hand, erect sensitive nipples pushing against his chest as she urged him on, biting his shoulder and then biting his bottom lip. 'Faster,' she breathed, 'yes, right there, oh God. Don't stop, Matt.'

'Like that?' he asked, tilting his face to look down into hers before gazing down at her body. 'You are so beautiful, Zoe.'

'You are too. Kiss me,' she ordered, tunnelling her hands into his hair and yanking his mouth to hers, 'kiss me.'

He did as she asked, tongue flicking against hers, hand moving faster and building the heat inside her to fever pitch. Her fingers clenched on his broad shoulders and his thighs trembled against hers in response.

'Tell me what you want,' he whispered, nuzzling her ear lobe. 'Tell me, Zoe. Harder? Faster?'

Nodding in agreement, she rolled her head on the pillow, skin going dewy. 'Yes. Yes, I'm going to co …' her voice got strangled in her throat as pulses starting racing outwards from her pelvis to the rest of her body. But it still wasn't enough. 'No. I want you inside me,' she whimpered, 'quickly, now.'

Pulling his hand away, she locked her legs around his back and jerked her hips up. She felt him prodding at her wet heat and then he was sliding all the way in and they were both groaning with pleasure.

'Zoe,' he groaned, sinking his face into her neck and pumping his hips.

Wrapping her arms around his shoulders, she hung on tight as he surged in and out, hard and fast, pounding into her almost roughly. She rocked with him, matching his movements, pleasure making her skin prickle and waves of shimmering warmth shooting through her and she was urging him on, moaning in his ear, telling him how unbelievably good it felt to have him inside her, racing to the finish line with him. Then he was kissing her desperately and the feeling was escalating and she was gasping, shaking and melting with an almost unbearable orgasm, calling his name over and over. Her inner muscles were pulsating and holding him tight and he said her name through gritted teeth and then fell over the edge into hot oblivion with her.

As they lay tangled together afterwards panting, Zoe took a deep, slow breath, waiting for Matt to do a runner. She was sure it was going to happen when he gently disengaged and shuffled to the end of the bed. But after disappearing into the bathroom for a moment, he slid back under the covers and gathered her close, tucking her into his manly, slightly sweaty body. With a satisfied murmur, he kissed her forehead and mumbled goodnight in a low, deep alcohol addled voice.

Her damp face creased in confusion. She wasn't sure how she felt about what'd happened. It had been mind-blowing and spine-tingling and that was based only on a quick, frantic tumble so who knew what would happen if they did it again taking their time—an explosion probably—but what did it mean? Where did they go from here? Was it just amazing sex or something more? Could they get past her deceit, the unanswered questions about Melody, and his grief for his late wife? Did they even want to?

Screwing her face up, she struggled to think clearly but failed.

A day of food, sunshine, endless glasses of wine and incredible, earth-shattering sex swept her towards sleep and even though she fought to stay awake to make sense of it all, with a murmur that echoed Matt's she snuggled into him and drifted away.

When she woke up in the morning with a pounding head, he was gone. Sitting up and clutching the covers around her, she swept her eyes around the room. Not a trace of him. So he hadn't done a runner last night, had probably been too drunk, but he had done one as the day had dawned.

'Fuck.' She dropped her face into her hands, shoulders slumping. He'd said he wouldn't regret it in the morning, had promised he was sure. Now she was here alone in her room and wished she could crawl back under the covers and never come out.

She'd had sex with him. It had been unbelievable, like nothing she'd ever experienced before, but with his absence a bolt of pain sliced through her. She felt tainted, uneasy. How was she going to face him after what had happened between them and he'd walked away without any explanation? She was living with him. Looking after his kids. Was he going to pretend it had never happened? She cringed. It would be excruciating.

Seeing her phone on the bedside cabinet, she scrambled towards it, forgetting about the hangover. As she saw a message icon on the screen hope soared in her chest, but when she opened the text it was from Frankie sent at half past midnight and thanking her for a nice night. *We liked Matt*, her friend had added on the end followed by two kisses.

Zoe winced, chucking her phone on the floor. Not a word from Matt. How could he? A note left on the bed saying 'speak later' or some other casual dismissal would have been better than him sneaking out of her bed without a word. Anything would have been better. She'd thought he respected her, that they'd built a friendship of sorts, even though they were supposed to be boss and employee. He'd told Aimee that they were friends. But this wasn't how you treated a friend. With friendship there was warmth, trust, respect, loyalty. Running away after having sex was none of those things.

'What the hell were you thinking?' she muttered out loud, pushing her shaking hands through her long knotted hair. Knotted from when she'd rolled her head back and forth on the pillow when he'd been sucking her nipples and—

'Stop it.' Lurching from the bed, not sure how much of the shaking was down to the alcohol from last night and how much was from anger and disappointment at Matt, she traipsed into the bathroom. Stepping into the shower, she turned it to the highest setting to scald away her shame and disillusionment. She'd thought Matt was better than this. She really had. More fool her. Stupid, stupid girl. She berated herself while shampooing her hair and scrubbing his smell from her body. How did she always get it so wrong when it came to men? First Henry, making her fall for him and then casting her aside after deciding he wasn't ready for a serious relationship. Then Greg cheating on her and sounding the death knell of their relationship, a cancelled wedding left in its wake. And now Matt, who she'd had no business getting involved with in the first place and had sorely misjudged.

What was wrong with her? Images of them in bed together the night before flittered through her mind. It had been so amazing, so intense. Surely he couldn't have looked at her that way, touched her like that if he didn't feel anything for her?

No. It had just been fantastic sex. That's all it was. That's all it could be.

Shaking her head vehemently as she turned the shower off made her groan. She had such a headache. What had she been thinking of drinking so much last night? If anything she should have been trying to keep a clear head given Rayne and Frankie's attendance at the party. It was because they'd been having so much fun she realised. Her and Matt, and the five couples who were all such lovely, good people. Wrapping a large bath towel around her and knotting it over her breasts, she brushed her teeth roughly while trying not to be sick and promised herself a couple of paracetamol ASAP. Striding into her bedroom, she dried off briskly even though it magnified the pain in her head by about a hundred and pulled on underwear, jeans and a loose, thin grey top. Sitting down on the edge of the bed, she tilted her head forward and used a hand towel to dry the ends of her hair.

'Oh,' a deep, surprised voice said above her head. 'Morning.'

Freezing, Zoe fought back a crashing wave of mixed emotions and took a deep breath. Some demons were best faced straight away. Flipping her head upright, she met Matt's eyes, desperate for the next few minutes to be over already. 'Hi.'

'I didn't think you'd be awake yet. It's only just gone nine and we had a late night.' He extended a tray full of mugs and plates towards her, his face pale. 'I went out to get us some pastries for breakfast. I needed some fresh air. I made us coffee too.'

'Oh,' now it was her turn to sound surprised. 'I woke up half an hour ago. Eight thirty is a lie-in for me compared to when I get up in the week.'

'Right.' Setting the tray down on the bedside cabinet, he joined her on the edge of the bed. 'But you got up straight away.' His eyes went to the pillow he'd slept on, the indent of his head still there. Dull colour seeped into his face. 'So you must have thought I'd left without saying anything. That I'd just left you.'

'I um … yeah, I guess I did,' she muttered, staring at the towel and twisting it between her hands. This was so awkward. Had she gotten it totally wrong?

'I'm sorry if that's what you thought, but that's not my style,' he pushed her thick damp hair behind her ear to see her face, then frowned and yanked his hand away as if the contact had burnt him. 'I thought you knew me well enough by now to know that, Zoe.'

'Sorry,' she said, gathering her courage and turning to look at him. His eyes fluttered away from hers, avoiding eye contact. 'But this wasn't supposed to happen, was it?' she pointed out. 'So you can hardly blame me for thinking the worst when I woke up and you'd gone.'

He sighed. 'I don't. I get it.' His shoulders slumped and he shifted away, a divide of wrinkled duvet appearing between them. 'Look, we need to talk.'

'Oh, Matt. Can't you come up with anything more original than that?' A huge lump lodged in her throat and she had to swallow twice to carry on. She wasn't sure she could bear this but at the same time knew that what he was about to say was probably the best for both of them under the circumstances. 'What are you going to say? It's not me, it's you? Or—'

'Hang on! Don't start making assumptions—'

'Of course I'm going to assume. You can't even look me in the eye. It's obvious you regret—'

'Don't tell me what's obvious!' Jumping up, he walked to the window, movements uncharacteristically jerky. Staring fixedly out of the window, he lowered his voice, 'You don't know how I feel or what I think. I walked to the bakery so I could get my head together before talking to you. I needed to get it all straight, needed to understand how I was feeling before I spoke to you. It's only fair.'

'Okay, so you've done that. Now tell me how you feel. Make it fair. You're saying you don't regret us sleeping together, but your body language is screaming with tension.' She breathed in, deep and slow, praying the answer to her next question would be no. 'Do you want me to leave, Matt? Is that it? Do you think it would be better but you're worried you'll come across as a bastard if you ask me to go now?'

'No. It's not regret, okay?' He span around to look at her, face flushed. 'It's guilt.'

She frowned. 'Guilt? Why on earth would you feel guilty? Okay, I was drunk but I knew what I was doing. It's been there between us for a while, hasn't it? So don't feel guilty on my account.'

He waved his hand to dismiss her words. 'No. It's not that.'

'What then?' she shot off the bed and marched over to him, grabbing his forearms, feeling the heat of his skin and the strength of his tense muscles beneath her fingers. 'Tell me. What is it?'

'Helen!' he ground out, a nerve pulsing in his jaw. 'It's Helen.'

'Oh, shit. I didn't think. I'm sorry.' Softening her voice, 'I know it's hard, but you shouldn't feel bad. She died three years ago. At some point you need to move on. I'm not saying you're doing that with me. I'm not asking you for anything, but its normal that ... What I mean is that when you love someone, are married and lose them—'

'Zoe.' He met her eyes. 'It's not that. She was my wife, yes. But this isn't me being afraid to move on because I'm still in mourning. I've tried to fight what's between us for so long, but I couldn't. Which is why I feel so bloody awful.'

'What is it then? Matt, what are you not telling me?'

'I don't deserve to be happy!' It burst out of him in a rush, his voice strangled.

'What?' She let out an astounded laugh. 'Don't be so stupid. Why on earth would you say that?'

'Because it's true,' he shouted, his breath hot on her cheek. 'It's true.'

'What?' She stepped back and released his arms, mouth dropping open at the fury in his voice.

'It's true, Zoe,' he repeated in an undertone. 'I'm sorry for yelling at you, but that's the way it is. I'm just being honest.'

She studied the pain on his face, the milky complexion under the ruddy cheekbones, the eyes filled with remorse, the tight lips. 'I'm sorry I didn't take you seriously,' she answered. 'I shouldn't have laughed. I didn't mean it in a ha-ha way, it was genuine disbelief. You're a good person,' pausing, she thought of what he'd done to Melody and how distant he'd been from the kids when she'd arrived, 'even though you may have made mistakes. But everybody does. It's what makes us human. We don't live in a vacuum. We live among other people and we're all messy, complex creatures.' Thinking of herself and of the plan she'd once had. 'So please tell me what you mean.'

542

He hesitated, expression torn between confusion and despair.

'Please, Matt,' she begged, sliding her hands around his wrists again to anchor him. She stroked them soothingly, reassuring him without words that no matter what, she was there.

Closing his eyes, he started talking. At first it was stilted and slow. 'I don't want to speak ill of the dead.'

'So don't. Just tell me the truth in your own words. I know it's hard, but focus on the facts. Besides, I'm not here to judge you.'

'All right,' he sighed. 'I … I told you that things were difficult between me and Helen towards the end. That she seemed to resent being a mum, and lost her way a bit. I explained to you that things were bad and then getting better. Or so I thought. The truth is, we'd simply found a way to rub along for the kids' sakes.'

Zoe winced. She'd seen on more than one occasion what staying together for the kids did. It caused two unhappy parents and equally miserable children. It was laudable to want to keep the family unit intact, but not at the expense of everyone in it.

'I thought I still loved her,' he continued, opening his eyes. 'I wanted things to work between us. I thought we were going through a rough patch. Sometimes we had spats, sometimes we virtually ignored each other, and sometimes there were these shitty, hideous silences. It went on for months. And then one night I tried to talk to her about what was going on between us and the way it was affecting us all. The way she only really seemed excited about shopping or seeing friends. How she'd been drinking more and more. It was no way to live.' Now that he'd started, it was like he couldn't stop, the words flowing out of him. 'She reacted badly. We had a massive argument and she was so unreasonable, almost hysterical. When I lost my temper and said maybe we should have a temporary separation, that I wanted her to take some time to go and figure out what she wanted, she freaked out. She was ranting and raving that I couldn't take it all away from her. Then she,' he gulped, eyes filling with horror, colour leeching from his skin so that it looked ash white, 'she grabbed the kids from their beds and ran out while I was in the kitchen at the back of the house. She put them in the Land Rover I'd bought for her and roared away. It scared the hell out of me. She'd come home after a few wines over lunch with friends, or at the time that's who I thought she was with, and had another few glasses over dinner.' He stared at Zoe sightlessly and she could tell he was lost in another time and place, re-living that harrowing night. She tightened her grip on his arms, stepping closer to him. Contrary to his usual heat, he felt cold, tremors wracking his body. 'When I realised what had happened I grabbed some shoes and looked for my car keys to follow her, but I couldn't find them.' His face paled further, lost in his own private agony. 'I couldn't find them and I didn't know what to think. I was frantic, couldn't breathe properly and didn't know whether to call the police or keep searching for the keys. I didn't think I'd ever see the kids again. I thought she was going to be one of those women who absconded with the children, or used them as weapons in some ugly war. But most of all I just kept thinking to myself, she's drinking and driving and my babies are in that car with her.'

'God, Matt.' She drew in a sharp breath, aching for him. So that was why he'd reacted so badly the day she'd got into the Prius to go to Longleat with the kids and he'd thought she was angry. She'd guessed there was something at the time, had asked outright about Helen and the accident, but he hadn't felt able to tell her. It must have brought it all back for him. That was also the first time they'd kissed, she realised. When he'd been vulnerable and hurting. So perhaps it wasn't about her, but about the comfort he'd needed that day.

She should let him go, break the physical contact between them but couldn't convince herself to release his arms just yet. So she simply listened as his sentences got shorter and shorter, racing through remembered pain.

'I eventually found the keys—she'd hidden them in one of Jasper's shoes—then ran out of the house. I leapt in the car and drove up the road. I wound the windows down. It was pouring with rain, even though it was June. Bloody British weather, I remember thinking. It was so strange and surreal. I was gasping in the warm air, praying to a God I never really believed in to keep them all safe when I heard the crash. I found out later it was over a quarter of a mile away.'

Her mouth fell open in dismay at the thought of the kids being hurt, and what it must have been like for him to hear the sound of the accident. It was so awful she could barely comprehend it.

'I got to the car and it was crumpled, concertinaed into a tree at the side of a residential road. It was starting to spark and smoke. I thought I'd lost them all,' his voice broke on the last word, 'and I felt as if someone had punched a hole straight through my chest. I ran over to the car, afraid to look, afraid of what I was going to see, afraid not to look. I- I saw Helen. She was badly injured. Her head was crushed against the windscreen and bleeding, her neck was at a weird angle and the airbag hadn't deployed. She'd talked about disabling it at some point but I didn't think she'd actually done it. She was in a bad way, but do you want to know what my first thought was? It wasn't that I should get her out, how I could help her, it was for the kids. I looked in the back seat and they weren't there. The kids weren't there.' His eyes were anguished, hands curling into fists and sending quivering ripples into her hands. 'I could smell petrol and the car was sparking. But still it was the kids that I was worried about. My brain knew they weren't in there, but I still ran around the car wrenching the doors open. Searching for them. Leaving Helen in the front, unconscious and bleeding. And then I heard Aimee calling me.' He ground his teeth, a vein pumping in his forehead. 'I spun around and she was standing further down the road holding Jasper's hand. There was a woman with them. I didn't know who she was or what was happening, so I started running toward them and then there was a clunking sound and a whoosh behind me and I was thrown to the floor by an explosion, straight onto my face. The fall broke my nose.' Freeing his arm from her hold, he rubbed the bridge of his nose with a trembling finger. It must be a constant reminder of the accident, Zoe thought, every time he looked in the mirror. 'When I stood up,' Matt continued, 'blood pouring down my top, the car was a burning wreck and Helen was dead.'

Zoe's eyes filled with tears, a sharp tingling sensation shooting down her nose. It was truly horrific, what this family had gone through. She didn't know what to say, or if she should say anything. All she knew was that she wanted to hold him and soothe him and take away his pain.

'The emergency services arrived only a few minutes later. The woman standing with the kids had called them. She lived nearby. She'd heard the crash and come out to help. When she'd found the kids she moved them away and kept them safe for me. If she hadn't …'

'But she did,' she whispered, picturing Aimee's shiny red hair in a neat ponytail as she bent over a book and Jasper's dark hair and green eyes full of excitement as he bopped up and down about something. Her heart swelled with affection and relief. She couldn't assimilate how close they had come to being hurt, or worse. 'They were fine, weren't they? They weren't injured?'

'They were fine, physically. It turned out that Helen had stopped and let the kids out at the side of the road. What she was thinking of abandoning them like that I don't know, and why she did it is a mystery too. Maybe she realised leaving me and having two children to look after wasn't going to be much fun. Or maybe it was because she was having an affair and thought the kids would be an inconvenience.'

'She had someone else?' she asked, astounded.

'Yes. A friend of a friend as it turned out. They'd run into each other at the gym. He came to see me after the funeral. I never forgave him for telling me. He should have kept quiet, said nothing. It was like a kick in the teeth on top of everything else. I haven't seen him since.'

So that's why when she'd confided in him about Greg cheating he'd been so understanding. He knew what it was like from personal experience. It was also possibly why he'd been so adamant after the newspaper article that he would never start something with someone if he was already in a relationship. She couldn't imagine why anyone would want to cheat on Matt. He was so warm, funny and caring. Not to mention gorgeous. Then again, if a person was unhappy, perhaps they could justify anything to themselves. So maybe it said more about the person who was being unfaithful, than the person they were cheating on. Maybe it wasn't about being unworthy, but about no longer being right for each other.

As for the other thing Matt had said … 'He may have thought you deserved to know the truth, Matt. So that you mourned the real person and not a wife you believed was loyal and faithful. Or maybe he was grieving too.'

'I suppose it's possible. I never thought of it like that. I was too angry.'

'But if you can't forgive other people, how can you get closure yourself and be happy? It'll always be hanging over you. And what you said about Helen taking the kids out of the car, have you ever considered that her mother's instinct kicked in? Perhaps she realised she was drunk and that they shouldn't be in the car with her. You told me before that even though she wasn't that emotionally invested you never normally worried about their safety with her.'

'It's possible. I never considered it that way. I just thought she was being irresponsible, but maybe it was the opposite. She did love them in her own way, I never doubted that. But why wouldn't she have simply pulled over and waited for me to catch up?'

'Who knows? We never will, because we can't ever know what was going through her head at the time, can we?'

'Well, what I do know from the Road Traffic Collision investigation is that she pulled straight into oncoming traffic and hit the tree at more than forty miles per hour when she swerved to

547

avoid a car. She was accelerating at the time. They said that she can't have been paying attention. She was nearly double the legal drink driving limit.' He dropped his chin, staring at the floor. 'I saw tears on her face when I found her in the wreck, Zoe.'

'And it's your fault,' she filled in softly, slowly putting it all together. The way he hardly ever talked about Helen to the kids, how uncomfortable he was around Helen's mum, the way he'd distanced himself from Aimee and Jasper. It was the guilt he'd referred to.

At her words, his head snapped up and back as if she'd slapped him. She could see the misery in his dark green eyes.

'It's your fault, that's what you think,' she expanded. 'You feel guilty and responsible and that's why you think you don't deserve to be happy.'

'I don't. I was responsible,' he gritted out. 'If I hadn't argued with her, she wouldn't have taken the kids and got in the car. I shouldn't have lost my temper!'

'Did you hit her, or threaten to?'

'No. Of course not.'

'Did you get in her face and make her feel afraid? Did she look scared?'

'No. I raised my voice but I didn't get in her space. She looked pissed off that I was suggesting we take a break, but that's all.'

'So you didn't drive her out of the house, did you? She wasn't fleeing for her life and I doubt she believed her or the kids were in imminent danger. She could have chosen one of any number of other options; gone to bed, gone to another part of the house, called someone to come and get her, or called a taxi. You need to think logically, remove yourself from the situation. She was drinking and she was angry. We make our own fate in life, Matt. The argument would have happened one way or another at some point. It was bound to if you were both unhappy. But there was no way you could have predicted it would end like that. Helen was the one who decided to drive under the influence. It was her who pulled out into traffic.'

'But I could have gotten her out of the car. I told you, I knew the kids weren't in there. I wasted time looking,' his voice, raw and twisted, broke again. 'I could have pulled her out. Should have.'

'And you could have caused her further injury, paralysed her if she'd hurt her neck or back,' she pointed out sharply, 'and you didn't know the car would go up so quickly, did you?'

'But I still can't help feeling I could have done something. If I hadn't been so focused on ...' he drifted off.

'What?' she inched nearer to him so that their chests were touching and she could stare up into his face. 'Looking for your children, who were God knows where and needed you? Who were what, two and four years old? Don't ever apologise for putting your children first! That's what parents are supposed to do. No,' she amended, 'that's what good parents do automatically.'

'But I wasn't a good parent. Because of me the kids lost their mum, because of me she died!' Screwing his face up, his shoulders shuddered on quick indrawn breaths, his eyes glazed with a sheen of tears.

'Yes, they did,' she nodded solemnly, pleading with her eyes for him to listen to her, and to take in what she was saying. 'But only because you care about them and love them so much. You were frantic, you said so yourself. What you've described, from arriving on scene, probably only happened in thirty seconds or so. You didn't have time to think, to weigh up the choices. You followed your instincts, which was to find and protect your children. It was unfortunate and sad that it ended as it did. It's a regret for you, obviously. But it's not one that should rule the rest of your life.' She freed one of his arms and lifted a hand to his face, stroking his jaw. 'Oh, Matt. Stop torturing yourself. You do know that Cynthia doesn't blame you, don't you?'

His expression turned shocked, pupils dilating. 'What do you mean? What do you know about what Cynthia thinks?'

'We spoke at the BBQ. She told me how good you've been,

letting her see the children. She also said that you blame yourself for Helen's death but shouldn't. She misses her daughter, Matt, and she'll always mourn her, but she doesn't hold you responsible and you shouldn't either. The only thing she's cross about is that you don't talk to the kids about their mum. That there are no photos of her here.'

'I thought it was for the best. They were so young when she died. I thought it was better not to remind them of what they were missing. What they'd lost.'

'Which would have also made you feel even guiltier,' she pointed out gently. 'They need to know they had a mum who loved them, and what she was like. It might make them sad that she's not around, but they need to know where they came from so they can understand themselves and their place in the world. It's absolutely vital for their self-esteem. I told Cynthia we've been going to Hyde Park, that you've been visiting the memorial plaque for Helen. I think that helped her feel a bit better. I do think it's been good for the three of you too. Remembering the good times, making some new ones together.'

'You're right, it has. We've done that with you. Because of you. Thank you.' He covered her hand with his, where it rested on his face, holding her fingers against his warm, stubbly cheek. Staring down at her, he nodded. 'Maybe you're right. Maybe I got it wrong. They should know their mother. It will be painful for me, but if it's what they need, of course I'll try.' Pausing. 'As for Cynthia, I haven't been able to look her in the eye for three years. I didn't dare. I guess I was afraid of what I would see.'

'I think you should talk to her. It would probably be cathartic for both of you. And I think that if you look in her eyes you might be surprised by what you see. Compassion. Understanding.' She smiled, a tiny hopeful hitch of her lips, 'You need to try and start moving on from this, Matt. Talk to someone professional maybe, see a counsellor or something. But please find a way to live with it. I mean really live, not this horrible half-life where you haven't been properly involved with the kids. It's getting better, don't get me wrong—you're more affectionate and more engaged—but there's still some way to go. I understand you've been feeling guilty for thinking you lost them their mum, but then in some respects you've taken their dad away as well. Give him back to them,' she pleaded, 'you all deserve more. You also deserve to move forward in your personal life. Don't let what happened hold you back. Three years is a long time, Matt.'

'Just like that?' he asked sadly, 'You think three years of feeling like shit about it is going to disintegrate overnight? That I'm suddenly going to feel fine?'

'No, I don't. But perhaps if you acknowledge it, if you make a conscious effort to start working through it, it'll get easier, until one day you'll realise the pain and guilt that used to tear you apart has faded to a dull ache. It'll be like a niggling little stone in your shoe. It's there and you can feel it but it doesn't stop you functioning. Do whatever you need to do, go to the basement and turn the music up loud and scream until you're hoarse, go and sit on Primrose Hill and watch the sun rise, or take a break from work and do something fun with the kids. Do anything you need to do that will help you deal with it and move on.'

'How do you know about dealing with grief? Oh, your parents,' he acknowledged. 'I guess you know what you're talking about.'

'I was a lot younger when I lost them. I didn't know what to think or feel. All I knew was that one day they were there and the next they were gone. It was like a chasm opened up under me and I was free-falling. I was powerless and needed control, so I got up every day, went to school and did everything I could to make them proud. To be honest, their deaths only really hit me in my mid-teens. I started acting out, coming home late, drinking, smoking and lying, but luckily before I could went too badly off course my teacher realised what was going on and referred me to a counsellor. It didn't bring them back, but talking about it and sorting through my feelings helped me cope when I had a bad day or felt overwhelmed by everything. It was the talking therapy that got me interested in doing a psychology degree, even though I ultimately ended up not using it. Counselling isn't the be all and end all, and it's not for everyone, but it's worth considering.'

'Okay, I'll think about it,' he said, eyes serious. 'But what about the guilt, what makes you the expert? You can't have blamed yourself for your parents' death, you weren't with them, were you?'

'No, it was just them in the car. But I live with guilt every day,' she admitted softly, knowing that after Matt had exposed himself so openly, had shared something so deeply personal, she had to tell him the truth now. No matter what the consequences might be. 'I left my younger sister to go to America, to make a new life for myself, to follow a man who ended up being worthless. I was heartbroken after my first serious boyfriend had dumped me. I shouldn't have gone. I shouldn't have left,' she reiterated. 'And no matter what she might say to me, I know I was selfish and hurt her and because I wasn't around, because she lived with my aunt who's not the type to talk about feelings, I feel like she didn't learn how to protect herself. She's naive. Trusts the wrong people and gets hurt. I've been trying to make up for it since.'

'It sounds like you're being a bit hard on yourself, Zoe, although I can appreciate that's going to sound a bit hypocritical given you feel I've been doing the same thing about Helen.' He narrowed his eyes. 'And I didn't know you had a sister. Why didn't I know that?'

She bit her lip. 'There's a lot that you don't know about me.' Sliding her hand from under his and letting go of his wrist, she backed away. She needed distance between them to do this. 'We all have our secrets, Matt.'

'Meaning?'

Taking a deep, shaky breath. 'Meaning I need to tell you something.'

'I knew it. I knew there was something. You've been seeing your ex, right?' He raked his hands through his hair, leaving it sticking up in uneven ruffles.

'My ex?' Shuddering at the thought of it. 'No, he lives in America. Why would you say that?'

'There have been times you've been twitchy about your phone and you've gone off to spend time with someone, but haven't said who. Obviously you don't have to tell me as your boss, but on a personal level I thought you might, and with what happened last night, I figured you'd come clean now ...' he trailed off, shaking his head. 'You stayed out last Saturday night, Zoe. All night. So I was sure you were with him. I've half been expecting you to hand your notice in. But then you don't seem the type to sleep with me if you're starting up with him again. Look, just level with me. Are you with him or not? Are you going back to America?'

'No! Urgh, I'd never go back to someone who cheated on me. Never,' she reiterated, edging backwards. 'The trust is gone and I don't feel I could ever get it back. He contacted me a few times by phone, but it was half hearted. He gave up after a couple of weeks when I ignored him. Maybe if this was a romance novel he'd turn up, beg my forgiveness and try to whisk me away but it's not. This is real life. This is *my* life. I haven't answered any of his messages. It's not him I've been talking to and seeing, I swear.'

'Come on, do you think I'm stupid? Your face says it all, you're literally a picture of guilt,' he stuffed his hands in his pockets, 'so don't bother denying it.'

'I'm not lying, Matt. I want to tell you the truth. I have done for some time, but at first I didn't trust you and then—'

'Didn't trust me? Why?' he demanded, but she just shrugged helplessly. 'And then, what?'

'I got in too deep,' she confessed, hoping he might find some way to understand what she'd done. 'The truth is,' she moved even further from him, putting her back against the window sill, bracing herself, 'the truth is that the younger sister I told you about? The one I abandoned? It's Melody.'

15

'Melody? As in my last nanny?'

'Yes,' she lifted her chin, dreading his reaction but ready for the blow, uneasiness curdling her stomach and making her hands curl into fists.

'Melody is your sister?' he said in disbelief. 'The sister who looked after my kids? The sister I fired and told to leave? When you came to the interview you didn't say anything. Why?' he demanded. 'Jesus, right from the beginning, it was always about that,' realisation dawned as he blurted out the words. Horror washed the colour out of his face and put a hardness in his beautiful green eyes that she hated. It was like looking at a stranger and Zoe gritted her teeth to stop from crying out at the loss. 'These last few months, living in my house, caring for my children and all along you were her sister. We talked about her, you asked about her and Stephen but still you said nothing. There was this ulterior motive the whole time. You betrayed us.' His face was screwed up in bewildered anger, trying to make sense of it. 'So, what is it you were after? What was it you wanted? Revenge? Or was it spite? Tell me. For fuck's sake, just say it.'

'I wanted answers,' she cried. 'I wanted to know why you would treat Melody so badly. I came here to confront you both, but Stephen was so cocky and left so quickly I didn't get a chance to say anything. He mentioned the interviews before he went and it was a way in so I used it. I held you largely responsible, so I wanted to have it out with you. Once I was inside the house you were so impatient, dismissive and—you might not like this—arrogant as well, that I didn't think you'd tell me what had happened, let alone be willing to explain yourself. You seemed so unaffected and oblivious to the consequences of what you'd done. I was furious with you and your brother, cut up on Mel's behalf because she was so devastated and clueless as to why you'd fire and chuck her out without explanation. I had to do something, she's my sister. I needed to get the answers for her, Matt.'

He didn't need to know what she'd intended, about the kiss and tell expose, *Plan Nannygate*. It didn't matter now and would only hurt him more. She took a breath, forcing calmness into her quivering, high pitched voice. 'I thought that if I worked for you, was here, you would open up and tell me. But instead I got sucked in. I didn't want to like you but somehow you grew on me.' She winced when he shook his head and muttered a swear word. 'It's true,' she insisted. 'You weren't what I was expecting. Not at all. I've grown to care about Jasper and Aimee so much, Matt. You have to believe that. I've never felt this way about children I've nannied before. There's a genuine bond there and I would never do anything to hurt them, I swear. I almost left a few times, nearly told you a few more, but after a while I didn't want to leave, and the timing was always off.' She spread her hands, desperate for him to listen, to understand. 'After getting to know you I realise you're not dismissive or arrogant. You were just stressed the day of the interviews and you disappear totally into your own world when you're concentrating or working on something. As for the answers I was looking for, obviously you think Mel did something wrong, something unforgivable which gave you grounds for your actions, but I never found out what because you always shied away from the details.' Shaking her head. 'You don't talk about things Matt, not how you should. You need to face things in life, confront them head on and deal with them. Not bury your head in the sand.'

'You're wrong. I wasn't shying away from it; I just had my reasons for keeping the details to myself. I have confronted things. You've made me. I trusted you!' He looked agonised, pacing the room back and forth, out of reach and then within reach but a thousand miles away. 'Jesus, Zoe, I confided in you and listened to you. And all time you were here because of Melody.'

'I was protecting her! I'm her big sister and I wasn't there for her. I left her to go to America because things were too painful here. I ran away and have felt guilty every single minute since, whatever she might say to try and make me feel better. That's why I said you have to face things, because I didn't and then it was too late. My sister and I, our relationship, it's not how it's used to be and that's my fault. So yes, I wanted to help her. I wanted to give her closure, help her understand why the boss she got on with so well and admired took everything away from her. I wanted to know why Stephen stopped taking her calls and cut himself off after they'd been so happy together.'

'Happy?' Matt froze, turning towards her. 'I don't think so. I told you, she broke his heart.' He shook his head. 'You may as well know the truth now. I don't see what there is to lose. If you tell anyone it's not as if you'll be a credible source given what you've done. Maybe you also have a right to know what kind of person your sister really is. Perhaps I owe you that much, given what you've done for me and the kids.'

She tried not to flinch at the condemnation in his words. 'So what is the truth?' she whispered, waiting breathlessly for the answer she'd first set out to discover.

'She tried to blackmail him.'

'What?' Her lips went numb with shock. 'No.'

'Yes. He came to me, begging for help. He didn't know what to do. She'd found out he had a criminal record for drug offences—'

'What?' Of all of the things she'd expected, it wasn't that. Drugs always seemed so sordid and dirty, not something an entitled playboy would be involved with.

'It happened during his time at private school. He and a few friends got caught doing some relatively low level dealing—not that I'm saying any dealing is right—when they were eighteen. They got expelled from school. Unfortunately, drugs can be rife among kids that age from privileged backgrounds,' the remark made it obvious he didn't count himself as part of that group, 'they like to party and think nothing of taking Class A drugs for recreational use. It wasn't that big a leap from Stephen and his mates taking them to supplying them to friends. The school wanted to cover it up to avoid damage to its reputation, because to a prestigious institution like that image is everything. However, the Crown Prosecution Service wanted to make an example of them and they could be tried as adults because of their age. I guess the thinking was, why should they get away with it just because their parents were rich? My parents didn't want to go to court, partly for Stephen's benefit and partly to protect the family name and their professional reputations, being senior civil servants. So he admitted the charges, sold out his supplier and got a warning. There was no custodial sentence because of mitigating circumstances and it being a first time offence, and we always managed to keep it quiet.' He stared at Zoe, eyes as unyielding as steel. 'Stephen told me Melody said she had evidence he was dealing again and would testify he'd supplied her drugs if he didn't give her hundreds of thousands of pounds. She threatened to go to the police and the press. He was frantic. Knew what it would look like with his background, and that he might not escape a sentence this time—'

'Bullshit,' she spat, 'Melody would never do anything like that. She's completely incapable of it. She's the most honest person I know. How could you believe it of her? Why the hell would she blackmail someone she was in love with? She's not into money and definitely isn't deceitful—'

'Not like her older sister, you mean? Your bar is hardly high seeing as you've lied to me for coming up to two months about

557

who you are.'

Her jaw clenched, fury started taking over from the hurt she'd caused him with her lies. 'Oh, don't give me that. You didn't know Mel was my sister but you know my name, my background, the way I've behaved with your kids, the hard work I've put in to bring them out of their shell and calm Jasper down. You know what I've done to build you a better relationship with them. It's no good being all self-righteous when you're the one who turfed a defenceless twenty-two year out on her arse without giving her a chance to understand why.'

'I had to,' he came towards her, face twisted. 'What did you expect me to do? He's my brother.'

She gazed at him, fingers clenching. It all made sense now. How out of character Matt's actions had seemed in relation to the person he actually was. 'You really believed him,' she said in amazement. 'So in your eyes, you were protecting him.'

'Of course I was. I couldn't let her do that to him. So I called her bluff and threw her out. I didn't even mention the money, I just told her to go and never come back. I figured that if I played the hard line, like it wasn't even worth discussing, she'd know there was no point in pursuing it. That we wouldn't give in to blackmail.'

A wave of relief crashed over Zoe. It was all a big mistake. Melody hadn't done anything wrong. Stephen was a liar and however misguided his actions had been, the only reason for Matt's actions was protecting his brother from something he perceived as a threat.

All along it had been about an older sibling driven to look out for a younger one. It was exactly what she'd done, so how the hell could she judge him for it? God, what a mess. 'But that also means you never asked her if it was true,' she pointed out, struggling to understand the way events had unfolded. 'You didn't give her a chance.' It didn't stack up. Why would Stephen make up such disgusting lies about Melody, who by all accounts he had genuinely cared for and changed for?

'It had to be done quickly,' Matt ground his back teeth, lip scar burning white. 'I was so furious I just wanted her gone and so did Stephen. We both felt betrayed and he was hurting, big time. I could have called the police you know. Blackmail is a criminal offence.'

She put a hand to her temple, massaging away the dull ache. 'But you didn't, even though you believed him,' she murmured as the fuzzy picture, the pieces that hadn't made sense started to slot together and come into focus. 'Why?'

He sighed, looking troubled. 'She was a nice girl until then and you were right a minute ago, we got on well. She was good to my kids. For some reason I couldn't just put that aside.'

'You didn't want to see her hauled through an investigation or face prison so you cut her loose as quickly as possible?'

'Perhaps. But more importantly if she left and didn't follow through on the threat of blackmail there would be no court case, no media circus and it wouldn't hurt my brother any more than it already had.'

In his own way Matt had tried to be fair, Zoe recognised. He had picked the least damaging option for Melody despite what he thought she'd done. An idea occurred to her. 'Or was it that there was a part of you that believed it might not be true?' she tilted her head, studying him thoughtfully. 'Don't tell me you never questioned whether Stephen might be lying?'

'No, I didn't.' He held his hands up. 'Wait. Just hang on a minute. Stephen's not perfect. He can be cocky, fickle and yeah, doesn't have the work ethic that I do or a history of stable relationships. And God knows he made a mess of it with those drug offences, but he was a screwed up kid at the time. At the end of the day he's my brother and wouldn't have any reason to lie.'

'Neither does Melody,' she put her hands on her hips. 'She has no clue about any of this; would be mortified and shocked at even a hint of it.' Her eyes flashed with heat and she stepped forward, jabbing him in the chest with one finger to emphasise her next point. 'She loves him and is as heartbroken as you claim he is. When I flew into Heathrow and found her at Jemima's she was in absolute bits. I had to take her home to our aunt's to recover. She's lost weight. Looks haunted.'

'Well, Stephen's gone AWOL somewhere in the Med,' Matt threw back, pushing her hand away, 'and I haven't heard from him in weeks. In fact I've put feelers out for him, have contacted a few of his friends and am starting to get seriously worried. But he's done this before when he's been in a bad place, so I'm hoping that he just doesn't want to be found at the moment. I'm afraid your sister hasn't got the monopoly on hiding away and hurting, Zoe.'

'No, I guess she hasn't, after all you've been doing it for three years right here in this house,' she lashed out unthinkingly, stung by the suggestion that her sister was somehow dramatising the situation, or not entitled to her heartache.

'Well at least I didn't run away to the other side of the Atlantic like a selfish child,' he retorted.

'What?' She couldn't believe it, the biggest regret of her life ripped open and used against her. 'You bastard. Well, if I'm so selfish you may as well watch me do it again,' she yelled, hardly knowing what she was saying, face flushed and chest tight with rolling anger. Racing over to her wardrobe she wrenched the doors open, yanked a case out of the bottom, unzipped it and began jerking clothes from hangers and flinging them into a haphazard pile.

'Fine by me. I wouldn't want you here after the way you've lied to me anyway.' Marching across the room, he slammed out of the door like it had personally injured him in some way. Just like she had.

Matt bolted down both spiral staircases and stormed into the garden, rage blazing through him. Sitting down on the wooden deck stairs, he leaned forward, elbows on thighs, head in hands. How could he not have seen it, not known that there was more to Zoe than met the eye? He'd suspected she was keeping something from him, but not this. He'd been convinced she was talking to her ex again but had hoped she wasn't, given how well the two of them had been getting on lately. Given the feelings he had tried to push aside but had failed to contain.

He thought back to the last accusation he'd thrown at her. She'd lied to him. He'd been fooled by another woman. Helen had been sneaking around behind his back for months and he'd been blind to it. Now Zoe had done the same. Well, not the same. But both situations had been betrayals. How could she do that to him, to them? Act like she was just there to do a job, when all the while she was trying to trip him up and catch him out?

Sighing, he rubbed the back of his neck, wishing he hadn't had so much to drink last night. His head was pounding and he felt sick. He supposed that could be as much to do with the emotional turmoil as the alcohol leaving his body.

Maybe he wasn't being fair to Zoe. He could see her side of the argument; it was reasonable to want to find out the truth. If Melody had genuinely acted like she didn't understand what'd happened, then of course Zoe would have been furious and puzzled on her sister's behalf. Also, unless Zoe was a Hollywood actress, the astonishment on her face about the blackmail had been sincere, as was the surprise at hearing about Stephen's criminal record. For the hundredth time, Matt wished Stephen had been a bit more focused and a bit less stupid and selfish as a teenager. Then again, everyone made mistakes and there were few things in life that you could never atone for, or come back from.

Screwing his eyes up, he went back over the last six weeks in his mind, scrutinising Zoe's behaviour, the initial anger subsiding as he picked it over and pulled it apart. He didn't get it. She'd hardly ever asked about Melody and what had happened. They'd only discussed Stephen a couple of times. She'd always seemed so focused on the job and getting to know the children, nurturing them and trying to help the three of them become a family again. Because they hadn't been one before she'd arrived. She was right. They had been going through the motions. At least, he had. He'd

561

kept a roof over his children's head, food on the table, made sure Melody looked after their basic needs, but he hadn't given them proper attention or affection. They hadn't been happy, he could see that now. Aimee had been withdrawn and hesitant, with Jasper bouncing off the walls. Zoe had changed that. He thought about the things she'd said about liking him and caring for the children. Reflected on how hard they'd worked together to make Jasper's party a success. How welcoming she'd been to his friends and family. How everything she'd done since her arrival appeared to have his family's best interests at heart.

From the first time he'd met her she'd challenged him on every level. Emotionally, mentally, even physically, because it had been torture keeping his hands off her and he'd had more cold showers over the summer than hot meals.

It had felt genuine. It had felt real. How long had it been since someone had engaged him, made him feel excited about getting up in the morning and spending time with his children? How long had it been since a woman had made him smile at the thought of coming home every day?

'Hello?'

Matt lifted his head at Cynthia's well-spoken tones.

'We tried the doorbell but no-one answered, so we used the side gate,' she explained, walking forward. 'Is everything all right? I'm sorry we're so early but Jasper kept talking about it being Sunday, the day for Hyde Park.' She looked worried, a frown creasing her forehead into lines.

'Yes,' the word came out croaky so he tried again, 'I mean, yes its fine.'

Jasper sprinted over, wrapping his arms round Matt's neck and squeezing tight.

'You okay, buddy?' Matt asked around the lump in his throat.

Jasper leaned back. 'Yep, we had fun with Nanny last night, but I wanted to come back. We're going for a picnic today, right Daddy? I love our picnics.' He gave his dad a big gappy grin.

It was Matt's favourite smile. One he might have been oblivious to if not for Zoe. He pulled Jasper back into the hug, savouring the warmth and sturdiness of his son's body. It was affection they might not be capable of if it wasn't for Zoe, coaxing them all along in the right direction.

'I love our picnics too,' he agreed.

He and his kids had been happy over the last month and a half. Because of Zoe. No matter that she'd lied to him, betrayed him in her own way, she had done a lot of good for them. She was a good person. No one could fake that so successfully and so intensely when living with a family twenty-four seven.

And while he couldn't forgive her right this minute for lying, he could see how it must have looked to an outsider who didn't know the situation. Her motives for coming here had been the same as his for making Mel leave. Love and loyalty for her family. How could he criticise her for that, or fail to empathise?

The truth was she'd done no harm other than hurting him and that was something he could get over. She'd told him the truth the first opportunity she'd had after they'd slept together. Plus, she could hardly have planned or wanted to get involved with a guy she thought had treated her sister so unjustly, a guy who must have looked like a cold uncaring bastard without knowing the context of Mel's behaviour.

What was less clear was what they could do about the situation when she was so adamant her sister would never do such a thing and he was equally adamant Stephen wouldn't fabricate a blackmail plot. The reality was that they might never know what had really happened between Melody and Stephen.

But maybe that's the way it should or would have to stay. Yeah, it would be difficult and no doubt awkward, but it didn't necessarily have to end what he and Zoe had started, did it? Whatever that was.

He wasn't sure. There was so much to process. All he knew was that there was a weird feeling in his chest at the idea of going to

Hyde Park alone with the kids, of waking up tomorrow and Zoe not being part of their home. It made him feel empty. It made him lose his breath.

Shit.

He couldn't let her go.

'Are you going to play with us?' Jasper wiggled away, eyes cajoling as he unknowingly pulled his father from his inner turmoil. 'I really like it when you do that.'

Matt put his best parent face on, smiling slightly and releasing his son. 'Yes, in a minute. Go and play on the bouncy castle for a few minutes first though, okay? The party equipment isn't being picked up by the hire company until tomorrow morning, so you may as well make the most of it.'

'Yay!' Jasper pelted off to the bottom of the garden, taking a running leap and disappearing into the depths of the yellow and red castle, a smiley face forming the entrance.

'What's the matter, Daddy?' Aimee traipsed over to him, a thick Harry Potter book in one hand and a pink rucksack on her back. 'You look upset.'

'I'm fine.' He stood up and gave her a quick hug. His acting skills must be woeful. 'Go and play with your brother for a minute, okay?'

'Sure,' she agreed, sliding the bag off her shoulder and handing it to him with her book.

Bemused, he looked down at the items as Aimee went to join her little brother, her striped skirt ruffled by the slight breeze that was stirring the leaves on the apple tree.

'Parents have many uses,' Cynthia said as she strolled over to him, having waited patiently while he greeted the kids, 'being a pack mule is one of them.' Taking Aimee's things from him she laid them on the nearest sun lounger and placed a slim, lined hand on his arm. 'What is it, Matthew? What's going on? You look terrible.'

He barked out a laugh, and looked at her. 'Thanks.' He almost dropped his gaze before remembering what Zoe had told him. There might not be the censure and accusation in her face that he was expecting. As he met Cynthia's blue eyes, the irises clear and so much like Helen's, he saw that Zoe was right. There was only curiosity and concern greeting him. No condemnation, no anger. The wave of relief made him feel dizzy. Zoe might be right about the guilt too. Could it be that Helen's death wasn't something he needed to torture himself with every day?

'I don't mean it like that. I just wondered if there's something I can do to help?' she asked hesitantly.

'Thank you, but no. It's very kind of you to offer though. It's more than I deserve. I'm afraid I've probably made a mess of something and I need to figure out how to fix it.' He craned his neck to glance up at Zoe's bedroom window, where she was no doubt busily packing. He'd been reeling, but he shouldn't have made that comment about her running away to America. It had been low and uncalled for. Although she'd been at fault too, with her comment about hiding. The difference was, he acknowledged, she'd been right.

Cynthia followed his gaze. 'She's quite lovely, isn't she? She also has a thing for you.'

Matt laughed again, this time in surprise. 'A thing for me? That doesn't sound like you.'

'You don't know me that well,' she rebuked gently. 'We never really got to know each other while you were married to Helen. As for what you deserve, it's as I told Zoe yesterday; you shouldn't be so hard on yourself. I know it might seem odd for me to be at peace with the prospect of you being with another woman given you were married to my daughter, but she's not coming back. It's taken me almost three years to accept that. At the end of the day, you never know what might be around the corner. You have to get on with it.' Squeezing his arm, 'You have a life to live with my grandchildren, Matthew.' The corners of her eyes drooped with sadness, but her smile was brave. 'So I'm sure you'll sort it out with your nanny, whatever it is you've done.'

He took a deep breath, shame flipping his stomach and making him trip over his own words. 'C-Cynthia, I'm so sorry if I haven't made it easy for you to talk to me since Helen died but I just felt so guilty.'

'Let's not do this today. Another time.' Lifting her chin, moisture gathered in her lower lashes. 'It's kept for the last few years so it will keep for another few days. Just knowing you're ready to start talking about it is enough for me. The only thing I'll say in parting is that she was my daughter and I loved her, but she wasn't always right in the things she did or the way she acted.' She sniffed. 'I'd better go. You have more pressing things to sort out.'

'Are you sure?'

'I am.' She dropped her hand from his arm, and straightened her pink satin blouse.

'Okay.' He started across the lawn with her, tucking his hands in his pockets, hardly able to believe how angry he'd been with Zoe less than ten minutes before and how much lighter he felt from Cynthia's accepting attitude. 'Thank you, Cynthia, for everything. For understanding. For having the kids last night too.'

'It was a pleasure,' she replied, turning to face him as she opened the gate, 'we'll have to do it more often so you can have a little more time for yourself. As for the other, I'm just pleased you've found someone who seems to understand what you're going through and who's so determined to make you all happy. She's marvellous with the children and they seem a lot more settled and confident. It's a gift when you find someone who loves you to the degree that your happiness is more important than their own, you know. So please don't do anything silly and throw it away.'

'Love?' His fingers gripped the black wrought-iron handle as he prepared to shut the gate behind her. 'I don't think so.'

'Don't you?' she answered, before slipping past him into the narrow, rose-lined alley.

He stared after her long after she'd gone, his heart pounding in his chest.

'Don't go.'

'Pardon?' Zoe fumbled in the act of packing another pair of shoes in the case, her hands still shaking with the emotional upheaval of their argument.

'You heard me.' Matt clicked the door shut behind him, walking over and sinking down onto the carpet next to her. 'Don't go.'

'You don't want me to leave? Why?' Afraid to look at him, she rearranged another pair of shoes, turning them so they were top to tail, slotting together perfectly. 'So I can look after the kids? So they're not losing a second nanny in the space of two months?' Shame, longing and dread rumbled through her and she couldn't look at him, too afraid of what she might see in his face or what he might read in hers.

'There is that, yeah. Of course. I love my kids and they need you.'

'Oh.' She gulped, lifting a cardigan up and refolding it.

'But I want you to stay for me as well.'

Her eyes flew to his. Suddenly she could look at him, and needed to know what was there. She clutched the cardigan to her chest, voice squeaking. 'Really? Even though I've lied to you for the last month and a half?'

'Really.' His face was deadly serious, his voice hushed. 'I'm not going to pretend I'm not bloody angry with you, because I am. But I can get past it if you can say there's nothing else I need to know, if you can get past what I did to Melody, and if we can put aside what she did,' he put a finger to her lips when she went to protest, 'or didn't do, to Stephen.'

'Right,' she said, her mouth moving against his finger, lips brushing his skin. She jerked her head away. Touching him made it harder to keep a clear head. This wasn't just about them, or what they wanted. There were children involved too. As well as her sister and his brother.

'What's the matter? Don't you want to stay? From what you said about liking me and caring for Aimee and Jasper, how upset you seemed, I thought you'd want to. I'm sorry for what I said about you running away to America. I didn't mean it. I promise I'll never throw that in your face again.'

'Thank you. But it's not that. I mean, it hurt a lot but I shouldn't have said what I did either. I'm sorry. Sorry for everything. I never should have moved in here. It was crazy, stupid and ill thought out. I shouldn't have kept who I was a secret for so long.' She shook her head. 'I do want to stay, but it's just so messy, isn't it? What we've both done, what happened between Stephen, Melody and you. I'm going to have to tell her what you think she did, Matt. It's going to hurt her so much. It'll be horrible. Plus it wasn't so long ago I was engaged to be married, and you've got those issues about Helen. We have to think about the kids too, we need to be careful.'

'I know it's complicated, but nothing of value is ever easy, is it? Stop that. Come here.' Prising the cardigan away and throwing it across the open case, he wrapped his arms around her waist, sliding her across the carpet and onto his lap.

She didn't put up much of a fight, the idea of staying here with him and his kids making her feel giddy, even though it shouldn't. This wasn't part of the plan. Now she knew the lies that Matt believed, she should leave. Except she didn't want to. But then again, when had life ever gone according to expectations? It was usually the unexpected things that made it interesting and worth living.

'I don't know, Matt.' She sighed, closing her eyes and inhaling his aftershave, the scent and sexiness she'd come to associate with him. It was all out in the open now. He knew who she was and why she had come here. Well, it was nearly all out in the open, but she definitely wasn't going to tell him her original intentions. There was no point. He'd asked if there was anything else he needed to know, and there wasn't. It was done with.

Maybe they could face the other issues together. Give whatever it was they had a chance. She just hoped Mel wouldn't see it as a betrayal. But the last time they'd spoken about it, her sister had said Matt wasn't a bastard and must have had good reason for chucking her out. At least Zoe would be able to confirm that was the case. That he wasn't a bad guy after all. She just hoped it didn't break her sister's heart again to hear what Stephen had accused her of and what Matt had believed.

'Stop making excuses,' he ordered, and she opened her eyes to look at him. 'I get that you're scared and the situation is hardly an ideal way to start a relationship and we don't even know what it is or where it's going to lead yet,' he continued, 'but come on, Zoe, we've been happy together, the four of us. I like being around you. We laugh together, have fun together, you challenge me and make me think. You make me a better dad.' His arms tightened around her as she fought and lost the war to rest her cheek on his chest. 'You're kind and caring,' stroking her hair, 'and then there's the bonus of the great sex,' he half-joked.

'Hey, easy buddy,' she answered, lifting her head and thumping him on the shoulder.

'Are you going to deny that last night was amazing, as well as bloody hot?' He pointed to the rumpled bed.

'No,' she said, 'I just don't want you to get a big head.'

'No chance of that with you around,' he mocked, 'you're always telling me how it is. And just think,' he added, a wicked glint in his eye, 'that was half drunk, fast and furious. Just imagine what it might be like if we were sober and were taking our time. Imagine me peeling off your clothes and covering your whole body with kisses, before sucking on your—'

Slapping a hand over his dirty mouth, she squirmed on his hard thighs and moaned. 'Stop. I heard Cynthia bring the children back. They're down in the garden, right? So we can't do anything now.'

He pulled a sorrowful expression. 'You're probably right.' He shifted so that she could feel the rigid length of him against her bum. 'It'll have to be a date for tonight,' he suggested, 'if that's what you want?'

She hesitated, thinking hard. 'It is. I do want to be with you, Matt. Even though it flies in the face of everything I should want

569

under the circumstances. But you're right, we have been happy. So let's just take it a day at a time and see what happens. Right?'

'Right,' he smiled. Then a shadow fluttered across his face. 'Are you going to be offended if I ask something?'

'We need to be discreet for the children's sakes,' she guessed the source of his concern, 'so I'll wait until they're in bed. Then you can come to my room or I can come to yours, but either way we go back to our rooms for morning. We mustn't confuse them, especially as we have so much to work through and figure out for ourselves. We're probably going to have to talk to Stephen and Melody at some point you know.'

'I know,' he said solemnly, before ruining it by grinning. 'You're so brilliant. Thank you for always putting the kids first.'

'I wouldn't have it any other way.' She looped her arms around his neck, kissing him gently, just once. 'I still can't believe you're okay with this.' The prospect of him finding out who she was had been a massive hurdle in her mind. She'd assumed he'd throw her straight out, but that fear hadn't materialised.

A warm feeling started to unfurl in her chest. He wanted her to stay. She made them happy. Though she hadn't wanted to admit her reluctance to leave even to herself, the truth was that they made her happy too. What should have been an awful time in her life with her break up, boxing up her old life and struggling to make a new one, had instead been an adventure.

'I told you,' he tapped her nose, 'I'm angry and hurt but I'll get over it. Of course, you may have to offer me some therapy for a while, just until I'm over the worst. You did suggest it might help.'

'What kind of therapy?' she asked suspiciously, wondering where this was going.

'I've heard that sex therapy is enormously beneficial. What do you think?'

'I think you're misquoting me,' she leaned in and bit his lower lip, before pulling away to watch his green eyes darken and smoulder, 'but I think we can experiment a bit and assess the results.'

'Great. Nine o'clock tonight? My room?'

Grinning, she wiggled around on his lap, making him groan. 'Perfect.'

He wrapped his arms around her and leaned in to kiss her, but with a laugh she jumped up and held out her hand. 'Enough of that. Come on, we have kids to see and a picnic to pack for.'

Groaning, he struggled to his feet, tugging his jeans away from his groin and linking his fingers with hers. 'Fine, you mad woman. Let's go and get ready to go to Hyde Park. But if Jasper jumps into the Serpentine again, you're on lifeguard duty.'

Rising on her tiptoes she planted a quick hard kiss on his mouth. 'Fine by me, as long as you buy us all ice-creams again.'

'Deal.' He swatted her bum as she let go of his hand and danced out ahead of him, the coffees and pastries on the bedside cabinet forgotten as they made their way down to the garden, the sunshine and his kids.

16

The next few days passed in a steamy haze of incredible sex and stolen kisses. Matt was sweet and attentive, helping her cook Jasper a special birthday dinner and spending the last few days of the kid's summer break at home, joining the three of them for lunch every day and even inviting them down into the basement to learn about the soundboard. Surprisingly, Jasper was a natural, with an ear for music and a fascination for the various buttons and functions that delighted his dad.

Zoe crept into Matt's room every night and left early every morning, but still managed to fall asleep in his arms. To her surprise he was a snuggler, enjoying the way her body tucked into the curve of his, complaining when her alarm went off at half past five and she left his bed, trying to tug her back in for just five more minutes, sounding like an older, more petulant version of his son. It made her smile, and melt.

They took the kids to school together on the first morning of term, waving Jasper off proudly as he started in Reception, the pretty brunette teacher talking to her new pupil reassuringly while making eyes at Matt.

Zoe had noticed all the women looking at him, surreptitiously finger combing their hair or dabbing on lipstick.

'What?' he'd asked innocently when she'd given him a dirty look.

She raised an eyebrow.

'Can I help it if they think I'm gorgeous?' he joked in a way she never would have imagined him capable of on the day of her interview.

'I suppose you're okay to look at,' she shrugged, 'but you might want to consider getting the nose fixed and the scar lasered. Some people might see them as flaws.'

'Good thing you don't,' he growled, yanking her into his arms, apparently not bothered by the people around them who were all staring avidly. 'I happen to know you find both sexy and adorable.'

'Bugger, I knew I shouldn't have told you that.'

'Well, we were in bed and I'd just rocked your world,' he whispered in her ear, making her knees fold. 'It's moments like that when women get all soft and gooey, isn't it?'

Pushing him away she's smacked his arm lightly. 'Not as bad as you, Mr Snuggles,' she said loudly. Grinning to herself she'd skipped off to the car, leaving him to trail along behind her muttering retribution.

After that they soon settled into a routine, Matt disappearing to his city office and studio every morning and Zoe doing the school runs each day and redecorating the kids' rooms in between. It was a task she'd begged for in order to occupy herself in the daytime and because it sorely needed doing. Although jam-packed with books and gizmo's respectively, Aimee and Jasper's bedrooms were as white and soulless as the rest of the place and needed some colour and personality. They were already enjoying sharing their ideas with her on themes and motifs and helping her pick things out of high end furniture catalogues.

Matt made a special effort to say goodbye to both children every morning and wish them a good day, and was always back by six to help them with their homework while Zoe made sandwiches for lunch boxes and cooked dinner. They were happy and it was working, although neither Matt nor Zoe had quite built up the nerve to tackle the question of Stephen and Melody yet. They were just enjoying what they had. Or maybe just hiding from reality and hoping for the best.

Until one morning when Zoe came home juggling wallpaper samples to find Matt in her bedroom, kneeling on the floor with an odd expression on his face.

'Hiya. What are you doing in here?' she asked. 'Why aren't you at the office? You didn't say anything about being here today when you left earlier.'

'I came back to let the delivery men in.' He said in a curt tone that she hadn't heard in weeks. 'I was getting a bespoke bookcase built for you.' He waved a hand at the new shiny oak shelves spanning one side of the room. 'It was supposed to be a surprise. I thought you'd be at the shops for longer. I started filling it with the books you'd unpacked. I was sorting them by genre and alphabetising them for you. You told me once that's how you liked them.'

'That's right.' She beamed at his sweet gesture. 'Thanks so much. It's such a lovely thought.' Flinging the samples down, she made to run across the room to him.

He stood up, holding his hands out, face washed of colour. 'Don't come any closer.'

'What? Why?' she frowned.

'Because I finally know what a lying, deceitful bitch you are and I don't want you anywhere near me. Or for that matter, my children.'

'What are you talking about?' She felt the blood seep out of her face and swayed. 'Why are you talking to me like this? You know about Melody. You said we could get past it.'

'I could. But you said there was no more, nothing else to tell me,' he hissed.

'Matt, what are you on about?'

He stalked towards her. 'This!' Thrusting a balled up piece of paper at her chest so hard that it would probably leave a bruise. He backed up rapidly, distaste curling his lip. 'You promised me once you weren't a journalist. And you're not. God, you're worse.

At least some of them are up front about who they are and what they're after.'

'I don't understand.'

'Read it,' he snarled. 'It might help jog your memory. I found it inside a book you were reading a few weeks ago.'

Slowly unfolding the piece of A4 paper, her mouth shaped a succinct, 'Shit,' as her eyes traced the words on the page.

The Truth About Matt Reilly

It's well known that infamous London-based music producer Matt Reilly is fiercely private and camera shy. He never gives interviews to the press, and seems uncomfortable at public events, preferring the focus to be on his artists. In an exclusive story, the girl who was his nanny for X months shares a kiss and tell story about his love life, his relationship with his two children and his ruthless work ethic ...

'Oh, fuck. No.' She remembered the night she'd printed the rough draft out, the way she'd read it and how lousy she'd felt, realising what a cow she was being. Tucking it into the back of a beach read she'd picked up in a street market one Saturday morning, she had forgotten all about it. 'Matt, hang on a minute. It's not what you think—'

'It's not?' he exclaimed in mock amazement. 'You mean you didn't write that? You're not the nanny that's quoted?'

Now was the moment for total and utter honesty. No more lies or half-truths. 'I did write it,' she met his gaze squarely, 'I am that nanny. But it was written a while ago, before I really knew you properly,' her voice grew pleading at the closed off expression on his face, one she hadn't seen since first arriving, even the day they'd argued when he found out she was Melody's sister. 'I was frustrated, angry, confused and venting one day, and yes, I'll level with you, it *was* my plan to do this originally,' she waved the crumpled piece of paper in the air, 'to expose the guy I thought had treated my little sister so despicably. A guy I thought was a heartless, immoral shit, but within a couple of weeks of being here I knew I couldn't do it. I didn't want the kids to get hurt, or later on, you.'

'Really? Is that what I'm supposed to believe?' he said, voice heavy with sarcasm.

'Yes,' she rushed across the room despite what he'd said about staying away, and stepped into his space, 'you have to understand that I wasn't in the right frame of mind when I set out to do this. I was heartbroken at Greg's deceit, or thought I was at the time, and how I'd lost five years with my sister for a cheating pig. Then Melody was so broken, so devastated, I lost it. But you have to believe me—'

'Let's get one thing clear.' His jaw was taut, lips as white as the plump roses in his garden. 'I believe fuck all of what you say.' He laughed bitterly, 'Jesus, now you'll be telling me it wasn't you that tipped off the press that day we were in Hyde Park when you were hung over.'

'It wasn't. Honestly, it was nothing to do with me. It's just a coincidence.'

'A coincidence? You must think I'm a complete idiot. It's a coincidence that an article that would have set you up so neatly as a credible source just happened to be published in a national newspaper weeks before you were going to do your sordid little kiss and tell about my sex life, and who knows what else?'

Flinching, she balled the paper back up and tossed it aside. 'I swear on my parent's graves that it was nothing to do with me and that the article I planned was never going to see the light of day. In fact, I wrote another one. That's the one you need to see.'

'Let me be clear. I have no interest in seeing anything you want to show me, or hearing anything either. That day, the one after Jasper's birthday party, when we'd slept together and you told me about Melody, I asked if there was anything else you needed to tell me. If there was anything else I needed to know. You said no, there was nothing. So why the hell should I believe you now when you tell me you were never going to use this? Why?' he shouted, eyes glinting, a vein pulsing in his forehead.

'You didn't need to know. I wasn't going to go through with it, so why hurt you by telling you?' she cried. 'As for why you should believe me, I don't know. I've given you every reason to distrust me, but I never meant any harm. Please, Matt. I love your kids, and I didn't think I'd feel this way about anyone so soon after Greg, but I do. The last few weeks have been amazing. Let's not throw that away.'

'You threw it away the moment you made the decision not to tell me. If you'd come clean, told me what you'd planned, shown the article to me but sworn it was never going to be used and destroyed it in front of me then I might have faith now. I might trust you. But you didn't. It's another betrayal.' He yanked his hands through his dark hair. 'You and your sister really are two peas in a pod, aren't you? You definitely share the same morals. To think what I've been exposing my children to. It makes me feel ill. All that publicity if the article goes out …'

'That's not fair! Don't bring Mel into it. She's done nothing wrong. This is on me. I made a mistake. We all make them, so please don't act as if you're immune. As for the kids, I told you, it's not going out. I swear. I would never do that.'

'Whatever.' He turned his back on her, staring fixedly out the window. 'You need to go. I'll arrange to send your stuff to you in a few days' time. Text me your address.'

'Matt?' she said uncertainly.

'I said, go.'

'You can't mean that.' Her eyes filled with tears.

'Can't I?' he gritted his teeth, broad shoulders tense and set. 'Get the hell out of my house, Zoe. Now.'

'You're repeating history. You're doing to me what you did to Mel. You were wrong then, and you're wrong now. Give me a chance to prove myself.'

'How exactly are you going to do that?' he asked without turning around.

She hesitated, thoughts whirring. 'I-I don't know right at this minute, but there must be a way.'

'I don't think so.' He dropped his hands to the window sill, clutching hold of the edge, knuckles pale. 'Leave.'

She could see he wasn't going to change his mind right now. He was too furious. Maybe if she gave him time, he might come around. 'But what about the kids? I dropped them off and they're expecting me to pick them up. I can't just leave without saying anything. They'll feel abandoned again after Helen and Melody—'

He span around, eyes wide, 'Don't you dare talk about Helen. And you don't deserve to say goodbye! You would have exposed them to the worst kind of ridicule at school with that article, would have marked them out for bullies. Did you ever think of that, or were you just too intent on getting revenge?'

'I've already told you I wasn't going to go through with it. Let me just see them, please. We can tell them I'm going away for a while, taking a holiday or something.'

'I'll tell them you had to attend to a sick relative. I'll say that you'll be gone for a while and then after a few weeks I'll tell them you had to leave for good. They'll understand. They'll get over it.'

She gulped, a sob lodged in her throat and a burning pain throbbing in her chest. 'But maybe I won't,' she whispered.

'What was that?'

'Nothing. I'm sorry. About everything. I'm telling you the truth though. One day you'll know that.'

'What I know is that you've got exactly five minutes to pack anything you can into a bag and get out of my house. You can take the BMW because right now I want you as far away from us as quickly as possible. I'll get it collected when your belongings are dropped off to you. But to be honest, at this moment I don't care if you keep it. I want you gone and it would be a small price to pay.' Marching across the room, he grabbed hold of the door handle and gave her a hard look. 'Don't bother coming to find me when you go. I'll be busy calling my solicitor. Goodbye, Zoe.' He slammed the door behind him with a scary finality.

She heard his footsteps recede as she stifled a sob, feeling numb and dazed at the same time. What had she done? How had she messed up so spectacularly and caused both of them so much pain?

Eyes glazed with moisture, she stumbled around the room, drunkenly stumbling from the bathroom to the bedroom and from one piece of furniture to another, hardly aware of what she was stuffing into a small vanity case. Holding it together, just, she lost it when she found a painting Jasper had given her, one of the four of them in Hyde Park sharing a picnic, a giant splodge of yellow sunshine in the upper right corner, lines of dark blue depicting a summer sky. Tears rolled down her cheeks and plopped onto her top as she carefully tucked a bookmark Aimee had made for her into the inside pocket of the case.

A minute later she was ready to go, but there was one last thing she did before leaving the house that had become her home in such a short time. Scrabbling around the lockable drawer of the bedside unit, she slid out the redraft of the kiss and tell article she'd written one night and sealed it in an envelope. Sneaking into Matt's room with guilt scorching her cheeks scarlet, she left it on the pillow she'd slept on for the last few nights, hoping he would understand what she was trying to tell him when she'd barely been able to put it into words herself. When she was only just in this moment realising what it was she was losing.

Zoe and Mel hugged tightly, a bulging backpack at their feet. The sisters had travelled into London from Southend together by train and had lunch before parting ways outside the gracefully arched building that housed Fenchurch Street Station. Zoe clutched Melody against her, desperate not to let go but knowing she had to. 'I'm going to miss you.' She laughed and sniffed at the same time as a few people jostled past them with the arrival of a train. It was mid-September and most of the tourists had returned home. She couldn't believe the summer was almost over. It was especially hard to process when the days were still so balmy and the evenings so light. They'd got the Indian summer that had been predicted after all. 'Are you sure this is the right thing to do?'

'Yes,' Melody drew back.

'Funny that this time it's not me running away, it's you,' Zoe remarked. 'That I'm the one staying put.'

'Living with Ruth will give you both a chance to keep on rebuilding your relationship.' Mel smiled, a sparkle in her dark eyes that Zoe hadn't seen in months. 'And I'm not running away. I'm going to find who I am.'

'You think travelling across Europe will give you that?'

'I think Jemima and I are going to have some wonderful adventures,' Mel said firmly, taking Zoe by surprise with how confident she sounded, 'and seeing the world will give me a chance to think, really think about what I want to do with my life and who I want to be. The last career decision I made was based on wanting to impress and be like you and while I still admire you loads I have to do something I'm passionate about. Plus it'll finally help me get over Stephen. We know he's back in the UK now,' they'd caught a snippet in the celebrity gossip pages the previous weekend which had included a tiny picture of her ex going into his Chelsea apartment, 'but he still hasn't been in touch and after what he told Matt about me, I don't want him anywhere near me anyway.' Pain and bewilderment scrunched up her face but with an effort she forced it away, relaxing her mouth and blinking away tears.

Zoe nodded, squeezing her sister's hands, 'Well, it's your decision. You have to do what's right for you. I'm not going to try and boss you around. I have learnt something from this whole mess.'

'Thanks, Sis. Thank you so much for the money too, I really appreciate it. I'll pay you back, I swear.'

'There's no need to, honestly. You deserve this, and I'm happy to share it with you. I saved up a lot when I was working for Liberty and I got back the share of the money I put into the wedding when I cancelled it. Ruth was pleased to help out too. She told me she's had no-one to spend it on since we've both been gone.' She smiled, thinking of her improved relationship with her aunt, one that meant she had somewhere to stay while she got her head together and tried to assimilate what she was going to do next. What the future may hold for her without Matt, Aimee and Jasper. 'Actually,' she shared, thinking of Ruth's future too, 'I was thinking that travelling and expanding her world might be good for her at some point. Maybe when you come back and tell us all about your adventures, we might persuade her to travel abroad?'

'That's a great idea. I've always thought she was too self-contained and should experience more of life. Not necessarily because she never got married or had kids of her own—after all, she had us—but more because she doesn't have many friends or go out much.'

'Well, I'll see what I can do about that while you're away,' Zoe said decisively.

'Good.' Melody nodded. 'You'll be fine, you know. You always are. I'm sure interviews and job offers will start flooding in soon.'

'Perhaps, if Matt even gives me a reference,' Zoe gulped, mouth twisting. 'I'm not that bothered about getting a job right now though, Mel. I don't need the money immediately and I've been thinking I might do something else for a while. It's just that I miss them so much. I should have handled things better. If only I'd told him the whole story when I told him I was your sister.' She had so many regrets. But on the other hand, she had her family back. She and Mel were more than okay and after two weeks at her aunt's home, coastal Southend was starting to feel comfortable.

She sighed. Actually, the truth was that she longed for London, the size and shape of it, the people and places, the buzz and the hum, the architectural marvels amongst the modern skyscrapers, the wide open green spaces in the middle of the teeming city. She'd left her heart here and she wasn't sure she'd ever get it back.

'I know you miss them,' Mel acknowledged. 'It's the sight of your moping face that's driven me to fly to Paris,' she teased, 'and even Ruth is beginning to feel sorry for you.'

Zoe's face fell.

'Hey, I was joking.' Melody's eyebrows pulled down in concern. 'Look, are you going to be all right? I should be leaving to meet Jemima soon. Our flight is only in a few hours.'

'I'll be fine. Go.' She didn't tell her sister she still hadn't brought herself to text Matt with Ruth's details. That she couldn't face the thought of all her stuff being dropped off to her, a tangible milestone that would signal the end of her relationship with him and the children for good. Clearing her throat, 'Don't forget I'm expecting regular Facebook posts and albums with anything too outrageous to share sent to me by email.'

'I know, I know.' Mel frowned, 'Do you know what the time is?'

'Hold on,' she bent her head to dig her mobile out of her handbag. Squinting at the phone, 'It's just gone two 'o' clock,' she said absently as she opened a text from Rayne.

> **You need to pick up a copy**
> **of The Telegraph. It'll be**
> **worth it, I promise.**
> **Let me know how it goes.**
>
> **xxx**

Wondering what on earth her friend was on about and if she should call her to find out, Zoe jerked her head up as Melody made a startled sound.

'Is that Matt?'

'What? Where?' Zoe asked breathlessly, spinning around.

'No. In the paper.' Her sister pointed at the front page on a pile of newspapers on a stand along the concourse from them, where a grizzled guy in a flat-cap was taking money and giving out folded up papers to passers-by.

'What the hell?' Zoe hurried over to the man, rooting around in her jeans pocket for the right change and practically throwing it at him, almost ripping the paper out of his hands in her haste to see it.

A picture of Matt sat under a bold headline. *The Truth About Matt Reilly; an exclusive interview.* The name of the journalist was one she recognised, a freelancer Rayne worked with sometimes.

Mel was on her heels as Zoe wrenched open the paper looking for the right page.

'An interview?' Mel said. 'I don't get it. Matt never gives interviews. He hates the press.'

'I know,' Zoe murmured as she found the article, hope soaring in her chest, the newspaper jumping up and down as her hands shook. She started reading.

I was lucky enough to interview a handsome, exhausted Matt Reilly yesterday, and he's not at all what I expected. Staring out at the beautiful garden of his multi-million pound property in Knightsbridge, the famous music producer who has a reputation with the ladies looks reflective and answers my questions candidly. Everything I ask him about (save for his children, who he is very protective of)—his career, his ambitions for the future, the death of his late wife, his love life—he responds to with a brutal honesty that takes me by surprise, given how fiercely guarded he's been in the past. The turnaround is surprising, but it soon becomes clear why he has chosen to make an exception. 'I've learnt a lot about myself over the last few months,' he states when I ask him what his biggest regret is, 'that I'm quick to judge; that I trust the wrong people sometimes, which regrettably may include family; that I am human and it's all right to make mistakes; and that I should follow my gut instinct and heart in knowing what's best for me and my kids. Most of all I've learnt that contrary to what I thought, it's okay to forgive myself for the things I can't change, and move on. My biggest regret is that the person I most want to move on with, the girl I love and who loves my children, is out there somewhere and I don't know where. So here I am, laying myself bare in the hope that she will read this and come find us. So that I can tell her how I feel, so that I can say sorry. If it's a Sunday afternoon, she'll know where we'll be.

'Oh my God,' Zoe breathed on a small sob, clutching the paper to her chest and gazing open mouthed at her sister. 'He loves me?' she said in wonder. 'He loves me. I can't believe he's done this. Rayne must have helped set it up, that's what the text was about.'

'It's you. It can't be anyone else.' Mel shook her head.

'It is me,' she whispered, starting to smile before faltering. 'But what about you?'

'Don't worry about me,' Mel grabbed her elbows, 'just because I don't get my happy ever after, it doesn't mean you can't have yours. Go to him. Go to them,' she pleaded 'You've been so miserable, there's no way you can ignore this. We know why he sacked me and chucked me out now. I don't bear any grudge against him. It wasn't his fault, he just believed his shit of a brother when he shouldn't have done. It's understandable. You would always believe me, wouldn't you?'

'Of course. I love you. But I can't do this again. You're my sister and he's a guy—'

'Uh-nuh. No way,' she started softly. 'You're not doing this. I know you feel guilty about the whole going to America thing after your break up with Henry, but I told you we're cool about that. Plus, this is not the same thing. You're not choosing Matt over me. I'm going travelling and I don't expect you to put your life on hold while I'm gone.' Her voice gained strength. 'As long as you promise that you'll stay in touch and that when I'm back we'll always make time for each other, then that's all we need.'

'I promise. Of course I do.'

'Good.' She pushed Zoe away almost roughly. It was uncharacteristic and Zoe realised the breakup had changed her sister. But maybe it wasn't a bad thing. Maybe it would make her more

584

resilient and less naive. 'Now get going,' Mel instructed. 'I have a plane to catch today and you have a family to reclaim. Tell them I said hello, by the way. That,' she waved at a red bus that had just pulled into station, 'is probably going to be your best bet at getting to them.'

'Thanks, sis. Love you heaps,' Zoe hugged Melody again, and started backing away, a sense of urgency filling her. 'Safe flight, text me when you take off and land. Don't forget to text Ruth too.'

'I won't,' Melody rolled her eyes at her sibling's bossiness. 'I'll see you in a couple of months. Love you too.'

Zoe turned to go but stopped at the last moment, studying her sister's face, memorising the curve of her cheek, the arch of her fine eyebrows, the dark eyes and blonde hair. 'Have a brilliant time, Mel. I hope you find what you're looking for and you're happy. That's all I wish for you.'

Welling up, Melody ran over and gave her one last hug. 'Thanks. Now you know I hate goodbyes, so please go.'

Zoe chuckled as they separated. 'We'll make it a *see you soon* then.' Blowing her a kiss, she sprinted to the bus and clambered on just as the driver was closing the doors. 'Wait,' she begged, 'there's somewhere I have to be.'

Zoe threw a shadow across Matt as she stood over him in the afternoon sunshine near the Princess Diana Memorial fountain. It reminded her of the first time she'd brought the kids here. It wasn't as roasting hot as it had been that day, but the air was still balmy and the sound of happy children rolled over her along with the tinkle and swish of water. Matt was lying on the familiar picnic blanket, eyes closed but looking far from relaxed with a crinkle between his eyebrows.

The newspaper was rolled up in her hand and she'd read the whole interview three times on the agonising, crawling half an hour journey to Hyde Park.

'Hi,' she said simply.

'Zoe.' His eyes flew open. 'Hi.' He leapt up, an uncertain expression on his gorgeous face. It was just like she'd remembered it. The crooked nose, the sexy scar, the beautiful green eyes. 'You came.'

'I did,' she agreed solemnly. 'Was I right to? Am I the girl?'

'What?' he looked dumbstruck. 'Of course you're the girl!'

'Good.' Now she was here, she wasn't sure what to say, how to act. She had missed them all so much. Why wasn't he grabbing her and kissing her senseless? 'Where are Aimee and Jasper?' she swivelled her head to search for them.

'Over there,' he gestured to a spot ten feet away where the kids were sitting on the stone edge kicking water at each other. 'I only had my eyes closed for a moment.'

She smiled. 'I'm sure you did. Don't worry, I won't call the police on you.'

'Great.'

'So.' Zoe shifted from one foot to another.

'So … shall we sit down?' Matt gestured to the blanket.

Why was he being so formal? 'No. This is bullshit, Matt. What's going on? You give this unbelievably romantic interview saying you love me and to come find you and when I come running, you act all weird.'

'You thought it was romantic?'

'Um, yeah,' she answered, 'any girl would.'

'Aren't you angry with me about making you leave? And that I believed Stephen over Melody?'

'Yes,' she said bluntly, taking a step towards him, desperate to feel his strong arms wrapped around her now she knew how he felt. 'And no. I was hurt and pissed off that you didn't listen, but once I calmed down I could see how it must have looked. Do I think you should have given me more of a chance to explain myself? Yes. Can I blame you for feeling betrayed or mistrusting me? No. I said so at the time and like you said in the interview, people make mistakes. As for Stephen, I understand why as his brother you would want to believe him. Mel and I have talked about it.

She doesn't have an issue with you, only him. She gets it. I do too.'

'Right,' he nodded slowly.

'So what did happen with Stephen? And how did you find out?'

Matt shoved his hands in his pockets. 'He popped up out of nowhere a week or so ago like he'd never been away and never worried me sick. When he saw the state I was in, he felt really guilty, got drunk one night and turned up on my doorstep at three in the morning. He started going on about loving Melody, rambling on about fucking it up and being scared,' he took a deep breath, 'and after a very painful hour, admitted to me he'd made the whole thing up because he was petrified of commitment and panicked. Would you believe it? He didn't want to break up with Melody because he'd fallen for her but he couldn't face the thought of settling down either. So he forced me to do his dirty work. He's a coward. I guess if it was me that made her leave, he could fool himself it wasn't his fault. He was miserable when he was away though and said he'd been a tosser. I didn't disagree. He shocked me by apologising for being stupid, selfish and causing us all a lot of pain. To be honest I think he wants her back but knows he's gone too far.'

'He has. I honestly don't think she could ever forgive him for it. God, what he did is really messed up,' Zoe muttered, wondering if it would be a good idea or a bad one for Mel to know that what had been an awful thing for Stephen to do had been fear borne out of the strongest emotion of all. Love. 'So what did you say to him?'

'I was too furious to say anything. I rang a taxi to take him back to his place in Chelsea and haven't spoken to him since. It's been a week. He's left a few messages but hasn't worked up the courage to come round yet.'

'What will you do when he does?'

'I don't know. All I know is that I'm so, so sorry for what I did to Melody.' He pushed his hands through his dark hair, looking wretched. 'I got it wrong and feel awful. I really want to talk to her, to try and make amends. At the very least she should get

587

some notice and holiday pay, right? I need to see her. Would that be okay, do you think?'

'I think it's too late for that, Matt.'

'Really? Shit. She hates me.'

'No, she doesn't,' she reassured him. 'She's gone travelling for a few months. But I'll happily let her know you'd like to see her when she gets back. Whatever happens after that is between the two of you, okay?'

'Yes. I'd appreciate that, thanks.' He hesitated. 'What do you think I should do about Stephen?'

Shrugging, she edged closer to him. 'I'm not sure. If you're looking for me to tell you never to see him again, never to forgive him, I won't. Firstly, because it's not my place to or my decision to make, and secondly because as much as he broke my sister's heart and I'll have a hard time reconciling that, life is too short to shut people out of it forever. I think it's like we agreed once when we were talking about us. You take it one day at a time, and see how you feel.'

'Sometimes that's not the right thing to do, though,' he answered, striding forward and finally scooping her up in his arms. He kissed her cheeks, her forehead, her neck, her mouth as she laughed. 'Sometimes you don't take it one day at a time,' he continued, 'because when you've found something that might last forever, you want to commit to it, make it yours. You never know what might happen or when it might be taken away.'

From the look on his face, Zoe could tell Matt was thinking about Helen. About how precarious and precious life was. 'Say it then,' she ordered.

'Say what?' he pulled a puzzled face, before burying his head in her neck and whispering, 'you smell so good. I've missed you so much.'

'Me too. Now say you love me.'

Lifting his head, he smiled down at her. 'I love you. I'm sorry I doubted you. When I read that other article you wrote and spoke to Rayne, I knew I was wrong. You never would have done that to us. Do you love me?' he demanded. 'Is that why you came?'

'Yes. As well as the fact that you still owe me an ice-cream.' She yelped when he pinched her bum. 'Okay, I love you too,' her lips curved, knowing it was the improbable, wonderful truth. She thought about the redraft of the kiss and tell story left on his pillow.

The Truth About Matt Reilly

There are many truths about Matt Reilly, infamous music producer. He is rich and doesn't mind spending his money on expensive cars. But he is also generous towards other people and thinks about their needs. He doesn't have many friends because he doesn't trust the people around him, but he is fiercely loyal to those he does have and their happiness is important to him. He is hard working and driven to be a positive role model for his children, and though this can mean he is distant and works long hours, you can't doubt his love for them. He gives himself a hard time when he shouldn't, but doesn't always hold a mirror up to himself when he should. He is funny, caring and an all-round nice guy with firm principles. The truth is, though he might not realise it, he is imminently lovable. The question is, will he let himself be loved?

'So you'll come back to mine? You'll be the kids' nanny again?' Stroking her hair off her face, Matt tucked it tenderly behind her ear.

She turned into his touch, revelling in it, feeling safe and loved. 'No. I won't be their nanny again.'

'What? Why?' he dropped his hand, confusion and distress creasing his face up.

She held a hand up to his stubbly cheek, delighting in the rasp of his whiskers. 'They don't really need me in that way now if they're both settled at school. But we'll tell them I'm their nanny and I'll move back into my old rooms until we're ready and they're ready for it to be more, if you want that?' She smiled at the relief on his face as he nodded emphatically. 'I'll do the school runs and help with homework in the evenings, but I'll be doing it because I want to, not for pay. And we'll redecorate their rooms together. While they're at school I'll be pursuing other career options. How does that sound?'

'That sounds perfect,' he hugged her close, laying his chin on top of her head and breathing in deeply. 'Let's do it.' Leaning back, he stared down at her. 'So what other options are you thinking of?

'I have some money put away, so I was thinking of training to be a counsellor. What do you think?' she held her breath, dreading the idea that he might laugh at her as Greg would have done.

'I think you'd be brilliant at it. I also think that whatever you want to do, I'm a hundred per cent behind you.'

'Thank you. That means a lot,' she grinned, knowing she'd found someone lovely. Someone who would always support her dreams. Someone who would always help her reach for the stars in the summer sky.

'Zoe! Zoe!' Jasper's excited cry greeted her at the same time as two extra pairs of arms did.

'Zoe,' Aimee's more sensible voice piped up. 'You're here.'

Zoe shrieked at the dampness seeping through her top. 'Jasper, you're soaking.'

'Sorry,' the little boy said sheepishly, moving back slightly.

Aimee shook her head at her brother, ponytail swishing. 'You'll make her leave again,' she tutted.

'Its fine,' Zoe reassured, hungrily taking in their adorable faces. 'I have missed you guys so much.' She looked at Matt, who nodded and mouthed *home*. 'I'm sorry I left but I'm not going anywhere. I'm back. How do you feel about that?'

Jasper let out a, 'Yay!' and delivered an air punch, while his sister gave a more sedate but equally enthusiastic nod.

'Great. What about a little rest before we have ice-cream? I don't know about you, but I'm a bit tired.'

'Kay,' Jasper dropped to the blanket, followed by Aimee. They both looked expectantly at their dad.

'I guess I'm the lucky one who gets to go underneath,' he said with a raised eyebrow, appearing far from horrified by the idea, green eyes warm and full of affection.

She winked at him, love swelling her heart and her chest. She was back where she belonged. 'I guess you do. If you're really lucky we can do that tonight too,' she said suggestively under her breath.

Without hesitation he lay down and waited for them to clamber over him and get comfortable.

Zoe grinned widely as she lay down and rested her head on Matt's flat stomach, her arms around his adorable but complicated children as they snuggled into both adults.

For the first time in a long time, she was hopeful that she would get her happily ever after. She was also certain that for many years to come they would enjoy picnics in beautiful, leafy Hyde Park.

Author Q&A with Nikki Moore

1. The #LoveLondon series is an interesting concept. Can you tell us what led you to write it?

The series was born out of me pitching my second full length novel *Picnics in Hyde Park* (a romance set in London) to my lovely editor Charlotte and her commissioning me to write a number of London based short romances linked to the novel and each other. I thought it was a brilliant and very exciting idea and couldn't wait to get started.

My debut *Crazy, Undercover, Love* was partly set in London and I've always loved the city and get a real buzz every time I visit, so I knew I wanted my second novel to be wholly set there. I find our capital endlessly fascinating because there's so much to see and do, and it's very diverse. I love the pace, architecture, nightlife, landmarks ... I think I could live in London and still never come closing to experiencing all of it. So when I had to fit in a few research trips for this series, I was very happy! It is totally true that I #LoveLondon.

2. How did you create each story to make it unique while linked and thematic?

The idea for the series evolved a number of times. Charlotte and I eventually settled on a series that would lead up to *Picnics at Hyde Park*, starting at Christmas with *Skating at Somerset House* with a story to follow roughly once a month to capture key dates or events in specific places in London, with one character in each novella either related to or friends with one of the main characters from Picnics. And so *New Year at The Ritz*, *Valentine's on Primrose Hill*, *Cocktails in Chelsea* and *Strawberries at Wimbledon* were created to follow my Christmas baby. :-)

In terms of the plots, these initially grew from the titles, covers, events and places and had to be about two people falling in love, or at least embarking on the possibility of it. What I found when I wrote the series was that each story was about a slightly different kind of, or source for, romantic love. One is about love unfolding from the differences between people and how those can strengthen the individuals; one is about choosing between old love versus new love; one is about love growing out of friendship; one is about love happening despite conflict and misunderstandings (a kind of modern comedy of errors); one is about revisiting first love, and one is about finding love when you least expect it. However, what really gave me the nitty gritty of ideas for the stories were the characters that came to me for each book and what they wanted or needed, what their hopes, dreams, challenges and fears were.

What I also found was that the setting and timing of each story naturally gave it a particular theme or 'feel.' For instance, *Skating at Somerset House* was set at Christmas and was more of a 'sweet' romance, whereas *Valentine's on Primrose Hill* asked questions about what love and romance really is, and was therefore deeper and strangely, darker. *Cocktails in Chelsea* had more of a sexy 'springtime fling' feel to it so was trendier and hotter. I'll leave you to make your mind up about the rest.

594

I have to admit that I really enjoyed catching up with the five couples from the novellas again in Picnics and seeing what they were up to. It was like visiting old friends, and I hope people who have read the rest of the series, or some of them, also enjoyed the chance to revisit some of those characters.

3. What's your writing schedule like? Where and when do you write?

I work full days in Human Resources over a nine day fortnight, meaning I get two Fridays off a month as dedicated writing time. I'm a single mum with two kids, one of them a teenager. They see their dad regularly but are with me day to day. Sometimes I write between 6.00 – 7.00 a.m. before the school run, but usually it's after my youngest has gone to bed from 9.00 p.m. until I fall asleep over the laptop. I do this at least three times a week but it can be closer to five or six evenings and weekends too if I'm up against a deadline.

Sometimes I fling food at the kids and tell them I'm neglecting them for a few hours, before closeting myself away. Mostly they accept this with good grace, as does my lovely boyfriend, who is more patient than I deserve. :-) My friends and family also accept falling by the wayside if I have a deadline. Equally, housework drops from my usual gold standard to bronze level. It's a delicate act to keep all the plates spinning but if I keep moving, I'm usually okay!

I do most of my writing either in my writing room (dining room at the front of the house) which contains my bookcase, laptops and a filing cabinet and has my book covers stuck up on the wall. I like writing in there because it's very light and airy. However, sometimes I write on the sofa or in bed when I want to be comfy and warm (really bad for the neck, back and shoulders though), in the staff room at work, on trains or even in cars. To be honest

I can write pretty much anywhere as long as I have my laptop and there's a plug handy, or if I have paper and a pen. Over the years I've learnt not to be precious about my writing time, or where I might do it, but to just do it whenever I get the chance.

4. Tell us a bit about your writing journey.

I've wanted to be a writer since I first learnt to read, at about five years old. I got addicted to getting lost in stories, being transported to different times and places, making new friends along the way in the characters. I thought it'd be amazing to be able to make up stories of my own for a living. I read a lot of romance novels in my teens and simply put, love writing about love. I was on the school newspaper at secondary school and my favourite subject was English, because I could write essays and short stories.

I first started writing seriously in my early twenties, when I wrote my first two novels which were romances targeted at Harlequin Mills and Boon. Shockingly (as when I look back at them now I cringe), the first one got as far as an acquisitions meeting with HM&B and the second had interest shown in it by another romance publisher but I didn't pursue that because I was uncomfortable with what they were asking me to do with the story (probably the right decision because they went out of business shortly afterwards). Writing took a back seat for eight or so years in the middle while I pursued a HR qualification and had my son, and I came back to writing in 2010.

I was a member of the Romantic Novelists Association New Writers Scheme for four years. I submitted two books for critiques (completed by an anonymous author/editor/agent), each of them twice. I can still remember the thrill of getting NWS reports that said my work was publishable, and giving me tips on how to improve it. The book I graduated to full RNA membership with in 2014 was my debut *Crazy, Undercover, Love* although it had a different title originally. I rewrote it several times, partially based on the reader's critiques that I received, and this definitely made it a much better book. When I was published I sent my readers' thank you cards.

Other highlights on my writing journey have been:

Getting an Honorable Mention for the RNA Elizabeth Goudge Trophy in 2010 and the phone call from Katie Fforde (one of my favourite authors, and the judge that year) that followed, congratulating me and telling me to keep writing.

Being offered my first publishing contract for my short story *A Night to Remember* published in the bestselling RNA/ Mills and Boon anthology in February 2014 alongside massive women's fiction authors such as Katie Fforde, Carole Matthews and Adele Parks.

Being offered a four book contract with HarperImpulse in October 2013 after meeting my editor Charlotte Ledger at the RNA Conference in July 2013. Thrilled doesn't even begin to cover it!

The day my debut novel *Crazy, Undercover, Love* was published in April 2014.

Being contacted by readers, bloggers and reviewers to say nice things about my stories or ask if I can write an article for them/ what I'm writing next/if I'm going to write a sequel.

Crazy, Undercover, Love being shortlisted for the RNA Joan Hessayon Award 2014 (for new writers) and attending the award ceremony in May 2015, where I was presented with a certificate and cheque alongside the other lovely finalists.

The success of the #LoveLondon series. :-)

There's not a day that goes by that I don't feel incredibly lucky and grateful to be doing something I love so much. Consequently, I always try and do what I can to encourage aspiring authors by offering them advice or sharing my experiences.

5. What's next for you?

Having written around 180,000 words over the past year and a half or so, alongside promoting the #LoveLondon series, the day job and the kids, I'm going to have a very short break from writing to spend some time exploring different marketing options for the #LoveLondon series. For instance, I'd love to try and do some magazine and radio interviews.

However, I also have a women's commercial fiction novel up my sleeve that I've been working on for some time, and I'm planning to get back to working on that in the autumn. And who knows what else I might do for HarperImpulse - I've always fancied writing a New Adult romance …!

Reader Q&A – Picnics in Hyde Park

1. Some people might find the idea of Zoe's plan for revenge uncomfortable. Do you think she was justified in what she originally intended to do? Why / why not?

2. What did you think of Melody, and the relationship between the two sisters?

3. Matt says that it's been 'complicated' since his wife died. What do you think he meant, and did you agree with Zoe that the reasons he gave were just excuses?

4. What impact do you think your childhood has on your adult life? How was this communicated through this story?

5. Before it was revealed, did you guess the reason Matt had for throwing Melody out? Were you surprised by the lie Stephen told and the reasons he did this?

6. What did you think of the end of the story? Did you find it was satisfying? What, if anything, would you change about the ending?

www.ingramcontent.com/pod-product-compliance
Ingram Content Group UK Ltd.
Pitfield, Milton Keynes, MK11 3LW, UK
UKHW022305180325
456436UK00003B/208